COLLECTED
STORIES

COLLECTED STORIES

V. S. Pritchett

RANDOM HOUSE NEW YORK

Many of these stories originally appeared in the following periodicals: *Encounter, Harper's*, the *New Statesman, The New Yorker, Queen* and *Playboy.*

Grateful acknowledgment is made the following for permission to reprint previously published material:
Alfred A. Knopf, Inc., and A. D. Peters and Co., Ltd.: Five stories from *When My Girl Comes Home.* Copyright © 1961 by V. S. Pritchett.
Random House, Inc., and Chatto & Windus, Ltd.: Five stories from *Blind Love.* Copyright © 1969 by V. S. Pritchett. Six stories from *The Camberwell Beauty.* Copyright © 1974 by V. S. Pritchett. Five stories from *On the Edge of the Cliff.* Copyright © 1979 by V. S. Pritchett.

Library of Congress Cataloging in Publication Data
Pritchett, V. S. (Victor Sawdon), 1900–
Collected stories.
I. Title.
PR6031.R7A15 1982   823'.912   81–48279
ISBN 0–394–52417–9   AACR2

Manufactured in the United States of America
2 4 6 8 9 7 5 3
First Edition

For Dorothy—always

Preface

To put together a substantial if not complete collection of the stories from the seven volumes I have written in the last fifty years is a startling experience in old age. One comes across a procession of vanished selves. In what room, in what town or country, did I write them? In what chair was I sitting and where did I get this or that fragment of a scene or a character? I see a crowd of fictions that have peculiar friends. How did the story change as I re-wrote it, perhaps four or five times, boiling down a hundred pages into twenty or thirty, as I still do? Story writing is exacting work. I fancy that if I took each story sentence by sentence, I would find that the now mingled minutes of personal experience taken arbitrarily from events or feelings (which in reality were far apart in my own life) had been turned by art into some other life, not my own. How was it that a commercial traveller in Enniskillen became another in the English Midlands and who told his own vernacular story when I had written it all before as an impersonal study? Certainly my original title was not "Sense of Humour"; he and the girl gave me that. So with every story I could go on: only once—and that was when I was twenty-three and beginning—did I take down the scene, the character and the conversation straight from life, as I listened to a man in Dublin trying to persuade a barman to give him a dozen oysters without paying for them. Since that lucky moment—never repeated—I have had to dig my stories out of myself and out of random events, re-imagined. Stories breed in the writer. "Real" life as it is, people as they are, are useless until art reveals what life merely suggested.

So, with astonishment, sometimes with a laugh of embarrassment, I have been exploring what I can only call my "other life." One or two details of period now amuse me. What extraordinary changes in society, manners, speech, ways of living, I have lived through; each decade has changed them. To live is to be out of date. There are those years which seem now unbelievable and which lasted until 1948 when I often lived in the country and worked by oil lamp and candlelight. Urban amenities had not reached the isolated places where I lived. And then, how comic, though true, are the sums of money my people talk about in my early stories. Sums that then seemed enormous, now seem trivial. Again, how much of speech was gilded by attempts at decorum— everyone being addressed as Mr., Mrs. or Miss—and how strange, even after World War I, that "bad" language was a still secret pleasure and limited, outside the soldiery. But of course respectability is always nominal; human beings have always done and said what they liked behind that screen—extravagantly, too.

The only volume of stories I have not drawn on is *The Spanish Virgin,* published in the 1920's and long out of print, in which I was learning my craft, seduced by many influences, and had not yet found a distinctive voice which is indispensable to the short-story writer and the poet. By the 1930's I had at any rate discovered my voice and that my native bent was to the designs of comedy and its ironies. For me comedy has a militant, tragic edge, even when I've proceeded to the purely comic or to farce. It has been said that many of my people are eccentrics. They do not seem so to me, but very native English in that they live for projecting the fantasies of their inner, imaginative life and the energies that keep them going. I have always thought it the duty of writers to justify their people, for we all feel that for good or ill, we are exceptional and justified in being what we are.

I began, in those early days, by writing anecdotal sketches of real people, because the newspapers liked that kind of thing. This taught me to look and listen and I was much helped by early editors. But soon the observer began to invent. I laboured at novels—two had some success and are still in print—but I was really attracted to concision, intensity, reducing possible novels to essentials. I love the intricacy of the short form, the speed with which it can change from scene to scene. I have always thought that the writer of short stories is a mixture of reporter, aphoristic wit, moralist and poet—though not "poetical"; he is something of a ballad-maker, and in the intricacy of his design is close to the writer of sonnets. He has to catch our attention at once, to get the opening line right. He has to be something of an architect. Except the very long stories, for which few periodicals exist, stories like "When My Girl Comes Home" (which is my favourite), "Blind Love" and "The Camberwell Beauty," the rest have appeared in English and American magazines. Although the short story is said to have lost its popularity, this is not my experience; thousands of addicts still delight in it because it is above all memorable and is not simply read, but re-read again and again. It is the glancing form of fiction that seems to be right for the nervousness and restlessness of contemporary life.

charles a. Brady says these are the
best stories:

Contents

CONTENTS

COLLECTED
STORIES

The Sailor

He was lifting his knees high and putting his hand up when I first saw him, as if, crossing the road through that stinging rain, he were breaking through the bead curtain of a Pernambuco bar. I knew he was going to stop me. This part of the Euston Road is a beat of the men who want a cup of tea or their fare to a job in Luton or some outlying town.

"Beg pardon, chum," he said in an anxious hot-potato voice. "Is that Whitechapel?"

He pointed to the traffic clogged in the rain farther down where the electric signs were printing off the advertisements and daubing them on the wet road. Coatless, with a smudged trilby hat on the back of his head so that a curl of boot-polish black hair glistered with raindrops over his forehead, he stood there squeezing the water in his boots and looking at me, from his bilious eyes, like a man drowning and screaming for help in two feet of water and wondering why the crowd is laughing.

"That's St. Pancras," I said.

"Oh, Gawd," he said, putting his hand to his jaw like a man with toothache. "I'm all messed up." And he moved on at once, gaping at the lights ahead.

"Here, wait," I said. "Which part of Whitechapel do you want? Where have you come from?"

"Surrey Docks," he said. "They said it was near Surrey Docks, see, but they put me wrong. I bin on the road since ten this morning."

"Acton," he read a bus sign aloud, recalling the bottom of the day's misery. "I bin there," and, fascinated, watched the bus out of sight.

The man's worried mouth dropped open. He was sodden. His clothes were black with damp. The smell of it came off him. The rain stained from the shoulders of his suit past the armpits over the ribs to the waist. It spread from dark blobs over his knees to his thighs. He was a greasy-looking man, once fat, and the fat had gone down unevenly like a deflating bladder. He was calming as I spoke to him.

A sailor, of course, and lost. Hopelessly, blindly lost. I calculated that he must have wandered twenty miles that day exhausting a genius for misdirection.

"Here," I said. "You're soaked. Come and have a drink."

There was a public house nearby. He looked away at once.

"I never touch it," he said. "It's temptation."

I think it was that word which convinced me the sailor was my kind of man. I am, on the whole, glad to say that I am a puritan and the word "temptation" went home, painfully, pleasurably, excitingly and intimately familiar. A most stimulating and austerely gregarious word, it indicates either the irresistible hypocrite or the fellow struggler with sin. I couldn't let him go after that.

Presently we were in a café drinking acrid Indian tea.

"Off a ship?" I said.

He looked at me as if I were a magician who could read his soul.

"Thank Gawd I stopped you," he said. "I kep' stopping people all day and they messed me up, but you been straight."

He gave me his papers, his discharge paper, his pension form, official letters, as he said this, like a child handing himself over. Albert Edward Thompson, they said, cook, born '96, invalided out of the service two years before. So he was not just off a ship.

"They're clean," he said suspiciously when I asked him about this. "I got ulcers, riddled with ulcers for fourteen years."

He had no job and that worried him, because it was the winter. He had ganged on the road, worked in a circus, had been a waiter in an Italian restaurant. But what worried him much more was getting to Whitechapel. He made it sound to me as though for two years he had been threshing about the country, dished by one job and another, in a less and less successful attempt to get there.

"What job are you going to do?" I said.

"I don't know," he said.

"It's a bad time," I said.

"I fall on my feet," he said, "like I done with you."

We sat opposite to each other at the table. He stared with his appalled eyeballs at the people in the café. He was scared of them and they looked scared too. He looked as though he was going to give a yell and spring at them; in fact, he was likelier to have gone down on his knees to them and to have started sobbing. They couldn't know this. And then he and I looked at each other and the look discovered that we were the only two decent, trustworthy men in a seedy and grabbing world. Within the next two hours I had given him a job. I was chum no longer, but "sir." "Chum" was anarchy and the name of any twisty bleeder you knocked up against, but "sir," for Thompson (out of the naval nursery), was hierarchy, order, payday, and peace.

I was living alone in the country in those days. I had no one to look after me. I gave Albert Thompson some money; I took him to Whitechapel and wrote down the directions for his journey to my house.

The bungalow where I lived was small and stood just under the brow of a hill. The country was high and stony there. The roads broke up into lanes, the lanes sank into woods, and cottages were few. The oak woods were naked and as green as canker. They stood like old men, and below them were sweet plantations of larch where the clockwork pheasants went off like toys in the rainy afternoons. At night you heard a farm dog bark like a pistol and the oceanic sound of the trees and sometimes, over an hour and half's walk away, the whistle of a train. But that was all. The few people looked as though they had grown out of the land, sticks and stones in cloth; they were old people chiefly. In the one or two bigger houses they were childless. It was derelict country; frost with its teeth fast in the ground, the wind running finer than sand through a changeless sky or the solitary dribble of water in the butts and the rain legging it over the grass—that was all one heard or saw there.

"Gawd!" said Thompson when he got there. "I thought I'd never strike the place." Pale, coatless again in the wet, his hat tipped back from a face puddingy and martyred, he came up the hill with the dancing step of a man treading on nails. He had been lost again. He had travelled by the wrong train, even by the wrong line, he had assumed that, as in towns, it was safest to follow the crowd. But country crowds soon scatter. He had been following people—it sounded to me —to half the cottages for miles around.

"Then I come to the Common," he said. "I didn't like the look of that. I kept round it."

At last some girl had shown him the way.

I calmed him down. We got to my house and I took him to his room. He sat down on the bed and told me the story again. He took off his boots and socks and looked at his blistered feet, murmuring to them as if they were a pair of orphans. There was a woman in the train with a kid, he said, and to amuse the kid he had taken out his jackknife. The woman called the guard.

After we had eaten and I had settled in, I went for a walk that afternoon. The pleasure of life in the country for me is in its monotony. One understands how much of living is habit, a long war to which people, plants, and animals have settled down. In the country one expects nothing of people; they are themselves, not bringers of gifts. In towns one asks too little or too much of them.

The drizzle had stopped when I went out, the afternoon was warmer and inert, and the dull stench of cattle hung over the grass. On my way down the hill I passed the bungalow that was my nearest neighbour. I could see the roof as pink as a slice of salt ham, from the top of my garden. The bungalow was ten years old. A chicken man had built it. Now the woodwork was splitting and shrinking, the garden was rank, two or three larches, which the rabbits had been at, showed above the dead grass, and there was a rosebush. The bush had one frozen and worm-eaten flower which would stick there half the winter. The history of the bungalow was written in the tin bath by the side door. The bath was full of gin, beer, and whisky bottles discarded after the weekend parties of many tenants. People took the place forever and then, after a month or two, it changed hands. A businessman, sentimental about the country, an invalid social worker, a couple with a motor bicycle, an inseparable pair of schoolteachers with big legs and jumping jumpers; and now there was a woman I hardly saw, a colonel's daughter, but the place was said to belong to a man in the Northampton boot trade.

A gramophone was playing when I walked by. Whenever I passed, the colonel's daughter was either playing the gramophone or digging in the garden. She was a small girl in her late twenties, with a big knowledgeable-looking head under tobacco-brown curls, and the garden fork was nearly as big as herself. Her gardening never lasted long. It consisted usually in digging up a piece of the matted lawn in order to bury tins; but she went at it intensely, drawing back the fork until her hair fell over her face and the sweat stood on her brow. She always had a cigarette in her mouth, and every now and then the carnation skin of her face, with its warm, dark-blue eyes, would be distorted and turned crimson by violent bronchial coughing. When this stopped she would straighten up, the delicacy came back to her skin, and she would say: "Oh, Christ. Oh, bloody hell," and you noticed at the end of every speech the fine right eyebrow would rise a little, and the lid of the eye below it would quiver. This wink, the limpid wink of the colonel's daughter, you noticed at once. You wondered what it meant and planned to find out. It was as startling and enticing as a fish rising, and you discovered when you went after it that the colonel's daughter was the hardest-drinking and most blasphemous piece of apparent childish innocence you had ever seen. Old men in pubs gripped their sticks, went scarlet, and said someone ought to take her drawers down and give her a tanning. I got a sort of fame from being a neighbour of the colonel's daughter. "Who's that piece we saw down the road?" people asked.

"Her father's in the Army."

"Not," two or three of them said, for this kind of wit spreads like measles, "the Salvation Army." They said I was a dirty dog. But I hardly knew the colonel's daughter. Across a field she would wave, utter her obscenity, perform her wink, and edge off on her slight legs. Her legs were not very good. But if we met face to face on the road she became embarrassed and nervous; this was one of her dodges. "Still alone?" she said.

"Yes. And you?"

"Yes. What do you do about sex?"

"I haven't got any."

"Oh, God, I wish I'd met you before."

When I had friends she would come to the house. She daren't come there when I was alone, she said. Every night, she said, she locked and bolted up at six. Then the wink—if it was a wink. The men laughed. She did not want to be raped, she said. Their wives froze and some curled up as if they had got the blight and put their hands hard on their husbands' arms. But the few times she came to the house when I was alone, the colonel's daughter stood by the door, the full length of the room away, with a guilty look on her face.

When I came back from my walk the gramophone had stopped. The colonel's daughter was standing at the door of her bungalow with her sleeves rolled up, a pail of water beside her, and a scrubbing brush in her hand.

"Hullo," she said awkwardly.

"Hullo," I said.

"I see you've got the Navy down here. I didn't know you were that way."

"I thought you would have guessed that straight away," I said.

"I found him on the Common crying this morning. You've broken his heart." Suddenly she was taken by a fit of coughing.

"Well," she said, "every day brings forth something."

When I got to the gate of my bungalow I saw that at any rate if Thompson could do nothing else he could bring forth smoke. It was travelling in thick brown funnel puffs from the short chimney of the kitchen. The smoke came out with such dense streaming energy that the house looked like a destroyer racing full steam ahead into the wave of hills. I went down the path to the kitchen and looked inside. There was Thompson, with not only his sleeves rolled up but his trousers also, and he was shovelling coal into the kitchener with the garden spade, the face of the fire was roaring yellow, the water was throbbing and sighing in the boiler, the pipes were singing through the house.

"Bunkering," Thompson said.

I went into the sitting-room. I thought I had come into the wrong house. The paint had been scrubbed, the floors polished like decks, the reflections of the firelight danced in them, the windows gleamed, and the room was glittering with polished metal. Doorknobs, keyholes, fire-irons, window-catches, were polished; metal that I had no idea existed flashed with life.

"What time is supper piped—er, ordered," said Thompson, appearing in his stockinged feet. His big round eyes started out of their dyspeptic shadows and became enthusiastic when I told him the hour.

A change came over my life after this. Before Thompson everything had been disorganized and wearying. He drove my papers and clothes back to their proper places. He brought the zest and routine of the Royal Navy into my life. He kept to his stockinged feet out of tenderness for those orphans, a kind of repentance for what he had done to them; he was collarless and he served food with a splash as if he allowed for the house to give a pitch or a roll that didn't come off. His thumbs left their marks on the plates. But he was punctual. He lived for "orders." "All ready, sir," he said, planking down the dish and looking up at the clock at the same moment. Burned, perhaps, spilling over the side, invisible beneath Bisto—but on time!

The secret of happiness is to find a congenial monotony. My own housekeeping had suffered from the imagination. Thompson put an end to this tiring chase of the ideal. "What's orders for lunch, sir?"

"Do you a nice fried chop and chips?" he said. That was settled. He went away, but soon he came back.

"What pudding's ordered, sir?" That stumped both of us, or it stumped me. Thompson watched me to time his own suggestion.

"Do you a nice spotted dick?" So it was. We had this on the second day and the third, we changed on the fourth, but on the fifth we came back to it. Then Thompson's mind gave a leap.

"Do you grilled chop, chips, spotted dick *and custard*?" he said. That became almost our fixed menu. There were bouts of blancmange, but spotted dick came back.

Thompson had been sinking towards semi-starvation, I to the insidious Oblomovism of the country. Now we were reformed and happy.

"I always fall on my feet," he said, "like I done with you." It was his refrain.

The winter dripped like a tap, the fog hardly left our hill. Winter in England has the colourless, steaming look of a fried-fish-shop window. But we were stoking huge fires, we bunkered, the garden spade went through coal by the hundredweight. We began to talk a more tangy dialect. Things were not put away; they were "stowed." String appeared in strange knots to make things "fast," plants were "lashed" in the dying garden, washing was "hoist" on the lines, floors were "swabbed." The kitchen became the "galley." The postman came "alongside," all meals were "piped," and at bedtime we "piped down." At night, hearing the wind bump in the chimneys and slop like ocean surf in the woods, looking out at the leather darkness, I had the sensation that we were creeping down the Mersey in a fog or lumping about in the Atlantic swell off Ushant.

I was happy. But was Thompson happy? He seemed to be. In the mornings we were both working, but in the afternoons there was little more to do. He sat on a low chair with his knees close to the bars of the range or on the edge of his bed, darning his clothes. (He lived in a peculiar muddle of his own and he was dirty in his own quarters.) In the evenings he did the same and sometimes we talked. He told me about his life. There was nothing in it at all. It was buried under a mumble of obscurity. His memories were mainly of people who hadn't "behaved right," a dejecting moral wilderness with Thompson mooching about in it, disappointed with human nature. He didn't stay to talk with me much. He preferred the kitchen, where, the oil lamp smoking, the range smoking, and himself smoking, he sat chewing it all over, gazing into the fire.

"You can go out, you know," I said, "whenever you want. Do what you like."

"I'm O.K.," he said.

"See some of the people," I said. Thompson said he'd just as lief stand by.

Everyone knows his own business best. But I was interested one night when I heard the sound of voices in the kitchen. Someone had come in. The voices went on and on other nights. Who was it? The milker from the farm probably or the cowman who cleaned out cesspits by lantern light at night and talked with nostalgia about burying bodies during the war. "If there hadn't been a war," this man used to say, "I wouldn't have seen nothing. It was an education."

I listened. Slow in question, slow in answer, the monotonous voices came. The woodcutter, the postman? I went into the kitchen to see who the profound and interminable crony was.

There was no one. There was only Thompson in the kitchen. Sitting close to the fire with all windows closed, a shallow, stupefied, oil-haired head in his own fug, Thompson was spelling out a story from a *Wild West Magazine.* It was old and dirty and his coal-blackened finger was moving from word to word.

So far Thompson had refused to go out of the house except as far as the coal-shed, but I was determined after this discovery that he should go out. I waited until payday.

"Here's your money," I said. "Take the afternoon off."

Thompson stepped back from the money.

"You keep it," he said, in a panic. "You keep it for me."

"You may need it," I said. "For a glass of beer or cigarettes or something."

"If I have it I'll lose it," he said. "They'll pinch it."

"Who?" I said.

"People," Thompson said. I could not persuade him.

"All right, I'll keep it for you," I said.

"Yes," he said eagerly. "If I want a bob I'll ask you. Money's temptation," he said.

"Well, anyway," I said, "take the afternoon off. It's the first sunny afternoon we've had. I'll tell you where to go. Turn to the right in the lane . . ."

"I don't like them lanes," said Thompson, looking suspiciously out of the window. "I'll stay by you."

"Well, take a couple of hours," I said. "We all need fresh air."

He looked at me as if I had suggested he should poison himself; indeed as if I were going to do the poisoning.

"What if I do an hour?" he began to bargain.

"No, the afternoon," I said.

"Do you half an hour?" he pleaded.

"All right, I don't want to force you," I said. "This is a free country. Go for an hour."

It was like an auction.

"Tell you what," he said, looking shifty. "I'll do you twenty minutes." He thought he had tricked me, but I went back into the kitchen and drove him to it. I had given him an overcoat and shoes, and it was this appeal to his vanity that got him. Out he went for his twenty minutes. He was going straight down the lane to where it met the main road and then straight back; it would take a smart walker about twelve minutes on a winter's day.

When an hour passed, I was pleased with myself. But when four hours had gone by and darkness came, I began to wonder. I went out to the gate. The land and the night had become one thing. I had just gone in again when I heard loud voices and saw the swing of a lamp. There came Thompson with a labourer. The labourer, a little bandy man known as Fleas, stood like a bent bush with a sodden sack on his shoulders, snuffling in the darkness, and he grinned at me with the malevolence of the land.

"He got astray," he said, handing Thompson over.

"Gawd," exclaimed Thompson, exhausted. His face was the familiar pale suety agony. He was full of explanations. He was sweating like a scared horse and nearly hysterical. He'd been on the wrong course. He didn't know where to steer. One thing looked like another. Roads and lanes, woods and fields, mixed themselves together.

"Woods I seen," he said in horror. "And that Common! It played me up proper."

"But you weren't anywhere near the Common," I said.

"Then what was it?" he said.

That night he sat by the fire with his head in his hands.

"I got a mood," he said.

The next morning cigarette smoke blew past my window and I heard coughing. The colonel's daughter was at the kitchen door talking to Thompson. "Cheero," I heard her say and then she came to my door and pushed it open. She stood there gravely and her eye winked. She was wearing a yellow jersey and looked as neat as a bird.

"You're a swine," she said.

"What have I done?"

"Raping women on the Common," she said. "Deserting your old friends, aren't you?"

"It's been too wet on the Common," I said.

"Not for me," she said. "I'm always hopeful. I came across last night. There was the minister's wife screaming in the middle of it. I sat on her head and calmed her down, and she said a man had been chasing her. 'Stop screaming,' I said. 'You flatter yourself, dear.' It was getting dark and I carried her shopping bag and umbrella for her and took her to her house. I often go and see her in the evenings. I've got to do something, haven't I? I can't stick alone in that bungalow all day and all night. We sit and talk about her son in China. When you're old you'll be lonely too."

"What happened on the Common?"

"I think I'm drunk," said the colonel's daughter, "but I believe I've been drunk since breakfast. Well, where was I? I'm losing my memory too. Well, we hadn't gone five minutes before I heard someone panting like a dog behind us and jumping over bushes. Old Mrs. Stour started screaming again. 'Stand still,' I said, and I looked and then a man came out of a tree about ten yards away. 'What the hell do you want?' I said. A noise came back like a sheep. 'Ma'am, ma'am, ma'am, ma'am,' it said."

"So that's where Thompson was," I said.

"I thought it was you," the colonel's daughter said. " 'There's a woman set about me with a stick on the Common,' he said. 'I didn't touch her, I was only following her,' he said. 'I reckoned if I followed her I'd get home.'

"When they got to the wood, Thompson wouldn't go into it and she had to take his hand; that was a mistake. He took his hand away and moved off. So she grabbed his coat. He struggled after this, she chased him into the thicket and told him not to be a fool but he got away and disappeared, running on to the Common.

"You're a damn swine," the colonel's daughter said to me. "How would you like to be put down in the middle of the sea?"

She walked away. I watched her go up the path and lean on the gate opposite to stroke the nose of a horse. She climbed into the field and the horses, like hairy yokels, went off. I heard her calling them, but they did not come.

When she was out of sight, the door opened behind me and Thompson came in.

"Beg pardon, sir," he said. "That young lady, sir. She's been round my kitchen door."

"Yes," I said.

He gaped at me and then burst out: "I didn't touch her, straight I didn't. I didn't lay a finger on her."

"She didn't say you did. She was trying to help you."

He calmed down. "Yes, sir," he said.

When he came back into the room to lay the table I could see he was trying to catch my eye.

"Sir," he said at last, standing at attention. "Beg pardon, sir, the young lady . . ."

His mouth was opening and shutting, trying to shape a sentence.

"The young lady—she'd had a couple, sir," he said in a rush.

"Oh," I said, "don't worry about that. She often has."

"It's ruination, sir," said Thompson evangelically.

She did not come to the house again for many days, but when she came I heard him lock both kitchen doors.

Orders at the one extreme, temptation at the other, were the good and evil of Thompson's life. I no longer suggested that he go out. I invented errands and ordered him to go. I wanted, in that unfortunate way one has, to do good to Thompson. I wanted him to be free and happy. At first he saw that I was not used to giving orders and he tried to dodge. His ulcers were bad, he said. Once or twice he went about barefoot, saying the sole was off one of his boots. But when he saw I meant what I said, he went. I used to watch him go, tilted forward on his toes in his half-running walk, like someone throwing himself blindly upon the mercy of the world. When he came back he was excited. He had the look of someone stupefied by incomprehensible success. It is the feeling a landsman has when he steps off a boat after a voyage. You feel giddy, canny, surprised at your survival after crossing that bridge of deep, loose water. You boast. So did Thompson—morally.

"There was a couple of tramps on the road," Thompson said. "I steered clear. I never talked to them," he said.

"Someone asked me who I was working for." He described the man. "I never told him," he said shrewdly. "I just said 'A gentleman.' Meaning you," he said.

There was a man in an allotment who had asked him for a light and wanted to know his business.

"I told him I didn't smoke," said Thompson. "You see my meaning —you don't know what it's leading up to. There warn't no harm, but that's how temptation starts."

What was temptation? Almost everything was temptation to Thompson. Pubs, cinemas, allotments, chicken-runs, tobacconists—in these, everywhere, the tempter might be. Temptation, like Othello's jealousy, was the air itself.

"I expect you'd like to go to church," I said. He seemed that kind.

"I got nothing *against* religion," Thompson said. "But best keep clear. They see you in church and the next thing they're after you."

"Who?" I asked.

"People," he said. "It's not like a ship."

I was like him, he said, I kept myself to myself. I kept out of temptation's way. He was glad I was like that, he said.

It was a shock to me that while I observed Thompson, Thompson observed me. At the same time one prides oneself, the moment one's character is defined by someone else, on defeating the definition. I kept myself to myself? I avoided temptation? That was all Thompson knew! There was the colonel's daughter. I might not see her very often; she might be loud, likeable, dreary or alarming by turns, but she was Temptation itself. How did he know I wasn't tempted? Thompson's remark made me thrill. I began to see rather more of the colonel's daughter.

And so I discovered how misleading he had been about his habits and how, where temptation was concerned, he made a difference between profession and practice. So strong was Thompson's feeling about temptation that he was drawn at once to every tempter he saw. He stopped them on the road and was soon talking about it. The postman was told. The shopkeepers heard all his business and mine. He hurried after tramps, he detained cyclists, he sat down on the banks with road-makers and ditchers, telling them the dangers of drink, the caution to be kept before strangers. And after he had done this he always ended by telling them he kept himself to himself, avoided drink, ignored women, and, patting his breast pocket, said that was where he kept his money and his papers. He behaved to them exactly as he had behaved with me two months before in the Euston Road. The colonel's daughter told me. She picked up all the news in that district.

"He's a decent, friendly soul," muttered the colonel's daughter thickly. "You're a prig. Keep your hair on. You can't help it. I expect you're decent, too, but you're like all my bloody so-called friends."

"Oh," I said hopefully, "are prigs your special line?"

I found out, too, why Thompson was always late when he came home from his errands. I had always accepted that he was lost. And so he was in a way, but he was lost through wandering about with people, following them to their doorsteps, drifting to their allotments, backyards, and all the time telling them, as he clung to their company, about the dangers of human intercourse. "I never speak to nobody"—it was untrue, but it was not a lie. It was simply a delusion.

"He lives in two worlds at once," I said to the colonel's daughter one morning. I had sent Thompson to the town to buy the usual chops, and I was sitting in her bungalow. This was the first time I had ever been in it. The walls were of varnished matchboarding like the inside of a gospel hall, and the room was heated by a paraffin stove which smelled like armpits. There were two rexine-covered chairs, a rug, and a table in the room. She was sorting out gramophone records as I talked and the records she did not like she dropped to the floor and broke. She was listening very little to what I said but walked to the gramophone, put on a record, stopped it after a few turns, and then, switching it off, threw the record away.

"Oh, you know a hell of a lot, don't you?" she said. "I don't say you're not an interesting man, but you don't get on with it, do you?"

"How old are you? Twenty-five?" I said.

Her sulking, ironical expression went. She was astonished.

"Good God!" she exclaimed with a smile of sincerity. "Don't be a damn fool." Then she frowned. "Or are you being professionally clever?

"Here," she said. "I was damn pretty when I was twenty-five. I'm thirty-nine. I've still got a good figure."

"I would have put you at twenty-seven at the most," I said truthfully.

She walked towards me. I was sitting on the armchair and she stood very close. She had never been as close to me before. I had thought her eyes were dark blue, but now I saw they were green and grey, with a moist lascivious haze in them and yet dead and clock-like, like a cat's on a sunless day. And the skin, which had seemed fresh to me, I saw in its truth for the first time. It was clouded and flushed, clouded with that thickened pimpled ruddiness which the skin of heavy drinkers has and which in middle age becomes bloated and mottled. I felt: This is why she has always stood the length of the room away before.

She saw what was in my mind and she sat down on the chair opposite me. The eye winked.

"Keep control of yourself," she said. "I came down here for a rest and now you've started coming round."

"Only in the mornings," I said.

She laughed. She went to a bookshelf and took down a bottle of whisky and poured out half a tumblerful.

"This is what you've done coming in here, early bird," she said. "Exciting me on an empty stomach. I haven't touched it for ten days. I had a letter this morning. From my old man."

"Your father?"

I had always tried to imagine the colonel. She gave a shout of cheerful laughter and it ended in coughing till tears came to her eyes.

"That's rich. God, that's rich. Keen observer of women! No, from my husband, darling. He's not my husband, damn him, of course, but when you've lived with someone for ten years and he pays the rent and keeps you, he is your husband, isn't he? Or ought to be. Ten years is a long time and his family thought he ought to be married. He thought so too. So he picked up a rich American girl and pushed me down here to take it easy in the country. I'm on the dole like your sailor boy. Well, I said, if he felt that way, he'd better have his head. In six months he'll tire of the new bitch. So I left him alone. I didn't want to spoil his fun. Well, now, he writes me, he wants to bring his fiancée down because she's heard so much about me and adores the country. . . ."

I was going to say something indignant.

"He's nice too," she said casually. "He sells gas heaters. You'd like him all the same. But blast that bloody woman," she said, raising her cool voice. "She's turned him into a snob. I'm just his whore now.

"Don't look so embarrassed," she said. "I'm not going to cry.

"For ten years," she said, "I read books, I learned French, educated myself, learned to say 'How d'you do?' instead of 'Pleased to meet you,' and look down my nose at everything in his sort of way. And I let him go about saying my father was in the Army too, but they were such bloody fools they thought he must be a colonel. They'd never heard of sergeant majors having children. Even my old man, bless his heart" — she smiled affectionately—"thought or let himself think as they did. I was a damn silly little snob."

"I don't know him," I said. "But he doesn't sound much good to me."

"That's where you're wrong," she said sharply. "Just weak, poor kid, that's all. You don't know what it is to be ashamed your mother's a housemaid. I got over it—but he didn't, that's all."

She paused and the wink gave its signal.

"This is more embarrassing than I thought," she said.

"I am very sorry," I said. "Actually I am in favour of snobbery, it is a sign of character. It's a bad thing to have, but it's a bad thing not to have had. You can't help having the diseases of your time."

"There you go," she said.

The suffering of others is incredible. When it is obscure it seems like a lie; when it is garish and raw, it is like boasting. It is a challenge to oneself. I got up from my chair and went towards her. I was going to kiss her.

"You are the sentimental type," she said.

So I didn't kiss her.

Then we heard someone passing the bungalow and she went to the window. Thompson was going by. The lock of black hair was curling over his sweating forehead and he gave a hesitant staggering look at the bungalow. There was a lump of fear on his face.

"He'd better not know where you've been," she said. She moved her lips to be kissed, but I walked out.

I was glad of the steady sense of the fresh grey air when I got outside. I was angry and depressed. I stood at the window of my house. Thompson came in and was very talkative. He'd been lost, of course. He'd seen people. He'd seen fields. He'd heard trees. He'd seen roads. I hardly listened. I was used to the jerky wobbling voice. I caught the words "legion" and "temptation," and thought he was quoting from the Bible. Presently I realized he was talking about the British Legion. The postman had asked him to go to a meeting of the British Legion that night. How simple other people's problems are! Yet "No" Thompson was saying. He was not going to the British Legion. It was temptation.

I ought to have made love to her and kissed her, I was thinking. She was right, I was a prig.

"You go," I said to Thompson, "if you want to. You'd enjoy it."

But how disgusting, obvious, stupid, to have made love to her then, I thought.

"Do as you like," I said.

"I'm best alongside you," said Thompson.

"You can't always be by me," I said. "In a month, perhaps less, as you know, I'll be leaving here and you'll have to go."

"Yes," he said. "You tol' me. You been straight. I'll be straight with you. I won't go to the Legion."

We ate our meal and I read.

"In every branch of our spiritual and material civilization we seem to have reached a turning point," I read. "This spirit shows itself not only in the actual state of public affairs . . ."

Well, I thought, I can ask her over tonight. I needn't be a fool twice. I went out for an hour. When I returned, Thompson was fighting Temptation hard. If he went to the Legion how would he get back? No, best not. He took the Legion on in its strength. (She is a type, I thought.) At four he was still at it. At five he asked me for his money. (Well, we are all types, I was thinking.) Very shortly he brought the money back and asked me to keep his pension papers. At half past six I realized this meant that Thompson was losing and the Legion and all its devils winning. (What is a prig, anyway?) He was looking out at the night. Yet, just when I thought he had lost, he had won. There was the familiar sound of the Wild West monologue in the kitchen. It was half past eight. The Legion was defeated.

I was disappointed in Thompson. Really, not to have had more guts than that! Restlessly I looked out of the window. There was a full moon spinning on the tail of a dying wind. Under the moonlight the fields were like wide-awake faces, the woods like womanish heads of hair upon them. I put on my hat and coat and went out. I was astonished by the circle of stars. They were as distinct as figures on a clock. I took out my watch and compared the small time in my hand with the wide time above. Then I walked on. There was a sour smell at the end of the wood, where, no doubt, a dead rabbit or pigeon was rotting.

I came out of the wood onto the metalled road. Suddenly my heart began to beat quickly as I hurried down the road, but it was a long way round now. I cut across fields. There was a cottage and a family were listening to a dance-band on the wireless. A man was going the rounds of his chickens. There was a wheelbarrow and there were spades and steel bars where a water mill was being built.

Then I crossed the last fields and saw the bungalow. My heart throbbed heavily and I felt all my blood slow down and my limbs grow heavy. It was only when I got to the road that I saw there were no lights in the bungalow. The colonel's daughter, the sergeant's daughter, had gone to bed early like a child. While I stood I heard men's voices singing across the fields. It must have gone ten o'clock and people were coming out of the public house. In all the villages of England, at this hour, loud-voiced groups were breaking up and dispersing into the lanes.

I got to my house and lit a candle. The fire was low. I was exhausted and happy to be in my house among my own things, as if I had got into my own skin again. There was no light in the kitchen. Thompson had gone to bed. I grinned at the thought of the struggles of poor Thompson. I picked up a book and read. I could hear still the sound of that shouting and singing. The beer was sour and flat in this part of the country, but it made people sing.

The singing voices came nearer. I put down the book. An argument was going on in the lane. I listened. The argument was nearing the cottage. The words got louder. They were going on at my gate. I heard the gate go and the argument was on my path. Suddenly—there could be no doubt—people were coming to the door. I stood up, I could recognize no voice. Loud singing, stumbling feet, then bang! The door broke open and crashed against the wall. Tottering, drunk, with their arms round each other, Thompson and the colonel's daughter nearly fell into the room.

Thompson stared at me with terror.

"Stand up, sailor," said the colonel's daughter, clinging to him.

"He was lonely," she said unsteadily to me. "We've been playing gramophone records. Sing," she said.

Thompson was still staring.

"Don't look at him. Sing," she said. Then she gave a low laugh and they fell bolt upright on the sofa like prim, dishevelled dolls.

A look of wild love of all the world came into Thompson's eyes and he smiled as I had never seen him smile before. He suddenly opened his twitching mouth and bawled:

> "You've robbed every tailor,
> And you've skinned every sailor,
> But you won't go walking Paradise Street no more."

"Go on. That's not all," the colonel's daughter cried and sang: "Go on—something—something, deep and rugged shore."

She put her arms round his neck and kissed him. He gaped at her with panic and looked at her skirt. It was undone.

He pointed at her leg in consternation. The sight sobered him. He pulled away his arms and rushed out of the room. He did not come back. She looked at me and giggled. Her eyes were warm and shining. She picked leaves off her skirt.

"Where's he gone? Where's he gone?" she kept asking.

"He's gone to bed," I said.

She started a fit of coughing. It strained her throat. Her eyes were dilated like an animal's caught in a trap, and she held her hand to her chest.

"I wish," she cried hysterically, pointing at me in the middle of her coughing, "I wish you could see your bloody face."

She got up and called out: "Thompson! Thompson!" And when he did not answer she sang out: "Down by the deep and rugged shore— ore-ore-ore."

"What's the idea?" I said.

"I want Thompson," she said. "He's the only man up here."

Then she began to cry. She marched out to his room, but it was locked. She was wandering through the other rooms calling him and then she went out, away up the path. She went calling him all the way down to her bungalow.

In the morning Thompson appeared as usual. He brought the breakfast. He came in for "orders." Grilled chop, did I think? And what about spotted dick? He seemed no worse. He behaved as though nothing had happened. There was no guilty look in his eyes and no apprehension. He made no apology. Lunch passed, teatime, and the day. I finished my work and went into the kitchen.

"Tell me," I said, "about last night."

Thompson was peeling potatoes. He used to do this into a bucket on the floor, as if he were peeling for a whole crew. He put down the clasp-knife and stood up. He looked worried.

"That was a terrible thing," Thompson said, as if it was something he had read about in the papers. "Terrible, sir. A young lady like that, sir. To come over here for me, an educated lady like that. Someone oughter teach her a lesson. Coming over and saying she wanted to play some music. I was took clean off my guard. It wasn't right," said Thompson. "Whichever way you look at it, it wasn't right. I told her she'd messed me up."

"I'm not blaming you. I want to know."

"And she waited till you was out," Thompson said. "That's not straight. She may class herself as an educated young lady, but do you know what I reckon she is? I reckon she's a jane."

I went down to the bungalow. I was beginning to laugh now. She was in the garden digging. Her sleeves were rolled up and she was sweating over the fork. The beds were thick with leaves and dead plants. I stood there watching her. She looked at me nervously for a moment. "I'm making the garden tidy," she said. "For Monday. When the bitch comes down."

She was shy and awkward. I walked on and, looking back, saw her go into the house. It was the last I ever saw of her. When I came back, the fork she had been using was stuck in the flower bed where she had left it. She went to London that night and did not return.

"Thank Gawd," Thompson said.

There was a change in Thompson after this and there was a change in me. Perhaps the change came because the dirty February days were going, the air softer and the year moving. I was leaving soon. Thompson mentioned temptation no more. Now he went out every day. The postman was his friend. They used to go to the pub. He asked for his money. In the public house the labourers sat around muttering in a language Thompson didn't understand. He stood them drinks. At his first pint he would start singing. They encouraged him. He stood them more drinks. The postman ordered them for him and then tapped him on the pocket book. They emptied his pockets every night. They despised him and even brought complaints to me about him after they had emptied his pockets.

Thompson came back across the Common alone, wild, enthusiastic, and moaning with suspicion by turns. The next day he would have a mood. All the countryside for ten miles round knew the sailor. He became famous.

Our last week came. He quietened down.

"What are you going to do?" I asked.

"I'll stay by you."

"You can't," I said. "I'll be going abroad."

"You needn't pay me," he said. "I'll stay by you." It was hard to make him understand he could not stay with me. He was depressed.

"Get me out of here safe," he pleaded at last. "Come with me to the station." He could not go on his own because all the people he knew would be after him. He had told them he was going. He had told them I was saving his pension and his last fortnight's pay. They would come creeping out of cottage doors and ditches for him. So I packed his things and got a taxi to call for us. How slowly we had lived and moved in these fields and lanes! Now we broke through it all with a rush as the car dropped down the hill and the air blew in at the window. As we passed the bungalow with the sun on its empty windows, I saw the fork standing in the neglected bed. Then we swept on. Thompson sat back in the car so that no one should see him, but I leaned forward to see everything for the last time and forget it.

We got to the town. As the taxi slowed down in the streets, people looked out of shops, doors; a potman nodded from the pub.

"Whatcha, Jack," the voices called.

The police, the fishmonger, boys going to school, dozens of people waved to him. I might have been riding with royalty. At the station a large woman sweeping down the steps of the bank straightened up and gave a shout.

"Hi, Jacko!" she called, bending double, went into shrieks of laughter and called across to a friend at a first-floor window. It was a triumph. But Thompson ignored them all. He sat back out of sight.

"Thank Gawd I've got you," he said. "They skin you of everything."

We sat in the train. It was a two-hour journey.

"Once I strike Whitechapel," he said in the voice of one naming Singapore, "I'll be O.K." He said this several times, averting his face from the passing horror of the green fields.

"Don't you worry," he said. "Don't fret yourself for me. Don't you worry." His optimism increased as mine dwindled as we got nearer London. By the time we reached London he was almost shouting. "I'll fall on my feet, don't you worry. I'll send you my address."

We stood on the kerb and I watched him walk off into the yellow rain and the clogged, grunting, and mewing traffic. He stepped right into it without looking. Taxis braked to avoid him. He was going to walk to Whitechapel. He reckoned it was safer.

The Saint

When I was seventeen years old I lost my religious faith. It had been
unsteady for some time and then, very suddenly, it went as the result
of an incident in a punt on the river outside the town where we lived.
My uncle, with whom I was obliged to stay for long periods of my life,
had started a small furniture-making business in the town. He was
always in difficulties about money, but he was convinced that in some
way God would help him. And this happened. An investor arrived who
belonged to a sect called the Church of the Last Purification, of
Toronto, Canada. Could we imagine, this man asked, a good and
omnipotent God allowing His children to be short of money? We had
to admit we could not imagine this. The man paid some capital into
my uncle's business and we were converted. Our family were the first
Purifiers—as they were called—in the town. Soon a congregation of
fifty or more were meeting every Sunday in a room at the Corn Exchange.

At once we found ourselves isolated and hated people. Everyone
made jokes about us. We had to stand together because we were
sometimes dragged into the courts. What the unconverted could not
forgive in us was first that we believed in successful prayer and, se-
condly, that our revelation came from Toronto. The success of our
prayers had a simple foundation. We regarded it as "Error"—our name

for Evil—to believe the evidence of our senses, and if we had influenza or consumption, or had lost our money or were unemployed, we denied the reality of these things, saying that since God could not have made them they therefore did not exist. It was exhilarating to look at our congregation and to know that what the vulgar would call miracles were performed among us, almost as a matter of routine, every day. Not very big miracles, perhaps; but up in London and out in Toronto, we knew that deafness and blindness, cancer and insanity, the great scourges, were constantly vanishing before the prayers of the more advanced Purifiers.

"What!" said my schoolmaster, an Irishman with eyes like broken glass and a sniff of irritability in the bristles of his nose. "What! Do you have the impudence to tell me that if you fell off the top floor of this building and smashed your head in, you would say you hadn't fallen and were not injured?"

I was a small boy and very afraid of everybody, but not when it was a question of my religion. I was used to the kind of conundrum the Irishman had set. It was useless to argue, though our religion had already developed an interesting casuistry.

"I *would* say so," I replied with coldness and some vanity. "And my head would not be smashed."

"You would not say so," answered the Irishman. "You would not say so." His eyes sparkled with pure pleasure. "You'd be dead."

The boys laughed, but they looked at me with admiration.

Then, I do not know how or why, I began to see a difficulty. Without warning and as if I had gone into my bedroom at night and had found a gross ape seated in my bed and thereafter following me about with his grunts and his fleas and a look, relentless and ancient, scored on his brown face, I was faced with the problem that prowls at the centre of all religious faith. I was faced by the difficulty of the origin of evil. Evil was an illusion, we were taught. But even illusions have an origin. The Purifiers denied this.

I consulted my uncle. Trade was bad at the time and this made his faith abrupt. He frowned as I spoke.

"When did you brush your coat last?" he said. "You're getting slovenly about your appearance. If you spent more time studying books"—that is to say, the Purification literature—"and less with your hands in your pockets and playing about with boats on the river, you wouldn't be letting Error in."

All dogmas have their jargon; my uncle as a businessman loved the trade terms of the Purification. "Don't let Error in" was a favourite one. The whole point about the Purification, he said, was that it was scientific and therefore exact; in consequence it was sheer weakness to admit discussion. Indeed, betrayal. He unpinched his pince-nez, stirred his tea, and indicated I must submit or change the subject. Preferably the latter. I saw, to my alarm, that my arguments had defeated my uncle. Faith and doubt pulled like strings round my throat.

"You don't mean to say you don't believe that what our Lord said was true?" my aunt asked nervously, following me out of the room. "Your uncle does, dear."

I could not answer. I went out of the house and down the main street to the river, where the punts were stuck like insects in the summery flash of the reach. Life was a dream, I thought; no, a nightmare, for the ape was beside me.

I was still in this state, half sulking and half exalted, when Mr. Hubert Timberlake came to the town. He was one of the important people from the headquarters of our church and he had come to give an address on the Purification at the Corn Exchange. Posters announcing this were everywhere. Mr. Timberlake was to spend Sunday afternoon with us. It was unbelievable that a man so eminent would actually sit in our dining-room, use our knives and forks, and eat our food. Every imperfection in our home and our characters would jump out at him. The Truth had been revealed to man with scientific accuracy—an accuracy we could all test by experiment—and the future course of human development on earth was laid down, finally. And here in Mr. Timberlake was a man who had not merely performed many miracles —even, it was said with proper reserve, having twice raised the dead —but had actually been to Toronto, our headquarters, where this great and revolutionary revelation had first been given.

"This is my nephew," my uncle said, introducing me. "He lives with us. He thinks he thinks, Mr. Timberlake, but I tell him he only thinks he does. Ha, ha." My uncle was a humorous man when he was with the great. "He's always on the river," my uncle continued. "I tell him he's got water on the brain. I've been telling Mr. Timberlake about you, my boy."

A hand as soft as the best quality chamois leather took mine. I saw a wide upright man in a double-breasted navy-blue suit. He had a pink square head with very small ears and one of those torpid, enamelled smiles which were said by our enemies to be too common in our sect.

"Why, isn't that just fine?" said Mr. Timberlake, who, owing to his

contacts with Toronto, spoke with an American accent. "What say we
tell your uncle it's funny he thinks he's funny."

The eyes of Mr. Timberlake were direct and colourless. He had the
look of a retired merchant captain who had become decontaminated
from the sea and had reformed and made money. His defence of me
had made me his at once. My doubts vanished. Whatever Mr. Timberlake believed must be true, and as I listened to him at lunch, I thought
there could be no finer life than his.

"I expect Mr. Timberlake's tired after his address," said my aunt.

"Tired?" exclaimed my uncle, brilliant with indignation. "How can
Mr. Timberlake be tired? Don't let Error in!"

For in our faith the merely inconvenient was just as illusory as a great
catastrophe would have been, if you wished to be strict, and Mr.
Timberlake's presence made us very strict.

I noticed then that, after their broad smiles, Mr. Timberlake's lips
had the habit of setting into a long depressed sarcastic curve.

"I guess," he drawled, "I guess the Al-mighty must have been tired
sometimes, for it says He re-laxed on the seventh day. Say, do you know
what I'd like to do this afternoon?" he said, turning to me. "While your
uncle and aunt are sleeping off this meal let's you and me go on the
river and get water on the brain. I'll show you how to punt."

Mr. Timberlake, I saw to my disappointment, was out to show he
understood the young. I saw he was planning a "quiet talk" with me
about my problems.

"There are too many people on the river on Sundays," said my uncle
uneasily.

"Oh, I like a crowd," said Mr. Timberlake, giving my uncle a tough
look. "This is the day of rest, you know." He had had my uncle
gobbling up every bit of gossip from the sacred city of Toronto all the
morning.

My uncle and aunt were incredulous that a man like Mr. Timberlake
should go out among the blazers and gramophones of the river on a
Sunday afternoon. In any other member of our church they would have
thought this sinful.

"Waal, what say?" said Mr. Timberlake. I could only murmur.

"That's fixed," said Mr. Timberlake. And on came the smile as
simple, vivid, and unanswerable as the smile on an advertisement.
"Isn't that just fine!"

Mr. Timberlake went upstairs to wash his hands. My uncle was
deeply offended and shocked, but he could say nothing. He unpinched
his glasses.

"A very wonderful man," he said. "So human," he apologized.

"My boy," my uncle said, "this is going to be an experience for you. Hubert Timberlake was making a thousand a year in the insurance business ten years ago. Then he heard of the Purification. He threw everything up, just like that. He gave up his job and took up the work. It was a struggle, he told me so himself this morning. 'Many's the time,' he said to me this morning, 'when I wondered where my next meal was coming from.' But the way was shown. He came down from Worcester to London and in two years he was making fifteen hundred a year out of his practice."

To heal the sick by prayer according to the tenets of the Church of the Last Purification was Mr. Timberlake's profession.

My uncle lowered his eyes. With his glasses off, the lids were small and uneasy. He lowered his voice too.

"I have told him about your little trouble," my uncle said quietly with emotion. I was burned with shame. My uncle looked up and stuck out his chin confidently.

"He just smiled," my uncle said. "That's all."

Then we waited for Mr. Timberlake to come down.

I put on white flannels and soon I was walking down to the river with Mr. Timberlake. I felt that I was going with him under false pretences; for he would begin explaining to me the origin of evil and I would have to pretend politely that he was converting me when already, at the first sight of him, I had believed. A stone bridge, whose two arches were like an owlish pair of eyes gazing up the reach, was close to the landing-stage. I thought what a pity it was the flannelled men and the sunburned girls there did not know I was getting a ticket for *the* Mr. Timberlake who had been speaking in the town that very morning. I looked round for him and when I saw him I was a little startled. He was standing at the edge of the water looking at it with an expression of empty incomprehension. Among the white crowds his air of brisk efficiency had dulled. He looked middle-aged, out of place, and insignificant. But the smile switched on when he saw me.

"Ready?" he called. "Fine!"

I had the feeling that inside him there must be a gramophone record going round and round, stopping at that word.

He stepped into the punt and took charge.

"Now I just want you to paddle us over to the far bank," he said, "and then I'll show you how to punt."

Everything Mr. Timberlake said still seemed unreal to me. The fact that he was sitting in a punt, of all commonplace material things, was

incredible. That he should propose to pole us up the river was terrifying. Suppose he fell into the river? At once I checked the thought. A
leader of our church under the direct guidance of God could not
possibly fall into a river.

The stream is wide and deep in this reach, but on the southern bank
there is a manageable depth and a hard bottom. Over the clay banks
the willows hang, making their basketwork print of sun and shadow on
the water, while under the gliding boats lie cloudy, chloride caverns.
The hoop-like branches of the trees bend down until their tips touch
the water like fingers making musical sounds. Ahead in midstream, on
a day sunny as this one was, there is a path of strong light which is hard
to look at unless you half close your eyes, and down this path on the
crowded Sundays go the launches with their parasols and their pen-
nants; and also the rowboats with their beetle-leg oars, which seem to
dig the sunlight out of the water as they rise. Upstream one goes, on
and on between the gardens and then between fields kept for grazing.
On the afternoon when Mr. Timberlake and I went out to settle the
question of the origin of evil, the meadows were packed densely with
buttercups.

"Now," said Mr. Timberlake decisively when I had paddled to the
other side. "Now I'll take her."

He got over the seat into the well at the stern.

"I'll just get you clear of the trees," I said.

"Give me the pole," said Mr. Timberlake, standing up on the little
platform and making a squeak with his boots as he did so. "Thank you,
sir. I haven't done this for eighteen years, but I can tell you, brother,
in those days I was considered some poler."

He looked round and let the pole slide down through his hands.
Then he gave the first difficult push. The punt rocked pleasantly and
we moved forward. I sat facing him, paddle in hand, to check any
inward drift of the punt.

"How's that, you guys?" said Mr. Timberlake, looking round at our
eddies and drawing in the pole. The delightful water sished down it.

"Fine," I said. Deferentially I had caught the word.

He went on to his second and his third strokes, taking too much
water on his sleeve, perhaps, and uncertain in his steering, which I
corrected, but he was doing well.

"It comes back to me," he said. "How am I doing?"

"Just keep her out from the trees," I said.

"The trees?" he said.

"The willows," I said.

"I'll do it now," he said. "How's that? Not quite enough? Well, how's this?"

"Another one," I said. "The current runs strong this side."

"What? More trees?" he said. He was getting hot.

"We can shoot out past them," I said. "I'll ease us over with the paddle."

Mr. Timberlake did not like this suggestion.

"No, don't do that. I can manage it," he said. I did not want to offend one of the leaders of our church, so I put the paddle down; but I felt I ought to have taken him farther along away from the irritation of the trees.

"Of course," I said, "we could go under them. It might be nice."

"I think," said Mr. Timberlake, "that would be a very good idea."

He lunged hard on the pole and took us towards the next archway of willow branches.

"We may have to duck a bit, that's all," I said.

"Oh, I can push the branches up," said Mr. Timberlake.

"It is better to duck," I said.

We were gliding now quickly towards the arch; in fact, I was already under it.

"I think I should duck," I said. "Just bend down for this one."

"What makes the trees lean over the water like this?" asked Mr. Timberlake. "Weeping willows—I'll give you a thought there. How Error likes to make us dwell on sorrow. Why not call them *laughing* willows?" discoursed Mr. Timberlake as the branch passed over my head.

"Duck," I said.

"Where? I don't see them," said Mr. Timberlake, turning round.

"No, your head," I said. "The branch," I called.

"Oh, the branch. This one?" said Mr. Timberlake, finding a branch just against his chest and he put out a hand to lift it. It is not easy to lift a willow branch and Mr. Timberlake was surprised. He stepped back as it gently and firmly leaned against him. He leaned back and pushed from his feet. And he pushed too far. The boat went on, I saw Mr. Timberlake's boots leave the stern as he took an unthoughtful step backwards. He made a last-minute grasp at a stronger and higher branch, and then there he hung a yard above the water, round as a blue damson that is ripe and ready, waiting only for a touch to make it fall. Too late with the paddle and shot ahead by the force of his thrust, I could not save him.

For a full minute I did not believe what I saw; indeed, our religion taught us never to believe what we saw. Unbelieving, I could not move. I gaped. The impossible had happened. Only a miracle, I found myself saying, could save him.

What was most striking was the silence of Mr. Timberlake as he hung from the tree. I was lost between gazing at him and trying to get the punt out of the small branches of the tree. By the time I had got the punt out, there were several yards of water between us, and the soles of his boots were very near the water as the branch bent under his weight. Boats were passing at the time but no one seemed to notice us. I was glad about this. This was a private agony. A double chin had appeared on the face of Mr. Timberlake and his head was squeezed between his shoulders and his hanging arms. I saw him blink and look up at the sky. His eyelids were pale like a chicken's. He was tidy and dignified as he hung there, the hat was not displaced, and the top button of his coat was done up. He had a blue silk handkerchief in his breast pocket. So unperturbed and genteel he seemed that as the tips of his shoes came nearer and nearer to the water, I became alarmed. He could perform what are called miracles. He would be thinking at this moment that only in an erroneous and illusory sense was he hanging from the branch of the tree over six feet of water. He was probably praying one of the closely reasoned prayers of our faith, which were more like conversations with Euclid than appeals to God. The calm of his face suggested this. Was he, I asked myself, within sight of the main road, the town recreation ground, and the landing-stage crowded with people, was he about to re-enact a well-known miracle? I hoped that he was not. I prayed that he was not. I prayed with all my will that Mr. Timberlake would not walk upon the water. It was my prayer and not his that was answered.

I saw the shoes dip, the water rise above his ankles and up his socks. He tried to move his grip now to a yet higher branch—he did not succeed—and in making this effort his coat and waistcoat rose and parted from his trousers. One seam of shirt with its pant-loops and brace-tabs broke like a crack across the middle of Mr. Timberlake. It was like a fatal flaw in a statue, an earthquake crack that made the monumental mortal. The last Greeks must have felt as I felt then, when they saw a crack across the middle of some statue of Apollo. It was at this moment I realized that the final revelation about man and society on earth had come to nobody and that Mr. Timberlake knew nothing at all about the origin of evil.

All this takes long to describe, but it happened in a few seconds as

I paddled towards him. I was too late to get his feet on the boat and the only thing to do was to let him sink until his hands were nearer the level of the punt and then to get him to change hand-holds. Then I would paddle him ashore. I did this. Amputated by the water, first a torso, then a bust, then a mere head and shoulders, Mr. Timberlake, I noticed, looked sad and lonely as he sank. He was a declining dogma. As the water lapped his collar—for he hesitated to let go of the branch to hold the punt—I saw a small triangle of deprecation and pathos between his nose and the corners of his mouth. The head resting on the platter of water had the sneer of calamity on it, such as one sees in the pictures of a beheaded saint.

"Hold on to the punt, Mr. Timberlake," I said urgently. "Hold on to the punt."

He did so.

"Push from behind," he directed in a dry business-like voice. They were his first words. I obeyed him. Carefully I paddled him towards the bank. He turned and, with a splash, climbed ashore. There he stood, raising his arms and looking at the water running down his swollen suit and making a puddle at his feet.

"Say," said Mr. Timberlake coldly, "we let some Error in that time."

How much he must have hated our family.

"I am sorry, Mr. Timberlake," I said. "I am most awfully sorry. I should have paddled. It was my fault. I'll get you home at once. Let me wring out your coat and waistcoat. You'll catch your death—"

I stopped. I had nearly blasphemed. I had nearly suggested that Mr. Timberlake had fallen into the water and that to a man of his age this might be dangerous.

Mr. Timberlake corrected me. His voice was impersonal, addressing the laws of human existence rather than myself.

"If God made water it would be ridiculous to suggest He made it capable of harming His creatures. Wouldn't it?"

"Yes," I murmured hypocritically.

"O.K.," said Mr. Timberlake. "Let's go."

"I'll soon get you across," I said.

"No," he said. "I mean let's go on. We're not going to let a little thing like this spoil a beautiful afternoon. Where were we going? You spoke of a pretty landing-place farther on. Let's go there."

"But I must take you home. You can't sit there soaked to the skin. It will spoil your clothes."

"Now, now," said Mr. Timberlake. "Do as I say. Go on."

There was nothing to be done with him. I held the punt into the bank and he stepped in. He sat like a bursting and sodden bolster in front of me while I paddled. We had lost the pole, of course.

For a long time I could hardly look at Mr. Timberlake. He was taking the line that nothing had happened and this put me at a disadvantage. I knew something considerable had happened. That glaze, which so many of the members of our sect had on their faces and persons, their minds and manners, had been washed off. There was no gleam for me from Mr. Timberlake.

"What's the house over there?" he asked. He was making conversation. I had steered into the middle of the river to get him into the strong sun. I saw steam rise from him.

I took courage and studied him. He was a man, I realized, in poor physical condition, unexercised and sedentary. Now the gleam had left him, one saw the veined empurpled skin of the stoutish man with a poor heart. I remember he had said at lunch:

"A young woman I know said: 'Isn't it wonderful? I can walk thirty miles in a day without being in the least tired.' I said: 'I don't see that bodily indulgence is anything a member of the Church of the Last Purification should boast about.' "

Yes, there was something flaccid, passive, and slack about Mr. Timberlake. Bunched in swollen clothes, he refused to take them off. It occurred to me, as he looked with boredom at the water, the passing boats, and the country, that he had not been in the country before. That it was something he had agreed to do but wanted to get over quickly. He was totally uninterested. By his questions—what is that church? Are there any fish in this river? Is that a wireless or a gramophone?—I understood that Mr. Timberlake was formally acknowledging a world he did not live in. It was too interesting, too eventful a world. His spirit, inert and preoccupied, was elsewhere in an eventless and immaterial habitation. He was a dull man, duller than any man I had ever known; but his dullness was a sort of earthly deposit left by a being whose diluted mind was far away in the effervescence of metaphysical matters. There was a slightly pettish look on his face as (to himself, of course) he declared he was not wet and he would not have a heart attack or catch pneumonia.

Mr. Timberlake spoke little. Sometimes he squeezed water out of his sleeve. He shivered a little. He watched his steam. I had planned, when we set out, to go up as far as the lock, but now the thought of another two miles of this responsibility was too much. I pretended I wanted to go only as far as the bend we were approaching, where one of the richest buttercup meadows was. I mentioned this to him. He turned and looked with boredom at the field. Slowly we came to the bank.

We tied up the punt and we landed.

"Fine," said Mr. Timberlake. He stood at the edge of the meadow just as he had stood at the landing-stage—lost, stupefied, uncomprehending.

"Nice to stretch our legs," I said. I led the way into the deep flowers. So dense were the buttercups there was hardly any green. Presently I sat down. Mr. Timberlake looked at me and sat down also. Then I turned to him with a last try at persuasion. Respectability, I was sure, was his trouble.

"No one will see us," I said. "This is out of sight of the river. Take off your coat and trousers and wring them out."

Mr. Timberlake replied firmly: "I am satisfied to remain as I am.

"What is this flower?" he asked, to change the subject.

"Buttercup," I said.

"Of course," he replied.

I could do nothing with him. I lay down full length in the sun; and, observing this and thinking to please me, Mr. Timberlake did the same. He must have supposed that this was what I had come out in the boat to do. It was only human. He had come out with me, I saw, to show me that he was only human.

But as we lay there I saw the steam still rising. I had had enough.

"A bit hot," I said, getting up.

He got up at once.

"Do you want to sit in the shade?" he asked politely.

"No," I said. "Would you like to?"

"No," he said. "I was thinking of you."

"Let's go back," I said. We both stood up and I let him pass in front of me. When I looked at him again, I stopped dead. Mr. Timberlake was no longer a man in a navy-blue suit. He was blue no longer. He was transfigured. He was yellow. He was covered with buttercup pollen, a fine yellow paste of it made by the damp, from head to foot.

"Your suit," I said.

He looked at it. He raised his thin eyebrows a little, but he did not smile or make any comment.

The man is a saint, I thought. As saintly as any of those gold-leaf figures in the churches of Sicily. Golden he sat in the punt; golden he sat for the next hour as I paddled him down the river. Golden and bored. Golden as we landed at the town and as we walked up the street back to my uncle's house. There he refused to change his clothes or to sit by a fire. He kept an eye on the time for his train back to London. By no word did he acknowledge the disasters or the beauties of the world. If they were printed upon him, they were printed upon a husk.

Sixteen years have passed since I dropped Mr. Timberlake in the river and since the sight of his pant-loops destroyed my faith. I have not seen him since, but today I heard that he was dead. He was fifty-seven. His mother, a very old lady with whom he had lived all his life, went into his bedroom when he was getting ready for church and found him lying on the floor in his shirt-sleeves. A stiff collar with the tie half inserted was in one hand. Five minutes before, she told the doctor, she had been speaking to him.

The doctor, who looked at the heavy body lying on the single bed, saw a middle-aged man, wide rather than stout and with an extraordinarily box-like thick-jawed face. He had got fat, my uncle told me, in later years. The heavy liver-coloured cheeks were like the chaps of a hound. Heart disease, it was plain, was the cause of the death of Mr. Timberlake. In death the face was lax, even coarse and degenerate. It was a miracle, the doctor said, that he had lived as long. Any time during the last twenty years the smallest shock might have killed him.

I thought of our afternoon on the river. I thought of him hanging from the tree. I thought of him indifferent and golden in the meadow. I understood why he had made for himself a protective, sedentary blandness, an automatic smile, a collection of phrases. He kept them on like the coat after his ducking. And I understood why—though I had feared it all the time we were on the river—I understood why he did not talk to me about the origin of evil. He was honest. The ape was with us. The ape that merely followed me was already inside Mr. Timberlake eating out his heart.

Many Are Disappointed

Heads down to the wind from the hidden sea, the four men were cycling up a deserted road in the country. Bert, who was the youngest, dreamed:

"You get to the pub, and there's a girl at the pub, a dark girl with bare arms and bare legs in a white frock, the daughter of the house, or an orphan—maybe it's better she should be an orphan—and you say something to her, or, better still, you don't say anything to her—she just comes and puts her arms round you, and you can feel her skin through her frock and she brings you some beer and the other chaps aren't there and the people don't say anything except laugh and go away, because it's all natural and she doesn't have a baby. Same at the next place, same anywhere, different place, different girl, or same girl —same girl always turning up, always waiting. Dunno how she got there. Just slips along without you knowing it and waiting like all those songs . . ."

And there the pub was. It stood on the crown of the long hill, straight ahead of them, a small red-brick house with outbuildings and a single chimney trailing out smoke against the strong white light which seemed to be thrown up by great reflectors from the hidden sea.

"There's our beer, Mr. Blake," shouted Sid on his pink racing tyres, who was the first to see it, the first to see everything. The four men glanced up.

Yes, there's our beer, they said. Our ruddy beer. They had been thinking about it for miles. A pub at the crossroads, a pub where the old Roman road crossed this road that went on to the land's end, a funny place for a pub, but a pub all right, the only pub for ten miles at Harry's ruddy Roman road, marked on the map which stuck out of the backside pocket of Harry's breeches. Yes, that was the pub, and Ted, the oldest and the married one, slacked on the long hill and said all he hoped was that the Romans had left a drop in the bottom of the barrel for posterity.

When they had left in the morning there had been little wind. The skylarks were over the fields, and the sun itself was like one of their steel wheels flashing in the sky. Sid was the first, but Harry with the stubborn red neck and the close dull fair curls was the leader. In the week he sat in the office making the plan. He had this mania for Roman roads. "Ask our Mr. Newton," they said, "the man with the big head and the brain." They had passed through the cream-walled villages and out again to pick up once more the singing of the larks; and then cloud had covered the sun like a grey hand, west of Handleyford the country had emptied, and it was astonishing to hear a bird. Reeds were in the small meadows. Hedges crawled uncut and there had been no villages, only long tablelands of common and bald wiry grass for sheep and the isolated farm with no ivy on the brick.

Well, they were there at last. They piled their bicycles against the wall of the house. They were shy before these country places. They waited for Ted. He was walking the last thirty yards. They looked at the four windows with their lace curtains and the varnished door. There was a chicken in the road and no sound but the whimper of the telegraph wire on the hill. In an open barn was a cart tipped down, its shaft white with the winter's mud, and last year's swallow nests, now empty, were under the eaves. Then Ted came and when he had piled his bicycle, they read the black sign over the door. "Tavern," it said. A funny old-fashioned word, Ted said, that you didn't often see.

"Well," Sid said, "a couple of pints all round?"

They looked to Harry. He always opened doors, but this door was so emphatically closed that he took off his fur gauntlet first and knocked before he opened it. The four men were surprised to see a woman standing behind the door, waiting there as if she had been listening to them. She was a frail, drab woman, not much past thirty, in a white blouse that drooped low over her chest.

"Good morning," said Sid. "This the bar?"

"The bar?" said the woman timidly. She spoke in a flat wondering voice and not in the singsong of this part of the country.

"Yes, the bar," Ted said. "It says 'Tavern,' " he said, nodding up at the notice.

"Oh, yes," she said, hesitating. "Come in. Come in here."

She showed them not into the bar but into a sitting-room. There was a bowl of tomatoes in the window and a notice said "Teas."

The four men were tall and large beside her in the little room and she gazed up at them as if she feared they would burst its walls. And yet she was pleased. She was trying to smile.

"This is on me," Sid said. "Mild and bitter four times."

"O.K., Mr. Blake," Ted said. "Bring me my beer."

"But let's get into the bar," said Bert.

Seeing an armchair, Ted sank into it and now the woman was reassured. She succeeded in smiling but she did not go out of the room. Sid looked at her, and her smile was vacant and faint like the smile fading on an old photograph. Her hair was short, an impure yellow, and the pale skin of her face and her neck and her breast seemed to be moist as if she had just got out of bed. The high strong light of this place drank all colour from her.

"There isn't a bar," she said. "This isn't a public house. They call it the Tavern, but it isn't a tavern by rights."

Very anxiously she raised her hands to her blouse.

"What!" they exclaimed. "Not a pub! Here, Harry, it's marked on your map." They were dumbfounded and angry.

"What you mean, don't sell beer," they said.

Their voices were very loud.

"Yes," said Harry. "Here it is. See? Inn."

He put the map before her face accusingly.

"You don't sell beer?" said Bert. He looked at the pale-blue-veined chest of the woman.

"No," she said. She hesitated. "Many are disappointed," she said, and she spoke like a child reciting a piece without knowing its meaning. He lowered his eyes.

"You bet they ruddy well are," said Ted from the chair.

"Where is the pub?" said Sid.

She put out her hand and a little girl came into the room and clung close to her mother. Now she felt happier.

"My little girl," she said.

She was a tiny, frail child with yellow hair and pale-blue eyes like her mother's. The four men smiled and spoke more quietly because of the resemblance between the woman and her child.

"Which way did you come?" she asked, and her hand moving over the child's hair got courage from the child. "Handleyford?" she said. "That's it. It's ten miles. The Queen's Arms, Handleyford, the way you came. That's the nearest pub."

"My God!" said Bert. "What a country!"

"The Queen's Arms," said Ted, stupefied.

He remembered it. They were passing through Handleyford. He was the oldest, a flat wide man in loose clothes, loose in the chin too, with watery rings under his eyes and a small golden sun of baldness at the back of his head. "Queen's Arms," he had called. "Here, what's the ruddy game?" But the others had grinned back at him. When you drop back to number four on the hills it comes back to you: they're single, nothing to worry about, you're married and you're forty. What's the hurry? Ease up, take what you can get. "Queen's Arms"—he remembered looking back. The best things are in the past.

"Well, that's that!" said Sid.

"Queen's Arms, Harry," Ted said.

And Bert looked at the woman. "Let's go on," he said fiercely. She was not the woman he had expected. Then he blushed and turned away from the woman.

She was afraid they were going and in a placating voice she said: "I do teas."

Sid was sitting on the arm of a chair, and the child was gazing at a gold ring he wore on his little finger. He saw the child was gazing and he smiled.

"What's wrong with tea?" Sid said.

"Ask the man with the brain," said Ted. "Ask the man with the map."

Harry said: "If you can't have beer, you'd better take what you can get, Mr. Richards."

"Tea," nodded Sid to the woman. "Make it strong."

The woman looked at Sid as if he had performed a miracle.

"I'll get you tea," she said eagerly. "I always do teas for people." She spoke with delight as if a bell had suddenly tinkled inside her. Her eyes shone. She would get them tea, she said, and bread and butter, but no eggs, because the man had not been that morning, and no ham. It was too early, she said, for ham. "But there are tomatoes," she said. And then, like a child: "I put them in the window so as people can see."

"O.K.," Sid said. "Four teas."

She did not move at once but still, like a shy child, stood watching them, waiting for them to be settled and fearful that they would not stay. But at last she put out her hand to the child and hurried out to the kitchen.

"Well, Mr. Blake," said Ted, "there's a ruddy sell."

"Have a gasper, Mr. Richards," said Sid.

"Try my lighter," said Ted.

He clicked the lighter, but no flame came.

"Wrong number," said Ted. "Dial O and try again." A steak, said Sid, had been his idea. A couple of pints just to ease the passage and then some real drinking, Ted said. But Bert was drumming on a biscuit tin and was looking inside. There was nothing in it. "Many," said Bert, "are disappointed."

They looked at the room. There were two new treacle-coloured armchairs. There was a sofa with a pattern of black ferns on it. The new plush was damp and sticky to the hands from the air of the hidden sea. There was a gun-metal fender and there was crinkled green paper in the fireplace. A cupboard with a glass door was empty except for the lowest shelf. On that was a thick book called *The Marvels of Science.*

The room was cold. They thought in the winter it must be damn cold. They thought of the ten drizzling miles to Handleyford.

They listened to the cold clatter of the plates in the kitchen and the sound of the woman's excited voice and the child's. There was the bare linoleum on the floor and the chill glass of the window. Outside was the road with blown sand at the edges and, beyond a wall, there were rows of cabbages, then a bit of field and the expressionless sky. There was no sound on the road. They—it occurred to them—had been the only sound on that road for hours.

The woman came in with a cup and then with a plate. The child brought a plate and the woman came in with another cup. She looked in a dazed way at the men, amazed that they were still there. It seemed to Ted, who was married, that she didn't know how to lay a table. "And now I've forgotten the sugar," she laughed. Every time she came into the room she glanced at Bert timidly and yet pityingly, because he was the youngest and had been the most angry. He lowered his eyes and avoided her look. But to Ted she said: "That's right, you make yourselves comfortable," and at Sid she smiled because he had been the kindest. At Harry she did not look at all.

She was very startled then when he stood at the door and said: "Where's this Roman road?"

She was in the kitchen. She told him the road by the white gate and showed him from the doorway of the house.

"There he goes," said Sid at the window. "He's looking over the gate."

They waited. The milk was put on the table. The woman came in at last with the bread and butter and the tea.

"He'll miss his tea next," Ted said.

"Well," Ted said, when Harry came back. "See any Romans?"

"It's just grass," Harry said. "Nothing on it." He stared in his baffled, bullnecked way.

"No beer and no Romans," Ted said.

The woman, who was standing there, smiled. In a faltering voice, wishing to make them happy, she said:

"We don't often get no Romans here."

"Oh, God!" Bert laughed very loudly and Ted shook with laughter too. Harry stared.

"Don't take any notice of them, missus," Sid said. And then to them: "She means gipsies."

"That come with brooms," she said, bewildered by their laughter, wondering what she had done.

When she had gone and had closed the door, Bert and Ted touched their heads with their fingers and said she was dippy, but Sid told them to speak quietly.

Noisily they had drawn up their chairs and were eating and drinking. Ted cut up tomatoes, salted them, and put them on his bread. They were good for the blood, he told them, and Harry said they reckoned at home his granddad got the cancer he died of from eating tomatoes day after day. Bert, with his mouth full, said he'd read somewhere that tea was the most dangerous drink on earth. Then the child came in with a paper and said her mother had sent it. Sid looked at the door when it closed again.

"Funny thing," he said. "I think I've seen that woman before."

That, they said, was Sid's trouble. He'd seen too many girls before.

He was a lanky man with a high forehead and a Hitler moustache and his lips lay over his mouth as if they were kissing the air or whispering to it. He was a dark, harsh-looking, cocksure man, but with a gentle voice, and it was hard to see his eyes under his strong glasses. His lashes were long and his lids often half-lowered, which gave him an air of seriousness and shyness. But he stuck his thumbs in his waistcoat and stuck out his legs to show his loud check stockings and he had that ring on his finger. "Move that up a couple and he'd be spliced," they said. "Not me," he said, "look at Ted." A man with no ideals, Bert thought, a man whose life was hidden behind the syrup-thick lens of his glasses. Flash Sid. See the typists draw themselves up, tilt back their heads, and get their hands ready to keep him off. Not a man with ideals. See them watch his arms and his hands, see them start tapping hard on the typewriter keys and pretending to be busy when he leaned over to tell them a story. And then, when he was gone, see them peep through the enquiry window to watch where he went, quarrel about him, and dawdle in the street when the office closed, hoping to see him.

"Well," said Harry when they had cleared the table and got out the map.

Sid said: "You gen'lemen settle it. I'll go and fix her up."

Sid's off, they said. First on the road, always leading, getting the first of the air, licking the cream off everything.

He found her in the kitchen and he had to lower his head because of the ceiling. She was sitting drably at the table, which was covered with unwashed plates and the remains of a meal. There were unwashed clothes on the backs of the chairs and there was a man's waistcoat. The child was reading a comic paper at the table and singing in a high small voice.

A delicate stalk of neck, he thought, and eyes like the pale wild scabious you see in the ditches.

Four shillings, she said, would that be too much?

She put her hand nervously to her breast.

"That's all right," Sid said, and put the money in her hand. It was coarsened by work. "We cleared up everything," he said.

"Don't get many people, I expect," he said.

"Not this time of year."

"A bit lonely," he said.

"Some think it is," she said.

"How long have you been here?" he said.

"Only three years. It seems," she said with her continual wonder, "longer."

"I thought it wasn't long," Sid said. "I thought I seen you some-where. You weren't in—in Horsham, were you?"

"I come from Ashford," she said.

"Ashford," he said. "I knew you weren't from these parts."

She brightened and she was fascinated because he took off his glasses and she saw the deep serious shadows of his eyes and the pale drooping of the naked lids. The eyes looked tired and as if they had seen many things and she was tired too.

"I bin ill," she said. Her story came irresistibly to her lips. "The doctor told us to come here. My husband gave up his job and everything. Things are different here. The money's not so good—" Her voice quickened. "But I try to make it up with the teas."

She paused, trying to read from his face if she should say any more. She seemed to be standing on the edge of another country. The pale-blue eyes seemed to be the pale sky of a faraway place where she had been living.

"I nearly died," she said. She was a little amazed by this fact.

"You're O.K. now," Sid said.

"I'm better," she said. "But it seems I get lonely now I'm better."

"You want your health, but you want a bit of company," Sid said.

"My husband says, 'You got your health, what you want company for?' "

She put this to Sid in case her husband was not right, but she picked up her husband's waistcoat from the chair and looked over its buttons because she felt, timorously, she had been disloyal to her husband.

"A woman wants company," said Sid.

He looked shy now to her, like Bert, the young one; but she was most astonished that someone should agree with her and not her husband.

Then she flushed and put out her hand to the little girl, who came to her mother's side, pressing against her. The woman felt safer and raised her eyes and looked more boldly at him.

"You and your friends going far?"

He told her. She nodded, counting the miles as if she were coming along with them. And then Sid felt a hand touch his.

It was the child's hand touching the ring on his finger.

"Ha!" laughed Sid. "You saw that before." He was quick. The child was delighted with his quickness. The woman put the waistcoat down at once. He took off the ring and put it in the palm of his hand and bent down so that his head nearly brushed the woman's arm. "That's lucky," he said. "Here," he said. He slipped the ring on the child's little finger. "See," he said. "Keeps me out of mischief. Keep a ring on your little finger and you'll be lucky."

The child looked at him without belief.

"Here y'are," he said, taking back the ring. "Your mother wants it," he said, winking at the woman. "She's got hers on the wrong finger. Little one luck, big one trouble."

She laughed and she blushed and her eyes shone. He moved to the door and her pale lips pouted a little. Then taking the child by the hand, she hurried over to him as if both of them would cling to him. Excitedly, avidly, they followed him to the other room.

"Come on, Mr. Blake," said Ted. The three others rose to their feet.

The child clung to her mother's hand and danced up and down. She was in the midst of them. They zipped up their jackets, stubbed their cigarettes, folded up the map. Harry put on his gauntlets. He stared at the child and then slowly took off his glove and pulled out a sixpence. "No," murmured Ted, the married man, but the child was too quick.

They went out of the room and stood in the road. They stretched themselves in the open air. The sun was shining now on the fields. The woman came to the door to see them. They took their bicycles from the wall, looked up and down the road, and then swung on. To the sea, the coast road, and then perhaps a girl, some girl. But the others were shouting.

"Good-bye," they called. "Good-bye."

And Bert, the last, remembered then to wave good-bye too, and glanced up at the misleading notice. When they were all together, heads down to the wind, they turned again. "Good God," they said. The woman and the child had come out into the middle of the road hand in hand and their arms were still raised and their hands were fluttering under the strong light of that high place. It was a long time before they went back into the house.

And now for a pub, a real pub, the three men called to Harry. Sid was ahead on his slim pink tyres getting the first of the new wind, with the ring shining on his finger.

Things as They Are

Two middle-class women were talking at half past eleven in the morning in the empty bar of a suburban public house in a decaying district. It was a thundery and smoky morning in the summer and the traffic fumes did not rise from the street.

"Please, Frederick," said Mrs. Forster, a *rentier* who spoke in a small, scented Edwardian voice. "Two more large gins. What were you saying, Margaret?"

"The heat last night, Jill. I tossed and I turned. I couldn't sleep—and when I can't sleep I scratch," said Margaret in her wronged voice. She was a barmaid and this was her day off.

Mrs. Forster drank and nodded.

"I think," said Margaret, "I mean I don't mean anything rude, but I had a flea."

Mrs. Forster put her grey head a little on one side and nodded again graciously under a flowered hat, like royalty.

"A flea, dear?" she said fondly.

Margaret's square mouth buckled after her next drink and her eyes seemed to be clambering frantically, like a pair of blatant prisoners behind her heavy glasses. Envy, wrong, accusation, were her life. Her black hair looked as though it had once belonged to an employer.

"I mean," she began to shout against her will, and Frederick, the elderly barman, moved away from her. "I mean I wouldn't have mentioned it if you hadn't mentioned it."

Mrs. Forster raised her beautiful arms doubtfully and touched her grey hair at the back and she smiled again.

"I mean when you mentioned when you had one yesterday you said," said Margaret.

"Oh," said Mrs. Forster, too polite to differ.

"Yes, dear, don't you remember, we were in here—I mean, Frederick! Were we in here yesterday morning, Frederick, Mrs. Forster and me . . ."

Frederick stood upright, handsome, old, and stupid.

"He's deaf, the fool, that's why he left the stage," Margaret said, glaring at him, knowing that he heard. "Jill, yesterday? Try and remember. You came in for a Guinness. I was having a small port, I mean, or were you on gin?"

"Oh, gin," said Mrs. Forster in her shocked, soft, distinguished way, recognizing a word.

"That was it, then," said Margaret, shaking an iron chin up and down four times. "It might have hopped."

"Hopped," nodded Mrs. Forster pleasantly.

"I mean, fleas hop, I don't mean anything vulgar." Margaret spread her hard, long bare arms and knocked her glass. "Distances," she said. "From one place to another place. A flea travels. From here, at this end of the bar, I don't say to the end, but along or across, I mean it could."

"Yes," said Mrs. Forster with agreeable interest.

"Or from a person. I mean, a flea might jump on you—or on me, it might jump from someone else, and then off that person, it depends if they are with someone. It might come off a bus or a tram." Margaret's long arms described these movements and then she brought them back to her lap. "It was a large one," she said. "A brute."

"Oh, large?" said Mrs. Forster sympathetically.

"Not large—I mean it must have been large, I could tell by the bites, I know a small flea, I mean we all do—don't mind my mentioning it—I had big bites all up my leg," said Margaret, stretching out a long, strong leg. Seeing no bites there, she pulled her tight serge skirt up with annoyance over her knee and up her thigh until, halted by the sight of her suspender, she looked angrily at Frederick and furtively at Mrs. Forster and pulled her skirt down and held it down.

"Big as pennies, horrible pink lumps, red, Jill," argued Margaret. "I couldn't sleep. Scratching doesn't make it any better. It wasn't a London flea, that I know, Jill. I know a London flea, I mean you know a London flea, an ordinary one, small beastly things, I hate them, but this must have been some great black foreign brute. Indian! Frederick! You've seen one of those things?"

Frederick went with a small business of finger-flicking to the curtains at the back of the bar, peeped through as if for his cue. All bars were empty.

"Never," he said contemptuously when he came back, and turning his back on the ladies, hummed at the shelves of bottles.

"It's easy," Margaret began to shout once more, swallowing her gin, shouting at her legs, which kept slipping off the rail of the stool and enraged her by jerking her body, "I mean, for them to travel. They get on ships. I mean those ships have been in the tropics, I don't say India necessarily, it might be in Egypt or Jamaica, a flea could hop off a native onto some sailor in the docks."

"You mean, dear, it came up from the docks by bus," said Mrs. Forster. "You caught it on a bus?"

"No, Jill," said Margaret. "I mean some sailor brought it up."

"Sailor," murmured Mrs. Forster, going pale.

"Ted," said Margaret, accusing. "From Calcutta. Ted could have brought it off his ship."

Mrs. Forster's head became fixed and still. She gazed mistily at Margaret and swayed. She finished her drink and steadied herself by looking into the bottom of the glass and waited for two more drops to come. Then she raised her small chin and trembled. She held a cigarette at the end of her thumb and her finger as if it were a stick of crayon and she were writing a message in blue smoke on the air. Her eyes closed sleepily, her lips sucked, pouted, and two tears rolled down her cheeks. She opened her large handbag and from the mess of letters, bills, money, keys, purses, and powder inside she took a small handkerchief and dabbed her eyes.

"Ah!" said Margaret, trying to get her arm to Mrs. Forster, but failing to reach her because her foot slipped on the rail again, so that she kicked herself. "Ah, Jill! I only mentioned it, I didn't mean anything, I mean when you said you had one, I said to myself: 'That's it, it's an Indian. Ted's brought it out of the ship's hold.' I didn't mean to bring up Ted, Jill. There's nothing funny about it, sailors do."

Mrs. Forster's cheeks and neck fattened amorously as she mewed and quietly cried and held her handkerchief tight.

"Here," said Margaret, mastering her. "Chin—chin, Jill, drink up, it will do you good. Don't cry. Here, you've finished it. Frederick, two more," she said, sliding towards Mrs. Forster and resting one breast on the bar.

Mrs. Forster straightened herself with dignity and stopped crying.

"He broke my heart," said Mrs. Forster, panting. "I always found one in the bed after his leave was over."

"He couldn't help it," said Margaret.

"Oh, no," said Mrs. Forster.

"It's the life sailors live," said Margaret. "And don't you forget, are you listening, Jill? Listen to me. Look at me and listen. You're among friends, Jill. He's gone, Jill, like you might say, out of your life."

"Yes," said Mrs. Forster, nodding again, repeating a lesson. "Out of my life."

"And good riddance, too, Jill."

"Riddance," murmured Mrs. Forster.

"Jill," shouted Margaret. "You've got a warm heart, that's what it is, as warm as Venus. I could never marry again after what I've been through, not whatever you paid me, not however much money it was you gave me, but you're not like me, your heart is too warm. You're too trusting."

"Trusting," Mrs. Forster repeated softly, squeezing her eyelids.

"I tell you what it was," Margaret said. "You were in love, Jill," said Margaret, greedy in the mouth. "Can you hear me?"

"Yes, dear."

"That's what I said. It was love. You loved him and you married him."

Margaret pulled herself up the bar and sat upright, looking with surprise at the breast that had rested there. She looked at her glass, she looked at Mrs. Forster's; she picked up the glass and put it down. "It was a beautiful dream, Jill, you had your beautiful dream and I say this from the bottom of my heart, I hope you will have a beautiful memory."

"Two months," sighed Mrs. Forster, and her eyes opened amorously in a grey glister and then sleepily half closed.

"But now, Jill, it's over. You've woke up, woken up. I mean, you're seeing things as they are."

The silence seemed to the two ladies to stand in a lump between them. Margaret looked into her empty glass again. Frederick lit a cigarette he had made, and his powdered face split up into twitches as he took the first draw and then put the cigarette economically on the counter. He went through his repertory of small coughs and then, raising his statesman-like head, he listened to the traffic passing and hummed.

Mrs. Forster let her expensive fur slip back from her fine shoulders and looked at the rings on her small hands.

"I loved him, Margaret," she said. "I really did love him."

"We know you loved him. I mean, it was love," said Margaret. "It's nothing to do with the age you are. Life's never over. It was love. You're a terrible woman, Jill."

"Oh, Margaret," said Mrs. Forster with a discreet glee, "I know I am."

"He was your fourth," said Margaret.

"Don't, Margaret," giggled Mrs. Forster.

"No, no, I'm not criticizing. I never criticize. Live and let live. It wasn't a fancy, Jill, you loved him with all your heart."

Jill raised her chin in a lady-like way.

"But I won't be hit," she whispered. "At my age I allow no one to strike me. I am fifty-seven, Margaret, I'm not a girl."

"That's what we all said," said Margaret. "You were headstrong."

"Oh, Margaret!" said Mrs. Forster, delighted.

"Oh, yes, yes, you wouldn't listen, not you. You wouldn't listen to me. I brought him up to the Chequers, or was it the Westmoreland? —no, it was the George—and I thought to myself, I know your type, young man—you see, Jill, I've had experience—out for what he could get—well, honest, didn't I tell you?"

"His face was very brown."

"Brown! Would you believe me? No, you wouldn't. I can see him. He came up here the night of the dance. He took his coat off. Well, we all sweat."

"But," sighed Mrs. Forster, "he had white arms."

"Couldn't keep his hands to himself. Put it away, pack it up, I said. He didn't care. He was after Mrs. Klebs and she went potty on him till Mrs. Sinclair came and then that Mr. Baum interfered. That sort lives for trouble. All of them mad on him—I bet Frederick could tell a tale, but he won't. Trust Frederick," she said with a look of hate at the barman, "upstairs in the billiard room, I shan't forget it. Torpedoed twice, he said. I mean Ted said: he torpedoed one or two. What happened to him that night?"

"Someone made him comfortable, I am sure," said Mrs. Forster, always anxious about lonely strangers.

"And you were quite rude with me, Jill, I don't mean rude, you couldn't be rude, it isn't in you, but we almost came to words. . . ."

"What did you say, Margaret?" said Mrs. Forster from a dream.

"I said at your age, fifty-seven, I said you can't marry a boy of twenty-six."

Mrs. Forster sighed.

"Frederick. Freddy, dear. Two more," said Mrs. Forster.

Margaret took her glass, and while she was finishing it Frederick held his hand out for it, insultingly rubbing his fingers.

"Hah!" said Margaret, blowing out her breath as the gin burned her. "You bowled over him, I mean you bowled him over, a boy of twenty-six. Sailors are scamps."

"Not," said Mrs. Forster, reaching to trim the back of her hair again and tipping her flowered hat forward on her forehead and austerely letting it remain like that. "Not," she said, getting stuck at the word.

"Not what?" said Margaret. "Not a scamp? I say he was. I said at the time, I still say it, a rotten little scamp."

"Not," said Mrs. Forster.

"A scamp," said Margaret.

"Not. Not with a belt," said Mrs. Forster. "I will not be hit with a belt.

"My husband," began Margaret.

"I will not, Margaret," said Mrs. Forster. "Never. Never. Never with a belt.

"Not hit, struck," Mrs. Forster said, defying Margaret.

"It was a plot, you could see it a mile off, it would make you laugh, a lousy, rotten plot," Margaret let fly, swallowing her drink. "He was after your house and your money. If he wasn't, what did he want to get his mother in for, a big three-storey house like yours, in a fine residential position? Just what he'd like, a little rat like that. . . ."

Mrs. Forster began a long laugh to herself.

"My grandfather," she giggled.

"What?" said Margaret.

"Owns the house. Not owns. Owned, I say, the house," said Mrs. Forster, tapping the bar.

"Frederick," said Mrs. Forster. "Did my grandfather own the house?"

"Uh?" said Frederick, giving his cuff links a shake. "Which house?"

"My house over there," said Mrs. Forster, pointing to the door.

"I know he owned the house, dear," Margaret said. "Frederick knows."

"Let me ask Frederick," said Mrs. Forster. "Frederick, you knew my grandfather."

"Uh?" said Frederick, leaning to listen.

"He's as deaf as a wall," Margaret said.

Frederick walked away to the curtain at the back of the bar and peeped through it. Nervously he came back, glancing at his handsome face in the mirror; he chose an expression of stupidity and disdain, but he spoke with a quiet rage.

"I remember this street," he raged, "when you could hardly get across it for the carriages and the footmen and the maids in their lace caps and aprons. You never saw a lady in a place like this."

He turned his back on them and walked again secretively to the curtain, peeped again, and came back stiffly on feet skewed sideways by the gravity of the gout and put the tips of his old, well-manicured fingers on the bar for them to admire.

"Now," he said, giving a socially shocked glance over the windows that were still half boarded after the bombing, "all tenements, flats, rooms, walls falling down, balconies dropping off, bombed out, and rotting," he said. He sneered at Margaret. "Not the same people. Slums. Riff-raff now. Mrs. Forster's father was the last of the old school."

"My grandfather," said Mrs. Forster.

"He was a gentleman," said Frederick.

Frederick walked to the curtains.

"Horrible," he muttered loudly, timing his exit.

There was a silence until he came back. The two women looked at the enormous empty public house, with its high cracked and dirty ceilings, its dusty walls unpainted for twenty years. Its top floor had been on fire. Its windows had gone, three or four times.

Frederick mopped up scornfully between the glasses of gin on the counter.

"That's what I mean," said Margaret, her tongue swelling up, her mouth side-slipping. "If you'd given the key to his mother, where would you have been? They'd have shut you out of your own house and what's the good of the police? All the scum have come to the top since the war. You were too innocent and we saved you. Jill, well, I mean if we hadn't all got together, the whole crowd, where were you? He was going to get into the house and then one night when you'd been over at the George or the Chequers or over here and you'd had one or two . . ."

Jill looked proudly and fondly at her glass, crinkled her childish eyes.

"Oh," said Jill in a little naughty-faced protest.

"I mean, I don't mean plastered," said Margaret, bewildered by the sound of her own voice and moving out her hand to bring it back.

"Not stinking, Jill, excuse me. I mean we sometimes have two or three. Don't we?" Margaret appealed to the barman.

"Uh?" said Frederick coldly. "Where was this?"

"Oh, don't be stupid," said Margaret, turning round suddenly and knocking her glass over, which Frederick picked up and took away. "What was I saying, Jill?"

A beautiful still smile, like a butterfly opening on an old flower, came onto Mrs. Forster's face.

"Margaret," she confided, "I don't know."

"I know," said Margaret, waving her heavy bare arm. "You'd have been signing papers. He'd have stripped you. He might have murdered you like that case last Sunday in the papers. A well-to-do woman like you. The common little rat. Bringing his fleas."

"He—was—not—common," said Mrs. Forster, sitting upright suddenly, and her hat fell over her nose, giving her an appearance of dashing distinction.

"He was off a ship," said Margaret.

"He was an officer."

"He *said* he was an officer," said Margaret, struggling with her corsets.

Mrs. Forster got down from her stool and held with one hand to the bar. She laughed quietly.

"He—" she began.

"What?" said Margaret.

"I shan't tell you," said Mrs. Forster. "Come here."

Margaret leaned towards her.

"No, come here, stand here," said Mrs. Forster.

Margaret stood up, also holding to the bar, and Mrs. Forster put her hands to Margaret's neck and pulled her head down and began to laugh in Margaret's ear. She was whispering.

"What?" shouted Margaret. "I can't hear. What is it?"

Mrs. Forster laughed with a roar in Margaret's ear.

"He—he—was a man, Margaret," she whispered. She pushed her away.

"You know what I mean, Margaret," she said in a stern clear voice. "You do, don't you? Come here again, I'll tell you."

"I heard you."

"No, come here again, closer. I'll tell you. Where are you?"

Mrs. Forster whispered again and then drew back.

"A man," she said boldly.

"And you're a woman, Jill."

"A man!" said Mrs. Forster. "Everything, Margaret. You know—everything. But not with a belt. I won't be struck." Mrs. Forster reached for her glass.

"*Vive la France!*" she said, holding up her glass, drank, and banged it down. "Well, I threw him out."

A lament broke from Margaret. She had suddenly remembered one of *her* husbands. She had had two.

"He went off to his work and I was waiting for him at six. He didn't come back. I'd no money in the house, that was seventeen years ago, and Joyce was two, and he never even wrote. I went through his pockets and gave his coats a shake, wedding rings poured out of them. What do you get for it? Your own daughter won't speak to you, ashamed to bring her friends to the house. 'You're always drunk,' she says. To her own mother. Drunk!" said Margaret. "I might have one or perhaps two. What does a girl like that know!"

With a soft, quick crumpling, a soft thump and a long sigh, Mrs. Forster went to the floor and full-length lay there with a beautiful smile on her face, and a fierce noise of pleasure came from her white face. Her hat rolled off, her bag fell down, open, and spilling with a loud noise.

"Eh," said Frederick, coming round from behind the counter.

"Passed out again. Get her up, get her up quick," said Margaret. "Her bag, her money.

"Lift her on the side," she said. "I will take her legs."

They carried Mrs. Forster to the broken leather settee and laid her down there. "Here's her bag," Margaret wrangled. "It's all there."

"And the one in your hand," said Frederick, looking at the pound note in Margaret's hand.

And then the crowd came in: Mrs. Klebs, Mrs. Sinclair, Mr. Baum, the one they called Pudding, who had fallen down the area at Christmas, and a lot more.

"What's this?" they said. "Not again? Frederick, what's this?"

"They came in here," Frederick said in a temper. "Ladies, talking about love."

Handsome Is
as Handsome Does

In the morning the Corams used to leave the pension, which was like a white box with a terracotta lid among its vines on the hill above the town, and walk through the dust and lavish shade to the beach. They were a couple in their forties.

He had never been out of England before, but she had spent half her youth in foreign countries. She used to wear shabby saffron beach pyjamas with a navy-blue top that the sun had faded. She was a short, thin woman, ugly yet attractive. Her hair was going grey, her face was clay-coloured, her nose was big and long, and she had long, yellowish eyes. In this beach suit she looked rat-like, with that peculiar busyness, inquisitiveness, intelligence, and even charm of rats. People always came and spoke to her and were amused by her conversation. They were startled by her ugly face and her shabbiness, but they liked her lazy voice, her quick mind, her graceful good manners, the look of experience and good sense in her eyes.

He was a year older. On the hottest days, when she lay bare-backed and drunk with sunlight, dozing or reading a book, he sat awkwardly beside her in a thick tweed jacket and a white hat pulled down over his eyes. He was a thick-set, ugly man; they were an ugly pair. Surly, blunt-speaking, big-boned, with stiff short fair hair that seemed to be struggling and alight in the sun, he sat frowning and glaring almost wistfully and tediously from his round blue eyes. He had big hands like a labourer's. When people came to speak to her, he first of all edged away. His instinct was to avoid all people. He wanted to sit there silently with her, alone. But if the people persisted, then he was rude to them, rude, uncouth, and quarrelsome. Then she had to smooth away his rudeness and distract attention from it. But he would ignore the person to whom she was talking and, looking down at her, would say: "What are you getting at me for, Julia?" There was a note of angry self-pity in his voice. She liked a man of spirit.

This started quarrels. They were always quarrelling. They quarrelled about their car, their food, where they would sit, whether on the beach or at cafés, whether they would read upstairs or downstairs. He did not really know he was quarrelling. The trouble was that everything seemed difficult to him. He had thoughts but he could not get them out. They were tied up in knots like snakes, squeezing and suffocating him. Whenever he made a suggestion or offered an opinion, his short brow became contorted with thick frowns, like a bull's forehead, and he coloured. He lowered his forehead, not as if he were going to charge with fury, but as if he were faced with the job of pushing some impossible rock uphill. He was helpless.

She would see this and, cunningly, tactfully, she would make things easy for him. They had no children and, because of the guilt she felt about this and because of the difficulties he saw everywhere, they had become completely dependent on each other.

First of all, they were alone at the pension. There were themselves and M. Pierre. He was the proprietor. At mealtimes they all sat together. M. Pierre was a plump grey man of sixty, with a pathetic, mean little mouth, a monocle in his eye. He was a short and vain little dandy and was given to boastfulness. The town was a gay place in the summer, like a pink flower opening by the peacock sea, and M. Pierre was the butterfly that flutters about it. He had the hips of a woman. He was full of learned little proverbs and precise little habits. Certain hours he would devote to lying on a couch and reading detective stories in a darkened room. At another time he would sit in his dining-room with a patent cigarette-making machine, winding the handle, meddling with the mechanism, turning out the cigarettes. He gave a lick to each one as it came out. "So he won't have to offer you one," Coram said.

In the afternoon M. Pierre made a great fuss. Appearing in yellow vest and red trousers, he took out a new bicycle done in grey enamel and glittering with plated bars, gears, brakes, acetylene lamps, and elaborate looped wires. He mounted by a tree and, talking excitedly as if he were about to depart on some dangerous journey to the Alps or the Himalayas, he would whiz giddily down to the beach with his towel and striped gown on the carrier.

"You are going to bathe this afternoon?" M. Pierre asked. "I am going." It was a question he put to the Englishman regularly at lunchtime. M. Pierre would boast of his love of the sea.

Coram frowned and coloured and a veil of wetness, as if tears were being generated by the struggle within, came to his eyes.

"What's he say?" he asked his wife at last, for he understood French poorly.

"He wants to know whether we are going to bathe with him."

"Him!" said Coram in a surly voice. "Him bathe! He can't swim. He can't swim a yard. He just goes down to look at the women."

"Please, Tom!" she said in a sharp lowered voice. "You mustn't say that in front of him. He understands more than you think."

M. Pierre sat at the head of the table, grey hair parted in the middle, monocle on expressionless face.

"He's a fraud," Coram said in his blunt grumbling voice. "If he understands English, why does he pretend he don't?"

"Parlez français, Monsieur Coram," came the neat, spinsterly correcting voice of the Frenchman.

"Oui," said the wife very quickly, smiling the long, enchanting smile that transformed her ugly face. "Il *faut.*"

M. Pierre smiled at her and she smiled at him. He liked her bad accent. And she liked him very much, but for her husband's sake she had to pretend to dislike him. Her life was full of pretences, small lies, and exaggerations which she contrived for her husband's sake.

But Coram disliked the Frenchman from the beginning. When M. Pierre saw the Corams had a car, he persuaded them to take him about the country; he would show them its beauties. Sitting like a little duke in the car, he pointed out the torrid towns raked together like heaps of earthenware in the mountain valleys, the pale stairways of olives going up hills where no grass grew and the valleys filled with vines. Driving in the fixed, unchanging sunlight, M. Pierre directed them to sudden sights of the sea in new bays more extravagant in colour. Coram frowned. It was all right for his wife. She had been to such places before. Her family had always been to such places. This was the thing that always awed him when he thought about her; pleasure had been natural to her family for generations. But for him it was unnatural. All this was too beautiful. He had never seen anything like it. He could not speak. At noon when the mountains of the coast seemed to lie head down to the sea like savage, panting, and silver animals, or in the evening when the flanks and summits were cut by sharp purple shadows and the sea became like some murmuring lake of milky opal, he felt the place had made a wound in him. He felt in his heart the suspended anger of a man torn between happiness and pain. After his life in the villas and chemical factories of the Midlands, where the air was like an escape of gas and the country brick-bruised and infected, he could not believe in this beautiful country. Incredulous, he mistrusted.

"Garsong!" (There was a café near the harbour where the Corams used to sit for an hour before dinner.) "Garsong—encore—drinks!" That was the only way he could melt his mistrust.

Coram could not explain why. He was thwarted like his country. All he could do was frown and take it out of M. Pierre.

"He's a mean squirt," Coram said.

"He's a liar," he said.

"Look at him making those cigarettes."

"We've known him a week and what's he do but cadge drinks and rides in the car. He's a fraud."

His wife listened. Her husband was a man without subtlety or wit, quite defenceless before unusual experience. He was a child. Every day she was soothing this smouldering aching struggle that was going on inside him.

After they had been there a week a newcomer arrived at the pension. He arrived one morning by the early train, walking down from the station with his new light suitcase. He was a young man in his twenties, tall, dark, aquiline, a Jew.

"We will call you Monsieur Alex," said M. Pierre with his French love of arranging things.

"That is charming," said the Jew.

He spoke excellent English, a little too perfect, a little too round in the vowels, and excellent French, almost too pure. He talked easily. He had heard, he said, that there were some excellent pictures in the churches of the mountain towns.

"Rather sweet, isn't he?" said Mrs. Coram. The Jew was grave and handsome. Coram was admiring too, but he was more cautious.

"Yeah. He looks all right," he said.

His mother was French, the young Jew told them on the first evening, his father German. But they had both come from Austria originally. He had cousins in every country in Europe. He had been edu-

cated in England. Slender, with long hands, a little coarse in complex-
ion in the Jewish way, he had grey and acute sepia eyes. He was so
boyish, so free in his talk about himself, so shy and eager in his laugh
—and yet—how could Mrs. Coram describe it?—he seemed ancient,
like some fine statue centuries old that has worn and ripened in the sun.
He was thick-lipped and had a slight lisping hesitance of speech and
this sense of the ancient and profound came perhaps from his habit of
pausing before he spoke as if judiciously cogitating. Mrs. Coram would
sit there expectant and curious. She was used to the hesitations, the
struggles with thought of her husband; but there was this difference:
when the Jew spoke at last, what he said was serious, considered, a
charming decoration of commentary upon their discussions.

M. Pierre always longed for fresh worlds to patronize; he was delighted with Alex. Too delighted for Coram and even for his wife. She
could not help being on the point of jealousy when Alex sat and talked
to the Frenchman. Coram bluntly wanted to rescue the young man
from "the fraud."

"You know what's wrong . . . with this place," Coram said to Alex.
"There's no industry."

"Oh, but surely agriculture, the wine," said Alex.

"Yeah, I know," said Coram. "I mean real industry. . . ."

"My husband's a chemist, industrial chemist," she explained.

"I mean," said Coram, grinding on and frowning quizzically, "they
just sit round and grow wine and batten on the visitors, like this fellow.
What a town like this wants is a couple of good whore shops and a
factory. . . ."

"Tom!" said Mrs. Coram. "How exotic you've become!"

"I expect ample provision has been made," said the Jew.

"No," said Coram, in his halting, muddling, bullying tone, "but you
see what I mean."

He screwed up his eyes. He wished to convey that he had not quite
found the words for what he had meant really to say.

The odd thing about the young Jew was that although he seemed
to be rich and was cultivated, he had no friends in the town. The young
always arrived in troops and carloads at this place. The elderly were
often in ones and twos, but the young—never. Mrs. Coram detected
a curious loneliness in him. Polite and formal, he sometimes seemed
not to be there. Why had he come? Why to this pension? It was a
cheap place and he obviously had money. Why alone? There were no
relations, no women. When he went out he saw no one, spoke to no

one. Why not? Alone he visited the mountain churches. He was equable, smiling, interested, happy—yet alone. He liked to be alone, it seemed, and yet when they spoke to him, when Coram—urged by her —asked him to come down to the beach or drive in the car, he came without hesitation, with the continuous effortless good manners and curious lack of intimacy that he always had. It baffled her. She wanted to protect and mother him.

"The Jewboy," Coram called him. His wife hated this. They quarrelled.

"Stop using that stupid expression," she said.

"He is," said her husband. "I've nothing against him. He's clever. But he's a Jewboy. That's all." He was not against the Jewboy. He even liked him. They talked together. Coram almost felt protective to him too.

"Aren't you being rather vulgar?" she said to her husband.

One effect the Jew had on them was to make them stop having this kind of quarrel in public. Coram did not change. He was as uncouth as ever. But his wife restrained herself. In mortification she heard his crude stumbling words and quickly interrupted them, smoothed them away hastily so that Alex should not notice them. Either she was brushing her husband away out of hearing, first of all, or she was working with every nerve to transform her husband in the young man's eyes. At the end of the day she was exhausted.

One evening when they went up to bed in the hot room at the top of the house, she said to her husband: "How old is he, Tom? Twenty-two?"

Coram stared at her. He did not know.

"Do you realize," she said, "we're nearly old enough to be his parents?" She had no children. She thought about him as her son.

She took off her clothes. The room was hot. She lay on the bed. Coram, slow and methodical, was taking off his shoes. He went to the window and emptied out the sand. He did not answer. He was working out how old he would have been if the young man had been his son. Before he found an answer, she spoke again.

"One forgets he must think we're old," she said. "Do you think he does? Do you think he realizes how much older we are? When I look at him it seems a century, and then other times we might all be the same age. . . ."

"Jews look older than they are," said Coram.

Her questioning voice stopped. Tom was hanging up his jacket.

Every time he took off a garment he walked heavily across the room. Her questions went on silently in her mind. Twenty-two? And she was forty. What did he think of her? What did he think of her husband? Did her husband seem crude and vulgar? Did he seem slow-minded? What did the young man think of both of them? Did he notice things? Did he notice their quarrels? And why did he like to spend time with them, talk to them, go about with them? What was he thinking, what was he feeling? Why was he so friendly and yet, ultimately, so unapproachable?

She lay on her side with her slight knees bent. Out of her shabby clothes her body was thin but graceful. Her shoulders were slender, but there were lines on her neck, a reddish stain spreading over her breastbone, a stain hard with exposure to years. Her small breasts were loose and slack over the ribs. The skin creasing under them was sallow. She ran her hands over her hips. She moved her hands round and round on her small flat belly, caressing herself where she knew her body was beautiful. It seemed only a few days ago that this had been the body of a young girl. She was filled with sadness for her husband and herself. She could hear the beating of her heart. She found herself listening for the steps of the young man on the stairs. Her heart beat louder. To silence it she said in an anxious voice to her husband, lowering her knees:

"Tom—you haven't stopped wanting me." She knew her voice was false.

He was taking off his shirt.

"What do you want?" he said.

His face looked grotesque as it looked out of the shirt top.

"Nothing," she said.

Tom took off his shirt and looked out of the window. You could see the white farms of the valley with their heavy walls from the window. The peasants kept their dogs chained, and when there was a moon they barked, a dozen or more of them, one after the other, all down the valley.

"If those dogs—start tonight—we won't sleep," he said. He came to the bed and waited for her to get under the sheet. She felt his big-boned body beside her and smelt his sharp, curious smell.

"God," he said. He felt stupefied in this place. In five minutes he was asleep. But she lay awake. Forty, she was thinking. A woman of forty with a son. No son. She heard, as she lay awake, the deep breathing of her husband, the curious whistlings of his breath. She lay think-

ing about her life, puzzling, wondering. Why had she no son? She
dozed. She awakened. She threw back the sheet and sleeplessly sighed.
If she slept, it was only in snatches and she woke up with her heart
beating violently and to find herself listening for the sound of a step
on the stairs. There was a sensation of inordinate hunger and breath-
lessness in her body.

Sometimes the young Jew waited for them in the morning and went
down with them to the beach. He carried her basket for her or her
book. He went back for things.

"Tom," she said in front of her husband, "has no manners."

She walked between them and talked excitedly to the young man
about characters in books, or foreign towns, or pictures. She laughed
and Coram smiled. He listened with wonder to them.

They sat on the beach. Under his clothes the Jew wore a black
bathing suit. He undressed at once and went into the water. His body
was alien and slender, the skin burned to the colour of dark corn. He
dived in and swam far out into the blue water, beyond the other
bathers. He did not laugh or wave or call back, but in his distant,
impersonal way he swam far out with long, easy strokes. After a mile
he lay floating in the sun. He seemed to pass the whole morning out
there. She could see his black head. To be young like that and lie in
the sea in the sun! And yet how boring to lie there for so long! She
would have sudden pangs of anxiety. She would talk of the cold current
that came out in the deeper water, from the harbour. She was always
glad and relieved when she saw his head moving towards the shore.
When he came out of the water he seemed to be dry at once, as if some
oil were in his skin. She would see only beads of water at the back of
his neck on the short black hair.

"You can swim!" she said.

He smiled.

"Not much," he said. "Why don't you?"

The question pleased her. She was astonished by the pleasure it gave
her.

"I'm not allowed," she said with animation. "Tell me what were you
doing out there. You were such a long time."

His dark eyes were large and candid as he turned to her and she
caught her breath. There were three or four black freckles on his skin.
Her older yellow eyes returned his innocent gaze. Good heavens, she

thought. With eyes like that he ought to be a girl. But she did not know and did not feel that her eyes were older than his.

"I was nearly asleep," he said. "The sea is like a mattress."

He and Coram had a scientific discussion about the possibility of sleeping on the sea.

It was absurd of her, she knew, but she was disappointed. Had he not thought of them, of her? She had been thinking of him all the time.

Coram sat beside them. He talked about the business scandals and frauds in the chemical trade. The quick-minded Jew understood all these stories long before Coram got to their elaborate end. Coram had an obsession with fraud. His slow mind was angry about that kind of quickness of mind which made fraud possible. Coram sat inert, uncomprehending, quite outside the gaiety on the beach. He was not gloomy or morose. He was not sulking. His blue eyes glistened and he had the wistful face of a dog trying to understand. He sat struggling to find words which would convey all that he had felt in this fortnight. He considered the sea and the young man for a long time. Then he undressed. Out of his dark-red bathing suit his legs were white and were covered with thick golden hairs. His neck was pink where the sun had caught it. He walked down awkwardly over the pebbles, scowling because of the force of the sun, and straddled knee-deep into the water. Then he flung himself on it helplessly, almost angrily, and began clawing at it. He seemed to swim with clenched fists. They could see him clawing and crawling as the slow blue swell lifted him up. For a hundred yards he would swim not in a straight line but make a half circle from the beach, as if he were incapable of swimming straight or of knowing where he was going. When he waded out with the water dripping from him there was a look of grievance on his face.

"That water's dirty," he said when he got back. The Mediterranean was a fraud: it was too warm, thick as syrup. He sat dripping on his wife's books.

One morning when he came back and was drying himself, rubbing his head with the towel, he caught sight of M. Pierre. The Frenchman was sitting not many yards away. Shortsighted, no doubt M. Pierre had not seen them. Beside him were his towels, his red slippers, his red swimming helmet, his cigarette case, his striped bathing gown, and his jar of coconut oil. He was in his bathing suit. More than ever, but for his short grey hair, he looked like a potbellied middle-aged woman as he rubbed coconut oil on his short brown arms. His monocle was in his eye. He looked like a lesbian in his monocle.

Coram scowled.

"You see," he blurted in a loud voice. "He hasn't been in. He won't go in either. He just comes—down here—all dolled up—to look at the women."

"Not so loud," his wife said. "Please." She looked with anxiety at the Jew. "Poor Monsieur Pierre," said Mrs. Coram. "Remember his age. He's sixty. Perhaps he doesn't want to go in. I bet you won't be swimming when you're sixty."

"He can swim very well," said the young Jew politely. "I went out with him a couple of days ago from the other beach." He pointed over the small headland. "He swam out to the ship in the bay. That is three miles."

"There, Tom!" cried his wife.

She was getting bored with these attacks on M. Pierre.

"He's a fraud, a rotten fraud," said Tom in his smouldering, struggling voice.

"But Alex was with him!" she said.

"I don't care who was with him," said Tom. "He's a fraud. You wait till you know him better," said Tom bluntly to the Jew. "Believe me, he's a rotten little blackmailer."

"Ssh. You don't know that. You mustn't repeat things," she said.

"Well, you know it as well as I do," Tom said.

"Quiet, Tom, please," his wife said. "He's sitting there."

"He blackmails his brother-in-law," Tom persisted. He was addressing himself to the Jew.

"Well, what of it?"

She was angry. M. Pierre could easily hear. And she was angry, trembling with anger, because she did not want the young man to see the uncouthness of her husband and her mortification at it.

"Pierre's sister married a motor millionaire. That's where Pierre gets his money. He waits till his brother-in-law has a new woman and then goes to his sister and pitches the tale to her. She goes to her husband, makes a jealous scene, and, to keep her quiet, he gives her what she wants for Pierre."

"You don't know that," she said.

"I know it as well as you do," he said. "Everyone in the town knows it. He's a fraud."

"Well, don't *shout*. And use some other word. It's a bore," she said.

"I've no respect for a man who doesn't earn his living," Coram said. (Oh, God, she thought, now he's going to quarrel with this boy.)

The Jew raised an eyebrow.

"Doesn't he keep the pension?" the Jew enquired calmly.

"You mean his servants keep it," blustered Coram. "Have you ever seen him do a stroke?"

"Well," his wife said, "we can't all be like you, Tom. My family never earned a penny in their lives. They would have been horrified at the idea."

She was speaking not with irony but with indignation. At once she knew she had gone too far. She had failed for once to soothe, to smooth away.

"Ay! Didn't want the dirty work," Coram said, dropping into his Midland accent. He was not angry. He was, from his own stolid point of view, reasonable and even genial. He wondered why she was "getting at" him.

"Why, dearest," she said, knowing how irony hurt his vanity. "You've hit it. You've hit it in one. Bravo. They had no illusions about the nobility of work." She was ridiculing him.

"You don't believe in the nobility of work, do you?" she said to the Jew. "My husband's got a slave's mind," she said.

"Working is a habit, like sleeping and eating," said the Jew seriously in his lazy and too perfect enunciation. It had the well-oiled precision of a complexity of small pistons in an impersonal machine. She had heard him speak French and German with an equal excellence. It was predestined.

Living with her husband, always dealing with the inarticulate, she had injured her own full capacity to speak. The Jew stirred her tongue and her lips. She felt an impulse to put her lips to his, not in love, but to draw some of the magic of exposition from him. She wanted her head to be joined to his head in a kiss, her brow to be against his. And then his young face and his dark hair would take the lines from her face and would darken her greyness with the dark, fresh, gleaming stain of youth. She could never really believe that her hair was grey. Her lips were tingling and parted as, lost in this imagination, she gazed at him; innocent and cool-eyed, he returned her look. She did not lower her eyes. How young she had been! A shudder of weakness took her shoulders and pain spread like a burn from her throat and over her breasts into the pit of her stomach. She moistened her lips. She saw herself driving in the August sun on an English road twenty years ago, a blue tarred road that ran dazzling like steel into dense trees and then turned and vanished. That day with its climate and the resinous smells of the country always came back when she thought of being young. She was overwhelmed.

The sun had gone in and the sea was grey and sultry and, in this light, the water looked heavier and momentous, higher and deeper at the shore, like a swollen wall. The sight of the small lips of foam was like the sight of thirst, like the sudden inexplicable thirst she had for his lips.

Then she heard Tom's voice. It was explanatory. Sitting with people who were talking, he would sometimes slowly come to conclusions about a remark that had struck him earlier in the conversation. He would cling to this, work upon it, struggle with it. She often laughed affectionately at this lagging of his tortoise mind.

The frowns were deep in the thick pink skin of his forehead, the almost tearful glare was in his eyes.

"They didn't want the dirty work," he said. He was addressing the young man. "They have butlers. They have a grown man to answer doorbells and bring letters. Her family had. They corrupt people by making them slaves. . . ."

The Jew listened politely. Coram felt he hadn't said what he meant. The frown deepened as the clear eyes of the Jew looked at his troubled face.

"I was on a jury," Coram said. "We had to try a man—"

"Oh, Tom, not that story about the butler who stole elevenpence. Yes, Tom was on a jury and a man got six months for obtaining a meal, value elevenpence, from an A.B.C. or a Lyons or some place. . . ."

"Yes," said Coram eagerly, his glaring eyes begging the Jew to see his point.

He wanted to explain that a man corrupts by employing servants. No, not that. What Coram really meant in his heart was that he would not forgive his wife for coming from a rich family. And yet something more than that too, something not so ridiculous, but more painful. He was thinking of some fatal difference between his wife and himself and their fatal difference from society. He was thinking of the wound which this place by the beautiful sea had made in him. He struggled, gave it up.

But she looked scornfully at him. She wiped him out of her sight. She was angry with him for exposing his stupidity before the young Jew. She had fought against it in the last few days; she had been most clever in concealing it. But now she had failed. The thing was public.

She got up angrily from the beach.

"Pick up my book," she said to her husband. The Jew did not quite hide his astonishment. She saw him gaze and was angrier still with herself. Tactfully he let her husband pick up the book.

They walked back to the pension. All the way along the road she scarcely spoke to her husband. Once in their room, she pulled off her hat and went to the mirror. She saw him reflected in the glass, standing with a look of heavy resentment on his face, bewildered by her.

She saw her own face. The skin was swollen with anger and lined too. Her grey hair was untidy. She was shocked by her physical deterioration. She was ugly. When she heard the young man's step on the stairs she could have wept. She waited: he did not close his door. This was more than she could bear. She turned upon her husband. She raised her voice. She wanted the young man to hear her rage.

Why had she married such an oaf, such a boor! Her family had begged her not to marry him. She mocked him. He failed at everything. There he was stuck at forty, stuck in his career, stuck for life.

Sometimes he blurted out things in the quarrel, but most of the time he was speechless. He stood at the foot of the bed with his tweed coat in his hand, looking at her with heavy blue eyes, his face reddening under the insults, his tongue struggling to answer, his throat moving. He was not cold, but hot with goading. Yet he did nothing. The forces inside him were locked like wrestlers at each other's throats, muddled, powerless. As the quarrel exhausted itself she sank on to the bed. She was fascinated by his hulking incapacity. She had always been fascinated. From the very beginning.

He had not moved during all this, but when she lay down on the bed with her head in the pillow he went quietly to the clothes peg and hung up his coat. He stood there rolling up his sleeves. He was going to wash. But she heard him move. She suddenly could not bear that he move away, even those two steps, from her. She could not bear that he should say to himself: "One of Julia's scenes. Leave her alone. She'll get over it," and, taking his opportunity, slip away and go on as if nothing had happened.

She sat up on the edge of the bed. Tears were stinging her cheeks.

"Tom!" she called out. "What are we going to do? What are we going to do?"

He turned guiltily. She had made him turn.

"I want a child, Tom. What are we going to do? I must have a child."

Her tone made his blood run cold. There was something wild and horror-struck in her voice. It sounded like a piercing voice crying out in a cavern far away from any other living creature, outraged, animal, and incomprehensible.

God, he thought. Are we going over all that again? I thought we'd resigned ourselves to that.

He wanted to say: "You're forty. You can't have a child." But he could not say that to her. He suspected that she was acting. He said instead what she so often said to him; it seemed to be the burden of their isolated lives.

"Quiet," he said. "People will hear."

"All you ever think of!" she cried out. "People. Drift. Do nothing."

They went down the tiled stairs to the dining-room. The sun had come out again, but it was weak. A thin film of cloud was rising in the east. The shutters of the dining-room were always closed early in the morning, and by noon the house was cool and dark. Before his guests came down, M. Pierre used to go round the room with a fly-swatter. Then the wine was brought in a bucket of water and he put it down beside his chair and waited. A clock clucked like some drowsy hen on the wall, and the coloured plates, like crude carnival wheels, glowed in the darkened room on the black carved shelves of the cupboard. Mrs. Coram came into the room and she heard the dust blowing outside in the breeze and the leaves moving in the vines. A bolt tapped on the shutters.

Their faces were dark in the room, all the faces except Mrs. Coram's. Her face was white and heavily powdered. She had been afraid that when she saw Alex she would be unable to speak, but would choke and have to run from the table. To her surprise, when she saw him standing by his chair in the room, with his brown bare arm on the chair top, she was able to speak. So easily that she talked a great deal.

"Red wine or white? The wishes of women are the wishes of God," said M. Pierre to her, paying himself a compliment at the same time.

She began to mock the young man. He laughed. He enjoyed the mockery. "The wishes of women are the sorrows of Satan," he said satanically. She went on to mockery of M. Pierre. He was delighted. She repeated in her own way the things that her husband said about him.

"Monsieur Pierre is a fraud," she said. "He goes to the beach. He pretends he goes there to swim. Don't you believe it! He goes there to look at the girls. And Alex—he has got a motor inside him. He goes straight out and anchors. You think he's swimming. But he's only floating."

"I can swim ten miles," said M. Pierre. He took a small mouthful of wine and boasted in a neat, deprecating way. "I once swam half across the Channel."

"Did you?" said the young man with genuine interest.

And once M. Pierre had started to boast, he could not be stopped. She egged him on.

"Challenge him," said Coram morosely to the young man, chewing a piece of meat.

"I challenge him," said M. Pierre.

But not at the town beach, he said, at the one beyond. It was true he rarely swam at the town beach. He liked to be alone when he swam . . . solitude . . . freedom. . . .

"You bet he does," grunted Coram.

"And Monsieur Coram too," said M. Pierre.

"I have been in once," Coram said.

"So have they!" she exclaimed.

When they got up from the table, Coram took his wife aside. He saw through it all, he said to her; it was a device of M. Pierre's to get a drive in his car. She was astonished at this remark. Before today she would not have been astonished, she would have tried to smooth away the difficulties he saw and the suspicions. But now everything was changed. He was like a stranger to her. She saw it clearly; he was mean. Men of his class who had worked their way up from nothing were often mean. Such a rise in the world was admired. She had once admired it. Now it amused her and made her contemptuous. Mean! Why had she never thought of that before? She had been blind.

When lunch was over, it was their habit in the house to go to their rooms and sleep. She waited. First M. Pierre went into his room, with his yellow novel. The Jew and her husband lingered. "The best thing about this place is the drinks," he was saying. "They're cheap. You can have as much as you like. Down at those hotels in the town they don't leave the bottle on the table." He was flushed and torpid. After a while he said: "I'm going up."

"I'm staying here. I shall take a deck chair outside. That room's too hot," she said.

He hesitated. "Go, go," she almost cried. She looked at the black shining hair of the young man, his full lips, the brown bare arms that came out of the blue vest, the large darker hands, redder with the flush of blood. They were spread on the table, stroking the cloth. She could feel, in imagination, those palms on her body. Her heart raced and shook her. She and he would be alone. She would talk to him, she would not listen to him, he should not have his own words, perfect, predestined, and impersonal. It was she who would talk. She would make him halt and stammer. She would break through this perfection of impersonal speech. She would talk and make him know her. She would bring herself close to him with words, and then with touch. She would touch him. He was young, he was without will: he would touch her. She saw in her mind the open door of his room. She thought all this as her husband hesitated, stupefied, by the table.

But when he went and she was alone with Alex, her heart stopped and there were no words in her throat. Her whole body was trembling, the bones of her knees were hard to her hands.

"I think," Alex suddenly said as he had often said before, "I think I shall go for a walk. I'll be back for the swim," he said.

She gasped. She looked with intent irony at him. She saw him get up from the table and, in his oddly studied way, as if there were meat in his solitude no one else could know, he went.

"You fool," she said to herself. But as she stared out of the open door and heard his cool footsteps on the gravel outside until the sound of the breeze in the vines licked them away, she felt lost with relief.

In a deck chair under the mulberry tree she thought about herself and her husband. It was the time of year when the fruit of the mulberry falls. The berries dropped on the gravel, into the tank where the frogs croaked at night and on the table. They broke there. Sometimes they dropped like small hard hearts into her lap, and when she picked them off they crushed in her fingers and the red juice ran out. She breathed deeply, almost panting in her chair.

She had married an outcast. Her relations had said that and they had been right. Some of those who had been right—her mother and father, for example—were dead. Tom's father had had a small boot-repairing business in Leicester. He worked in the front room of their house, with its bay window. "Coram. Repairs While You Wait." That man and his wife had had seven children. Imagine such a life! Tom had studied, won scholarships, passed examinations. All his life he had been different from his brothers and sisters. Now his job was chemistry. Once he was going to be a famous chemist. Instead he got commercial jobs in the laboratories of big firms. He did not belong to the working class any more. He did not belong to her class. He did not belong to the class of the comfortable professional people he now met. He did not belong anywhere. He was lost, rough, unfinished, ugly, unshaped by the wise and harmonious hand of a good environment.

And she had really been the same. That was what had brought them together. He was ugly in life, she was ugly in body; two ugly people cut off from all others, living in their desert island.

Her family were country gentry, not very rich, with small private incomes and testy, tiresome genteel habits. The males went into the Army. The females married into the Army. You saw one and you had seen them all. She had always been small and thin; her long nose, her long mouth, her almost yellowish eyes and dead clay skin made her ugly. She had to be clever and lively, had to have a will or no one would have noticed her. At one time she supposed she would marry one of those tedious young men with dead eyes and little fair moustaches who were "keen" on gunnery and motor cars. She had thrown herself at them—thrown herself at them, indeed, like a bomb. That didn't suit the modern militarists. They had the tastes of clerks. They fingered their moustaches, looked dead and embarrassed at her, said they couldn't bear "highbrow" girls, and got away as quickly as they could. They were shocked because she didn't wear gloves. The naked finger seemed an indecency to them. "I could be a general's wife by now if I'd worn gloves," she used to say. Before they could throw her out and treat her as the bright, noisy, impossible woman who appears in every family, she threw them out.

So she married Tom. She got away from her home, went to live with a friend, met Tom, and married him. There was a row. "The toothpaste man," her relations called him. Thought she was going to live in a chemist's shop. He became a stick to beat her family with; he was going to be a great man, a great scientist—she flogged them. He was going to be a much greater man than those "keen" subalterns with their flannel bags, dance records, and little moustaches or those furtive majors, guilty with self-love.

She looked back on these days. She had always expected something dramatic and sudden to happen. But—what was it?—Tom had not become a great man. The emergence from his class had become really an obsession, and a habit. He was struggling to emerge long after he had emerged. He was always spending his energy on reacting from something that no longer existed. He lived—she could never quite understand it—in the grip of some thwarting inward conflict; his energy went into this invisible struggle. The veins and the muscles swelled as if they would burst. Torn between dealing with her—that is, with the simple business of giving her simple natural happiness—and himself, he was paralysed. And they had had no children. Whose fault was that? At first it was a mercy, because they were poor, but later? She slept with him. Her body had grown old trying to tear a child from him. Afterwards she attacked him. He listened stupefied.

Why had this happened to her? And why had she this guilt towards him so that now she pitied him and spent all her day coming between him and difficulty? She had sown her disappointment in him, he had sown his frustration in her. Why? And why did they live in a circle they could not break? Why did they live so long in it until suddenly she was forty, a grey-haired woman?

She went over these things, but she was not thinking and feeling them only. There was the soft stroke of a pulse between her breasts, making her breathless with every throb. Movement came to her blood from the sight of the blowing vines and the red soil of the olive fields and out of the wind-whitened sky. Her lips parted in thirst for the articulate lips of the young Jew. She could not sleep or read.

At last she went into the cool house. The flies, driven indoors by the wind, were swimming in the darkness. She went up the stairs to her room.

"Get up," she said to her husband. "We must go."

He couldn't go in these clothes, she said. He must get the car. She bullied him. She changed into a green dress. Grumbling, he changed.

She looked out of the window. Alex was not coming. She could see the valley and the trees flowing and silvered by the wind. Dust was blowing along the roads between the earth and sun, giving it a weird and brilliant light like the glitter of silica in granite.

Tom went downstairs. His clothes were thrown all over the room.

"We're waiting," he said when she came down. The black car was there and M. Pierre. He stood by it as if he owned it.

"Women," said M. Pierre, "are like the bon Dieu. They live not in time but in eternity."

Coram glared at him. Alex was there, tall and impersonal. He had come back, he said, some other way. He gravely considered M. Pierre's remark. He made a quotation from a poet. This was obscure to her and everyone.

"Where the hell's this picnic going to be?" said Coram.

They disputed about where they should sit. That is, she said one

thing and her husband another. At last M. Pierre was in front and she
and the young man were at the back. Coram got in and sulked. No one
had answered his question. "If anyone knows where they're going
they'd better drive," he said.

"The far beach," she called out.

"Well, in God's name!" he muttered. Still, he drove off.

"Are you crowded at the back?" he said later in a worried voice. A
sudden schoolgirl hilarity took her.

"We like it," she cried loudly, giggling. And pressed her legs against
Alex.

She was immediately ashamed of her voice. Before she could stop
herself she cried out: "I've got my young man."

She swaggered her arm through his and laughed loudly close to his
face. She was horrified at herself. He laughed discreetly, in a tolerant
elderly way at her. So they bumped and brushed over the bad roads to
the beach. Coram swore it would break the springs of his car, this damn
fool idea. She could see the sweat on her husband's thick pink neck.
She goaded him. She called to him not to crawl, not to bump them
about, not to take the town road but the other. Coram turned angrily
to her.

She wanted to show the young man: "You see, I don't care. I don't
care how revolting I am. I don't care for anything, I hate everything
except a desire that is in me. There is nothing but that."

The car topped the hill and she turned her head to look back upon
the town. She was surprised. Two belfries stood above the roofs. She
had never seen them before. The clay-coloured houses were closely
packed together by the hills, and those that were in the sun stood out
white and tall. The roofs went up in tiers, and over each roof a pair
of windows stared like foreign eyes. The houses were a phalanx of white
and alien witnesses. She was startled to think that she had brought her
life to a place so strange to her. She and her husband had lived in the
deeply worn groove of their lives even in this holiday and had not
noticed the place. Her mood quietened.

The outlying villas of this side of the town were newer, and the air
burned with the new resinous odour of the pines and the two flames
of sea and sky.

"I often come this way," said the Jew, "because there is more air.
Do you know the waiter in the café by the harbour? On one hot day
last year he chased his wife's lover down the street, loosing off a
revolver. He breaks out once a year. The rest of the time he is the

perfectly contented complaisant husband. If the café were up here, it would not happen. Or perhaps he might only be complaisant once a year. Probably our whole emotional life is ruled by temperature and air currents."

She looked at him. "You have read your Huxley," she said dryly, "haven't you?" But afterwards she felt repentant because she thought if he was showing off, it was because he was young. "*I* could cure him of that."

Presently the car stopped. They had got to the beach. They sat for a minute in the car studying it. It was a long beach of clean sand, looped between two promontories of rock, a wilder beach than the one by the town where people came to picnic. Now there was no one on it. And here the sea was not the pan of enamelled water they had known, but was open and stood up high from the beach like a loose tottering wall, green, wind-torn, sun-shot, and riotous. The sky was whitened on the horizon. The lighthouse on the red spit eight miles across the bay seemed to be racing through the water like a periscope. The whole coast was like groups of reddened riders driving the waves into a corral.

"The east wind," said M. Pierre, from his window, considering it.

They got out of the car. They walked on the sand, and the waves unrolled in timed relay along the shore. The three men and Mrs. Coram stood singly, separated by the wind, gazing at the tumult. They spoke and then turned to see where their words had gone. The wind had swept them from their lips and no one could hear.

Alex stayed behind, but soon he ran forward in his bathing suit.

"You're not going!" Tom said. The sea was too wild. The Jew did not hear him and ran down to the shore.

"Oh!" Mrs. Coram said anxiously, and moved to Pierre.

Without a word the Jew had dived in. Now he was swimming out. She held Pierre's arm tightly, and then slowly the grip of her fingers relaxed. She smiled and then she laughed. It was like watching a miracle to see Alex rise and sink with those tall waves, strike farther out, and play like some remote god with their dazzling falls. Sometimes he seemed to drop like a stone to the sea's floor and then up he shot again as if he had danced to the surface. She watched him, entranced.

"He's fine," she called. She looked for Tom. He was standing back from them, looking resentfully, confusedly, at the sea. Suddenly all her heart was with the swimmer and her mind felt clean by the cleansing sea. Her fear for him went. She adored his danger in the water and the way he sought it, the way he paused and went for the greatest waves and sailed through.

"Tom!" she called.

Before he knew what she wanted, Coram said, "I'm not going out in that."

"Pierre is," she called. "Aren't you?"

The old man sat down on the shingle. Yes, he was going in, he said.

Alex came back. He came out and stood by the water, unable to leave it. He was fifty yards from them. Suddenly he had dived in again. Then he came out once more and stood throwing stones into the sea. She saw him crouch and his long arm fling out as he threw the stone. He was smiling when he came back to them.

They sat down and talked about the rough water. They were waiting for Pierre to go. He did nothing. He sat down there and talked. The Jew eyed him. Eagerly he wanted Pierre to come. The time passed and Pierre said this sea was nothing. He began to boast of a time when he had been in a yacht that had been dismasted in a gale. "I looked death in the face," he said. Coram glowered, and winked at the Jew.

The Jew grew tired of waiting and said he was going to try the other end of the beach. She watched him walk away over the sand. Like a boy he picked up stones to throw as he went. She was hurt that he went away from her and yet she admired him more for this. She leaned back on her elbow; the soft stroke of pleasure and pain was beating between her breasts, a stroke for every step of his brown legs across the sand, a stroke for every fall of the sea on the shore. She saw him at last run down to the water and go in. He went far out of sight until there was a crest of fear to every breath of longing in her. He has gone far enough, she thought, far enough away from me.

She stood up. If she could fly in this wind over the sea and, like a gull, call to him from overhead and, pretending to be pursued, make him follow her to the shore! Then, to her surprise, he was suddenly on the shore again, standing as he had done before, studying the waves he had just been through. He stood there a long time and afterwards sat down and watched them. She called to him. It was too far. Timelessly he lived in his faraway youth. What was he doing, what was he thinking as he sat there remote in the other world of his youth?

Now M. Pierre had the beach to himself and there were no near competitors, he walked away and undressed. Presently he came back, short and corpulent in his bathing suit and his red slippers. He asked particularly that Mrs. Coram should be careful with his eyeglass. He fastened his helmet. Dandified, deprecating, like the leading dancer in a beauty chorus he stood before them.

"I float naturally in the sea," he observed as if he were a scientific exhibit, "because the balance of displacement in my case is exact."

He went to the sea's edge like royalty, pausing every few yards to nod.

"Look," she said.

It was odd, for the moment, to be alone with her husband, to feel that just he and she saw this as they alone had seen many other things in the world.

"He won't go in," said Coram.

M. Pierre had reached the sea's edge. Impertinently a large wave broke and he stood, surprised, like an ornament in a spread lace doily of surf. It swilled his ankles. He waited for it to seethe back a little and then he bent and wetted his forehead. He paused again. A green wave stood up on end, eight feet high, arched and luminous like a carved window in a cathedral. It hung waiting to crash. But before it crashed an astonishing thing happened. The fat little man had kicked up his heels and dived clean through it. They saw the soles of his red rubber shoes as he went through and disappeared. There he was on the other side of the wave in the trough and then, once again, he dived through the next wave and the next, clambering over the surf-torn ridges like a little beetle. The foam spat round him, suds of it dabbed his face. Now his head in its red bathing helmet bobbed up in dignified surprise at the top of a wave, now he was trudging out farther and farther into the riotous water.

"He's floating," said Tom.

"He's swimming," she said.

They talked and watched. She looked down the beach for Alex. He was lying full length in the sun.

Pierre was far out. How far they could not tell. Sometimes they saw the head bobbing in the water, sometimes they could not see him. They lost him. It was difficult to see against the flash of the sun. Nearer to them the emerald water fell in its many concussions on the shore and the shingle sang as the undertow drew back. She saw with surprise the lighthouse still racing, periscope-like, through the waves, dashing through the water and yet going nowhere. Why does he stay there, why doesn't he come back? She looked avidly to the young man stretched on the shore.

"Let's go up to the car and have a drink," said Tom.

"No," she said. "Wait."

She looked up for Pierre. He was not straight ahead of them.

"Where is Pierre?"

Ah, there he was; he was far out, swimming as far as they could see parallel to the beach.

She got up and walked along the beach. The mounting chaos of the sea was like the confusion of her heart. The sea had broken loose from the still sky and the stable earth; her life was breaking loose too from everything she had known. Her life was becoming free and alarmed. The prostration of each wave upon the sand mocked her with the imagination of desire forever fulfilling and satiate; satiate and fulfilling. She walked dazed and giddily towards Alex as if she were being blown towards him. Her dress blew and the wind wetted her eyes. She lifted her arms above her head and the wind blew into her legs, drove back her skirts. She paused. Did he see her? Did he see her miming her passion, with the wind?

She marched back to her husband. The wind caught and blew her almost unwillingly fast towards him.

"Tom!" she said. "I shall have a child by someone else."

He looked at her, in his habitual startled stupor. He hated this sea, this beach, this extraordinary country. He simply did not believe in it. Those words seemed like the country, wild and incredible. He just did not believe them, any more than he believed that the wind could speak. God, he thought she'd had her scene for the day and had got over it.

He was struggling.

"I have decided," she said. It was an ultimatum.

He smiled because he could not speak.

"You don't believe me."

"If you say so, I believe you."

She had terrified him. He was like a man blundering about a darkened room. Say? What could he say? She'd be crying before the night was out that she could never leave him. Or would she? He was relieved to see her walk away and to sink back into his habitual stupor. When she had gone he wanted to seize her and shake her. He saw another man lying naked on her; the picture enraged him and yet it gave him the happiness of an inexpressible jealousy. Then tears came to his eyes and he felt like a child.

She was walking away looking for Pierre and thinking: He doesn't believe me. He's a lout.

She watched Pierre as she walked. An old man, a nice old man, a funny old man. And very brave. Two unconcerned men, making no fuss, one old and one young: Pierre and the Jew.

The grace of the Jew, the comic strength of Pierre—they belonged to a free, articulate world. She was opposite to Pierre now. The sea was heavy in his course, the waves weightier there, and once or twice a roller cracked at the crest as he was swimming up it. But he was coming in, she saw, very slowly coming in. He was coming in much farther down. She came back to Tom.

"Look," she jeered. She seemed to have forgotten her earlier words. "You said he couldn't swim!" Coram screwed up his eyes. She walked down once more to the place where Pierre would land. The roar of the waves was denser and more chaotic. Tom followed her down. Pierre hardly seemed nearer. It was long waiting for him to come in.

At this end of the beach there was rock. It ran out from the promontory into the water. She climbed up to get a better view.

Suddenly she called out in a controlled voice: "Tom. Come here. Look."

He climbed up and followed her. She was looking down. When he got there he looked down too. "Hell," he said.

Below them was a wide cavern worn by the sea, with two spurs of rock running out into the water from either side of it. The enormous waves broke on the outer spurs and then came colliding with each other and breaking against the tables of rock submerged in the water, jostled, punched, and scattered in green lumps into the cave. With a hollow boom they struck and then swept back on the green tongue of the undertow. The place was like a wide gulping mouth with jagged teeth. Mr. and Mrs. Coram could not hear themselves speak, though they stood near together looking down at the hole with wonder and fear.

"Tom," she said, clutching his arm. He pulled his arm away. He was frightened too.

"Tom!" she said. "Is he all right?"

"What?"

"Pierre—he's not coming in here?" she said.

He looked at the hole and drew back.

"Tom, he is. He is!" she cried out suddenly in a voice that stopped his heart. "He's drifting. He's drifting in here. These rocks will kill him."

Tom glared at the sea. He could see it as plainly as she. He backed away.

"The damn fool," Tom said. "He's all right."

"He's not. Look."

He was drifting. He had been drifting all the time they had talked.

They had thought he was swimming parallel to the beach but all the time he had been drifting.

They could see M. Pierre plainly. In five minutes he would be borne beyond the first spur and would be carried into the hole.

As he came nearer they saw him at battle. They saw him fighting and striking out with his arms and legs. His cap had come loose and his grey hair was plastered over his head. His face had its little air of deprecation, but he was gasping and spitting water, his eyes were stern and bewildered as if he had not time to decide which of the waves that slapped him on the face was his opponent. He was like a man with dogs jumping up at his waving arms. The Corams were above him on the rock and she called out and signalled to him, but he did not look up.

"Are you all right?" she called.

"Course he's all right," said Coram.

It seemed to her that Pierre refused to look up but kept his eyes lowered. Increasingly, as he got into the outer breakers he had the careless, dead look of a body that cannot struggle any more and helplessly allows itself to be thrown to its pursuers. The two watchers stood hypnotized on the rock. Then Mrs. Coram screamed. A wave, larger than the rest, seemed to dive under Pierre and throw him half out of the water. His arms absurdly declaimed in space, and a look of dazed consternation was on his face as he dropped into the trough. The sun in the sky flashed like his own monocle upon him and the rich foam.

"Quick. He is going," she cried to her husband, clambering down the rock to the beach.

"Come on," she said. He followed her down. She ran towards the surf. "We'll make a chain. Quick. Take my hand. He's finished. We'll get him before he goes."

She stretched out her hand.

"Get Alex," she said. "Run and get him. We'll make a chain. Quickly run and get him."

But Tom drew back. He drew back a yard, two yards, he retreated up the beach, backing away.

"No," he said angrily, waving his arm as though thrusting her away. Yet she was not near him or touching him.

"Tom!" she called. "Quick. You can swim. I'll come."

"No," he said.

She did not see for a moment that the look of angry stupor on his face was fear, that he was prepared to let Pierre drown; and then as he half ran up the beach she saw it. He would not go in himself. He would not fetch Alex. He was going to stand there and let Pierre drown. "Tom," she called. She saw his thick red glistening face, his immovable glowering struggling stare. He stood like a chained man. He would stand there like that doing nothing and let Pierre drown. She was appalled.

So she ran. She ran down the beach, calling, waving to the Jew.

It happened that he had got up and was wandering idly along the surf towards them. He heard her cry and thought she was calling out with the excitement of the wind. Then he saw.

"Quick," she called. "Pierre is drowning."

She clutched his arm as the Jew came up to her. He gave a glance, jerked away her arm, and ran swiftly along the beach. She followed him. She saw him smile as he ran, the slight gleam of his teeth. When he got near the rock he broke into a short laugh of joy and rushed into the water. In two strokes he was there.

She feared for both of them. She saw a wave rise slowly like an animal just behind Pierre and a second greater one, green as ice and snowy with fluttering spume, following it closely. The two swimmers stared with brief, almost polite surprise at each other. Then the Jew flung himself bodily upon Pierre. An arm shot up. Their legs were in the air. They were thrown like two wrestlers in the water. There was a shout. The Jew came up, his arm went out, and his hand—the big hand she had seen upon the table that morning in the pension—caught the old man under the armpit. They were clear of the rock. They swayed like waltzing partners and then the enormous wave picked them both up, tossed them to its crest, and threw them headlong over and over on the shore. The falling wave soaked Mrs. Coram as they fell.

M. Pierre crawled dripping up the shingle and sank down panting. His face was greenish in colour, his skin purple with cold. He looked astonished to be out of the sea. The Jew had a lump the size of an egg on his shin.

"I thought I was finished," Pierre said.

"I'll get some brandy," Mrs. Coram said.

"No," he said. "It is not necessary."

"You saved his life," she said excitedly to the Jew.

"It was nothing," he said. "I found myself the current out there is strong."

"I could do nothing against the current," Pierre said. "I was finished. That," he said in his absurd negligent way, "is the second time I have looked death in the face."

"Rub yourself with the towel," she said.

He did not like being treated as an old man.

"I'm all right," he said. After all, once he had attempted to swim the Channel. Perhaps they would believe now he was a swimmer.

"It is always you good swimmers who nearly drown," she said tactfully.

"Yes," Pierre boasted, becoming proud as he warmed up. "I nearly drowned! I nearly drowned! Ah yes, I nearly drowned."

The emotion of the rescue had driven everything else from her mind. The scene was still in front of her. She looked with fear still at the careless water by the rock where only a few minutes ago she had seen him nearly go. Never would she forget his expressionless head in the water. With the eyelids lowered it had looked grave, detached, like a guillotined head. She was shivering; her fingers were still tightly clenched. Supposing now they had M. Pierre dead beside them. How near they had been to death! She shuddered. The sea, green and dark as a blown shrub, with its slop of foam, sickened her.

He is not very grateful, she thought. And she said aloud: "Monsieur Pierre, but for Alex you would be dead."

"Ah yes," said M. Pierre, turning to the Jew not very warmly. "I must express my warmest thanks to you. That is the second time I have looked . . ."

"You get no credit," she said to Alex in English just in her husband's way. It was odd how she had his habit in a time of stress. "He thinks he's immortal."

"Parlez français," said M. Pierre.

"She says," said Alex quickly, "that you are immortal."

All this time she was standing up. One side of her dress had been soaked by the wave that had borne them in. As she talked she could see Tom standing forty yards off. He was standing by the car as if for protection and half turned from the sight of the sea. She was still too much in the excitement of the rescue, going over it again and again, to realize that she was looking at him or to know what she thought of him.

"We must get you home," she said to M. Pierre, "quickly."

"There is no hurry," he said with dignity. "Sit down, madame. Calm yourself. When one has looked death in the face . . ."

She obeyed. She was surprised they thought her not calm. She sat next to Alex as all the afternoon, when he had gone off, she had wished to do. She looked at his arms, his chest, and his legs as if to find the courage shining on his body.

"It was nothing." She could see that this was true. It had been nothing to him. One must not exaggerate. He was young. His black hair was thick and shining and young. His eyes were young too. He had, as she had always thought, that peculiarly ancient and everlasting youth of the Greek statues that are sometimes unearthed in this Mediterranean soil. He was equable and in command of himself, he was at the beginning of everything, at the beginning of the mind and the body. There was no difficulty anywhere, it was all as easy as that smile of his when he ran into the water. Had she been like that when she was young? How had she been? Had everything been easy? No, it had been difficult. She could not remember truly, but she could not believe she had ever been as young as he was young. Without knowing it she touched his bare leg with two of her fingers and ran them down to his knee. The skin was firm.

"You're cold," she said. The coldness startled her. He had probably never slept with a woman. She found herself, as she touched that hard body which did not move under her touch, pitying the woman who might have slept with this perfect, impersonal, impenetrable man.

There was resentment against his perfection, his laugh in the water, his effortless achievement. He showed no weakness. There was no confusion in him. There was no discernible vice. She could not speak.

And now, as she calmed down and saw Tom, her heart started. She saw, really saw him for the first time since the rescue and went up the tiring shingle to him. He was still standing against the car.

"The damn fool," Coram said before his wife could speak. "Trying to drown others beside himself. They're all alike."

"It is no thanks to you that we saved him," she said. "Leave it to me! You ran away!" she said angrily.

"I didn't," he said. "Drown myself for a fool like that. What do you take me for? He wasn't drowning anyway."

"He was," she said. "And you ran away. You wouldn't even go for Alex. I had to go."

"No need to shout," he said. She stood below him on the shingle and he winced as if she were throwing stones at him. "These people get me down in this place," he said, "going into a sea like that."

"You ran away when I called," she insisted.

"Are you saying I'm a coward?" he said.

He looked at her small, shrilling figure. She was ugly when she was in a temper, like a youth, gawky, bony, unsensual. Now she had joined all the things that were against him. The beauty of this country was a fraud, a treachery against the things he had known. He saw the red street of his childhood, heard the tap of his father's hammer, the workers getting off the trams with their packages and little bags in their hands, the oil on their dungarees. He heard the swing door of his laboratory, the drum of machines, and smoke drooping like wool through the Midland rain, saw the cold morning placards. That was his life. The emeralds and ultramarine of this sea and the reddened, pine-plumed coast made him think of those gaudy cocottes he had seen in Paris. The beauty was corruption and betrayal.

He did not know how to say this. It was confused in his mind. He blustered. He glared. She saw through the glowering eyes the piteous struggle, the helpless fear. He was ugly. He stood there blustering and alone with his dust-covered car, an outcast.

"I'm saying you could have helped," she said.

She looked in anger at him. Her heart was beating loudly, her blood was up. It was not the rescue—she half realized now—which had stirred her—but the failure to rescue. From the very moment when he had run away, something in her had run after him, clamouring for him, trying to drag him back. Now his muddle seemed to drag her in too.

"Help that swine!" he said.

M. Pierre and Alex came to the car carrying their towels.

"You think of no one but yourself," she said to her husband in front of them. "For God's sake let's get home."

Everyone looked at her apprehensively. Coram got into the car and she, determined not to let him escape one moment of her contempt, sat beside him. Pierre and Alex were at the back. In silence they drove from the beach and over the hill from which the white town could be seen stacked closely in the sun, like a pack of tall cards. As the car crawled through the narrow streets, which were crowded in the evenings with holiday-makers and workers who came up from the harbour or down from the fields, Pierre put his head out of the window. He waved to friends sitting in cafés.

"I nearly drowned!" he called out. "I nearly drowned."

"Drowned?" People laughed, getting up from their tables.

"For the second time in my life," he called, "I have looked death in the face."

"Tiens!"

"Yes, I nearly . . ."

Coram trod on the accelerator. M. Pierre fell back into his seat, his little scene cut short, as they swerved up the dusty road to the pension.

Coram was silent. They got out and he went to put the car away.

Pierre went to his room and she and Alex went up the stairs of the shuttered house to their rooms. She was ahead of him. When she got to his landing she saw his door was open. She turned and said:

"May I see what you are like?"

"Of course," he said.

She went into his room and he followed her. The shutters were closed and the room was dark and cool. There was the white shape of the bed, the pile of books by its side, the white enamel basin on its iron stand, and his suitcase on a chair. He went to push open the shutters.

"Oh, don't do that," she said. But one shutter slipped open. Her face was white and hard, tragically emptied of all expression as she looked at his polite face.

There was nothing.

She went over and lay on the bed. He raised his eyebrows slightly. She saw him raise them.

"They are hard in this house," she said. "The beds."

"A bit," he said.

She leaned up on one elbow.

"You were plucky," she said, "this afternoon. But my husband ran away."

"Oh, no," he said. "He had not changed. He had not been in."

"He ran away," she said. "He wouldn't even go and fetch you."

"One could not expect . . ." Alex began.

"You mean you are young?" she said.

"Yes," said Alex.

"My husband is my age," she said in a hard voice. "Turned forty.

"I admired what you did," she said.

He murmured something politely. She got up and sat on the edge of the bed.

"My skirt," she said, "was soaked. Look."

She pulled it above her knees. "Feel it," she said.

He came close to her and felt the frock. She stared into his eyes as he touched the cloth. She was shivering.

"Close the door," she said suddenly. "I must take it off. I don't want Monsieur Pierre to see me." He closed the door. While his back was turned she picked up the hem of her frock and pulled it over her head. She stood bare-legged in her white underclothes. The shoulder strap slipped over her arm. She knew that he saw her white breast.

"In England this might be misunderstood," she said, with a loud nervous laugh. "But not in France." She laughed and stared, frightened at him.

"I'm old enough to be your mother, aren't I?"

"Well, not quite," he said.

She was nearly choking. She could nearly scream. She was ugly and hideous. She had wanted to show him what she was. "Feel how cold I am," she said, putting out her leg. He put his hand on her white thigh. It was soft and warm. He was puzzled.

"Do you mind?" she said. She lay back on the bed. Tears came into her eyes when she spoke.

"You are young," she said. "Come and sit here."

He came and sat on the edge of the bed beside her. He was very puzzled. She took his hand. But there was no desire in her. It had gone. Where had it gone? She dropped his hand and stared helplessly at him. She saw that he did not want her and that it had not occurred to him to want her. If she had drawn his head down to her breast she would have been cold to his touch. There was no desire, but only shame and anger in her heart.

"I suppose," she said suddenly, with a false yawn, "that this is a little unconventional."

To her astonishment, he got up.

"Have you ever been in love?" she asked in a mocking voice to call him back. "Hardly, I expect, not yet. You are only a child." Before he could answer she said, "Too young to sleep with a woman."

Now he looked embarrassed and angry. She laughed. She got up. She was delighted she had made him angry.

She took her frock and waited. Perhaps he would attempt to kiss her. She stood waiting for him. But he did not move. Slowly a horror of what she was doing came over her. There was no desire. She saw too a remote fear of her in his brown eyes.

"Thank you," she said. She put the frock against her breast and went to the door. She hoped for one more humiliation when she opened it: that she should be seen, half naked, leaving his room. But there was no one on the stairs.

From the landing window as she went up she saw the familiar picture. The military rows of the vines in the red soil. The shadow-pocked mountains, the pines. It was like a postcard view taken in the sun, the sun not of today but of other days, a sun that was not warm but the indifferent, hard, dead brilliance of the past itself, surrounding her life.

She lay down on her bed and sobbed with misery and shame as a broken creature will abase itself before a bloodless, unapproachable idol. She sobbed because of her ugliness and of the ugliness of having no desire. She had abased and humiliated herself. When had the desire gone? Before Alex had rushed to the rescue into the sea it had been there. When?

It had gone when she had heard her husband's refusal and had seen the fear and helplessness in his eyes, the muddle in his heart. Her desire had not gone winged after the rescuer, but angry, hurt, astounded, and shocked towards her husband. She knew this.

She stopped weeping and listened for him. And in this clarity of the listening mind she knew she had not gone to Alex's room to will her desire to life or even to will it out of him, but to abase herself to the depths of her husband's abasement. He dominated her entirely, all her life; she wished to be no better than he. They were both of them like that; helpless, halted, tangled people, outcasts in everything they did.

She heard him coming up the stairs.

"Tom," she called. "Tom."

She went avidly to the door.

That evening in the quietness after dinner some friends of M. Pierre's came in to hear about his escape. He wore his yachting cap that night. Death, he said, had no terrors for him, nor had the sea. In his case the balance of displacement was exact; once already he had looked death in the face. . . . He was the hero. He did not once refer to his rescuer. Two of the guests were English, a colonel and his wife, and to them Coram, also, told the story. He stumbled over his words. He lumbered on. They sat under the massed black leaves of the mulberry tree.

Mrs. Coram sat there, calm, clever, and experienced, as she always was. Here and there, as she always did, she helped her husband over the story. "Let me tell you what happened," she said, smiling. They turned to her with relief and Coram himself was grateful.

Wonderful story she always tells, they said. Ought to write. Why didn't she take it up? "Go on, Mrs. Coram, give us the lowdown."

They all laughed, except Pierre, under the trees. He was out of his depth in so much quick English.

It was ridiculous, she said, in her quickest voice, glancing at Alex, to go out in a sea like that. She described the scene.

"Tom tried to persuade him not to go, but he would. You know how vain they are," she said. "And then," she said as they laughed with approval and caught the excitement of her story, "poor Tom had to go in and rescue him."

She looked at them. Her eyes were brilliant, her whole body alive with challenge as she glanced from her visitors to Alex and Tom.

"B—" Tom began.

"Alex was at the other end of the beach and Tom had to go in and rescue him," she repeated.

She looked at all of them with defiance and a pause of pity for Alex; at Tom, like a cracking whip before a too docile lion. The Corams against the world.

You Make Your Own Life

Upstairs from the street a sign in electric light said "Gent's Saloon."
I went up. There was a small hot back room full of sunlight, with hair
clippings on the floor, towels hanging from a peg, and newspapers on
the chairs. "Take a seat. Just finishing," said the barber. It was a lie.
He wasn't anywhere near finishing. He had in fact just begun a shave.
The customer was having everything.

In a dead place like this town you always had to wait. I was waiting
for a train, now I had to wait for a haircut. It was a small town in a
valley with one long street, and a slow mud-coloured river moving
between willows and the backs of houses.

I picked up a newspaper. A man had murdered an old woman, a
clergyman's sister was caught stealing gloves in a shop, a man who had
identified the body of his wife at an inquest on a drowning fatality met
her three days later on a pier. Ten miles from this town the skeletons
of men killed in a battle eight centuries ago had been dug up on the
Downs. That was nearer. Still, I put the paper down. I looked at the
two men in the room.

The shave had finished now, the barber was cutting the man's hair.
It was glossy black hair and small curls of it fell on the floor. I could
see the man in the mirror. He was in his thirties. He had a swarthy skin
and brilliant long black eyes. The lashes were long too and the lids when

he blinked were pale. There was just that suggestion of weakness. Now he was shaved, there was a sallow glister to his skin like a Hindu's, and as the barber clipped away and grunted his breaths, the dark man sat engrossed in his reflection, half smiling at himself and very deeply pleased.

The barber was careful and responsible in his movements, but nonchalant and detached. He was in his thirties too, a young man with fair receding hair, brushed back from his forehead. He did not speak to his customer. His customer did not speak to him. He went on from one job to the next silently. Now he was rattling his brush in the jar, wiping the razor, pushing the chair forward to the basin. Now he gently pushed the man's head down, now he ran the taps and was soaping the head and rubbing it. A peculiar look of amused affection was on his face as he looked down at the soaped head.

"How long are you going to be?" I said. "I've got a train."

He looked at the clock. He knew the trains.

"Couple of minutes," he said.

He wheeled a machine on a tripod to the back of the man. A curved black thing like a helmet enclosed the head. The machine was plugged to the wall. There were vials with coloured liquids in them and soon steam was rushing out under the helmet. It looked like a machine you see in a Fun Fair. I don't know what happened to the man or what the barber did. Shave, hot towels, haircut, shampoo, this machine, and then yellow liquid like treacle out of a bottle—that customer had everything.

I wondered how much he would have to pay.

Then the job was over. The dark man got up. The clippers had been over the back of his neck and he looked like a guardsman. He was dressed in a square-shouldered grey suit, very dandyish for this town, and he had a silk handkerchief sticking out of his breast pocket. He wore a violet and silver tie. He patted it as the barber brushed his coat. He was delighted with himself.

"So long, Fred." He smiled faintly.

"Cheero, Albert," said the upright barber, and his lips closed to a small, hardly perceptible smile too. Thoughtfully, ironically, the barber watched his handiwork go. The man hadn't paid.

I sat in the chair. It was warm, too warm, where the man had sat. The barber put the sheet round me. The barber was smiling to himself like a man remembering a tune. He was not thinking about me.

The barber said that machine made steam open the pores. He

glanced at the door where the man had gone. "Some people want everything," he said, "some want nothing." You had to have a machine like that.

He tucked in the cotton wool. He got out the comb and scissors. His fingers gently depressed my head. I could see him in the mirror bending to the back of my head. He was clipping away. He was a dull young man with pale-blue eyes and a look of ironical stubbornness in him. The small dry smile was still like claw marks at the corners of his lips.

"Three bob a time," he said. He spoke into the back of my neck and nodded to the door. "He has it every week."

He clipped away.

"His hair's coming out. That's why he has it. Going bald. You can't stop that. You can delay it but you can't stop it. Can't always be young. He thinks you can." He smiled dryly but with affection.

"But he wasn't so old."

The barber stood up.

"That man!" he said. He mused to himself with growing satisfaction. He worked away in long silence as if to savour every possible flavour of my remark. The result of his meditation was to make him change his scissors for a finer pair.

"He ought to be dead," he said.

"T.B.," he said with quiet scorn.

He looked at me in the mirror.

"It's wonderful," he said, as if to say it was nothing of the sort.

"It's wonderful what the doctors can do," I said.

"I don't mean doctors," he said. "Consumptives! Tuh! They're wonderful." As much as to say a sick man can get away with anything —but you try if you're healthy and see what happens!

He went on cutting. There was a glint in his pale-blue eyes. He snipped away amusedly as if he were attending to every individual hair at the back of my head.

"You see his throat?" he said suddenly.

"What about his throat?" I asked.

"Didn't you notice anything? Didn't you see a mark a bit at the side?" He stood up and looked at me in the mirror.

"No," I said.

He bent down to the back of my neck again. "He cut his throat once," he said quietly. "Not satisfied with T.B.," he said with a grin. It was a small, firm, friendly grin. So long, Fred. Cheero, Albert. "Tried to commit suicide."

"Wanted everything," I said.

"That's it," he said.

"A girl," the barber said. "He fell in love with a girl."

He clipped away.

"That's an item," said the barber absently.

He fell in love with a local girl who took pity on him when he was in bed, ill. Nursed him. Usual story. Took pity on him but wasn't interested in him in that way.

"A very attractive girl," said the barber.

"And he got it badly?"

"They get it badly, consumptives.

"Matter of fact," said the barber, stepping over for the clippers and shooting a hard sideways stare at me, "it was my wife.

"Before she was my wife," he said. There was a touch of quiet, amused resolution in him.

He'd known that chap since he was a kid. Went to school with him. Used to be his best friend. Still was. Always a lad. Regular nut. Had a milk business, was his own guv'nor till he got ill. Doing well.

"He knew I was courting her." He smiled. "That didn't stop him." There was a glint in his eye.

"What did you do?" I asked.

"I lay low," he said.

She had a job in the shop opposite. If you passed that shop you couldn't help noticing her at the cash desk near the door. "It's not for me to say—but she was the prettiest girl in this town," he said. "Still is," he mused.

"You've seen the river? You came over it by the station," he said. "Well, he used to take her on the river when I was busy. I didn't mind. I knew my mind. She knew hers. I knew it was all right.

"I knew him." He grinned. "But I knew her. 'Let him take you on the river,' I said."

I saw the barber's forehead and his dull blue eyes looking up for a moment over my head in the mirror.

"Damp river," he said reflectively. "Damp mists, I mean, on the river. Very flat, low-lying, unhealthy," he said. "That's where he made his mistake. It started with him taking her on the river.

"Double pneumonia once," he said. "Sixty cigarettes a day, burning the candle at both ends."

He grunted.

"He couldn't get away with it," he said.

When he got ill, the girl used to go and look after him. She used to go and read to him in the afternoons. "I used to turn up in the evenings too when we'd closed."

The barber came round to the front and took the brushes lazily. He glanced sardonically at the door as if expecting to see the man standing there. That cocksure irony in the barber seemed to warm up.

"Know what he used to say to her?" he said sharply and smiled when I was startled. " 'Here, Jenny,' he used to say, 'tell Fred to go home and you pop into bed with me. I'm lonely.' " The young barber gave a short laugh.

"In front of me," he said.

"What did you say?"

"I told him to keep quiet or there'd be a funeral. Consumptives want it, they want it worse than others, but it kills them," he said.

"I thought you meant *you'd* kill him," I said.

"Kill him?" he said. "Me kill him?" He smiled scornfully at me: I was an outsider in this. "He tried to kill *me,*" he said.

"Yeah," he said, wiping his hands on a towel. "Tried to poison me. Whisky. It didn't work. Back O.K.?" he said, holding up a mirror. "I don't drink.

"I went to his room," he said. "I was his best friend. He was lying on the bed. Thin! All bones and blue veins and red patches as if he'd been scalded and eyes as bright as that bottle of bath salts. Not like he is now. There was a bottle of whisky and a glass by the side of the bed. He wanted me to have a drop. He knew I didn't drink.

" 'I don't want one,' I said. 'Yes, you do,' he said. 'You know I never touch it,' I said. 'Well, touch it now,' he said. 'I tell you what,' he said; 'you're afraid.' 'Afraid of what?' I said. 'Afraid of catching what I've got.' 'Touch your lips to it if you're not afraid. Just have a sip to show.'

"I told him not to be a fool. I took the bottle from him. He had no right to have whisky in his state. He was wild when I took it. 'It'll do some people a bit of good,' I said, 'but it's poison to you.'

" 'It *is* poison,' he said.

"I took the bottle away. I gave it to a chap in the town. It nearly finished him. We found out it *was* poison. He'd put something in it."

I said I'd have a singe. The barber lit the taper. I felt the flame warm against my head. "Seals up the ends," the barber said. He lifted up the hair with the comb and ran the flame along. "See the idea?" he said.

"What did you do?"

"Nothing," he said. "Just married my girl that week," the barber said. "When she told him we were going to get married, he said: 'I'll give you something Fred won't give you.' We wondered what it would be. 'Something big,' he said. 'Best man's present,' he said. He winked at her. 'All I've got. I'm the best man.' That night he cut his throat." The barber made a grimace in the mirror, passed the scissors over his throat, and gave a grin.

"Then he opened the window and called out to a kid in the street to fetch *her*. The kid came to me instead. Funny present," he said. He combed, he patted, he brushed. He pulled the wool out of the back of my neck. He went round it with the soft brush. Coming round to the front he adroitly drew off the sheet. I stood up.

"He got over it," he said. "Comes round and plays with my kids on Sundays. Comes in every Friday, gets himself up. See him with a different one every week at the pictures. It's a dead place this; all right in the summer on the river. You make your own life. The only thing is he don't like shaving himself now, I have to go over every morning and do it for him."

He stood with his small grin, his steady eyes amused and resolute. "I never charge him," he said. He brushed my coat, he brought my hat.

The Voice

A message came from the rescue party, who straightened up and leaned on their spades in the rubble. The policeman said to the crowd: "Everyone keep quiet for five minutes. No talking, please. They're trying to hear where he is."

The silent crowd raised their faces and looked across the ropes to the church which, now it was destroyed, broke the line of the street like a decayed tooth. The bomb had brought down the front wall and the roof, the balcony had capsized. Freakishly untouched, the hymnboard still announced the previous Sunday's hymns.

A small wind blew a smell of smouldering cloth across people's noses from another street where there was another scene like this. A bus roared by and heads turned in passive anger until the sound of the engine had gone. People blinked as a pigeon flew from a roof and crossed the building like an omen of release. There was dead quietness again. Presently a murmuring sound was heard by the rescue party. The man buried under the debris was singing again.

At first difficult to hear, soon a tune became definite. Two of the rescuers took up their shovels and shouted down to encourage the buried man, and the voice became stronger and louder. Words became clear. The leader of the rescue party held back the others, and those who were near strained to hear. Then the words were unmistakable:

> "Oh Thou whose Voice the waters heard,
> And hushed their raging at Thy Word."

The buried man was singing a hymn.

A clergyman was standing with the warden in the middle of the ruined church.

"That's Mr. Morgan all right," the warden said. "He could sing. He got silver medals for it."

The Reverend Frank Lewis frowned.

"Gold, I shouldn't wonder," said Mr. Lewis dryly. Now he knew Morgan was alive, he said: "What the devil's he doing in there? How did he get in? I locked up at eight o'clock last night myself."

Lewis was a wiry, middle-aged man, but the white dust on his hair and his eyelashes, and the way he kept licking the dust off his dry lips, moving his jaws all the time, gave him the monkeyish, testy, and suspicious air of an old man. He had been up all night on rescue work in the raid and he was tired out. The last straw was to find the church had gone and that Morgan, the so-called Reverend Morgan, was buried under it.

The rescue workers were digging again. There was a wide hole now and a man was down in it filling a basket with his hands. The dust rose like smoke from the hole as he worked.

The voice had not stopped singing. It went on, rich, virile, masculine, from verse to verse of the hymn. Shooting up like a stem through the rubbish, the voice seemed to rise and branch out powerfully, luxuriantly, and even theatrically, like a tree, until everything was in its shade. It was a shade that came towards one like dark arms.

"All the Welsh can sing," the warden said. Then he remembered that Lewis was Welsh also. "Not that I've got anything against the Welsh," the warden said.

The scandal of it, Lewis was thinking. Must he sing so loud, must he advertise himself? I locked up myself last night. How the devil did he get in? And he really meant: How did the devil get in?

To Lewis, Morgan was the nearest human thing to the devil. He could never pass that purple-gowned figure, sauntering like a cardinal in his skull cap on the sunny side of the street, without a shudder of distaste and derision. An unfrocked priest, his predecessor in the church, Morgan ought in strict justice to have been in prison, and would have been but for the indulgence of the bishop. But this did not prevent the old man with the saintly white head and the eyes half closed by the worldly juices of food and wine from walking about dressed in his vestments, like an actor walking in the sun of his own vanity, a hook-nosed satyr, a he-goat significant to servant girls, the crony of the public house, the chaser of bookmakers, the smoker of cigars. It was terrible, but it was just that the bomb had buried him; only the malice of the Evil One would have thought of bringing the punishment of the sinner upon the church as well. And now, from the ruins, the voice of the wicked man rose up in all the elaborate pride of art and evil.

Suddenly there was a moan from the sloping timber, slates began to skate down.

"Get out. It's going," shouted the warden.

The man who was digging struggled out of the hole as it bulged under the landslide. There was a dull crumble, the crashing and splitting of wood, and then the sound of brick and dust tearing down below the water. Thick dust clouded over and choked them all. The rubble rocked like a cakewalk. Everyone rushed back and looked behind at the wreckage as if it were still alive. It remained still. They all stood there, frightened and suspicious. Presently one of the men with the shovel said, "The bloke's shut up."

Everyone stared stupidly. It was true. The man had stopped singing. The clergyman was the first to move. Gingerly he went to what was left of the hole and got down on his knees.

"Morgan!" he said in a low voice.

Then he called out more loudly: "Morgan!"

Getting no reply, Lewis began to scramble the rubble away with his hands.

"Morgan!" he shouted. "Can you hear?" He snatched a shovel from one of the men and began digging and shovelling the stuff away. He had stopped chewing and muttering. His expression had entirely changed. "Morgan!" he called. He dug for two feet and no one stopped him. They looked with bewilderment at the sudden frenzy of the small man grubbing like a monkey, spitting out the dust, filing down his nails. They saw the spade at last shoot through the old hole. He was down the hole widening it at once, letting himself down as he worked. He disappeared under a ledge made by the fallen timber.

The party above could do nothing. "Morgan," they heard him call. "It's Lewis. We're coming. Can you hear?" He shouted for an axe and presently they heard him smashing with it. He was scratching like a dog or a rabbit.

A voice like that to have stopped, to have gone! Lewis was thinking. How unbearable this silence was. A beautiful proud voice, the voice of a man, a voice like a tree, the soul of a man spreading in the air like the cedars of Lebanon. "Only one man I have heard with a bass like that. Owen the Bank, at Newtown before the war. Morgan!" he shouted. "Sing! God will forgive you everything, only sing!"

One of the rescue party following behind the clergyman in the tunnel shouted back to his mates.

"I can't do nothing. This bleeder's blocking the gangway."

Half an hour Lewis worked in the tunnel. Then an extraordinary thing happened to him. The tunnel grew damp and its floor went as soft as clay to the touch. Suddenly his knees went through. There was a gap with a yard of cloth, the vestry curtain or the carpet at the communion rail was unwound and hanging through it. Lewis found himself looking down into the blackness of the crypt. He lay down and put his head and shoulders through the hole and felt about him until he found something solid again. The beams of the floor were tilted down into the crypt.

"Morgan. Are you there, man?" he called.

He listened to the echo of his voice. He was reminded of the time he had talked into a cistern when he was a boy. Then his heart jumped. A voice answered him out of the darkness from under the fallen floor. It was like the voice of a man lying comfortably and waking up from a snooze, a voice thick and sleepy.

"Who's that?" asked the voice.

"Morgan, man. It's Lewis. Are you hurt?" Tears pricked the dust in Lewis's eyes, and his throat ached with anxiety as he spoke. Forgiveness and love were flowing out of him. From below, the deep thick voice of Morgan came back.

"You've been a hell of a long time," it said. "I've damn near finished my whisky."

"Hell" was the word which changed Mr. Lewis's mind. Hell was a real thing, a real place for him. He believed in it. When he read out the word "Hell" in the Scriptures he could see the flames rising as they rise out of the furnaces at Swansea. "Hell" was a professional and poetic word for Mr. Lewis. A man who had been turned out of the church had no right to use it. Strong language and strong drink, Mr. Lewis hated both of them. The idea of whisky being in his church made his soul rise like an angered stomach. There was Morgan, insolent and comfortable, lying (so he said) under the old altar-table, which was propping up the fallen floor, drinking a bottle of whisky.

"How did you get in?" Lewis said sharply from the hole. "Were you in the church last night when I locked up?"

The old man sounded not as bold as he had been. He even sounded shifty when he replied, "I've got my key."

"*Your* key. I have the only key of the church. Where did you get a key?"

"My old key. I always had a key."

The man in the tunnel behind the clergyman crawled back up the tunnel to the daylight.

"O.K.," the man said. "He's got him. They're having a ruddy row."

"Reminds me of ferretting. I used to go ferretting with my old dad," said the policeman.

"You should have given that key up," said Mr. Lewis. "Have you been in here before?"

"Yes, but I shan't come here again," said the old man.

There was the dribble of powdered rubble, pouring down like sand in an hour-glass, the ticking of the strained timber like the loud ticking of a clock.

Mr. Lewis felt that at last after years he was face to face with the devil, and the devil was trapped and caught. The tick-tock of the wood went on.

"Men have been risking their lives, working and digging for hours because of this," said Lewis. "I've ruined a suit of . . ."

The tick-tock had grown louder in the middle of the words. There was a sudden lurching and groaning of the floor, followed by a big heaving and splitting sound.

"It's going," said Morgan with detachment from below. "The table leg." The floor crashed down. The hole in the tunnel was torn wide and Lewis grabbed at the darkness until he caught a board. It swung him out and in a second he found himself hanging by both hands over the pit.

"I'm falling. Help me," shouted Lewis in terror. "Help me." There was no answer.

"Oh, God," shouted Lewis, kicking for a foothold. "Morgan, are you there? Catch me. I'm going."

Then a groan like a snore came out of Lewis. He could hold no longer. He fell. He fell exactly two feet.

The sweat ran down his legs and caked on his face. He was as wet as a rat. He was on his hands and knees gasping. When he got his breath again, he was afraid to raise his voice.

"Morgan," he said quietly, panting.

"Only one leg went," the old man said in a quiet grating voice. "The other three are all right."

Lewis lay panting on the floor. There was a long silence. "Haven't you ever been afraid before, Lewis?" Morgan said. Lewis had no breath to reply. "Haven't you ever felt rotten with fear," said the old man calmly, "like an old tree, infested and worm-eaten with it, soft as a rotten orange? You were a fool to come down here after me. I wouldn't have done the same for you," Morgan said.

"You would," Lewis managed to say.

"I wouldn't," said the old man. "I'm afraid. I'm an old man, Lewis, and I can't stand it. I've been down here every night since the raids got bad."

Lewis listened to the voice. It was low with shame, it had the roughness of the earth, the kicked and trodden choking dust of Adam. The earth of Mr. Lewis listened for the first time to the earth of Morgan. Coarsened and sordid and unlike the singing voice, the voice of Morgan was also gentle and fragmentary.

"When you stop feeling shaky," Morgan said, "you'd better sing. I'll do a bar, but I can't do much. The whisky's gone. Sing, Lewis. Even if they don't hear, it does you good. Take the tenor, Lewis."

Above in the daylight the look of pain went from the mouths of the rescue party, a grin came on the dusty lips of the warden.

"Hear it?" he said. "A ruddy Welsh choir!"

Sense of Humour

It started one Saturday. I was working new ground and I decided I'd stay at the hotel the weekend and put in an appearance at church.

"All alone?" asked the girl at the cash desk.

It had been raining since ten o'clock.

"Mr. Good has gone," she said. "And Mr. Straker. He usually stays with us. But he's gone."

"That's where they make their mistake," I said. "They think they know everything because they've been on the road all their lives."

"You're a stranger here, aren't you?" she said.

"I am," I said. "And so are you."

"How do you know that?"

"Obvious," I said. "Way you speak."

"Let's have a light," she said.

"So's I can see you," I said.

That was how it started. The rain was pouring down on the glass roof of the office.

She'd a cup of tea steaming on the register. I said I'd have one, too. What's it going to be and I'll tell them, she said, but I said just a cup of tea.

"I'm T.T.," I said. "Too many soakers on the road as it is."

I was staying there the weekend so as to be sharp on the job on

Monday morning. What's more, it pays in these small towns to turn up at church on Sundays, Presbyterians in the morning, Methodists in the evening. Say "Good morning" and "Good evening" to them. "Ah!" they say. "Churchgoer! Pleased to see that! T.T., too." Makes them have a second look at your lines in the morning. "Did you like our service, Mr.—er—er?" "Humphrey's my name." "Mr. Humphrey." See? It pays.

"Come into the office, Mr. Humphrey," she said, bringing me a cup. "Listen to that rain."

I went inside.

"Sugar?" she said.

"Three," I said. We settled to a very pleasant chat. She told me all about herself, and we got on next to families.

"My father was on the railway," she said.

" 'The engine gave a squeal,' " I said. " 'The driver took out his pocket-knife and scraped him off the wheel.' "

"That's it," she said. "And what is your father's business? You said he had a business."

"Undertaker," I said.

"Undertaker?" she said.

"Why not?" I said. "Good business. Seasonable like everything else. High-class undertaker," I said.

She was looking at me all the time wondering what to say, and suddenly she went into fits of laughter.

"Undertaker," she said, covering her face with her hands and went on laughing.

"Here," I said, "what's up?"

"Undertaker!" She laughed and laughed. Struck me as being a pretty thin joke.

"Don't mind me," she said. "I'm Irish."

"Oh, I see," I said. "That's it, is it? Got a sense of humour."

Then the bell rang and a woman called out "Muriel! Muriel!" and there was a motorbike making a row at the front door.

"All right," the girl called out. "Excuse me a moment, Mr. Humphrey," she said. "Don't think me rude. That's my boyfriend. He wants the bird turning up like this."

She went out, but there was her boyfriend looking over the window ledge into the office. He had come in. He had a cape on, soaked with rain, and the rain was in beads in his hair. It was fair hair. It stood up on end. He'd been economizing on the brilliantine. He didn't wear a hat. He gave me a look and I gave him a look. I didn't like the look of him. And he didn't like the look of me. A smell of oil and petrol and rain and mackintosh came off him. He had a big mouth with thick lips. They were very red. I recognized him at once as the son of the man who ran the Kounty Garage. I saw this chap when I put my car away. The firm's car. Locked up, because of the samples. Took me ten minutes to ram the idea into his head. He looked as though he'd never heard of samples. Slow—you know the way they are in the provinces. Slow on the job.

"Oh, Colin," says she. "What do you want?"

"Nothing," the chap said. "I came in to see you."

"To see me?"

"Just to see you."

"You came in this morning."

"That's right," he said. He went red. "You was busy," he said.

"Well, I'm busy now," she said.

He bit his tongue and licked his big lips over and took a look at me. Then he started grinning.

"I got the new bike, Muriel," he said. "I've got it outside. It's just come down from the works," he said.

"The laddie wants you to look at his bike," I said. So she went out and had a look at it.

When she came back she had got rid of him.

"Listen to that rain," she said. "Lord, I'm fed up with this line," she said.

"What line?" I said. "The hotel line?"

"Yes," she said. "I'm fed right up to the back teeth with it."

"And you've got good teeth," I said.

"There's not the class of person there used to be in it," she said. "All our family have got good teeth."

"Not the class?"

"I've been in it five years and there's not the same class at all. You never meet any fellows."

"Well," said I, "if they're like that half-wit at the garage, they're nothing to be stuck on. And you've met me."

I said it to her like that.

"Oh," says she. "It isn't as bad as that yet."

It was cold in the office. She used to sit all day in her overcoat. She was a smart girl with a big friendly chin and a second one coming, and her forehead and nose were covered with freckles. She had copper-coloured hair too. She got her shoes through the trade from Duke's traveller and her clothes, too, off the Hollenborough mantle man. I told her I could do her better stockings than the ones she'd got on. She got a good reduction on everything. Twenty-five or thirty-three and a third. She had her expenses cut right back. I took her to the pictures that night in the car. I made Colin get the car out for me.

"That boy wanted me to go on the back of his bike. On a night like this," she said.

"Oh," she said, when we got to the pictures. "Two shillings's too much. Let's go into the one-and-sixes at the side and we can nip across into the two-shillings when the lights go down."

"Fancy your father being an undertaker," she said in the middle of the show. And she started laughing as she had laughed before.

She had her head screwed on all right. She said:

"Some girls have no pride once the lights go down."

Every time I went to that town I took a box of something. Samples, mostly, they didn't cost me anything.

"Don't thank me," I said. "Thank the firm."

Every time I took her out I pulled the blinds in the back seat of the car to hide the samples. That chap Colin used to give us oil and petrol. He used to give me a funny look. Fishy sort of small eyes he'd got. Always looking miserable. Then we would go off. Sunday was her free day. Not that driving's any holiday for me. And, of course, the firm paid. She used to take me down to see her family for the day. Start in the morning, and taking it you had dinner and tea there, a day's outing cost us nothing. Her father was something on the railway, retired. He had a long stocking somewhere, but her sister, the one that was married, had had her share already.

He had a tumour after his wife died and they just played upon the old man's feelings. It wasn't right. She wouldn't go near her sister and I don't blame her, taking the money like that. Just played upon the old man's feelings.

Every time I was up there Colin used to come in looking for her.

"Oh, Colin," I used to say. "Done my car yet?" He knew where he got off with me.

"No, now, I can't, Colin. I tell you I'm going out with Mr. Humphrey," she used to say to him. I heard her.

"He keeps on badgering me," she said to me.

"You leave him to me," I said.

"No, he's all right," she said.

"You let me know if there's any trouble with Colin," I said. "Seems to be a harum-scarum sort of half-wit to me," I said.

"And he spends every penny he makes," she said.

Well, we know that sort of thing is all right while it lasts, I told her, but the trouble is that it doesn't last.

We were always meeting Colin on the road. I took no notice of it first of all and then I grew suspicious and awkward at always meeting him. He had a new motor bicycle. It was an Indian, a scarlet thing that he used to fly over the moor with, flat out. Muriel and I used to go out over the moor to Ingley Wood in the firm's Morris—I had a customer out that way.

"May as well do a bit of business while you're about it," I said.

"About what?" she said.

"Ah-ha!" I said. "That's what Colin wants to know," I said.

Sure enough, coming back we'd hear him popping and backfiring close behind us, and I put out my hand to stop him and keep him following us, biting our dirt.

"I see his little game," I said. "Following us."

So I saw to it that he did follow. We could hear him banging away behind us, and the traffic is thick on the Ingley road in the afternoon.

"Oh, let him pass," Muriel said. "I can't stand those dirty things banging in my ears."

I waved him on and past he flew with his scarf flying out, blazing red into the traffic. "We're doing fifty-eight ourselves," she said, leaning across to look.

"Powerful buses those," I said. "Any fool can do it if he's got the power. Watch me step on it."

But we did not catch Colin. Half an hour later he passed us coming back. Cut right in between us and a lorry—I had to brake hard. I damn nearly killed him. His ears were red with the wind. He didn't wear a hat. I got after him as soon as I could, but I couldn't touch him.

Nearly every weekend I was in that town seeing my girl, that fellow was hanging round. He came into the bar on Saturday nights, he poked his head into the office on Sunday mornings. It was a sure bet that if we went out in the car he would pass us on the road. Every time we would hear that scarlet thing roar by like a horse-stinger. It didn't matter where we were. He passed us on the main road, he met us down the side roads. There was a little cliff under oak trees at May Ponds, she said, where the view was pretty. And there, soon after we got there, was Colin on the other side of the water, watching us. Once we found him sitting on his bike, just as though he were waiting for us.

"You been here in a car?" I said.

"No, motorbike," she said, and blushed. "Cars can't follow in these tracks."

She knew a lot of places in that country. Some of the roads weren't roads at all and were bad for tyres and I didn't want the firm's car scratched by bushes, but you would have thought Colin could read what was in her mind. For nine times out of ten he was there. It got on my nerves. It was a red, roaring, powerful thing and he opened it full out.

"I'm going to speak to Colin," I said. "I won't have him annoying you."

"He's not annoying me," she said. "I've got a sense of humour."

"Here, Colin," I said one evening when I put the car away. "What's the idea?"

He was taking off his overalls. He pretended he did not know what I was talking about. He had a way of rolling his eyeballs, as if they had got wet and loose in his head, while he was speaking to me, and you never knew if it was sweat or oil on his face. It was always pale, with high colour on his cheeks and very red lips.

"Miss MacFarlane doesn't like being followed," I said.

He dropped his jaw and gaped at me. I could not tell whether he was being very surprised or very sly. I used to call him "Marbles" because when he spoke he seemed to have a lot of marbles in his mouth.

Then he said he never went to the places we went to, except by accident. He wasn't following us, he said, but we were following him. We never let him alone, he said. Everywhere he went, he said, we were there. Take last Saturday, he said, we were following him for miles down the bypass, he said. "But you passed us first and then sat down in front," I said. "I went to Ingley Wood," he said. "And you followed me there." No, we didn't, I said, Miss MacFarlane decided to go there.

He said he did not want to complain, but fair was fair. "I suppose you know," he said, "that you have taken my girl off me. Well, you can leave *me* alone, can't you?"

"Here," I said. "One minute! Not so fast! You said I've taken Miss MacFarlane from you. Well, she was never your girl. She only knew you in a friendly way."

"She was my girl" was all he said.

He was pouring oil into my engine. He had some cotton wool in one hand and the can in the other. He wiped up the green oil that had overflowed, screwed on the cap, pulled down the bonnet, and whistled to himself.

I went back to Muriel and told her what Colin had said.

"I don't like trouble," I said.

"Don't you worry," she said. "I had to have someone to go to all these places with before you came. Couldn't stick in here all day Sunday."

"Ah," I said. "That's it, is it? You've been to all these places with him?"

"Yes," she said. "And he keeps on going to them. He's sloppy about me."

"Good God," I said. "Sentimental memories."

I felt sorry for that fellow. He knew it was hopeless, but he loved her. I suppose he couldn't help himself. Well, it takes all sorts to make a world, as my old mother used to say. If we were all alike it wouldn't do. Some men can't save money. It just runs through their fingers. He couldn't save money, so he lost her. I suppose all he thought of was love.

I could have been friends with that fellow. As it was, I put a lot of business his way. I didn't want him to get the wrong idea about me. We're all human after all.

We didn't have any more trouble with Colin after this until Bank Holiday. I was going to take her down to see my family. The old man's getting a bit past it now and has given up living over the shop. He's living out on the Barnum Road, beyond the tram stop. We were going down in the firm's car, as per usual, but something went wrong with the mag and Colin had not got it right for the holiday. I was wild about this. What's the use of a garage who can't do a rush job for the holidays! What's the use of being an old customer if they're going to let you down! I went for Colin bald-headed.

"You knew I wanted it," I said. "It's no use trying to put me off with a tale about the stuff not coming down from the works. I've heard that one before."

I told him he'd got to let me have another car, because he'd let me down. I told him I wouldn't pay his account. I said I'd take my business away from him. But there wasn't a car to be had in the town because of the holiday. I could have knocked the fellow down. After the way I'd sent business to him.

Then I saw through his little game. He knew Muriel and I were going to my people and he had done this to stop it. The moment I saw this I let him know that it would take more than him to stop me doing what I wanted.

I said: "Right. I shall take the amount of Miss MacFarlane's train fare and my own from the account at the end of the month."

I said: "You may run a garage, but you don't run the railway service."

I was damned angry going by train. I felt quite lost on the railway after having a car. It was crowded with trippers too. It was slow—stopping at all the stations. The people come in, they tread all over your feet, they make you squeeze up till you're crammed against the window, and the women stick out their elbows and fidget. And then the expense! a return for two runs you into just over a couple of quid. I could have murdered Colin.

We got there at last. We walked up from the tram stop. Mother was at the window and let us in.

"This is Miss MacFarlane," I said.

And Mother said: "Oh, pleased to meet you. We've heard a lot about you.

"Oh," Mother said to me, giving me a kiss, "are you tired? You haven't had your tea, have you? Sit down. Have this chair, dear. It's more comfortable."

"Well, my boy," my father said.

"Want a wash," my father said. "We've got a washbasin downstairs," he said. "I used not to mind about washing upstairs before. Now I couldn't do without it. Funny how your ideas change as you get older.

"How's business?" he said.

"Mustn't grumble," I said. "How's yours?"

"You knew," he said, "we took off the horses: except for one or two of the older families we have got motors now."

But he'd told me that the last time I was there. I'd been at him for years about motor hearses.

"You've forgotten I used to drive them," I said.

"Bless me, so you did," he said.

He took me up to my room. He showed me everything he had done to the house. "Your mother likes it," he said. "The traffic's company for her. You know what your mother is for company."

Then he gives me a funny look.

"Who's the girl?" he says.

My mother came in then and said: "She's pretty, Arthur."

"Of course she's pretty," I said. "She's Irish."

"Oh," said the old man. "Irish! Got a sense of humour, eh?"

"She wouldn't be marrying me if she hadn't," I said. And then I gave *them* a look.

"Marrying her, did you say?" exclaimed my father.

"Any objection?" I said.

"Now, Ernest dear," said my mother. "Leave the boy alone. Come down while I pop the kettle on."

She was terribly excited.

"Miss MacFarlane," the old man said.

"No sugar, thank you, Mrs. Humphrey. I beg your pardon, Mr. Humphrey?"

"The Glen Hotel at Swansea, I don't suppose you know that?" my father said. "I wondered if you did, being in the catering line."

"It doesn't follow she knows every hotel," my mother said.

"Forty years ago," the old man said, "I was staying at the Glen in Swansea and the headwaiter—"

"Oh, no, not that one. I'm sure Miss MacFarlane doesn't want to hear that one," my mother said.

"How's business with you, Mr. Humphrey?" said Muriel. "We passed a large cemetery near the station."

"Dad's Ledger," I said.

"The whole business has changed so that you wouldn't know it, in my lifetime," said my father. "Silver fittings have gone clean out. Everyone wants simplicity nowadays. Restraint. Dignity," my father said.

"Prices did it," my father said.

"The war," he said.

"You couldn't get the wood," he said.

"Take ordinary mahogany, just an ordinary piece of mahogany. Or teak," he said. "Take teak. Or walnut."

"You can certainly see the world go by in this room," I said to my mother.

"It never stops," she said.

Now it was all bicycles over the new concrete road from the gun factory. Then traction engines and cars. They came up over the hill where the A.A. man stands and choked up round the tram stop. It was mostly holiday traffic. Everything with a wheel on it was out.

"On this stretch," my father told me, "they get three accidents a week." There was an ambulance station at the crossroads.

We had hardly finished talking about this—in fact, the old man was still saying that something ought to be done—when the telephone rang.

"Name of MacFarlane?" the voice said on the wire.

"No. Humphrey," my father said. "There is a Miss MacFarlane here."

"There's a man named Colin Mitchell lying seriously injured in an accident at the Cottage Hospital, gave me the name of MacFarlane as his nearest relative." ·

That was the police. On to it at once. That fellow Colin had followed us down by road.

Cry, I never heard a girl cry as Muriel cried when we came back from the hospital. He had died in the ambulance. Cutting in, the old game he used to play on me. Clean off the saddle and under the Birmingham bus. The blood was everywhere, they said. People were still looking at it when we went by. Head on. What a mess! Don't let's talk about it.

She wanted to see him, but they said no. There wasn't anything recognizable to see. She put her arms round my neck and cried, "Colin, Colin," as if I were Colin, and clung to me. I was feeling sick myself. I held her tight and I kissed her and I thought: Holiday ruined.

Damn fool man, I thought. Poor devil, I thought.

"I knew he'd do something like this."

"There, there," I said to her. "Don't think about Colin."

Didn't she love me, I said, and not Colin? Hadn't she got me? She said yes, she had. And she loved me. But, "Oh, Colin! Oh, Colin!" she cried. "And Colin's mother," she cried. "Oh, it's terrible." She cried and cried.

We put her to bed and I sat with her, and my mother kept coming in.

"Leave her to me," I said. "I understand her."

Before they went to bed they both came in and looked at her. She lay sobbing with her head in the pillow.

I could quite understand her being upset. Colin was a decent fellow. He was always doing things for her. He mended her electric lamp and he riveted the stem of a wineglass so that you couldn't see the break. He used to make things for her. He was very good with his hands.

She lay on her side with her face burning and feverish with misery and crying, scalded by the salt, and her lips shrivelled up. I put my arm under her neck and I stroked her forehead. She groaned. Sometimes she shivered and sometimes she clung to me, crying: "Oh, Colin! Colin!"

My arm ached with the cramp and I had a crick in my back, sitting in the awkward way I was on the bed. It was late. There was nothing to do but to ache and sit watching her and thinking. It is funny the way your mind drifts. When I was kissing her and watching her I was thinking out who I'd show our new Autumn range to first. Her hand held my wrist tight, and when I kissed her I got her tears on my lips. They burned and stung. Her neck and shoulders were soft and I could feel her breath hot out of her nostrils on the back of my hand. Ever noticed how hot a woman's breath gets when she's crying? I drew out my hand and lay down beside her and "Oh, Colin, Colin," she sobbed, turning over and clinging to me. And so I lay there, listening to the traffic, staring at the ceiling, and shivering whenever the picture of Colin shooting right off that damned red thing into the bus came into my mind—until I did not hear the traffic any more, or see the ceiling any more, or think any more, but a change happened—I don't know when. This Colin thing seemed to have knocked the bottom out of everything and I had a funny feeling we were going down and down and down in a lift. And the further we went, the hotter and softer she got. Perhaps it was when I found with my hands that she had very big breasts. But it was like being on the mail steamer and feeling engines start under your feet, thumping louder and louder. You can feel it in every vein of your body. Her mouth opened and her tears dried. Her breath came through her open mouth and her voice was blind and husky. Colin, Colin, Colin, she said, and her fingers were hooked into me. I got out and turned the key in the door.

In the morning I left her sleeping. It did not matter to me what my father might have heard in the night, but still I wondered. She would hardly let me touch her before that. I told her I was sorry, but she shut me up. I was afraid of her. I was afraid of mentioning Colin. I wanted to go out of the house there and then and tell someone everything. Did she love Colin all the time? Did she think I was Colin? And every time I thought of that poor devil covered over with a white sheet in the hospital mortuary, a kind of picture of her and me under the sheets with love came into my mind. I couldn't separate the two things. Just as though it had all come from Colin.

I'd rather not talk any more about that. I never talked to Muriel about it. I waited for her to say something, but she didn't. She didn't say a word.

The next day was a bad day. It was grey and hot and the air smelt of oil fumes from the road. There's always a mess to clear up when things like this happen. I had to see to it. I had the job of ringing up the boy's mother. But I got round that, thank God, by ringing up the garage and getting them to go round and see the old lady. My father is useless when things are like this. I was the whole morning on the phone: to the hospital, the police, the coroner—and he stood fussing beside me, jerking up and down like a fat indiarubber ball.

I found my mother washing up at the sink and she said: "That poor boy's mother! I can't stop thinking of her."

Then my father comes in and says—just as though I was a customer: "Of course if Mrs. Mitchell desires it we can have the remains of the deceased conveyed to his house by one of our new specially sprung motor hearses and can, if necessary, make all the funeral arrangements."

I could have hit him because Muriel came into the room when he was saying this. But she stood there as if nothing had happened.

"It's the least we can do for poor Mrs. Mitchell," she said. There were small creases of shadow under her eyes, which shone with a soft strong light I had never seen before. She walked as if she were really still in that room with me, asleep. God, I loved that girl! God, I wanted to get all this over, this damned Colin business that had come right into the middle of everything like this, and I wanted to get married right away. I wanted to be alone with her. That's what Colin did for me.

"Yes," I said. "We must do the right thing by Colin."

"We are sometimes asked for long-distance estimates," my father said.

"It will be a little something," my mother said.

"Dad and I will talk it over," I said.

"Come into the office," my father said. "It occurred to me that it would be nice to do the right thing by this friend of yours."

We talked it over. We went into the cost of it. There was the return journey to reckon. We worked it out that it would come no dearer to old Mrs. Mitchell than if she took the train and buried the boy here. That is to say, my father said, if I drove it.

"It would look nice," my father said. "Saves money and it would look a bit friendly," my father said. "You've done it before."

"Well," I said. "I suppose I can get a refund on my return ticket from the railway."

But it was not as simple as it looked, because Muriel wanted to come. She wanted to drive back with me and the hearse. My mother was very worried about this. It might upset Muriel, she thought. Father thought it might not look nice to see a young girl sitting by the coffin of a grown man.

"It must be dignified," my father said. "You see, if she was there, it might look as though she were just doing it for the ride—like these young women on bakers' vans."

My father took me out into the hall to tell me this because he did not want her to hear. But she would not have it. She wanted to come back with Colin.

"Colin loved me. It is my duty to him," she said. "Besides," she said suddenly, in her full open voice—it had seemed to be closed and carved and broken and small—"I've never been in a hearse before."

"And it will save her fare too," I said to my father.

That night I went again to her room. She was awake. I said I was sorry to disturb her, but I would go at once only I wanted to see if she was all right. She said, in the closed voice again, that she was all right.

"Are you sure?" I said.

She did not answer. I was worried. I went over to the bed.

"What is the matter? Tell me what is the matter," I said.

For a long time she was silent. I held her hand, I stroked her head. She was lying stiff in the bed. She would not answer. I dropped my hand to her small white shoulder. She stirred and drew up her legs and half turned and said, "I was thinking of Colin. Where is he?" she asked.

"They've brought him round. He's lying downstairs."

"In the front room?"

"Yes, ready for the morning. Now be a sensible girl and go back by train."

"No, no," she said. "I want to go with Colin. Poor Colin. He loved me and I didn't love him." And she drew my hands down to her breasts.

"Colin loved me," she whispered.

"Not like this," I whispered.

It was a warm grey morning like all the others when we took Colin back. They had fixed the coffin in before Muriel came out. She came down wearing the bright-blue hat she had got off Dormer's millinery man and she kissed my mother and father good-bye. They were very sorry for her. "Look after her, Arthur," my mother said. Muriel got in beside me without a glance behind her at the coffin. I started the engine. They smiled at us. My father raised his hat, but whether it was to Muriel and me or to Colin, or to the three of us, I do not know. He was not, you see, wearing his top hat. I'll say this for the old boy, thirty years in the trade have taught him tact.

After leaving my father's house you have to go down to the tram terminus before you get on the bypass. There was always one or two drivers, conductors, or inspectors there, doing up their tickets, or changing over the trolley arms. When we passed I saw two of them drop their jaws, stick their pencils in their ears, and raise their hats. I was so surprised by this that I nearly raised mine in acknowledgement, forgetting that we had the coffin behind. I had not driven one of my father's hearses for years.

Hearses are funny things to drive. They are well-sprung, smooth-running cars, with quiet engines, and if you are used to driving a smaller car, before you know where you are, you are speeding. You know you ought to go slow, say twenty-five to thirty maximum, and it's hard to keep it down. You can return empty at seventy if you like. It's like driving a fire engine. Go fast out and come back slow—only the other way round. Open out in the country, but slow down past houses. That's what it means. My father was very particular about this.

Muriel and I didn't speak very much at first. We sat listening to the engine and the occasional jerk of the coffin behind when we went over a pothole. We passed the place where poor Colin—but I didn't say anything to Muriel, and she, if she noticed—which I doubt—did not say anything to me. We went through Cox Hill, Wammering, and Yodley Mount, flat country, don't care for it myself. "There's a wonderful lot of building going on," Muriel said at last.

"You won't know these places in five years," I said.

But my mind kept drifting away from the road and the green fields and the dullness, and back to Colin—five days before, he had come down this way. I expected to see that Indian coming flying straight out of every corner. But it was all bent and bust up properly now. I saw the damned thing.

He had been up to his old game, following us, and that had put the end to following. But not quite; he was following us now, behind us in the coffin. Then my mind drifted off that and I thought of those nights at my parents' house, and Muriel. You never know what a woman is going to be like. I thought, too, that it had put my calculations out. I mean, supposing she had a baby. You see I had reckoned on waiting eighteen months or so. I would have eight hundred then. But if we had to get married at once, we should have to cut right down. Then I kept thinking it was funny her saying "Colin!" like that in the night; it was funny it made her feel that way with me, and how it made me feel when she called me Colin. I'd never thought of her in that way, in what you might call the "Colin" way.

I looked at her and she looked at me and she smiled but still we did not say very much, but the smiles kept coming to both of us. The light-railway bridge at Dootheby took me by surprise and I thought the coffin gave a jump as we took it.

"Colin's still watching us," I nearly said.

There were tears in her eyes.

"What was the matter with Colin?" I said. "Nice chap, I thought. Why didn't you marry him?"

"Yes," she said. "He was a nice boy. But he'd no sense of humour.

"And I wanted to get out of that town," she said.

"I'm not going to stay there, at that hotel," she said.

"I want to get away," she said. "I've had enough."

She had a way of getting angry with the air, like that. "You've got to take me away," she said. We were passing slowly into Muster, there was a tram ahead and people thick on the narrow pavements, dodging out into the road. But when we got into the Market Square, where they were standing round, they saw the coffin. They began to raise their hats. Suddenly she laughed. "It's like being the King and Queen," she said.

"They're raising their hats," she said.

"Not all of them," I said.

She squeezed my hand and I had to keep her from jumping about like a child on the seat as we went through.

"There they go."

"Boys always do," I said.

"And another.

"Let's see what the policeman does."

She started to laugh, but I shut her up. "Keep your sense of humour to yourself," I said.

Through all those towns that run into one another as you might say, we caught it. We went through, as she said, like royalty. So many years since I drove a hearse, I'd forgotten what it was like.

I was proud of her, I was proud of Colin, and I was proud of myself. And after what had happened, I mean on the last two nights, it was like a wedding. And although we knew it was for Colin, it was for us too, because Colin was with both of us. It was like this all the way.

"Look at that man there. Why doesn't he raise his hat? People ought to show respect for the dead," she said.

The Wheelbarrow

"Robert," Miss Freshwater's niece called down from the window of the dismantled bedroom, "when you have finished that, would you mind coming upstairs a minute? I want you to move a trunk."

And when Evans waved back from the far side of the rumpled lawn where he was standing by the bonfire, she closed the window to keep out the smoke of slow-burning rubbish—old carpeting, clothes, magazines, papers, boxes—which hung about the waists of the fir trees and blew towards the house. For three days the fire had been burning, and Evans, red-armed in his shirt-sleeves and sweating along the seams of his brow, was prodding it with a garden fork. A sudden silly tongue of yellow flame wagged out: some inflammable piece of family history—who knew what? Perhaps one of her aunt's absurd summer hats or a shocking year of her father's daydream accountancy was having its last fling. She saw Evans pick up a bit of paper from the outskirts of the fire and read it. What was it? Miss Freshwater's niece drew back her lips and opened her mouth expectantly. At this stage all family privacy had gone. Thirty, forty, fifty years of life were going up in smoke.

Evans took up the wheelbarrow and swaggered back with it across the lawn towards the house, sometimes tipping it a little to one side to see how the rubber-tyred wheel was running and to admire it. Miss Freshwater's niece smiled. With his curly black hair, his sun-reddened face, and his vacant blue eyes, and the faint white scar or chip on the side of his nose, he looked like some hard-living, hard-bitten doll. "Burn this? This lot to go?" was his cry. He was an impassioned and natural destroyer. She could not have found a better man. "Without you, Robert," she said on the first day and with real feeling, "I could never have faced it."

It was pure luck getting him, but, lazy, smiling and drifting, she always fell on her feet. She had stepped off the morning train from London at the beginning of the week and had stood on the kerb in the station yard, waiting for one of the two or three taxi drivers who were talking there to take notice of her. Suddenly Evans drove in fast from the street outside, pulled up beside her, pushed her in, and drove off. It was like an abduction. The other taxi drivers shouted at him in the bad language of law-abiding men, but Evans slowly moved his hand up and down, palm downwards, silently and insultingly telling them to shut up and keep their hair on. He looked very pious as he did this. It made her laugh out loud.

"They are manner-less," he said in a slow, rebuking voice, giving each syllable its clear value as if he were speaking the phrase of a poem. "I am sorry I did not ask you where you want me to take you."

They were going in the wrong direction, and he had to swing round the street. She now saw him glance at her in the mirror and his doll's eyes quickly changed from shrewd pleasure to vacancy: she was a capture.

"This is not the first time you are here, I suppose?" he said.

"I was born here," she said. "I haven't been here for twenty-five years—well, perhaps just for a day a few years ago. It has changed. All this building!"

She liked friendly conversations.

They were driving up the long hill out of the town towards her aunt's house. Once there had been woodland here, but now, like a red hard sea flowing in to obliterate her memory, thousands of sharp villas replaced the trees in angular waves.

"Yes," he said simply. "There is money everywhere."

The car hummed up the long, concrete hill. The villas gave way to ribbons of shacks and bungalows. The gardens were buzzing with June flowers. He pointed out a bungalow that had a small grocery shop in the lean-to at the side, a yard where a couple of old cars stood, and a petrol pump. That was his place, he said. And then, beyond that, were the latest municipal housing estates built close to the Green, which was only half a mile from her aunt's house. As they passed, she saw a white marquee on the Green and a big sagging white banner with the words "Gospel Mission" daubed on it.

"I see the Gospellers still keep it up," she said. For it was all bad land outside the town, a place for squatters, poor craftsmen, smallholders, little men with little sheds, who in their flinty way had had for generations the habit of breaking out into little religious sects.

"Oh, yes," said Evans in a soft voice, shocked that she could doubt it. "There are great openings. There is a mighty coming to the Lord. I toil in the vineyard myself. You are Miss Freshwater's niece?" he said. "She was a toiler too. She was a giantess for the Lord."

She saw she had been reckless in laughing. She saw she was known. It was as if he had knowingly captured her.

"You don't come from these parts, do you?" she said.

"I am from Wales," he said. "I came here from the mines. I objected to the starvation."

They arrived at the ugly yellow house. It could hardly be seen through the overgrown laurels and fir trees which in some places fingered the dirty windows. He steadied her as she got out, for she had put on weight in the last year or so, and while she opened her bag to find some money, he walked to the gate and looked in.

"It was left to you in the will, I suppose?" he said.

"Yes," she said. She was a woman always glad to confide. "I've come down to clear up the rubbish before the sale. Do you know anyone here who would give me a hand?"

"There are many," he pronounced. "They are too handy." It was like a line from an anthem. He went ahead, opened the gate, and led the way in, and when she opened the front door, splitting it away from the cobwebs, he went in with her, walking into the stale, sun-yellowed rooms. He looked up the worn carpet of the stairs. He looked at the ceilings, measuring the size of everything.

"It will fetch a high price," he said in a sorrowful voice and then, looking over her figure like a farmer at the market, in case she might go with the property, he added enthusiasm to his sorrow.

"The highest!" he said. "Does this door go to the back?" She lost him for a while. When she found him he was outside, at the back of the house, looking into sheds. He had opened the door of one that contained gardening tools and there he was, gazing. He was looking at a new green metal wheelbarrow with a red wheel and a rubber tyre and he had even pulled it out. He pushed it back, and when he saw her he said accusingly:

"This door has no lock. I do not like to see a door without a lock. I will bring one this afternoon."

It was how she knew he had appointed himself.

"But who will do your taxi work?"

"My son will do that," he said.

From that moment he owned her and the house.

"There will be a lot of toil in this vineyard," she said to him maliciously and wished she had not said it; but Evans's eyes lost their vacancy again and quickened and sparkled. He gave a shout of laughter.

"Oh, boy, there will!" he said, admiring her. And he went off. She walked from room to room opening windows, and from an upper one she saw distantly the white sheet of the Gospel tent through the fir trees. She could settle to nothing.

It was an ugly house of large mean rooms, the landings dark, the stairs steep. The furniture might have come out of old-fashioned hotels and had the helpless look of objects too large, ill-met commercially, and too gregarious. After her mother's death, her father had moved his things into his sister's house. Taste had not been a strong point in the family. The books, mainly sermons, were her grandfather's; his son had lived on a hoard of engineering textbooks and magazines. The sister read chiefly the Bible and the rest of her time changed her clothes, having the notion that she might be going out.

What paralysed Miss Freshwater's niece was the emptiness of the place. She had expected to disturb ghosts if she opened a drawer. She had expected to remember herself. Instead, as she waited for Evans to come on the first day she had the sensation of being ignored. Nothing watched in the shadows, nothing blinked in the beams of sunlight slanting across the room. The room she had slept in meant nothing. To fit memories into it was a task so awkward and artificial that she gave up trying. Several times she went to the window, waiting for Evans to walk in at the gate and for the destruction to begin.

When he did come he seized the idea at once. All files marked "A.H.F."—that was her father—were "rubbish."

"Thorpe?" he said. "A.H.F., more A.H.F.! Burn it?" He was off with his first load to lay the foundation to the fire.

"And get this carpet up. We shall trip on it: it is torn," she said. He ripped the carpet off the stairs. He tossed the doormats, which were worn into holes, outside. By the barrowload out went the magazines. Every now and then some object took his eye—a leather strap, a bowl, a pipe rack—which he put into a little heap of other perquisites at the back door.

But to burn was his passion, to push the wheelbarrow his joy. He swaggered with it. He unloaded it carefully at the fire, not putting it down too near or roughly tipping it. He often tried one or two different grips on the handles before he started off. Once, she saw him stop in the middle of the lawn and turn it upside down and look it over carefully and make the wheel spin. Something wrong? No, he lovingly wiped the wheel with a handful of grass, got an oilcan from his pocket, and gave the wheel a squirt. Then he righted the wheelbarrow and came on with it round the house, singing in a low and satisfied voice. A hymn, it sounded like. And at the end of the day, when she took him a cup of tea and they stood chatting, his passion satisfied for the time being, he had a good look at her. His eye was on the brooch she was carelessly wearing to fasten her green overall. He came closer and put his hand to the brooch and lifted it.

"Those are pearls, I shouldn't wonder?" he said.

"Yes," she said. He stepped nimbly away, for he was as quick as a flea.

"It is beautiful," he said, considering the brooch and herself together. "You would not buy it for fifty pounds, nor even a hundred, I suppose. A present, I expect?" And before she could answer, he said gravely: "Half past five! I will lock the sheds. Are you sleeping here? My wife would go off her head, alone in the house. When I'm at the mission, she's insane!"

Evans stared at Miss Freshwater's niece, waiting for a response to his drama. She did not know what to do, so she laughed. Evans gave a shout of laughter too. It shook the close black curls of his hair and the scar on the side of his nose went white.

"I have the key," he said seriously, and went off.

"Robert!" Miss Freshwater's niece opened the window and called again. "Can you come now? I can't get on."

Evans was on his way once more to the house. He stamped quickly up the bare stairs.

"I'm in here," she called. "If you can get in!"

There was a heap of old brown paper knee-high at the door. Some of the drawers of a chest had been taken out, others were half open; a wardrobe's doors were open wide. There were shoes, boxes, and clothes piled on the bed, which was stripped. She had a green scarf in a turban round her head, and none of her fair hair could be seen. Her face, with its strong bones and pale skin marked by dirty fingers, looked hard, humorous, and naked. Her strong lips were dry and pale with dust.

They understood each other. At first he had bossed her, but she had fought back on the second day and they were equals now. She spoke to him as if they were in a conspiracy together, deciding what should be "saved" and what should be "cast into the flames." She used those words purposely, as a dig of malice at him. She was taller than he. She couldn't get over the fact that he preached every night at the mission and she had fallen into the habit of tempting him by some movement of arm or body, when she caught him looking at her. Her aunt had used the word "inconvenient," when her niece was young, to describe the girl's weakness for dawdling about with gardeners, chauffeurs, errand boys. Miss Freshwater's niece had lost the sense of the "convenient" very early in life.

"I've started upstairs now," she said to Evans. "It's worse than downstairs. Look at it."

Evans came a step further into the room and slowly looked round, nodding his head.

She leaned a little forward, her hands together, eagerly waiting for him to laugh so that they could laugh together.

"She never threw away a scrap of paper. Not even paper bags. Look at this," she said.

He waded into the heap and peeped into a brown paper bag. It contained a bun, as hard as stone.

"Biscuits too," she said. "Wrapped up! Like a larder. They must have been here for years. In the top drawer."

Evans did not laugh.

"She feared starvation," he said: "old people are hungry. They are greedy. My grandmother nibbled like a little rat, all day. And in the night too. They wake up in the night and they are afraid. They eat for comfort. The mice did not get in, I hope," he said, going to look in the drawer.

"She was eighty-four," she said.

"My grandmother was ninety," he said. "My father's mother. She liked to hear a mouse. It was company, she said."

"I think my aunt must have been fond of moths," she said. "They came out in clouds from that wardrobe. Look at all those dresses. I can hardly bear to touch them."

She shook a couple of dresses in the wardrobe and then took them out. "There you are, did you see it? There goes one."

She held up an old-fashioned silk dress.

"Not worn for twenty years, you can see by the fashion. There!" She gave the dress a pull. "Did you hear? Perished. Rotten. They are all like that. You can't give them away. They'd fall off you."

She threw the dresses on the floor and he picked up one and he saw where moths had eaten it.

"It is wicked," he said. "All that money gone to waste."

"Where moth and dust doth corrupt," she mocked him, and took an armful of the clothes and threw them on the floor. "Why did she buy them if she did not want them? And all those hats we had to burn? You haven't seen anything yet. Look at this."

On the bed was lying a pile of enormous lace-up corsets. Evans considered them.

"The men had patience," he said.

"Oh, she was not married," she said.

He nodded.

"That is how all the property comes to you, I suppose," he said. There was a shrewd flash in his blue eyes and she knew he had been gazing at her all this time and not at the clothes; but even as she caught his look the dissembling, still, vacant light slid back into it.

"Shoes!" she said with excitement. "Do you want any shoes?" A large number of shoes of all kinds, little worn or not worn at all, were rowed in pairs on the bed and some had been thrown into a box as well.

"Fifty-one pairs I counted," she said. "She never went out but she went on ordering them. There's a piece of paper in each pair. Have a look. Read it. What does it say?"

He took a piece of paper out of a shoe.

" 'Comfortable for the evening,' " he read out. He took another. " 'For wet weather.' Did it rain indoors?"

She took one and read out: " 'With my blue dress'! Can you imagine? 'Sound walking pair.' " She laughed, but he interrupted her.

"In Wales they lacked them," he said. "In the bad times they were going barefoot. My sisters shared a pair for dances."

"What shall I do with them?" she asked. "Someone could wear them."

"There are good times now. They have the money," he said, snubbing her. "They buy new."

"I mean—anyone," she said. "They are too big for me. I'll show you."

She sat down on a packing case and slipped her foot into a silver evening shoe.

"You can see, my feet are lost in them," she said.

"You have small feet," he said. "In Wales the men would be chasing you."

"After chapel, I've no doubt," she said. "Up the mountain—what was the name of it? You told me."

"It has the best view in Wales. But those who go up it never see it," he laughed. "Try this pair," he said, kneeling down and lifting her foot. "Ah no, I see. But look at those legs, boy!"

Miss Freshwater's niece got up.

"What size does your wife take?" she asked.

"I don't know," he said, very pleased with himself. "Where is this trunk you said we had to move?"

"Out in the landing cupboard. I'll show you. I can't move it."

She led the way to the landing and bent down to tug at it.

"You must not do that," he said, putting his hands on her waist and moving her out of the way. He heaved at the trunk and tipped it on end. She wanted it, she said, in the light, where she could see.

"Here on the chest," she said.

He lifted it up and planked it down on the chest.

"Phew!" he said. "You have a small waist for a married woman. Soft. My wife is a giantess, she weighs thirteen stone. And yet you're big, too, oh, yes, you are. But you have light bones. With her, now, it is the bones that weigh. Shall we open it?"

She sat down on a chair and felt in her pocket for a mirror.

"Why didn't you tell me I looked such a sight?" she said, wiping her face. "Yes, open it."

The trunk was made of black leather; it was cracked, peeling, stained, and squashed by use. Dimly printed on it was her father's fading name in white, large letters. The trunk had been pitched and bumped and slithered out of ships' holds and trains, all over the world. Its lid, now out of the true, no longer met the lock and it was closed by a strap. It had lain ripening and decaying in attics and lofts for half a lifetime.

"What is in it?" she called, without looking from her mirror.

"Clothes," he said. "Books. A pair of skates. Did the old lady go skating?"

He pulled out a Chinese hat. There was a pigtail attached to it and he held it up.

"Ah," he called. "This is the job." He put the hat on his head and pulled out a mandarin coat.

Miss Freshwater's niece stared and then she flushed.

"Where did you get that?" she cried, jumping up, taking the hat from his head and snatching the coat. "They're mine! Where were they?"

She pushed him aside and pulled one or two things from the trunk. "They're mine!" she accused him. "All mine."

She aged as she looked at him. A photograph fell to the floor as she lifted up a book. " 'To darling Laura,' " she read out. "Tennyson."

"Who is this?" he said, picking up the photograph.

She did not hear. She was pulling out a cold, sequined evening dress that shrank almost to nothing as she picked it up.

"Good God," she said and dropped it with horror. For under the dress was an album. "Where," she said, sharply possessive, "did you put the skates?" She opened the album. She looked at a road deep in snow leading to a hotel with eaves a yard wide. She had spent her honeymoon there.

"Kitzbühel," she said. "Oh, no!"

She looked fiercely at him to drive him away. The house, so anonymous, so absurd, so meaningless and ghostless, had suddenly got her. There was a choke of cold wonder in her throat.

She turned on him. "Can't you clear up all that paper in the room?" She did not want to be seen by him.

Evans went to the door of the bedroom and, after a glance inside, came back. He was not going to leave her. He picked up the book of poems, glanced at a page or two, and then dropped it back in the trunk.

"Everyone knows," he said scornfully, "that the Welsh are the founders of all the poetry of Europe."

She did not hear him. Her face had drained of waking light. She had entered blindly into a dream in which she could hardly drag herself along. She was looking painfully through the album, rocking her head slowly from side to side, her mouth opening a little and closing on the point of speech, a shoulder rising as if she had been hurt, and her back moving and swaying as she felt the clasp of the past like hands on her. She was looking at ten forgotten years of her life, her own life, not her family's, and she did not laugh when she saw the skirts too long, the top-heavy hats hiding the eyes, her face too full and fat, her plainness so sullen, her prettiness too open-mouthed and loud, her look too grossly sly. In this one, sitting at the café table by the lake when she was nineteen, she looked masterful and at least forty. In this garden picture she was theatrically fancying herself as an ancient Greek in what looked like a nightgown! One of her big toes, she noticed, turned up comically in the sandal she was wearing. Here on a rock by the sea, in a bathing dress, she had got thin again—that was her marriage—and look at her hair! This picture of the girl on skis, sharp-faced, the eyes narrowed—who was that? Herself—yet how could she have looked like that! But she smiled a little at last at the people she had forgotten. This man with the crinkled fair hair, a German—how mad she had been about him. But what pierced her was that in each picture of herself she was just out of reach, flashing and yet dead; and that really it was the things that burned in the light of permanence—the chairs, the tables, the trees, the car outside the café, the motor launch on the lake. These blinked and glittered. They had lasted and were ageless, untouched by time, and she was not. She put the album back into the trunk and pulled out an old tweed coat and skirt. Under it was an exercise book with the word "Diary" written on it in a hand more weakly rounded than the hand she wrote today. Part of a letter fell out of the diary, the second page, it seemed, of a letter of her own. She read it.

" . . . the job at any rate," she read. "For a whole week he's forgotten his chest, his foot, his stomach. He's not dying any more!!! He conde (crossed out) congratulates himself and says it just shows how doctors are all fools. Inner self-confidence is what I need, he tells me!! It means giving up the flat and that's what I keep thinking—Oxford will be much more difficult for you and me. Women, he says, aren't happy unless they're sacrificing themselves. Darling, he doesn't know: it's the thought of You that keeps . . ."

She turned over the page. Nothing. She looked through the diary. Nothing. She felt sick and then saw Evans had not gone and was watching her. She quickly put the letter back into the diary.

"Ah," she said nervously. "I didn't know you were here. I'll show you something." She laughed unnaturally and opened the album until she found the most ludicrous and abashing picture in the book, one that would humiliate her entirely. "Here, look at this."

There was a see-saw in the foreground surrounded by raucously laughing people wearing paper hats and looking as though they had been dipped in glycerine: she was astride at the higher end of the see-saw, kicking her legs, and on the lower end was a fat young man in a pierrot costume. On her short, fuzzy, fair hair was a paper hat. She showed the picture to Evans and picked out the terrible sequin dress from the trunk.

"That's the dress!" she said, pointing to the picture. "I was engaged to him. Isn't it terrible?" And she dropped the dress back again. It felt cold and slippery, almost wet. "I didn't marry him."

Evans scowled.

"You were naked," he said with disgust.

"I remember now. I left it all here. I kept that dress for years. I'll have to go through it all." And she pulled down the lid.

"This photograph fell out," he said.

It was the picture of another young man.

"Is this your husband?" Evans asked, studying the man.

"My husband is dead," she said sharply. "That is a friend." And she threw the picture back into the trunk. She realized now that Evans had been holding her arm a long time. She stepped away from him abruptly. The careless friendliness, the sense of conspiracy she had felt while they worked together, had gone. She drew away and said, in the hostile voice of unnecessary explanation:

"I mean," she said, "my husband died a few years ago. We were divorced. I mustn't waste any more time."

"My wife would not condescend to that," he said.

"She has no reason, I am sure," said Miss Freshwater's niece severely, and returned to the bedroom.

"Now! We can't waste time like this. You'd better begin with what is on the bed. And when you've cleared it you can put the kettle on."

When Evans had gone downstairs with his load, she went to the landing and glared at the trunk. Her fists were clenched; she wished it was alive and that she could hit it. Glancing over the banisters to be sure she was alone, she opened it again, took out the photograph and the letter from her diary and put them in her handbag. She thought she was going to be sick or faint, for the past was drumming, like a train coming nearer and nearer, in her head.

"My God," she said. And when she saw her head in its turban and her face hardened by shock and grief in her aunt's absurd dressing-table mirror, she exclaimed with real horror. She was crying. "What a mess," she said and pulled the scarf off her head. Her fair, thick hair hung round her face untidily. Not once, in all those photographs, had a face so wolfish with bitterness and without laughter looked back at her.

"I'm taking the tea out," Evans called from below.

"I'm just coming," she called back and hurriedly tried to arrange her hair and then, because she had cried a little, she put on her glasses. Evans gave a keen look at the change in her when she got downstairs and walked through the hall to the door.

He had put the tray on the grass near a yew hedge in the hot corner at the side of the house and was standing a few yards away drinking his tea. In the last two days he had never drunk his tea near her but had chatted from a distance.

In her glasses and with her hair girlishly brushed back, Miss Freshwater's niece looked cold, tall, and grand, like a headmistress.

"I hope we shan't get any more smoke here," she said. "Sit down. You look too restless."

She was very firm, nodding to the exact place on the lawn on which she required him to sit. Taken aback, Evans sat precisely in that place. She sat on the grass and poured herself a cup of tea.

"How many souls came to Jesus last night?" she asked in her lady-like voice. Evans got up and squatted cheerfully but watchfully on his heels.

"Seventeen," he said.

"That's not very good," she said. "Do you think you could save mine?"

"Oh, yes," he said keenly.

"You look like a frog," she said, mocking. He had told her miners always squat in this way after work. "It's too late," she went on. "Twenty years too late. Have you always been with the mission?"

"No," he said.

"What was it? Were you converted, did you see the light?" she mocked, like a teacher.

"I had a vision," he said seriously.

"A vision!" she laughed. She waved her hand. "What do you mean —you mean, you—well, where? Up in the sky or something?"

"No," he said. "It was down the mine."

"What happened?"

He put down his cup and he moved it away to give himself more room. He squatted there, she thought, not like a frog at all, but like an imp or a devil, very grave and carven-faced. She noticed now how wide his mouth was and how widely it opened and how far the lips drew back when he spoke in his declamatory voice. He stared a long time waiting for her to stop fidgeting. Then he began.

"I was a drunkard," he declaimed, relishing each syllable separately. "I was a liar. I was a hypocrite. I went with women. And married women, too!" His voice rose. "I was a fornicator. I was an adulterer. Always at the races, too, gambling: it was senseless. There was no sin the Devil did not lead me into; I was like a fool. I was the most noteworthy sinner in the valley; everyone spoke of it. But I did not know the Lord was lying in wait for me."

"Yes, but what happened?" she said.

He got to his feet and gazed down at her and she was compelled to look up at him.

"I will tell you," he said. "It was a miracle." He changed his manner, and after looking round the garden, he said in a hushing and secretive voice:

"There was a disaster in the mine," he said. "It was in June. I was twenty-three and I was down working and I was thinking of the sunlight and the hills and the evening. There was a young girl called Alys Davies, you know, two or three had been after her and I was thinking I would take her up the rock, that is a quiet place, only an old mountain ram would see you—"

"You were in the mine," she said. "You are getting too excited about this Alys Jones—"

"Davies," he said with a quick grin. "Don't worry about her. She is married now." He went back to his solemn voice.

"And suddenly," he said, "there was a fall, a terrible fall of rock like thunder and all the men shouting. It was at eleven in the morning when we stopped work for our tea. There were three men in there working with me and they had just gone off. I was trapped alone."

"Were you hurt?" she said anxiously.

"It was a miracle, not a stone touched me. I was in a little black cave. It was like a tomb. I was in that place alone for twelve hours. I could hear them working to get at me, but after the first fall there was a second and then I thought I was finished. I could hear nothing."

"What did you do? I would have gone out of my mind," she said. "Is that how you got the scar on your nose?"

"That was in a fight," he said, off-hand. "Madness is a terrible thing. I stared into the blackness and I tried to think of one thing to stop my mind wandering but I could not at first for the fear, it was chasing and jumping like a mad dog in my head. I prayed, and the more I prayed, the more it chased and jumped. And then suddenly it stopped. I saw in my mind a picture. I saw the mantelpiece at home and on it a photograph of our family—my father and mother, my four sisters and my brother. And we had an aunt and uncle just married; it was a wedding photograph. I could see it clearly as if I had been in my home. They were standing there looking at me and I kept looking at them and thinking about them. I held on to them. I kept everything else out of my mind; wherever I looked that picture was before my eyes. It was like a vision. It saved me."

"I have heard people say they hear voices," said Miss Freshwater's niece, kindly now.

"Oh, no! They were speechless," said Evans. "Not a word! I spoke to them," he said. "Out loud. I promised God in front of all my family that I would cleanse my soul if I got out."

Evans stood blazing in his trance and then he picked up his cup from the grass and took it to her.

"May I please have some more tea?" he said.

"Of course," she said. "Sit down."

He considered where he should sit and then put himself beside her.

"When I saw you looking at your photographs," he said, "I thought: She is down the mine."

"I have never been down a mine in my life. I don't know why. We lived near one once when I was in the north," she evaded.

"The mine of the past," he said. "The dark mine of the past."

"I can see why you are a preacher, Robert." She smiled. "It's funny how one cannot get one's family out of one's head. I could feel mine inside me for years—but not now."

She had entirely stopped mocking him.

"I can't say they ever saved me," she said. "I think they nearly ruined me. Look at that ugly house and all that rubbish. Did you ever see anything like their furniture? When I was a girl I used to think: Suppose I got to look like that sideboard! And then money was all they ever talked about—and good and nice people, and nice people always had money. It was like that in those days; thank God that has gone. Perhaps it hasn't. I decided to get away from it and I got married. They ought to have stopped me—all I wanted was to get away—but they thought my husband had money, too. He just had debts and a bad stomach. When he spent all my money, he just got ill to punish me. . . . You don't know anything about life when you're young, and when you are old it's too late . . .

"That's a commonplace remark," she went on, putting her cup on the tray and reaching for his. "My mother used to make it." She picked up her scarf and began to tie it on her head, but as she was tying it Evans quickly reached for it and pulled it off. His hand held the nape of her neck gently.

"You are not old," he shouted, laughing and sparkling. "Your hair is golden, not a grey one in it, boy."

"Robert, give me that scarf. It is to keep out the dust," she said, blushing. She reached for the scarf and he caught her wrist.

"When I saw you standing at the station on Monday, I said: 'Now, there is a woman! Look at the way she stands, a golden woman, that is the first I have seen in this town, she must be a stranger,' " he said.

"You know all the others, I expect," she said with amusement.

"Oh, indeed, yes I do! All of them!" he said. "I would not look at them twice."

His other hand slipped from her neck to her waist.

"I can trust myself with them, but not with you," he said, lowering his voice and speaking down to her neck. "In an empty house," he whispered, nodding to the house, letting go of her hand and stroking her knee.

"I am far past that sort of thing," said Miss Freshwater's niece, choosing a lugubrious tone. She removed his arm from her waist. And she stood up, adroitly picking up the tray, and from behind that defence, she looked round the garden. Evans sprang up, but instead of coming near her, he jumped a few yards away and squatted on his heels, grinning at her confidently.

"You look like the Devil," she said.

He had placed himself between her and the way to the house.

"It is quiet in the garden, too," he said with a wink. And then she saw the wheelbarrow, which he had left near the fire.

"That barrow ought to go well in the sale," she said. "It is almost new. How much do you think it will fetch?"

Evans stood up at once and his grin went. An evasive light, almost the light of tears, came into his hot blue eyes and he stared at her with an alarm that drove everything else out of his head.

"They'll put it with the tools, you will not get much for it."

"I think every man in the town will be after it," she said, with malice.

"What price did you want for it?" he said, uncertain of her.

"I don't know what they cost," she said carelessly and walked past him very slowly back to the house, maddening him by her walk. He followed her quickly, and when she turned, still carrying the tray, to face him in the doorway, she caught his agitation.

"I will take the tray to the kitchen," he said politely.

"No," she said, "I will do that. I want you to go upstairs and fetch down all those shoes. And the trunk. It can all go."

And she turned and walked through the house to the kitchen. He hesitated for a long time; at last she heard him go upstairs and she pottered in the kitchen, where the china and pans were stacked on the table, waiting for him to come down. He was a very long time. He came down with the empty trunk.

"It can all go. Burn it all. It's no good to anyone, damp and rotten. I've put aside what I want," she said.

He looked at her sullenly. He was startled by her manner and by the vehemence of her face, for she had put on the scarf and her face looked strong-boned, naked, and ruthless. She was startled herself.

His sullenness went; he returned to his old excitement and hurried the barrow to the fire and she stood at the door impatiently waiting for the blaze. When he saw her waiting he came back.

"There it goes," he said with admiration.

The reflection of the flame danced in points of light in her eyes; her mouth was set, hard and bitter. Presently the flame dropped and greenish smoke came out thickly.

"Ah!" she gasped. Her body relaxed and she smiled at Evans, tempting him again.

"I've been thinking about the barrow," she said. "When we've finished up here, I'll make you a present of it. I would like to give it to you, if you have a use for it?"

She could see the struggle going on inside him as he boldly looked at her; and she saw his boldness pass into a small shrug of independent pride and the pride into pretence and dissembling.

"I don't know," he said, "that I have a use—well, I'll take it off you. I'll put the shoes in it, it will save bringing the car." He could not repress his eagerness any longer. "I'll put the shoes into it this evening. Thank you." He paused. "Thank you, ma'am," he said.

It was the first time he had called her "ma'am." The word was like a blow. The affair was over. It was, she realized, a dismissal.

An hour later she heard him rumbling the barrow down the path to the gate. The next day he did not come. He had finished with her. He sent his son up for his money.

It took Miss Freshwater's niece two more days to finish her work at the house. The heavy jobs had been done, except for putting the drawers back into the chests. She could have done with Evans's help there, and for the sweeping, which made her hot, but she was glad to be alone because she got on more quickly with the work. She hummed and even sang as she worked, feeling light and astonishingly happy. Once or twice, when she saw the white sheet of the mission tent distantly through the trees, she smiled.

"He got what he wanted! And I'm evidently not as old as I look."

The last hours buzzed by and she spun out the time, reluctant to go. She dawdled, locking the sheds, the windows and doors, until there was nothing more to keep her. She brought down a light suitcase in which she had put the few things she wanted to take away and she sat in the dining-room, now as bare as an office, to go through her money. After the destruction she was having a fit of economy and it had occurred to her that instead of taking a taxi to the station, she could walk down to the bus stop on the Green. She knew that the happiness she felt was not ebbing, but had changed to a feeling she had not had for many years—the feeling of expectancy—and as this settled in her, she put her money and her papers back into her bag. There was a last grain of rubbish here: with scarcely a glance at them, she tore up the photograph and the unfinished letter she had found in the trunk.

I owe Evans a lot, she thought.

Nothing retained her now.

She picked up her case. She left the house and walked down the road in the strong shade of the firs and the broad shade of the oak trees, whose leaves hardened with public contentment in the long evening light. When she got to the open Green, children were playing round the Gospel tent and, in twos and threes, people were walking from the houses across the grass towards it. She had twenty minutes to wait until her bus arrived. She heard the sound of singing coming from the tent. She wondered if Evans would be there.

I might give him the pleasure of seeing what he missed, she thought.

She strolled across to the tent.

A youth who had watered his hair and given it a twirl with a comb was standing in his best clothes at the entrance to the tent.

"Come to Jesu! Come to Jesu!" he said to her as she peeped inside.

"I'm just looking for someone," she said politely.

The singing had stopped when she looked in, but the worshippers were still standing. They were packed in the white light of the tent and the hot smell of grass and somewhere at the far end, invisible, a man was shouting like a cheap jack selling something at an auction. He stopped suddenly and a high, powerful, country voice whined out alone: "Ow in the vale . . ." and the congregation joined in for another long verse.

"Is Mr. Evans here tonight?" she asked the youth.

"Yes," he said. "He's witnessing every night."

"Where is he? I don't see him."

The verse came to an end and once more a voice began talking at the other end of the tent. It was a woman's voice, high and incomprehensible and sharp. The hymn began again and then spluttered into an explosive roar that swept across the Green.

"They've fixed it. The loudspeaker!" the youth exclaimed. Miss Freshwater's niece stepped back. The noises thumped. Sadly she looked at her watch and began to walk back to the bus stop. When she was about ten yards from the tent, the loudspeaker gave a high whistle and then, as if God had cleared his throat, spoke out with a gross and miraculous clearness.

"Friends," it said, sweeping right across the Green until it struck the furthest houses and the trees. "My friends . . ."

The word seemed to grind her and everyone else to nothing, to mill them all into the common dust.

"When I came to this place," it bellowed, "the serpent . . ."—an explosion of noise followed, but the voice cleared again—" . . . heart. No bigger than a speck it was at first, as tiny as a speck of coal grit in your eye . . ."

Miss Freshwater's niece stopped. Was it Evans's voice? A motor coach went by on the road and drowned the next words, and then she heard, spreading into an absurd public roar:

"I was a liar. I was an adulterer. Oh my friends, I was a slave of the strange woman the Bible tells about, the whore of Babylon, in her palace where moth and dust . . ." Detonations again.

But it was Evans's voice. She waited and the enormously magnified voice burst through.

"And then by the great mercy of the Lord I heard a voice cry out: 'Robert Evans, what are you doing, boy? Come out of it. . . .' " But the voice exploded into meaningless concussions, suddenly resuming:

" . . . and burned the adulteress in the everlasting fire, my friends—and all her property."

The hymn started up again.

"Well, not quite all, Robert," said Miss Freshwater's niece pleasantly aloud, and a child eating an ice cream near her watched her walk across the grass to the bus stop.

The Fall

It was the evening of the annual dinner. More than two hundred accountants were at that hour changing into evening clothes, in the flats, villas, and hotel rooms of a large, wet, Midland city. At the Royal was Charles Peacock, slender in his shirt, balancing on one leg and gazing with frowns of affection in the wardrobe mirror at the other leg as he pulled his trouser on; and then with a smile of farewell as the second went in. Buttoned up, relieved of nakedness, he visited other mirrors—the one at the dressing table, the two in the bathroom, assembling the scattered aspects of the unsettled being called Peacock "doing," as he was apt to say, "not so badly" in this city that smelt of coal and where thirty-eight years ago he had been born. When he left his room there were mirrors in the hotel lift and down below in the foyer and outside in the street. Certain shop windows were favourable and assuring. The love affair was taken up again at the Assembly rooms by the mirrors in the tiled corridor leading towards the bullocky noise of two hundred-odd chartered accountants in black ties, taking their drinks under the chandeliers that seemed to weep above their heads.

Crowds or occasions frightened Peacock. They engaged him, at first sight, in the fundamental battle of his life: the struggle against nakedness, the panic of grabbing for clothes and becoming someone. An acquaintance in a Scottish firm was standing near the door of the packed room as Peacock went in.

"Hullo, laddie," Peacock said, fitting himself out with a Scottish accent as he went into the crowded, chocolate-coloured buffet.

"What's to do?" he said, passing on to a Yorkshireman.

"Are you well now?" he said in his Irish voice. And, gaining confidence, "Whatcha cock!" to a man up from London, until he was shaking hands in the crowd with the President himself, who was leaning on a stick and had his foot in plaster.

"I hope this is not serious, sir," said Peacock in his best southern English, nodding at the foot.

"Bloody serious," said the President, sticking out his peppery beard. "I caught my foot in a grating. Some damn fools here think I've got gout."

No one who saw Peacock in his office, in boardrooms, on committees, at meetings, knew the exhausting number of rough sketches that had to be made before the naked Peacock could become Peacock dressed for his part. Now, having spoken to several human beings, the fragments called Peacock closed up. And he had one more trick up his sleeve if he panicked again: he could drop into music-hall Negro.

Peacock got a drink at the buffet table and pushed his way to a solitary island of carpet two feet square, in the guffawing corral. He was looking at the back of the President's neck. Almost at once the President, on the crest of a successful joke he had told, turned round with appetite.

"Hah!" he shouted. "Hah! Here's friend Peacock again." Why "again"? thought Peacock.

The President looked Peacock over.

"I saw your brother this afternoon," shouted the President. The President's injured foot could be said to have made his voice sound like a hilarious smash. Peacock's drink jumped and splashed his hand. The President winked at his friends.

"Hah!" said the President. "That gave our friend Peacock a scare!"

"At the Odeon," explained a kinder man.

"Is Shelmerdine Peacock your brother? The actor?" another said, astonished, looking at Peacock from head to foot.

"Shelmerdine Peacock was born and bred in this city," said the President fervently.

"I saw him in *Waste*," someone said. And others recalled him in *The Gun Runner* and *Doctor Zut*.

Four or five men stood gazing at Peacock with admiration, waiting for him to speak.

"Where is he now?" said the President, stepping forward, beard first. "In Hollywood? Have you seen him lately?"

They all moved forward to hear about the famous man.

Peacock looked to the right—he wanted to do this properly—but there was no mirror in that direction; he looked to the left, but there was no mirror there. He lowered his head gravely and then looked up, shaking his head sorrowfully. He brought out the old reliable Negro voice.

"The last time I saw l'il ole brudder Shel," he said, "he was being thrown out of the Orchid Room. He was calling the waiters 'goat-herds.'"

Peacock looked up at them all and stood, collected, assembled, whole at last, among their shouts of laughter. One man who did not laugh and who asked what the Orchid Room was, was put in his place. And in a moment a voice bawled from the door: "Gentlemen. Dinner is served." The crowd moved through two anterooms into the great hall, where, from their portraits on the wall, mayors, presidents, and justices looked down with the complacent rosiness of those who have dined and died. It was gratifying to Peacock that the President rested his arm on his shoulder for a few steps as they went into the hall.

Shel often cropped up in Peacock's life, especially in clubs and at dinners. It was pleasing. There was always praise; there were always questions. He had seen the posters about Shel's film during the week on his way to his office. They pleased, but they also troubled. Peacock stood at his place at table in the great hall and paused to look round, in case there was one more glance of vicarious fame to be collected. He was enjoying one of those pauses of self-possession in which, for a few seconds, he could feel the sensations Shel must feel when he stepped before the curtain to receive the applause of some great audience in London or New York. Then Peacock sat down. More than two hundred soup spoons scraped.

"Sherry, sir," said the waiter.

Peacock sipped.

He meant no harm to Shel, of course. But in a city like this, with Shel appearing in a big picture, with his name fifteen feet long on the hoardings, talked about by girls in offices, the universal instinct of family disparagement was naturally tickled into life. The President might laugh and the crowd admire, but it was not always agreeable for the family to have Shel roaming loose—and often very loose—in the world. One had to assert the modesty, the anonymity of the ordinary assiduous Peacocks. One way of doing this was to add a touch or two to famous scandals: to enlarge the drunken scrimmages and add to the divorces and the breaches of contract, increase the overdoses taken by flighty girls. One was entitled to a little rake-off—an accountant's charges—from the fame that so often annoyed. One was entitled, above all, because one loved Shel.

"Hock, sir?" said the waiter.

Peacock drank. Yes, he loved Shel. Peacock put down his glass, and the man opposite him spoke across the table, a man with an amused mouth, who turned his sallow face sideways so that one had the impression of being enquired into under a loose lock of black hair by one sharp, serious eye only.

"An actor's life is a struggle," the man said. Peacock recognized him: it was the man who had not laughed at his story and who had asked what the Orchid Room was, in a voice that had a sad and puncturing feeling for information sought for its own sake.

Peacock knew this kind of admirer of Shel's and feared him. They were not content to admire, they wanted to advance into intimacy, and collect facts on behalf of some general view of life's mysteriousness. As an accountant Peacock rejected mystery.

"I don't think l'il ole brudder Shel has struggled much," said Peacock, wagging his head from side to side carelessly.

"I mean he has to dedicate himself," said the man.

Peacock looked back mistrustfully.

"I remember some interview he gave about his school days—in this city," said the man. "It interested me. I do the books for the Hippodrome."

Peacock stopped wagging his head from side to side. He was alert. What Shel had said about his early life had been damned tactless.

"Shel had a good time," said Peacock sharply. "He always got his own way."

Peacock put on his face of stone. He dared the man to say out loud, in that company, three simple English words. He dared him. The man smiled and did not say them.

"Volnay, sir," said the waiter as the pheasant was brought. Peacock drank.

"Fried fish shop," Peacock said to himself as he drank. Those were the words. "Shel could have kept his mouth shut about that. I'm not a snob, but why mention it? Why, after they were all doing well, bring ridicule upon the family? Why not say simply: 'Shop'? Why not say, if he had to, 'Fishmonger'? Why mention frying? Why add: '*Bankrupt* fried fish shop'?"

It was swinish, disloyal, ungrateful. Bankrupt—all right; but some of that money, Peacock said, hectoring the pheasant on his plate, paid for Shel's years at the Dramatic school. It was unforgivable.

Peacock looked across at the man opposite, but the man had turned to talk to a neighbour. Peacock finished his glass and chatted with the man sitting to his right, but he felt like telling the whole table a few facts about dedication.

"Dedication," he would have said. "Let us take a look at the figures. An example of Shel's dedication in those fried fish shop days he is so fond of remembering to make fools of us. Saturday afternoon. Father asleep in the back room. Shel says: 'Come down the High Street with me, Tom. I want to get a record.' Classical, of course. Usual swindle. If we get into the shop he won't have the money and will try and borrow from me. 'No,' I say. 'I haven't got any money.' 'Well, let's get out of this stink of lard and fish.' He wears me down. He wore us all down, the whole family. He would be sixteen, two years older than me. And so we go out and at once I know there is going to be trouble. 'I saw the Devil in Cramer's,' he says. We go down the High Street to Cramer's—it's a music shop—and he goes up to the girl to ask if they sell bicycle pumps or rubber heels. When the girl says no, he makes a terrible face at her and shouts out 'Bah.' At Hook's, the stationer's, he stands at the door and calls to the girl at the cash desk: 'You've got the Devil in here. I've reported it,' and slams the door. We go on to Bond's, the grocer's, and he pretends to be sick when he sees the bacon. Goes out. 'Rehearsing,' he says. The Bonds are friends of Father's. There is a row. Shel swears he was never anywhere near the place and goes back the following Saturday and falls flat on the floor in front of the Bond daughter, groaning: 'I've been poisoned. I'm dying. Water! Water! Falls flat on his back . . .' "

"Caught his foot in a grating, he told me, and fell," the man opposite was saying. "Isn't that what he told you, Peacock?"

Peacock's imaginary speech came suddenly to an end. The man was smiling as if he had heard every word.

"Who?" said Peacock.

"The President," said the man. "My friend, Mr. McAlister, is asking me what happened to the President. Did he fall in the street?"

Peacock collected himself quickly and to hide his nakedness became Scottish.

"Ay, mon." He nodded across the table. "A wee bit of a tumble in the street."

Peacock took up his glass and drank.

"He's a heavy man to fall," said the man called McAlister.

"He carries a lot of weight," said his neighbour. Peacock eyed him. The impression was growing that this man knew too much, too quietly. It struck him that the man was one of those who ask what they know already, a deeply unbelieving man. They have to be crushed.

"Weight makes no difference," said Peacock firmly.

"It's weight and distance," said the Scotsman. "Look at children."

Peacock felt a smile coming over his body from the feet upwards.

"Weight and distance make no difference," Peacock repeated.

"How can you say that?"

An enormous voice, hanging brutally on the air like a sergeant's, suddenly shouted in the hall. It was odd to see the men in the portraits on the wall still sitting down after the voice sounded. It was the voice of the toastmaster.

"Gen-tle-men!" it shouted. "I ask you. To rise to. The toast of Her. Maj-es-ty. The Queen."

Two hundred or more accountants pushed back their chairs and stood up.

"The Queen," they growled. And one or two, Peacock among them, fervently added: "God bless her," and drained his glass.

Two hundred or more accountants sat down. It was the moment Peacock loved. And he loved the Queen.

"Port or brandy, sir?" the waiter asked.

"Brandy," said Peacock.

"You were saying that weight and distance make no difference. How do you make that out?" the sidelong man opposite said in a sympathetic and curious voice that came softly and lazily out.

Peacock felt the brandy burn. The question floated by, answerable if seized as it went and yet, suddenly, unanswerable for the moment. Peacock stared at the question keenly as if it were a fly that he was waiting to swat when it came round again. Ah, there it came. Now! But no, it had gone by once more. It was answerable. He knew the answer. Peacock smiled, loosely biding his time. He felt the flame of authority, of absolute knowledge burn in him.

There was a hammering at the President's table, there was handclapping. The President was on his feet and his beard had begun to move up and down.

"I'll tell you later," said Peacock curtly across the table. The interest went out of the man's eye.

"Once more," the President's beard was saying, and it seemed sometimes that he had two beards. "Honour," said one beard; "privilege," said the other; "old friends," said both beards together. "Speeches . . . brief . . . reminded of story . . . shortest marriage service in the world . . . Tennessee . . ."

"Hah! Hah! Hah!" shouted a pack of wolves, hyenas, hounds in dinner jackets.

Peacock looked across at the unbeliever who sat opposite. The interest in weight and distance had died away in his face.

"Englishman . . . Irishman . . . Scotsman . . . train . . . Englishman said . . . Scotsman said . . . Och, says Paddy . . ."

"Hah! Hah! Hah!" from the pack.

Over the carnations in the silver-plated vases on the table, over the heads of the diners, the cigar smoke was rising sweetly and the first-level indigo shafts of it were tipping across the middle air and turning the portraits of the past masters into daydreams. Peacock gazed at it. Then a bell rang in his ear, so loudly that he looked shyly to see if anyone else had heard it. The voice of Shel was on some line of his memory, a voice richer, more insinuating than the toastmaster's or the President's, a voice utterly flooring.

"Abel?" Shel was saying. "Is that you, Abel? This is Cain speaking. How's the smoke? Is it still going up straight to heaven? Not blowing about all over the place? . . ."

The man opposite caught Peacock's eye for a second, as if he too had heard the voice, and then turned his head away. And just at the very moment when once more Peacock could have answered that question about the effect of weight and distance, the man opposite stood up; all the accountants stood up. Peacock was the last. There was another toast to drink. And immediately there was more hammering and another speaker. Peacock's opportunity was lost. The man opposite had moved his chair back from the table and was sitting sideways to the table, listening, his interest in Peacock gone for good.

Peacock became lonely. Sulkily he played with matchsticks and arranged them in patterns on the tablecloth. There was a point at annual dinners when he always did this. It was at that point when one saw the function had become fixed by a flash photograph in the gloss of celebration and when everyone looked sickly and old. Eyes became hollow, temples sank, teeth loosened. Shortly the diners would be carried out in coffins. One waited restlessly for the thing to be over. Ten years of life went by and then, it seemed, there were no more speeches. There was some business talk in groups; then twos and threes left the table. Others filed off into a large chamber next door. Peacock's neighbours got up. He, who feared occasions, feared even more their dissolution. It was like that frightening ten minutes in a theatre when the audience slowly moves out, leaving a hollow stage and row after row, always increasing, of empty seats behind them. In a panic Peacock got up. He was losing all acquaintance. He had even let the man opposite slip away, for that man was walking down the hall with some friends. Peacock hurried down his side of the long table to meet them at the bottom, and when he got there he turned and barred their way.

"What we were talking about," he said. "It's an art. Simply a matter of letting the breath go, relaxing the muscles. Any actor can do it. It's the first thing they learn."

"I'm out of my depth," said the Scotsman.

"Falling," said Peacock. "The stage fall." He looked at them with dignity, then he let the expression die on his face. He fell quietly full length to the floor. Before they could speak he was up on his feet.

"My brother weighs two hundred and twenty pounds," he said with condescension to the man opposite. "The ordinary person falls and breaks an arm or a foot because he doesn't know. It's an art."

His eyes conveyed that if the Peacocks had kept a fried fish shop years ago, they had an art.

"Simple," said Peacock. And down he went, thump, on the carpet again, and lying at their feet he said:

"Painless. Nothing broken. Not a bruise. I said 'an art.' Really one might call it a science. Do you see how I'm lying?"

"What's happened to Peacock?" said two or three men joining the group.

"He's showing us the stage fall."

"Nothing," said Peacock, getting up and brushing his coat-sleeve and smoothing back his hair. "It is just a stage trick."

"I wouldn't do it," said a large man, patting his stomach.

"I've just been telling them—weight is nothing. Look." Peacock fell down and got up at once.

"You turn. You crumple. You can go flat on your back. I mean, that is what it looks like," he said.

And Peacock fell.

"Shel and I used to practise it in the bedroom. Father thought the ceiling was coming down," he said.

"Good God, has Peacock passed out?" A group standing by the fireplace in the hall called across. Peacock got up and, brushing his jacket again, walked up to them. The group he had left watched him. There was a thump.

"He's done it again," the man opposite said.

"Once more. There he goes. Look, he's going to show the President. He's going after him. No, he's missed him. The old boy has slipped out of the door."

Peacock was staring with annoyance at the door. He looked at other groups of twos and threes.

"Who was the casualty over there?" someone said to him as he walked past.

Peacock went over to them and explained.

"Like judo," said a man.

"No!" said Peacock indignantly, even grandly. And in Shel's manner. Anyone who had seen Shelmerdine Peacock affronted knew what he looked like. That large white face trod on you. "Nothing to do with judo. This is the theatre. . . ."

"Shelmerdine Peacock's brother," a man whispered to a friend.

"Is that so?"

"It's in the blood," someone said.

To the man who had said "judo," Peacock said: "No throwing, no wrestling, no somersaulting or fancy tricks. That is not theatre. Just . . . simply . . ." said Peacock. And crumpling, as Shel might have done in *Macbeth* or *Hamlet*, or like some gangster shot in the stomach, Peacock once more let his body go down with the cynicism of the skilful corpse. This time he did not get up at once. He looked up at their knees, their waists, at their goggling faces, saw under their double chins and under their hairy eyebrows. He grinned at their absurdity. He saw that he held them. They were obliged to look at him. Shel must always have had this sensation of hundreds of astonished eyes watching him lie, waiting for him to move. Their gaze would never leave the body. He never felt less at a loss, never felt more completely himself. Even the air was better at carpet level; it was certainly cooler and he was glad of that. Then he saw two pairs of feet advancing from another group. He saw two faces peep over the shoulders of the others, and heard one of them say:

"It's Peacock—still at it."

He saw the two pairs of boots and trousers go off. Peacock got to his feet at once and resentfully stared after them. He knew something, as they went, that Shel must have known: the desperation, the contempt for the audience that is thinning out. He was still brushing his sleeve and trousers legs when he saw everyone moving away out of the hall. Peacock moved after them into the chamber.

A voice spoke behind him. It was the quiet, intimate voice of the man with the loose lock of black hair who had sat opposite him.

"You need a drink," the man said.

They were standing in the chamber, where the buffet table was. The man had gone into the chamber and, clearly, he had waited for Peacock. A question was going round as fast as a catherine wheel in Peacock's head and there was no need to ask it: it must be so blindingly obvious. He looked for someone to put it to, on the quiet, but there were only three men at the buffet table with their backs turned to him. Why (the question ran) at the end of a bloody good dinner is one always left with some awful drunk, a man you've never liked—an unbeliever?

Peacock mopped his face. The unbeliever was having a short, disgusting laugh with the men at the bar and now was coming back with a glass of whisky.

"Sit down. You must be tired," said the unbeliever.

They sat down. The man spoke of the dinner and the speeches. Peacock did not listen. He had just noticed a door leading into a small anteroom and he was wondering how he could get into it.

"There was one thing I don't quite get," the man said: "perhaps it was the quickness of the hand deceiving the eye. I should say 'feet.' What I mean is—do you first take a step, I mean like in dancing? I mean is the art of falling really a paradox—I mean the art of keeping your balance all the time?"

The word "paradox" sounded offensive to Peacock.

The man looked too damn clever, in Peacock's opinion, and didn't sit still. Wearily Peacock got up.

"Hold my drink," he said. "You are standing like this, or facing sideways—on a level floor, of course. On a slope like this . . ."

The man nodded.

"I mean—well, now, watch carefully. Are you watching?"

"Yes," said the man.

"Look at my feet," said Peacock.

"No," said the man hastily, putting out a free hand and catching

Peacock by the arm. "I see what you mean. I was just interested in the theory."

Peacock halted. He was offended. He shook the man's arm off.

"Nothing theoretical about it," he said, and, shaking his sleeves, added: "No paradox."

"No," said the man, standing up and grabbing Peacock so that he could not fall. "I've got the idea." He looked at his watch. "Which way are you going? Can I give you a lift?"

Peacock was greatly offended. To be turned down! He nodded to the door of the anteroom. "Thanks," he said. "The President's waiting for me."

"The President's gone," said the man. "Oh well, good night." And he went away. Peacock watched him go. Even the men at the bar had gone. He was alone.

"But thanks," he called after him. "Thanks."

Cautiously Peacock sketched a course into the anteroom. It was a small, high room, quite empty and yet, one would have said, packed with voices, chattering, laughing, and mixed with music along the panelled walls, but chiefly coming from behind the heavy green velvet curtains that were drawn across the window at one end. There were no mirrors, but Peacock had no need of them. The effect was ornate— gilded pillars at the corners, a small chandelier rising and falling grace- fully from a carven ceiling. On the wall hung what at first sight seemed to be two large oil paintings of queens of England, but on going closer, Peacock saw there was only one oil painting—of Queen Victoria. Peacock considered it. The opportunity was enormous. Loyally, his face went blank. He swayed, loyally fell, and loyally got to his feet. The Queen might or might not have clapped her little hands. So encour- aged, he fell again and got up. She was still sitting there.

"Shel," said Peacock aloud to the Queen, "has often acted before royalty. He's in Hollywood now, having left me to settle all his tax affairs. Hundreds of documents. All lies, of course. And there is this case for alimony going on. He's had four wives," he said to Queen Victoria. "That's the side of theatre life I couldn't stand, even when we were boys. I could see it coming. But—watch me," he said.

And delightfully he crumpled, the perfect backwards spin. Leaning up on his elbow from where he was lying, he waited for her to speak.

She did not speak, but two or three other queens joined her, all crowding and gossiping together, as Peacock got up. The royal box! It was full. Cars hooting outside the window behind the velvet curtains had the effect of an orchestra and then, inevitably, those heavy green curtains were drawn up. A dark, packed, and restless auditorium opened itself to him. There was dense applause.

Peacock stepped forward in awe and wholeness. Not to fall, not to fall, this time, he murmured. To bow. One must bow and bow and bow and not fall, to the applause. He set out. It was a strangely long uphill journey towards the footlights, and not until he got there did it occur to him that he did not know how to bow. Shel had never taught him. Indeed, at the first attempt the floor came up and hit him in the face.

When My Girl Comes Home

She was kissing them all, hugging them, her arms bare in her summer dress, laughing and taking in a big draught of breath after every kiss, nearly knocking old Mrs. Draper off her feet, almost wrestling with Mrs. Fulmino, who was large and tall. Then Hilda broke off to give another foreign-sounding laugh and plunged at Jack Draper ("the baby") and his wife, at Mr. Fulmino, who cried out: "What, again?" and at Constance, who did not like emotion; and after every kiss, Hilda drew back, getting her breath and making this sound like "Hah!"

"Who is this?" she said, looking at me.

"Harry Fraser," Mr. Fulmino said. "You remember Harry?"

"You worked at the grocer's," she said. "I remember you."

"No," I said, "that was my brother."

"This is the little one," said Mrs. Fulmino.

"Who won the scholarship," said Constance.

"We couldn't have done anything without him," said Mr. Fulmino, expanding with extravagance as he always did about everything. "He wrote to the War Office, the Red Cross, the Prisoners of War, the American government, all the letters. He's going to be our head librarian."

Mr. Fulmino loved whatever had not happened yet. His forecasts were always wrong. I left the library years ago and never fulfilled the future he had planned for me. Obviously Hilda did not remember me. Thirteen years before, when she married Mr. Singh and left home, I was no more than a boy.

"Well, I'll kiss him too," she said. "And another for your brother."

That was the first bad thing to happen, the first of many signs of how her life had had no contact with ourselves.

"He was killed in the war, dear," said Mrs. Fulmino.

"She couldn't know," said Constance.

"I'm sorry," said Hilda.

We all stood silent, and Hilda turned to hold on to her mother, little Mrs. Johnson, whose face was coquettish with tears and who came up only to Hilda's shoulder. The old lady was bewildered. She was trembling as though she were going to shake to pieces like a tree in the autumn. Hilda stood still, touching her tinted brown hair, which was done in a tight, high style and still unloosened, despite all the hugs and kissings. Her arms looked as dry as sand, her breasts were full in her green, flowered dress, and she was gazing over our heads now from large yellow eyes that had almost closed into two blind, blissful curving lines. Her eyebrows seemed to be lacquered. How Oriental she looked on that first day! She was looking above our heads at old Mrs. Draper's shabby room and going over the odd things she remembered, and while she stood like that, the women were studying her clothes. A boy's memory is all wrong. Naturally, when I was a boy I had thought of her as tall. She was really short. But I did remember her bold nose: it was like her mother's and old Mrs. Draper's; those two were sisters. Otherwise I wouldn't have known her. And that is what Mr. Fulmino said when we were all silent and incredulous again. We had Hilda back. Not just "back," either, but "back from the dead," reborn.

"She was in the last coach of the train, wasn't she, Mother?" Mr. Fulmino said to Mrs. Johnson. He called her "Mother" for the occasion, celebrating her joy.

"Yes," said Mrs. Johnson. "Yes." Her voice scraped and trembled.

"In the last coach, next the van. We went right up the platform, we thought we'd missed her, didn't we? She was," he exclaimed with acquisitive pride, "in the first class."

"Like you missed me coming from Penzance," said Mrs. Fulmino, swelling powerfully and going that thundery violet colour which old wrongs gave her.

"Posh!" said Hilda. And we all smiled in a sickly way.

"Don't you ever do it again, my girl! Don't you ever do it again," said her mother, old Mrs. Johnson, clinging to her daughter's arm and shaking it as if it were a bell rope.

"I was keeping an eye on my luggage," Hilda said, laughing.

Ah! That was a point! There was not only Hilda, there was her luggage. Some of it was in the room, but the bigger things were outside on the landing, piled up, looking very new, with the fantastic labels of hotels in Tokyo, San Francisco, and New York on it, and a beautiful jewel box in white leather on top like a crown. Old Mrs. Draper did not like the luggage being outside the room in case it was in the way of the people upstairs. Constance went out and fetched the jewel box in. We had all seen it. We were as astonished by all these cases as we were by Hilda herself. After thirteen years, six of them war, we recognized that the poor ruined woman we had prepared for had not arrived. She shone with money. Later on, one after the other of us, except old Mrs. Draper, who could not walk far, went out and looked at the luggage and came back to study Hilda in a new way.

We had all had a shock. She had been nearly two years coming home from Tokyo. Before that there was the occupation; before that the war itself. Before that there were the years in Bombay and Singapore, when she was married to an Indian they always called Mr. Singh. All those years were lost to us. None of us had been to India. What happened there to Mr. Singh? We knew he had died—but how? Even if we had known, we couldn't have imagined it. None of us had been to Singapore, none of us to Japan. People from streets like Hincham Street do go to such places: it is not past belief. Knock on the doors of half the houses in London and you will find people with relations all over the world. But none of *us* had. Mention these places to us, we look at our grey skies and see boiling sun. Our one certainty about Hilda was what, in fact, the newspaper said the next day, with her photograph and the headline: A MOTHER'S FAITH. FOUR YEARS IN JAPANESE TORTURE CAMP. LONDON GIRL'S ORDEAL. Hilda was a terrible item of news, a gash in our lives, and we looked for the signs of it on her body, in the way she stood, in the lines on her face, as if we were expecting a scream from her mouth like the screams we were told Bill Williams gave out at night in his sleep, after he had been flown back home when the war ended. We had had to wait and wait for Hilda. At one time —there was a postcard from Hawaii—she was pinned like a butterfly in the middle of the Pacific Ocean; soon after there was a letter from Tokyo saying she couldn't get a passage. Confusing. She was travelling backwards. Letters from Tokyo were still coming after her letters from San Francisco.

We were still standing, waiting for Constance to bring in the teapot, for the tea was already laid. The trolley buses go down Hincham Street. It is a mere one hundred and fifty yards of a few little houses and a few little shops, which has a sudden charmed importance because the main road has petered out at our end by the Lord Nelson and an enormous public lavatory, and the trolley buses have to run down Hincham Street before picking up the main road again, after a sharp turn at the convent. Hincham Street is less a street than an interval, a disheartened connection. While we stood in one of those silences that follow excitement, a trolley bus came by and Hilda exclaimed:

"You've still got the old trams. Bump! Bump! Bump!" Hilda was ecstatic about the sound. "Do you remember I used to be frightened the spark from the pole would set the lace curtains on fire when I was little?"

For as the buses turned, the trolley arms would come swooping with two or three loud bumps and a spit of blue electricity, almost hitting Mrs. Draper's sitting-room window, which was on the first floor.

"It's trolleys now, my girl," said old Mrs. Draper, whose voice was like the voice of time itself chewing away at life. "The trams went years ago, before the war."

Old Mrs. Draper had sat down in her chair again by the fire that always burned winter and summer in this room; she could not stand for long. It was the first remark that had given us any sense of what was bewildering all of us: the passing of time, the growing of a soft girl into a grown, hard-hipped woman. For old Mrs. Draper's mind was detached from events round her and moved only among the signal facts and conclusions of history.

Presently we were, as the saying is, "at our teas." Mr. Fulmino, less puzzled than the rest of us, expanded in his chair with the contentment of one who had personally operated a deeply British miracle. It was he who had got Hilda home.

"We've got all the correspondence, haven't we, Harry?" he said. "We kept it—the War Office, Red Cross, Prisoner of War Commission—everything, Hilda. I'll show it to you."

His task had transformed him and his language. Identification, registration, accommodation, communication, rehabilitation, hospitalization, administration, investigation, transportation—well, we had all dreamt of Hilda in our different ways.

"They always said the same thing," Mrs. Fulmino said reproachfully. "No one of the name of Mrs. Singh on the lists."

"I wrote to Bombay," said Mr. Fulmino.

"He wrote to Singapore," said Mrs. Fulmino.

Mr. Fulmino drank some tea, wiped his lips, and became geography. "All British subjects were rounded up, they said," Mrs. Fulmino said.

We nodded. We had made our stand, of course, on the law. Mrs. Fulmino was authority.

"But Hilda was married to an Indian," said Constance.

We glanced with a tolerance we did not usually feel for Constance. She was always trying to drag politics in.

"She's a British subject by birth," said Mrs. Fulmino firmly.

"Mum," Hilda whispered, squeezing her mother's arm hard, and then looked up to listen, as if she were listening to talk about a faraway stranger. "I was in Tokyo when the war started," she said. "Not Singapore."

"Oh, Tokyo," exclaimed Mr. Fulmino, feeling in his waistcoat for a pencil to make a note of it and, suddenly, realizing that his note-taking days were over.

"Whatever the girl has done she has been punished for it," came old Mrs. Draper's mournful voice from the chair by the fire; but in the clatter no one heard her, except old Mrs. Johnson, who squeezed her daughter's arm and said:

"My girl is a jewel."

Still, Hilda's words surprised us. We had worked it out that after she and Mr. Singh were married and went to Bombay, he had heard of a better job in the state railway medical service and had gone to Singapore, where the war had caught her. Mrs. Fulmino looked affronted. If Mr. Fulmino expanded into geography and the language of state— he worked for the Borough Council—Mrs. Fulmino liked a fact to be a fact.

"We got the postcards," said Mrs. Fulmino, sticking to chronology.

"Hawaii," Mr. Fulmino said. "How'd you get there? Swim, I suppose." He added: "A sweet spot, it looks. Suit us for a holiday—palms."

"Coconuts," said young Jack Draper, who worked in a pipe factory, speaking for the first time.

"Be quiet," said his wife.

"It's an American base now," said Constance with her politically sugared smile.

We hesitated but let her observation pass. It was simple to ignore her. We were happy.

"I suppose they paid your fare," said Jack Draper's wife, a north-country woman.

"Accommodation, transportation," said Mr. Fulmino, "food, clothing. Everything. Financed by the international commission."

This remark made old Mrs. Johnson cry a little. In those years none of us had deeply believed that Hilda was alive. The silence was too long; too much time had gone by. Others had come home by the thousand with stories of thousands who had died. Only old Mrs. Johnson had been convinced that Hilda was safe. The landlord at the Lord Nelson, the butcher, anyone who met old Mrs. Johnson as she walked by like a poor, decent ghost with her sewing bundles, in those last two years, all said in war-staled voices:

"It's a mother's faith, that's what it is. A mother's faith's a funny thing."

She would walk along with a cough, like someone driving tacks. Her chest had sunk and under her brown coat her shoulder blades seemed to have sharpened into a single hump. Her faith gave her a bright, yet also a sly, dishonest look.

"I'm taking this sewing up to Mrs. Tracy's. She wants it in a hurry," she might say.

"You ought to rest, Mrs. Johnson, like the doctor said."

"I want a bit of money for when my girl comes home," she said. "She'll want feeding up."

And she would look round, perhaps, for a clock, in case she ought by this time to have put a pot on the stove.

She had been too ill, in hospital, during the war, to speak about what might have happened to Hilda. Her own pain and fear of dying deafened her to what could be guessed. Mrs. Johnson's faith had been born out of pain, out of the inability—within her prison of aching bones and crushed breathing—to identify herself with her daughter. Her faith grew out of her very self-centredness. And when she came out from the post office every week, where she put her savings, she looked demure, holy, and secretive. If people were too kind and too sympathetic with her, she shuffled and looked mockingly. Seven hospitals, she said, had not killed *her*.

Now, when she heard Mr. Fulmino's words about the fare, the clothes, the food, the expense of it all, she was troubled. What had she worked for—even at one time scrubbing in a canteen—but to save

Hilda from a charity so vast in its humiliation, from so blank a herding mercy. Hilda was hers, not theirs. Hilda kept her arm on her mother's waist, and while Mr. Fulmino carried on with the marvels of international organization (which moved Mrs. Fulmino to say hungrily: "It takes a war to bring it out"), Hilda ignored them and whispered to comfort her mother. At last the old lady dried her eyes and smiled at her daughter. The smile grew to a small laugh; she gave a proud jerk to her head, conveying that she and her Hil were not going to kowtow in gratitude to anyone, and Hilda at last said out loud to her mother what no doubt she had been whispering.

"He wouldn't let me pay anything, Mum. Faulkner, his name was. Very highly educated. He came from California. We had a fancy-dress dance on the ship and he made me go as a geisha. . . . He gave me these. . . ." And she raised her hand to show her mother the bracelets on it.

Mrs. Johnson laughed wickedly. "Did he . . . ? Was he . . . ?" said Mrs. Johnson.

"No. Well, I don't know," said Hilda. "But I kept his address."

Mrs. Johnson smiled round at all of us, to show that in spite of all, being the poorest in the family and the ones that had suffered most, she and Hilda knew how to look after themselves.

This was the moment when there was that knock on the door. Everyone was startled and looked at it.

"A knock!" said Mr. Fulmino.

"A knock, Constance," said young Mrs. Draper, who had busy north-country ears.

"A knock," several said.

Old Mrs. Draper made one of her fundamental utterances again, one of her growls from the belly of the history of human indignation.

"We are," she said, "in the middle of our teas. Constance, go and see and tell them."

But before Constance got to the door, two young men, one with a camera, came right into the room, without asking. Some of us lowered our heads and then, just as one young man said "I'm from the *News*," the other clicked his camera.

Jack Draper said, nearly choking: "He's taken a snap of us eating."

While we were all staring at them, old Mrs. Draper chewed out grandly: "Who may they be?"

But Hilda stood up and got her mother to her feet, too. "Stand up, all of us," she said eagerly. "It's for the papers."

It was the Press. We were in confusion. Mrs. Fulmino pushed Mr.

Fulmino forward towards the reporter and then pulled him back. The reporter stood asking questions and everyone answered at once. The photographer kept on taking photographs and, when he was not doing that, started picking up vases and putting them down and one moment was trying the drawer of a little table by the window. They pushed Hilda and her mother into a corner and took a picture of them, Hilda calling to us all to "come in" and Mr. Fulmino explaining to the reporters. Then they went, leaving a cigarette burning on one of old Mrs. Draper's lace doilies under the fern and two more butts on the floor. "What did they say? What did they say?" we all asked one another, but no one could remember. We were all talking at once, arguing about who had heard the knock first. Young Mrs. Draper said her tea was spoiled, and Constance opened the window to let the cigarette smoke out and then got the kettle. Mr. Fulmino put his hand on his wife's knee because she was upset, and she shook it off. When we had calmed down, Hilda said:

"The young one was a nice-looking boy, wasn't he, Mum?" and Mr. Fulmino, who almost never voiced the common opinion about any-thing but who had perhaps noticed how the eyes of all the women went larger at this remark, laughed loudly and said:

"We've got the old Hilda back!"

I mention this because of the item in the papers next day: A MOTHER'S FAITH. FOUR YEARS IN JAPANESE TORTURE CAMP. LONDON GIRL'S ORDEAL.

Wonderful, as Mr. Fulmino said.

To be truthful, I felt uncomfortable at old Mrs. Draper's. They were not my family. I had been dragged there by Mr. Fulmino, and by a look now and then from young Mrs. Draper and from Constance, I had the feeling that they thought it was indecent for me to be there when I had only been going with Iris, Mr. Fulmino's daughter, for two or three months. I had to be tolerated as one more example of Mr. Fulmino's uncontrollable gift—the gift for colonizing.

Mr. Fulmino had shot up from nothing during the war. It had given him personality. He was a short, talkative, heavy man of forty-five with a wet gold tooth and glossy black hair that streamlined back across his head from an arrow point, getting thin in front. His eyes were anxious, overworked, and puddled; indeed, if you had not known him you would have thought he had had a couple of black eyes that had never got right. He bowled along as he walked, like someone absorbed by fondness for his own body. He had been in many things before he got to work for the council—the Army (but not a fighting soldier) in the war, in auctions, and at the bar of a club. He was very active, confiding and enquiring.

When I first met him I was working at the counter of the public library, during the war, and one day he came over from the council officers and said importantly: "Friend, we've got a bit of a headache. We've got an enquiry from the War Office. Have you got anything about Malaya—with maps?"

In the next breath he was deflating himself.

"It's a personal thing. They never tell you anything. I've got a niece out there."

Honesty made him sound underhand. His manner suggested that his niece was a secret fortification somewhere east of Suez. Soon he was showing me the questionnaire from the Red Cross. Then he was telling me that his wife, like the rest of the Drapers, was very handsome—"A lovely woman" in more ways, his manner suggested, than one—but that since Hilda had gone, she had become a different woman. The transition from handsome to different was, he suggested, a catastrophe that he was obliged to share with the public. He would come in from fire-watching, he said, and find her demented. In bed, he would add. He and I found ourselves fire-watching together, and from that time he started facetiously calling me "my secretary."

"I asked my secretary to get the sand and shovel out," he would say about our correspondence, "and he wrote the letter."

So I was half a stranger at Hilda's homecoming. I looked round the room or out at the shops opposite, and when I looked back at the family several times I caught Hilda's eyes wandering too. She also was out of it. I studied her. I hadn't expected her to come back in rags, as old Mrs. Draper had, but it was a surprise to see she was the best-dressed woman in the room and the only one who looked as if she had ever been to a hairdresser. And there was another way in which I could not match her with the person Mr. Fulmino and I had conjured up. When we thought of everything that must have happened to her, it was strange to see that her strong face was smooth and blank. Except for the few minutes of arrival and the time the reporters came, her face was vacant and plain. It was as vacant as a stone that had been smoothed for centuries in the sand of some hot country. It was the face of someone to whom nothing had happened; or perhaps so much had happened to her that each event wiped out what had happened before. I was dis-

turbed by something in her—the lack of history, I think. We were
worm-eaten by it. And that suddenly brought her back to me as she
had been when she was a schoolgirl and when my older brother got into
trouble for chasing after her. She was now sharper in the shoulders and
elbows, no longer the swollen schoolgirl, but, even as a girl, her face
had had the same quality of having been fixed and unchangeable
between its high cheekbones. It was disturbing, in a face so anonymous,
to see the eyes move, especially since she blinked very little; and if she
smiled it was less a smile than an alteration of the two lines at the
corners of her lips.

The party did not settle down quite in the same way after the
reporters had been, and there was talk of not tiring Hilda after her long
journey. The family would all be meeting tomorrow, the Sunday, as
they always did, when young Mrs. Jack Draper brought her children.
Jack Draper was thinking of the pub, which was open now, and asking
if anyone was going over. And then something happened. Hilda walked
over to the window to Mr. Fulmino and said, just as if she had not been
there at the time:

"Ted, what did that man from the *News* ask you—about the food?"

"No," said Mr. Fulmino, widening to a splendid chance of not giving
the facts. "No—he said something about starving the prisoners. I was
telling him that in my opinion the deterioration in conditions was
inevitable after the disorganization in the camps resulting from air
operations. . . ."

"Oh, I thought you said we starved. We had enough."

"What?" said Mr. Fulmino.

"Bill Williams was a skeleton when he came back. Nothing but a
bowl of rice a day. Rice!" said Mrs. Fulmino. "And torture."

"Bill Williams must have been in one of those labour camps," said
Hilda. "Being Japanese, I was all right."

"Japanese!" said Mr. Fulmino. "You?"

"Shinji was a Japanese," said Hilda. "He was in the Army."

"You married a Japanese!" said Mrs. Fulmino, marching forward.

"That's why I was put in the American camp, when they came. They
questioned everyone, not only me. That's what I said to the reporter.
It wasn't the food, it was the questions. What was his regiment? When
did you hear from him? What was his number? They kept on. Didn't
they, Mum?"

She turned to her mother, who had taken the chance to cut herself
another piece of cake and was about to slip it into her handkerchief,

I think, to carry to her own room. We were all flabbergasted. A trolley bus went by and took a swipe at the wall. Young Mrs. Draper murmured something, and her young husband, Jack, hearing his wife, said loudly:

"Hilda married a Nip!"

And he looked at Hilda with astonishment. He had very blue eyes.

"You weren't a prisoner!" said Mrs. Fulmino.

"Not of the Japanese," said Hilda. "They couldn't touch me. My husband was Japanese."

"I'm not stupid. I can hear," said young Mrs. Draper to her husband. She was a plainspoken woman from the Yorkshire coalfields, one of a family of twelve.

"I've nowt to say about who you married, but where is he? Haven't you brought him?" she said.

"You were married to Mr. Singh," said Mrs. Fulmino.

"They're both dead," said Hilda, her vacant yellow eyes becoming suddenly brilliant like a cat's at night. An animal sound, like the noise of an old dog at a bone, came out of old Mrs. Draper by the fire.

"Two," she moaned.

No more than that. Simply, again: "Two."

Hilda was holding her handbag and she lifted it in both hands and covered her bosom with it. Perhaps she thought we were going to hit her. Perhaps she was going to open the bag and get out something extraordinary—documents, letters, or a handkerchief to weep into. But no—she held it there very tight. It was an American handbag; we hadn't seen one like that before, cream-coloured, like the luggage. Old Mrs. Johnson hesitated at the table, tipped the piece of cake back out of her handkerchief onto a plate, and stepped to Hilda's side and stood, very straight for once, beside her, the old blue lips very still.

"Ted," accused Hilda. "Didn't you get my letters? Mother"—she stepped away from her mother—"didn't you tell them?"

"What, dear?" said old Mrs. Johnson.

"About Shinji. I wrote you. Did Mum tell you?" Hilda appealed to us and now looked fiercely at her mother.

Mrs. Johnson smiled and retired into her look of faith and modesty. She feigned deafness.

"I put it all in the post office," she said. "Every week," she said. " 'Until my girl comes home,' I said. 'She'll need it.' "

"Mother!" said Hilda, giving the old lady a small shake. "I wrote to you. I told you. Didn't you tell them?"

"What did Hilda say?" said Mr. Fulmino gently, bending down to the old lady.

"Sh! Don't worry her. She's had enough for today. What did you tell the papers, Ted?" said Mrs. Fulmino, turning on her husband. "You can't ever keep your big mouth shut, can you? You never let me see the correspondence."

"I married Shinji when the war came up," Hilda said.

And then old Mrs. Draper spoke from her armchair by the fire. She had her bad leg propped up on a hassock.

"Two," said Mrs. Draper savagely again.

Mr. Fulmino, in his defeat, lost his nerve and let slip a remark quite casually, as he thought, under his voice, but everyone heard it—a remark that Mrs. Fulmino was to remind him of in months to come.

"She strikes like a clock," he said.

We were stupefied by Mr. Fulmino's remark. Perhaps it was a relief.

"Mr. Fraser!" Hilda said to me. And now her vacant face had become dramatic and she stepped towards me, appealing outside the family. "You knew, you and Ted knew. You've got all the letters. . . ."

If ever a man looked like the captain going down with his ship and suddenly conscious, at the last heroic moment, that he is not on a ship at all, but standing on nothing and had hopelessly blundered, it was Mr. Fulmino. But we didn't go down, either of us. For suddenly old Mrs. Johnson couldn't stand straight any longer; her head wagged and drooped forward, and but for a chair, she would have fallen to the ground.

"Quick! Constance! Open the window," Mrs. Fulmino said. Hilda was on her knees by her mother.

"Are you there, Hilly?" said her mother.

"Yes, I'm here, Mum," said Hilda. "Get some water—some brandy." They took the old lady next door to the little room Hilda was sharing with her that night.

"What I can't fathom is your aunt not telling me, keeping it to herself," said Mr. Fulmino to his wife as we walked home that evening from Mrs. Draper's, and we had said good-bye to Jack Draper and his wife.

He was not hurt by Mrs. Johnson's secretiveness but by an extraordinary failure of co-operation.

It was unwise of him to criticize Mrs. Fulmino's family.

"Don't be so smug," said Mrs. Fulmino. "What's it got to do with you? She was keeping it from Gran: you know Gran's tongue. She's her sister." They called old Mrs. Draper "Gran" or "Grandma" sometimes.

But when Mr. Fulmino got home he asked me in so that we could search the correspondence together. Almost at once we discovered his blunder. There it was in the letter saying a Mrs. Singh or Shinji Kobayashi had been identified.

"Shinji!" exclaimed Mrs. Fulmino, putting her big index finger on the page. "There you are, plain as dirt."

"Singh," said Mr. Fulmino. "Singh, Shinji, the same name. Some Indians write Singh, some Shinji."

"And what is Kobayashi? Indian too? Don't be a fool."

"It's the family name or Christian name of Singh," said Mr. Fulmino, doing the best he could.

"Singh, Shinji, Shinji, Singh," he murmured to himself, and he walked about trying to convince himself by incantation and hypnosis. He lashed himself with Kobayashi. He remembered the names of other Indians, Indian cities, mentioned the Ganges and the Himalayas; had a brief, brilliant couple of minutes when he argued that Shinji was Hindu for Singh. Mrs. Fulmino watched him with the detachment of one waiting for a bluebottle to settle so that she could swat it.

"*You* thought Kobayashi was Indian, didn't you, Harry?" he appealed to me. I did my best.

"I thought," I said weakly, "it was the address."

"Ah, the address!" Mr. Fulmino clutched at this, but he knew he was done for. Mrs. Fulmino struck.

"And what about the Sunday papers, the man from the *News?*" she said. "You open your big mouth too soon."

"Christ!" said Mr. Fulmino. It was the sound of a man who has gone to the floor.

I will come to that matter of the papers later on. It is not very important.

When we went to bed that night we must all have known in our different ways that we had been disturbed in a very long dream. We had been living on inner visions for years. It was an effect of the long war. England had been a prison. Even the sky was closed, and, like convicts, we had been driven to dwelling on fancies in our dreary minds. In the cinema the camera sucks some person forward into an enormous close-up and holds a face there yards wide, filling the whole screen, all holes and pores, like some sucking octopus that might eat up an audience many rows at a time. I don't say these pictures aren't beautiful sometimes, but afterwards I get the horrors. Hilda had been a close-up like this for us when she was lost and far away. For myself, I could hardly remember Hilda. She was a collection of fragments of my childhood and I suppose I had expected a girl to return.

My father and mother looked down on the Drapers and the Johnsons. Hincham Street was "dirty," and my mother once whispered that Mr. Johnson had worked "on the line," as if that were a smell. I remember the old man's huge, crinkled, white beard when I was a child. It was horribly soft and like pubic hair. So I had always thought of Hilda as a railway girl, in and out of tunnels, signal boxes, and main-line stations, and when my older brother was "chasing" her, as they said, I admired him. I listened to the quarrels that went on in our family: how she had gone to the convent school and the nuns had complained about her; and was it she or some other girl who went for car rides with a married man who waited round the corner of Hincham Street for her? The sinister phrase "The nuns have been to see her mother" stuck in my memory. It astonished me to see Hilda alive, calm, fat, and walking after that, as composed as a railway engine. When I grew up and Mr. Fulmino came to the library, I was drawn into his search because she brought back those days with my brother, those clouts on the head from some friend of his, saying: "Buzz off. Little pigs have big ears," when my brother and he were whispering about her.

To Mrs. Fulmino, a woman whose feelings were in her rolling arms, flying out from one extreme to another as she talked, as if she were doing exercises, Hilda appeared in her wedding clothes and all the sexuality of an open flower, standing beside her young Indian husband, who was about to become a doctor. There was trouble about the wedding, for Mr. Singh spoke a glittering and palatial English—the beautiful English a snake might speak, it seemed to the family—that made a few pockmarks on his face somehow more noticeable. Old Mrs. Draper alone, against all evidence—Mr. Singh had had a red racing car —stuck to it that he was "a common Lascar off a ship." Mrs. Fulmino had been terrified of Mr. Singh, she often conveyed, and had "refused to be in a room alone with him." Or "How can she let him touch her?" she would murmur, thinking about that, above all. Then whatever vision was in her mind would jump forward to Hilda captured, raped, tortured, murdered in front of her eyes. Mrs. Fulmino's mind was voluptuous. When I first went to Mr. Fulmino's house and met Iris and we talked about Hilda, Mrs. Fulmino once or twice left the room and he lowered his voice. "The wife's upset," he said. "She's easily upset."

We had not all been under a spell. Not young Jack Draper or his wife, for example. Jack Draper had fought in the war, and whereas we thought of the war as something done to us and our side, Jack thought of it as something done to everybody. I remember what he said to his wife before the Fulminos and I said good night to them on the Saturday Hilda came home.

"It's a shame," said Jack, "she couldn't bring the Nip with her."

"He was killed," said his wife.

"That's what I mean," said Jack. "It's a bleeding shame she couldn't."

We walked on and then young Mrs. Draper said, in her flat, northern, laconic voice:

"Well, Jack, for all the to-do, you might just as well have gone to your fishing."

For Jack had made a sacrifice in coming to welcome Hilda. He went fishing up the Thames on Saturdays. The war for him was something that spoiled fishing. In the Normandy landing he had thought mostly of that. He dreamt of the time when his two boys would be old enough to fish. It was what he had had children for.

"There's always Sunday," said his wife, tempting him. Jack nodded. She knew he would not fall. He was the youngest of old Mrs. Draper's family, the baby, as they said. He never missed old Mrs. Draper's Sundays.

It was a good thing he did not, a good thing for all of us that we didn't miss, for we would have missed Hilda's second announcement.

Young Mrs. Draper provoked it. These Sunday visits to Hincham Street were a ritual in the family. It was a duty to old Mrs. Draper. We went there for our tea. She provided, though Constance prepared for it as if we were a school, for she kept house there. We recognized our obligation by paying sixpence into the green pot on the chiffonier when we left. The custom had started in the bad times when money was short; but now this money was regarded as capital, and Jack Draper used to joke and say: "Who are you going to leave the green pot to, Mum?" Some of Hilda's luggage had been moved by the afternoon into her mother's little room at the back, and how those two could sleep in a bed so small was a question raised by Mrs. Fulmino, whose night

with Mr. Fulmino required room for struggle, as I know, for this
colonizing man often dropped hints about how she swung her legs over
in the night.

"Have you unpacked yet, Hilda?" Mrs. Fulmino was asking.

"Unpacked!" said Constance. "Where would she put all that?"

"I've been lazy," said Hilda. "I've just hung up a few things because
of the creases."

"Things do crease," said Mrs. Fulmino.

"Bill Williams said he would drop in later," said Constance.

"That man suffered," said Mrs. Fulmino, with meaning.

"He heard you were back," said Constance.

Hilda had told us about Shinji. Jack Draper listened with wonder.
Shinji had been in the jute business, and when the war came he was
called up to the Army. He was in Stores. Jack scratched with delight
when he heard this. "Same as I tried to work it," Jack said. Shinji had
been killed in an air raid. Jack's wife said, to change the subject, she
liked that idea, the idea of Jack "working" anything; he always let
everyone climb up on his shoulders. "First man to get wounded. I knew
he would be," she said. "He never looks where he's going."

"Is that the Bill Williams who worked for Ryan, the builder?" said
Hilda.

"He lives in the Culverwell Road," young Mrs. Draper said.

Old Mrs. Draper, speaking from the bowels of history, said: "He got
that Sellers girl into trouble."

"Yes," exclaimed Hilda, "I remember."

"It was proved in court that he didn't," said Constance briskly to
Hilda. "You weren't here."

We were all silent. One could hear only the sounds of our cups on
the saucers and Mrs. Fulmino's murmur: "More bread and butter?"
Constance's face had its neat, pink, enamelled smile, and one saw the
truthful blue of her small eyes become purer in colour. Iris was next
to me and she said afterwards something I hadn't noticed, that Constance hated Hilda. It is one of the difficulties I have in writing, that,
all along, I was slow to see what was really happening, not having a
woman's eye or ear. And being young. Old Mrs. Draper spoke again,
her mind moving from the past to the present with that suddenness
old people have.

"If Bill Williams is coming, he knows the way," she said.

Hilda understood that remark, for she smiled and Constance flushed.
(Of course, I see it now: two women in a house! Constance had ruled

old Mrs. Draper and Mrs. Johnson for years and her money had made a big difference.) They knew that one could, as the saying is, "trust Gran to put her oar in."

Again, young Mrs. Draper changed the subject. She was a nimble, tarry-haired woman, impatient of fancies, excitements, and disasters. She liked things flat and factual. While the family gaped at Hilda's clothes and luggage, young Mrs. Draper had reckoned up the cost of them. She was not avaricious or mean, but she knew that money is money. You know that if you have done without. So she went straight into the important question, being (as she would say) not like people in the south, double-faced Wesleyans, but honest, plain, and straight out with it, what are they ashamed of? Jack, her husband, was frightened by her bluntness, and had the nervous habit of folding his arms across his chest and scratching fast under his armpits when his wife spoke out about money; some view of the river, with his bait and line and the evening flies, came into his panicking mind. Mr. Fulmino once said that Jack scratched because the happiest moments of his life, the moments of escape, had been passed in clouds of gnats.

"I suppose, Hilda, you'll be thinking of what you're going to do?" young Mrs. Draper said. "Did they give you a pension?"

I was stroking Iris's knee but she stopped me, alerted like the rest of them. The word "pension" is a very powerful word. In this neighbourhood one could divide the world into those who had pensions and those who hadn't. The phrase "the old pensioner" was one of envy, abuse, and admiration. My father, for example, spoke contemptuously of pensioners. Old Mrs. Draper's husband had had a pension, but my father would never have one. As a librarian, Mr. Fulmino pointed out, I would have a pension and thereby I had overcome the first obstacle in being allowed to go out with his daughter.

"No," said Hilda, "nothing."

"But he was your husband, you said," said Constance.

"He was in the Army, you say," said young Mrs. Draper.

"Inflation," said Mr. Fulmino grandly. "The financial situation."

He was stopped.

"Then," said young Mrs. Draper, "you'll have to go to work."

"My girl won't want for money," said old Mrs. Johnson, sitting beside her daughter as she had done the day before.

"No," said young Mrs. Draper, "that she won't while you're alive, Mrs. Johnson. We all know that, and the way you slaved for her. But Hilda wants to look after you, I'm sure."

It was, of course, the question in everyone's mind. Did all those clothes and cases mean money or was it all show? That is what we all wanted to know. We would not have raised it at that time and in that way. It wasn't our way; we would have drifted into finding out—Hilda was scarcely home. But young Mrs. Draper had been brought up hard, she said, twelve mouths to feed.

"*I'm* looking after *you*, Mum," said Hilda, smiling at her mother.

Mrs. Johnson was like a wizened little girl gazing up at a taller sister.

"I'll take you to Monte Carlo, Mum," Hilda said.

The old lady tittered. We all laughed loudly. Hilda laughed with us.

"That gambling place!" the old lady giggled.

"That's it," laughed Hilda. "Break the bank."

"Is it across water?" said the old lady, playing up. "I couldn't go on a boat. I was so sick at Southend when I was a girl."

"Then we'll fly."

"Oh!" the old lady screeched. "Don't, Hil—I'll have a fit."

"The man who broke the bank at Monte Carlo," Mr. Fulmino sang. "You might find a boyfriend, Mrs. Johnson."

Young Mrs. Draper did not laugh at this game; she still wanted to know; but she did smile. She was worried by laughter. Constance did not laugh but she showed her pretty white teeth.

"Oh, she's got one for me," said Mrs. Johnson. "So she says."

"Of course I have. Haven't I, Harry?" said Hilda, talking across the table to me.

"Me? What?" I said, completely startled.

"You can't take Harry," said Iris, half frightened. Until then I did not know that Iris was interested in me.

"Did you post the letter?" said Hilda to me.

"What letter?" said Iris to me. "Did she give you a letter?"

Now, there is a thing I ought to have mentioned! I had forgotten all about the letter. When we were leaving the evening before, Hilda had called me quietly to the door and said:

"Please post this for me. Tonight."

"Hilda gave me a letter to post," I said.

"You did post it?" Hilda said.

"Yes," I said.

She looked contentedly round at everyone.

"I wrote to Mr. Gloster, the gentleman I told you about, on the boat. He's in Paris. He's coming over at the end of the week to get a car. He's taking Mother and me to France. Mr. Gloster, Mum, I told you.

No, not Mr. Faulkner. That was the other boat. He was in San Francisco."

"Oh," said Mrs. Johnson, a very long "oh," and wriggling like a child listening to a story. She was beginning to look pale, as she had the evening before when she had her turn.

"France!" said Constance in a peremptory voice.

"Who is Mr. Gloster? You never said anything," said Mrs. Fulmino.

"What about the currency regulations?" said Mr. Fulmino.

Young Mrs. Draper said: "France! He must have money."

"Dollars," said Hilda to Mr. Fulmino.

Dollars! There was a word!

"The almighty dollar," said Constance, in the cleansed and uncorrupted voice of one who has mentioned one of the Commandments. Constance had principles; we had the confusion of our passions.

And from sixteen years or more back in time, or perhaps it was from some point in history hundreds of years back and forgotten, old Mrs. Draper said: "And is this Indian married?"

Hilda, to whom no events, I believe, had ever happened, replied: "Mr. Gloster's an American, Gran."

"He wants to marry her," said old Mrs. Johnson proudly.

"If I'll have him!" said Hilda.

"Well, he can't if you won't have him, can he, Hilda?" said Mrs. Fulmino.

"Gloster. G–L–O–S–T–E–R?" asked Mr. Fulmino.

"Is he in a good job?" asked young Mrs. Draper.

Hilda pointed to a brooch on her blouse. "He gave me this," she said.

She spoke in her harsh voice and with a movement of her face which in anyone else one would have called excited, but in her it had a disturbing lack of meaning. It was as if Hilda had been hooked into the air by invisible wires and was then swept out into the air and back to Japan, thousands of miles away again, and while she was on her way, she turned and knocked us flat with the next item.

"He's a writer," she said. "He's going to write a book about me. He's very interested in me. . . ."

Mrs. Johnson nodded.

"He's coming to fetch us, Mum and me, and take us to France to write this book. He's going to write my life."

Her life! Here was a woman who had, on top of everything else, a life.

"Coming *here*?" said Mrs. Fulmino with a grinding look at old Mrs.

Draper and then at Constance, trying to catch their eyes and failing; in despair she looked at the shabby room, to see what must be put straight, or needed cleaning or painting. Nothing had been done to it for years, for Constance, teaching at her school all day and very clean in her person, let things go in the house, and young Mrs. Draper said old Mrs. Draper smelt. All the command in Mrs. Fulmino's face collapsed as rapidly, on her own, she looked at the carpets, the lino, the curtains.

"What's he putting in this book?" said young Mrs. Draper cannily.

"Yes," said Jack Draper, backing up his wife.

"What I tell him," Hilda said.

"What she tells him," said old Mrs. Johnson, sparkling. Constance looked thoughtfully at Hilda.

"Is it a biography?" Constance asked coldly. There were times when we respected Constance and forgot to murmur "Go back to Russia" every time she spoke. I knew what a biography was and so did Mr. Fulmino, but no one else did.

"It's going to be made into a film," Hilda replied.

"A film," cried Iris.

Constance gleamed.

"You watch for American propaganda," said Constance. There you are, you see: Constance was back on it!

"Oh, it's about me," said Hilda. "My experiences."

"Very interesting," said Mr. Fulmino, preparing to take over. "A Hollywood production, I expect. Publication first and then they go into production." He spread his legs.

None of us had believed or even understood what we heard, but we looked at Mr. Fulmino with gratitude for making the world steady again.

Jack Draper's eyes filled with tears because a question was working in him but he could not get it out.

"Will you be in this film?" asked Iris.

"I'll wait till he's written it," said Hilda with that lack of interest we had often noticed in her after she had made some dramatic statement.

Mrs. Fulmino breathed out heavily with relief and after that her body seemed to become larger. She touched her hair at the back and straightened her dress, as if preparing to offer herself for the part. She said, indeed:

"I used to act at school."

"She's still good at it," said Mr. Fulmino with daring to Jack Draper, who always appreciated Mr. Fulmino, but, seeing the danger of the moment, hugged himself and scratched excitedly under both armpits, laughing.

"You shouldn't have let this Mr. Gloster go," said Constance.

Hilda was startled by this remark and looked lost. Then she shrugged her shoulders and gave a low laugh, as if to herself.

Mr. Fulmino's joke had eased our bewilderment. Hilda had been our dream, but now she was home she changed as fast as dreams change. She was now, as we looked at her, far more remote to us than she had been all the years when she was away. The idea was so far beyond us. It was like some story of a bomb explosion or an elopement or a picture of bathing girls one sees in the newspapers—unreal and, in a way, insulting to being alive in the ordinary daily sense of the word. Or she was like a picture one sees in an art gallery which makes you feel sad because it is painted.

After tea, when Hilda took her mother to the lavatory, Constance beckoned to Iris and let her peep into the room Hilda was sharing, and young Mrs. Draper, not to be kept out of things, followed. They were back in half a minute.

"Six evening dresses," Iris said to me.

"She said it was Mr. Faulkner who gave her the luggage, not this one who was going to get her into pictures," said Mrs. Fulmino.

"Mr. Gloster, you mean," said Constance.

Young Mrs. Draper was watching the door, listening for Hilda's return.

"Ssh," she said at the sound of footsteps on the stairs, and to look at us—the men on one side of the room and the women on the other, silent, standing at attention, facing each other—we looked like soldiers.

"Oh," said Constance. The steps we had heard were not Hilda's. It was Bill Williams who came in.

"Good afternoon, one and all," he said. The words came from the corner of a mouth that had slipped down at one side. Constance drew herself up; her eyes softened. She had exact, small, round breasts. Looking round, he said to Constance: "Where is she?"

Constance lowered her head when she spoke to him, though she held it up shining, admiring him, when he spoke to us, as if she were displaying him to us.

"She'll be here in a minute," she said. "She's going into films."

"I'll take a seat in the two-and-fourpennies," said Bill Williams, and he sat down at his ease and lit a cigarette.

Bill Williams was a very tall, sick-faced man who stooped his shoulders as if he were used to ducking under doors. His dry black hair, not oiled like Mr. Fulmino's, bushed over his forehead, and he had the shoulders, arms, and hands of a lorry driver. In fact, he drove a light van for a textile firm. His hazel eyes were always watching and wandering, and we used to say he looked as though he was going to snaffle something, but that may simply have been due to the restlessness of a man with a poor stomach. Laziness, cunning, and aches and pains were suggested by him. He was a man taking his time. His eyebrows grew thick and the way one brow was raised, combined with the side slip of his mouth, made him look like some shrewd man about to pick up a faulty rifle, hit the bull's-eye five times running at a fair, and moan afterwards. He glanced a good deal at Constance. He was afraid of his manners before her, we thought, because he was a rough type.

"Put it here," said Constance, bringing him an ashtray. That was what he was waiting for, for he did not look at her again.

Bill Williams brought discomfort with him whenever he came on Sundays, and we were always happier when he failed to come. If there was anything private to say, we tried to get it over before he came. How a woman like Constance, a true, clean, settled schoolteacher who even spoke in the clear, practical, and superior manner of someone used to the voice of reason, who kept her nails so beautifully, could have taken up with him baffled us. He was very often at Mrs. Draper's in the week, eating with them, and Constance, who was thirty-five, quarrelled like a girl when she was getting things ready for him. Mrs. Fulmino could not bear the way he ate, with his elbows out and his face close to the plate. The only good thing about the affair was that, for once, Constance was overruled.

"Listen to her," Bill Williams would say with a nod of his head. "A rank-red Communist. Tell us about Holy Russia, Connie."

"Constance is my name, not Connie," she said.

Their bickering made us die. But we respected Constance even when she was a trial. She had been twice to Russia before the war, and though we argued violently with her, especially Mr. Fulmino, who tried to take over Russia and populate it with explanations, we always boasted that she'd been there, to other people.

"On delegations," Mr. Fulmino would say.

But we could *not* boast that she had taken up with Bill Williams. He had been a hero when he came back from Japan, but he had never kept a job since, he was rough, and his lazy, zigzagging habits in his work made even Constance impatient. He had for her the fascination a teacher feels for a bad pupil. Lately their love affair had been going better because he was working outside London and sometimes he worked at weekends; this added to the sense of something vague and secretive in his life that had attracted Constance. For there was much that was secret in her, or so she liked to hint: it was political. Again, it was the secretiveness of those who like power; she was the schoolmistress who has the threat of inside knowledge locked up in the cupboard. Once Mrs. Fulmino went purple and said to her husband (who told me; he always told me such things) that she believed Constance had lately started sleeping with Bill Williams. That was because Constance had once said to her:

"Bill and I are individuals."

Mrs. Fulmino had a row with Iris after this and stopped me seeing her for a month.

Hilda came back into the room alone. Bill Williams let his mouth slip sideways and spoke a strange word to her, saying jauntily to us: "That's Japanese."

Hilda wasn't surprised. She replied with a whole sentence in Japanese.

"That means—" Bill Williams was beaten, but he passed it off. "Well, I'd best not tell them what it means," he said.

"East meets East," Mr. Fulmino said.

"It means," said Hilda, "you were on the other side of the fence, but now the gate is open."

Bill Williams studied her inch by inch. He scratched his head. "Straight?" he said.

"Yes," she said.

"Stone me, it was bloody closed when we were there," said Bill Williams offensively, but then said: "They fed her well, didn't they, Constance? Sit down." Hilda sat down beside him.

"Connie!" he called. "Seen these? Just the job, eh?" He was nodding at Hilda's stockings. Nylons. "Now," he said to Hilda, looking closely at her. "Where were you? It got a bit rough at the finish, didn't it?"

Jack Draper came close to them to hear, hoping that Hilda would say something about what moved him the most: the enemy. Bill Williams gave him a wink and Hilda saw it. She looked placidly at Bill Williams, considering his face, his neck, his shoulders, and his hands, which were resting on his knees.

"I was okey doke," she said.

Bill Williams dropped his mouth open and waggled the top of his tongue in a back tooth in his knowing manner. To our astonishment Hilda opened her mouth and gave a neat twist to her tongue in her cheek in the same way.

Bill Williams slapped his knee and, to cover his defeat in this little duel, said to all of us: "This little girl's got yellow eyes."

All the colour had gone from Connie's face as she watched the meeting.

"They say you're going to be in pictures," said Bill Williams.

And then we had Hilda's story over again. Constance asked what papers Mr. Gloster wrote for.

"I don't know. A big paper," said Hilda.

"You ought to find out," Constance said. "I'll find out."

"Um," said Hilda with a nod of not being interested.

"I could give him some of my experience," said Bill Williams. "Couldn't I, Connie? Things I've told you—you could write a ruddy book."

He looked with challenge at Hilda. He was a rival.

"Gawd!" he exclaimed. "The things."

We heard it again, how he was captured, where his battery was, the long march, Sergeant Harris who was hanged, Corporal Rowley bayoneted and left to die in the sun, the starvation, the work on the road that killed half of them. But there was one difference between this story and the ones he had told before. The sight of Hilda altered it.

"You had to get round the guards," he said with a wink. "If you used your loaf a bit, eh? Scrounge round, do a bit of trade. One or two had Japanese girls. Corporal Jones went back afterwards trying to trace his, wanted to marry her."

Hilda listened and talked about places she had lived in, how she had worked in a factory.

"That's it," said Bill Williams, "you had to know your way round and talk a bit of the lingo."

Jack Draper looked with affection and wonder at the talk, lowering his eyes if her eyes caught his. Every word entered him. The heat! she said. The rain. The flowers. The telegraph poles! Jack nodded.

"They got telegraph poles." He nodded to us.

You sleep on the floor. Shinji's mother, she mentioned. She could have skinned her. Jack, brought up among so many women, lost interest, but it revived when she talked of Shinji. You could see him mouthing his early marvelling sentence: "She married a Nip," but not saying it. She was confirming something he had often thought of in Normandy; the men on the other side were married too. A bloody marvel. Why hadn't she brought him home? He would have had a friend.

"Who looked after the garden when Shinji was called up?" he asked. "Were they goldfish, ordinary goldfish, in the pond?"

Young Mrs. Draper shook her head. "Eh," she said. "If he'd a known he'd have come over to change the water. Next time we have a war you just let him know."

Mrs. Fulmino, who was throbbing like a volcano, said: "We better all go next time by the sound of it."

At the end, Bill Williams said: "I suppose you're going to be staying here."

"No," said Constance quickly, "she isn't. She's going to France. When is it, Hilda? When is Mr. Gloster coming?"

"Next week, I don't know," said Hilda.

"You shouldn't have let him go!" laughed Bill Williams. "Those French girls will get him in Paree."

"That is what I have been saying," said Constance. "He gave her that brooch."

"Oh, ah! It's the stockings I'm looking at," said Bill Williams. "How did you get all that stuff through the customs? Twenty cases, Connie told me."

"Twelve," said Hilda.

Bill Williams did not move her at all. Presently she got up and started clearing away the tea things. I will say this for her: she didn't let herself be waited on.

Iris, Mr. and Mrs. Fulmino, and the young Drapers and their children and myself left Hincham Street together.

"You walk in front with the children, Iris," said Mrs. Fulmino. Then they turned on me. What was this letter, they wanted to know. Anyone would have thought by their questions that I ought to have opened it and read it.

"I just posted it at the corner." I pointed to the pillar box. Mrs. Fulmino stopped to look at the pillar box and I believe was turning over in her mind the possibility of getting inside it. Then she turned on her husband and said with contemptuous suspicion: "Monte Carlo!" As if he had worked the whole thing in order to go there himself.

"Two dead," she added in her mother's voice, the voice of one who would have been more than satisfied with the death of one.

"Not having a pension hasn't hurt her," said Mrs. Draper.

"Not a tear," said Mrs. Fulmino.

Jack and Mr. Fulmino glanced at each other. It was a glance of surreptitious gratitude: tears—they had escaped that.

Mr. Fulmino said: "The Japanese don't cry."

Mrs. Fulmino stepped out, a bad sign; her temper was rising.

"Who was the letter to?" she asked me. "Was the name Gloster?"

"I didn't look," I said.

Mrs. Fulmino looked at her husband and me and rolled her eyes. Another of our blunders!

"I don't believe it," she said.

But Mrs. Fulmino *did* believe it. We all believed and disbelieved everything at once. I said I would come to the report in the *News*. It was in thick lettering like mourning, with Hilda's picture: A MOTHER'S FAITH. FOUR YEARS IN JAPANESE TORTURE CAMP. LONDON GIRL'S ORDEAL.

And then an account of how Hilda had starved and suffered and been brainwashed by questioners. Even Hilda was awed when she read it, feeling herself drain away, perhaps, and being replaced by this fantasy; and for the rest of us, we had become used to living in a period when events reduced us to beings so trivial that we had no strong feeling of our own existence in relation to the world round us. We had been bashed first one way, then the other, by propaganda until we were indifferent. At one time people like my parents or old Mrs. Draper could at least trust the sky and feel that it was certain, and before it they could have at least the importance of being something in the eye of heaven.

Constance read the newspaper report and it fulfilled her.

"Propaganda," she said. "Press lies."

"All lies," Mr. Fulmino agreed with wonder. The notion that the untrue was as effective as the true opened to him vast areas to his powers. It was like a temptation.

It did not occur to us that we might be in a difficult situation in the neighbourhood when the truth came out until we heard Constance and Bill Williams had gone over to the Lord Nelson with the paper and Constance had said: "You can't believe a word you read in the capitalist press."

Alfred Levy, the proprietor and a strong Tory, agreed with her. But was Hilda criticized for marrying an enemy? The hatred of the Japanese was strong at this time. She was not. Constance may not have had the best motives for spreading the news, we said, but it did no harm at all. That habit of double vision affected everyone publicly. We lived in the true and the untrue, comfortably and without trouble. People picked up the paper, looked at her picture, and said: "That's a shocking thing. A British subject," and even when they knew, even from Hilda's own lips, the true story, they said, congratulating themselves on their cunning: "The papers make it all up."

Of course, we were all in that stage where the forces of life, the desire to live, were coming back, and although it was not yet openly expressed, we felt that curiosity about the enemy that ex-soldiers like Jack Draper felt when he wondered if some Japanese or some Germans were as fed up as he was on Saturdays by missing a day's fishing. When people shook Hilda's hand they felt they gave her life. I do not say there were not one or two mutterings afterwards, for people always went off from the Lord Nelson when it closed in a state of moralization: beer must talk; the louts singing and the couples saying this or that "wasn't right." But this gossip came to nothing because, sooner or later, it came to a closed door in everybody's conscience. There were the men who had shot off trigger fingers, who had got false medical certificates, deserters, ration frauds, black marketeers, the pilferers of Army stores. And the women said a woman is right to stand by her husband and, looking at Hilda's fine clothes, pointed out to their husbands that that kind of loyalty was sometimes rewarded. Mrs. Fulmino, indeed, asserted it ought to be—by law.

We had been waiting for Hilda; now, by a strange turn, we were waiting for Hilda's Mr. Gloster. We waited for a fortnight and it ran on into three weeks. George Hartman Gloster. I looked up the name on our cards at the library, but we had no books of his. I looked up one or two catalogues. Still nothing. It was not surprising. He was an American who was not published in this country. Constance came in and looked too.

"It is one of those names the Americans don't list," she said. Constance smiled with the cool air of keeping a world of meaningful secrets on ice.

"They don't list everything," she said.

She brought Bill Williams with her. I don't think he had ever been in a public library before, because his knowing manner went and he was overawed. He said to me:

"Have you read all these books? Do you buy them second-hand? What's this lot worth?"

He was a man always on the look-out for a deal; it was typical of him that he had come with Constance in his firm's light-green van. It was not like Constance to travel in that way. "Come on," he said roughly.

The weather was hot; we had the sun blinds down in the library. We were in the middle of one of those brassy fortnights of the London summer when English life as we usually know it is at a standstill, and everyone changes. A new, grinning, healthy race, with long red necks sticking out of open shirts and blouses, appears, and the sun brings out the variety of faces and bodies. Constance might have been some trim nurse marching at the head of an official procession. People looked calm, happy, and open. There was hardly ever a cloud in the sky, the slate roofs looked like steel with the sun's rays hitting them, and the side streets were cool in sharp shadow. It was a pleasant time for walking, especially when the sky went whitish in the distances of the city in the evening and when the streets had a dry, pleasant smell and the glass of millions of windows had a motionless but not excluding stare. Even a tailor working late above a closed shop looked pleased to be going on working while everyone else was out, wearing out their clothes.

Iris and I used to go to the park on some evenings, and there every blade of grass had been wire-brushed by sunlight; the trees were heavy with still leaves, and when darkness came they gathered into soft black walls and their edges were cut out against the nail varnish of the city's night. During the day the park was crowded. All over the long sweeps of grass the couples were lying, their legs at careless angles, their bottoms restless as they turned to the horseplay of love in the open. Girls were leaning over the men rumpling their hair, men were tickling the girls' chins with stalks of grass. Occasionally they would knock the wind out of each other with plunging kisses; and every now and then a girl would sit up and straighten her skirt at the waist, narrowing her eyes in a pretence of looking at some refining sight in the distance, until she was pulled down again and, keeping her knees together, was caught again. Lying down, you smelt the grass and listened to the pleasant rumble of the distant traffic going round like a wheel that never stopped.

I was glad to know the Fulminos and to go out with Iris. We had both been gayer before we met each other, but seriousness, glumness, a sadness came over us when we became friends—that eager sadness that begins with thoughts of love. We encouraged and discouraged these thoughts in each other, yet were always hinting, and the sight of so much love round us turned us naturally away from it to think about it privately the more. She was a beautifully formed girl, as her mother must have once been, but slender. She had a wide laugh that shook the curls of her thick black hair. She was being trained at a typing school.

One day when I was sitting in the park and Iris was lying beside me, we had a quarrel. I asked her if there was any news of Mr. Gloster— for she heard everything. She had said there was none and I said, sucking a piece of grass:

"That's what I would like to do. Go round the world. Anywhere. America, Africa, China."

"A chance is a fine thing," said Iris, daydreaming.

"I could get a job," I said.

Iris sat up. "Leave the library?" she said.

"Yes," I said. "If I stay there I won't see anything." I saw Iris's face change and become very like her mother's. Mrs. Fulmino could make her face go larger and her mouth go very small. Iris did not answer. I went on talking. I asked her what she thought. She still did not answer.

"Anything the matter?" She was sulking. Then she said, flashing at me:

"You're potty on that woman too. You all are. Dad is, Jack is—and look at Bill Williams. Round at Hincham Street every day. He'll be having his breakfast there soon. Fascinated."

"He goes to see Constance."

"Have you seen Constance's face?" she jeered. "Constance could kill her."

"She came to the library."

"Ah." She turned to me. "You didn't tell me that."

"She came in for a book, I told you. For Mr. Gloster's books. Bill Williams came with her."

Iris's sulk changed into satisfaction at this piece of news.

"Mother says if Constance's going to marry a man like Mr. Williams," she said, "she'll be a fool to let him out of her sight.

"I'll believe in Mr. Gloster when I see him," Iris said. It was, of course, what we were all thinking. We made up our quarrel and I took Iris home. Mrs. Fulmino was dressed up, just putting the key in the door of her house. Iris was astonished to see her mother had been out and asked where she had been.

"Out," said Mrs. Fulmino. "Have I got to stay in and cook and clean for you all day?"

Mrs. Fulmino was even wearing gloves, as if she had been to church.

And she was wearing a new pair of shoes. Iris went pale at the sight of them. Mrs. Fulmino put her gloves down on the sitting-room table and said:

"I've got a right to live, I suppose?"

We were silenced.

One thing we all agreed on while we waited for Mr. Gloster was that Hilda had the money and knew how to spend it. The first time she asked the Fulminos and young Drapers to the cinema, Mrs. Fulmino said to her husband:

"You go. I've got one of my heads."

"Take Jack," young Mrs. Draper said. "I've got the children."

They were daring their husbands to go with her. But the second time, there was a party. Hilda took some of them down to Kew. She took old Mrs. Johnson down to Southend—and who should they meet there but Bill Williams, who was delivering some goods there, spoiling their day, because old Mrs. Johnson did not like his ways. And Hilda had given them all presents. And two or three nights a week she was out at the Lord Nelson.

It was a good time. If anyone asked: "Have you heard from Mr. Gloster yet?" Hilda answered that it was not time yet, and as a dig at Constance which we all admired, she said once: "He has business at the American embassy." And old Mrs. Johnson held her head high and nodded.

At the end of three weeks we became restless. We noticed old Mrs. Johnson looked poorly. She said she was tired. Old Mrs. Draper became morose. She had been taught to call Mr. Gloster by his correct name, but now she relapsed.

"Where is this Indian?" she uttered.

And another day, she said, without explanation:

"Three."

"Three what, Gran?"

"There've been two, that's enough."

No one liked this, but Mrs. Johnson understood.

"Mr. Gloster's very well, isn't he, Hil? You heard from him yesterday?" she said.

"I wasn't shown the letter," said old Mrs. Draper. "We don't want a third."

"We don't," said Mrs. Fulmino. With her joining in "on Gran's side," the situation changed. Mrs. Fulmino had a low voice and the sound of it often sank to the floor of any room she was in, travelling under chairs and tables, curling round your feet, and filling the place from the bottom as if it were a cistern. Even when the trolley bus went by, Mrs. Fulmino's low voice prevailed. It was an undermining voice, breaking up one's uppermost thoughts and stirring up what was underneath them. It stirred us all now. Yes, we wanted to say, indeed, we wanted to shout, where is this Mr. Gloster, why hasn't he come, did you invent him? He's alive, we hope? Or is he also, as Gran suggests, dead?

Even Mr. Fulmino was worried. "Have you got his address?" he asked.

"Yes, Uncle dear," said Hilda. "He'll be staying at the Savoy. He always does."

Mr. Fulmino had not taken out his notebook for a long time, but he did so now. He wrote down the name.

"Has he made a reservation?" said Mr. Fulmino. "I'll find out if he's booked."

"He hasn't," said Bill Williams. "I had a job down there and I asked. Didn't I, Connie?"

Mrs. Fulmino went a very dark colour; she wished she had been as cunning as Williams. Hilda was not offended, but a small smile clipped her lips as she glanced at Connie.

"I asked Bill to do it," she said.

And then Hilda, in that harsh, lazy voice which she had always used for announcements:

"If he doesn't come by Wednesday you'll have to speak for me at your factory, Mr. Williams. I don't know why he hasn't come, but I can't wait any more."

"Bill can't get you a job. You have to register," said Constance.

"Yes, she'll have to do that," said Mr. Fulmino.

"I'll fix it. Leave it to me," said Bill Williams.

"I expect," said young Mrs. Draper, "his business has kept him." She was sorry for Hilda.

"Perhaps he's gone fishing," said Jack Draper, laughing loudly in a kind way. No one joined in.

"Fishing for orders," said Bill Williams.

Hilda shrugged her shoulders and then she made one of those remarks that Grandma Draper usually made: I suppose the gift really ran through the family.

"Perhaps it was a case," she said, "of ships that pass in the night."

"Oh, no, dear," said Mrs. Johnson, trembling, "not ships." We went to the bus stop afterwards with the Fulminos and the Johnsons. Mrs. Fulmino's calm had gone. She marched out first, her temper rising.

"Ships!" she said. "When you think of what we went through during the war. Did you hear her? Straight out?"

"My brother Herbert's wife was like that. She's a widow. Take away the pension and they'll work like the rest of us. I had to."

"Job! Work! I know what sort of work she's been doing. Frank, walk ahead with Iris."

"Well," said young Mrs. Draper. "She won't be able to go to work in those clothes and that's a fact."

"All show," said Mrs. Fulmino triumphantly. "And I'll tell you something else: she hasn't a penny. She's run through her poor mother's money."

"Ay, I don't doubt," said young Mrs. Draper, who had often worked out how much the old lady had saved.

Mr. Gloster did not come on Wednesday or on any day, but Hilda did not get a job either, not at once. And old Mrs. Johnson did not go to Monte Carlo. She died. This was the third, we understood, that old Mrs. Draper had foreseen.

Mrs. Johnson died at half past eight in the morning just after Constance had gone off to school, the last day of the term, and before old Mrs. Draper had got up. Hilda was in the kitchen wearing her blue Japanese wrap when she heard her mother's loud shout, like a man selling papers, she said, and when Hilda rushed in, her mother was sitting up in bed. She gripped Hilda with the ferocity of the dying, as if all the strength of her whole life had come back and she was going to throw her daughter to the ground. Then she died. In an hour she looked like a white leaf that has been found after a lifetime pressed between the pages of a book and as delicate as a saint. The death was not only a shock; from the grief that spread from it staining all of us, I trace the ugly events that followed. Only the frail figure of old Mrs. Johnson, with her faith and her sly smile, had protected us from them until then, and when she went, all defence went with her.

I need not describe her funeral: it was done by Bickerson's; Mr. Fulmino arranged it. But one thing astonished us: not only our families but the whole neighbourhood was affected by the death of this woman who, in our carelessness, we thought could hardly be known to anyone. She had lived there all her life, of course, but people come and go in London; only a sluggish residue stay still; and I believe it was just because a large number of passing people knew just a little about her, because she was a fragment in their minds, that her death affected them. They recognized that they themselves were not people but fragments. People remembered her going into shops now and then, or going down to the bus stop, passing down a street. They remembered the bag of American cloth she used to carry containing her sewing; they spoke for a long time afterwards about this bag, more about it, indeed, than about herself. Bickerson's is a few doors from the Lord Nelson, so that when the hearse stood there covered with flowers, everyone noticed it, and although the old lady had not been in that public house for years since the death of her husband, all the customers came out to look. And they looked at Hilda sitting in her black in the car when the hearse moved slowly off, and all who knew her story must have felt that the dream was burying the dreamer. Hilda's face was dirty with grief and she did not turn her head to right or left as they drove off. I remember a small thing that happened when we were all together at old Mrs. Draper's, after we had got her back with difficulty up the stairs.

"Bickerson's did it very well," said Mr. Fulmino, seeking to distract the old lady, who, swollen with sadness, was uncomfortable in her best clothes. "They organize everything so well. They gave me this."

He held up a small brass disc on a little chain. It was one of those identity discs people used to wear on their wrists in the war.

"She had never taken it off," he said. It swung feebly on its chain. Suddenly, with a sound like a shout, Mr. Fulmino broke into tears. His face caved in and he apologized.

"It's the feeling," he said. "You have the feeling. You feel." And he looked at us with panic, astonished by this discovery of an unknown self, spongy with tears, that had burst out and against which he was helpless. Mrs. Fulmino said gently: "I expect Hilda would like to have it."

"Yes, yes. It's for her," he said, drying his eyes, and Hilda took it from him and carried it to her room. While she was there (and perhaps she was weeping, too), Mr. Fulmino looked out from his handkerchief and said, still sobbing:

"I see that the luggage has gone."

None of us had noticed this and we looked at Constance, who said in a whisper: "She is leaving us. She has found a room of her own." That knocked us back. "Leaving!" we exclaimed. It told against Hilda, for although we talked of death being a release for the dead person, we did not like to think of it as a release for the living; grief ought to hold people together, and it seemed too brisk to have started a new life so soon. Constance alone looked pleased by this. We were whispering but stopped when we heard Hilda coming back.

Black had changed her. It set off her figure, and although crying had hardened her, the skin of her neck and her arms and the swell of her breasts seemed more living than they had before. She looked stronger in body perhaps because she was shaken in mind. She looked very real, very present, more alive than ourselves. She had not heard us whispering, but she said, to all of us, but particularly to Mr. Fulmino:

"I have found a room for myself. Constance spoke to Bill Williams for me: he's good at getting things. He found me a place and he took the luggage round yesterday. I couldn't sleep in that bed alone any more."

Her voice was shaky.

"She didn't take up much room. She was tiny and we managed. It was like sleeping with a little child."

Hilda smiled and laughed a little.

"She used to kick like a kid."

Ten minutes on the bus from Hincham Street and close to the centre of London is a dance hall called the Temple Rooms. It has two bands, a low gallery where you can sit, and a soft-drink bar. Quite a few West Indians go there, mainly students. It is a respectable place; it closes at eleven and there is never any trouble. Iris and I went there once or twice. One evening we were surprised to see Constance and Bill Williams dancing there. Iris pointed to them. The rest of the people were jiving, but Bill Williams and Constance were dancing in the old-fashioned way.

"Look at his feet!" Iris laughed.

Bill Williams was paying no attention to Constance, but looking round the room over her head as he stumbled along. He was tall.

"Fancy Auntie Constance!" said Iris. "She's getting fed up because he won't listen."

Constance Draper dancing! At her age! Thirty-eight!

"It's since the funeral," said Mr. Fulmino over our usual cup of tea. "She was fond of the old lady. It's upset her."

Even I knew Mr. Fulmino was wrong about this. The madness of Constance dated from the time Bill Williams had taken Hilda's luggage round to her room and got her a job at the reception desk in the factory at Laxton. It dated from the time a week later when, standing at old Mrs. Draper's early one evening, Constance had seen Hilda get out of Bill Williams's van. He had given her a lift home. It dated from words that passed between Hilda and Constance soon afterwards. Hilda said Williams hung round for her at the factory and wanted her to go to a dance. She did not want to go, she said, and here came the fatal sentences—both of her husbands had been educated men. Constance kept her temper but said coldly:

"Bill Williams is politically educated."

Hilda had her vacant look. "Not his hands aren't," she said.

The next thing, Constance, who hardly went into a pub in her life, was in the Lord Nelson night after night, playing bar billiards with Bill Williams. She never let him out of her sight. She came out of school and instead of going home, marking papers, and getting a meal for herself and old Mrs. Draper, she took the bus out to the factory and waited for him to come out. Sometimes he had left on some job by the time she got there and she came home, beside herself, questioning everybody. It had been her habit to come twice a week to change her library books. Now she did not come. She stopped reading. At the Temple Rooms, when Iris and I saw her, she sat out holding hands with Bill Williams and rubbing her head into his shoulder, her eyes watching him the whole time. We went to speak to them and Constance asked:

"Is Hilda here tonight?"

"I haven't seen her."

"She's a whore," said Constance in a loud voice. We thought she was drunk.

It was a funny thing, Mr. Fulmino said to me, to call a woman a whore. He spoke as one opposed to funny things.

"If they'd listened to me," he said, "I could have stopped all this trouble. I offered to get her a job in the council office, but"—he rolled his eyes—"Mrs. F. wouldn't have it, and while we were arguing about it, Bill Williams acts double quick. It's all because this Mr. Gloster didn't turn up."

Mr. Fulmino spoke wistfully. He was, he conveyed, in the middle of a family battle; indeed, he had a genuine black eye the day we talked about this. Mrs. Fulmino's emotions were in her arms.

This was a bad period for Mr. Fulmino because he had committed a folly. He had chosen this moment to make a personal triumph. He had got himself promoted to a much better job at the council offices and one entitling him to a pension. He had become a genuine official. To have promoted a man who had the folly to bring home a rich whore with two names, so causing the robbery and death of her mother, and to have let her break Constance's heart was, in Mrs. Fulmino's words, a crime. Naturally, Mr. Fulmino regarded his mistakes as mere errors of routine and even part of his training for his new position.

"Oh, well," he said when we finished our tea and got up to pay the bill. "It's the British taxpayer that pays." He was heading for politics. I have heard it said, years later, that if he had had a better start in life he would have gone to the top of the administration. It is a tragic calling.

If Hilda was sinister to Constance and Mrs. Fulmino, she made a different impression on young Mrs. Draper. To call a woman a whore was neither here nor there to her. Up north where she came from, people were saying that sort of thing all day long as they scrubbed floors or cleaned windows or did the washing. The word gave them energy and made things come up cleaner and whiter. Good money was earned hard; easy money went easy. To young Mrs. Draper, Hilda seemed "a bit simple," but she had gone to work, she earned her living. Cut off from the rest of the Draper family, Hilda made friends with this couple. Hilda went with them on Saturday to the zoo with the children. They were looking at a pair of monkeys. One of them was dozing and its companion was awake, pestering and annoying it. The children laughed. But when they moved on to another cage, Hilda said sulkily:

"That's one thing. Bill Williams won't be here. He pesters me all the time."

"He won't if you don't let him," said young Mrs. Draper.

"I'm going to give my notice if he doesn't stop," said Hilda. She hunched a shoulder and looked round at the animals.

"I can't understand a girl like Constance taking up with him. He's not on her level. And he's mean. He doesn't give her anything. I asked if he gave her that clip, but she said it was Gran's. Well, if a man doesn't give you anything he doesn't value you. I mean she's a well-read girl."

"There's more ways than one of being stupid," said young Mrs. Draper.

"I wonder she doesn't see," said Hilda. "He's not delivering for the firm. When he's got the van out, he's doing something on the side. When I came home with him, there was stuff at the back. And he keeps on asking how much things cost. He offered to sell my bracelet."

"You'd get a better price in a shop if you're in need," said young Mrs. Draper.

"She'd better not be with him if he gets stopped on the road," said

Jack, joining in. "You wouldn't sell that. Your husband gave it you."

"No. Mr. Faulkner," said Hilda, pulling out her arm and admiring it.

Jack was silent and disappointed; then he cheered up. "You ought to have married that earl you were always talking about when you were a girl. Do you remember?" he said.

"Earls—they're a lazy lot," said young Mrs. Draper.

"I did, Jack," said Hilda. "They were as good as earls, both of them."

And to young Mrs. Draper she said: "They wouldn't let another man look at me. I felt like a woman with both of them."

"I've nowt against that if you've got the time," said young Mrs. Draper. She saw that Hilda was glum.

"Let's go back and look at the giraffes. Perhaps Mr. Faulkner will come for you now Mr. Gloster hasn't," young Mrs. Draper said.

"They were friends," said Hilda.

"Oh, they knew each other!" said young Mrs. Draper. "I thought you just . . . met them. . . ."

"No, I didn't meet them together, but they were friends."

"Yes. Jack had a friend, didn't you?" said Mrs. Draper, remembering.

"That's right," said Jack. He winked at Hilda. "Neck and neck, it was." And then he laughed outright.

"I remember something about Bill Williams. He came out with us one Saturday and you should have seen his face when we threw the fish back in the water."

"We always throw them back," said young Mrs. Draper, taking her husband's arm, proudly.

"Wanted to sell them or something. Black-market perch!"

"He thinks I've got dollars," said Hilda.

"No, fancy, Jack—Mr. Gloster and Mr. Faulkner being friends. Well, that's nice."

And she looked sentimentally at Hilda.

"She's brooding," young Mrs. Draper said to Mrs. Fulmino after this visit to the zoo. "She won't say anything." Mrs. Fulmino said she had better not or *she* might say something. "She knows what I think. I never thought much of Bill Williams, but he served his country. She didn't."

"She earns her living," said Mrs. Draper.

"Like we all do," said Mrs. Fulmino. "And it's not men, men, men all day long with you and me."

"One's enough," said young Mrs. Draper, "with two children round your feet."

"She doesn't come near me," said Mrs. Fulmino.

"No," Mr. Fulmino said sadly, "after all we've done."

They used to laugh at me when I went dancing with Iris at the Temple Rooms. We had not been there for more than a month and Iris said:

"He can't stop staring at the band."

She was right. The beams of the spotlights put red, green, violet, and orange tents on the hundreds of dancers. It was like the Arabian nights. When we got there, Ted Custer's band was already at it like cats on dustbins and tearing their guts out. The pianist had a very thin neck and kept wagging his head as if he were ga-ga; if his head had fallen off he would have caught it in one of his crazy hands and popped it on again without losing a note; the trumpet player had thick eyebrows that went higher and higher as he tried and failed to burst; the drummers looked doped; the saxophone went at it like a man in bed with a girl who had purposely left the door open. I remember them all, especially the thin-lipped man, very white-faced, with the double bass drawing his bow at knee level, to and fro, slowly, sinful. They all whispered, nodded, and rocked together, telling dirty stories until bang, bang, bang, the dancers went faster and faster, the row hit the ceiling or died out with the wheeze of a balloon. I was entranced.

"Don't look as though you're going to kill someone," Iris said.

That shows how wrong people are. I was full of love and wanted to cry.

After four dances I went off to the soft-drink bar and there the first person I saw was Bill Williams. He was wearing a plum-coloured suit and a red and silver tie and he stood, with his dark hair, dusty-looking and spouting forward as if he had just got out of bed and was ducking his head on the way to the lavatory.

"All the family here?" he asked, looking all round.

"No," I said. "Just Iris and me."

He went on looking round him.

"I thought you only came Saturdays," he said suspiciously. He had a couple of friends with him, two men who became restless on their feet, as if they were dancing, when I came up.

"Oh," said Bill Williams. Then he said, "Nicky pokey doda—that's Japanese, pal, for 'keep your mouth shut.' Anyone say anything, you never see me. I'm at Laxton, get me? Bill Williams? He's on night shift. You must be barmy. Okay? Seeing you," he said. "No sign of Connie."

And he walked off. His new friends went a step or two after him, dancing on their pointed shoes, and then stopped. They twizzled round, tapping their feet, looking all round the room until he had got to the carpeted stairs at the end of the hall. I got my squash, and when I turned round, the two men had gone also.

But before Bill Williams had got to the top of the stairs he turned round to look at the dancers in one corner. There was Hilda. She was dancing with a young West Indian. When I got back to our table she was very near.

I have said that Hilda's face was eventless. It was now in a tranced state, looking from side to side, to the floor, in the quick turns of the dance, swinging round, stepping back, stepping forward. The West Indian had a long jacket on. His knees were often nearly bent double as though he were going to do some trick of crawling towards her; then he recovered himself and turned his back as if he had never met her and was dancing with someone else. If Hilda's face was eventless, it was the event itself, it was the dance.

She saw us when the dance was over and came to our table breathlessly. She was astonished to see us. To me she said, "And fancy you!" She did not laugh or even smile when she looked at me. I don't know how to describe her look. It was dead. It had no expression. It had nothing. Or rather, by the smallest twitch of a muscle, it became nothing. Her face had the nakedness of a body. She saw that I was deaf to what Iris was saying. Then she smiled, and in doing that, she covered herself.

"I am with friends over there"—we could not tell who the friends were—and then she leaned towards us and whispered:

"Bill Williams is here, too."

Iris exclaimed.

"He's watching me," Hilda said.

"I saw him," I said. "He's gone."

Hilda stood up, frowning. "Are you sure? Did you see him? How long ago?"

I said it was about five minutes before.

She stood as I remember her standing in Mrs. Draper's room on the first day when she arrived and was kissing everyone. It was a peculiar stance because she usually stood so passively; a stance of action and, I now saw, a stance of plain fright. One leg was planted forward and bent at the knee like a runner at the start and one arm was raised and bent at the elbow, the elbow pushed out beyond her body. Her mouth was open and her deep-set yellow eyes seemed to darken and look tired.

"He was with some friends," I said, and, looking back at the bar: "They've gone now."

"Hah!" It was the sound of a gasp of breath. Then suddenly the fright went and she shrugged her shoulders and talked and laughed to all of us. Soon she went over to her friends, the coloured man and a white couple; she must have got some money or the ticket for her handbag from one of them, for presently we saw her walking quickly to the cloakroom.

Iris went on dancing. We must have stayed another half an hour, and when we were leaving we were surprised to see Hilda waiting in the foyer. She said to me:

"His car has gone."

"Whose?"

"Bill Williams's car."

"Has he got a car?" Iris said.

"Oh, it's not his," said Hilda. "It's gone. That's something. Will you take me home? I don't want to go alone. They followed me here."

She looked at all of us. She was frightened.

I said: "Iris and I will take you on our way."

"Don't make me late," said Iris crossly. "You know what Mum is." I promised. "Did you come with him?"

"No, with someone else," Hilda said, looking nervously at the revolving glass door. "Are you sure his friends went too? What did they look like?"

I tried to describe them.

"I've seen the short one," she said, frowning, "somewhere."

It was only a quarter of an hour's ride at that hour of the night. We walked out of the Temple Rooms and across the main road to the bus stop and waited under the lights that made our faces corpse-like. I have always liked the hard and sequined sheen of London streets at night, their empty-dockyard look. The cars come down them like rats. The red trolley bus came up at last, and when we got in, Hilda sat between us. The busload of people stared at her and I am not surprised. I have not said what she looked like—the hair built up high, her bright-green wrap and red dress. I don't know how you would describe such clothes. But the people were not staring at her clothes. They were staring at her eyebrows. I said before that her face was an extension of her nakedness. I say it again. Those eyebrows of hers were painted and looked like the only things she had on; they were like a pair of beetles with turned-up tails that had settled on her forehead. People laughed behind their hands and two or three youths at the front of the bus turned round and guffawed and jostled and whistled; but Hilda, remember, was not a girl of sixteen gone silly, but a woman, hard rather than soft in the face, and the effect was one of exposure, just as a mask has the effect of exposing. We did not talk, but when the trolley arm thumped two or three times at a street junction, Hilda said with a sigh: "Bump! Bump! Bump!" She was thinking of her childhood in old Mrs. Draper's room at Hincham Street. We got off the bus a quarter of a mile further on, and as she was stepping off, Hilda said, speaking of what was in her mind, I suppose, during the ride:

"Shinji had a gold wristwatch with a gold strap and a golden pen. They had gone when he was killed. They must have cost him a hundred pounds. Someone must have stolen them and sold them.

"I reported it," Hilda said. "I needed the money. That is what you had to do—sell. Everything. I had to eat."

And the stare from her mask of a face stated something of her life that her strangeness had concealed from us. We walked up the street.

She went on talking about that watch and how particular Shinji was about his clothes, especially his shirts. All his collars had to be starched, she said. Those had gone too, she said. And his glasses. And his two gold rings. She walked very quickly between us. We got to the corner of her street. She stopped and looked down it.

"Bill Williams's van!" she said.

About thirty houses down the street we could indeed see a small van standing.

"He's waiting for me," she said.

It was hard to know whether she was frightened or whether she was reckoning, but my heart jumped. She made us stand still and watch. "My room's in the front," she said. I crossed over to the other side of the street and then came back.

"The light is on," I said.

"He's inside," she said.

"Shall I go and see?" I said.

"Go," said Iris to me.

Hilda held my wrist. "No," she said.

"There are two people, I think, in the front garden," I said.

"I'm going home with you," Hilda said to Iris decisively. She rushed

off and we had to race after her. We crossed two or three streets to
the Fulminos' house. Mrs. Fulmino let us in.

"Now, now, Hilda, keep your hair on. Kill you? Why should he? This
is England, this isn't China. . . ."

Mr. Fulmino's face showed his agony. His mouth collapsed, his eyes
went hard. He looked frantic with appeal. Then he turned his back on
us, marched into the parlour, and shouted as if he were calling across
four lines of traffic:

"Turn the wireless off."

We followed him into the room. Mrs. Fulmino, in the suddenly
silent room, looked like a fortress waiting for a flag to fall.

We all started talking at once.

"Can I stay with you tonight?" she said. "Bill Williams has broken
into my house. I can't go there. He'll kill me." The flag fell.

"Japan," said Mrs. Fulmino, disposing of her husband with her first
shot. Then she turned to Hilda; her voice was coldly rich and rumbling.
"You've always a home here, as you well know, Hilda," she went on,
giving a very unhomely sound to the word. "And," she said, glancing
at her neat curtains, to anyone who might be in ambush outside the
window, "if anyone tries to kill you, they will have to kill"—she nodded
to her husband—"Ted and me first. What have you been doing?"

"I was down at the Temple. Not with Bill Williams," said Hilda.
"He was watching me. He's always watching me."

"Now, look here, Hilda, why should Bill Williams want to kill you?
Have you encouraged him?"

"Don't be a fool," shouted Mrs. Fulmino.

"She knows what I mean. Listen to me, Hilda. What's going on
between you and Bill Williams? Constance is upset, we all know."

"Oh, keep your big mouth shut," said Mrs. Fulmino to her husband.
"Of course she's encouraged him. Hilda's a woman, isn't she? I encouraged *you,* didn't I?"

"I know how to look after myself," said Hilda, "but I don't like that
van outside the house at this hour of night. I didn't speak to him at
the dance."

"Hilda's thinking of the police," ventured Mr. Fulmino.

"Police!" said Mrs. Fulmino. "Do you know what's in the van?"

"No," said Hilda. "And that's what I don't want to know. I don't
want him on my doorstep. Or his friends. He had two with him. Harry
saw them."

Mrs. Fulmino considered.

"I'm glad you've come to us. I wish you'd come to us in the first place," she said. Then she commanded Mr. Fulmino: "You go up there at once with Harry," she said, "and tell that man to leave Hilda alone. Go on, now. I can't understand you"—she indicated me—"running off like that, leaving a van there. If you don't go, I'll go myself. I'm not afraid of a paltry . . . a paltry . . . What does he call himself? You go up."

Mrs. Fulmino was as good a judge of the possibilities of an emotional situation as any woman on earth: this was her moment. She wanted us out of the house and Hilda to herself.

We obeyed.

Mr. Fulmino and I left the house. He looked tired. He was too tired to put on his jacket. He went out in his shirt-sleeves.

"Up and down we go, in and out, up and down," said Mr. Fulmino. "First it's Constance, now it's Hilda. And the pubs are closed.

"There you are, what did I tell you?" said Mr. Fulmino when we got to Hilda's street. "No van, no sign of it, is there? You're a witness. We'll go up and see, all the same."

Mr. Fulmino had been alarmed, but now his confidence came back. He gave me a wink and a nod when we got to the house.

"Leave it to me," he said. "You wait here."

I heard him knock at the door and after a time knock again. Then I heard a woman's voice. He was talking a long time. He came away.

He was silent for a long time as we walked. At last he said:

"That beats all. I didn't say anything. I didn't say who I was. I didn't let on. I just asked to see Hilda. 'Oh,' says the landlady, 'she's out.' 'Oh,' I said, 'that's a surprise.' I didn't give a name. 'Out, you say? When will she be back?' 'I don't know,' said the landlady, and this is it, Harry —'she's paid her rent and given her notice. She's leaving first thing in the morning,' the landlady said. 'They came for the luggage this evening.' Harry," said Mr. Fulmino, "did Hilda say anything about leaving?"

"No."

"Bill Williams came for her luggage."

We marched on. Or rather we went stealthily along like two men walking a steel wire of suspicion. We almost lost our balance when two cats ran across the street and set up howls in a garden, as if they were howling us down. Mr. Fulmino stopped.

"Harry!" he said. "She's playing us up. She's going off with Bill Williams."

"But she's frightened of him. She said he was going to kill her."

"I'm not surprised," said Mr. Fulmino. "She's been playing him up. Who was she with at the dance hall? She's played everyone up. Of course she's frightened of him. You bet. I'm sorry for anyone getting mixed up with Bill Williams: he'll knock some sense into her. He's rough. So was her father."

"Bill Williams might have just dropped by to have a word," I said.

Mr. Fulmino marched forward again.

"Funny word at half past eleven at night," said Mr. Fulmino. "When I think of all that correspondence, all those forms—War Office, State Department, United Nations—we did, it's been a poor turnout. You might say"—he paused for an image sufficiently devastating—"a waste of paper, a ruddy wanton waste of precious paper."

We got back to his house. I have never mentioned I believe that it had an iron gate that howled and a clipped privet hedge like a moustache to the tiny garden.

We opened the gate, the gate howled, Mrs. Fulmino's nose appeared at the curtains.

"Don't say a word," said Mr. Fulmino.

Tea—the room smelt of that, of course. Mrs. Fulmino had made some while we were out. She looked as though she had eaten something, too. A titbit. They all looked sorry for Mr. Fulmino and me. And Mrs. Fulmino *had* had a titbit! In fact I know from Iris that the only thing Mrs. Fulmino had got out of Hilda was the news that she had had a postcard from Mr. Faulkner from Chicago. He was on the move.

"Well?" said Mrs. Fulmino.

"It's all right, Hilda," said Mr. Fulmino coldly. "They've gone."

"There," said Mrs. Fulmino, patting Hilda's hand.

"Hilda," said Mr. Fulmino, "I've been straight with you. I want you to be straight with me. What's going on between you and Bill Williams? . . ."

"Hilda's told me," Mrs. Fulmino said.

"I asked Hilda, not you," said Mr. Fulmino to his wife, who was so surprised that she went very white instead of her usual purple.

"Hilda, come on. You come round here saying he's going to kill you. Then they tell me you've given your notice up there."

"She told me that. I think she's done the right thing," Mrs. Fulmino said.

"And did you tell her why you gave your notice?" asked Mr. Fulmino.

"She's given her notice at the factory, too," said Mrs. Fulmino.

"Why?" said Mr. Fulmino.

Hilda did not answer.

"You are going off with Bill Williams, aren't you?"

"Ted!" Hilda gave one of her rare laughs.

"What's this?" cried Mrs. Fulmino. "Have you been deceiving me? Deceit I can't stand, Hilda."

"Of course she is," said Mr. Fulmino. "She's paid her rent. He's collected her luggage this evening. Where is it to be? Monte Carlo? Oh, it's all right, sit down." Mr. Fulmino waved Mrs. Fulmino back. "They had a row at the dance this evening."

But Hilda was on her feet.

"My luggage!" she cried, holding her bag with both hands to her bosom as we had seen her do once before when she was cornered. "Who has touched my luggage?"

I thought she was going to strike Mr. Fulmino.

"The dirty thief. Who let him in? Who let him take it? Where's he gone?"

She was moving to the door. We were stupefied.

"Bill Williams!" she shouted. Her rage made those artificial eyebrows look comical, and I expected her to pick them off and throw them at us. "Bill Williams, I'm talking about. Who let that bloody war hero in? That bitch up there . . ."

"Hilda," said Mrs. Fulmino. "We don't want language."

"You fool," said Mrs. Fulmino in her lowest, most floor-sweeping voice to her husband. "What have you been and done? You've let Bill Williams get away with all those cases, all her clothes, everything. You let that spiv strip her."

"Go off with Bill Williams!" Hilda laughed. "My husband was an officer.

"I knew he was after something. I thought it was dollars," she said suddenly.

She came back from the door and sat down at the table and sobbed.

"Two hundred and fifty pounds he's got," she sobbed. It was a sight to see Hilda weeping. We could not speak.

"It's all I had," she said.

We watched Hilda. The painted eyebrows made the grimace of her weeping horrible. There was not one of us who was not shocked. There was in all of us a sympathy we knew how to express but it was halted —as by a fascination—with the sight of her ruin. We could not help contrasting her triumphant arrival with her state at this moment. It was as if we had at last got her with us as we had, months before, expected her to be. Perhaps she read our thoughts. She looked up at us and she had the expression of a person seeing us for the first time. It was like an inspection.

"You're a mean lot, a mean respectable lot," she said. "I remember you. I remember when I was a girl. What was it Mr. Singh said? I can't remember—he was clever—oh well, leave it, leave it. When I saw that little room they put my poor mother in, I could have cried. No sun. No warmth in it. You just wanted someone to pity. I remember it. And your faces. The only thing that was nice was"—she sobbed and laughed for a moment—"was bump, bump, bump, the trolley." She said loudly: "There's only one human being in the whole crew—Jack Draper. I don't wonder he sees more in fish."

She looked at me scornfully. "Your brother—he was nice," she said. "Round the park at night! That was love."

"Hilda," said Mrs. Fulmino without anger. "We've done our best for you. If we've made mistakes I hope you haven't. We haven't had your life. You talk about ships that pass in the night. I don't know what you mean, but I can tell you there are no ships in this house. Only Ted."

"That's right," said Mr. Fulmino quietly too. "You're overwrought."

"Father," said Mrs. Fulmino, "hadn't you better tell the police?"

"Yes, yes, dear," agreed Mr. Fulmino. "We'd better get in touch with the authorities."

"Police," said Hilda, laughing in their faces. "Oh, God. Don't worry about that. You've got one in every house in this country." She picked up her bag, still laughing, and went to the door.

"Police," she was saying, "that's ripe."

"Hilda, you're not to go out in the street looking like that," said Mrs. Fulmino.

"I'd better go with her," said Mr. Fulmino.

"I'll go," I said. They were glad to let me.

It is ten years since I walked with Hilda to her lodgings. I shall not forget it, and the warm, dead, rubbery city night. It is frightening to walk with a woman who has been robbed and wronged. Her eyes were half closed as though she was reckoning as she walked. I had to pull her back onto the pavement or she would have gone flat into a passing car. The only thing she said to me was:

"They took Shinji's rings as well."

Her room was on the ground floor. It had a divan and a not very clean dark-green cover on it. A pair of shoes were sticking out from under it. There was a plain deal cupboard and she went straight to it. Two dresses were left. The rest had gone. She went to a table and opened the drawer. It was empty except for some letters.

I stood not knowing what to say. She seemed surprised to see me there still.

"He's cleared the lot," she said vacantly. Then she seemed to realize that she was staring at me without seeing me, for she lowered her angry shoulders.

"We'll get them back," I said.

"How?" she said, mocking me, but not unkindly.

"I will," I said. "Don't be upset."

"You!" she said.

"Yes, I will," I said.

I wanted to say more. I wanted to touch her. But I couldn't. The ruin had made her untouchable.

"What are you going to do?" I said.

"Don't worry about me," she said. "I'm okey doke. You're different from your brother. You don't remember those days. I told Mr. Gloster about him. Come to that, Mr. Faulkner too. They took it naturally. That was a fault of Mr. Singh"—she never called him by his Christian name—"jealousy."

She kicked off her shoes and sat down on the cheap divan and frowned at the noise it made and she laughed.

"One day in Bombay I got homesick and he asked me what I was thinking about, and I was green, I just said, 'Sid Fraser's neck. It had a mole on it.' You should have seen his face. He wouldn't talk to me for a week. It's a funny thing about those countries. Some people might rave about them, I didn't see anything to them."

She got up.

"You go now," she said, laughing. "I must have been in love."

I dreamt about Hilda's face all night, and in the morning I wouldn't have been surprised to see London had been burned out to a cinder. But the next night her face did not come and I had to think about it. Further and further it went, and became a little less every day, and I did not seem to notice when someone said Bill Williams had been picked up by the police, or when Constance had been found half dead with aspirins, and when, in both cases, Mr. Fulmino told me he had to "give assistance in the identification," for Hilda had gone. She left the day after I took her to her room. Where she went no one knew. We guessed. We imagined. Across water, I thought, getting further and further away, in very fine clothes and very beautiful. France, Mr. Fulmino thought, or possibly Italy. Africa, even. New York, San Francisco, Tokyo, Bombay, Singapore. Where? Even one day six months after she had left, when he came to the library and showed me a postcard he had had from her, the first message, it did not say where she was and someone in the post office had pulled off the stamp. It was a picture of Hilda herself on a seat in a park, sitting with Mr. Faulkner and Mr. Gloster. You wouldn't recognize her.

But Mr. Gloster's book came out. Oh yes. It wasn't about Japan or India or anything like that. It was about us.

Citizen

I wonder if you go to picture exhibitions and if you saw the drawings at the W Gallery a month or so ago. Italian drawings, by a woman— Effie Alldraxen. Very good notices, the critics gave her. Very gratifying to me. She is my daughter. There was one large drawing that several of our friends mentioned—typically Italian, the picture of one of those *palazzo* courtyards in Rome with a statue in it. It was one she called *The Father*. She caught the feeling that you have in Rome, of statues being everywhere—stone people (do you know?) threatening, appealing, almost walking about, crowding in, pushing the living off the pavement. One of the critics said she made the figure live—a curious statement, I thought, because stone and bronze are dead, aren't they? Of course, I don't know anything about art. I'm just a layman, a doctor. My business is illness. What interested me when I went to look at Effie's show was that the child was ill when she was doing the best of that stuff. I say "child"—a father's slip of the tongue; she is turned forty.

I hope not to sound harsh, but Effie has not been an easy child. I would describe myself as detached. I see so many sick people. She has been sending us telegrams all her life, and before I opened the one she sent from Rome, where she was doing that picture, I thought: Now what mess has she got into? Effie's telegrams read as though she is doing her face in the mirror—a dab here, a dab there, but with words. It went: "In hospital, motor accident. No bones, not serious, don't worry, just bad breakdown. Can you come immediately, not to bother, please if possible. Very well."

Children tear at one's bowels. In eight hours I was out of the London rain and sitting by Effie's bedside in Rome, listening to her childish voice. She had not been in a motor accident. She had been pushed by the bumper of a slow-moving car in the Corso and had been knocked down by a bicycle.

"I think—" she said after we had gone over the incident several times. "I think," she said, stubbornly putting up her chin, "I must have been trying not to get married."

Effie is a small woman, and although she is growing plump, she looks younger than she is. She will be forty-one next June. She was sitting up in bed, and she had the pleased, shining, new, ashamed look, rather wet and cunning, of a golden spaniel that has been dressed up in shawls by children and is presently going to make a bolt for it into the garden.

"To Mr. Wilkins," she said.

"And who is he?" I asked.

"He was on the train when you saw me off from London. Schoolmaster," she said. For testing one out, she has a small, high, plaintive voice.

"I don't remember him," I said. "But what's the matter? Is he married already?" One of the difficulties of Effie's life has been her love of other women's husbands.

"Oh, no!" said Effie, giving a squeal of pleasure. She loved this kind of conversation. "He hasn't got a wife." Then she looked at me slyly. Effie is proud of her turbulent history. "I suppose his not being married is the trouble," she said.

Effie has two voices and two kinds of laughter. Her usual voice is small and sweet—the matter-of-fact voice of a girl of five—and she uses it for things that are true. The laughter that goes with it is the high squeal that used to enchant us when she was little. This voice is, no doubt, too arch for a woman of her age. Her other voice is dry, abrupt, grown-up, bold, and mannish, and it drops to short, doggish barks of laughter. In this voice, Effie does not often tell the truth. I knew now that Effie was going to tell me a lie next, because she arranged her bedclothes and looked me gruffly in the eye.

"You are going to be cross with me," she said in the brisk manner. "I've started doing it again."

"What?"

"Making happenings," she said. She blushed.

I did not answer.

"I'm being followed," said Effie.

"By Mr. Wilkins?" I said, guessing.

"Oh, no, no," she barked.

"By some Italian?" I said.

Effie was so startled that she stopped laughing. I could see that I had put an idea into her head, perhaps for use in the future. There is something innocent about her. She had been a fortnight in Italy and it had not occurred to her that an Italian might follow her in the street, though she knew they followed other women. She had not thought of this because it was she who, in her daydreams, was always the follower.

"Oh, no," she said. "Not a man." And then she added primly, correcting me: "Not followed. Accompanied."

After a moment, she went on. "Everywhere," she said. "In the street. I have to make room. I have to step out of the way. That's how I got knocked down. There wasn't room."

Effie stared at my stare. "I can't see whether you're looking at me, Daddy," she said. "The light is on your glasses."

"But who accompanies you?" I said.

"Oh, I knew you'd understand! Give me my drawings from the table," she said. "I'll show you. No, all of them. Not this one. Not this —flowers, rather nice, don't you think? Here it is. This one." She pointed. "It comes with me."

There was simply a drawing of the courtyard of a Roman palace, but there was no one in it.

"The statue," she said. "It walks with me everywhere I go." There was certainly a statue in the foreground of the drawing. She broke into real tears. "Silly?" she sniffed. "It came . . . here . . . this morning. But it's gone, now you're here. Not a fool—I, not you. I mean me—I'm not. It's true." And then she said, with a touch of aesthetic shame: "It's bronze, very late, 1884."

I suppose I owe my great influence with my daughter to the fact that I have made it an absolute rule to believe everything she says. I have never known her to be unpractical. She is brisk and domestic—a drawer-tidier, a sock-darner, a saucepan-buyer (one would say)—and she is pretty. Her fair hair is duller than it used to be, and she has eyes the colour of dark ginger. A poet might call them "orbs." She dresses oddly, as spinsters do, but that is because her practical instinct makes her do a little something different with everything. She was now doing something with a statue.

"It must make a terrible noise," I said.

"Frightful," she said. "And such a bad period."

The effect that Italy has upon Anglo-Saxons is always impressive. In a couple of days, when Effie's temperature was down, I went to look at her persecutor. The *palazzo* is on the street that leads to the bridge you cross to get to Sant' Angelo. There is a wide entrance smelling of cold candle smoke, and then one walks between double rows of columns into the courtyard beyond, where the colonnade continues on three sides of the building. On the fourth is the higher brick wall of some large house, relieved by creepers and fountains. After the hot street, this courtyard is cool and enchanting. Which of the figures had Effie's wanton mind chosen? I looked at them. The statues were set off in arches or placed among shrubs. They stood amid the dark gloss of creepers and beside fountains. The chief fountain was against the back wall, where three Tritons, the mask of disaster upon their spreading mouths, spouted into the tank beneath them; in the corners of the court two other pipes of water spoke out in higher voice beneath the hanging foliage. The air was as still and cool and golden as white wine; the place was filled with the sounds of water notes, high and low, like faraway talk and quiet laughing. One could fancy that this sound was the classical jargon of the figures standing near or posed under the twenty arches of the colonnade. Apollo, conceited in cheek and buttocks—was it he Effie had chosen? Or Mercury, off on one of his record flights? The Venus, vacant-minded, or that careerist Diana? Which of all those white, finger-pointing gods and goddesses, those stooping nymphs and skilful boys, with their grubby, blind eyes and stone-deaf ears? As I entered the courtyard, my steps seemed to have frozen the movements of immortals, who, once my back was turned, would resume their irreconcilable and impossible lives.

I come out of this disturbing episode in the life of my family so much better than anyone else that I have no reluctance now about describing the large bronze statue that was obviously Effie's. It stood on a high plinth in the middle of the courtyard. Bronze. More than life-size, it was the naked figure of a man; on the pedestal were boldly cut out a name and, beneath it, the words *"Cittadino Esemplare"*—"The Exemplary Citizen." He was a man in the prime of life—a merchant, a burgher, a city father of some kind. His features were strong, his body muscular, boldly veined, broad-chested, overbearing. The legs were powerful; the expression of the face tragic, jealous, authoritative, unreasonable, and morose. The large hands were the open hands of a maker —a breadwinner's hands, which could stun an enemy or drive a woman.

The Citizen was the not-to-be-questioned head of a large family (one would guess), a master of the marriage bed, the married man in absolute degree.

Mr. Wilkins came with me on this visit to the courtyard—the Mr. Wilkins Effie had spoken of when I got to the hospital, and whom I had made it my business to get in touch with. I glanced at Mr. Wilkins. I stared again at the statue. What a rival!

I must describe Mr. Wilkins. If my portrait appears to be unfavourable, it is because Mr. Wilkins was one of those men who enter enthusiastically into the art of making an unfavourable impression. He was a tall man, fortyish, with dry hair, wearing a light-grey suit and a school tie. He had a difficulty with the letter "i." We first met in the bar of my hotel to drink what he called "a glass of wain."

"Ai run a school," he said. He bent down and up from his thin waist as he talked—a habit picked up from talking to little boys—keeping his hands fidgeting frivolously in his pockets as he did so. A friendly man, fizzing with descriptive talk, he was always in steadily rising spirits, but before he reached his limit, something checked him, his throat gave a click, and tears of apology came into his eyes. Unfairly, this suggested the shadiness of a double life.

I would have known him from Effie's account of him; she is a cruel mimic. He had been on the train when it left London, and on the motor coach from Paris across the Alps. They were in sight of Turin, she said, when Wilkins, who was sitting behind her, put his hand round the side of the high seat and tapped her on the shoulder. "Castle," said Wilkins. There are often white chapels on the tops of the steep hills of the lower Alpine valleys.

Effie bent forward to look up. "Shrine, I think," said Effie, who was working on her guidebook.

"Bai Jove!" said Wilkins. "You're raight, shraine."

A little later there was another tap. Then another. From Turin to Milan, and then on to Bologna and Florence, she said, Mr. Wilkins must have tapped away at her shoulder dozens of times. First she had to twist her neck towards him as he put his face round the side of the seat; then she had to turn her back and twist forward, craning to see what he was talking about; after that she had to twist back towards him to make a comment. She would see a head of dry hair, and the head would be zigzagging, nose down, towards her, behind a ragged moustache. Her replies were usually corrections, for, in an educated way, Mr. Wilkins was often mildly wrong in his information. In moments of rest, she would hear him making a sishing noise behind her. He made this sound, she discovered later, by rubbing his hands up and down the thighs of his trousers, like a boy who is just about to be caned. After Florence, her neck was stiff and her right shoulder was hunched inward at an uncomfortable angle from her efforts to avoid Mr. Wilkins's tap. In her hotel, when she undressed, she looked on her delicate skin for the mark.

I understood Wilkins at once. His distortion of the letter "i" was not due to affectation. It sounded like a family piety, a deference to a dear dead cultured sister; or it may have been due to catarrh, for he spoke like a person holding an inhaler to one nostril in order to keep on terms with a distant cold. A woman can conceal her life, but Wilkins could not hide his out-of-date appearance, his overfriendly guiltiness. In his one-sided way, he had an air, but pinned to his back there seemed to hang a notice that Effie must have read at once: "Frantically desires some woman to pull him together."

From shoulder-tapping, Effie said, Wilkins moved to a feeble squeezing of the upper arm. Effie likes a strong hand. In Milan, the party they were travelling with went to the opera, and Wilkins slept through the first act, making a personal sound, with his free nostril, that was just above the note of the violins.

"Ai feah," Wilkins apologized to Effie, "Ai overdid the wain at luncheon."

They went to the cathedral in Milan. "Ai adore baroque," said Wilkins.

"Gothic," Effie said sharply.

"Mai word, Miss Alldraxen," Wilkins said with appetite, "Ai love it when you are severe. You're taking me in hand."

Before Leonardo da Vinci in Bologna it was: "Now you're going to put me through it." And in Rome, to the party at large as they sat at luncheon, Wilkins announced: "Bai Jove, Miss Alldraxen gave me some punishment in the Vatican this morning. It is what Ai need."

The actual proposal of marriage was made, Effie said, in the Colosseum at night. The floodlighting there penetrates the upper arches and turns the high brick colander into a place of strong-smelling shadows. There is a hoarse whispering of voices from invisible tourists. Across the brown darkness came the nasal syllables of guides.

"Torn—er—to pieces—er—by wild—er—animalls," a guide was saying as Wilkins took Effie's hand.

Effie said: "Don't be stupid," and got back, in a temper, to the motor coach, which was hooting for them. She has told me that the moment Wilkins declared himself, a sharp pain went into her shoulder and stayed there like a nail. It was, so to say, his last tap, and he had driven it home. She was annoyed as she took her seat in the coach, and then the annoyance went. I can see her looking with pride at the women of the party, who were already gossiping about Mr. Wilkins and herself. "My rheumatism," her expression would signal to them. "I knew it would come."

I have seen Effie in love a great many times. I do not mean that she was now in love, but she was—as she likes to be—adjacent to love. When this happens, her nature changes; she even changes shape. Her bosom rises, her back straightens, she puffs out softly. Her voice becomes sad and wise, and has a peculiar soft hoot, a flute-like sound. Glumly, her head is raised. She feels she has the weight of the air before a thunderstorm upon her, the oppression that makes people complain of their heads, retire to a darkened room, and sicken. For to Effie love is illness. The sacred illness. Attentive doctors and pained nurses gather about an imaginary bed, which is not the bed of ecstasy but the bed of some satisfying ailment.

I will skip the passions of her childhood, but there was Mr. Lucas at the art school when she was eighteen. Mr. Lucas's wife would not divorce him; Effie became ill with a strained heart. Then there was a man called Bobby, who said: "It was only a passade." Effie with a year's neuralgia. Sinclair, wife and three: bronchitis. Allardyce, Roman Catholic, judicial separation: migraines. Macdonald, wife in India: imaginary pregnancy. I could go on. If there was an unmarriageable man in love with someone else, Effie's hospital instinct would find him at once. If an unmarried man fell in love with her, as Wilkins did, she bit his head off.

Effie knows all this very well. I had it out with her six or seven years ago—once and for all, as I thought—after she had sat for three days with a packed suitcase containing towels, sheets, and dishcloths on the stairs outside the studio of a painter called Gotloff, whom she planned to move in on, but who had gone off in time to Paris. I found her in hospital recovering from what she pretended was an attempt at suicide. I shall not forget the long, promiscuous smile on her face and the bark of satisfied laughter she gave as I went to her bedside. "It is really marriage I am in love with, not men," she said then.

So Effie was well equipped for the Wilkins affair. At luncheon on the day after Wilkins had proposed, she was telling the party about "my

old pain"—the pain in her shoulder. The women were soon offering
her remedies. After each suggestion, the pain would change its nature.
It shot from shoulder to head, from head to stomach, from stomach
to knees. Was it the food? Was it the wine? Was it the water? Was
it the Tiber, or Roman fever, or the drains? The women gave orders
to Wilkins, who went out to the pharmacy and came back with a
collection of medicines—poultices, headache pills, throat pastilles, in-
digestion tablets, liver pills, drugs, purges, and tonics. Also a kilo of
cotton wool—his own idea. The party went to the catacombs in the
afternoon, and Effie and Wilkins stayed behind at the hotel. "No
thermometer!" she said. Out Wilkins went again. When he got back,
Effie said, she was alone in the lounge.

"I am dying of thirst," she said. "Is there any mineral water?"

Hearing a precise request, Wilkins was impelled to go it one better.
He sent for a brandy. When it was brought, he sat beside Effie, with
his hands on his long thighs, regarding her with enthusiasm; illness in
women was a form of surrender. In actual fact, of course, *he* was
surrendering. In her bounteous complaints, Effie was giving him something to surrender to. He saw—I have no doubt—a house, a lifetime
marked by journeys up and downstairs to the body of the holy object,
with trays and bottles. He may even have imagined the spit of temper
and reprimand.

The brandy improved Effie; its subtle medicinal evocation of the
beauty of past illnesses must have warmed her. She looked at Mr.
Wilkins, who was waiting for more punishment.

"I suddenly saw," she said to me, "that he really meant it. I mean,
he really did want to marry me." He was, to all appearances, what she
had been looking for all her life since the age of three—a husband.
They sat in the lounge on a deep, hot sofa. Holding her glass, leaning
her head back and looking at the ceiling, she talked. Out of imitative
sympathy, aroused by his love, Wilkins leaned back and looked at the
ceiling also. They exchanged untrue versions of their own early lives.
Mr. Wilkins stopped looking at the ceiling and gazed at Effie with
headlong admiration.

"Bai Jove!" he exclaimed. "Ai have never had a past."

It was not a boast; it was not a confession. It was said in the dashing
and reckless manner of one who, as far as pasts were concerned, was
agog to spend the future living in hers. I am pretty certain that until
this sentence of his Effie had no interest at all in Mr. Wilkins; the
unlucky man had been damned in her eyes by his marriageable condi-

tion. But now he had revealed a difficulty; he was too utterly marriageable, and difficulty was indispensable to her.

I listened to Effie as she sat up in bed telling her story in her evasive,
upside-down way. Her wet handkerchief was screwed up in one hand.
She was laughing one minute and dabbing her eyes the next while the
nun kept coming into the room at the wrong moment and the Italian
cars changed gears on the hill outside. She told me that Mr. Wilkins's
words had made her compare their two cases. She must have paused
to consider whether to re-edit her life story and to appear no longer in
the role of the victim of other people's marriages but as an innocent
waiting, neatly and circumspectly, for "love to come" at last. Effie was
as good as any woman at altering the play she was acting in. I don't
know—she didn't tell me this—but I don't mind betting that Effie
replied, "I haven't had a real past, either."

But I wasn't there to speculate, so I asked her: "Yes, but what did
you say to him? Did you tell him you would marry him?"

"Oh, no!" She squealed with the pleasure of maddening me. "You
are funny. I told him I would have to think."

Everyone who has heard Effie say the word "think" agrees it has a
musical sound that takes all suggestion of the process called "thought"
out of it. To see her "thinking" is delightful. She looks as though she
is listening to a voice singing on a distant mountain. But she is practical.
Oh, always practical. She went off into the streets of Rome with her
sketchbook, looking for something—some person, some place on which
to drape her thoughts. She found the *palazzo* and its courtyard. Why
did she choose the courtyard?

"It was so quiet, so expectant," she said to me.

Yes, I thought, and it had an obvious difficulty and flaw—The
Exemplary Citizen. There was something terribly wrong about *Cittadino Esemplare*, 1884. He was an aesthetic mistake—the wrong
period, on the wrong scale. Wherever one stood, that gloomy, dictato-
rial male rose like an implacable obstacle.

She sat down to draw. "I had a really big think," she said. "About
Mr. Wilkins, about me—about everything." As her pencil worked, her
mind undoubtedly set off on a number of short trips into Wilkins's
future life. She was in Warwickshire, the headmaster's wife; she was
wearing a new sage-green tweed, with a yellow scarf, unmistakably
smarter than the wives of the masters. She saw her shoes—red, I
expect, to make people talk. At the school, she introduced progressive
ideas—mixed-coloured sweaters for the boys, perhaps a French after-

noon in her drawing-room, more Creative Art. There was a master—
young, satanic, modern languages, shadows under his eyes, unhappy
with a wife not quite his class. He avoided Effie at first. She said: "Why
do you avoid me?" Frankly, he looked as though he would kill her, and
then suddenly "it all came out." They watched football matches while
he told her, under his breath, things that (she told him) he ought not
to say. Difficult. She looked at his dark palm; the lines of two major
love affairs were deeply cut under the little finger.

She shifted her thoughts to the matrons. One of them had to go—
one whose nose was out of joint. The woman had obviously been in love
with Mr. Wilkins for years, and besides, where did the sherry go? There
was also a sad one who made a hysterical scene about the school
secretary and "poured out her heart" into Effie's lap. Effie was also
getting to know the Christian names of the boys, tiptoeing in to give
a pat to a pillow of a new boy who was crying. One who stole she saved,
by timely psychiatry, from kleptomania.

It was twelve o'clock in the *palazzo* courtyard, Effie told me. She
had heard the midday siren of some factory. The morning had passed
quickly, and art is exhausting. She had been sitting on a stone step, and
she was stiff. She got up and looked at the enormous statue from a new
angle and then at her drawing. It was wrong. It was awful. Apart from
anything else, the feet were wrong. She had not made them stand
squarely on the plinth; the figure was half in the air. I have no doubt
she was giddy with hunger, but she felt, she said, that she was going
to cave in with a sense of incompetence and failure. She walked to the
plinth and looked at the Citizen's feet, and saw the sculptor had easily
succeeded where she had failed.

"Damn! I can't even draw now! I shall have to marry him!" she said
aloud, in an irritable and snapping voice.

She must have spoken louder than she knew, for she was startled to
hear the walls of the courtyard echo her words. Among those statues,
she had the impression of being overheard. She was even more startled
to feel one of those well-known taps on her shoulder. She was horrified.
Mr. Wilkins! He had followed her! He had heard!

"I was so ashamed I couldn't move," Effie said. "I mean I really
couldn't move. I was fixed to the spot. He was holding me. He was
hurting. I could hardly turn my head, and when I did, I saw—"

Effie began to cry again. I think *I* had better describe what she says
she saw. The hand on her shoulder was not the familiar hand of the
schoolmaster. It was not a pink and playful human hand. It was far too

large. The fingers were of metal, glossy and greenish-black; the back of
the hand was black, polished, and had bold, sculptured veins. It was the
hand of the Citizen. And at once, leaning half his weight on her, he
got clumsily down from his plinth, with a clang loud enough to bring
all that part of Rome to its windows. Moving his hand to her neck, he
gave her a shove forward and, without pause, marched her stumbling
out of the courtyard and onto the pavement, naked and twice life-size
as he was, clang, clang, clang, through half a mile of street, he made
for the hotel. It was lunchtime. The crowds on the pavement and street
corners were thick, the sunlight was blinding and sickening, but the
exemplary male barged on. Effie had to step out into the street to save
herself from being trodden on by him. She collided with people. And
they, the whole lunchtime crowd, treated the thing in the traditional
manner of the Italian nation: they stared at the woman, not at the man.
At last the Citizen got her to the Corso and made to cross over to the
Galleria, where—and how she dreaded it!—Mr. Wilkins was to be
waiting. The traffic was heavy and fast, but the Citizen, that ungovern-
able married man, marched deafeningly across, now pushing his way
ahead. He hauled her into the middle of the street, right in front of
a car, and trod clean through a bicycle—a father not to be obstructed.

"But Mr. Wilkins—didn't he help? Didn't he see? What did he
do?" I asked.

Mr. Wilkins did not have a chance. Nor did the police, the crowd,
or the ambulance men. The statue even got into the ambulance when
she was picked up.

"No one could stop him," Effie sobbed. "He came to the hospital.
He came to this room. He was here all the time. He wouldn't let Mr.
Wilkins in."

Effie stopped crying and lowered her eyes demurely. "He told me—
Mr. Wilkins," she said, "that I'd overdone the wine."

She raised her eyes again. Even Effie must have seen that she had
gone too far. She quickly put out her hand and took mine.

"I'm sorry, Daddy dear," she said. "He's gone. It's over. You came,
and he went."

The Key to
My Heart

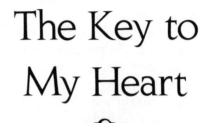

When Father dropped dead and Mother and I were left to run the business on our own, I was twenty-four years old. It was the principal bakery in our town, a good little business, and Father had built it up from nothing. Father used to wink at me when Mother talked about their "first wedding." "How many times have you been married? Who was it that time?" he used to say to her. She was speaking of the time they first ventured out of the bakery into caterings for weddings and local dances. For a long time, when I was a child, we lived over the shop; then Mother made Father take a house down the street. Later still, we opened a café next door but two to the shop, and our idea was to buy up the two little places in between. But something went wrong in the last years of Father's life. Working at night in the heat and getting up at the wrong time of day disorganized him. And then the weddings were his downfall. There is always champagne left over at weddings, and Father got to like it and live on it. And then brandy followed. When Mr. Pickering, the solicitor, went into the will and the accounts, there was muddle everywhere, and bills we had never heard of came in.

"Father kept it all in his head," Mother said, very proud of him for that. Mr. Pickering and I had to sort it all out, and one of the things we discovered was that what we owed was nothing to what people owed us. Mother used to serve in the shop and do the books. She did it, we used to say, for the sake of the gossip—to daydream about why the schoolmistress ordered crumpets only on Thursdays, or guessing, if someone ordered more of this kind of cake or that, who was going to eat it with them. She was generally right, and she knew more about what was going on in the town than anyone else. As long as the daily and weekly customers paid their books, she didn't bother; she hated sending bills, and she was more pleased than upset when Mr. Pickering told her there was a good six hundred pounds owing by people who either hadn't been asked to pay or who were simply not troubling themselves. In a small business, this was a lot of money. It was the rich and the big pots in the country who were the worst of these debtors. Dad and Mother never minded being owed by the rich. They had both grown up in the days when you were afraid of offending people, and to hear my mother talk, you would have thought that by asking the well-off to fork out you were going to kill the goose that lays the golden egg, knock the bottom out of society, and let a Labour government in.

"Think of what they have to pay in taxes," she would say, pitying them. "And the death duties!" And when I did what Mr. Pickering said, and sent out accounts to these people, saying politely that it had no doubt been overlooked, Mother looked mournful and said getting a commission in the Army had turned my head. The money came in, of course. When Colonel Williams paid up and didn't dispute it, Mother looked at his cheque as if it were an insult from the old gentleman and in fact "lost" it in her apron pocket for a week. Lady Littlebank complained, but she paid all the same. A few did not answer, but when I called at their houses they paid at once. But the look on Mother's face was as much as to say I was a son ruining her lifework and destroying her chances of holding her head up in society. At the end of two or three months, there was only one large account outstanding—a Mrs. Brackett's. Mrs. Brackett did not answer, and you can guess Mother made the most of this. Mother spoke highly of Mrs. Brackett, said she was "such a lady, came of a wonderful family," and once even praised her clothes. She was the richest woman in the county, and young. She became my mother's ideal.

Mrs. Brackett was married to a pilot and racing motorist known in the town as Noisy Brackett; it was she, as my mother said, nodding her head up and down, who "had the money." Noisy was given a couple of cars and his pocket money, but having done that, Mrs. Brackett paid as little as she could, as slowly as she could, to everyone else. When I talked about her account to other shopkeepers in the town, they put on their glasses, had a look at their books, sniffed, and said nothing. Every shopkeeper, my father used to say, woke up in the early hours of the morning thinking of how much she owed him, and dreaming of her fortune. You can work out how long her bill with us had run on when I say it was nearly two hundred and thirty pounds. The exact sum was two hundred and twenty-eight pounds, fourteen and fourpence. I shall always remember it.

The first time I made out Mrs. Brackett's bill, I gave it to Noisy. He often came into the café to flirt with the girls, or to our shop to see Mother and get her to cash cheques for him. He was a thin little man, straight as a stick and looked as brittle, and covered (they said) with scars and wounds from his crashes. He had the curly, shining black hair of a sick gipsy, and the lines of a charmer all over his face. His smiles quickly ended in a sudden, stern twitching of his left cheek and eye, like the crack of a whip, which delighted the women. He was a dandy, and from Mother he had the highest praise she could give to any man. He was, she said, "snobby."

When I gave Noisy our bill, he handed it back to me at once. "Be a sweetie-pie," he said, "and keep it under your hat until the day after tomorrow. Tomorrow's my payday, and I don't want the Fairy Queen to get her mind taken off it—d'you follow? Good! Fine! Splendid fellow! Bang on!" And with a twitch he was back in his long white Bentley. "Bring it yourself," he said, looking me up and down. I am a very tall man, and little Noisy had a long way to look. "It'll do the trick."

Noisy did not hide his dependence on his wife. Everyone except the local gentry liked him.

So on the Thursday, when the shop was closed and I could leave the café to the waitresses—a good pair of girls, and Rosie, the dark one, very pretty—I took the station wagon and drove up to Heading Mount, four miles out of the town. It was June; they were getting the hay in. The land in the valley fetches its price; you wouldn't believe it if I told you what a farm fetches there. Higher up, the land is poor, where the oak woods begin, and all that stretch used to belong to old Mr. Lucas, Mrs. Brackett's father, who had made a fortune out of machine tools. The estate was broken up when he died. I came out of the oak woods and turned into the drive, which winds between low stone walls and tall rhododendron bushes, so that it is like a damp, dark, sunken lane, and very narrow. Couples often walked up on Sundays in June to see the show of rhododendrons on the slopes at Heading; the bushes were in flower as I drove by. I was speeding to the sharp turn at the end of the drive, before you come to the house, when I had to brake suddenly. Mrs. Brackett's grey Bentley was drawn broadside across it, blocking the drive completely. I ought to have seen this was a bad omen.

To leave a car like that, anywhere, was typical of Mrs. Brackett. If there was a traffic jam in the town, or if someone couldn't get into the market, nine times out of ten Mrs. Brackett's car was the cause. She just stepped out of it wherever it was, as if she were dropping her coat off for someone else to pick up. The police did nothing. As she got back in, she would smile at them, raise one eyebrow, wag her hips, and let them see as much of her legs as she thought fit for the hour of the day, and drive off with a small wave of her hand that made them swell with apologies and blow up at someone else. Sometimes she went green with a temper that was terrifying coming from so small a person.

Now, in her driveway, I left my wagon and walked round her car towards the house. It was an old L-shaped house, sheltered by sycamores and built in the grey flaking stone of our part of the country. They say her father paid only twelve thousand pounds for it, and that included two or three cottages and farm buildings. The kitchens and servants' rooms and garages were at one side of the L—modern buildings, screened by laurels. Not that there were often any servants there. There was a small circle of lawn in the front of the house, with a statue in the middle of it.

As I walked across the lawn, I realized I had missed the back lane to the house, and that I ought to have driven along a wire-fenced road across the fields to the farm and the kitchen, where the housekeeper lived. But I had not been up there for several years and had forgotten it. As I walked towards the white front door, I kicked a woman's shoe —a shoe for a very small foot. I picked it up. I was a few yards from the door when Mrs. Brackett marched out, stopped on the steps, and then, as sharp as a sergeant, shouted: "Jimmy!" She was looking up at the sky, as though she expected to bring her husband down out of it.

She was barefooted, wearing a blue-and-white-checked shirt and dusty jeans, and her short, fair hair untidy, and she was making an ugly mouth, like a boy's, on her pretty face. I was holding out the shoe as I went forward. There was no answer to her shout. Then she saw me and stared at the shoe.

"Who are you? What are you doing with that?" she asked. "Put it down."

But before I could answer, from the other side of the buildings there was the sound of a car starting and driving off on the back road. Mrs. Brackett heard this. She turned and marched into the house again, but in a few seconds she returned, running past me across the lawn. She jumped into her car, backed up—and then she saw mine blocking the drive. She sounded her horn, again and again. A dog barked, and she jumped out and bawled at me. "You bloody fool!" she shouted. "Get that van of yours out of the way!"

The language that came out of her small mouth was like what you hear in the cattle market on Fridays. I slowly went up and got into my van. I could hear her swearing and the other car tearing off; already it must have turned into the main road. I got into mine, and there we sat, face to face, scowling at each other through our windscreens. I reversed down the long, winding drive, very fast, keeping one eye on her all the time, and turned sharply off the road at the entrance. I don't mind saying that I was showing off. I can reverse a car at speed and put it anywhere to within an inch of where I want to. I saw her face change as she came on, for in her temper she was coming fast down the drive straight at me, radiator to radiator. At the end, she gave one glance of surprise at me, and I think held back a word she had ready as she drove past. At any rate, her mouth was open. Half a dozen cows started from under the trees and went trotting round the field in panic as she went, and the rooks came out of the elms like bits of black paper.

By bad luck, you see, I had arrived in the middle of one of the regular Brackett rows. They were famous in the neighbourhood. The Bracketts chased each other round the house, things came out of windows— clothes, boots, anything. Our roundsman said he had once seen a portable radio, playing full on, come flying out, and that it had fallen, still playing, in the roses. Servants came down to the town and said they had had enough of it. Money was usually at the bottom of the trouble. There was a tale going round that when a village girl who worked there got married, Mrs. Brackett gave her a three-shilling alarm clock for a wedding present.

The rows always went the same way. A car would race out of the drive with Noisy in it, and five minutes later Mrs. Brackett would be in her car chasing him, and no one was safe on the roads for twenty miles round. Sometimes it might end quietly in a country pub, with Mrs. Brackett in one bar and Noisy in the other, white-faced and playing hymns on the piano to mock her until she gave in. Other times it might go on through the night. Noisy, who raced cars, was the better driver, but she was wilder. She would do anything; she once cut through the footpath of the cemetery to catch him on the other side. She sometimes caught him, but more than once her meanness about money would leave her standing. There would be a telephone call to Briggs's garage: Mrs. Brackett had run out of petrol. She was too mean ever to have much more than a gallon in the tank.

"Bless her," Noisy used to say if anyone mentioned these chases to him. "I always rely on the Fairy Queen to run out of gas."

Noisy was a woman hater. His trouble was his habit of saying "Bless you" to the whole female sex.

"Well, I hope you're satisfied," my mother said when I got home. I put Mrs. Brackett's shoe on the table.

"I've made some progress," I said.

My mother looked at the shoe for a long time. Now that I had got something out of Mrs. Brackett, Mother began to think a little less of her. "You'd think a woman with feet like that would dress better," she said.

But what annoyed me was that at some stage in the afternoon's chase Noisy had slipped in and got Mother to cash him a cheque for twenty pounds.

June is the busy time of the year for us. There are all the June weddings. Noisy and Mrs. Brackett must have settled down again somehow, because I saw them driving through the town once or twice. I said to myself: "You wait till the rush is over."

In July, I went up to the Bracketts' house a second time. Rosie, the dark girl who works in our café, came with me, because she wanted to meet her aunt at the main-line station, three or four miles over the hill beyond Heading Mount, and I was taking her on there after I had spoken to Mrs. Brackett. I drove up to the house. The rhododendrons had died, and there were pods on them already going brown. The sun struck warm in front of the house. It was wonderfully quiet.

I left the girl in the car, reading a book, and was working out a sentence to say, when I saw Mrs. Brackett kneeling by a goldfish pond, at the far side of the great lawn. She turned and saw me. I did not know whether to go over the lawn to her or to wait where I was. I decided to go over, and she got up and walked to me. Mother was right about her clothes. This time she was wearing a gaudy tomato-coloured cotton dress that looked like someone else's, and nothing on underneath it. I do not know why it was—whether it was because I was standing on the grass she was walking over, whether it was my anxiety about how to begin the conversation, or whether it was because of her bare white arms, the dawdling manner of her walk, and the inquisitiveness of her eyes—but I thought I was going to faint. When she was two yards away, my heart jumped, my throat closed, and my head was swimming. Although I had often seen her driving through the town, and though I remembered our last meeting all too well, I had never really looked at her before. She stopped, but I had the feeling that she had not stopped but was invisibly walking on until she walked clean through me. My arms went weak. She was amused by the effect she had on me.

"I know who you are," she said. "You are Mr. Fraser's son. Do you want to speak to me?"

I did, but I couldn't. I forgot all the sentences I had prepared. "I've come about our cheque," I said at last. I shouted it. Mrs. Brackett was as startled by my shout as I was. She blushed at the loudness and shock of it—not a light blush but a dark-red flooding blush on her face and her neck that confused her and made her lower her head like a child caught stealing. She put her hands behind her back like a child. I blushed, too. She walked up and down a yard or two, her head still down, thinking. Then she walked away to the house.

"You'd better come inside," she called back in an off-hand way.

You could have put our house into the hall and sitting-room of Heading Mount. I had been in that room when I was a boy, helping the waitress when my father was there doing the catering for a party. I do not know what you'd have to pay for the furniture there—thousands, I suppose. She led me through the room to a smaller room beyond it, where there was a desk. I felt I was slowly walking miles. I have never seen such a mess of papers and letters. They were even spread on the carpet. She sat down at the desk.

"Can you see the bill?" she muttered, not looking at me and pointing to the floor.

"I've got it here," I said, taking the bill out of my pocket. She jerked her head. The flush had gone, and now she looked as keen as needles at me.

"Well, sit down," she said.

She took the bill from me and looked at it. Now I could see that her skin was not white but was really pale and clay-coloured, with scores of little cracks in it, and that she was certainly nearer forty than thirty, as Mother always said.

"I've paid this," she said, giving the bill a mannish slap. "I pay every quarter."

"It has been running for three and a half years," I said, more at ease now.

"What?" she said. "Oh, well, I paid something, anyway. This isn't a bill. It's a statement."

"Yes," I said. "We have sent you the bills."

"Where's the date? This hasn't got any date on it."

I got up and pointed to the date.

"It ought to be at the top," she said.

My giddiness had gone. Noisy came into the room. "Hullo, Bob," he said. "I've just been talking to that beautiful thing you have got in the car." He always spoke in an alert, exhausted way about women, like someone at a shoot waiting for the birds to come over. "Have you seen Bob's girl, darling?" he said to her. "I've just offered her the key to my heart." And he lifted the silk scarf he was wearing in the neck of his canary-coloured pullover, and there was a piece of string round his neck with a heavy old door key hanging from it. Noisy gave a twitch to one side of his face.

"Oh, God, that old gag," said Mrs. Brackett.

"Not appreciated, old boy," said Noisy to me.

"Irresistible," said Mrs. Brackett, with an ugly mouth. She turned and spoke to me again, but glanced shrewdly at Noisy as she did so. "Let me try this one on you," she said. "You've already got my husband's cheque for this bill. I send him down to pay you, and he just cashes them?"

"I'm afraid not, Mrs. Brackett," I said. "That wouldn't be possible."

"You can't get away with that one, my pet," said Noisy. "Are you ready to go out?" He looked at her dress, admiring her figure. "What a target, Bob," he said.

"I don't think we will ask Mr. Fraser's opinion," she said coldly, but very pleased. And she got up and started out of the room, with Noisy behind her.

"You had better send me the bills," she called back to me, turning round from the door.

I felt very, very tired. I left the house and slammed the car door when I got in. "Now she wants the damn bills," I said to Rosie as I drove her up to Tolton station. I did not speak to her the rest of the way. She irritated me, sitting there.

When I got home and told my mother, she was short with me. That was the way to lose customers, she said. I was ruining all the work she and Dad had put into the business. I said if Mrs. Brackett wanted her bills she could come and get them herself. Mother was very shocked.

She let it go for a day or two, but she had to bring it up again. "What are you sulking about?" she said to me one afternoon. "You upset Rosie this morning. Have you done those bills for Mrs. Brackett yet?"

I made excuses, and got in the car and went over to the millers and to the people who make our boxes, to get away from the nagging. Once I was out of the town, in the open country, Mrs. Brackett seemed to be somewhere just ahead of me, round a corner, over a hill, beyond a wood. There she was, trying to make me forget she owed us two hundred and twenty-eight pounds, fourteen and fourpence. The moment she was in my head, the money went out of it. When I got back, late in the evening, Mother was onto me again. Noisy had been in. She said he had been sent down by his wife to ask why I had not brought the bills.

"The poor wing commander," my mother said. "Another rumpus up there." (She always gave him his rank if there was a rumour of another quarrel at Heading.) "She never gives him any peace. He's just an errand boy. She does what she likes with him."

"He's been offering you the key to his heart, Mother," I said.

"I don't take any stock of him," Mother said. "Or that pansy 'sweetheart' stuff. Dad was the one and only for me. I don't believe in second marriages. I've no time for jealous women; they're always up to something, like Mrs. Doubleday thinking I spoke to her husband in the bank and she was caught with the chemist, but you always think the Fairy Prince will turn up—it's natural."

It always took a little time getting at what was in Mother's mind, yet it was really simple. She was a good churchwoman, and she thought Noisy was not really married to Mrs. Brackett, because he had been divorced by his first wife. She did not blame Noisy for this—in fact, she admired it, in a romantic way—but she blamed Mrs. Brackett because, by Mother's theories, Mrs. Brackett was still single. And Mother never knew whether to admire single women for holding out or to suspect them of being on the prowl. One thing she was certain of. "Money talks," she said. The thing that made Noisy respectable for her, and as good as being married in church, was that he had married Mrs. Brackett for her money.

She talked like this the night we sat up and did that month's bills, but the next day—and this was the trouble with Mother—it ended in a row. I sent the bills up to Mrs. Brackett by our delivery van.

"That is not the way to behave," Mother said. "You should have taken them yourself."

And before the day was out, Mother was in a temper again. Mrs. Brackett had spoken to her on the telephone and said she had been through the bills and that we had charged her for things she hadn't had, because she'd been in the South of France at the time.

"I told you to go," Mother said to me.

I was angry, too, at being called dishonest. I got out the van and said I was going up at once.

"Oh, that's how it is," said my mother, changing round again. "Her Ladyship snaps her fingers and you go up at once. She's got you running about for her like Noisy. If I ask you to do anything, you don't pay any attention to me. But Mrs. Brackett—she's the Queen of England. Two of you running after her."

Mother was just like that with Father when he was alive. He took no notice. Neither did I. I went up to Heading. A maid let me in, and I sat there waiting in the drawing-room. I waited a long time, listening to the bees coming down the chimney, circling lower and lower and then roaring out into the room, like Noisy's car. I could hear Mrs. Brackett talking on the telephone in her study. I could hear now and then what she was saying. She was a great racing woman, and from words she said here and there I would say she was speaking to a bookmaker. One sentence I remember, because I think it had the name of a horse in it, and when I got back home later I looked up the racing news to see if I could find it. "Tray pays on," she said. She came out into the room with the laughter of her telephone call still on her face. I was standing up, with our account book in my hand, and when she saw me the laughter went.

I was not afraid of her any more. "I hear there is some trouble about the bills," I said. "If you've got them, you can check them with the book. I've brought it."

Mrs. Brackett was a woman who watched people's faces. She put on her dutiful, serious, and obedient look, and led me again to the little room where the papers were. She sat down and I stood over her while we compared the bills and the book. I watched the moving of her back as she breathed. I pointed to the items, one by one, and she nodded and ticked the bills with a pencil. We checked for nearly half an hour.

The only thing she said was in the middle of it—"You've got a double-jointed thumb: so have I"—but she went right on.

"I can see what it is," I said at the end. "You've mistaken 1953 for '54."

She pushed the book away and leaned back in the chair against my arm, which was resting on it.

"No, I haven't," she said, her small, unsmiling face looking up into mine. "I just wanted you to come up."

She gazed at me a long time. I thought of all the work Mother and I had done, and then that Mother was right about Mrs. Brackett. I took my hand from the chair and stepped back.

"I wanted to ask you one or two things," she said confidingly, "about that property next to the shop. I'll be fair with you. I'm interested in it. Are you? All right, don't answer. I see you are."

My heart jumped. Ever since I could remember, Father and Mother had talked of buying this property. It was their daydream. They simply liked little bits of property everywhere, and now I wanted it so that we could join the shop and the café.

"I asked because . . ." She hesitated. "I'll be frank with you. The bank manager was talking about it to me today."

My fright died down. I didn't believe that the bank manager—he was Mr. Pickering's brother-in-law—would let my mother down and allow the property to go to Mrs. Brackett without giving us the offer first.

"We want it, of course," I said. And then I suspected this was one of her tricks. "That is why I have been getting our bills in," I said.

"Oh, I didn't think that was it," she said. "I thought you were getting married. My husband says you are engaged to the girl you brought up here. He said he thought you were. Has she any money?"

"Engaged!" I said. "I'm not. Who told him that?"

"Oh," she said, and then a thought must have struck her. I could read it at once. In our town, if you cough in the High Street the chemist up at the Town Hall has got a bottle of cough mixture wrapped up and waiting for you; news travels fast. She must have guessed that when Noisy came down dangling the key to his heart, he could have been round the corner all the time, seeing Rosie.

"I'm glad to hear you're not engaged," Mrs. Brackett said tenderly. "I like a man who works. You work like your father did—God, what an attractive man! You're like him. I'm not flattering you. I saw it when you came up the first time."

She asked me a lot of questions about the shop and who did the baking now. I told her I didn't do it and that I wanted to enlarge the restaurant. "The machine bakeries are getting more and more out into the country," I said. "And you've got to look out."

"I don't see why you shouldn't do catering for schools," she said. "And there's the works" (her father's main factory). "Why don't you get hold of the catering there?"

"You can only do that if you have capital. We're not big enough," I said, laughing.

"How much do you want?" she said. "Two thousand? Three? I don't see why we couldn't do something."

The moment she said "we," I came to my senses. Here's a funny turnout, I thought. She won't pay her bills, but first she's after these shops, and now she's waving two thousand pounds in my face. Everyone in our town knew she was artful. I suppose she thought I was green.

"Not as much as two thousand," I said. "Just the bill," I said, nodding at it.

Mrs. Brackett smiled. "I like you. You're interested in money. Good. I'll settle it." And taking her cheque-book from the top of the desk, she put it in her drawer. "I never pay these accounts by cheque. I pay in cash. I'll get it tomorrow at the bank. I'll tell you what I'll do. You've got a shoe of mine. Bring it up tomorrow evening at, say, half past eight. I'll be back by then and you can have it." She paused, and then, getting up, added quickly, "Half tomorrow, half in October."

It was like dealing with the gipsies that come to your door.

"No, Mrs. Brackett," I said. "I'd like all of it. Now." We stared at each other. It was like that moment months ago when she had driven at me in her car and I had reversed down the drive with one eye watching her and one on the road as I shot back. That was the time, I think, I first noticed her—when she opened her mouth to shout a word at me and then did not shout. I could have stayed like this, looking into her small, pretty, miser's blue eyes, at her determined head, her chopped-off fair hair, for half an hour. It was a struggle.

She was the first to speak, and that was a point gained to me. Her voice shook a little. "I don't keep that amount of money in the house," she said.

I knew that argument. Noisy said she always had two or three hundred pounds in the safe in the wall of her study, and whether this was so or not, I could not help glancing towards it.

"I don't like being dictated to," she said, catching my glance. "I have told you what I will do."

"I think you could manage it, Mrs. Brackett," I said.

I could see she was on the point of flying into one of her tempers, and as far as I was concerned (I don't know why), I hoped she would. Her rows with Noisy were so famous that I must have wanted to see one for myself. And I didn't see why she should get away with it. At the back of my mind, I thought of all the others down in the town and how they would look when I said I had got my money out of Mrs. Brackett.

Yet I wasn't really thinking about the money at all, at this moment. I was looking at her pretty shoulders.

But Mrs. Brackett did not fly into a temper. She considered me, and then she spoke in a quiet voice that took me off my guard. "Actually," she said, lowering her eyes, "you haven't been coming up here after money at all, have you?"

"Well—" I began.

"Sh-h-h!" she said, jumping up from her chair and putting her hand on my mouth. "Why didn't you ring me and tell me you were coming? I am often alone."

She stepped to the door and bawled out: "Jimmy!" as if he were a long way off. He was—to my surprise, and even more to hers—very near.

"Yes, ducky?" Noisy called back from the hall.

"Damn," she said to me. "You must go." And squeezing my hand, she went through the drawing-room into the hall.

"What time do we get back tomorrow evening?" she said boldly to Noisy. "Half past eight? Come at half past eight," she said, turning to me, for I had followed her. "I'll bring back the cash."

The sight of Noisy was a relief to me, and the sound of the word "cash" made Noisy brighten.

"Not lovely little bits of money!" he exclaimed.

"Not you," said Mrs. Brackett, glaring at him.

"How did you work it, old boy?" said Noisy later, giving me one of his most quizzical twitches as he walked with me to my van. When I drove off, I could see him still standing there, watching me out of sight.

I drove away very slowly. My mind was in confusion. About half a mile off, I stopped the car and lit a cigarette. All the tales I had heard about Mrs. Brackett came back into my mind. It was one thing to look at her, another thing to know about her. The one person I wished I had with me was Noisy. He seemed like a guarantor of safety, a protection. To have had my thoughts read like that by her filled me with fear.

I finished my cigarette. I decided not to go straight home, and I drove slowly all along the lower sides of the oak woods, so slowly and carelessly that I had to swerve to avoid oncoming cars. I was making, almost without knowing it, for The Green Man, at Mill Cross. There was a girl there I had spoken to once or twice. No one you would know. I went in and asked for a glass of beer. I hardly said a word to her, except about the weather, and then she left the bar to look after a baby in the kitchen at the back. That calmed me. I think the way she gave me my change brought me back to earth and made me feel free of Mrs. Brackett's spell. At any rate, I put the threepence in my pocket and swallowed my beer. I laughed at myself. Mrs. Brackett had gypped me again.

When I got home, it was late, and my mother was morose. She was wearing a black dress she often wore when she was alone, dressed up and ready to go out, yet not intending to, as if now that my father was dead she was free if someone would invite her. Her best handbag was beside her. She was often waiting like this, sitting on the sofa, doing nothing but listening to the clock tick, and perhaps getting up to give a touch to some flowers on the table and then sitting down again. Her first words shook me.

"Mrs. Brackett was down here looking for you," she said sharply. "I thought you were with her. She wants you to be sure to go up tomorrow evening to collect some money when she comes back from Tolton. Where have you been?"

"Let the old bitch post it or bring it in," I said.

Mother was horrified at the idea of Mrs. Brackett soiling her hands with money.

"You'll do as I tell you," she said. "You'll go up and get it. If you don't, Noisy will get his hands on it first. You'd think a woman with all that money would go to a decent hairdresser. It's meanness, I suppose."

And then, of course, I saw I was making a lot of fuss about nothing. Noisy would be there when I went up to Heading. Good old Noisy, I thought; thank God for that. And he'll see I get the money, because she said it in front of him.

So the next evening I went. I put my car near the garage, and the first person I saw was Noisy, standing beside his own car. He had a suitcase in his hand. I went over to him.

"Fairy Queen's been at work," he said. He nodded at his tyres. They were flat. "I'm doing some quick thinking."

At that moment, a top window of the house was opened and someone emptied a suitcase of clothes out of it, and then a shower of
cigarettes came down.

"She's tidying," he said. "I've got a quarter of an hour to catch the
London train. Be a sweetie-pie and run me over there."

I had arrived once more in the middle of one of the Brackett rows.
Only this time Noisy was leaving it to me. That is how I felt about it.
"Hop in," I said.

And when we were off and a mile from Heading, he sat up in the
seat and looked round. "Nothing on our tail," he said.

"Have you ever heard of a horse called Tray?" I asked him. "Tray
pays something? Tray pays on—that can't be it."

"Tray pays on?" repeated Noisy. "Is it a French horse?"

"I don't know," I said.

"Bloody peasant? Could be," said Noisy. "Sounds a bit frog to me."

We got to Tolton station. Noisy was looking very white and set with
hatred. Not until he was standing in the queue getting his ticket did
it occur to me what Noisy was doing.

"The first time I've travelled by train for fifteen years," he called to
me across from the queue. "Damned serious. You can tell her if you
see her"—people stared—"the worm has turned. I'm packing it in for
good."

And as he went off to the train, he called, "I suppose you are going
back? No business of mine, but I'll give you a tip. If you do, you won't
find anything in the kitty, Bob." He gave me his stare and his final
twitch. It was like the crack of a shot. Bang on, as he would have said.
A bull's-eye.

I walked slowly away as the London train puffed out. I took his
advice. I did not go back to Heading.

There were rows and rows between the Bracketts, but there was none
like this one. It was the last. The others were a chase. This was not.
For only Mrs. Brackett was on the road that night. She was seen, we
were told, in all the likely places. She had been a dozen times through
the town. Soon after ten o'clock she was hooting outside our house.
Mother peeped through the curtains, and I went out. Mrs. Brackett got
out of her car and marched at me. "Where have you been?" she
shouted. "Where is my husband?"

"I don't know," I said.

"Yes, you do," she said. "You took him to Tolton, they told me."

"I think he's gone to London," I said.

"Don't be a damn liar," she said. "How can he have? His car is up there."

"By train," I said.

"By train," she repeated. Her anger vanished. She looked at me with astonishment. The rich are very peculiar. Mrs. Brackett had forgotten people travel by train. I could see she was considering the startling fact. She was not a woman to waste time staying in one state of mind for long. Noisy used to say of her: "That little clock never stops ticking."

"I see," she said to me sarcastically, nodding out the words. "That's what you and Jimmy have been plotting." She gave a shake to her hair and held her chin up. "You've got your money and you don't care," she said.

"What money is that?" I said.

"What money!" she exclaimed sharply, going over each inch of my face. What she saw surprised her at first. Until then she had been fighting back, but now a sly look came to her; it grew into a smile; the smile got wider and wider, and then her eyes became two curved lines, like crow's wings in the sky, and she went into shouts of laughter. It sounded all down the empty street. She rocked with it.

"Oh, no!" she laughed. "Oh, no, that's too good! That's a winner. He didn't give you a penny! He swiped the lot!"

And she looked up at the sky in admiration of that flying man. She was still grinning at me when she taunted breathlessly: "I mean to say —I mean to say—"

I let her run on.

"It was all or nothing with you, wasn't it?" she said. "And you get nothing, don't you?"

I am not sure what I did. I may have started to laugh it off and I may have made a step towards her. Whatever I did, she went hard and prim, and if ever a woman ended anything, she did then. She went over to the car, got in, and slammed the door.

"You backed the wrong horse when you backed Jimmy," she called out to me.

That was the last of her. No more Mrs. Brackett at the shop. "You won't hear another word from her," my mother said.

"What am I supposed to do—get her husband back?" I said.

By the end of the week, everyone in the town was laughing and winking at me.

"You did the trick, boy," the grocer said.

"You're a good-looking fellow, Bob," the ironmonger said.

"Quite a way with the girls," the butcher said. "Bob's deep."

For when Mrs. Brackett went home that night, she sat down and paid every penny she owed to every shopkeeper in the town. Paid everyone, I say. Bar me.

Blind Love

"I'm beginning to be worried about Mr. 'Wolverhampton' Smith," said Mr. Armitage to Mrs. Johnson, who was sitting in his study with her notebook on her knee and glancing from time to time at the window. She was watching the gardener's dog rooting in a flower bed. "Would you read his letter again: the second paragraph about the question of a partnership?"

Since Mr. Armitage was blind it was one of Mrs. Johnson's duties to read his correspondence.

"He had the money—that is certain; but I can't make out on what conditions," he said.

"I'd say he helped himself. He didn't put it into the business at Ealing—he used it to pay off the arrears on the place at Wolverhampton," she said in her cheerful manner.

"I'm afraid you're right. It's his character I'm worried about," said Mr. Armitage.

"There isn't a single full stop in his letter—a full page on both sides. None. And all his words are joined together. It's like one word two pages long," said Mrs. Johnson.

"Is that so?" said Mr. Armitage. "I'm afraid he has an unpunctuated moral sense."

Coming from a blind man whose open eyes and face had the fixed gleam of expression you might have seen on a piece of rock, the word "unpunctuated" had a sarcasm unlike an ordinary sarcasm. It seemed, quite delusively, to come from a clearer knowledge than any available to the sighted.

"I think I'll go and smell out what he's like. Where is Leverton Grove? Isn't it on the way to the station? I'll drop in when I go up to London tomorrow morning," said Mr. Armitage.

The next morning he was driven in his Rolls-Royce to Mr. Smith's house, one of two or three little villas that were part of a building speculation that had come to nothing fifty years before. The yellow-brick place was darkened by the firs that were thick in this district. Mrs. Johnson, who had been brought up in London houses like this, winced at the sight of them. (Afterwards she said to Mr. Armitage, "It brings it back." They were talking about her earlier life.) The chauffeur opened the car door, Mrs. Johnson got out, saying "No kerb," but Armitage waving her aside, stepped out unhelped and stood stiff with the sainted upward gaze of the blind; then, like an Army detail, the party made a sharp right turn, walked two paces, then a sharp left to the wooden gate, which the chauffeur opened, and went forward in step.

"Daffodils," said Mrs. Johnson, noting a flower bed. She was wearing blue to match her bold, practical eyes, and led the way up the short path to the door. It was opened before she rang by an elderly, sick-looking woman with swollen knuckles who half hid behind the door as she held it, to expose Smith standing with his grey jacket open, his hands in his pockets—the whole man an arrangement of soft smiles from his snowball head to his waistcoat, from his fly to his knees, sixteen stone of modest welcome with nothing to hide.

"It is good of you to come," he said. He had a reverent voice.

"On my way to the station," said Armitage.

Smith was not quite so welcoming to Mrs. Johnson. He gave her a dismissive frown and glanced peremptorily at his wife.

"In here?" said Mrs. Johnson, briskly taking Armitage's arm in the narrow hall.

"Yes," he said.

They all stood just inside the doorway of the front room. A fir tree darkened it. It had, Mrs. Johnson recorded at once, two fenders in the fireplace, and two sets of fire-irons; then she saw two of everything—two clocks on the fireplace, two small sofas, a dining table folded up, even two carpets on the floor, for underneath the red one, there was the fringe of a worn yellow one.

Mr. Smith saw that she noted this and, raising a grand chin and now unsmiling, said, "We're sharing the 'ouse, the house, until we get into something bigger."

And at this, Mrs. Smith looked with the searching look of an agony in her eyes, begging Mrs. Johnson for a word.

"Bigger," echoed Mrs. Smith and watched to see the word sink in. And then, putting her fingers over her face, she said, "Much bigger," and laughed.

"Perhaps," said Mr. Smith, who did not care for his wife's laugh, "while we talk—er . . ."

"I'll wait outside in the car," said the decisive Mrs. Johnson, and when she was in the car she saw Mrs. Smith's gaze of appeal from the step.

A half an hour later, the door opened and Mrs. Johnson went to fetch Mr. Armitage.

"At this time of the year the daffodils are wonderful round here," said Armitage as he shook hands with Smith, to show that if he could not see there were a lot of things he knew. Mr. Smith took the point and replaced his smiling voice with one of sportive yet friendly rebuke, putting Mr. Armitage in his place.

"There is only one eye," he stated as if reading aloud. "The eye of God."

Softly the Rolls drove off, with Mrs. Smith looking at it fearfully from the edge of the window curtain.

"Very rum fellow," said Armitage in the car. "I'm afraid he's in a mess. The Inland Revenue are after him as well. He's quite happy because there's nothing to be got out of him. Remarkable. I'm afraid his friends have lost their money."

Mrs. Johnson was indignant.

"What's he going to do down here? He can't open up again."

"He's come here," Armitage said, "because of the chalk in London water. The chalk, he says, gets into the system with the result that the whole of London is riddled with arthritis and nervous diseases. Or rather the whole of London is riddled with arthritis and nervous diseases because it believes in the reality of chalk. Now, chalk has no reality. We are not living on chalk or even on gravel: we dwell in God. Mr. Smith explains that God led him to manage a chemist's shop in Wolverhampton, and to open one of his own in Ealing without capital. He now realizes that he was following his own will, not the will of God. He is now doing God's work. Yesterday he had a cable from California.

He showed it to me. 'Mary's cancer cured gratitude cheque follows.' He's a faith healer."

"He ought to be in jail," said Mrs. Johnson.

"Oh, no. He's in heaven," said Armitage. "I'm glad I went to see him. I didn't know about his religion, but it's perfect: you get witnesses like him in court every day, always moving on to higher things."

The Rolls arrived at the station and Mr. Armitage picked up his white stick.

"Cancer today. Why not blindness tomorrow? Eh?" he said. Armitage gave one low laugh from a wide mouth. And though she enjoyed his dryness, his rare laugh gave a dangerous animal expression to a face that was usually closed. He got out of the car and she watched him walk into the booking hall and saw knots of people divide to make way for him on the platform.

In the damp town at the bottom of the hills, in the shops, at the railway station where twice a week the Rolls waited for him to come back from London, it was agreed that Armitage was a wonder. A gentleman, of course, they said; he's well-off, that helps. And there is that secretary-housekeeper, Mrs. Johnson. That's how he can keep up his legal business. He takes his stick to London, but down here he never uses it. In London he has his lunch in his office or in his club, and can manage the club stairs which worry some of the members when they come out of the bar. He knows what's in the papers—ever had an argument with him?—of course Mrs. Johnson reads them to him.

All true. His house stood, with a sudden flash of Edwardian prosperity, between two larch coppices on a hill five miles out and he could walk out on to the brick terrace and smell the lavender in its season and the grass of the lawns that went steeply down to his rose garden and the blue tiles of his swimming pool boxed in by yew.

"Fabian Tudor. Bernard Shaw used to come here—before our time, of course," he would say, disparaging the high, panelled hall. He was really referring to his wife, who had left him when he was going blind twenty-two years ago. She had chosen and furnished the house. She liked leaded windows, brass, plain velvet curtains, Persian carpets, brick fireplaces and the expensive smell of wood smoke.

"All fake," he would say, "like me."

You could see that pride made him like to embarrass. He seemed to know the effect of jokes from a dead face. But, in fact, if he had no animation—Mrs. Johnson had soon perceived in her commonsensical way—this was because he was not affected, as people are, by the movements on other faces. Our faces, she had learned from Armitage, threw their lives away every minute. He stored his. She knew this because she stored hers. She did not put it like this, in fact what she said appeared to contradict it. She liked a joke.

"It's no good brooding. As Mother used to say, as long as you've got your legs you can give yourself an airing."

Mrs. Johnson had done this. She had fair hair, a good figure, and active legs, but usually turned her head aside when she was talking, as if to an imaginary friend. Mrs. Johnson had needed an airing very badly when she came to work for Mr. Armitage.

At their first interview—he met her in the panelled hall: "You do realize, don't you, that I am totally blind. I have been blind for more than twenty years," he said.

"Yes," she said. "I was told by Dr. James." She had been working for a doctor in London.

He held out his hand and she did not take it at once. It was not her habit to shake hands with people; now, as always, when she gave in she turned her head away. He held her hand for a long time and she knew he was feeling the bones. She had heard that the blind do this, and she took a breath as if to prevent her bones or her skin passing any knowledge of herself to him. But she could feel her dry hand coming to life and she drew it away. She was surprised that, at the touch, her nervousness had gone.

To her, Armitage's house was a wonderful place. The space, the light made friendly by the small panes of the tall leaded windows, charmed her.

"Not a bit like Peckham," she said cheerfully.

Mr. Armitage took her through the long sitting-room, where there were yellow roses in a bowl, into his study. He had been playing a record and put it off.

"Do you like music?" he said. "That was Mozart."

"I like a bit of a singsong," she said. "I can't honestly say I like the classical stuff."

He took her round the house, stopped to point to a picture or two and, once more down in the long room, took her to a window and said, "This is a bad day for it. The haze hasn't lifted. On a clear day you can see Sevenham Cathedral. It's twelve miles away. Do you like the country?"

"Frankly I've never tried it."

"Are you a widow, Mrs. Johnson?"

"No. I changed my name from Thompson to Johnson and not for the better. I divorced my husband," said Mrs. Johnson crisply.

"Will you read something to me—out of the paper?" he said. "A court case."

She read and read.

"Go on," he said. "Pick out something livelier."

"Lonely monkeys at the zoo?"

"That will do."

She read again and she laughed.

"Good," he said.

"As Father used to say, 'Speak up . . .' " she began, but stopped. Mr. Armitage did not want to hear what Father said.

"Will you allow me," Armitage said, getting up from his desk, "would you allow me to touch your face?"

Mrs. Johnson had forgotten that the blind sometimes asked this.

She did not answer at once. She had been piqued from the beginning because he could not see her. She had been to the hairdresser's. She had bought a blouse with a high frilled neck which was meant to set off the look of boyish impudence and frankness of her face. She had forgotten about touch. She feared he would have a pleading look, but she saw that the wish was part of an exercise for him. He clearly expected her to make no difficulty about it.

"All right," she said, but she meant him to notice the pause, "if you want to."

She faced him and did not flinch as his hand lightly touched her brow and cheek and chin. He was, she thought, "after her bones," not her skin, and that, though she stiffened with resistance, was "O.K. by her." But when, for a second, the hand seemed about to rest on her jaw, she turned her head.

"I weigh eight stone," she said in her bright way.

"I would have thought less," he said. That was the nearest he came to a compliment. "It was the first time," she said afterwards to her friend Marge in the town, "that I ever heard of a secretary being bought by weight."

She had been his secretary and housekeeper for a long time now. She had understood him at once. The saintly look was nonsense. He was neither a saint nor a martyr. He was very vain; especially he was vain of never being deceived, though in fact his earlier secretaries had not been a success. There had been three or four before her. One of them

—the cook told her—imagined him to be a martyr because she had a taste for martyrdom and drank to gratify it; another yearned to offer the compassion he hated, and muddled everything. One reckoning widow lasted only a month. Blatantly she had added up his property and wanted to marry him. The last, a "lady," helped herself to the household money, behind a screen of wheezing grandeur and name-dropping.

Remembering the widow, the people who came to visit Mr. Armitage when he gave a party were relieved after their meeting with Mrs. Johnson.

"A good honest-to-God Cockney" or "Such a cheery soul." "Down to earth," they said. She said she had "knocked about a bit." "Yes, sounds as if she had": they supposed they were denigrating. She was obviously not the kind of woman who would have any dangerous appeal to an injured man. And she, for her part, would go to the pictures when she had time off or simply flop down in a chair at the house of her friend Marge and say, "Whew, Marge. His nibs has gone to London. Give me a strong cuppa. Let's relax."

"You're too conscientious."

"Oh, I don't mind the work. I like it. It occupies your mind. He has interesting cases. But sometimes I get keyed up."

Mrs. Johnson could not herself describe what "keyed her up"— perhaps being on the watch? Her mind was stretched. She found herself translating the world to him and it took her time to realize that it did not matter that she was not "educated up to it." He obviously liked her version of the world, but it was a strain having versions. In the mornings she had to read his letters. This bothered her. She was very moral about privacy. She had to invent an impersonal, uninterested voice. His lack of privacy irked her; she liked gossip and news as much as any woman, but here it lacked the salt of the secret, the whispered, the found out. It was all information and statement. Armitage's life was an abstraction for him. He had to know what he could not see. What she liked best was reading legal documents to him.

He dressed very well and it was her duty to see that his clothes were right. For an orderly, practical mind like hers, the order in which he lived was a new pleasure. They lived under fixed laws: no chair or table, even no ashtray must be moved. Everything must be in its place. There must be no hazards. This was understandable: the ease with which he moved without accident in the house or garden depended on it. She did not believe when he said, "I can hear things before I get to them.

A wall can shout, you know." When visitors came she noticed he stood in a fixed spot: he did not turn his head when people spoke to him and among all the head-turning and gesturing he was the still figure, the lawgiver. But he was very cunning. If someone described a film they had seen, he was soon talking as if he had been there. Mrs. Johnson, who had duties when he had visitors, would smile to herself, at the surprise on the faces of people who had not noticed the quickness with which he collected every image or scene or character described. Some-times, a lady would say to her, "I do think he's absolutely marvellous," and, if he overheard this—and his hearing was acute—Mrs. Johnson would notice a look of ugly boredom on his face. He was, she noted, particularly vain of his care of money and accounts. This pleased Mrs. Johnson because she was quick to understand that here a blind man who had servants might be swindled. She was indignant about the delinquency of her predecessor. He must have known he was being swindled.

Once a month Mrs. Johnson would go through the accounts with him. She would make out the cheques and take them to his study and put them on his desk.

The scene that followed always impressed her. She really admired him for this. How efficient and devious he was! He placed the cheque at a known point on his blotter. The blunt fingers of his hairless hands had the art of gliding and never groping, knowing the inches of dis-tance; and then, as accurately as a geometrician, he signed. There might be a pause as the fingers secretly measured, a pause alarming to her in the early days, but now no longer alarming; sometimes she detected a shade of cruelty in this pause. He was listening for a small gasp of anxiety as she watched.

There was one experience which was decisive for her. It occurred in the first month of her employment and had the lasting stamp of a revelation. (Later on, she thought he had staged the incident in order to show her what his life was like and to fix in her mind the nature of his peculiar authority.) She came into the sitting-room one evening in the winter to find a newspaper and heard sharp, unbelievable sounds coming from his study. The door was open and the room was in darkness. She went to it, switched on the light, and saw he was sitting there typing in the darkness. Well, she could have done that if she had been put to it—but now she *saw* that for him there was no difference between darkness and light.

"Overtime, I see," she said, careful not to show surprise.

This was when she saw that his mind was a store of maps and measured things; a store of sounds and touches and smells that became an enormous translated paraphernalia.

"You'd feel sorry for a man like that," her friend Marge said.

"He'd half kill you if you showed you were sorry," Mrs. Johnson said. "I don't feel sorry. I really don't."

"Does he ever talk about his wife?"

"No."

"A terrible thing to do to leave a man because he's blind."

"She had a right to her life, hadn't she?" said Mrs. Johnson flatly. "Who would want to marry a blind man?"

"You are hard," Marge said.

"It's not my business," said Mrs. Johnson. "If you start pitying people you end up by hating them. I've seen it. I've been married, don't forget."

"I just wish you had a more normal life, dear."

"It suits me," said Mrs. Johnson.

"He ought to be very grateful to you."

"Why should he be? I do my job. Gratitude doesn't come into it. Let's go and play tennis."

The two women went out and played tennis in the park and Mrs. Johnson kept her friend running from court to court.

"I smell tennis balls and grass," said Mr. Armitage when she returned.

In the March of her third year a bad thing happened. The winter was late. There was a long spell of hard frost and you could see the cathedral tower clearly over the low-lying woods on most days. The frost coppered the lawns and scarcely faded in the middle of the day. The hedges were spiked and white. She had moved her typing table into the sitting-room close to the window to be near a radiator and when she changed a page she would glance out at the garden. Mr. Armitage was out there somewhere and she had got into the habit of being on the watch. Now she saw him walk down the three lawns and find the brick steps that led to the swimming pool. It was enclosed by a yew hedge and was frozen over. She could see Armitage at the far side of it pulling at a small fallen branch that had been caught by the ice. His foot had struck it. On the other side of the hedge, the gardener was cutting cabbage in the kitchen garden and his dog was snuffling about. Suddenly a rabbit ran out, ears down, and the dog was yelping after it. The rabbit ran through the hedge and almost over Armitage's feet with the dog nearly on it. The gardener shouted. The next moment Armitage, who was squatting, had the dog under his legs, lost his balance, and fell full length through the ice into the pool. Mrs. Johnson saw this. She saw the gardener drop his knife and run to the gap in the hedge to help Armitage out. He was clambering over the side. She saw him wave the gardener's hand away and shout at him and the gardener step away as Armitage got out. He stood clawing weed off his face, out of his hair, wringing his sleeves and brushing ice off his shirt as he marched back fast up the garden. He banged the garden door in a rage as he came in.

"That bloody man. I'll have that dog shot," shouted Armitage. She hurried to meet him. He had pulled off his jacket and thrown it on a chair. Water ran off his trousers and sucked in his shoes. Mrs. Johnson was appalled.

"Go and change your things quickly," she said. And she easily raced him to the stairs to the landing and to his room. By the time he got there she had opened several drawers, looking for underclothes, and had pulled out a suit from his cupboard. Which suit? She pulled out another. He came squelching after her into the room.

"Towel," she cried. "Get it all off. You'll get pneumonia."

"Get out. Leave me alone," shouted Armitage, who had been tugging his shirt over his head as he came upstairs.

She saw then that she had done a terrible thing. By opening drawers and putting clothes on the bed, she had destroyed one of his systems. She saw him grope. She had never seen him do this before. His bare white arms stretched out in a helpless way and his brown hands pitiably closed on air. The action was slow and his fingers frightened her.

"I told you to leave me alone," he shouted.

She saw she had humiliated him. She had broken one of the laws. For the first time she had been incompetent.

Mrs. Johnson went out and quietly shut the door. She walked across the landing to the passage in the wing where her own room was, looking at the wet marks of his muddy shoes on the carpet, each one accusing her. She sat down on the edge of her bed. How could she have been such a fool! How could she have forgotten his rule? Half naked to the waist, hairy on the chest and arms, he shocked because the rage seemed to be not in his mind but in his body like an animal's. The rage had the pathos of an animal's. Perhaps when he was alone he often groped; perhaps the drilled man she was used to, who came out of his bedroom or his study, was the expert survival of a dozen concealed disasters?

Mrs. Johnson sat on her bed listening. She had never known Armitage to be angry; he was a monotonously considerate man. The shout abashed her and there was a strange pleasure in being abashed; but her mistake was not a mere mistake. She saw that it struck at the foundation of his life and was so gross that the surface of her own confidence was cracked. She was a woman who could reckon on herself, but now her mind was scattered. Useless to say to herself, "What a fuss about nothing," or "Keep calm." Or, about him, "Nasty temper." His shout, "Get out. I told you to leave me alone," had, without reason (except that a trivial shame is a spark that sets fire to a long string of greater shames), burned out all the security of her present life.

She had heard those words, almost exactly those words, before. Her husband had said them. A week after their wedding.

Well, *he* had had something to shout about, poor devil. She admitted it. Something a lot more serious than falling into a pool and having someone commit the crime of being kind to you and hurting your silly little pride.

She got up from the bed and turned on the tap of the washbasin to cool down her hot face and wash her hands of the dirt of the jacket she had brought upstairs. She took off her blouse and as she sluiced her face she looked through the water at herself in the mirror. There was a small birthmark the size of a red leaf which many people noticed and which, as it showed over the neck of the high blouses she usually wore, had the enticement of some signal or fancy of the blood; but under it, and invisible to them, were two smaller ones and then a great spreading ragged liver-coloured island of skin which spread under the tape of her slip and crossed her breast and seemed to end in a curdle of skin below it. She was stamped with an ineradicable bloody insult. It might have been an attempt to impose another woman on her. She was used to seeing it, but she carried it about with her under her clothes, hiding it and yet vaunting.

Now she was reaching for a towel and inside the towel, as she dried herself, she was talking to Armitage.

"If you want to know what shame and pride are, what about marrying a man who goes plain sick at the sight of your body and who says 'You deceived me. You didn't tell me.' "

She finished drying her face and put the towel on the warm rail and went to her dressing table. The hairbrush she picked up had been a wedding present and at each hard stroke of the brush on her lively fair hair, her face put up a fight, but it exhausted her. She brushed the image of Armitage away and she was left staring at the half-forgotten but never-forgotten self she had been.

How could she have been such a fool as to deceive her husband? It was not through wickedness. She had been blinded too—blinded by love; in a way, love had made her so full of herself that perhaps she had never seen *him.* And her deceptions: she could not stop herself smiling at them, but they were really pitiable because she was so afraid of losing him and to lose him would be to lose this new beautifully deluded self. She ought to have told him. There were chances. For example, in his flat with the grey sofa with the spring that bit your bottom going clang, clang at every kiss, when he used to carry on about her wearing dresses that a man couldn't get a hand into. He knew very well she had had affairs with men, but why, when they were both "worked up," wouldn't she undress and go to the bedroom? The sofa was too short. She remembered how shocked his face looked when she pulled up her skirts and lay on the floor. She said she believed in sex before marriage, but she thought some things ought to wait: it would be wrong for him to see her naked before their wedding day. And to show him she was no prude—there was that time they pretended to be looking out of the window at a cricket match; or Fridays in his office when the staff was gone and the cleaners were only at the end of the passage.

"You've got a mole on your neck," he said one day.

"Mother went mad with wanting plums when she was carrying me. It's a birthmark."

"It's pretty," he said and kissed it.

He kissed it. He kissed it. She clung to that when after the wedding they got to the hotel and she hid her face in his shoulder and let him pull down the zip of her dress. She stepped away, and pretending to be shy, she undressed under her slip. At last the slip came off over her head. They both looked at each other, she with brazen fear and he— she couldn't forget the shocked blank disgust on his face. From the neck over the left shoulder down to the breast and below, and spreading like a red tongue to the back was this ugly blob—dark as blood, like a ragged liver on a butcher's window, or some obscene island with ragged edges. It was as if a bucket of paint had been thrown over her.

"You didn't tell me," he said. If only she had told him, but how could she have done? She knew she had been cursed.

"That's why you wouldn't undress, you little hypocrite."

He himself was in his underpants with his trousers on the bed and

with his cuff links in his hand, which made his words absurd and awful.
His ridiculous look made him tragic and his hatred frightening. It was
terrible that for two hours while they talked he did not undress and
worse that he gave her a dressing gown to cover herself. She heard him
going through the catalogue of her tricks.

"When . . ." he began in a pathetic voice. And then she screamed
at him.

"What do you think? Do you think I got it done, that I got myself
tattooed in the Waterloo Road? I was born like it."

"Ssh," he said. "You'll wake the people in the next room."

"Let them hear. I'll go and show them," she screamed. It was kind
of him to put his arm round her. When she had recovered, she put on
her fatal, sporty manner. "Some men like it," she said.

He hit her across the face. It was not then but in the following weeks
when pity followed and pity turned to cruelty he had said, "Get out.
Leave me alone."

Mrs. Johnson went to her drawer and got out a clean blouse.

Her bedroom in Armitage's house was a pretty one, far prettier than
any she had ever had. Up till now she had been used to bed-sitters since
her marriage. But was it really the luxury of the house and the power
she would have in it that had weighed with her when she had decided
to take on this strange job? She understood now something else had
moved her in the low state she had been in when she came. As a
punished and self-hating person she was drawn to work with a punished
man. It was a return to her girlhood: injury had led her to injury.

She looked out of the window at the garden. The diamond panes
chopped up the sight of the frozen lawns and the firs that were frost-
whiskered. She was used to the view. It was a view of the real world;
that, after all, was her world, not his. She saw that gradually in three
years she had drifted out of it and had taken to living in Armitage's
filed memory. If he said, for example, "That rambler is getting wild.
It must be cut back," because a thorn caught his jacket, or if he made
his famous remark about seeing the cathedral on a clear day, the
landscape limited itself to these things and in general reduced itself to
the imposed topographical sketch in his mind. She had allowed him,
as a matter of abnegation and duty, to impose his world on hers. Now
this shock brought back a lost sense of the right to her own landscape;
and then to the protest that this country was not hers at all. The
country bored her. The fir trees bored her. The lanes bored her. The

view from this window or the tame protected view of the country from
the Rolls-Royce window bored her. She wanted to go back to London,
to the streets, the buses and the crowds, to crowds of people with eyes
in their heads. And—her spirits rising—"To hell with it, I want people
who can *see* me."

She went downstairs to give orders for the carpet to be brushed.

In the sitting-room she saw the top of Armitage's dark head. She had
not heard him go down. He was sitting in what she called the cathedral
chair facing the window and she was forced to smile when she saw a
bit of green weed sticking to his hair. She also saw a heavy glass ashtray
had fallen off the table beside him. "Clumsy," she said. She picked it
up and lightly pulled off the piece of weed from his hair. He did not
notice this.

"Mr. Armitage," she said in her decisive manner, "I lost my head.
I'm sorry."

He was silent.

"I understand how you feel," she said. For this (she had decided in
her room) was the time for honesty and for having things out. The
impersonality could not go on, as it had done for three years.

"I want to go back to London," she said.

"Don't be a damn fool," he said.

Well, she was not going to be sworn at. "I'm not a damn fool," she
said. "I understand your situation." And then, before she could stop
herself, her voice shaking and loud, she broke out with: "I know what
humiliation is."

"Who is humiliated?" said Armitage. "Sit down."

"I am not speaking about you," she said stiffly.

That surprised him, she saw, for he turned his head.

"I'm sorry, I lost my temper," he said. "But that stupid fellow and
his dog . . ."

"I am speaking about myself," she said. "We have our pride, too."

"Who is *we?*" he said, without curiosity.

"Women," she said.

He got up from his chair, and she stepped back. He did not move
and she saw that he really had not recovered from the fall in the pool,
for he was uncertain. He was not sure where the table was.

"Here," he said roughly, putting out a hand. "Give me a hand out
of this."

She obediently took him by the arm and stood him clear of the table.

"Listen to me. You couldn't help what happened and neither could

I. There's nothing to apologize for. You're not leaving. We get on very well. Take my advice. Don't be hard on yourself."

"It is better to be hard," she said. "Where would you have been if you had not been hard? I'm not a girl. I'm thirty-nine." He moved towards her and put his hand on her right shoulder and she quickly turned her head. He laughed and said, "You've brushed your hair back." He knew. He always knew.

She watched him make for his study and saw him take the wrong course, brush against the sofa by the fireplace, and then a yard or two further, he shouldered the wall.

"Damn," he said.

At dinner, conversation was difficult. He offered her a glass of wine which she refused. He poured himself a second glass and as he sat down he grimaced with pain.

"Did you hurt your back this afternoon?" she asked.

"No," he said. "I was thinking about my wife."

Mrs. Johnson blushed. He had scarcely ever mentioned his wife. She knew only what Marge Brook had told her of the town gossip: how his wife could not stand his blindness and had gone off with someone and that he had given her a lot of money. Someone said, ten thousand pounds. What madness! In the dining-room Mrs. Johnson often thought of all those notes flying about over the table and out of the window. He was too rich. Ten thousand pounds of hatred and rage, or love, or madness. In the first place, she wouldn't have touched it.

"She made me build the pool," he said.

"A good idea," she said.

"I don't know why. I never thought of throwing her into it," he said.

Mrs. Johnson said, "Shall I read the paper?" She did not want to hear more about his wife.

Mrs. Johnson went off to bed early. Switching on the radio in her room and then switching it off because it was playing classical music, she said to herself, "Well, funny things bring things back. What a day!" and stepped yawning out of her skirt. Soon she was in bed and asleep.

An hour later she woke up, hearing her name.

"Mrs. Johnson. The water got into my watch, would you set it for me?" He was standing there in his dressing gown.

"Yes," she said. She was a woman who woke up alert and clear-headed.

"I'm sorry. I thought you were listening to a program. I didn't know you were in bed," he said. He was holding the watch to his ear.

"Would you set it for me and put my alarm right?" He had the habit of giving orders. They were orders spoken into space—and she was the space, nonexistent. He gave her the watch and went off. She put on her dressing gown and followed him to his room. He had switched on the light for her. She went to the bedside table and bent down to wind the clock. Suddenly she felt his arms round her, pulling her upright, and he was kissing her head. The alarm went off suddenly and she dropped the clock. It went on screeching on the floor at her feet.

"Mr. Armitage," she said in a low angry voice, but not struggling. He turned her round and he was trying to kiss her on the lips. At this she did struggle. She twisted her head this way and that to stop him, so that it was her head rather than her body that was resisting him. Her blue eyes fought with all their light, but his eyes were dead as stone.

"Really, Mr. Armitage. Stop it," she managed to mutter. "The door is open. Cook will hear."

She was angry at being kissed by a man who could not see her face, but she felt the shamed insulted woman in her, that blotched inhabitant, blaze up in her skin.

The bell of the alarm clock was weakening and then choked to a stop and in her pettish struggle she stepped on it; her slipper had come off.

"I've hurt my foot." Distracted by the pain she stopped struggling, and Armitage took his opportunity and kissed her on the lips. She looked with pain into his sightless eyes. There was no help there. She was terrified of being drawn into the dark where he lived. And then the kiss seemed to go down her throat and spread into her shoulders, into her breasts and branch into all the veins and arteries of her body and it was the tongue of the shamed woman who had sprung up in her that touched his.

"What are you doing?" she was trying to say, but could only groan the words. When he touched the stained breast she struck back violently, saying, "No, no."

"Come to bed with me," he said.

"Please let me go. I've hurt my foot."

The surprising thing was that he did let her go, and as she sat panting and white in the face on the bed to look at her foot, she looked mockingly at him. She forgot that he could not see her mockery. He sat beside her but did not touch her and he was silent. There was no scratch on her foot. She picked up the clock and put it back on the table.

Mrs. Johnson was proud of the adroitness with which she had kept men away from her since her marriage. It was a war with the inhabitant of the ragged island on her body. That creature craved for the furtive, for the hand that slipped under a skirt, for the scuffle in the back seat of a car, for a five-minute disappearance into a locked office.

But the other Mrs. Johnson, the cheerful one, was virtuous. She took advantage of his silence and got quickly up to get away; she dodged past him, but he was quick too. He was at the closed door. For a moment she was wily. It would be easy for her to dodge him in the room. And then she saw once more the sight she could not bear that melted her more certainly than the kisses which had filled her mouth and throat: she saw his hands begin to open and search and grope in the air as he came towards the sound of her breathing. She could not move. His hand caught her. The woman inside her seemed to shout, "Why not? You're all right. He cannot see." In her struggle she had not thought of that. In three years he had made her forget that blindness meant not seeing.

"All right," she said, and the virtue in Mrs. Johnson pouted. She gently tapped his chest with her fingers and said with the sullenness of desire, "I'll be back in a minute."

It was a revenge: that was the pleasure.

"Dick," she called to her husband, "look at this," when the man was on top of her. Revenge was the only pleasure and his excitement was soon over. To please him she patted him on the head as he lay beside her and said, "You've got long legs." And she nearly said, "You are a naughty boy" and "Do you feel better?" but she stopped herself and her mind went off on to what she had to do in the morning; she listened and wondered how long it would be before he would fall asleep and she could stealthily get away. Revenge astonished by its quickness.

She slyly moved. He knew at once and held her. She waited. She wondered where Dick was now. She wished she could tell him. But presently this blind man in the bed leaned up and put both his hands on her face and head and carefully followed the round of her forehead, the line of her brow, her nose and lips and chin, to the line of her throat and then to her nape and shoulders. She trembled, for after his hands had passed, what had been touched seemed to be new. She winced as his hand passed over the stained shoulder and breast and he paused, knowing that she winced, and she gave a groan of pleasure to deceive him; but he went on, as if he were modelling her, feeling the pit under the arms, the space of ribs and belly and the waist of which she was proud, measuring them, feeling their depth, the roundness of her legs, the bone in her knees until, throwing all clothes back, he was holding her ankle, the arch of her foot, and her toes. Her skin and her bones became alive. His hands knew her body as she had never known it. In her brief love affairs, which had excited her because of the risk of being caught, the first touch of a man stirred her at once and afterwards left her looking demurely at him; but she had let no one know her with a pedantry like his. She suddenly sat up and put her arms round him, and now she went wild. It was not a revenge now; it was a triumph. She lifted the sad breast to his lips. And when they lay back she kissed his chest and then— with daring—she kissed his eyes.

It was six o'clock before she left him, and when she got to her room the stained woman seemed to bloom like a flower. It was only after she had slept and saw her room in daylight again that she realized that once more she had deceived a man.

It was late. She looked out of the window and saw Armitage in his city clothes talking to the chauffeur in the garden. She watched them walk to the garage.

"O.K.," she said dryly to defend herself. "It was a rape." During the day there would be moments when she could feel his hands moving over her skin. Her legs tingled. She posed as if she were a new-made statue. But as the day went on she hardened and instead of waiting for him to return she went into the town to see Marge.

"You've put your hair up," Marge said.

"Do you like it?"

"I don't know. It's different. It makes you look severe. No, not severe. Something. Restless."

"I am not going back to dinner this evening," she said. "I want a change. Leonard's gone to London."

"Leonard!" said Marge.

Mrs. Johnson wanted to confide in Marge, but Marge bored her. They ate a meal together and she ate fast. To Marge's astonishment she said, "I must fly."

"You *are* in a mood," Marge said.

Mrs. Johnson was unable to control a longing to see Armitage. When she got back to the house and saw him sitting by the fire she wanted him to get up and at least put his arms round her; but he did not move, he was listening to music. It was always the signal that he wanted to be alone.

"It is just ending," said Armitage.

The music ended in a roll of drums.

"Do you want something, Helen?" he said.

She tried to be mocking, but her voice could not mock and she said seriously, "About last night. It must not happen again. I don't want to be in a false position. I could not go on living in the house."

She did not intend to say this; her voice, between rebuke and tenderness, betrayed this.

"Sit down."

She did not move.

"I have been very happy here," she said. "I don't want to spoil it."

"You are angry," he said.

"No, I'm not," she said.

"Yes, you are; that is why you were not here when I got back," he said.

"You did not wait for me this morning," she said. "I was glad you didn't. I don't want it to go on."

He came nearer to her and put his hand on her hair.

"I like the way your hair shows your ears," he said. And he kissed them.

"Now, please," she said.

"I love you," he said and kissed her on the forehead and she did not turn her head.

"Do you? I'm glad you said that. I don't think you do. When something has been good, don't spoil it. I don't like love affairs," she said.

And then she changed. "It was a party. Good night."

"You made me happy," he said, holding on to her hand.

"Were you thinking about it a long time?" she said in another voice, lingering for one more word.

"Yes," he said.

"It is very nice of you to say that. It is what you ought to say. But I mean what I said. Now, really, good night. And," giving a pat to his arm, she said, "keep your watch wound up."

Two nights later he called to her loudly and curtly from the stairs:

"Mrs. Johnson, where are you?" and when she came into the hall he said quietly, "Helen."

She liked that. They slept together again. They did not talk.

Their life went on as if nothing had happened. She began to be vain of the stain on her body and could not resist silently displaying, almost taunting him, when she undressed, with what he could not see. She liked the play of deceiving him like this; she was paying him out for not being able to see her; and when she was ashamed of doing this the shame itself would rouse her desire: two women uniting in her. And fear roused her too; she was afraid of his blindness. Sometimes the fear was that the blind can see into the mind. It often terrified her at the height of her pleasure that she was being carried into the dark where he lived. She knew she was not but she could not resist the excitement of imagining it. Afterwards she would turn her back to him, ashamed of her fancies, and as his finger followed the bow of her spine she would drive away the cynical thought that he was just filing this affair away in one of the systems of his memory.

Yet she liked these doubts. How dead her life had been in its practical certainties. She liked the tenderness and violence of sexual love, the simple kindness of the skin. She once said to him, "My skin is your skin." But she stuck to it that she did not love him and that he did not love her. She wanted to be simply a body: a woman like Marge who was always talking about love seemed to her a fool. She liked it that she and Armitage were linked to each other only by signs. And she became vain of her disfigurement, and looking at it, even thought of it as the lure.

I know what would happen to me if I got drunk, she thought at one of Armitage's cocktail parties, I'm the sort of woman who would start taking her clothes off. When she was a young woman she had once started doing so, and someone, thank God, stopped her.

But these fancies were bravado.

They were intended to stop her from telling him.

On Sundays Mrs. Johnson went to church in the village near the house. She had made a habit of it from the beginning, because she thought it the proper thing to do: to go to church had made her feel she need not reproach herself for impropriety in living in the same house as a man. It was a practical matter: before her love affair the tragic words of the service had spoken to her evil. If God had done this to her, He must put up with the sight of her in His house. She was not a religious woman; going to church was an assertion that she had as much right to fair play as anyone else. It also stopped her from being "such a fool" as to fall to the temptation of destroying her new wholeness by telling him. It was "normal" to go to church and normality had been her craving ever since her girlhood. She had always taken her body, not her mind, to church.

Armitage teased her about her churchgoing when she first came to work for him; but lately his teasing became sharper: "Going to listen to Dearly Beloved Brethren?" he would say.

"Oh, leave him alone," she said.

He had made up a tale about her being in love with the vicar; at first it was a joke, but now there was a sharp edge to it. "A very respectable man," he said.

When the church bells rang on Sunday evening he said, "He's calling to you." She began to see that this joke had the grit of jealousy in it; not of the vicar, of course, but a jealousy of many things in her life.

"Why do you go there? I'd like to understand, seriously," he said.

"I like to get out," she said.

She saw pain on his face. There was never much movement in it beyond the deepening of two lines at the corners of his mouth; but when his face went really dead, it was as sullen as earth in the garden. In her sense, she knew, he never went out. He lived in a system of tunnels. She had to admit that when she saw the grey church she was glad, because it was not his house. She knew from gossip that neither he nor his wife had ever been to it.

There was something else in this new life; now he had freed her they were both more watchful of each other. One Sunday in April she saw his jealousy in the open. She had come in from church and she was telling him about the people who were there. She was sitting on the sofa beside him.

"How many lovers have you had?" he said. "That doctor you worked for, now?"

"Indeed not," she said. "I was married."

"I know you were married. But when you were working for those people in Manchester? And in Canada after the war?"

"No one else. That was just a trip."

"I don't believe you."

"Honestly, it's true."

"In court I never believe a witness who says 'Honestly.'"

She blushed, for she had had three or four lovers, but she was defending herself. They were no business of his.

The subject became darker.

"Your husband," he said. "He saw you. They all saw you."

She knew what he meant, and this scared her.

"My husband. Of course he saw me. Only my husband."

"Ah, so there were others."

"Only my husband saw me," she said. "I told you about it. How he walked out of the hotel after a week."

This was a moment when she could have told him, but to see his jealousy destroy the happiness he had restored to her made her indignant.

"He couldn't bear the sight of me. He had wanted," she invented, "to marry another woman. He told me on the first night of our marriage. In the hotel. Please don't talk about it."

"Which hotel was this?" he said.

The triviality of the question confused her. "In Kensington."

"What was the name?"

"Oh, I forget, the something Royal . . ."

"You don't forget."

"I do honestly . . ."

"Honestly!" he said.

He was in a rage of jealousy. He kept questioning her about the hotel, the length of their marriage. He pestered for addresses, for dates, and tried to confuse her by putting his questions again and again.

"So he didn't leave you at the hotel!" he said.

"Look," she said. "I can't stand jealous men and I'm not going to be questioned like one of your clients."

He did not move or shout. Her husband had shouted and paced up and down, waving his arms. This man sat bolt upright and still, and spoke in a dry, exacting voice.

"I'm sorry," he said.

She took his hand, the hand that groped like a helpless tentacle and that had modelled her; it was the most disturbing and living thing about him.

"Are you still in love with your husband?"

"Certainly not."

"He saw you and I have never seen you." He circled again to his obsession.

"It is just as well. I'm not a beautiful woman," she laughed. "My legs are too short, my bottom is too big. You be grateful—my husband couldn't stand the sight of me."

"You have a skin like an apple," he said.

She pushed his hand away and said, "Your hands know too much."

"*He* had hands. And he had eyes," he said in a voice grinding with violence.

"I'm very tired. I am going to bed," she said. "Good night."

"You see," he said. "There is no answer."

He picked up a braille book and his hand moved fast over the sheets.

She went to her room and kicked off her shoes and stepped out of her dress.

I've been living in a dream, she thought. Just like Marge, who always thinks her husband's coming back every time the gate goes. It is a mistake, she thought, living in the same house.

The jealous fit seemed to pass. It was a fire, she understood, that flared up just as her shame used to flare, but two Sundays later the fit came on again. He must hate God, she thought, and pitied him. Perhaps the music that usually consoled him had tormented him. At any rate, he stopped it when she came in and put her prayer book on the table. There was a red begonia, which came from the greenhouse, on the table beside the sofa where he was sitting very upright, as if he had been waiting impatiently for her to come back.

"Come and sit down," he said and began kindly enough. "What was church like? Did they tell you what to do?"

"I was nearly asleep," she said. "After last night. Do you know what time it was?" She took his hand and laughed.

He thought about this for a while. Then he said, "Give me your hands. No. Both of them. That's right. Now spit on them."

"Spit!"

"Yes, that is what the church tells you."

"What *are* you talking about?" she said, trying to get her hands away.

"Spit on them." And he forced her hands, though not roughly, to her lips.

"What are you doing?" She laughed nervously and spat on her fingers.

"Now—rub the spittle on my eyes."

"Oh, no," she said.

He let go of her wrist.

"Do as I tell you. It's what your Jesus Christ did when he cured the blind man."

He sat there waiting and she waited.

"He put dust or earth or something on them," he said. "Get some."

"No," she said.

"There's some here. Put your fingers in it," he said shortly. She was frightened of him.

"In the pot," he insisted as he held one of her wrists so that she could not get away. She dabbed her wet fingers in the earth of the begonia pot.

"Put it on my eyes."

"I can't do that. I really can't," she said.

"Put it on my eyes," he said.

"It will hurt them."

"They are hurt already," he said. "Do as I tell you." She bent to him and, with disgust, she put her dirty fingers on the wet eyeballs. The sensation was horrible, and when she saw the dirty patches on his eyes, like two filthy smudges, she thought he looked like an ape.

"That is what you are supposed to do," he said. Jealousy had made him mad.

I can't stay with a mad man, she thought. He's malicious. She did not know what to do, but he solved that for her. He reached for his braille book. She got up and left him there. The next day he went to London.

His habits changed. He went several times into the nearby town on his own and she was relieved that he came back in a silent mood which seemed happy. The horrible scene went out of her mind. She had gone so far as to lock her bedroom door for several nights after that scene, but now she unlocked it. He had brought her a bracelet from London; she drifted into unguarded happiness. She knew so well how torment comes and goes.

It was full undreaming June, the leaves in the garden still undarkened, and for several days people were surprised when day after day the sun was up and hot and unclouded. Mrs. Johnson went down to the pool. Armitage and his guests often tried to persuade her to go in but she always refused.

"They once tried to get me to go down to Peckham Baths when I was a kid, but I screamed," she said.

The guests left her alone. They were snobbish about Peckham Baths.

But Mrs. Johnson decided to become a secret bather. One afternoon when Armitage was in London and the cook and gardener had their day off, she went down with the gardener's dog. She wore a black bathing suit that covered her body and lowered herself by the steps into the water. Then she splashed at the shallow end of the pool and hung on to the rail while the dog barked at her. He stopped barking when she got out and sniffed round the hedge where she pulled down her bathing dress to her waist and lay down to get sun-drunk on her towel.

She was displaying herself to the sun, the sky and the trees. The air was like hands that played on her as Armitage did and she lay listening to the snuffles of the dog and the humming of the bees in the yew hedge. She had been there an hour when the dog barked at the hedge. She quickly picked up a towel and covered herself and called to the dog: "What is it?"

He went on barking and then gave up and came to her. She sat down. Suddenly the dog barked again. Mrs. Johnson stood up and tried to look through one of the thinner places in the hedge. A man who must have been close to the pool and who must have passed along the footpath from the lane, a path used only by the gardener, was walking up the lawns towards the house carrying a trilby hat in his hand. He was not the gardener. He stopped twice to get his breath and turned to look at the view. She recognized the smiling grey suit, the wide figure and snowball head: it was "Wolverhampton" Smith. She waited and saw him go on to the house and ring a bell. Then he disappeared round the corner and went to the front of the house. Mrs. Johnson quickly dressed. Presently he came back to look into the windows of the sitting-room. He found the door and for a minute or two went into the house and then came out.

"The cheek," she said. She finished dressing and went up the lawn to him.

"Ah, there you are," he said. "What a sweet place this is. I was looking for Mr. Armitage."

"He's in London."

"I thought he might be in the pool," he said. Mr. Smith looked rich with arch, smiling insinuation.

"When will he be back?"

"About six. Is there anything I can do?"

"No, no, no," said Mr. Smith in a variety of genial notes, waving a hand. "I was out for a walk."

"A long walk—seven miles."

"I came," said Mr. Smith, modestly lowering his eyes in financial confession, "by bus."

"The best way. Can I give you a drink?"

"I never touch it," Mr. Smith said, putting up an austere hand.

"Well, a glass of water perhaps. As the Americans say, 'I'm mighty thirsty.' My wife and I came down here for the water, you know. London water is chalky. It was very bad for my wife's arthritis. It's bad for everyone, really. There's a significant increase in neuralgia, neuritis, arthritis in a city like London. The chalky water does it. People don't realize it"—and here Mr. Smith stopped smiling and put on a stern excommunicating air—"If you believe that man's life is ruled by water. I personally don't."

"Not by water only, anyway," said Mrs. Johnson.

"I mean," said Mr. Smith gravely, "if you believe that the material body exists." And when he said this, the whole sixteen stone of him looked scornfully at the landscape which, no doubt, concealed thousands of people who believed they had bodies. He expanded: he seemed to threaten to vanish.

Mrs. Johnson fetched a glass of water. "I'm glad to see you're still there," she laughed when she came back.

Mr. Smith was resting on the garden seat. "I was just thinking— thank you—there's a lot of upkeep in a place like this," he said.

"There is."

"And yet—what is upkeep? Money—so it seems. And if we believe in the body, we believe in money, we believe in upkeep, and so it goes on," said Mr. Smith sunnily, waving his glass at the garden. And then sharply and loftily, free of this evil: "It gives employment." Firmly telling her she was employed. "But," he added, in warm contemplation, putting down his glass and opening his arms, gathering in the landscape, "but there is only one employer."

"There are a hell of a lot of employers."

Mr. Smith raised an eyebrow at the word "hell" and said, "Let me correct you there. I happen to believe that God is the only employer."

"I'm employed by Mr. Armitage," she said. "Mr. Armitage loves this place. You don't have to see to love a garden."

"It's a sweet place," said Mr. Smith. He got up and took a deep breath. "Pine trees. Wonderful. The smell! My wife doesn't like pine trees. She is depressed by them. It's all in the mind," said Mr. Smith. "As Shakespeare says. By the way, I suppose the water's warming up in the pool? June—it would be. That's what I should like—a swim."

He *did* see me! thought Mrs. Johnson.

"You should ask Mr. Armitage," she said coldly.

"Oh, no, no," said Mr. Smith. "I just *feel* that to swim and have a sunbathe would be the right idea. I should like a place with a swimming pool. And a view like this. I feel it would suit me. And, by the way," he became stern again, "don't let me hear you say again that Mr. Armitage enjoys this place although he doesn't see it. Don't tie his blindness on him. You'll hold him back. He *does* see it. He reflects all-seeing God. I told him so on Wednesday."

"On Wednesday?"

"Yes," he said. "When he came for treatment. I managed to fit him in. Good godfathers, look at the time! I've to get the bus back. I'm sorry to miss Mr. Armitage. Just tell him I called. I just had a thought to give him, that's all. He'll appreciate it."

"And now," Mr. Smith said sportively, "I must try and avoid taking a dive into that pool as I go by, mustn't I?"

She watched his stout marching figure go off down the path.

For treatment! What on earth did Mr. Smith mean? She knew the rest when Armitage came home.

"He came for his cheque," he said. "Would you make out a cheque for a hundred and twenty pounds—"

"A hundred and twenty pounds!" she exclaimed.

"For Mr. Smith," he repeated. "He is treating my eyes."

"Your eyes! He's not an ophthalmic surgeon."

"No," said Armitage coldly. "I have tried those."

"You're not going to a faith healer!"

"I am."

And so they moved into their second quarrel. It was baffling to quarrel with Armitage. He could hear the firm ring of your voice but he could not see your eyes blooming wider and bluer with obstinacy; for her, her eyes were herself. It was like quarrelling with a man who had no self, or perhaps with one that was always hidden.

"Your church goes in for it," he said.

"Proper faith healing," she said.

"What is proper?" he said.

She had a strong belief in propriety.

"A hundred and twenty pounds! You told me yourself Smith is a fraud. I mean, you refused his case. How can you go to a fraud?"

"I don't think I said fraud," he said.

"You didn't like the way he got five thousand pounds out of that silly young man."

"Two thousand," he said.

"He's after your money," she said. "He's a swindler."

In her heart, having been brought up poor, she thought it was a scandal that Armitage was well-off; it was even more scandalous to throw money away.

"Probably. At the end of his tether," he said. He was conveying, she knew, that he was at the end of his tether too.

"And you fall for that? You can't possibly believe the nonsense he talks."

"Don't you think God was a crook? When you think of what He's done?"

"No, I don't." (But in fact the stained woman thought He was.)

"What did Smith talk about?"

"I was in the pool. I think he was spying on me. I forget what he was talking about—water, chalky water, was it?"

"He's odd about chalk!" Armitage laughed. Then he became grim again: "You see—even Smith can see *you*. You see people, you see Smith, everyone sees everything, and so they can afford to throw away what they see and forget. But I have to remember everything. You know what it is like trying to remember a dream. Smith is right, I'm dreaming a dream," Armitage added sardonically. "He says that I'm only dreaming I cannot see."

She could not make out whether Armitage was serious.

"All right. I don't understand, but all right. What happens next?"

"You can wake up."

Mr. Armitage gave one of his cruel smiles. "I told you. When I used to go to the courts I often listened to witnesses like Smith. They were always bringing 'God is my witness' into it. I never knew a more religious lot of men than dishonest witnesses. They were always bringing in a higher power. Perhaps they were in contact with it."

"You don't mean that. You are making fun of me," she said. And then vehemently: "I hate to see you going to an ignorant man like that. I thought you were too proud. What has happened to you?"

She had never spoken her mind so forcibly to him before.

"If a man can't see," he said, "if *you* couldn't see, humiliation is what you'd fear most. I thought I ought to accept it."

He had never been so open with her.

"You couldn't go lower than Mr. Smith," she said.

"We're proud. That is our vice," he said. "Proud in the dark. Everyone else has to put up with humiliation. You said you knew what it was —I always remember that. Millions of people are humiliated: perhaps it makes them stronger because they forget it. I want to join them."

"No, you don't," she said.

They were lying in bed and leaning over him she put her breast to his lips, but he lay lifeless. She could not bear it that he had changed her and that she had stirred this profound wretchedness in him. She hated confession: to her it was the male weakness—self-love. She got out of bed.

"Come to that," she said. "It's you who are humiliating me. You are going to this quack man because we've slept together. I don't like the compliment."

"And you say you don't love me," he said.

"I admire you," she said. She dreaded the word "love." She picked up her clothes and left the room. She hadn't the courage to say she hadn't the courage. She stuck to what she had felt since she was a child: that she was a body. He had healed it with his body.

Once more she thought, I shall have to go. I ought to have stuck to it and gone before. If I'd been living in the town and just been coming up for the day it would have been O.K. Living in the house was your mistake, my girl. You'll have to go and get another job. But of course when she calmed down, she realized that all this was self-deception: she was afraid to tell him. She brusquely drove off the thought, and her mind went to the practical.

That hundred and twenty pounds! She was determined not to see him swindled. She went with him to Mr. Smith's next time. The roof of the Rolls-Royce gleamed over the shrubbery of the uncut hedge of Mr. Smith's house. A cat was sitting on the window sill. Waiting on the doorstep was the little man, wide-waisted and with his hands in his optimistic pockets, and changing his smile of welcome to a reminder of secret knowledge when he saw her. Behind the undressing smile of Mr. Smith stood the kind, cringing figure of his wife, looking as they all walked into the narrow hall.

"Straight through?" said Mrs. Johnson in her managing voice. "And leave them to themselves, I suppose?"

"The back gets the sun. At the front it's all these trees," said Mrs. Smith, encouraged by Mrs. Johnson's presence to speak out in a weak voice, as if it was all she did get. "I was a London girl."

"So am I," said Mrs. Johnson.

"But you've got a beautiful place up there. Have you got these pine trees too?"

"A few."

"They give me the pip," said Mrs. Smith. "Coffee? Shall I take your coat? My husband said you'd got pines."

"No, thank you, I'll keep it," said Mrs. Johnson. "Yes, we've got pines. I can't say they're my favourite trees. I like to see leaves come off. And I like a bit of traffic myself. I like to see a shop."

"Oh, you would," said Mrs. Smith.

The two women looked with the shrewd London look at each other.

"I'm so busy up there I couldn't come before. I don't like Mr. Armitage coming alone. I like to keep an eye on him," said Mrs. Johnson, set for attack.

"Oh, yes, an eye."

"Frankly, I didn't know he was coming to see Mr. Smith."

But Mrs. Johnson got nothing out of Mrs. Smith. They were both half listening to the rumble of men's voices next door. Then the meeting was over and they went out to meet the men. In his jolly way Mr. Smith said to Mrs. Johnson as they left, "Don't forget about that swim!"

Ostentatiously to show her command and to annoy Armitage, she armed him down the path.

"I hope you haven't invited that man to swim in the pool," said Mrs. Johnson to Mr. Armitage on the way home.

"You've made an impression on Smith," said Armitage.

"No, *I* haven't."

"Poor Mrs. Smith," said Mrs. Johnson.

Otherwise they were silent.

She went a second, then a third time to the Smiths' house. She sat each time in the kitchen talking and listening to the men's voices in the next room. Sometimes there were long silences.

"Is Mr. Smith praying?" Mrs. Johnson asked.

"I expect so," said Mrs. Smith. "Or reading."

"Because it *is* prayer, isn't it?" said Mrs. Johnson.

Mrs. Smith was afraid of this healthy downright woman and it was an effort for her to make a stand on what evidently for most of her married life had been poor ground.

"I suppose it is. Prayer, yes, that is what it would be. Dad . . ."— she changed her mind—"my husband has always had faith." And with this, Mrs. Smith looked nervously at being able loyally to put forward the incomprehensible.

"But what does he actually *do*? I thought he had a chemist's shop," pursued Mrs. Johnson.

Mrs. Smith was a timid woman who wavered now between the relics of dignity and a secretive craving to impart.

"He has retired," said Mrs. Smith. "When we closed the shop he took this up." She said this, hoping to clutch a certainty.

Mrs. Johnson gave a bustling laugh. "No, you misunderstand me. What I mean is, what does he actually *do*? What is the treatment?"

Mrs. Smith was lost. She nodded, as it were, to nothingness several times.

"Yes," she said. "I suppose you'd call it prayer. I don't really understand it."

"Nor do I," said Mrs. Johnson. "I expect you've got enough to do keeping house. I have my work cut out too."

They still heard the men talking. Mrs. Johnson nodded to the wall.

"Still at it," said Mrs. Johnson. "I'll be frank with you, Mrs. Smith. I am sure your husband does whatever he does do for the best . . ."

"Oh, yes, for the best," nodded Mrs. Smith. "It's saved us. He had a writ out against him when Mr. Armitage's cheque came in. I know he's grateful."

"But I believe in being open . . ."

"Open," nodded Mrs. Smith.

"I've told him and I've told Mr. Armitage that I just don't believe a man who has been blind for twenty-two years—"

"Terrible," said Mrs. Smith.

"—can be cured. Certainly not by—whatever this is. Do you believe it, Mrs. Smith?"

Mrs. Smith was cornered.

"Our Lord did it," she said desperately. "That is what my husband says . . ."

"I was a nurse during the war and I have worked for doctors," said Mrs. Johnson. "I am sure it is impossible. I've knocked about a lot. You're a sensible woman, Mrs. Smith. I don't want to offend you, but you don't believe it yourself, do you?"

Mrs. Johnson's eyes grew larger and Mrs. Smith's older eyes were helpless and small. She longed for a friend. She was hypnotized by Mrs. Johnson, whose face and pretty neck grew firmly out of her frilled and high-necked blouse.

"I try to have faith . . ." said Mrs. Smith, rallying to her husband. "He says I hold him back. I don't know."

"Some men need to be held back," said Mrs. Johnson, and she gave a fighting shake to her healthy head. All Mrs. Smith could do in her panic was to watch every move of Mrs. Johnson's, study her expensive shoes and stockings, her capable skirt, her painted nails. Now, at the shake of Mrs. Johnson's head, she saw on the right side of the neck the small petal of the birthmark just above the frill of the collar.

"None of us are perfect," said Mrs. Smith slyly.

"I have been with Mr. Armitage four years," Mrs. Johnson said.

"It is a lovely place up there," said Mrs. Smith, eager to change the subject. "It must be terrible to live in such a lovely place and never see it . . ."

"Don't you believe it," said Mrs. Johnson. "He knows that place better than any of us, better than me."

"No," groaned Mrs. Smith. "We had a blind dog when I was a girl. It used to nip hold of my dress to hold me back if it heard a car coming when I was going to cross the road. It belonged to my aunt and she said 'That dog can see. It's a miracle.' "

"He heard the car coming," said Mrs. Johnson. "It's common sense."

The words struck Mrs. Smith.

"Yes, it is, really," she said. "If you come to think of it."

She got up and went to the gas stove to make more coffee and new courage came to her. We know why she doesn't want Mr. Armitage to see again! She was thinking: the frightening Mrs. Johnson was really weak. Housekeeper and secretary to a rich man, sitting very pretty up there, the best of everything. Plenty of money, staff, cook, gardener, chauffeur, Rolls-Royce—if he was cured where would her job be? Oh, she looks full of herself now, but she is afraid. I expect she's got round him to leave her a bit.

The coffee began to bubble up in the pot and that urgent noise put excitement into her and her old skin blushed.

"Up there with a man alone. As I said to Dad, a woman can tell! Where would she get another man with that spot spreading all over? She's artful. She's picked the right one." She was telling the tale to herself.

The coffee boiled over and hissed on the stove and a sudden forgotten jealousy hissed up in Mrs. Smith's uncertain mind. She took the pot to the table and poured out a boiling-hot cup and, as the steam clouded up from it, screening her daring stare at the figure of Mrs. Johnson, Mrs. Smith wanted to say: "Lying there stark naked by that swimming pool right in the face of my husband. What was he doing up there anyway?"

She could not say it. There was not much pleasure in Mrs. Smith's life; jealousy was the only one that enlivened her years with Mr. Smith. She had flown at him when he came home and had told her that God had guided him, that prayer always uncovered evil and brought it to the surface; it had revealed to him that the Devil had put his mark on Mrs. Johnson, and that he wouldn't be surprised if that was what was holding up the healing of Mr. Armitage.

"What were you doing," she screamed at him, "looking at a woman?"

The steam cleared and Mrs. Smith's nervousness returned as she saw that composed face. She was frightened now of her own imagination and of her husband's. She knew him. He was always up to something.

"Don't you dare say anything to Mr. Armitage about this!" she had shouted at him.

But now she fell back on admiring Mrs. Johnson again.

Settled for life, she sighed. She's young. She is only fighting for her own. She's a woman.

And Mrs. Smith's pride was stirred. Her courage was fitful and weakened by what she had lived through. She had heard Mrs. Johnson was divorced and it gave Mrs. Smith strength as a woman who had "stuck to her husband." She had not gone round taking up with men as she guessed Mrs. Johnson might have done. She was a respectable married woman.

Her voice trembled at first but became stronger.

"Dad wanted to be a doctor when he was a boy," Mrs. Smith was saying, "but there wasn't the money so he worked in a chemist's but it was always church on Sundays. I wasn't much of a one for church myself. But you must have capital and being just behind the counter doesn't lead anywhere. Of course I tried to egg him on to get his diploma and he got the papers—but I used to watch him. He'd start his studying and then he'd get impatient. He's a very impatient man and he'd say 'Amy, I'll try the ministry'—he's got a good voice— 'church people have money.' "

"And did he?"

"No, he always wanted to, but he couldn't seem to settle to a church —I mean a religion. I'll say this for him, he's a fighter. Nixon, his first guv'nor, thought the world of him: quick with the sales. Nixon's Cough Mixture—well, he didn't invent it, but he changed the bottles and the labels, made it look—fashionable, dear—you know? A lot of Wesleyans took it."

Mrs. Smith spread her hands over her face and laughed through her fingers.

"When Nixon died someone in the church put up some money, a very religious, good man. One day Dad said to me—I always remember it—'It's not medicine. It's faith does it.' He's got faith. Faith is—well, faith."

"In himself?" suggested Mrs. Johnson.

"That's it! That's it!" cried Mrs. Smith with excitement. Then she quietened and dabbed a tear from her cheek. "I begged him not to come down here. But this Mrs. Rogers, the lady who owns the house, she's deaf and on her own, he knew her. She believes in him. She calls him Daniel. He's treating her for deafness, she can't hear a word, so we brought our things down after we closed up in Ealing, that's why it's so crowded, two of everything, I have to laugh."

"So you don't own the house?"

"Oh, no, dear—oh, no," Mrs. Smith said, frightened of the idea. "He wants something bigger. He wants space for his work."

Mrs. Smith hesitated and looked at the wall through which the sound of Mr. Smith's voice was coming. And then, fearing she had been disloyal, she said, "She's much better. She's very funny. She came down yesterday calling him. 'Daniel. Daniel. I hear the cuckoo.' Of course I didn't say anything: it was the man calling out "Coal." But she is better. She wouldn't have heard him at all when we came here."

They were both silent.

"You can't live your life from A to Z," Mrs. Smith said, waking up. "We all make mistakes. We've been married for forty-two years. I expect you have your troubles too, even in that lovely place."

After the hour Mr. Smith came into the kitchen to get Mrs. Johnson.

"What a chatter!" he said to her. "I never heard such a tittle-tattle in my life."

"Yes, we had a fine chat, didn't we?"

"Oh, yes," said Mrs. Smith boldly.

"How is it going on?" said Mrs. Johnson.

"Now, now," Mr. Smith corrected her. "These cases seemingly take time. You have to get to the bottom of it. We don't intend to, but we keep people back by the thoughts we hold over them."

And then, in direct attack on her—"I don't want you to hold no wrong thoughts over me. You have no power over divine love." And he turned to his wife to silence her.

"And how would I do that?" said Mrs. Johnson.

"Cast the mote out of thine own eye," said Smith. "Heal yourself. We all have to." He smiled broadly at her.

"I don't know what all this talk about divine love is," said Mrs. Johnson. "But I love Mr. Armitage as he is."

Smith did not answer.

Armitage had found his way to the door of the kitchen. He listened and said, "Good-bye, Mrs. Smith." And to Mr. Smith: "Send me your bill. I'm having the footpath closed."

They drove away.

"I love Mr. Armitage as he is." The words had been forced out of her by the detestable man. She hated that she had said to him what she could not say to Armitage. They surprised her. She hoped Armitage had not heard them.

He was silent in the car. He did not answer any of her questions.

"I'm having that path closed," he repeated.

I know! she thought. Smith has said something about me. Surely not about "it"!

When they got out of the car at the house he said to the chauffeur, "Did you see Mr. Smith when he came up here three weeks ago? It was a Thursday. Were you down at the pool?"

"It's my afternoon off, sir."

"I know that. I asked whether you were anywhere near the pool. Or in the garden?"

"No, sir."

Oh, God, Mrs. Johnson groaned. Now he's turned on Jim.

"Jim went off on his motorbike. I saw him," said Mrs. Johnson.

They went into the house.

"You don't know who you can trust," Armitage said and went across to the stairs and started up. But instead of putting his hand to the rail which was on the right, he put it out to the left, and not finding it, stood bewildered. Mrs. Johnson quietly went to that side of him and nudged him in the right direction.

When he came down to lunch he sat in silence before the cutlets on his plate.

"After all these years! I know the rail is on the right and I put out my left hand."

"You just forgot," she said. "Why don't you try forgetting a few more things?"

She was cross about the questioning of the chauffeur.

"Say, one thing a day," she said.

He listened and this was one of those days when he cruelly paused a long time before replying. A minute went by and she started to eat.

"Like this?" he said, and he deliberately knocked his glass of water over. The water spread over the cloth towards her plate.

"What's this silly temper?" she said, and lifting her plate away, she lifted the cloth and started mopping with her table napkin and picked up the glass.

"I'm fed up with you blind people," she said angrily. "All jealousy and malice, just childish. You're so clever, aren't you? What happened? Didn't that good Mr. Smith do the magic trick? I don't wonder your wife walked out on you. Pity the poor blind! What about other people? I've had enough. You have an easy life; you sail down in your Rolls and think you can buy God from Mr. Smith just because—I don't know why—but if he's a fraud you're a fraud." Suddenly the wronged inhabitant inside her started to shout: "I'll tell you something about that Peeping Jesus: he saw the lot. Oh, yes, I hadn't a stitch on. The lot!" she was shouting. And then she started to unzip her dress and pull it down over her shoulder and drag her arm out of it. "You can't see it, you silly fool. The whole bloody Hebrides, the whole plate of liver."

And she went to his place, got him by the shoulder and rubbed her stained shoulder and breast against his face.

"Do you want to see more?" she shouted. "It made my husband sick. That's what you've been sleeping with. And"—she got away as he tried to grip her and laughed—"you didn't know! *He* did."

She sat down and cried hysterically with her head and arms on the table.

Armitage stumbled in the direction of her crying and put his hand on her bare shoulder.

"Don't touch me! I hate your hands." And she got up, dodged round him to the door and ran out sobbing; slower than she was, he was too late to hear her steps. He found his way back to the serving hatch and called to the cook.

"Go up to Mrs. Johnson. She's in her room. She's ill," he said.

He stood in the hall waiting; the cook came downstairs and went into the sitting-room.

"She's not there. She must have gone into the garden." And then she said at the window, "She's down by the pool."

"Go and talk to her," he said.

The cook went out of the garden door and on to the terrace. She was a thin round-shouldered woman. She saw Mrs. Johnson move back to the near side of the pool; she seemed to be staring at something in the water. Then the cook stopped and came shouting back to the house.

"She's fallen in. With all her clothes on. She can't swim. I know she can't swim." And then the cook called out, "Jim! Jim!" and ran down the lawns.

Armitage stood helpless.

"Where's the door?" he called. There was no one there.

Armitage made an effort to recover his system, but it was lost. He found himself blocked by a chair, but he had forgotten which chair. He waited to sense the movement of air in order to detect where the door was, but a window was half open and he found himself against glass. He made his way feeling along the wall, but he was travelling away from the door. He stood still again, and smelling a kitchen smell he made his way back across the centre of the long room and at last found the first door and then the door to the garden. He stepped out, but he was exhausted and his will had gone. He could only stand in the breeze, the disorderly scent of the flowers and the grass mocking him. A jeering bird flew up. He heard the gardener's dog barking below and a voice, the gardener's voice, shouting "Quiet!" Then he heard voices coming slowly nearer up the lawn.

"Helen," called Armitage, but they pushed past him. He felt her wet dress brush his hand and her foot struck his leg; the gardener was carrying her.

"Marge," Armitage heard her voice as she choked and was sick.

"Upstairs. I'll get her clothes off," said the cook.

"No," said Armitage.

"Be quiet," said the cook.

"In my room," said Armitage.

"What an idea!" said the cook. "Stay where you are. Mind you don't slip on all this wet."

He stood, left behind in the hall, listening, helpless. Only when the doctor came did he go up.

She was sitting up in bed and Armitage held her hand.

"I'm sorry," she said. "You'd better fill that pool up. It hasn't brought you any luck."

Armitage and Mrs. Johnson are in Italy now; for how long it is hard to say. They themselves don't know. Some people call her Mrs. Armitage, some call her Mrs. Johnson; this uncertainty pleases her. She has always had a secret and she is too old, she says, to give up the habit now. It still pleases Armitage to baffle people. It is impossible for her to deny that she loves Armitage, because he heard what she said to Smith; she has had to give in about that. And she does love him because his system has broken down completely in Italy. "You are my eyes," he says. "Everything sounds different here." "I like a bit of noise," she says.

Pictures in churches and galleries he is mad about and he likes listening to her descriptions of them and often laughs at some of her remarks, and she is beginning, she says, to get "a kick out of the classical stuff" herself.

There was an awkward moment before they set off for Italy when he made her write out a cheque for Smith and she tried to stop him.

"No," he said. "He got it out of you. I owe you to him."

She was fighting the humiliating suspicion that in his nasty prying way Smith had told Armitage about her before *she* had told him. But Armitage said, "I knew all the time. From the beginning. I knew everything about you."

She still does not know whether to believe him or not. When she does believe, she is more awed than shamed; when she does not believe she feels carelessly happy. He depends on her entirely here. One afternoon, standing at the window of their room and looking at the people walking in the lemonish light across the square, she suddenly said, "I love you. I feel gaudy!" She notices that the only thing he doesn't like is to hear a man talk to her.

A Debt of Honour

Mrs. Thwaite got off the bus and turned the street corner, holding her key ready to get into her new flat. Every evening, for months now, she was eager to be home, to sniff the new paint and to stand looking at the place, wanting to put her arms round it. She ran up the stairs, let herself in and threw her old fur coat on the divan in the sitting-room, put the gas poker in the fire and drew the curtains which did not quite meet, as if—by her intention—they had been carelessly made so as to let a little of the shabby Square and a stare of the London night into the flat. Then she went into the bedroom to see to the bed she had left unmade all day; almost at once she was sitting on the edge of it laughing, and telephoning to dear Argo—as she called him—to ask him to guess what she had found: his wristwatch under the pillow! And in a lower voice: "Oh, wasn't it lovely?"

She was swinging the wristwatch in her hand, Argo was saying he would be round, as usual, at half past seven, and just then the doorbell gave its ugly little buzz.

"Hold on a minute, darling. Someone at the door."

When she got there, still dangling the watch, she saw a man with his hat in his hand standing there, a short figure with silver hair brushed straight back and wearing a silvery-grey overcoat. His face looked like a white blown-out paper bag. Long afterwards, she used to say he had the gleam of a simulacrum or a ghost. Then the paper bag burst and he showed his teeth in a smile. She instantly hid the watch in her hand. The teeth were unmistakable. They were not false teeth, but they looked false because they were not closely set; they were a squad of slight gaps, but the gaps were a little wider now than they had been nine years ago in her short married life. Her husband was standing there.

"Hullo, Phoebe," he said, and with that he marched in past her across the little hall into the middle of the sitting-room. He was much shorter than she was. She was a very tall woman and instinctively she stooped (as she had always done with him) when she followed the gleam of his overcoat into the room.

He turned round and said at once, "Nice place. Newly decorated. Frankly I didn't expect it in a neighbourhood like this." He marked at once his disappointment with her. After nine years, he conveyed, she had gone downhill.

Mrs. Thwaite could not speak. A long scream seemed to be frozen in her. The shock was that, but for his teeth, Charles Thwaite was unrecognizable. She might have been telling lies about him for years.

He had been a bland little dark-haired pastry-fed fellow from the North when they had first gone off together, her fur-coat collar sticking to the frost inside the window of the night train. What a winter that was! He was a printer but had given that up, a man full of spit when he talked and his black eyebrows going up like a pair of swallows. The kind of man who said, "When I believe in a thing I put everything on it. Every penny in the bank, house, wife, children, shirt—everything." Even in those days his face had been blown out. Under the eyebrows there were a pair of earnest eyes fixed in an upward look, the eyes of a chapel-going boy caught with a finger in the jam pot; under them were curious, almost burned scoops of brown shadow—trademarks of a fate, the stamp of something saleable, they had seemed to her. She could never stop wondering what it was.

But now, as she stood there with her hands clenched upon Argo's watch, and looking down at her husband she saw that age had efficiently smoothed him. The stains were like hard coins; his effect was metallic. He looked collected, brisk and dangerous. And she had forgotten how short he was, for her Argo was a tall man.

What came back to her in the instant of this meeting was the forgotten, indignant girlish feeling—which living with Argo had cured her of—that she was lanky and exposed. If she had been able to move from where she was standing, she would have made a grab at her coat in order to cover herself and especially to cover her legs. She had the sensation that she had become a joke once more.

For, to start with, her height had always been ridiculous. Men passing in the street turned to look up at her, startled and in dismay, and she was not a beauty; her features were too large. And jokes attract jokes; only stumpy little fellows—her husband was one of them—ever looked twice at her, and with a very trying ambition or impudence puffing themselves out. She had had the timid impression that men were playing a game of hide-and-seek round her, as boys playing in the street sometimes did still. This made her either stare crushingly over their heads or droop like a schoolgirl. In her early meetings with Charles she had got into the habit of finding a long low seat and at a distance from him where she could sit down, draw up her long legs, and listen, an equal on the same level. Being tall had turned her into a believer and listener, listening being a kind of apology; and she would look covertly down at her legs with a reproach that would change to a pout; for—when she had been with Charles—she was proud of the dashing way in which her legs had rushed her into this love affair and marriage and had disorganized her life. Nowadays, even with Argo, she would look at her legs with fear, thinking they belonged to someone else or were a pair of fine but disobedient daughters. What they had done to her, carrying her into that story of disaster! But the story itself, of course, had attracted Argo, and she had come to feel that she had the grand distinction of being a woman to whom happiness and good luck were pettily irrelevant.

One Sunday Argo looked at his feet sticking out boastfully from the bottom of the bed and said, "Don't talk nonsense. Nine years is a long time. Your husband may be dead."

"Oh, no!" She still wanted her husband to be alive—and not for the sake of vengeance only.

"If he were, we could get married. Anyway, the law could presume death . . ." Argo went on.

She was happy with Argo after years of misery. But she wouldn't have *that.* She did not quite want to lose the gamble, the incompleteness—so breathlessly necessary to her—of her history.

History was standing there at ease, looking at the flat.

"I've given you a surprise," her husband said.

"What do you want?" She could speak at last. "I can't have you here. I have people coming."

"May I take my coat off?" he said, and taking it off put it down beside hers on the divan.

"New?" he said, looking at hers.

At that her courage returned to her. "That's the only thing you left me with," she almost shouted and was ready to fly at him if he touched it. For in this frightened moment the coat, poor as it was, seemed to be her whole life—more than the office she worked in, more than Argo, more than her marriage. It was older than any of them. It was herself; it had known her longer than anything in the room.

Her husband turned away contemptuously, and while she un-clenched her hands and put Argo's watch on the mantelpiece he sat down in an armchair. As his eyes stripped the room, he said, "Very nice, very nice. Kitchen there, I suppose. Bedroom through the door. Is that rug Chinese? I'm glad you're comfortable. You haven't changed. I must say you're very beautiful. By the way, I think you've left the telephone off in the bedroom—I can hear it crackling. Put it back, will you? Naturally I want to say a few words, to explain . . ."

"Say a few words"—how the phrase came back! There would be a lot of phrases.

She was determined not to sit down. The crackling of the telephone made her feel Argo was near.

An explanation! She wanted to demand it, rage for it, but she could not get the word out. She wanted to say, "Why? I just want to know why you left me. Don't imagine that I care, but I have a right to know. Then go."

"I found the address in the telephone book," he said, noting how well the world was organized. Then he made his announcement. It was more; it was a pronouncement, made with the modesty of an enormous benefactor.

"I have come back to you," he said.

"Argo, he's going to kill us," she wanted to cry out, and moved behind her chair for protection. The chair, the whole room seemed to be sickening, sliding her into the past, out of the window, into the flat she and her husband had had—the flat at the top of the small hotel she had bought for them with her own money—to those terrible scenes, to the sight of him opening the drawers of her desk in the little office, to that morning when she had unlocked the safe and found all the money gone—eight hundred pounds. Two of her father's pictures as well—but he left the frames behind!—and with them the foreign girl in Number 7. She held the chair tightly to hold the drifting room still. There he sat and, by merely sitting, occupied more and more of the room until only the few inches where she stood belonged to her. Nothing in the room, the pictures, the tables, the curtains, chairs, not even the little blue pot on the mantelpiece with pencils in it, came to her help. She would have to pass him to shout from the window.

"You are a very beautiful woman," he said in his praying, looking-skyward manner, but now the look was obsequious. "You are the most beautiful woman I have ever known. You are the only woman I have been in love with."

"You cannot break into my life like this," she said. "I have never been taken in by flattery."

"You are my wife," he said.

"I am certainly not," she said. "What is it you want?" And then she felt tears on her cheeks; ruinous tears, for this was the moment when he would get up and put his arms round her and she would be helpless. She tried to glare through her tears and did not know that this made her look brilliant, savage and frightening, indeed not helpless at all.

"I want *you*," he said, without moving.

It was so wonderfully meaningless to hear him say this. Her tears stopped and she laughed loudly and did not know she was laughing. The laughter chased the fright out of her body. The joke restored her. That was the rock she stood on: a joke had been played on her when she was a child. She must put up with being a collection of jokes, but this joke was so preposterous that it drove all the others out. She could feel her laughter swallowing the little man up. It was wonderful also to see how her laughter took him aback and actually confused him so that he raised his chin and held up his hand to silence her. He had a small white hand. She remembered that this meant he was going to make a moral statement.

"I am a man who has sacrificed himself to women," he said, pointing to this as one of his unanswerable historic benefactions.

Another of his sayings! How she longed for Argo to come in and hear it. Charles was a man who had always gone blandly back to first principles. Argo never quite believed the things she said about her marriage.

" 'I am a man who has sacrificed myself to women'—it was one of the first things he said to me when I met him. It was that cold winter, the worst winter for seventeen years—I told you my coat stuck to the frosty window in the train—shall I tell you about it? You don't mind? There was an election. He was—you won't believe, but it is true, it was one of his 'ideas'—standing for Parliament. Can you see him? He was standing as an Independent Republican—can you imagine it—in England, in the twentieth century! A gang of youths went round his meetings and sang 'Yankee Doodle' when he was speaking. Of course he didn't get in. He got two hundred and thirty-five votes. He lost his deposit. There was a row in the town. They were afraid he was splitting the vote. Splitting—he didn't even touch it! I was staying at the only hotel, a freezing-cold place. I had gone north to see my brother, who was in hospital. Charles was always rushing in and out of the hotel, telephoning to his wife in London, who was behaving very well—they were being divorced but she was holding the divorce up to stop the scandal—and to his mistress, who was very tiresome. You could hear what he was saying all over the hotel because the telephone box was in the hall and he came out of it one evening and knew that I had heard. I was sitting wrapped up because I couldn't get near the fire.

" 'You look warm,' he said, and then he looked back at the telephone box and said—well, that sentence. His set piece: 'I've sacrificed myself to women.' "

(What she did not tell Argo was that the remark was true. The scoundrel had "sacrificed" himself to women and that this was what had attracted her. She really had wanted in her naïve way to be the chief altar.)

"I told my brother when I went to the hospital. He said, 'He certainly doesn't sacrifice himself to anything else.' "

Now as he sat there in her flat and her laughter was warming her, Charles went one better.

"Everything I have done," he said, "I have done for you. Oh, yes, I have. You have been the cause and inspiration of it. You are the only woman who has influenced my mind. You changed my life. You were the making of me. When I went to South America . . ."

"Not South America!" she said. "Really! Think of something better than that. Monte Carlo. Cape Town."

"Buenos Aires first of all, then Chile—the women have beautiful voices there: it is the German and English influence," he went on, taking no notice of her. "Colombia—there's a culture that has collapsed. Bolivia, an extreme revolutionary situation, Ecuador, Indians in trilby hats looking like wood. I met the President. I've just come from Barranquilla. I flew."

"With that girl?" she said. A bad slip. He'd be the first to note her jealousy and mock it.

"Of course not," he said. He had a flat Yorkshire accent. "I have always been interested, as you know, in the Republican experience. You remember the book you made me write?"

"You didn't write it!" she said.

It was fabulous, after nine years, to see again his blank, baby-like effrontery, to hear his humourless, energetic innocence. He wasn't joking: the scoundrel *was* seriously, very seriously interested in republics! In a moment, he would tell her that he had stolen eight hundred pounds from her and deserted her out of a pure, disinterested passion for a harem of republics in South America!

The dangerous thing was that he was manoeuvring her back to the time of their marriage. She could feel him re-creating their marriage, against all her resistance, so that the room was filling with it. She feared he would wait for some sign of weakness, and then leap at her; the little man was very strong. She saw that he was already undressing the years from her and taking her back to her naked folly and credulity; until, if she was not careful, he would bring her to the point of the old passion. The Republic—it was incredible to remember—he had caught her with it.

It was a shock to her to remember what she had been like in those days—for example, how for years she had nursed her mother and had no friends. Every day she pushed the old lady down the sea front in her chair. Men looked at her or rather stepped back in half-grinning astonishment at a young woman so lanky, so gauche and shy and craving. The sight of her scared them. When her mother died, she got away to London. She had a little money which she knew she must be careful with and tried to find a job. Living alone, she simply read. Her tallness made her crave, and since no man came near her she craved for an idea.

So she was divided now between impatience and the memory he was rousing in her. She saw a half-empty room in that Town Hall in the North and him on the platform, uttering the fatal word, at the end of his speech. Republic—all men equal—equal height, perhaps that was the lure?—and so on: Republic. Quoted Plato even: "Love the beloved Republic." In a small industrial town, the war just over, snow frozen to black rock for six weeks on the pavements outside; and the small audience of men just back from the war, breaking up, drifting out, the gang of louts singing their "Yankee Doodle." She saw herself, exalted, turning in anger on the bored people around who were so rudely getting out and clattering their chairs; and gazing back at him, she signalled to him, "Yes, yes, yes, the Republic!" And when he lost, she really felt *she* would be the Republic! She had told Argo about this. "How I hate that word now. I can't even bear to read it in the newspapers. I was mad," she said. Argo could be very nasty sometimes. He said, "I thought it was only men who went to bed with an idea."

She had to admit, as she listened, that dear Argo knew little about women. She had had two triumphs in her marriage: she had won a short period of power over her husband by persuading him that if he thought so much about republics he ought to write a book about them. She put her money into a small London hotel and drove him off to the British Museum to write it. If she had thought, she would have seen it was the ideal place for picking up foreign girls; but never mind about that. The other triumph was more important. She had beaten those two women, his wife in London and his mistress who was there in the North working for him. She—and the winter—had frozen them out.

Her husband was now in San Tomás—was it?—and in the midst of the mulatto problem.

"Where did you get the money?" she said coldly.

"Money?" he said. "I went back to the printing trade."

It was the first hint of reproach. She had persuaded him to give up that trade. Once she had got him she had been going to turn him into a political thinker. She had always said grandly to her friends: "He's in politics." Now she noticed a little colour come to his face and that he was patting his small hand up and down on the arm of the chair in a dismissing way, as he had always done when money was mentioned. She had asked, she knew, the right question: indifference had made her intelligent.

"The heat was awful," he was saying. "When you go out into the street it is like a wall standing against you—I was glad you weren't there"—he had the nerve to say—"it shuts you in. I used to change my clothes four or five times a day . . ."

"Expensive," she said. "I couldn't have afforded it." He ignored this: no irony ever touched him.

"The only air-conditioned place was the casino and the cinema. The printing press was always breaking down. I was doing repairs half the time. I've not much use for casinos but I used to go there to cool off."

He raised his eyes seriously in the manner of the schoolboy now licking the spoon—who was he raising them to? Some feared school-master, preacher or father?—and she remembered with pleasure that this presaged the utterance of some solemn, earnestly believed untruth.

"I have never been a gambling man," he said, "as you know—but there the casino is packed every night. You have to get a permit, of course. Thousands change hands. I used to watch the tables and then go home along the shore road. I used to listen to the sea; you couldn't see the waves, except sometimes a flash of white, like Robin Hood's Bay on a rough night—remember, lass?"—dropping into broad Yorkshire —"Listen to this. One night when I went to the casino I had a shock: I saw *you*. I could have sworn it was you. You were standing there by one of the tables with a man, some politician: I knew him, the cousin of a man who owned one of the local papers. It was you, tall, beautiful, even the way you do your hair. I shan't forget the look in your eyes when you saw me. I thought: My God. I didn't do the right thing by her. I took her money. I have been a swine. I'll get the money and go back to her. I'll go down on my knees and beg her to take me back. You don't know what remorse is."

"Oh, so you've come to pay me back?" she said.

"I knew it wasn't you, but it showed how you've haunted my mind every night for the last nine years," he said. "I couldn't take my eyes off that woman. She was playing. I went close to her and I played. I followed her play and won. I kept winning. Her husband came and joined us and we were all winning and I thought all the time: This is for her. For her."

"For whom?" asked Mrs. Thwaite.

"For you."

"Did you sleep with her?"

"You can't sleep with those women. I was sleeping with an Indian girl," he said impatiently. "Don't interrupt me. It was for you. And then we started losing. I borrowed from her husband—he was excited like me. We all were. I'm not hiding anything. I lost everything I had. More than I had. A very large sum. I was ruined. Well, people are rich there. There was a thunderstorm that night. I couldn't pay for a taxi. The rain came down in sheets and the lightning was dancing about over the water in the streets. The whole place looked violet and yellow. I never saw anything like it. I wish you could have seen it. I stood there watching. You could see the sea, waves shooting up high, like hands. I thought, What have I done? What have I done to her?"

"Who?" she said.

"*You.* I thought, My God, suppose she is dead! I've never spent such a night in my life. At the door of the casino I heard that woman's voice. I thought it was yours. I went out. I went searching among the cars."

"And she wasn't there?"

"I was drenched. I was out in it for half an hour. I didn't know what I was doing."

"How did you pay back the money?" she said. "*Did* you pay it back?"

"Naturally," he said with stupendous coldness. "I had borrowed it from her husband. It was a debt of honour."

"Oh, honour," she said. "And what about the lady?" It shocked her that she felt that not quite conquerable disloyalty of the body when he mentioned the woman.

She had long ago admitted to herself that jealousy had been the foundation of her love for him. At the first sight of him in that hotel in the North, she had seen him sitting with three or four people near the fire. There was a cheerful vulgar fellow with drink-pimpled skin— his agent, no doubt. There was an elderly man who looked at him with a noble pathos and two grey-haired women who watched him with mistrust. They were talking about the meeting in the Town Hall and one said, "In this weather there'll be a poor turnout." A very thin young woman in a cheap black coat came in from the street kicking snow off her shoes and carrying a roll of posters which were packed in wet newspaper. Her stockings were wet. He went up to her quickly, scowling (but smiling too), and after taking the posters, he led the wretched girl by the arm not to the fire, but to the street door, speaking in a loud official voice about canvassing in the morning; at the door, he lowered his voice and said, shadily and sharply and intimately, looking into her defiant eyes: "I told you not to come here."

An intrigue! She heard it. A flare of desire to be part of it, and of jealousy, went through her, a sudden hungry jealousy. She had never felt like this until then, not at any rate since she was a child. She felt she had been set alight.

Now, nine years later, she said, "I don't know what you want. Why you're telling me this tale. It's all a lot of lies, I know. I never wanted to see you again, but now I'm glad you've come. Where are you staying? Give me your address. I want a divorce. I shall divorce you. It's not a question of what you want. It is what I want now."

She was fighting for Argo and herself.

"Just a moment," he said. "I haven't come to talk about divorces."

"You can't stay here," she said. "I won't have you here."

"Let me speak," he said. "I haven't come here to quarrel." And shyly
—how extraordinary to see him shy, for once—"I want your help. I
know I must have made you suffer. You have something rare in a
woman: integrity. You tell the truth."

"I'm certainly not going to help you about anything," she said.

"Divorce," he said. "Of course, I hadn't thought of that. It's natural,
of course: I'm a Catholic, but still . . ."

"Yes?" she said.

He tapped one of his teeth with his finger thoughtfully.

"Let's get to the point. I'm in a little difficulty. Let me go on with
what I was telling you. I've saved the printers a great deal of money
—the firm in San Tomás. They were going to be forced to buy a new
machine in New York, but I told them to wait, to let me work on it.
That's what I've been doing. I've saved them thousands. These South
Americans are no good at machinery. They just say, 'Buy a new one'
—like that. They've got piles of money."

Perhaps he *has* come to pay me back? Is that the idea—buying me
back? she wondered. The white hand went slowly up and down on the
arm of the chair.

"What is it you really came here for?" she said reasonably. A full
smile of pure, admiring pleasure made his white skin shine, a smile of
polite tenderness and discreet thanks.

"I want twelve hundred pounds," he said. "I had to borrow it from
the firm to pay that man—as I told you just now. I want it rather
quickly. The accountants come in at the end of the month. I want you
to lend it to me."

He said this in a voice of stupefying kindness and seriousness, as if
he were at last atoning for what he had done, unasked, in real friendship
and generosity. It would, he gravely conveyed, be the most binding of
ties. It would remind her of those happy days—ah, he too wished them
to return!—when he had had money from her before. He conveyed
that she would instinctively see the beauty of it—that he had come to
her, the perfect woman, a second time; that she was, in truth, the only
woman in his life, that of no one else would he ask such a thing.

And the strange part of it was that as she gasped at the preposterous
suggestion and was about to turn on him a small thrill went through
her. She was a prudent woman, if anything a shade mean about the
little money left to her, but he brought back to her the sense of
unreason and danger that had turned her head when she had first met

him. He brought back to her the excitement of the fact that he was
—as she knew—unbelievable. It enhanced some quality in her own
character: she was the kind of woman to whom mad things happened.
And she saw herself running to Argo with her astounded mouth open
and telling him, telling everyone. And, for a few seconds, she admired
her husband. Twelve hundred pounds! In nine years his price had gone
up!

"You stole twelve hundred pounds?" she said. "Fiddled the books?"

"Stole?" he said. "I don't like to hear you use a word like that. I
borrowed it. I told you. It was a debt of honour."

"You must be mad to think I would be such a fool. I haven't got
twelve hundred pence. I've never had such a sum in my life."

Stole! Arrest! Prison! Perhaps he had already been in prison? Was
that why he was so pale? She was not frightened, but his case seemed
to taint herself.

"But you can raise it," he said briskly, dismissing what she said.

"I work for my living. I go to my office every day. I've had to. Where
do you think I could get the money?"

There was a silence filled by the enormity of that sum. He was
proposing to come here, settle here, and tie that huge debt to her neck,
like a boulder. Argo must turn him out. He must come and turn him
out.

"I was very sorry to see—when was it? I saw an English paper over
there—that your aunt had died," he said in a changed and sorrowful
voice. "I think you *can* raise it," he said suddenly, coolly threatening.

"Ah!" She woke up to it. "*Now* I see why you have come back to
me. You thought I had just come into her money. You saw it in the
paper and you came rushing back."

"It was coming to you. I remember you telling me. And I am your
husband."

"Well, if you want to know, it did *not* come to me. When you left
me, she blamed me, not you. But do you think even if I had, I would
give it to you? She left it to her brother."

"Your brother?" he said sharply.

"No, *her* brother," she said triumphantly.

"Is that true?"

"Ask him."

He took out a pocket notebook and turned over a page or two. "The
one in Newcastle?" he said. He had obviously been checking her family.

"You got nothing at all?" he said.

"No." And this time she really did shout at him.

"I can't believe it," he said curtly. "I just can't believe you can have been such a damn fool."

She could see he was affronted and injured. "I offer you everything," he seemed to say. "And you give me nothing."

There was a sneer on his papery face. The sneer, she knew, concealed desperation and she felt the beginnings of pity, but she knew now—what she had not known nine years ago—that this pity was dangerous to her; he would see it at once, and he would come towards her, grip her arm, press upon her, ignoring her mind but moving her body. He had a secret knowledge of her, for he had been the first to know that her body was wild.

She was frightened of herself. She had to get out of the room, but each room was a trap. The only hope was the most dangerous room: the bedroom. It had a telephone in it.

"Argo, Argo, please come. Hurry," she was crying to herself. But her husband did not step towards her, he went over to the mantelpiece and he was looking at something on it. He picked up Argo's watch. She moved to snatch it from him, but he closed his hand. She actually touched his sleeve: touching him made her feel sick.

"Beginning all over again, I see," he said. "Does he live here?"

"That's my business."

"Snug under the coat?" He laughed and let the watch dangle by its strap. She was blushing, and almost gasping, fearing he would now attack her.

But he did not.

"You realize, I hope, that you are committing adultery?" he said stiffly. "I don't understand what has happened to you. You seem to have gone to pieces since I left you. I was surprised to see you living in a low-class district like this—what is he? Some clerk? You can't even manage your own money. Left it to her brother! How often I've told you—you never had any sense of reality. And by the way," he went on angrily, "if you had not left all your money in the safe, none of this would have happened. You should have paid it into the bank."

"He is not a clerk," she said. "He's a professor in the university."

He laughed. "That's what you wanted me to be. You are just romantic. The printing trade was not good enough for the lady."

"I didn't want you to be a professor."

"Write about the Republic. What republic?" he jeered.

"It was your idea," she said.

"Sitting in the British Museum, coming round to you for my money. I sacrificed myself to you. Why? I have always sacrificed myself to women. I loved you and you ruined me."

"I don't believe you ever went to the museum," she said, "except to pick up girls."

"To think of my wife committing adultery!" he exclaimed. And—she could not believe her luck—he put the watch back on the mantelpiece with disgust. He ran his fingers on the mantelpiece and saw dust on his fingers.

"You don't look after your things. There are cigarette burns on this mantelpiece. I don't like your pictures—one, two, three nudes. Indecent. I don't like that. I suppose that is how you see yourself."

He mooched about the flat and pointed at the frayed lining of her coat on the divan.

"That ought to have gone to the furrier's," he said. He stared at the coat and his temper quietened.

"It was a very cold winter, wasn't it?" he said. "The worst winter for years. It cut down the canvassing, I couldn't get people to the polls. It wasn't that, though. Do you know what lost me that election? Your coat. That was a true thing Jenny said after you saw me tell her to keep out of the hotel. 'We're up against those hard-faced Tory women in their mink.' "

"It's not mink," she said.

"Whatever it is. Of course she was suspicious. But that wasn't the trouble. She was just freezing cold. Her room was an icebox. She couldn't stand it. She was coughing even when we started. She went off."

He suddenly laughed. "She was frozen out. You had a fur coat, she hadn't. Your coat won. Fourteen Purser Street, do you remember?—it kept us warm, after she had gone?"

"She didn't go for a week," she said. After all, she had sat her rival out. But Mrs. Thwaite was watching for her opportunity. How to get past him and snatch back the watch? She saw her chance and grabbed it. He was taken by surprise and did not, as she feared he would, catch her arm.

"I feel sick," she said and rushed with her handkerchief to her mouth to the bedroom.

She sat on the bed and heard the crackling of the telephone receiver, which she had not replaced. She put it back and then took it off to dial Argo's number, looking in fear at the door she had left open.

"Darling, darling. Charles has come back. My husband, yes. Yes, he's here. I am frightened. He won't go. I can't get him out. Please come, he's horrible. What are we to do? No, if he sees you he will go. Call the police? How can I do that? He's my husband. He's in the sitting-room, he's moving about. I can hear him. Get a taxi. I'm afraid. I'm afraid of what he'll do. I can't tell you. Get him out? How can I? Oh, please, thank you, darling, thank you, I love you . . . He's horrible."

She put down the telephone and moved away, standing with her back to the window. If he came into the bedroom she would open the window and jump out. But he did not. He seemed to be picking up things in the sitting-room. She went back boldly now. He had picked up her coat and was holding it by the shoulders.

"Get out. Put that down. Get out. I have my own life now. I never want to set eyes on you again. I'm going to divorce you. I have rung for help." She was astonished by her own power and the firmness of her voice.

"Yes, I heard you," he said. He had put his overcoat on again.

"And put my coat down!" she shouted again.

They stood outstaring each other. He was half smiling with passing admiration.

"No," he said, "I'll take it with me. A souvenir. Good-bye."

She was flabbergasted to see him walk past her out of the room, open the door of the flat and go downstairs with her coat on his arm.

"Charles." She ran to the door. "Charles." He went on.

"Charles, come back here."

She was down at the street door, but already he was twenty yards away, crossing the street. He looked not so much ridiculous as luxurious carrying the coat. She felt he was carrying her off too. She shouted again but not loudly, for she did not want people to stare at them in the street. She was about to run after him when she saw the blind man who lived further down come tapping towards her with his white stick. He slowed down, sensing disturbance. He paused like a judgement. And in her pause of indecision, she saw her husband get to the bus stop and instantly, as if he were in league with buses and had bribed one or got it by some magic, a bus floated up beside him and he was off on it.

He had taken the last thing she had, he had taken twenty years of her life with him. She watched the bus until it was out of sight.

She went back to her door and she climbed the stairs and got inside and looked at the room where he had stood; it seemed to her that it was stripped of everything, even of herself. It seemed to her that she was not there. "Why are women so mad about furs?" he had once said to her. "To keep warm? No, so that they can feel naked." One of his "sayings." But that was what she felt as she sat waiting for Argo to come; her husband had taken her nakedness.

Argo found her sitting there. When she stopped crying in his arms he said, "He won't come back. I'll get on to the police."

"Oh, no."

"He'll sell it. He was just after anything he could get. He might get fifty pounds for it."

"He was very jealous. He used to try to make me say some man had given it to me." She was proud of that. "He's a funny man. He may not sell it."

"You mean," said Argo who, though placating, had his nasty side, "he'll give it to one of his girl friends?"

"No," she said angrily. She was not going to have that! An old feeling, one she used to have, that there was something stupid about very tall men like Argo, came back to her.

In the night she lay awake, wondering where her husband was. Perhaps everything he said had been true: that he did love her more than any of the women he had known, that he did want to be forgiven, that she had been hard and was to blame from the beginning. He had remembered Purser Street. Perhaps he *had* been in South America. She wished she had had twelve hundred pounds to give him. She would never forgive herself if he was arrested. Then her thoughts changed and she fell into thinking in his melodramatic way: he had taken her youth, her naked youth, with him and left her an old woman. She got up in the night and went to her mirror to see how much grey there was in her hair. She was not very much younger than Charles. She went back cold to bed and put her arms round Argo.

"Love me. Love me," she said.

She hated Argo for saying that her husband had given the coat to another woman.

In the morning she went to her office.

"Someone walked into my flat yesterday and stole my fur coat," she said.

What a life, they said, that poor woman has had; something is always happening to her. It never ends. But they saw her eyes shining brilliantly within their gloom.

The Cage Birds

Just as he was getting ready to go to his office, the post came.

"A card from Elsie," Mrs. Phillips said. " 'Come on Wednesday. All news when we meet. I've got Some Things. Augusta.' " She turned the card over. There was a Mediterranean bay like a loud blue wide-open mouth, a small white town stretching to a furry headland of red rocks. A few villas were dabbed in and a large hotel. The branch of a pine tree stretched across the foreground of the picture, splitting the sea in two. Her husband had been brushing his jacket and stopped to look at the card: he started brushing again. In ten years, it seemed to her, he had brushed half the suit away: it was no longer dark grey but a parsimonious gleam.

They looked at each other, disapproving of the foreign scene; also of the name Elsie had given herself: Augusta. They had never got used to it.

"Ah-ha! The annual visit! You'd better go," he said. And then he laughed in his unnatural way, for he laughed only when there was no joke, a laugh that turned the pupils of his eyes into a pair of pinheads. "Before her maid gets hold of the things."

"I'll have to take the boy. It's a school holiday."

"Half fare on the bus," he said. "She always gives you something for the fare."

And he laughed at this too.

"She forgot last year," she said.

He stopped laughing. He frowned and reflected.

"You shouldn't let her forget. Fares have gone up. All across London! When I was a boy you could do it for sixpence. Get off at Baker Street—that'll save fourpence."

He put the brush down. He was a youngish man whose sleeves were too short, and he was restlessly rubbing his red hands together now, glistering at the thought of the economy; but she stood still, satisfied. When they were first married his miserliness had shocked her, but now she had fallen into abetting it. It was almost their romance; it was certainly their Cause. When she thought of the mess the rest of her family was in, she was glad to have years of girlhood anxiety allayed by a skinflint. She knew the sharp looks the shopkeepers and neighbours gave him when his eyes filled with tears as he haggled over a penny or two, and counted the change in his open martyred hand. But she stood by him obstinately, raising her chin proudly when, giving his frugal laugh, he cringed at a counter or a ticket office. He had the habit of stroking his hands over the legs of his trousers and smiling slyly at her when he had saved a penny, and she, in ten years of marriage, had come to feel the same small excited tingle in her own skin as he felt in his.

"Get out of my way. We're going to Auntie's tomorrow," she said to the boy when he came back from school in the afternoon. "Here" —and she gave him the postcard—"look at this."

She was in the kitchen, a room darkened by the dark blobs of the leaves of a fig tree hanging their tongues against the window. It was an old tree, and every year it was covered with fruit that looked fresh and hopeful for a few weeks, and then turned yellow and fell onto the grass, because of the failure of the London sun. The dirty-minded woman next door said those leaves put ideas into your head, but Mrs. Phillips couldn't see what she meant. Now she was ironing a petticoat to put on for the visit tomorrow and the boy was looking at the mole on her arm as it moved back and forth, her large grey eyes watching the iron like a cat. First the black petticoat, then her brassière, then her knickers; the boy watched restlessly.

"Mum. Where is Auntie's house?" the boy said, looking at the card.

"There," she said, straightening up and dashing a finger at random on the card.

"Can I swim?"

"No, I told you. We're not going there. We haven't got the money for holidays. That's where Auntie Elsie lives in the summer."

"Where's Uncle Reg?"

That was the trouble: the kid asking questions.

"I told you. He's gone to China, Africa—somewhere. Stop kicking your shoes. They're your school shoes. I can't afford any more."

Then she put down the iron with a clump and said, "Don't say anything about Uncle Reg tomorrow, d'you hear? It upsets Auntie."

"When are we going to see her?"

"Tomorrow. I keep telling you."

"On a bus?"

"On a bus. Here," she said, "give me those shirts of yours."

The boy gave her the pile of shirts and she went on working. She was a woman who scarcely ever sat down. She was wearing a black petticoat like the one she had ironed, her arms were bare, and when she lifted up a garment he could see the hair in her armpits; hair that was darker than the tawny hair that was loose over her sweating forehead. What disturbed the boy was the way she changed from untidy to tidy and especially when she put on her best blouse and skirt and got ready to go out. The hours he had to wait for her when, going to the cupboard and looking at the dresses hanging there, she changed herself into another woman!

She was this other woman the next day when they went off to the bus stop. She was carrying a worn, empty suitcase and walked fast, so he had almost to run to keep up with her. She was wearing a navy-blue dress. She had tied a grey-and-white scarf round her head, so that the pale face looked harder, older, and emptier than it was. The lips were long and thin. It was a face set in the past; for the moment it was urging her to where she was going but into the past it would eventually fall back. At the bus stop she simply did not see the other people standing there. The boy looked at her raised chin with anxiety, and when the bus came, she came down out of the sky and pushed the boy on and put the case under the stairs.

"You sit there," she said. "And see no one takes it."

The annual visit! Her sister had come over from that island in June this year, early for her. It used to be Christmas in Reg's time and, for that matter, in the time of that other man she had never met. This new one had lasted three years; he was called Williams and he was buying the headland on the postcard, and he was a June man. He couldn't stand the mosquitoes. Her sister said, "They suck his blood. He's like beef to them." But who was the bloodsucker? You ask *him*! Those women have to get it while they can. At the Ritz one minute—and the next where are they? She called herself Augusta now. But Grace stuck to calling her Elsie: it was virtuous.

London was cabbaged with greenery. It sprouted in bunches along the widening and narrowing of the streets, bulging at corners, at the awkward turnings that made the streets look rheumatic. There were wide pavements at empty corners, narrow ones where the streets were packed. Brilliant traffic was squeezing and bunching, shaking, spurting, suddenly whirling round bends and then dawdling in short disorderly processions like an assortment of funerals. On some windows the blinds of a night worker were drawn and the milk bottle stood untouched at the door; at the Tube, papers and cigarette litter blowing, in the churchyards women pushing prams. The place was a fate, a blunder of small hopes and admired defeats. By the river one or two tall new buildings stuck up, prison towers watching in the midst of it. The bus crossed the river and then gradually made north to the park and the richer quarters.

"There's your dad's shop," she said to the boy. They passed a large store.

"There's his window, first floor," she pointed up. That was where he worked in the week.

Now the streets were quieter, the paint was fresher, the people better dressed. By a church with a golden statue of St. George and the Dragon outside it, she got the boy off the bus and walked to a new building where there was a man in blue uniform at the door.

In this instant the boy saw his mother change. She stopped, and her grey eyes glanced to right and then to left fearfully. Usually so bold, she cringed before the white building and its balconies that stuck out like sun decks. She lowered her head when the porter with the meaty despising nose opened the door into the wide hall. She was furtive, and in the lift she tried to push the suitcase out of sight behind the boy; she felt ashamed. She also nervously trembled, fearing to be suspected of a crime.

"Take your cap off in the lift when you're with a lady," she said to the boy, asserting to the porter that she was respectable. With both hands the startled boy clawed the cap off his head.

The porter was not going to let them out of his sight. On the eleventh floor the doors slid open. Across another hall of carpet and mirrors which made her feel she was a crowd of women at many doors and not one, he led her to the door. The boy noticed it had no knocker. No bang, bang, bang, iron on iron, as on their door at home; a button was pressed and a buzz like hair spray at the barber's could be heard.

There were, he noticed, white bars behind the figured glass on the door where ferns were frosted.

Presently a maid wearing a pretty apron opened the door and let them in, looking down at their shoes. A green carpet, mirrors framed in mirror again, hotel flowers, lilies chiefly, on a glass-topped table of white metal: the flat was like the hall outside. It smelt of scent and the air stood warm and still. Then they were shown into a large room of creamy furniture, green and white satin chairs. There were four wide windows, also with white metal strips on them, beyond which the fat trees of the park lolled. Did Auntie own them? At one end of the room was a small bar of polished bamboo. Then out of another room came Auntie herself, taking funny short steps which made her bottom shake, calling in a little girl's voice, "Grace!" She bent down low to kiss him with a powdery face, so that he could see the beginning of her breasts. Her brooch pricked his jersey, catching it. "Oh, we're caught." She disentangled it.

"It's torn my jersey," the boy whined.

"There you are. Look. I'll take it off and put it here." She put the brooch on the table.

"Umph. Umph," she said, going back to him and kissing him again. Auntie had the tidiness of a yellow-haired doll. She was as pink as a sugared almond and her kiss tasted of scent and gin.

"You've lost a lot, Grace," she said to her sister. "Look at me. It's that French food. I've put on seven pounds. It shows when you're small. Mr. Williams is coming today. I flew in yesterday from Paris. I've got some lovely things. It's no good anyone thinking they can leave me in Paris on my own."

"Is Uncle Reg in Paris?" said the boy.

His mother blushed.

"Keep quiet. I told you," she said with a stamp.

Elsie's round blue eyes looked at the boy and her lips pouted with seductive amusement. She wriggled a shoulder and moved her hips. The boy grew up as she looked at him.

"What do you like for tea? I've got something for you. Come with me and see Mary. Sit down, Grace."

When the boy had gone the two sisters took up what they felt to be their positions in the room. Grace refused to take off her scarf and refused also out of dread of contamination from the expense of the satin to sit back on the sofa; she kept to the edge from where she could get a good view of everything. Elsie sat with her beautiful silk legs drawn up on the seat of a chair and lit a cigarette and touched the hair that had been made into a golden crust of curls that morning.

Grace said, "The carpet's new."

"They never last more than a year," Elsie said with a cross look. She was pretty, therefore she could be cross. "People drop cigarettes. I had the whole place done." And with that she restlessly got up and shut a window.

"The curtains as well. Mr. Williams paid five hundred pounds for the curtains alone! I mean—you've got to be kind to yourself. No one else will be. We only live once. He spent nearly as much on the bedroom. I saw the bills. Come and look at it."

She got up and then sat down again. "We'll see it in a minute."

"You're all barred in," Grace said.

"We had burglars again. I just got in—Mr. Williams took me to Ascot. He likes a bit of racing—and I rushed back, well, to tell you the truth I must have eaten something that didn't agree with me, duck pâté I think that's what it was, and I had to rush. He must have followed me in, this man, I mean, and when I came out my handbag was open and he had cleared a hundred and fifty pounds. Just like that." She lowered her voice. "I don't like the man on the lift. Then at Christmas when we were on the island they came in again. The staff here were off duty, but you'd have thought people would see. Or hear . . . That's what staff is like these days."

"What happened?"

"They took my mink coat and the stole, and a diamond clasp, a diamond necklace and Mr. Williams's coat, a beautiful fur-lined coat —he carried on, I can tell you—and all my rings. Well, not all. We got insurance but I don't keep anything here now except what I'm wearing. The brooch—did you see it? Mr. Williams gave it to me as a consolation, I was so upset. Pictures, that's where he puts his money usually. Everything's going up. You want to put your money into things. That's why we put those bars on the door and the windows. And —come here, I'll show you."

They walked into the bedroom and on the door that gave on to the balcony there was a steel grille that closed like a concertina.

"You're caged in," said Grace.

Elsie laughed.

"It's what Mr. Williams said. Funny you should say it. He likes a joke—Reg could never see one, d'you remember? 'Birdie—we'll keep you in a cage.' Ah now"—she pointed to the white bed where dresses were laid out—"here it all is. I've picked them all out."

But Grace was looking at a white cupboard with a carved and gilded top to it. The doors were open and thrown inside was a pile of summery hats; some had fallen out onto the violet carpet of the bedroom. Half of them were pink—"My colour."

"Oh," said Elsie in a bored voice, already tired of them. "That's what I got in Paris. I told you. On the way back."

Elsie led her sister out of the bedroom again.

The cringing had gone; Grace sat stiffly, obstinately, hardened, without curiosity, looking at the luxury of the room.

"I heard from Birmingham the day before yesterday," she said in a dead voice.

Elsie's pretty face hardened also.

"Mother's ill," said Grace.

"What is it?" said Elsie.

"Her legs."

"I hope you didn't tell her this address," Elsie accused.

"I haven't written yet."

"Grace," said Elsie in a temper, "Mother has her life. I have mine. And she never writes."

She went to the bar, saying in the middle of her temper, "This is new. I know it's no good asking you," and she poured herself a glass of gin and vermouth and then resumed her temper, raising her small plump doll's chin so that Grace should know why her chin and throat and shoulders could, when her lips pouted and her eyes moistened, draw men's eyes to the hidden grave gaze of her breast. Men would lower their heads as if they were going to jump and she kept her small feet nimble and ready to dodge. It was a dogma in the minds of both sisters that they were (in different but absolute ways) who they were, what they were, on their own and immovable in unwisdom. This was their gift, the reward for a childhood that had punished them.

"Listen," said Elsie in her temper, "you haven't seen me. 'How is Elsie?' 'I don't know. I don't know where she is.' I've got my life. You've got yours. If Dad had been alive things would be different."

"I never say anything," said Grace grimly. "I mind my own business. I wouldn't want to say anything."

Suddenly Elsie became secretive.

"Mary," she nodded to the room where the maid and the boy were, "always has her eye on the clothes. I don't trust anybody. You know these girls. You have to watch them. 'Where's my red dress?' 'At the cleaner's, ma'am.' I wasn't born yesterday. But you can *use* them, Grace, I *know*. Let's go and look."

Gay and confiding, she took Grace back to the bedroom and looked at the dresses spread out on the bed. She held up a blue one.

"It's funny, I used to be jealous of your clothes. When we went to church," Elsie said. "Do you remember your blue dress, the dark-blue one with the collar? I could have killed you for it and the bank manager saying, 'Here comes the bluebird of happiness.' Aren't kids funny? When you grew out of it and it came down to me, I hated it. I wouldn't put it on. It was too long. You were taller than me then, we're the same now. Do you remember?"

"And here is a black," she said, holding up another. "Well, every picture tells a story. Mr. Williams threw it out of the window when we were in Nice. He has a temper. I was a bit naughty. This one's Italian. It would suit you. You never wear anything with flowers though, do you?"

She was pulling the dresses off the bed and throwing them back again.

"Reg was generous. He knew how to spend. But when his father died and he came into all that money, he got mean—that's where men are funny. He was married—well, I knew that. Family counted for Reg. Grace, how long have you been married?"

"Ten years," said Grace.

Elsie picked up a golden dress that had a paler metallic sheen to it, low in the neck and with sleeves that came an inch or two below the elbow. She held it up.

"This would suit you, Grace. You could wear this colour with your hair. It's just the thing for cocktails. With your eyes it would be lovely. Mr. Williams won't let me wear it, he hates it, it looks hard, sort of brassy on me—but you, look!"

She held it against her sister.

"Look in the mirror. Hold it against yourself."

Against her will Grace held it to her shoulders over her navy woollen dress. She saw her body transformed into a sunburst of light.

"Grace," said Elsie in a low voice. "Look what it does to you. It isn't too big."

She stepped behind and held the dress in at the waist. Grace stood behind the dress and her jaw set and her bones stiffened in contempt at first and then softened.

"There's nothing to be done to it. It's wonderful," said Elsie.

"I never go to cocktail parties," said Grace.

"Look. Slip it on. You'll see."

"No," said Grace and let go of a shoulder. Elsie pulled it back into place.

"With the right shoes," Elsie said, "that will lift it. Slip it on. Come on. I've never seen anything like it. You remember how things always looked better on you. Look."

She pulled the dress from Grace and held it against herself. "You see what I look like.

"No," she went on, handing it back. She went to the bedroom door and shut it and whispered, "I paid two hundred and forty pounds for it in Paris—if you're not going to wear it yourself you can't have it. I'll give it to Mary. She's had her eye on it."

Grace looked shrewdly at Elsie. She was shocked by her sister's life. From her girlhood Elsie had wheedled. She had got money out of their aunt; she drew the boys after her but was soon the talk of the town for going after the older men, especially the married. She suddenly called herself Augusta. It baffled Grace that men did not see through her. She was not beautiful. The blue eyes were as hard as enamel and she talked of nothing but prices and clothes and jewellery. From this time her life was a procession through objects to places which were no more than objects, from cars to yachts, from suites to villas. The Mediterranean was something worn in the evening, a town was the setting for a ring, a café was a looking-glass, a nightclub was a price. To be in the sun on a beach was to have found a new man who had bought her more of the sun.

Once she giggled to Grace: "When they're doing it—you know what I mean—that's when I do my planning. It gives you time to yourself."

Now, as Grace held the golden dress and Elsie said in her cold baby voice, "If you don't keep it to wear I'll give it to Mary," Grace felt their kinship. They had been brought up poor. They feared to lose. She felt the curious pleasure of being a girl again, walking with Elsie in the street and of being in the firm humouring position of the elder sister of a child who at that time simply amused them all by her calculations. Except for their father, they were a calculating family. Calculation was their form of romance. If I put it on, Grace thought, that doesn't mean I'll keep it for myself. I'll sell it with the rest.

"All right. I'll just try it," she said.

"I'll unzip you," said Elsie, but she let Grace pull her dress over her head, for the navy wool disgusted her. And Grace in her black slip pouted shyly, thinking, Thank heavens I ironed it yesterday. To be untidy underneath in an expensive flat like this—she would have been shamed.

She stepped into the golden dress and pulled it up and turned to the long mirror as she did this, and at once to her amazement she felt the gold flowing up her legs and her waist, as if it were a fire, a fire which she could not escape and which, as Elsie fastened it, locked her in. The mirror she looked in seemed to blaze.

"It's too long."

"We're the same height. Stand on your toes. Do you see?"

Grace felt the silk with her fingers.

"Take off your scarf."

Grace pulled it off. Her dead hair became darker and yet it, too, took on the yellow glint of the flame.

"It's too full," said Grace, for her breasts were smaller than Elsie's.

"It was too tight on me. Look!" Elsie said. She touched the material here and there and said, "I told you. It's perfect."

Grace half smiled. Her face lost its empty look and she knew that she was more beautiful than her sister. She gazed, she fussed, she pretended, she complained, she turned this way and that. She stretched out an arm to look at the length of the sleeve. She glowed inside it. She saw herself in Elsie's villa. She saw herself at one of those parties she had never been to. She saw her whole life changed. The bus routes of London were abolished. Her own house vanished and inside herself she cried angrily, looking at the closed door of the bedroom, so that her breasts pushed forward and her eyes fired up with temper: "Jim, where are you? Come here! Look at this."

At that very moment, the bedroom door was opened. The boy walked in and a yard behind him, keeping not quite out of sight, was a man.

"Mum," the child called, with his hands in his pockets, "there's a man."

The boy looked with the terror of the abandoned at the new woman he saw and said, "Where's Mum?" looking at her in unbelief.

She came laughing to him and kissed him. He scowled mistrustfully and stepped back.

"Don't you like it?"

As she bent up from the kiss she had a furtive look at the man in the room: Was it Mr. Williams? He was gazing with admiration at her.

But Elsie was quick. She left Grace and went into the sitting-room and Grace saw her sister stop suddenly and heard her say, in a voice she had never heard before—a grand stagy voice spoken slowly and arrogantly as if she had a plum in her mouth, her society voice: "Oh, you! I didn't invite you to call this afternoon." The man was dark and young and tall, dandified and sunburned. He was wearing a white polo-neck jersey and he was smiling over Elsie's golden head at Grace, who turned away at once.

Elsie shut the bedroom door. As she did so, Grace heard her sister say, "I have got my dressmaker here. It's very inconvenient."

To hear herself being called "my dressmaker" and not "my sister," and in that artificial voice, just at the moment of her stupefying glory, to have the door shut in her face! She stared at the door that separated them, and then in anger went over to the door and listened. The boy spoke.

"Ssh," said Grace.

"I am annoyed with you. I told you to telephone," Elsie was saying. "Who let you in?"

Grace heard him say, "Get rid of her. Send her away."

But Elsie was saying nervously, "How *did* you get in?"

And quite clearly the man said, "The way I went out last night, through the kitchen."

Grace heard a chair being pushed and Elsie say, "Don't, I tell you. Mr. Williams will be here. Stop."

"Here, help me," said Grace to the boy. "Pick them up." She had the suitcase on the bed and quickly started to push the dresses into her case. "Come on."

She tried to unzip the yellow dress but she could not reach.

"Damn this thing," she said.

"Mum, you said a word," said the boy.

"Shut up," she said. And giving up, she pushed the navy dress she had taken off into the case, just as Elsie came back into the room and said to the boy, "Go and talk to the gentleman." The boy walked backwards out of the room, gaping at his mother and his aunt until Elsie shut the door on him.

"Grace," she said in an excited, low voice, wheedling, "don't pack up. What are you doing? You're not going? You mustn't go."

"I've got to get my husband his supper," said Grace sharply. Elsie opened her handbag and pulled out a five-pound note and pushed it into Grace's hand. "There's time. That's for a taxi. Something awkward's happened. Mr. Williams will be here in a minute and I can't get rid of this man. I don't know what to do. It is a business thing about the villa and he's pestering me and Mr. Williams loathes him. I met him on the plane. I was very, very silly. If Mr. Williams comes, I'll say he's come with you from the dress shop. And you can leave with him."

"You *said* Mr. Williams knew him," said Grace with contempt.

"Did I? I was a bit silly," Elsie wheedled. "You know what a fool I am—I let this gentleman drive me from the airport—well, that's harmless, I mean . . . Grace, you look wonderful in that dress. I only mean go out of the flat *with* him." She looked slyly and firmly at Grace.

Into Grace's mind came that scene from their girlhood outside their school when Elsie made her stand with a young man and hold his arm to prevent him getting away while she fetched a new red coat. The young man had a marvellous new motorbike. It was the first time Grace had held a young man's arm. She would never forget the sensation and the youth saying: "She's a little bitch. Let's go."

And how, just as she was going to say wildly, "Oh, yes," and he squeezed her arm, Elsie came running back and pulled him to the motorbike and shouted to Grace, "So long!"

Grace hesitated now, but then she remembered Elsie's society voice: "My dressmaker." And with that she had a feeling that was half disgust and half fear of being mixed up in Elsie's affairs. For Grace the place was too grand. The lies themselves were too grand. And there was this revelation that for years, in every annual visit, Elsie had concealed and denied that they were sisters, just as she denied the rest of the family.

"No, Elsie," Grace said. "I've got to get back to Harry."

She was tempted to leave the suitcase, but she thought, She'd only think I'm a fool if I leave it.

"I'll take the case and I'd best go. Thanks, though, for the taxi."

"Good-bye, ma'am," she said to Elsie in a loud, proud voice as they went into the sitting-room.

"Come on," she called to the child. "Where are you?"

He was sitting on a chair staring at the man, and particularly at his jacket, as if his eyes were microscopes. The man had walked over to the window.

Grace took the boy by the hand.

"Say good-bye to the lady," Grace said, pulling the boy, who, scared still by the strangeness of his mother in her glory, said, "Good-bye, Auntie."

They sat in the taxi.

"Sit down," said Grace to the boy. He had never been in a taxi before. He took a timid look at her. She was overpowering.

"I haven't been in a taxi since your dad and I came back from our honeymoon," she said. London had changed. There were only doors to look at, doors at first of the rich houses in the park and herself arriving at them, being taken into drawing-rooms. She wished her suitcase was not so shabby. She would go into the doorways of hotels; palaces seemed familiar; streets wider; she looked at the windows of shoeshops. She looked at the handbags women were carrying. The taxi came to the river and there she gleamed as she passed over the sad, dirty, dividing water, but through the poorer streets, past the factories, the railway arches, the taxi went fast, passing the crowded buses. She was indignant with traffic lights that stopped them.

"Mum," said the boy.

She was daydreaming about the effect she would have on her husband when she opened the gate of her house.

"Do you like it?" she said.

"Yes. But, Mum . . ."

"Look," she said, excited, "we're nearly there. There's Woolworth's. There's Marks's. Look, there's Mrs. Sanders. Wave to Mrs. Sanders. I wonder if she saw us."

Then the taxi stopped at the house. How mean it looked!

"Your dad is home," she said as she paid the driver and then opened the gate and looked at the patch of flower bed. "He's been watering the garden." But when she was paying the taxi driver the door of the house opened and her husband stood there with his eternal clothes brush held in horror in the air. He gaped at her. His eyes became small.

"You took a cab!" he said, and looked as if he were going to run after it as it grunted off. "How much did you give him?"

"She paid," she said.

"Come in," he said. "Come in." And he went into the dark hall, put the brush down, and rubbed his hands as she lifted the suitcase into the house. The boy crept past them.

"What did he charge?" her husband said.

Not until then did he see the dress.

"Couldn't you get it into the case?" he said when they were in the small room that was darkened by the drooping bodies of the leaves of the fig tree. "That colour marks easily."

"That's why I took the cab."

She watched her husband's eyes as she posed, her own eyes getting larger and larger, searching him for praise.

"It wants the right shoes," she said. "I saw some as we came back just now, in Walton's."

She looked at him and the ghost of her sister's wheedling attitude came into her head as she let it droop just a little to one side.

"And my hair done properly. It blew about in the taxi. Jim was at the window all the time."

Her husband's eyeballs glistered with what looked like tears.

"You're not thinking of keeping it for yourself?" he said, his face buckling into smiles that she knew were not smiles at all.

"Why not?" she said, understanding him. "There's eighty pounds' worth in the case there."

"You're rich," he said.

She opened the case.

"Look," she said.

"You'd better get it off, you'll mark it cooking," he said, and went out of the room.

From her bedroom she saw him in the back garden spraying his roses and brushing the green fly off with his finger. He was shaking the syringe to see if there was a drop more in it and she heard him ask the boy if he had been playing with the thing and wasting the liquid.

She gave a last look at herself in the mirror. She despised her husband. She remembered the look of admiration on the face of the man in her sister's flat. She took off the dress and pulled her woollen one out of the case and put it on. The golden woman had gone.

That evening as they sat at their meal, her husband was silent. He grunted at her account of the visit. She did not tell him she had been called "the dressmaker." Her husband was sulking. He was sulking about the dress. She tried to placate him by criticizing her sister.

"There was a man there, someone she picked up on the plane. She was trying to get rid of him because this man with all the property, Mr. Williams, was expected. I don't envy her. She lives in a cage. Two burglaries they've had."

"They're insured." His first words.

She could still feel some of the gold of the dress on her skin, but as she went on about her sister, the grey meanness which in some way was part of her life with her husband, which emanated from him and which, owing to the poverty of her life as a girl, seemed to her like a resource—this meanness crept over her and coated her once more.

"And you talk of wearing the dress of a woman like that," he said. And then the boy said, with his mouth full of potato: "The man took Auntie's brooch off the table. I saw him. The pin was sticking out of his pocket. I saw it. It tore my best jersey."

"Tore your jersey!" said her husband.

"What's this?" they both said together, united. And they questioned the child again and again.

Husband and wife studied each other.

"That wasn't a pin," the father said to the boy.

"No," said his wife, in her false voice. "She'd got the brooch on." And she signalled to her husband, but her husband said to the boy, "Did he come in the taxi with you?"

"No," said the boy and his mother together.

"I asked the boy."

"No," said the boy.

"Just as well," he said to his wife. "You see what they might say when they find out. I told you I don't like you going to that place. You lose your head."

The next day she packed the gold dress with the rest and sold them all, as usual, to the dealers.

The Skeleton

Awful things happen to one every day: they come without warning and
—this is the trouble, for who knows?—the next one may be the Great
Awful Thing. Whatever that is.

At half past seven, just as the new day came aching into the London
sky, the waiter-valet went up in the old-fashioned lift of the Service
Flats with a tray of tea to Mr. Clark's flat on the top floor. He let
himself in and walked down the long, tiled hallway, through part of Mr.
Clark's picture collection, into the large sitting-room and, putting the
tray down on the desk, drew back the curtains and looked down on the
roofs. Arrows of fine snow had shot along the slate, a short sight of the
Thames between the buildings was as black as iron, the trees stuck out
their branches like sticks of charcoal, and a cutting wind was rumbling
and occasionally squealing against the large windows. The man wiped
his nose and then went off to switch on one bar of the electric fire—
he was forbidden to put on two—and moved the tray to a table by the
fire. He had often been scolded for putting the tray upon Clark's
valuable Chippendale desk, and he looked round to see if anything else
was out of place in this gentlemanly room where every flash of polish
or glass was as unnerving to him as the flash of old George Clark's
glasses.

With its fine mahogany, its glazed bookcases which contained a crack regiment of books on art in dress uniform, its Persian rugs, its bronzes, figurines and silken-seated chairs and deep sofa that appeared never to have been sat on, and on the walls some twenty-five oil paintings, the room had the air of a private museum. The valet respected the glass. He had often sat for a while at Mr. Clark's desk, gossiping with one of the maids while he saw to it that she did not touch the bronze and the Chinese figures—"He won't allow anyone to touch them. They're worth hundreds—thousands"—and making guesses at what the lot would fetch when the old man died. He made these guesses about the property of all the rich old people who lived in the flats.

The girls, an ignorant lot, Irish mainly these days, gaped at the pictures.

"He's left them all to the Nation," the valet would say importantly. He could not disguise his feeling that the poor old Nation had a lot to put up with from the rich. He could always get in a sexy word to the maids when they looked at the cylindrical nude with a guitar lying across her canister-like knees. But the other pictures of vegetation— huge fruits, enormous flowers that looked tropical, with gross veins and pores on stalk and leaves—looked humanly physical and made him feel sick. The flowers had large evil sucking mouths; there were veined intestinal marrows; there was a cauliflower like a gigantic brain that seemed to swell as you looked at it. Nature, to this painter, was a collection of clinical bodies and looked, as Seymour said, "nood." The only living creature represented—apart from the cylindrical lady—was a fish, but it, too, was oversized and gorged. Its scales, minutely enumerated, gave Seymour "the pip." It was hung over the central bookcase.

"It doesn't go with the furniture," Seymour had often said. The comforting thing to him was that, at any rate, the collection could not move and get at him. Like the books, the pictures, too, were cased behind glass.

"All by the same man. Come into the bedroom. Come on. And don't touch anything there because he'll notice. He sees everything," he'd say.

In the bedroom he would show the girls the small oil painting of the head of a young man with almost white hair standing on end and large blue eyes.

"That's the bloke," the valet would say. "He did it himself. Self-portrait. John Flitestone—see, the name's at the bottom—cut his throat. You watch—his eyes follow you," he would say, steering the girl. "He used to come here with the old man."

"Oh," the girls were apt to gasp.

"Stop it, Mr. Seymour," they added, taken off their guard.

"Years ago," Seymour said, looking pious after the pinch he'd given them.

The valet left the room and went down the passage to George Clark's bedroom. Carpet stopped at the door of the room. Inside the room the curtains were blowing, the two sparse rugs lifting in the draught on the polished floor and snow spitting on the table beside the bed. He caught the curtains and drew them back and tried to shut the heavy window. The room contained a cheap yellow wardrobe and chest of drawers which old George Clark had had since he was a boy. The sitting-room was luxurious but his bedroom was as bleak as a Victorian servant's. On a very narrow iron bedstead he lay stiff as a frozen monk and still as a corpse, so paper-thin as to look bodiless, his wiry black hair, his wiry black moustache and his greenish face and cold red nose showing like a pug's over the sheet. It sneered in sleep.

"Seven-thirty, sir. Terrible morning," he said. There was no answer. "By God," the valet said after a pause, "the old man's dead." In death —if that was what it was—the face on the pillow looked as if it could bite. Then the old man gave a snuffle.

The old man opened a wicked eye.

"The old bastard," murmured the valet. Often the old boy had terrified and tricked him with his corpse-like look. It was Clark's open-ing victory in a day, indeed a life, devoted to victory. Then he woke up fully, frightened, reaching for his glasses, to see Seymour's blood-coloured face looking down at him.

"What?" George Clark said. And then the valet heard him groan. These groans were awful.

"Oh my God!" George Clark groaned, but spoke the words in a whisper.

"It's a terrible morning. Shall I put on the fire?"

"No." The old man sat up.

The valet sighed. He went and fetched a cup of tea.

"You'll need this." He put on his bullying voice. "Better drink it hot in here. You'd better have your lunch here today. Don't you go to the club. It's snowing, the wind's terrible."

George Clark got out of bed in his flannel pyjamas. He stepped barefooted to the window, studying the driving grey sky, the slant of snow and the drift of chimney smoke.

"Who closed the window?" he said.

Oh, dear, said the valet to himself, now he's going to begin. "The snow was coming in, Mr. Clark. You'll get pneumonia. Please, sir."

Clark was upright and tall. His small head jerked when he talked on a long, wrinkled neck. His voice was naturally drawling but shortness of breath was in conflict with the drawl and the sounds that came out were jerky, military, and cockerel-like. At eighty-two he looked about sixty, there was hardly any grey in his moustache, the bridge of his gold-framed glasses cut into his red nose. Seymour, who was fifty, was humped and lame and looked seventy. In a fight old George would win and he gave a sniff that showed he knew it. In fact, he got up every day to win; Seymour knew that and accepted it.

What reduced him to misery was that the old man would *explain* his victories. He was off on that now.

"No, I won't get pneumonia," old George snapped. "You see, Seymour, it's a north wind. The north wind doesn't touch me. There's no fat on me, I'm all bones. I'm a skeleton, there's nothing for it to bite on."

"No, sir," said Seymour wretchedly. Ten to one George Clark would now mention his family. He did.

"My father was thin, so was my grandfather, we're a thin family. My youngest sister—she's seventy-eight—she's all bones like me."

Oh, God (Seymour used to moan to himself), I forgot—he's got a sister! Two of them! He moved to get out of the room, but the old man followed him closely, talking fast.

"One day last week I thought we were going to catch it, oh, yes. Now we're going to get it, I said! Awful thing! That clean white light in the sky, stars every night, everything clear, everything sparkling. I saw it and said, Oh, no! No, no. I don't like this, oh, no."

He had now got Seymour in the doorway. "You see—I know what *that* means."

"Yes, sir."

"East wind," said George victoriously.

"That's it, sir."

"Ah, then you've got to look out, Seymour. Oh, yes. Awful business. That's what finishes old people. Awful thing." He drove Seymour forward into the sitting-room and went to this window, studying the sky, and sniffed two or three times at it.

"We're all right, Seymour. You see, I was right. It's in the north. I shall have lunch at the club. Bring my cup in here. Why did you take it to the bedroom?"

It was a cold flat. George Clark took a cold bath, as he had done ever since his schooldays. Then he ate a piece of toast and drank a second cup of tea and looked eagerly to see what was annoying in the papers —some new annoyance to add to a lifetime's accumulation of annoyances. It was one of the calamities of old age that one's memory went and one forgot a quite considerable number of exasperations and awful things in which, contrary to general expectation, one had been startlingly right. This forgetting was bad—as if one were the Duke of Wellington and sometimes forgot one had won the Battle of Waterloo.

In fact, George sat in comfort in a flat packed with past rows, annoyances, and awful things, half forgotten. It was an enormous satisfaction that many of his pictures annoyed the few people who came to see him nowadays. The Flitestones annoyed violently. They had indeed annoyed the Nation to such an extent that, in the person of a "nasty little man" called Gaiterswell, the Nation had refused them. (Seymour was wrong there.) George was very proud of this: his denunciation of Gaiterswell was one of the major victories of his life. George had been the first to buy Flitestones and even Flitestone himself, and had warned the vain and swollen-headed young man against Gaiterswell, years and years ago. "Modish, Jack, he's merely modish. He'll drop you when it suits him."

At twelve o'clock George walked across the park to one of his clubs. He belonged to three. The park was empty. He blew across it like a solitary late leaf. The light snow was turning Whitehall black, and spat on his gold glasses, but he arrived, a little breathless, but ready to deal with that bugbear of old men: protective sympathy.

"George! You ought not to be out on a day like this!" several said. One put his arm round his shoulder. They were a sneezing and coughing lot with slack affectionate faces and friendly overburdened bellies, talking of snowed-up roads, late trains and scrambles for taxis.

"You *walked* through this! Why didn't you make your chauffeur bring you?"

"No car."

"Or a cab?"

"Fares have gone up. I'm too mean."

"Or a bus?"

"Oh, no, no, you see," said George, glittering at them. "I don't know if I told you"—he had told them innumerable times—"when you're brought up by a rich brute of a father, as I was—oh, yes, he was very rich—you get stingy. I'm very stingy. I must have told you about my father. Oh, well, now, there's a story," he began eagerly. But the bar was crowded; slow to move, George Clark found his listener had been pushed away and had vanished. He stood suddenly isolated in his autobiography.

"Oh, God," he groaned loudly, but in a manner so sepulchral and private that people moved respectfully away. It was a groan that seemed to come up from the earth, up from his feet, a groan of loneliness that was raging and frightening to the men round him. He had one of those moments which, he had to admit, were much commoner than they used to be, when he felt dizzy; when he felt he was lost among unrecognizable faces, without names, alone, in the wrong club, at the wrong address even, with the tottering story of his life, a story which he was offering or, rather, throwing out as a lifeline for help. His hand shook as he finished his glass of sherry. The moment passed and, recovering and trembling, he aged as he left the bar and crossed the hall to the dining-room, saying aloud to himself, in his fighting drawl: "Now, now, now, we must be careful."

The side tables were already taken but there were gaps at the two long tables. George stood blinking at the battlefield. He had in the last years resigned from several clubs. Sometimes it was because of bridge, central heating, ventilation, smoking, about house committees, food, and servants, usually over someone who unknowingly had become for a period uncommonly like the Arch Enemy, but who turned out to be no more than an understudy for the part. After a year or so George would rejoin the club. For him the dining-room was one more aspect of the general battlefield. Where should he place his guns? Next to Doyle? No, he was "a Roman." George hated "Romans." He hated "Protestants" too. He was an atheist who never found anyone sufficiently atheistical. George was tired of telling Doyle how he had happened to be in Rome in '05 staying with one of the great families ("she was a cousin of the Queen's") and had, for a year, an unparalleled inside view of what was going on in the Vatican. "Oh, yes, you see, a Jesuit, one of their relations, became a great friend and exposed the whole hocus-pocus to me. You see, I have often been in a position to know more of what is going on than most people. I was close to Haig in the war." There was Gregg, the painter—but it was intolerable to listen to

Academicians; there was Foster who had been opposed to Munich and George could not stand that. There was Macdonald—but Scots climb. Look at Lang! There was Jeffries, such a bore about divorce reform: the bishops want it but daren't say so. "I told the Archbishop in this club that the moment you drag in God you lose your reason. My mother ought to have got a divorce. You should have seen his face. Oh, no, oh, no, he didn't like it. Not a bit."

George looked at the tops of heads and the tableloads of discarded enemies, casualties of his battles, with a grin. At last, glancing round him, he chose a seat beside a successful, smirking pink man of fifty whose name he had forgotten. "Pretty harmless," muttered George. "He thinks Goya a great painter when we all know he is just a good painter of the second rank. Ah, he's eating oysters." This stirred a memory. The man was talking to a deaf editor but on the other side there were empty chairs. It was against George's military sense to leave an exposed flank, but the chance of attacking the club oysters was too good to miss.

"I see you've risked the oysters. I never eat oysters in this club," said George, sitting down. "Poisonous. Oh, yes, yes—didn't I tell you? Oh, you see, it was an awful thing, last year—"

"Now, George," said the man, "you told me that story before."

"Did I? Nothing in that," sniffed George. "I always repeat myself, you see I make a point of telling my stories several times. I woke up in the night—"

"Please, George," said the man more sternly, "I want to enjoy my lunch."

"Oh, ah, ah, ah," said George, sniffing away. "I'll watch your plate. I'll warn you if I see a bad one."

"Oh, really, George!" said the young man.

"You're interrupting our conversation, George," the editor called across. " I was telling Trevor something very interesting about my trip to Russia."

"I doubt if it is interesting," said George in a loudish whisper to the other man. "Interesting! I never found a Whig interesting."

"Dear George is old. He talks too much," said the deaf editor, speaking louder than he knew.

"Not a lot of rot," said George in a loud mutter.

"What's he say?" said the deaf editor.

"You see," George continued to interrupt, "I talk a lot because I live alone. I probably talk more than anyone in this club and I am more interesting than most people. You see, I've often been in a position to know more than most people here. I was in Rome in '05 . . ."

But George looked restlessly at the vacant chair beside him. "I hope," he said, suddenly nervous, "some awful bore is not going to sit here. You never know who, who—oh, no, oh, no, no . . ."

It happened as simply as that, when one was clean off one's guard. Not a single awful thing: but the Great Awful Thing. He saw a pair of small, polished, sunburned hands with soft black hair on them pull back the chair and then a monkeyish man of seventy, with wretched eyes and an academic heaving up of the right shoulder, sit beside him. And heard the voice: "Good morning, George," uttering the name George as if it contained a lifetime's innuendo.

"Oh, God," George said.

The man was the Arch Enemy and in a form he had never expected. Out of the future he should have come, a shape at a slowly opening door, pausing there, blocking it, so that one could not get out. Who he would be, what he would be, was unknown: he was hidden in next week, next year, as yet unborn.

But this man was known. He had sneaked in not from the future, but from the past. It was Gaiterswell.

"Just the man I want to speak to," said Gaiterswell, picking up the menu in hands that George could only think of as thieving.

"I didn't know you were a member," George choked out in words like lead shot.

"Just elected."

George gave a loud sniff.

"Monstrous," said George, but holding on to manners said it under his breath. He grasped his table napkin, ready to fly off and at once resign. It was unbelievable that the Committee, knowing his feelings as they must do, had allowed this man in. Gaiterswell, who had stolen Flitestone from him; who had turned down Flitestone; who had said in the *Times*—in a letter, above all—that George's eccentric tastes had necessarily taught him nothing about the chemical composition of oil paint; Gaiterswell of the scandalous official appointment!

George had forgotten these Waterloos; but now the roar of them woke up in his brain. The fusillades he had let off in committees were heard again. The letters to the *Times* were shot off once more. Gaiterswell had said there were too many "gentlemen" in the art world. It was a pity (he was known to have said), it was a pity that the Empire had gone and there were no more natives for them to pester. George had replied, around the clubs, that "the nasty little man" suffered glaringly from merit and the path of the meritorious was strewn with the bodies they had kicked down the ladder as they climbed.

After he had said things like this, George considered that Gaiterswell was dead. The body could no doubt be found still lying, after twenty-five years, in that awful office of his with the fake Manet—of course it was a fake—on the wall.

"Just the man I want to speak to," Gaiterswell said to the menu. (You noticed he never looked you in the face.)

"Wants to speak to me. For no good reason," George murmured loudly to the man sitting on the other side of him.

"I bet you won't guess who came to see me the other day," Gaiterswell said. "Gloria Archer, Stokes that was. She's married to a Frenchman called Duprey. You remember her? What are you eating? The pie? Is it any good? She's got a lot of poor Jack Flitestone's letters. She's short of money. You wrote the memoir, didn't you, George? Charming little book, charming. I told her to drop in on you. I said you'd be delighted to see her."

George was about to put a piece of pie into his mouth. He put his fork down. He was shaking. He was choking.

"Drop in!" he said, astounded. "Drop in?"

"Look here," he called out, pushing his chair from the table. "Oh, this is monstrous." And he called to one of the waiters, who rushed past and ignored him. "Look here, I say, why do we have to have meat like this in this club . . . It's uneatable . . . I shall find the secretary . . ."

And getting up, with his table napkin waving from his hand, he hurried to the end of the room, the light tossing in his glasses, and then after wild indecision, left the room.

"Where has George Clark gone?" said an old gentleman who had been sitting opposite. "He never finishes a meal."

"It's his teeth," the deaf editor said.

George had made for the Morning Room of the club, where he circled like a dog.

"What manners!" he said to the portraits of the dead members on the wall. Happier than he, they were together; he was alone. He was older than most of them had been, and with a flick of ironic pride which never quite left him in any distress, he could not but notice that he was rather better connected and had more inside knowledge than most of them had had. He addressed them again: "Drop in! What manners! I shall resign."

The Arch Enemy had appeared in a fashion unpredictable: from the Past—and now he saw—not as a male but as a female. Gloria Archer —as he had always said: "What a name!" It recalled (as he firmly pronounced it), the "Kinema," striking a blow for classical scholarship. Her portrait, if one could call it that, was in his sitting-room, cylindrical and naked. It had been there for over twenty-five years, with the other Flitestones, and he had long ago stopped remembering her or even Flitestone himself as human beings he had known. They were not life; they were art—not even art now, but furniture of his self-esteem. He had long ago closed his mind to them as persons. They had become fossilizations of mere anecdote. Now that damn little shot-up official, Gaiterswell, who had been polished off long ago, had brought first Gloria back to life, and the name of Gloria had brought Flitestone back. The seals of anecdote were broken; one of the deepest wounds of George's existence was open and raw again. A woman's work: it was Gloria who had shown how dangerous Flitestone was to him; it was Gloria who had shown him the chaos of his heart.

He left the Morning Room, got his hat and coat, buttoned himself up to the neck, and walked out into the street, where the snow was coming in thicker shots. At once he felt something like a film of ice form between his shirt and his bony chest and he stepped back, afraid.

"No, no," he said very loudly, and passersby raised their ducked heads, thinking he was talking to them. But he was speaking to the wind: it had gone round to the east.

Seymour met him in the lift at the flat. Seymour smelt of beer.

"You shouldn't have gone out, sir," said Seymour. He looked murderous with self-righteousness.

George sat down on his sofa, frightened and exhausted. He was assaulted by real memories and was too weak to fend them off: he had felt frightened to death—he now admitted—in that so enjoyable 1914 war. Flitestone's pictures took on life. Flitestone, too. The cliché vanished—"Not a bad minor painter, like a good many others ruined by the school of Paris": the dangerous Flitestone appeared. George saw again the poor boy from a Scottish mill town, with gaunt cheeks, light-blue eyes and almost white hair that stood up like a dandelion clock ("took hours brushing it, always going to expensive hairdressers"). A pedant, too, with morbid and fanatical patience: it took him longer to paint a picture than anyone George Clark had ever known; the young man was rather deaf, which made him seem to be an unworldly, deeply innocent listener, but there was—as George Clark saw—nothing innocent about him, there was a mean calculating streak ("After all, he realized I was a rich man"—George swaggered), and he was soon taken up by wealthy people. He was clever and made them laugh. He was in trouble all the time with women, chasing them like a maniac and painting them with little heads and large bottoms, like pairs of enormous pink poppies. ("Now, there's a bloody fine bottom, George.")

Very annoying he was, too, especially when he got into Society. That was one thing George Clark knew all about and to be told about Lord This or That or a lot of duchesses, by a crude young genius from the slums, was infuriating.

"He's got five bloody great castles . . ."

"Only one. Forstairs and Aldbaron belong to his half brother who married Glasnevin's sister. Jack, I wish you wouldn't pick your teeth at meals. I can't bear it. It's such frightful manners."

"Lord Falconer does. He's got a gold toothpick."

But these squabbles were merely annoying. Flitestone was the only human being George ever loved. Jealously loved. He was his prize and his possession. And the boy liked him. Here was the danger. George had dreaded to be liked. You lose something when people like you. You are in danger of being stripped naked and of losing a skin. With Flitestone he felt—ah, there was the danger: he did not know what he felt except that it was passion. He could listen to him for hours. For eleven years, George had the sensation that he had married late in life someone who fortunately did not exist, and that Flitestone was their fantastic, blindly invented son. Like a son he clawed at George's bowels.

His love affairs? Well, one had to avert the eye. They were, nevertheless, an insurance against George's instant jealous fear: that Flitestone would marry. The thought of that made George shrink. "Marriage will ruin you"—he nagged at it. And that was where Gloria came in.

When Gaiterswell spoke of Gloria, a shot of jealous terror and satisfaction had gone through George. She bored him, of course. Yet in the last years of their friendship, Flitestone's insane love for this girl who would have nothing to do with him was the real guarantee. George even admired the young girl for the cruelty of her behaviour, for being so complete an example of everything that made women impossible. He was so absorbed in this insurance that he forgot the obvious: that

Gloria might marry. She did. In a month on the rebound, Flitestone had married some milky student girl whose first act was to push her husband into the influence of Gaiterswell. For Gaiterswell was the Nation. A breach with George was inevitable.

He went to his desk and started writing to Gaiterswell.

"I shall be obliged if you will inform Miss Stokes, Mrs. Archer, or whatever her name is, that I have no desire to meet her or enter into correspondence . . ." His hand shook. He could not continue.

"Awful business" was all he could say. The Arch Enemy had deprived him even of the power to talk to himself.

The east wind. Impossible to go out to any of his clubs that night. After dinner, he poured himself a very large whisky and left the bottle, uncorked, on his desk—a sinister breach of habit, for he always locked up his drink.

"I always reckon to be rather drunk every evening," George used to say. It was a gesture to the dignity of gentlemanly befuddlement. But now he felt his legs go; he was rapidly very drunk. He tottered to his bedroom, dropped his clothes on the floor, and got into bed with his shirt, collar, and tie on and was asleep at once. Often at night he had enjoyable dreams of social life at Staff H.Q. in the 1914 war. Haig, Ronnie Blackwater and others would turn up. A bit of gunfire added an interest; but this night he had a frightful dream. He dreamt that at the club, before all the members, he had kissed the teeth of George V.

This woke him up and he saw that it was daylight. His heart was racing. He could not find his glasses. He got out of bed. The room was getting light; he wondered if he were dead and he pulled back the curtain and what he saw convinced him that he was. The snow had stopped, the sky was hard and clear, and the sun was coming up in a gap between two high buildings. It was still low and this made it an enormous raw yellow football that someone had kicked there, without heat or radiance yet. It looked like a joke or some aimless idea; one more day (George realized as he became more conscious) had begun its unsolicited course over the blind slates of the city. "Old men are lonely," he often said, but now he saw a greater loneliness than his own.

"I want those letters." The desire came out before he could stop it. "I must see Gloria. I must get Gaiterswell's dirty little hands off them." He was longing for the past. Then he saw he was wearing his day shirt, his collar and tie.

"Oh, God," he said. And he got into his pyjamas and back into bed before Seymour should catch him.

At half past seven Seymour let himself into the flat. His demeanour was of one whose expectations were at last being fulfilled. He had warned several of the old people in the flats about the weather; he had seen Mr. Clark come back yesterday exhausted when against all advice he had gone to the club. Reaching the sitting-room, Seymour saw a decanter of whisky standing on the table. This was a sight that he had thirsted for for years and he gazed at it entranced, unbelieving and with suspicion. He listened. There was no sound. Seymour made a grab at the decanter and took a long swig, letting a drop rest on his chin while he replaced what he had drunk with water from the hot-water pot on the tea tray. He stood still, trying to lick the drip off his chin but, failing, he wiped it off with his sleeve, and after looking at the letters on Mr. Clark's desk, walked confidently to Mr. Clark's bedroom.

"Good morning, Seymour. Half past seven," said George. He was sitting up in bed. Seymour heard this reversal of their usual greeting with alarm. He stood well away and slopped the tea in its saucer. He was even more alarmed to see Mr. Clark had switched on his own fire and that his clothes were dropped in a muddle on the floor. George caught his glance and got out of bed to show that he was properly dressed and stood with one foot on his rumpled jacket. Panic and the whisky brought guilt into Seymour's face: he suddenly remembered he had made a disastrous mistake. He had forgotten to give Mr. Clark a message.

"A lady rang last night, sir, when you were at dinner."

"A lady—why didn't you tell me?"

"The headwaiter took the call. He said you were out. She didn't leave a name."

To distract an angry question, Seymour looked at the clothes on the floor.

"Dear, dear, dear, what a way to leave a suit." He pulled the trouser leg from under George's foot and held the trousers up. "Look at it."

"What lady?" said George.

"She didn't leave a name. She said she'd drop in."

"Drop in!" The horrible phrase.

"That's what she said, she'd drop in."

"Who was it?"

"I don't know, sir. I never took the message. I told you—it was the new headwaiter."

"Don't stand there waving my trousers about like a fool, Seymour. It's your business to know."

"They're all foreigners downstairs."

George had his glasses on now and Seymour stepped away. In his panic, he took a gamble.

"Might have been Miss Stokes," he said. He had read the name on George's unfinished letter. The gamble was a mistake.

"Archer!" cried George. "Where is the headwaiter?" And hurrying to the sitting-room, he started banging the telephone. There was no answer.

"What time do the servants come on?" he called to Seymour. Seymour came in and listened to George banging away. He was very scared now. He dreaded that the headwaiter would answer.

"They come when it suits them now. They suit themselves," said Seymour, putting on a miserable manner. And then he got in his blow, the sentence he often used to the old people in the flats when they got difficult. It always silenced them.

"Might just as well sell the place," he said.

"Sell!" George was silenced, too. He stared at Seymour, who straightened himself and said accusingly, "Where's the jacket of this! Dear, dear, I suppose that's on the floor too," and walked out, leaving George shivering where he stood.

"Sell?" said George.

On a long ledge of the stained building opposite, thirty or forty dirty pigeons were huddled, motionless, with puffed-out feathers, too cold to fly.

"Out on the street! Homeless." Like Stebbing-Walker, crippled and deaf, who had married Kempton's half sister—she was a Doplestone—and now lay in his nursing home, or Ronnie Blackwater, who sat paralysed in the Army infirmary. Sell—it was the awful word anxiously whispered in the lift by the old ladies as they went up and down to their meals. Was the place being sold? Were the rents going up? Were they going to pull the whole place down? For months there would be silence; everyone breathed again; then once more, mostly from Seymour, the rumours began. Fear made them sly and they believed Seymour rather than the management. He moved among them like a torment.

George Clark went down early to luncheon, to get in before the restaurant vanished; rushed upstairs afterwards to barricade himself, so to speak, in his flat. There were few pigeons on the ledge now. What? Had tenancy gone out of Nature too? At seven o'clock he went to dinner. Instead of the two or three tables of old doll-like couples in the middle of the room, there was a large table at which ten large young men, loud and commercial, were laughing together. One or two had briefcases with them. Obviously this was the group who were going to pull down the flats. George raced through the meal, feeling that possibly even before the apples and custard, he might be sitting out alone on a vacant site. George's fighting spirit revived over his wine. "Ha," he sneered at them as he left the table and went to the lift, "I'll be dead before you can turn me out."

The lift wheezed and wobbled upwards, making the sound of all the elderly throats in the building. He was startled to see the door of his flat open and, for a moment, thought the men had broke in already; but Seymour was standing in the cold hall. His heavy face looked criminal. In an insinuating, lugubrious voice he said, "The lady's waiting to see you, sir."

"Seymour, I've told you, never . . ." George hurried to his sitting-room. Gloria was standing by his desk reading the letter he had begun so often.

"Dear Gaiterswell, I would have thought that common decency . . ."

"Oh, oh, no, no, I say," said George, greeting her, but was stopped.

A fur coat and a close-fitting black hat like a faded turban with brass-coloured hair sticking out of it rushed at him; a hot powdery face kissed him with a force that made him crack in his joints like a stick.

"Oh, George, darling, I dropped in," Gloria shouted at him through large stained teeth and laughed.

All he could see was these teeth and lipstick and blue eyes and she was laughing and laughing as she wiped the lipstick off his face.

"Oh, well," he said, "they're selling the place . . ."

Then she stood back in a pair of cracking shoes. "George," she said in a Cockney voice, "it's marvellous. You haven't changed at all. You're not a day older."

And she let her fur coat fall open and slip back on her shoulders and he saw the cigarette ash and one or two marks on the bosom of her black dress. She was a big woman.

"Oh." George recovered and gave a victorious sniff. "I'm eighty-two."

"You're a boy," she cried.

"Oh, no, don't think I'm deceived by that sort of talk—er, well, you see, I mean . . ." George nearly smiled. By his reckoning she was in her fifties and he could see what she wanted, what all women wanted, compliments. He was not, at his age, going to fall for that old game. She sat down on the sofa so as to show off her fine legs.

"Did you recognize me?" she asked.

"Oh, well, you know . . ."

"Oh, come on, George."

"I daresay I—er—might have done. You see, I forget names and faces, it's an awful business . . . old people . . . they're selling this place . . ."

"Oh, you crusty old thing. What do you mean—selling?" she said. "You always were crusty. I knew you'd be at dinner, so I got that man to bring me up. What is his name? Is he all right? I didn't feel very comfortable with him in the lift."

She moved her body and pouted.

"When your lady friends call, you ought to tell them to keep an eye —well, George, how are you? How many years is it? It must be twenty-five. You weren't living here then."

"It was the beginning of the war," said George, but he could not remember. He had discarded memory as useless a long time back. He had seen her a lot, yet one of his few clear recollections was of sitting with Flitestone in the old Café Royal waiting for her to come in and arguing with him that she was not a woman who would stick to any man: he remembered her really as an absence.

"You've put on weight," he said. But she hadn't changed much.

"Yes," she said. "I like it, don't you?"

The Cockney voice came warm and harsh out of the wide mouth. Her skin was rougher and was now looser on her bones but still had a wide-pored texture and the colourlessness which Flitestone used to say was like linen. One spot of colour in her cheeks and Flitestone would probably never have fallen for her. "She's like a canvas. I'd like to paint on her," Flitestone used to say to George. He did remember. The bare maleness of face on a girlish body was still there on the body of the full woman.

George stood, shaking at the sight of her.

"You're still an old bachelor, George?" she said. "You didn't marry?"

"No," said George with a grin of victory. "You see, in my day, one never met any girls, everyone was chaperoned, you couldn't speak and we had no one to the house, oh, no, my father wouldn't allow anyone and then the war, and all that. I told you about my father, oh, now, there's a story—"

"Oh, I've been. Three times," she cut in, parading herself.

"Oh, three! Well, that's interesting. Or I suppose it is. It doesn't surprise me. Please sit down. Let me get you a drink. Now, let me see, keys. I have to keep it locked—well, with the servants it isn't fair to leave drink about. Ah, in this pocket. I keep them here."

He fussed at the cupboard and brought out a bottle of whisky and a bottle of sherry.

"Oh, gin, please," she said. "Can I help?"

"No, no, it's here. I keep it at the back. I'll put this bottle down here, yes, that's the way . . ." he chattered to himself.

Gloria walked across the room to look at the pictures, but stopped instead to look at her reflection in the glass of the bookcases and to rearrange the neck of her dress. Then she looked up at the large picture of the fish.

"George! You've got my fish."

"Ah, yes, the fish. He painted four fish pictures. One is in the Tate, one is . . . now, where is it?"

"*My* fish, I mean," she said. "Don't you remember, it's the one I made you carry to Jack's place and the paper came off . . ."

"No, no," said George.

"Yes, you must remember. You're not still cross, are you? You looked so funny."

She took a deep breath in front of the picture, inhaling it.

"I don't know why we didn't eat it."

"Ah yes. Awful business. Café Royal," said George, a memory coming back.

She turned to the cylindrical woman in a shift, with enormous column-like legs, who was playing a guitar, and looked with flirtatious annoyance at it, paying off an old score.

"That's me," she said.

"Oh, no," said George sarcastically. He was beginning to enjoy himself. "It was done in Paris."

"It's me," said Gloria. "But they're Violet's legs." Gloria turned abruptly away, insulted, and taking her drink from George went back to the sofa. Once more she gave a large sigh and gazed with admiring calculation at the room. She leaned her head to one side and smiled at George.

"You are a dear, George. How cosy you are. It's wonderful to see old friends," said Gloria sweetly. "It brings it all back."

She got up and put more gin in her drink and then leaned over his chair as she passed him and kissed the top of his head.

"Dear George," she said and sat down. "And you live here, all alone! Well, George, I've brought the letters, all Jack's letters to me. I didn't know I had them. It's a funny thing: François found them, my husband, he's French. We live in France and he has an antique business. He said 'They ought to fetch a bit,' you know what the French are about money, so I remembered Monkey—"

"Monkey?"

"Monkey Gaiterswell, I always used to call him Monkey. We used," said Gloria very archly, "to be friends and he said, 'Sell them to America.' Do you think he's right—I mean Monkey said you'd written a book about Jack and you'd know? He said I'd get five hundred pounds for them. I mean they're all about painting, famous people, the whole circle . . ."

Ah, it was a plot!

"Five hundred," said George. "You won't get five pounds. No one has ever heard of Flitestone in America. None of his pictures went there."

"But the letters are very *personal,* George. Naturally you're in them."

"I doubt it."

"Oh, you are. I remember. I know you are. You were his best friend. And you wrote so beautifully about him. Monkey says so."

Obviously there was a plot between Monkey and Gloria.

"I've no doubt they are full of slanders. I should tear them up," said George shortly.

"George," she appealed. "I need the money. François has gone off with some woman and I'm broke. Look."

She opened her black shopping bag and took out a parcel of crumpled brown paper and put it on George's desk.

"Open it. I'll leave them with you to look at. You'll see."

"Oh, no. I can't do that," said George. "I don't care to be responsible. It leads to all sorts of awful business."

"Read them. Open it. Here."

She put down her empty glass and untied the string. A pile of letters of all sizes in Flitestone's large hand, each word formed carefully like the words of a medieval manuscript, slid onto George's desk.

George was sitting there and he withdrew his hand so as not to touch the letters. They brought Jack Flitestone into the room. George wanted them. He knew now what was meant when she said *he* was in them. It was not what *she* meant. The letters contained the to-him-affronting fact that he had not after all succeeded in owning his own life and closing it to others; that he existed in other people's minds and that all people dissolved in this way, becoming fragments of one another, and nothing in themselves. He had known that once, when Jack Flitestone had brought him to life. He knew, too, that he had once lived or nearly lived. Flitestone, in his dangerous way, had lived for him. One letter had fallen to the floor and Gloria read aloud:

". . . Archie's car broke down outside Medley and we didn't get to Gorse until the middle of dinner. La Tarantula was furious and I offered to eat in the kitchen and the Prime Minister who was already squiffy . . .

"There you are, George. The Prime Minister," cried Gloria.

George took the letter in the tips of his fingers and Gloria helped herself to another drink.

"Jack was an awful snob," said George, but admiringly, putting the letter back. "No manners, writing about people when he was a guest."

"Oh, come off it, George," said Gloria, picking out one or two more. "You know, I haven't read them for years. Actually Jack frightened me. So morbid. Here's one. Oh, this is good. It's about the time you and Jack went to Chartres. The tie drawer, George!"

The new blow from the past struck him. He remembered it: the extraordinary thing about small French hotels—they never gave you a drawer for your ties. He took the letter and read:

". . . George surpassed himself this morning . . ."

He had walked down the corridor to Flitestone's room and knocked.

"Here. I say, Jack. I want to speak to you."

"What is it?" Flitestone had called. Ordinary manners, one would have thought, would at least have led Flitestone to open the door. Jack was so *thoughtless*.

"Jack, Jack, I've no tie drawer in my room."

Flitestone came to the door naked and pushed a drawer from his wardrobe into George's hand. "Take mine."

"Jack, here, I say, dear fellow. Chambermaid."

"Umph," said George to Gloria. "Inaccurate."

He reached out for the next letter she offered to him. He looked at it distantly, read a few lines, and stopped.

"Here, I say, I can't read this. It is to you." He sneered a little.

"They're all to me."

"Yes, but this is—er—private, personal."

George looked quizzically and sternly at her; it was "not done" to look into another's moral privacy. It was also shameless and woman-like to show letters like these to him. But the phrases he had run into head-on had frightened him, they brought back to him the danger he had once lived in: his heart had been invaded, he had been exposed once to a situation in which the question of a victory or a defeat vanished.

"You see," he said, turning his head away nervously from her as he handed back the letter to her.

Gloria took it. She put on her glasses and read. Immediately she smiled. The smile became wider and she gave pleased giggles. She was blushing.

"Jack ought to have been a writer," she said. "I hated his paintings. It's quite true what he says, George. I was very attractive. I had marvellous legs."

She turned to look at her reflection in the glass of the bookcase and took her fur coat off and posed. Gradually she lifted her skirt above her knees and, pleased by what she saw, she lifted her skirt higher, putting one leg forward, then the other.

"Look, George," she said. "Look. They're still good. There aren't many women of my age with legs like these. They're damn fine, George. You've never seen a pair like that." She turned sideways and pranced with pleasure.

"Gloria, please," said George sharply.

But she marched over to the picture of the woman with cylindrical legs and said, "I could have killed him for that. What's the matter with painters? Didn't he have enough to eat when he was a boy? He was always carrying on about his hard times."

She lowered her dress and sat down to go on reading the letter.

"The pink peony, did you get to that?" she said. "Really, Jack's ideas! Not very nice, is it? I mean, not in a letter. He wasn't very . . ." She stopped and was sad. "No," she checked herself. "I'll tell you something, George: we only went to bed together once . . ."

"Gloria," said George in agitation. "Give me the letter. I'll put it with the others . . ."

She was making Flitestone far too alive.

"It was your fault, George. It was the dinner you gave us that night, the night I bought the fish. You say you don't remember? At the Café

Royal. I made you go off to the Café Royal kitchen and get the largest fish they had. I don't know why. I wanted to get rid of you and I thought it would annoy you. I was getting plastered. Don't you remember? I said, 'Tell them we want it for our cat. Our cat is enormous. It eats a salmon a day.' And Jack kept on saying—we were both drunk —'I want to paint a large salmon. You're bloody stingy, George, you won't buy me a salmon.' "

"Awful business," snapped George. "Jack never understood money."

"You remember! Isn't that wonderful?" cried Gloria, pulling off her hat and looking into her empty glass.

"You followed us out of the restaurant, all up Shaftesbury Avenue, and he was going to show me his new pictures. You had no tact, George. He was carrying the fish and he suddenly gave it to you and made you carry it and the paper blew off. George," she said, "do you mind if I have just a teeny-weeny one? There's a letter about it."

And she pushed him aside and got at the parcel on his desk.

"I think you've had enough, Gloria."

"For old times' sake," said Gloria, filling her glass. She unfolded the parcel again and scattered the letters. George looked at the clock.

"I can't find it," she said. "It's here somewhere."

"Gloria, I don't want drink spilled on my desk. I've forbidden Seymour . . ."

Gloria stopped and, now red in the face, smiled amorously.

"That man?" she said. "Is he here?"

"Gloria," said George. "I'll have to—er—I'll have to— It's eleven o'clock, I . . ."

Gloria replied with dignity. "Jack had no sense of behaviour. I could see it was spoiling your suit. I begged him, begged him," she said grandly, "to carry it himself. I was furious with him. He could see you had an umbrella as well, you always carried one and wore a bowler hat. He said, 'Stick it on the umbrella.' I was terribly upset when he slammed the door in your face when we got to the studio. We had a terrible row and I made him swear to go round to your flat and apologize. It was awful, George. What did you do?"

"I took a cab, of course," said George.

"Well, I mean, you couldn't leave a salmon in the street," said Gloria. "It was a suit like the one you are wearing now, dark grey. That isn't the one, is it? It can't be."

"Gloria, I am sorry, but . . ."

Gloria frowned.

"I am sure it's there," she said and went to the letters on the desk again. "No, not that. Not that," she began throwing the letters on the floor. "Ah, here."

She waved the letter and looked through it in silence until she read aloud:

". . . I apologized to George and he said he had left the fish with the hall porter, so I went down there. We had a bit of a row about my low-class manners. I said I thought half the salmon in England had been to Eton. He told me to ask Seymour, the hall porter, for it—"

"Inaccurate," interrupted George. "Seymour was never hall porter."

". . . I said I have called for the specimen I loaned to Sir George Clark, the marine biologist, who is doing research on spawn . . .

"You see, George," she said. She went back to the sofa. "Come and sit here, George, don't be so stuffy. We can talk, can't we, after all these years? We are friends. That is what we all need, George, friends. I'm serious, George." She had tears in her eyes.

"It was wicked of Jack to call you stingy. You gave him money. You bought his pictures."

"But I *am* stingy," said George. "You see, rich people never give their children a penny. We never had anyone to the house at Maddings . . ."

"It was his jealousy," said Gloria darkly. "He was jealous of you."

"Oh, well, class envy—" George began.

"No, of you and me," she said. "Oh, yes, George, he really was. That's why he tried to shake you off, that night, that's why we had such terrible scenes . . . You were rich . . ."

"Don't be ludicrous, Gloria."

"Letters by every post, pursuing, bombarding me, I couldn't stand it."

"Nonsense."

"It isn't nonsense. You were very blind, George. And so you live in this place, alone. Jealous men are so *boring*, George. I've had four. I said 'Oh, to hell' and I went off to France. Vive de Gaulle! You know?" she said, raising her glass.

"To *les feuilles mortes d'automne,*" she said. "That's what my husband says."

He bent to take her glass to prevent her drinking more and she stroked his spiky hair. He put the glass away out of reach.

"That is why Jack married that stupid student girl," she said in a suddenly sharp calculating voice. "That broke up you and Jack, didn't it?"

"I don't wish to talk about it," said George. "It ruined him. Marriage is the ruin of painters."

"George, come clean. After all, we all know it. You were in love with him, weren't you?"

There was a silence.

"Weren't you?" she persisted.

He recovered and achieved his worldly drawl. "Oh, I know there's a lot of that sort of thing about, was in my time, too. I paid no attention to it . . . Women don't understand talent. I understood Jack's talent. Women ruined it."

"Jack said you'd never been to bed with a woman in your life," she said.

"It wasn't possible, it wasn't possible," said George angrily, "not in my day. Not for a gentleman." And he turned on her. "I won't be questioned. I should burn those letters. You treated him badly. You killed his imagination. It's obvious in his work."

He looked at the clock.

"George," she said. "You don't mean that. You don't know what you are saying. You were always so sweet to me."

"I do mean what I said. Read your letters," said George. And briskly he collected them off the floor and packed them up and tied the parcel. He was going to turn her out now.

She was staring stupidly.

"You don't want them?" she said. "Monkey said you'd jump at them."

"You've got one in your hands," he said. "No," he added, "I won't give a penny for them. I won't be blackmailed."

Gloria got up to give the letter to him. She could not walk and put her hand on the table beside the sofa. It fell over, carrying her glass with it.

"What's that man Seymour doing in here? Tell him to get out. Out with Seymour," she suddenly shouted. "Out. Out. What d'you mean? Stop playing the innocent. You've never lived. That's you, George, that fish." And she tried to point at the picture.

"Gloria, I won't have this," shouted George. "You're drunk."

"You won't have it? You've never had it. My coat, who's taken that?"

But when she turned she fell heavily onto the sofa, twisted her body and fell asleep instantly with her skirt above her knees and one majestic leg trailing on the floor.

"Gloria. How dare you! In my house!"

"Darling," she smiled.

"Women," George always said, glittering dryly, "they contribute nothing." She was contributing a stentorian snore.

He had couples up after dinner sometimes, elderly friends, and you could see how it was: they either couldn't let their husbands speak—poor Caldicott, for instance—or they sat as stupid as puddings. The men aged as they sat: rather them than me. Eighty-two and not a day's illness.

Gloria was contributing more than a snore. She was contributing an enormous haunch, an indecent white thigh—"Really." He would have to cover it. Couldn't she pull her skirt down? Couldn't she be drunk like a—like a lady? She contributed brutality, an awful animality, to the room.

He went over and tried to pull her skirt down.

"Gloria," he shouted.

He couldn't move the skirt. He gave her a shake. It stirred an enormous snore and a voluptuous groan and it seemed that she was going to roll off the sofa onto the floor. He couldn't have women lying on the floor in his flat. He could never get her up. He moved a chair against the sofa.

He sat down and waited. Gaiterswell was responsible for this. In the promiscuous Bohemian set he had lived in, the dirty little man would be used to it.

George could not ring for Seymour. Think of the scandal. She had trapped him. He hated her for what she had done to Jack, driving him out of his mind with jealousy of other men, encouraging him, evading him, never letting go. She, more than his expensive wife, was responsible for Jack's suicide. Gloria had paralysed him. You could see it in his paintings, after they had broken up: the paintings had become automatic, academic, dead, without air, without life. There were ten drawings of that fish. He had become obsessed with it.

It was a death of the heart: of George's heart as well. This body lying in the room was like the brutal body of his father. The old brute with his rages and his passions, his disgraceful affairs with governesses and maids in the very next room to where he slept as a boy—awful business —he would never forget that—the manners!—the shouts, his terrible behaviour to his wife: it had paralysed the whole family. They all hated him so violently, with a violence that so magnetized them all, that none of them had heart for others. He had killed their hearts; not one of them had been able to love. For a moment George left these memories and went off into anecdotes about how he fought back against his father, sniffing triumphantly, as he did at the club. But the sight of Gloria there smashed the anecdotal in him. He recognized that he had *not* fought back and had *not* been victorious. He had risked nothing. He had been whipped into the life of a timid, self-absorbed scholar.

He poured himself a large whisky. It was gone midnight. Perhaps by the time he checked up on the windows in the flat and saw all the doors were closed she would wake up. He carried his glass to his bedroom and put it by the bedside; and there exhaustion drove him to his habits. He took off his watch and put it on the table. He forgot why he had come into the room. It was not what he intended to do, but he was tired, and murmuring to himself, "Coat, hanger, shirt, trousers, shoes, socks," he undressed, and shivering he got into bed. He finished his whisky, turned out the light and—Gloria forgotten—he was at once asleep. And at once dreaming he was back in the sitting-room, parcelling the letters, watching her. He dreamt that he called Seymour, who got a taxi, and they hauled her into it. But as fast as they got her into the cab she was back upstairs on the sofa, and his father and Jack were there too, but ignoring him, standing a yard or two away, though he shouted at them to help. And then the awful thing happened. He picked her up himself. He was at a railway station; he could go no further; he dropped her. With an appalling noise, the enormous body fell just as a train came, steaming, blasting, wheels grinding, a massive black engine, advancing upon him. He gave a shout. It had hit him and crushed him. He was dying. He had had a heart attack. He screamed and he woke up shouting, sitting up in bed.

In the bedroom Gloria was standing in her stockinged feet and her petticoat, holding her skirt in her hand, her hair in disorder.

"What's the matter, George?" she said thickly.

George could not speak.

"What is it? I woke up. I heard you shout." Her breathing was heavy, it was the sound of the engine he had heard. George gaped at her.

"Are you ill?" she said. "I passed out."

"I . . . I . . . I . . ." He could say nothing more. He got out of bed. George was shuddering. "What's the time?"

"Get into bed. You're freezing. You're ill." She came over and took him by the arm and he allowed himself to be put back to bed.

"What an icebox," she said. She shut the window, switched on the fire.

"I'd better get a doctor," she said.

"No," said George. "I'm all right." He was panting. She felt his head.

"Where is my watch."

"It's half past three nearly. George, for God's sake, don't do that again. Have you got any aspirins? What happens when you're alone and there is no one here?"

"Ah, you see, I have an arrangement with the . . ."

"What? The doctor?"

"The telephone," said George.

"The telephone? What the hell's the good of that? You might die, George. Where are those aspirins, be a dear and tell me. I'm sorry, George. You screamed. God, I hadn't time to put a skirt on," she said archly.

"Oh, well, so I see," said George sarcastically.

"Ah, thank God," said Gloria, sighing. "Now you sound more like yourself. You gave me a turn. I would have fallen on the floor if you hadn't put the chair there. I'll make you a cup of tea. Can you make tea in this awful museum?"

"No," said George victoriously. "You can't. I never keep tea here. Tea, I never make it. Seymour brings it."

"Well, my God, how you live, George, in this expensive barn," she said, sitting on the bed.

"Awful business. Awful dream," said George, coming round. "I had an awful dream the other night, oh, yes . . ."

"You look green, George. I'll get you a drink."

She brought it to him and watched him drink it.

"I've been round your flat. There are no beds. If you don't mind I'll go back to the sofa. Now, stop talking."

For George was off on some tale of a night in the war.

"This is the only bed," he said. "I used to keep a spare bed but I stopped that. People exploit you. Want to stay the night. It upsets the servants here."

"There's not room for two in it, George," she said. George stopped his drink.

"Gloria," he stammered in terror of her large eyes. She came closer and sat on the bed. She took his free hand.

"You're cold," she said.

"No," he said. "I'm not. All bone, you see, skeleton. My sister . . ."

She stood up and then bent over him and kissed him.

"I'll find a blanket," she said. "I'll go back to the sofa. I'm terribly sorry, George. George, I really am."

"Well," said George.

"George, forgive me," she said and suddenly kneeled at the bed and put her arms round him. "Let me warm you."

"Oh, no, no. No. Awful business," said George.

She went away. George heard her opening cupboards, looking for blankets. He listened to every movement. He thought, Seymour will find her in the morning. Where could he hide her? Could he make her go to the bathroom and stay there till Seymour left? No, Seymour always ran his bath. He was trapped. He heard her go to the sitting-room. It was six before he fell asleep again.

At half past seven she came to his room with Seymour.

"My brother was taken very ill in the night," she was saying to Seymour. "I cannot find out who his doctor is. He oughtn't to be alone like this. At his age."

"No, ma'am," said Seymour, looking guilty.

"Bring me his tea. Where does he keep his thermometer? Get me one."

"I told him not to go out, ma'am," said Seymour.

"Thank heaven I came in."

When Seymour left she said to George, "Don't talk. It's tiring. A little scandal would have done you good, George, but not at your age."

"Umph," said George. "That man knows my sister. She's as thin as a pole. She's meaner than me," he cackled. "She never tips anyone."

"I told him I was the fat one," she said. "You stay there. I'm calling a doctor."

Waiting for him to come was a nuisance. "Awful business" having a woman in the house. They spend half their lives in the bathroom. You can't get into it. When George did get to it he was so weak he had to call for her. She was sitting in a chair reading Flitestone's letters and smiling. She had—George had to admit—made herself presentable.

"You're right, George," she said. "I'm going to keep them. He was so full of news. They're too . . ." she said demurely, "personal."

And then the doctor came.

At the club George was sitting at luncheon.

"You're looking well, George," said the academician, who had just passed him the decanter.

"I never drink until the evening. I always reckon to drink a bottle of wine at dinner, a couple of glasses of port. I usually have a whisky here and one more back at the flat when I get home. I walk home, taxis are expensive and oh, oh, oh, I don't like the underground. Oh, no, I don't like that."

"You're looking fine."

"I have been very ill. I had pneumonia. I was taken very ill a month ago, in the night. Luckily my sister has been looking after me. That is the trouble with old people who live alone, no one knows. They can't reach the bell. I told you about that awful night when I ate the oysters—"

"George, not now, please. I didn't know you had a sister?"

"Oh, yes, oh, yes. Two," said George sharply. "One is very thin, all bones like me, the other very fat."

"But you're better? You look fine. I hear, by the way, that Sanders is getting married."

"Oh, I knew about that. I advised him to, at his age. I warned him about the loneliness of bachelors in old age. I'm used to it. Keep occupied. See people. That's the secret. Oh, yes, I worked it out. My father lived till he was ninety. You see, when I was young one never met any women. Just girls at deb parties, but speak to them, oh dear no. Not done. That's a big change. The bishops don't like sex, though Canterbury is beginning to come round. The Pope will have to make a move, he's been the stumbling block. A scandal. Oh, yes, I happened to be in Rome in '05, staying with a papal count and, well, I was able to tell him the whole inside story at the Vatican, you see I knew a very able Jesuit who was very frank about it privately—"

"What happened about Gloria?" said a voice. It was the Arch Enemy, sitting opposite.

"Hah," said George. "I recommended her not to sell. She offered to give me the letters, but I didn't care to take them. They were very intimate, personal."

"I thought her husband had left her and she was short of money?"

"That's not the worst thing to be short of," sniffed George.

"The trouble with Gloria was that she was always so sentimental," said the Arch Enemy. "The moment she sees a man her mind simply goes. Still does, and she must be sixty if she's a day," he said, looking at George.

By God, George thought, the Arch Enemy is a fool.

The Speech

"It's a funny turnout. You don't know what front to take up for the best," the chatty doorman replied to the big-bellied woman as he opened the door and let her and the other speakers into the hall.

"You'd better bloody well make your mind up or you'll be dead," she said to him with a grin over her shoulder as she passed and followed the others up the steps onto the cold, dusty platform. And she said to the young man with heavy fair hair who was next to her when they sat down: "That's this place for you. Did you hear him? It's dead. They've had the bomb already."

A man's voice shouted from the audience, just before Lord Birt got up to introduce the speakers: "Good old Sally."

No smile of pleasure moved her double chin, nor did she nod. She was counting. That one shout echoed. It revealed the emptiness of the hall. It would hold eight hundred; she had seen in her time twice that number fighting their way in. Now (she reckoned it up) there were no more than fifty or sixty.

The weather, the sleet whipping across all day—the secretary had said—not having had longer notice, couldn't get through to headquarters on the phone. A lot of people on short time. Excuses. They had even spelled her name wrong on the notice outside: Sally Proser, leaving out the second "s," and the sleet spitting on it made the red ink run into the blue as if the poster were sobbing and ashamed of them all. They couldn't get her name right, even in her own town.

Lord Birt had sat down. The first speaker was up.

"Friends," he was saying, "I shall not take up your time . . ."

She looked at her watch. "We'll be here half the night," she said to the young man next to her. He was trying to keep a piercing look on his face. "Who is he?"

"Doctor," hissed the young man, crossing his legs. "Quaker. Liberal."

"God," she said very audibly.

It was a large hall, a yawning historic fake in a Gothic baronial style, built out of cotton profits a hundred years before, shabbied by hundreds, thousands, of meetings, the air staled and exhausted by generations of preachers, mayors and politicians. The damp had brought out a smell made of floorboards, the municipal disinfectants, the sweet, sooty cellulose effluence of the city. It was a smell provided by a dozen mills whose tall chimneys pencilled the pink fume of the sky, and by something of the fouled, milky green industrial river and the oily canal. A mist hung across the middle of the hall like breath left behind for years, and although all the chandeliers were lit, the light fell yellowish and weak on the audience sitting in their overcoats in the first five rows and on the long funereal stretch of empty chairs behind. One person after another turned round in discomfort, looking at the distant glass doors at the back and then at the side, to see where the arctic draught came from; and then, reproaching themselves, lifted their chins stiffly and stared with resentment at the platform.

The doctor was still going on. He was a tall, very thin man, vain of his eagle face, his blossom of white hair, his gentle, high-pitched, doubting vocables. They were moving equably out of "the situation before all of us today"; then went on derisively to "the international plane" and "the lessons of history": (his past); to what he had said "in this very hall" (references to local elections thirty years ago), and emerged into the benignancy of the "moral issue" and circled impatiently to what he had "always said." Beside him sat young Lord Birt, ace flyer, Matisse owner, lecturer in America, with a dark, prompt electric black moustache, like a too-recent political decision, and next to him the very young man.

"It's a scandal, a meeting like this," Mrs. Prosser was saying to him audibly through the doctor's speech. "I'll take it up with headquarters. Where have they put you up—in an hotel? I was out last night, God knows where, in the treasurer's house, and there's been a death in the family. Imagine the atmosphere."

"Someone just died?" said the young man, astonished.

"Twenty-five years ago!" she said sarcastically. "I've made fourteen speeches on this tour, in the last six days, and they hadn't the decency to put me into a hotel. It's all wrong."

And Mrs. Prosser's head, mouth, and jaws, even her big arms, seemed to gather themselves together until she looked like a fist.

"What about Hungary?" shouted a man from the audience.

"Yes, what about Hungary?" shouted two or three others.

"They're waking up," said the young man.

"I'm glad you asked me that question," said the doctor, going on.

"No, it's nothing," she said, giving an experienced glance at the shouters. "They're dead. How did you get here? They didn't even have a car, borrowed it from the treasurer's son, it broke down. We sat on the road for half an hour, on a night like this. Ah, well, the old bastard is drying up. It's you."

The young man got up.

"Ladies and gentlemen," he began.

(Oh, God, thought Mrs. Prosser, but forgave him.) He had learned his speech, he was sawing it off, it fell in lumps to the floor. The women looked sympathetically, the men looked ironical, one or two of the shouters leaned forward to egg him on at first, and then leaned back, with their hands on their knees, giving up. Handsome, his hair flopping, he seemed to have some invisible opponent in front of him whom he was angrily trying to push away so that he could see the audience. He struggled and at last he stopped struggling. He came to an end, looked back nervously to see if his chair was still there, and when the audience clapped he looked back at them with suspicion and anger.

"I made a mess of it," he murmured to Mrs. Prosser as he sat down.

"Here we go." Mrs. Prosser ignored him. "Watch me, if I don't wet my drawers before I've done with this bloody lot . . ."

She was up, adroitly slipping her old fur coat off her shoulders and into the hands of the young man, stepping in one stride to the edge of the platform. She stared at the audience, let them have a good look at her. She was a short woman of forty-seven. Robust. She was wearing a tan jumper that was low on her strong neck and pulled on anyhow, and a shabby green skirt. She had big breasts, which she had been ashamed of in her young days, wanting to hide them, but that was before she joined the Movement; a stout belly, hard as a drum, which made her laugh when she got up in the morning. Her face was round and she had a double chin and the look on her face said: Go on! Take a good look. It's your last chance.

Suddenly she let out her voice.

"Fellow workers," she shouted. The words, slow, deep, and swinging in delivery, rocked them. They stopped fidgeting and coughing. She heard with pleasure her full plain northern voice sweep out over them and to the back of the hall, filling it to the baronial beams and spreading over the seats and into the empty galleries.

"Good old Sally," shouted a man.

"Come on, Sally," shouted another, wet-lipped with love at the sight of her and nudging his neighbour. She paused in the middle of her sentence and smiled fully at him—the first broad smile of the night.

She loved these opening minutes of her speeches. I'm an old potato, she thought, but my hair is brown and alive and I've got a voice. I can do anything with it. It was as powerful as a man's, yet changeable. Now it was soft, now violent; riotous in argument yet simple; always firm and disturbing. It could be blunt and brutal and yet it throbbed. It had sloshed its way through strikes and mass meetings; it had rebounded off factory walls, it had romped and somersaulted over thousands of heads. It had rung bitterly out through the Spanish War, when she was a young woman; through the rows of the Second Front, the peace campaigns, the Hungarian quarrel; it was all out now for Banning the Tests. It had never worn out, never coarsened, never aged; in these first few minutes it was her blood, the inner, spontaneous fountain of her girlhood, something virginal she would never lose. At every meeting it was reborn.

Even her shrewd brown eyes were bemused by her utter pleasure in hearing this voice, so that all of her early sentences surprised her by their clarity and the feeling that was in them; she was proud to feel her lungs heave, to watch the next thought form in her brain, the next argument assemble, the words, the very vowels and consonants fall into place. It was thrilling to pause and throw in a joke, a flash of hate or a line of wit that would sometimes recklessly jump into her head and make it itch with pleasure. This was the moment when she caught the crowd, played with them and made them hers. It was the time, for her, of consciousness, like a sudden falling in love, when the eyes of the audience answered her signals, when she could look carelessly from face to face, watching her words flick like an angler's line over them, looking for the defaulter. And, picking this man or this woman out, she would pause, as it were, to ask the audience to watch her make her catch, as if she had come down off the platform to be down among them with an intimacy that teased them and made their minds twist and flick and curl with fear and pleasure.

And then—it happened: the break, almost painful for her. The virginal voice that was so mysteriously herself would separate from her and perform alone as if it had nothing to do with her at all. It became, simply, the Voice. It left her—a plain, big-bellied, middle-aged woman —a body, to stand there exposed in all the woundedness of her years, while it went off like some trained dog barking round the audience, rounding them up, fetching in some stray from the back, flinging itself against the rows of empty chairs.

"And I say and I say again: we've got to stop these tests! We tell the Americans to stop these tests. We tell this Tory government that if it does not stop these tests . . ."

Now it was barking down derisively from the gallery at the end of the hall, barking at the City Arms, at fire extinguishers, at the Roll of Honour in gold, at the broom left by the cleaner, at the draught coming in at the doors, it was barking round walls below and the feet of the audience.

The light went out of Mrs. Prosser's face. She let the Voice carry on and she looked with boredom at the people. There was the elderly man, deaf and impatient; there was the big married woman with folded arms who kept glancing down her row to see everyone was listening, like a policewoman. There were the two girls, shoulder to shoulder, with pretty false faces, waiting for a chance to whisper. There was a woman with mouth open, ravenous, as if she were going to rush the platform and kiss her. There were the threes or fours of men frosted with self-respect. There was the man who seemed nowadays to come to all her meetings, a man neither young nor old, listening with one ear and sly, who sat at the end of the row with one bent leg sticking out of the neat block of audience and who glanced often at the side door, as if he were waiting his chance or for a sign to make a bolt for it. For what? For the pubs before they closed, for the last tram, to meet someone, even just to stand in the street—why? Had he got—a life? It always troubled her. She wanted to follow him. And there was that swing-door, which kept gulping like a sob as someone pushed in and gave a glance at the meeting and then went out and the door gave another gulp like the noise of a washbasin, as if all the words of that

Voice of hers were going down a drain. She heard the Voice go on:

"For you can take it from me, if the Americans don't stop these tests, if the Russians don't stop these tests, if the Tory party just sits on its bum . . ."

Loud cheers. That was a word made for the North. Mrs. Prosser grinned at the Voice's joke. She had a good big bum herself.

The Voice went on. It carried nearly thirty years of her life. At a meeting like this—no, not like this, but much larger and in the open streets, in the Blackshirt days—she had met her husband. There was a shouting, arm-wrenching, tearing, kicking fight with the police. What solid lumps their bodies were! She (when she remembered it) had felt as light as air. A gale had lifted her suddenly so that she, like the rest of the scattering and re-forming crowd, was blown about and with a force in her big arms and body that was exalted. Bodies swung about like sacks of meal. The houses and all their windows seemed to buckle and bulge towards her, the cobbled street heaved up and down like a sea. You could pick up the street in your hands. A young man near her gave a shout and she shouted, too, and her shout was his and his was hers; for an extraordinary few moments they had the same body. A policeman struck at the young man, the blow fell on his neck, and *she* felt the pain. She could not remember how—but she was clawing at the policeman and the young man's blood struck her cheek. They spent that night in prison.

The pupil teacher at the Adderdale Road School (Girls) to be in prison! That was when the hate started—her mother saying she would never hold her head up again; they had always been decent people. The father saying: "All stuck-up with those books and too good for her own family." And now she had disgraced them. If young Prosser, the little weed, came round the house again—the father said—he'd belt him. In this very city. They sacked her from the school. From that time on her life had been committees, lectures, meetings. Always travelling, always on platforms, her husband at one end of the country and she at the other. He with the shout on his face and she with the shout on hers, a drawing back of the lips over the teeth: that was their love, too. Love a shout, marriage a shout. They saw each other for an hour or two, or a day or two, eating anything, anywhere, usually a sandwich or a few bars of chocolate. It was the chocolate that had made her put on weight. "I'm a fighting sweetshop." At first, he had been the nimble one, the leader, wearing himself out and often ill; he had the ideas; then one week when he was sick with an ulcer, she had taken a meeting—

and the Voice, this strange being inside her, came out and now it was she who commanded not only him but audiences by the hundreds, then the thousands. The Voice took over her own and her husband's life.

And they stick me at a place nine miles outside the city (her body, her bullying breasts and affronted belly were saying), in weather like this! I don't say I wasn't comfortable. That'd be a lie. I was glad to see a coal fire. Three-piece suite too and the telly on, very nice. You wouldn't have seen that in our home when I was a girl. We had a laugh too about Lord Birt's house, all those chimneys. Mrs. Jenkins was a maid there when she was a girl and they used to bless those chimneys! My husband and I did our courting up there in the woods above. Mrs. Jenkins and I had a good laugh about old times.

And then the old lady, Mr. Jenkins's mother, got restless. "Eh," says Mrs. Jenkins, "Mother wants her telly. We turned it off when you came. She sits there in front of it, tapping her toes on the floor when the cowboys go by, rocking up and down."

"You want to get on your horse and ride the range, Gran, don't you?" says Harry Jenkins, the lad. "Gran's in her saddle, reaching for her gun when the Westerns come on. She gets excited, don't you, Gran?"

Of course, the old lady was stone-deaf and couldn't hear a word he said. But she looks at me and says, suddenly, "That's Sally Gray." Just like that, her eyes like pistols. "That's Sally Gray."

"No, Gran, that's Mrs. Prosser. Excuse her, Mrs. Prosser, the mind . . . she's failing."

"It's Sally Gray," says the old lady.

"Now, Gran!" says Mrs. Jenkins. "You be a good girl."

"It's the girl that killed our Leslie. It's Sally Gray that sent our boy to Spain and killed him."

"Gran," says Mrs. Jenkins, "stop that. I won't have you upset us. Excuse her, Mrs. Prosser. My husband's brother was killed in the Spanish War. She doesn't forget it."

"It's Sally Gray, the schoolteacher, who went to prison and got her name in the papers and broke poor Mrs. Gray's heart." The old lady stands flapping her little hands about and turning round and round like a dog.

The atmosphere—you can imagine it!

"Now, Gran, Mrs. Prosser didn't do anything to Les. It's a long time ago."

"Tuesday, we heard," the old lady said.

"Gran," says the lad, taking the old lady's arm to steady her, "don't carry on. It'd be a bad day for the workers if they didn't fight for themselves. Uncle Les was an idealist."

Nine miles outside the town in weather like this.

"I'm sorry, Mrs. Prosser," says Mrs. Jenkins. "Switch on the telly, Harry. She's a great problem. Definitely. I could kill her," says Mrs. Jenkins, standing up stiff. And she suddenly picks up the teapot and rushes out of the room, crying.

"Excuse us," says Mr. Jenkins, giving the old lady a shake.

What a committee to put me in a house like that with a mad old woman. Where's the consideration? And they bring me here in a borrowed car that breaks down and we stand there on the moor, with the sleet coming through my stockings. And they spell your name wrong and scrape up an audience of ten or twenty people.

There was a cheer from the audience. The Voice had got into them. Mrs. Prosser paused: she was startled herself. She paused for the cheer and the Voice cracked a thin joke about the Foreign Secretary: "They fly about from Bonn to Washington, from Washington to London; you don't see them flying down here. They're afraid of getting their feathers dirty," and got a laugh from them, a dirty, draughty laugh, which gave the man at the end of the row a chance to inch his leg out further and get ready to make a bolt for it; and at that very second she saw the dead-white face of the clock at the end of the hall, its black hands like a jackknife opening.

Twenty to nine! Her husband down at Plymouth, the other end of the country. And Jack? Where is Jack? But as her Voice picked up its freedom again and sailed on, she silently asked the audience: Where's my son? What have you done with my son? A year ago I could tell you what he was doing. He'd come home from school, get himself some supper, that boy could cook, oh, yes, and clean up afterwards—and then settle to his homework. He could look after himself better than a grown man. From the age of nine he could manage on his own. My husband and I could leave him a week at a time and he didn't mind. And I'll tell you something else: a boy with a real political conscience!

You've done it—her body was shouting to the audience—*you've* done it! For twenty-five years my husband and I have been fighting for *you*, fighting the class enemy, getting justice for you, and you sit there —what is left of you—pulling in the big money, drunk on hire purchase, mesmerized by your tellys and your pools—and what do you do for *us*? When I knew I was going to have that boy I said to my husband,

"We won't let this stop the work." And we didn't. But you and your rotten society just did nothing. A year ago he was the best boy in this country and you couldn't stand it. No. You had to get him out and start him drinking with a lot of thieving hooligans, you put a knife in his hand. You know what he said to his father? "Well, you were in prison, you and Mother, you told me." "Son," his father said, "we were fighting for justice for the people." "Oh, that crap!" he says. That's what the great British people did while we were working for them. Those people out there lost a son twenty-five years ago in Spain. I want to tell you I lost mine last year—killed by his own side.

"Good old Sally," the audience shouted. "Hit 'em. Listen to her."

Mrs. Prosser paused with a smile of victory.

"But, my friends, you will say to me," the Voice suddenly became quiet and reasonable, "this government cannot act alone. It has got to consider the American government and the Russian government. You will say the British people cannot isolate itself from the human family . . ."

But Mrs. Prosser was saying to them: Before I came here this evening they took me to this Lord Birt's house, the one I told you about with all those chimneys; very friendly those chimneys looked when we were courting in the woods above. My husband and I used to look down at the house. And the time I liked the best was when the smoke was going up straight from them in the autumn. Some weekends when there was company at the house the smoke went up from many of them like it does from his lordship's mills, but pleasanter, homey. You'd see rooks turning round and round over it and hear a dog drag its chain and bark, or hear pails clash where they were washing the car or swooshing out the yard at the back: I always wanted to see inside when I was a girl. Well, today I saw it. Oh, yes! There I was inside sitting by the fire with a cat on my knees. Can you see me with a cat? There were some people there and after we'd had our meal this young man who just made that bad speech was there looking at the books in the white bookcases. And there was a young girl, plump with brown hair, talking to him about them. Lord Birt asked him where they'd been that morning and they said, "Up in the woods at the back." I'll tell you something. I was jealous. I was jealous of that young girl talking to that young man. I felt old and ugly and fat. Mind you, I don't like the way these girls wear trousers, so that they look as naked as the tadpoles we used to catch when we were kids. I'd split them myself, you'd have a laugh—but it wasn't that that made me jealous. I couldn't *talk* about anything. That lad can't make a speech, but he can talk and so could the girl. I sat there dumb and stupid. Every day, morning and evening, year after year, generation after generation, this was a home and they could talk about a subject in it. If you talked about a subject in my home when I was a girl they'd call you stuck-up. All I can do is to make bloody fine speeches in bloody empty halls like this.

There was coughing in the audience and now the Voice was quieter. The man sitting at the end of the row with his leg out made up his mind. He got both legs out, and bending slightly, thinking to make himself invisible, he slowly tiptoed out across the bare space to the door at the side. And half those forty or fifty heads, in the midst of their coughing, turned to watch, but not that widely smiling woman who was still looking ravenously up at the platform as if she were going to rush at Mrs. Prosser and swallow her.

Mrs. Prosser saw the man tiptoeing out to that life of his and she did what she always could do at any meeting, startle it out of its wits with a sudden shout, and make any escaper stop in his absurd delinquent steps.

"Fellow workers (the Voice rang out), don't kid yourselves. You won't escape. It is you and your children who are being betrayed by this cowardly government. It is you . . ."

But her life was the forty-seven-year-old body with the big white mournful bottom saying to them: And if you want to know what I thought when I passed the long mirror in the hall of Lord Birt's house when we were getting in the car to come to this place where I was born and brought up and where you can't even spell my name, if you want to know what I thought, I can tell you. It's you have made me ugly! Working for you! You never gave me a minute to read a book, look at a picture, or feed the spirit inside me. It was you who made me sit dumb as an old cow back there. You fight for justice and you lose half your life. You're ugly and you've made me as ugly as you are.

The applause went up sharp and short near the platform and echoed in the emptiness behind the audience. Chairs shifted. Mrs. Prosser sat down. Lord Birt and the young man congratulated her. She looked scornfully and boastfully at them.

"I've wet them," she said to the young man as they walked away down the steps off the platform. Out of the little crowd of people who had stayed behind to talk to the speakers, the young girl came forward and secretively, not to embarrass him, squeezed the young man's arm and said, "You were wonderful." He hardly listened but was looking eagerly into the crowd that surrounded Mrs. Prosser.

"We'll wait for her," he said fiercely. "She had them"—he held out his cupped hand—"like that." And he clenched his fist.

The Camberwell Beauty

August's? On the Bath road? Twice-Five August—of course I knew
August: ivory man. And the woman who lived with him—her name was
Price. She's dead. He went out of business years ago. He's probably
dead too. I was in the trade only three or four years but I soon knew
every antique dealer in the South of England. I used to go to all the
sales. Name another. Naseley of Close Place? Jades, Asiatics, never
touched India. Alsop of Ramsey? Ephemera. Marbright, High Street,
Boxley? Georgian silver. Fox? Are you referring to Fox of Denton or
Fox of Camden—William Morris, art nouveau—or the Fox Brothers
in the Portobello Road?—the eldest stuttered. They had an uncle in
Brighton who went mad looking for old Waterford. Hindmith? No, he
was just a copier. Ah now, Pliny! He was a very different cup of tea:
Caughley ware. (Coalport took it over in 1821.) I am speaking of
specialties: furniture is the bread and butter of the trade. It keeps a man
going while his mind is on his specialty, and within that specialty there
is one object he broods on from one year to the next, most of his life:
the thing a man would commit murder to get his hands on if he had
the nerve, but I have never heard of a dealer who had. Theft perhaps.
A stagnant lot. But if he does get hold of that thing he will never let
it go or certainly not to a customer— dealers only really like dealing
among themselves—but every other dealer in the trade knows he's got

it. So they sit in their shops reading the catalogues and watching one another. Fox broods on something Alsop has. Alsop has his eye on Pliny and Pliny puts his hands to one of his big red ears when he hears the name of August. At the heart of the trade is lust, but a lust that is a dream paralysed by itself. So paralysed that the only release, the only hope, as everyone knows, is disaster: a bankruptcy, a divorce, a court case, a burglary, trouble with the police, a death. Perhaps then the grip on some piece of treasure will weaken and fall into the watcher's hands and even if it goes elsewhere he will go on dreaming about it.

What was it that Pliny, Gentleman Pliny, wanted of a man like August, who was not much better than a country junk dealer? When I opened up in London I thought it was a particular Staffordshire figure, but Pliny was far above that. These figures fetch very little, though one or two are hard to find: "The Burning of Cranmer," for example. Very few were made; it never sold and the firm dropped it. I was young and eager and one day when a collector, a scholarly man, as dry as a stick, came to my shop and told me he had a complete collection except for this piece, I said in my innocent way: "You've come to the right man. I'm fairly certain I can get it for you—at a price." This was a lie; but I was astonished to see the old man look at me with contempt, then light up like a fire, and when he left, look back furtively at me: he had betrayed his lust.

You rarely see an antique shop standing on its own; there are always three or four together watching each other. I asked the advice of the man next door who ran a small boatyard on the canal in his spare time and he said, "Try Pliny down the Green: he knows everyone." I went "over the water," to Pliny; he was closed, but I did find him at last at a sale room. Pliny was marking his catalogue and waiting for the next lot to come up and he said to me in a scornful way, slapping a young man down, "August's got it." I saw him wink at the man next to him as I left.

I had bought myself a small red car that annoyed the older dealers and I drove down the other side of Steepleton on the Bath road. August's was one of four shops opposite the Lion Hotel on the main road at the end of the town where the country begins again, and there I got my first lesson. The shop was closed. I went across to the bar of the hotel, and August was there, a fat man of fifty in wide trousers and a drip to his nose who was paying for drinks from a bunch of dirty notes in his jacket pocket and dropping them on the floor. He was drunk and very offended when I picked a couple up and gave them to him. He'd just come back from Newbury races. I humoured him but he kept rolling about and turning his back to me half the time and so I blurted out, "I've just been over at the shop. You've got some Staffordshire, I hear."

He stood still and looked me up and down and the beer swelled in him.

"Who may you be?" he said with all the pomposity of drink. I told him. I said right out, "Staffordshire. 'Cranmer's Burning.' " His face went dead and the colour of liver.

"So is London," he said, and turned away to the bar.

"I'm told you might have it. I've got a collector," I said.

"Give this lad a glass of water," said August to the barmaid. "He's on fire."

There is nothing more to say about the evening or the many other visits I made to August's except that it has a moral to it and that I had to help August over to his shop, where an enormous woman much taller than he in a black dress and a little girl of fourteen or so were at the door waiting for him. The girl looked frightened and ran a few yards from the door as August and his woman collided belly to belly.

"Come back," called the woman.

The child crept back. And to me the woman said, "We're closed," and having got the two inside, shut the door in my face.

The moral is this: if "The Burning of Cranmer" was August's treasure, it was hopeless to try and get it before he had time to guess what mine was. It was clear to him I was too new to the trade to have one. And in fact I don't think he had the piece. Years later, I found my collector had left his collection complete to a private museum in Leicester when he died. He had obtained what he craved: a small immortality in being memorable for his relation to a minor work of art.

I know what happened at August's that night. In time his woman, Mrs. Price, bellowed it to me, for her confidences could be heard down the street. August flopped on his bed, and while he was sleeping off the drink she got the bundles of notes out of his pockets and counted them. She always did this after his racing days. If he had lost she woke him up and shouted at him; if he had made a profit she kept quiet and hid it under her clothes in a chest of drawers. I went down from London again and again, but August was not there.

Most of the time these shops are closed. You rattle the door handle; no reply. Look through the window, and each object inside stands gleaming with something like a smile of malice, especially on porcelain and glass. The furniture states placidly that it has been in better houses than you will ever have, the brass speaks of vanished servants. Everything speaks of the dead hands that have touched it; even the dust is like the dust of vanished families. In the shabby places—and August's was shabby—the dealer is like a toadstool that has grown out of the unwanted. There was only one attractive object in August's shop—as I say, he went in for ivories, and on a table at the back was a set of white and red chessmen set out on a board partly concealed by a screen. I was tapping my feet impatiently and looking through the window when I was astonished to see two of the chessmen had moved; then I saw a hand, a long, thin work-reddened hand appear from behind the screen and move one of the pieces back. Life in the place! I rattled the door handle again and the child came from behind the screen. She had a head loaded with heavy black hair to her shoulders and a white heart-shaped face and wore a skimpy dress with small pink flowers on it. She was so thin that she looked as if she would blow away in fright out of the shop, but instead, pausing on tiptoe, she swallowed with appetite: her sharp eyes had seen my red car outside the place. She looked back cautiously at the inner door of the shop and then ran to unlock the door. I went in.

"What are you up to?" I said. "Playing chess?"

"I'm teaching my children," she said, putting up her chin like a child of five. "Do you want to buy something?"

At once Mrs. Price was there, shouting, "Isabel, I told you not to open the door. Go back into the room."

Mrs. Price went to the chessboard and put the pieces back in their places.

"She's a child," said Mrs. Price, accusing me.

And when she said this, Mrs. Price blew herself out to a larger size; then her sullen face went blank and babyish as if she had travelled out of herself for a beautiful moment. Then her brows levelled and she became sullen.

"Mr. August's out," she said.

"It is about a piece of Staffordshire," I said. "He mentioned it to me. When will he be in?"

"He's in and out. No good asking. He doesn't know himself."

"I'll try again."

"If you like."

There was nothing to be got out of Mrs. Price.

In my opinion, the antique trade is not one for a woman, unless she is on her own. Give a woman a shop and she wants to sell something: even the little girl at August's wanted to sell. It's instinct. It's an excitement. Mrs. Price, August's woman, was living with a man exactly like the others in the trade; he hated customers and hated parting with anything. By middle age these women have dead blank faces, they look with resentment and indifference at what is choking their shops; their eyes go smaller and smaller as the chances of getting rid of it become rarer and rarer and they are defeated. Kept out of the deals their husbands have among themselves, they see even their natural love of intrigue frustrated. This was the case of Mrs. Price, who must have been handsome in a big-boned way when she was young, but who had swollen into a drudge. What allured the men did not allure her at all. The trade feeds on illusions. If you go after Georgian silver you catch the illusion, while you are bidding, that you are related to the rich families who owned it. You acquire imaginary ancestors. Or, like Pliny with the piece of Meissen he never got his hands on, you drift into German history and become a secret curator of the Victoria and Albert Museum—a place he often visited. August's lust for "the ivories" gave to his horse-racing mind a private Oriental side: he dreamt of rajahs, sultans, harems, and lavish gamblers, which, in a man as vulgar as he was, came out in sad reality as a taste for country girls and the company of bookies. Illusions lead to furtiveness in everyday life and to sudden temptations: the trade is close to larceny, to situations where you don't ask where something has come from, especially for a man like August, whose dreams had landed him in low company. He had started at the bottom, and very early he "received" and got twelve months for it. This frightened him. He took up with Mrs. Price, and though he resented it, she had made a fairly honest man of him. August was to be *her* work of art.

But he did not make an honest woman of her. No one disapproved of this except herself. Her very size, growing year by year, was an assertion of virtue. Everyone took her side in her public quarrels with him. And as if to make herself more respectable, she had taken in her sister's little girl when the sister died: the mother had been in Music Hall. Mrs. Price petted and prinked the little thing. When August became a failure as a work of art, Mrs. Price turned to the child. Even August was charmed by her when she jumped on his knee and danced about showing him her new clothes. A little actress, as everyone said —exquisite.

It took me a long time to give up the belief that August had the

Cranmer piece, and as I know now, he hadn't got it; but at last I did see I was wasting my time and settled into the routine of the business. I sometimes saw August at country sales, and at one outside Marlborough something ridiculous happened. It was a big sale and went on till late in the afternoon and he had been drinking; after lunch the auctioneer had put up a china cabinet and the bidding was strong. Some outsider was bidding against the dealers, a thing that made them close their faces with moral indignation: the instinctive hatred of customers united them. Drink always stirred August morally; he was a rather despised figure and he was, I suppose, determined to speak for all. He entered the bidding. Up went the price: 50,5,60,5,70,5,80,5,90. The outsiders were a young couple with a dog.

"Ninety, ninety?" called the auctioneer.

August could not stand it. "Twice-five," he shouted.

There is not much full-throated laughter at sales: it is usually shoppish and dusty. But the crowd in this room looked round at August and shouted with a laughter that burst the gloom of trade. He was put out for a second and then saw his excitement had made him famous. The laughter went on: the wonder had for a whole minute stopped the sale. "Twice-five!" He was slapped on the back. At sixty-four the man who had never had a nickname had been christened. He looked round him. I saw a smile cross his face and double the pomposity that beer had put into him and he redoubled it that evening at the nearest pub. I went off to my car, and Alsop of Ramsey, the ephemera man who had picked up some Victorian programs, followed me and said out of the side of his mouth, "More trouble tonight at August's."

And then to change the subject and speaking for every dealer south of the Trent, he offered serious news. "Pliny's mother's dead—Pliny of the Green."

The voice had all the shifty meaning of the trade. I was too simple to grasp the force of this confidence. It surprised me in the following weeks to hear people repeat the news, "Pliny's mother's dead," in so many voices, from the loving-memory-and-deepest-sympathy manner as much suited to old clothes, old furniture, and human beings indiscriminately as to the flat statement that an event of business importance had occurred in my eventless trade. I was in it for the money and so, I suppose, were all the rest—how else could they live?—but I seemed to be surrounded by a dreamy freemasonry who thought of it in a different secretive way.

On a wet morning the following spring I was passing through Salisbury on market day and stopped in the square to see if there was anything worth picking up at the stalls there. It was mostly junk, though I did find a pretty Victorian teapot—no mark, I agree—with a chip in the spout for a few shillings, because the fever of the trade never quite leaves one even on dull days. (I sold the pot five years later for eight pounds when prices started to go mad.) I went into one of the pubs on the square—I forget its name—and I was surprised to see Marbright and Alsop there and, sitting near the window, Mrs. Price. August was getting drinks at the bar.

Alsop said to me, "Pliny's here. I passed him a minute ago."

Marbright said, "He was standing in Woolworth's doorway. I asked him to come and have one, but he wouldn't."

"It's hit him hard, his mother going," Marbright said. "What's he doing here? Queen Mary's dead."

It was an old joke that Gentleman Pliny had never been the same since the old Queen had come to his shop some time back—everyone knew what she was for picking up things. He only opened on Sundays now and a wealthy crowd came there in their big cars—a new trend, as Alsop said. August brought the drinks and stood near, for Mrs. Price spread herself on the bench and never left much room for anyone else to sit down. He looked restless and glum.

"Where will Pliny be without his mother," Mrs. Price moaned into her glass and, putting it down, glowered at August. She had been drinking a good deal.

August ignored her and said, sneering, "He kept her locked up." There is always a lot of talking about "locking up" in the trade; people's minds go to their keys.

"It was a kindness," Mrs. August said, "after the burglars got in at Sampson's, three men in a van loading it up in broad daylight. Any woman of her age would be frightened."

"It was nothing to do with the burglary," said August, always sensitive when crime was mentioned. "She was getting soft in the head. He caught her giving his stuff away when she was left on her own. She was past it."

Mrs. Price was a woman who didn't like to be contradicted.

"He's a gentleman," said Mrs. Price, accusing August. "He was good to his mother. He took her out every Sunday night of his life. She liked a glass of stout on Sundays."

This was true, though Mrs. Price had not been to London for years and had never seen this event; but all agreed. We live on myths.

"It was her kidneys," moaned Mrs. Price; one outsize woman was mourning another, seeing a fate.

"I suppose that's why he didn't get married, looking after her," said Marbright.

"Pliny! Get married! Don't make me laugh," said August with a defiant recklessness that seemed to surprise even himself. "The last Saturday in every month like a clock striking he was round the pubs in Brixton with old Lal Drake."

And now, as if frightened by what he said, he swanked his way out of the side door of the pub on his way to the gents'.

We lowered our eyes. There are myths, but there are facts. They all knew—even I had heard—that what August said was true, but it was not a thing a sensible man would say in front of Mrs. Price. And—mind you—Pliny standing a few doors down the street. But Mrs. Price stayed calm among the thoughts in her mind.

"That's a lie," she said peacefully, though she was eyeing the door waiting for August to come back.

"I knew his father," said Alsop. We were soon laughing about the ancient Pliny, the Bermondsey boy who began with a barrow shouting "Old iron" in the streets, a man who never drank, never had a bank account—didn't trust banks—who belted his son while his mother "educated him up"—she was a tall woman and the boy grew up like her, tall with a long arching nose and those big red ears that looked as though his parents had pulled him now this way, now that, in their fight over him. She had been a housekeeper in a big house and she had made a son who looked like an old family butler, Cockney to the bone, but almost a gentleman. Except, as Alsop said, his way of blowing his nose like a foghorn on the Thames, but sharp as his father. Marbright said you could see the father's life in the store at the back of the shop: it was piled high with what had made the father's money—every kind of old-fashioned stuff.

"Enough to furnish two or three hotels," Alsop said. Mrs. Price nodded.

"Wardrobes, tables . . ." she said.

"A museum," said Marbright. "Helmets, swords. Two fourposters the last time I was there."

"Ironwork. Brass," nodded Mrs. Price mournfully.

"Must date back to the Crimean War," said Marbright.

"And it was all left to Pliny."

There was a general sigh.

"And he doesn't touch it. Rubbish, he calls it. He turned his back on it. Only goes in for the best. Hepplewhite, marquetries, his consoles, Regency."

There was a pause.

"And," I said, "his Meissen."

They looked at me as if I were a criminal. They glanced at one another as if asking whether they should call the police. I was either a thief or I had publicly stripped them of all their clothes. I had publicly announced Pliny's lust.

Although Mrs. Price had joined in the conversation, it was in the manner of someone talking in her sleep, for when this silence came she woke up and said in a startled voice, "Lal Drake." And screwing up her fists she got up, and pausing to get ready for a rush, she heaved herself fast to the door by which August had left for the gents' down the alley a quarter of an hour before.

"The other door, missis," someone shouted. But she was through it.

"Drink up," we said and went out by the front door. I was the last and had a look down the side alley and there I saw a sight: August with a hand doing up his fly buttons and the other arm protecting his face. Mrs. Price was hitting out at him and shouting. The language!

"You dirty sod. I knew it. The girl told me." She was shouting. She saw me, stopped hitting and rushed at me in tears and shouted back at him. "The filthy old man."

August saw his chance and got out of the alley and made for the cars in the square. She let me go, to shout after him. We were all there, and in Woolworth's doorway was Pliny. Rain was still falling and he looked wet and all the more alone for being wet. I walked off, and, I suppose, seeing me go and herself being alone and giddy in her rage she looked all round and turned her temper on me. "The girl has got to go," she shouted.

Then she came to her senses.

"Where is August?" August had got to his car and was driving out of the square. She could do nothing. Then she saw Pliny. She ran from me to Pliny, from Pliny to me.

"He's going after the girl," she screamed.

We calmed her down and it was I who drove her home. (This was when she told me, as the wipers went up and down on the windshield, that she and August were not married.) Her tears were like the hissing water we splashed through on the road. "I'm worried for the child. I told her, 'Keep your door locked.' I see it's locked every night. I'm afraid I'll forget and won't hear him if I've had a couple. She's a kid. She doesn't know anything." I understood that the face I had always thought was empty was really filled with the one person she loved: Isabel.

August was not there when we got to their shop. Mrs. Price went in, and big as she was, she did not knock anything over.

"Isabel?" she called.

The girl was in the scullery and came out with a wet plate that dripped on the carpet. In two years she had changed. She was wearing an old dress and an apron, but also a pair of silver high-heeled evening shoes. She had become the slut of the house and her pale skin looked dirty.

"You're dripping that thing everywhere. What have you got those shoes on for? Where did you get them?"

"Uncle Harry, for Christmas," she said. She called August "Uncle Harry." She tried to look jaunty, as if she had put all her hope in life into those silly evening shoes.

"All right," said Mrs. Price weakly, looking at me to keep quiet and say nothing.

Isabel took off her apron when she saw me. I don't know whether she remembered me. She was still pale, but had the shapeliness of a small young woman. Her eyes looked restlessly and uncertainly at both of us; her chin was firmer but it trembled. She was smiling too, and because I was there and the girl might see an ally in me, Mrs. Price looked with half kindness at Isabel. But when I got up to go, the girl looked at me as if she would follow me out the door. Mrs. Price got up fast to bar the way. She stood on the doorstep of the shop watching me get into the car, puffing with the inability to say "Thank you" or "Good-bye." If the girl was a child, Mrs. Price was ten times a child, and both of them standing on the doorstep were like children who don't want anyone to go away.

I drove off, and for a few miles I thought about Mrs. Price and the girl, but once settled into the long drive to London, the thought of Pliny supplanted them. I had been caught up in the fever of the trade. Pliny's mother was dead. What was going to happen to Pliny and all that part of the business Pliny had inherited from his father, the stuff he despised and had not troubled himself with very much in his mother's time? I ought to go "over the water"—as we say in London —to have a look at it sometime.

In a few days I went there; I found the idea had occurred to many others. The shop was on one of the main bus routes in South London, a speckled early Victorian place with an ugly red-brick store behind it. Pliny's father had had an eye for a cosy but useful bit of property. Its windows had square panes (1810) and to my surprise the place was open and I could see people inside. There was Pliny with his nose which looked servile rather than distinguished, wearing a long biscuit-coloured tweed jacket with leather pads at the elbows like a Cockney sportsman. There, too, was August with his wet eyes and drinker's shame, Mrs. Price swelling over him in her best clothes, and the girl. They had come up from the country and August had had his boots cleaned. The girl was in her best, too, and was standing apart touching things in the shop and on the point of merriment, looking with wonder at Pliny's ears. He often seemed to be talking at her when he was talking to Mrs. Price. I said, "Hullo! Up from the country? What are you doing here?"

Mrs. Price was so large that she had to turn her whole body and place her belly in front of everyone who spoke to her.

"Seeing to his teeth," she said, nodding at August, and from years of habit, August turned, too, when his wife turned, in case it was just as well not to miss one of her pronouncements, whatever else he might dodge. One side of August's jaw was swollen. Then Mrs. Price slowly turned her whole body to face Pliny again. They were talking about his mother's death. Mrs. Price was greedy, as one stout woman thinking of another, for a melancholy tour of the late mother's organs. The face of the girl looked prettily wise and holidayfied because the heavy curls of her hair hung close to her face. She looked out of the window, restless and longing to get away while her elders went on talking, but she was too listless to do so. Then she would look again at Pliny's large ears with a child's pleasure in anything strange: they gave him a dog-like appearance, and if the Augusts had not been there, I think she would have jumped at him mischievously to touch them but remembered in time that she had lately grown into a young lady. When she saw him looking at her she turned her back and began writing in the dust on a little table standing next to a cabinet which had a small jug in it. She was writing her name in the dust I S A B . . . And then stopped. She turned round suddenly because she saw I had been watching.

"Is that old Meissen?" she called out, pointing to the jug in the cabinet. They stopped talking. It was comic to see her pretending, for my benefit, that she knew all about porcelain.

"Cor! Old Meissen!" said August, pulling his racing newspaper out of his jacket pocket with excitement, and Mrs. Price fondly swung her big handbag; all laughed loudly—a laugh of lust and knowledge. They knew, or thought they knew, that Pliny had a genuine Meissen piece somewhere, probably upstairs where he lived. The girl was pleased to have made them laugh at her; she had been noticed.

Pliny said decently, "No, dear. That's Caughley. Would you like to see it?"

He walked to the cabinet and took the jug down and put it on a table.

"Got the leopard?" said August knowingly. Pliny showed the mark of the leopard on the base of the jug and put it down again. It was a pretty, shapely jug with a spray of branches and in the branches a pair of pheasants were perching, done in transfer. The girl scared us all by picking it up in both hands, but it was charming to see her holding it up and studying it.

"Careful," said Mrs. Price.

"She's all right," said Pliny. Then—it alarmed us—she wriggled with laughter.

"What a funny face," she said.

Under the lip of the jug was the small face of an old man with a long nose looking sly and wicked.

"They used to put a face under the lip," Pliny said.

"That's right," said August.

The girl held it out at arm's length, and looking from the jug to Pliny, she said, "It's like you, Mr. Pliny."

"Isabel!" said Mrs. Price. "That's rude."

"But it is," said Isabel. "Isn't it?" She was asking me. Pliny grinned. We were all relieved to see him take the jug from her and put it back in the cabinet.

"It belonged to my mother," he said. "I keep it there."

Pliny said to me, despising me because I had said nothing and because I was a stranger, "Go into the back and have a look round if you want to. The light's on."

I left the shop and went down the steps into the long storeroom, where the whitewashed walls were grey with dust. There was an alligator hanging by a nail near the steps, a couple of cavalry helmets and a dirty drum that must have been there since the Crimean War. I went down into streets of stacked-up furniture. I felt I was walking into an inhuman crypt or, worse still, one of those charnel houses or ossuaries I had seen pictures of in one of my father's books when I was a boy. Large as the store was, it was lit by a single electric light bulb hanging from a girder in the roof, and the yellow light was deathly. The notion of "picking up" anything at Pliny's depressed me, so that I was left with a horror of the trade I had joined. Yet feelings of this kind are never simple. After half an hour I left the shop.

I understood before that day was over and I was back in the room over my own place that what had made me more wretched was the wound of a sharp joy. First, the sight of the girl leaving her name unfinished in the dust had made my heart jump; then when she held the vase in her hands I had felt the thrill of a revelation: until then I had never settled what I should go in for, but now I saw it. Why not collect Caughley? That was it. Caughley: it was one of those inspirations that excite one so that every sight in the world changes—even houses, buses, streets, and people are transfigured and become unreal as desire carries one away—and then, cruelly, it passes and one is left exhausted. The total impossibility of an impatient young man like myself collecting Caughley, which hadn't been made since 1821, became brutally clear. Too late for Staffordshire, too late for Dresden, too late for Caughley and all the beautiful things. I was savage for lack of money. The following day I went to the Victoria and Albert and there I saw other far more beautiful things enshrined and inaccessible. I gazed with wonder. My longing for possession held me, and then I was elevated to a state of worship, as if they were idols, holy and never to be touched. Then I remembered the girl's hands and a violent daydream passed through my head: it lasted only a second or two, but in that time I smashed the glass case, grabbed a treasure, and bolted with it. It frightened me that such an idea could have occurred to me. I left the museum and I turned against my occupation, against Marbright, Alsop and, above all, Pliny and August, and it broke my heart to think of that pretty girl living among such people and drifting into the shabbiness of the trade. I S A B—half a name, written by a living finger in dust.

One has these brief sensations when one is young. They pass and one does nothing about them. There is nothing remarkable about Caughley —except that you can't get it. I did not collect Caughley for a simple reason: I had to collect my wits. The plain truth is that I was incompetent. I had only to look at my bank account. I had bought too much.

At the end of the year it seemed like the bankruptcy court unless I had a stroke of luck. Talk of trouble making the trade move: I was trouble myself; dealers could smell it coming and came sniffing into my shop—and at the end of the year I sold up for what I could get. It would have been better if I could have waited for a year or two when the boom began. For some reason I kept the teapot I had bought in Salisbury to remind me of wasted time. In its humble way it was pretty.

In the next six months I changed. I had to. I pocketed my pride and got a dull job at an auctioneer's; at least it took me out of the office when I got out keys and showed people round. The firm dealt in house property and developments. The word "develop" took hold of me. The firm was a large one and sometimes "developed" far outside London. I was told to go and inspect some of the least important bits of property that were coming into the market. One day a row of shops in Steeple-ton came up for sale. I said I knew them. They were on the London road opposite the Lion Hotel at the end of the town. My boss was always impressed by topography and the names of hotels and sent me down there. The shops were in the row where August and one or two others had had their business, six of them.

What a change! The Lion had been repainted; the little shops seemed to have got smaller. In my time the countryside had begun at the end of the row. Now builders' scaffolding was standing in the fields beyond. I looked for August's. A cheap café had taken over his place. He had gone. The mirror man who lived next door was still there but had gone into beads and fancy art jewellery. His window was full of hanging knick-knacks and mobiles.

"It's the tourist trade now," he said. He looked ill.

"What happened to August?"

He studied me for a moment and said, "Closed down," and I could get no more out of him. I crossed the street to the Lion. Little by little, a sentence at a time in a long slow suspicious evening, I got news of August from the barmaid as she went back and forth serving customers, speaking in a low voice, her eye on the new proprietor in case the next sentence that came out of her might be bad for custom. The sentences were spoken like sentences from a judge summing up, bit by bit. August had got two years for receiving stolen goods; the woman—"She wasn't his wife"—had been knocked down by a car as she was coming out of the bar at night—"not that she drank, not really drank; her weight, really"—and then came the final sentence that brought back to me the alerting heat and fever of the trade's secrets: "There was always trouble over there. It started when the girl ran away."

"Isabel?" I said.

"I dunno—the girl."

I stood outside the hotel and looked to the east and then to the west. It was one of those quarters of an hour on a main road when, for some reason, there is no traffic coming either way. I looked at the now far-off fields where the February wind was scything over the grass, turning it into waves of silver as it passed over them. I thought of Isab . . . running with a case in her hand, three years ago. Which way? Where do girls run to? Sad.

I went back to London. There are girls in London too, you know. I grew a beard, reddish; it went with the red car, which I had managed to keep. I could afford to take a girl down to the south coast now and then. Sometimes we came back by the Brixton road, sometimes through Camberwell, and when we did this I often slowed down at Pliny's and told the girls, "That man's sitting on a gold mine." They never believed it or, at least, only one did. She said: "Does he sell rings? Let us have a look."

"They're closed," I said. "They're always closed."

"I want to look," she said, so we stopped and got out.

We looked into the dark window—it was Saturday night—and we could see nothing, and as we stared we heard a loud noise coming, it seemed, from the place next door or from down the drive-in at the side of Pliny's shop, a sound like someone beating boxes or bathtubs at first until I got what it was: drums. Someone blew a bugle, a terrible squeaky sound. There was heavy traffic on the street, but the bugle seemed to split it in half.

"Boys' Brigade, practicing for Sunday," I said. We stood laughing with our hands to our ears as we stared into the dark. All I could make out was something white on a table at the back of the shop. Slowly I saw it was a set of chessmen. Chess, ivories, August—perhaps Pliny had got August's chessmen.

"What a din!" said the girl. I said no more to her, for in my mind there was the long-forgotten picture of Isabel's finger on the pieces, at Steepleton.

When I've got time, I thought, I will run over to Pliny's; perhaps he will know what happened to the girl.

And I did go there again, one afternoon, on my own. Still closed. I rattled the door handle. There was no answer. I went to a baker's next door, then to a butcher's, then to a pub. The same story. "He only opens on Sundays" or "He's at a sale." Then to a tobacconist's. I said it was funny to leave a shop empty like that, full of valuable stuff. The tobacconist became suspicious.

"There's someone there, all right. His wife's there."

"No, she's not," his wife said. "They've gone off to a sale. I saw them."

She took the hint.

"No one in charge to serve customers," she said.

I said I'd seen a chessboard that interested me and the tobacconist said: "It's dying out. I used to play."

"I didn't know he got married," I said.

"He's got beautiful things," said his wife. "Come on Sunday."

Pliny married! That made me grin. The only women in his life I had ever heard of were his mother and the gossip about Lal Drake. Perhaps he had made an honest woman of *her.* I went back for one last look at the chessmen and, sure enough, as the tobacconist's wife had hinted, someone *had* been left in charge, for I saw a figure pass through the inner door of the shop. The watcher was watched. Almost at once I heard the tap and roll of a kettledrum; I put my ear to the letter box and distinctly heard a boy's voice shouting orders. Children! All the drumming I had heard on Saturday had come from Pliny's—a whole family drumming. Think of Pliny married to a widow with kids: he had not had time to get his own. I took back what I had thought of him and Lal Drake. I went off for an hour to inspect a house that was being sold on Camberwell Green, and stopped once more at Pliny's on the way back, on the chance of catching him, and I went to the window. Standing in the middle of the shop was Isabel.

Her shining black hair went to her shoulders. She was wearing a red dress with a schoolgirlish white collar to it. If I had not known her by her heart-shaped face and her full childish lips, I would have known her by her tiptoe way of standing like an actress just about to sing a song or do a dance when she comes forward on the stage. She looked at me daringly. It was the way, I remembered, she had looked at everyone. She did not know me. I went to the door and tipped the handle. It did not open. I saw her watching the handle move. I went on rattling. She straightened and shook her head, pushing back her hair. She did not go away: she was amused by my efforts. I went back to the window of the shop and asked to come in. She could not hear, of course. My mouth was opening and shutting foolishly. That amused her even more. I pointed to something in the window, signalling that I was interested in it. She shook her head again. I tried pointing to other things: a cabinet, an embroidered fire screen, a jar three feet high. At each one she shook her head. It was like a guessing game. I was smiling, even laughing, to persuade her. I put my hands to my chest and

pretended to beg like a dog. She laughed at this and looked behind, as
if calling to someone. If Pliny wasn't there, his wife might be, or the
children, so I pointed upwards and made a movement of my hands,
imitating someone turning a key in a lock. I was signalling "Go and get
the key from Mrs. Pliny," and I stepped back and looked up at a
window above the shop. When I did this, Isabel was frightened; she
went away shouting to someone. And that was the end of it; she did
not come back.

I went away thinking, Well, that is a strange thing! What ideas
people put into your head and you build fancies yourself: that woman
in the bar at Steepleton telling me Isabel had run away and I imagining
her running in those poor evening shoes I'd once seen, in the rain down
the Bath road, when—what was more natural in a trade where they all
live with their hands in one another's pockets—Pliny had married, and
they had taken the girl on at the shop. It was a comfort to think of.
I hadn't realized how much I had worried about what would happen
to a naïve girl like Isabel when the break-up came. Alone in the world!
How silly. I thought, One of these Sundays I'll go up there and hear
the whole story. And I did.

There was no one there except Pliny and his rich Sunday customers.
I even went into the store at the back, looked everywhere. No sign of
Isabel. The only female was a woman in a shabby black dress and not
wearing a hat who was talking to a man testing the door of a wardrobe,
making it squeak, while the woman looked on without interest, in the
manner of a dealer's wife: obviously the new Mrs. Pliny. She turned
to make way for another couple waiting to look at it. I nearly knocked
over a stack of cane chairs as I got past.

If there was no sign of Isabel, the sight of Pliny shocked me. He had
been a dead man, permanently dead as wood, even clumsy in his big
servile bones, though shrewd. Now he had come to life in the strangest,
excited way—much older to look at, thinner and frantic as he looked
about him this way and that. He seemed to be possessed by a demon.
He talked loudly to people in the shop and was suspicious when he was
not talking. He was frightened, abrupt, rude. Pliny married! Marriage
had wrecked him or he was making too much money; he looked like
a man expecting to be robbed. He recognized me at once. I had felt
him watching me from the steps going down to the store. As I came
back to the steps to speak to him he spoke to me first—distinctly, in
a loud voice, "I don't want any of August's men here, see?"

I went red in the face. "What do you mean?" I said.

"You heard me," he said. "You know what he got."

Wells of Hungerford was standing near, pretending not to listen. Pliny was telling the trade that I was in with August—publicly accusing me of being a fence. I controlled my temper.

"August doesn't interest me," I said. "I'm in property. Marsh, Help, and Hitchcock. I sold his place, the whole street."

And I walked past him looking at a few things as I left.

I was in a passion. The dirty swine—all right when his mother kept an eye on him, the poor old woman, but now he'd gone mad. And that poor girl! I went to the tobacconist's for the Sunday paper in a dream, put down my money and took it without a word and was almost out the door when the wife called out, "Did you find him? Did you get what you wanted?" A friendly London voice. I tapped the side of my head.

"You're telling me," the wife said. "Well, he has to watch everything now. Marrying a young girl like that, it stands to reason," she said in a melancholy voice.

"Wears him out, at his age," suggested the tobacconist.

"Stop the dirty talk, Alfred," said the wife.

"You mean he married the *girl*?" I said. "Who's the big woman without a hat—in the store?"

"What big woman is that?" asked the tobacconist's wife. "He's married to the girl. Who else do you think—there's no one else."

The wife's face went as blank as a tombstone in the sly London way.

"She's done well for herself," said the tobacconist. "Keeps her locked up like his mother, wasn't I right?"

"He worships her," said the woman.

I went home to my flat. I was nauseated. The thought of Isabel in bed with that dressed-up servant, with his wet eyes, his big raw ears, and his breath smelling of onions! Innocent? No, as the woman said, "She has done well for herself." Happy with him too. I remembered her pretty face laughing in the shop. What else could you expect, after August and Mrs. Price.

The anger I felt with Pliny grew to a rage, but by the time I was in my own flat, Pliny vanished from the picture in my mind. I was filled with passion for the girl. The fever of the trade had come alive in me: Pliny had got something I wanted. I could think of nothing but her, just as I remember the look August gave Pliny when the girl asked if the jug was Meissen. I could see her holding the jug at arm's length, laughing at the old man's face under the lip. And I could see that Pliny was not mad: what was making him frantic was possessing the girl.

I kept away from Pliny's. I tried to drive the vision out of my mind, but I could not forget it. I became cunning. Whenever my job allowed it—and even when it didn't—I started passing the time of day with any dealer I had known, picked up news of the sales, studied catalogues, tried to find out which ones Pliny would go to. She might be with him. I actually went to Newbury but he was not there. Bath he couldn't miss and, sure enough, he was there and she wasn't. It was ten in the morning and the sale had just started.

I ran off and got into my car. I drove as fast as I could the hundred miles back to London and cursed the lunchtime traffic. I got to Pliny's shop and rang the bell. Once, then several long rings. At once the drum started beating and went on as if troops were marching. People passing in the street paused to listen too. I stood back from the window and I saw a movement at a curtain upstairs. The drumming was still going on, and when I bent to listen at the letter box I could hear the sound become deafening and often very near and then there was a blast from the bugle. It was a misty day south of the river, and for some reason or other I was fingering the grey window and started writing her name, I S A B . . . hopelessly, but hoping that perhaps she might come near enough to see. The drumming stopped. I waited and waited and then I saw an extraordinary sight: Isabel herself in the dull-red dress, but with a lancer's helmet on her head and a side drum on its straps hanging from her shoulders and the drumsticks in her hand. She was standing upright like a boy playing soldiers, her chin up and puzzling at the sight of the letters ᗺ A S I on the window. When she saw me she was confused. She immediately gave two or three taps to the drum and then bent almost double with laughter. Then she put on a straight face and played the game of pointing to one thing after another in the shop. Every time I shook my head, until at last I pointed to her. This pleased her. Then I shouted through the letter box, "I want to come in."

"Come in," she said. "It's open." The door had been open all the time: I had not thought of trying it. I went inside.

"I thought you were locked in."

She did not answer but wagged her head from side to side.

"Sometimes I lock myself in," she said. "There are bad people about, August's men."

She said this with an air of great importance, but her face became ugly as she said it. She took off the helmet and put down the drum.

"So I beat the drum when Mr. Pliny is away," she said. She called him Mr. Pliny.

"What good does that do?"

"It is so quiet when Mr. Pliny is away. I don't do it when he's here. It frightens August's men away."

"It's as good as telling them you are alone here," I said. "That's why I came. I heard the drum and the bugle."

"Did you?" she said eagerly. "Was it loud?"

"Very loud."

She gave a deep sigh of delight.

"You see!" she said, nodding her head complacently.

"Who taught you to blow the bugle?" I said.

"My mother did," she said. "She did it on the stage. Mr. Pliny— you know, when Mr. Pliny fetched me in his motor car—I forgot it. He had to go back and get it. I was too frightened."

"Isab . . ." I said.

She blushed. She remembered.

"I might be one of August's men," I said.

"No, you're not. I know who you are," she said. "Mr. Pliny's away for the day but that doesn't matter. I am in charge. Is there something you were looking for?"

The child had gone when she put the drum aside. She became serious and practical: Mrs. Pliny! I was confused by my mistake in not knowing the door was open and she busied herself about the shop. She knew what she was doing and I felt very foolish.

"Is there something special?" she said. "Look around." She had become a confident woman. I no longer felt there was anything strange about her. I drifted to look at the chessmen and I could not pretend to myself that they interested me, but I did ask her the price. She said she would look it up and went to a desk where Pliny kept his papers, and after going through some lists of figures which were all in code she named the sum. It was enormous—something like two hundred and seventy-five pounds—and I said "What!" in astonishment. She put the list back on the desk and said firmly, "My husband paid two hundred and sixty pounds for it last Sunday. It was carved by Dubois. There are only two more like it. It was the last thing he did in 1785."

(I found out afterwards this was nonsense.)

She said this in Pliny's voice; it was exactly the sort of casual sentence he would have used. She looked expressionless and not at all surprised when I said, "Valuable," and moved away.

I meant, of course, that she was valuable, and in fact her mystery having gone, she seemed conscious of being valuable and important herself, the queen and owner of everything in the shop, efficiently in charge of her husband's things. The cabinet in the corner, she said, in an off-hand way, as I went to look at it, had been sold to an Australian. "We are waiting for the packers." We! Not to feel less knowing than she was, I looked round for some small thing to buy from her. There were several small things, like a cup and saucer, a little china tray, a christening mug. I picked things up and put them down listlessly, and from being indifferent she became eager and watched me. The self-important, serious expression she had had vanished, she became child-ish suddenly, and anxious: she was eager to sell something. I found a little china figure on a shelf.

"How much is this?" I said. It was Dresden: the real thing. She took it and looked at the label. I knew it was far beyond my purse and I asked her the price in the bored hopeless voice one puts on.

"I'll have to look it up," she said.

She went to the desk again and looked very calculating and thought-ful and then said, as if naming an enormous sum, "Two pounds."

"It can't be," I said.

She looked sad as I put it back on the shelf and she went back to the desk. Then she said, "I tell you what I'll do. It's got a defect. You can have it for thirty-five shillings."

I picked it up again. There was no defect in it. I could feel the huge wave of temptation that comes to one in the trade, the sense of the incredible chance, the lust that makes one shudder first and then breaks over one so that one is possessed, though even at that last moment, one plays at delay in a breathless pause now that one is certain of one's desire.

I said, "I'll give you thirty bob for it."

Young Mrs. Pliny raised her head and her brown eyes became bril-liant with naïve joy.

"All right," she said.

The sight of her wrapping the figure, packing it in a box and taking the money so entranced me, that I didn't realize what she was doing or what I had done. I wasn't thinking of the figure at all; I was thinking of her. We shook hands. Hers were cold and she waved from the shop door when I left. And when I got to the end of the street and found myself holding the box I wondered why I had bought it. I didn't want it. I had felt the thrill of the thief and I was so ashamed that I once or twice thought of dropping it into a litter box. I even thought of going back and returning it to her and saying to her, "I didn't want it. It was a joke. I wanted you. Why did you marry an awful old man like Pliny?"

And those stories of Pliny going off once a month in the old days, in his mother's time, to Lal Drake, that old whore in Brixton, came back to me. I didn't even unpack the figure but put it on the mantelpiece in my room, then on the top shelf of a cupboard which I rarely used. I didn't want to see it. And when in the next months—or even years —I happened to see it, I remembered her talking about the bad people, August's men.

But though I kept away from Pliny's on Sundays, I could not resist going back to the street and eventually to the shop—just for the sight of her.

And after several misses I did see her in the shop. It was locked. When I saw her she stared at me with fear and made no signals and quickly disappeared—I suppose, into the room at the back. I crossed the main road and looked at the upper part of the house. She was upstairs, standing at a window. So I went back across the street and tried to signal, but of course she could only see my mouth moving. I was obsessed by the way I had cheated her. My visits were a siege, for the door was never open now. I did see her once through the window and this time I had taken the box and offered it to her in dumb show. That did have an effect. I saw she was looking very pale, her eyes ringed and tired, and whether she saw I was remorseful or not I couldn't tell, but she made a rebuking yet defiant face. Another day I went and she looked terrified. She pointed and pointed to the door, but as I eagerly stepped towards it she shook her head and raised a hand to forbid me. I did not understand until, soon, I saw Pliny walking about the shop. I moved off. People in the neighbourhood must often have seen me standing there and the tobacconist I went to gave me a look that suggested he knew what was going on.

Then, on one of my vigils, I saw a doctor go to the side door down the goods entrance and feared she was ill, but the butcher told me it was Pliny. His wife, they said, had been nursing him. He ought to convalesce somewhere. "A nice place by the sea. But he won't. It would do his wife good. The young girl has worn herself out looking after him. Shut up all day with him." And the tobacconist said what his wife had said a long time back. "Like his poor mother. He kept *her* locked in too. Sunday evening's the only time she's out. It's all wrong."

I got sick of myself. I didn't notice the time I was wasting, for one day passed like a smear of grey into another and I wished I could drag myself away from the district, especially now that Pliny was always there. At last one Saturday I fought hard against a habit so useless and

I had the courage to drive past the place for once and not park my car up the street. I drove on, taking side streets (which I knew, nevertheless, would lead me back), but I made a mistake with the one-ways and got on the main Brixton road and was heading north to freedom from myself.

It was astonishing to be free. It was seven o'clock in the evening, and to celebrate I went into a big pub where they had singers on Saturday nights; it was already filling up with people. How normal, how cheerful they were, a crowd of them, drinking, shouting and talking: the human race! I got a drink and chose a quiet place in a corner and I was taking my first mouthful of the beer, saying to myself: "Here's to yourself, my boy," as though I had just met myself as I used to be. And then, with the glass still at my lips, I saw in a crowd at the other end of the bar Pliny, with his back half turned. I recognized him by his jug-handle ears, his white hair, and the stoop of a tall man. He was not in his dressy clothes but in a shabby suit that made him seem disguised. He was listening to a woman with a large handbag who had bright blond hair and a big red mouth; she was telling him a joke and she banged him in the stomach with her bag and laughed. Someone near me said, "Lal's on the job early this evening." Lal Drake. All the old stories about Pliny and his woman came back to me and how old Castle of Westbury said that Pliny's mother had told him, when she was saying what a good son he was to her, that the one and only time he had been seen with a woman he had come home and told her and put his head in her lap and cried "like a child" and promised on the Bible he'd never do such a thing again. Castle swore this was true.

I put down my beer and got out of the pub fast without finishing it. Not because I was afraid of Pliny. Oh, no! I drove straight back to Pliny's shop. I rang the bell. The drum started beating a few taps and then a window upstairs opened.

"What do you want?" said Isabel in a whisper.

"I want to see you. Open the door."

"It's locked."

"Get the key."

She considered me for a long time.

"I haven't got one," she said, still in a low voice, so hard to hear that she had to say it twice.

"Where have you been?" she said.

We stared at each other's white faces in the dark. She had missed me!

"You've got a key. You must have," I said. "Somewhere. What about the back door?"

She leaned on the window, her arms on the sill. She was studying my clothes.

"I have got something for you," I said. This changed her. She leaned forward, trying to see more of me in the dark. She was curious. Today I understand what I did not understand then: she was looking me over minutely, inch by inch—what she could see of me in the sodium light of the street lamp—not because I was strange or unusual but because I was not. She had been shut up either alone or with Pliny without seeing another soul for so long. He was treating her like one of his collector's pieces, like the Meissen August had said he kept hidden upstairs. She closed the window. I stood there wretched and impatient. I went down the goods entrance ready to kick the side door down, break a window, climb in somehow. The side door had no letter box or glass panes, no handle even. I stood in front of it and suddenly it was opened. She was standing there.

"You're *not* locked in," I said.

She was holding a key.

"I found it," she said.

I saw she was telling a lie.

"Just now?"

"No. I know where he hides it," she said, lowering her frank eyes. It was a heavy key with an old piece of frayed used-up string on it.

"Mr. Pliny does not like me to show people things," she said. "He has gone to see his sister in Brixton. She is very ill. I can't show you anything."

She recited these words as if she had learned them by heart. It was wonderful to stand so near to her in the dark.

"Can I come in?" I said.

"What do you want?" she said cautiously.

"You," I said.

She raised her chin.

"Are you one of August's men?" she said.

"You know I'm not. I haven't seen August for years."

"Mr. Pliny says you are. He said I was never to speak to you again. August was horrible."

"The last I heard he was in prison."

"Yes," she said. "He steals." This seemed to please her: she forgave him that easily. Then she put her head out of the doorway as if to see if August were waiting behind me.

"He does something else too," she said.

I remembered the violent quarrel between August and poor Mrs. Price when she was drunk in Salisbury—the quarrel about Isabel.

"You ran away," I said.

She shook her head.

"I didn't run away. Mr. Pliny fetched me," she said and nodded primly, "in his car. I told you."

Then she said, "Where is the present you were bringing me?"

"It isn't a present," I said. "It's the little figure I bought from you. You didn't charge me enough. Let me in. I want to explain."

I couldn't bring myself to tell her that I had taken advantage of her ignorance, so I said, "I found out afterwards that it was worth much more than I paid you. I want to give it back to you."

She gave a small jump towards me. "Oh, please, please," she said and took me by the hand. "Where is it?"

"Let me come in," I said, "and I will tell you. I haven't got it with me. I'll bring it tomorrow—no, not tomorrow—Monday."

"Oh, please," she pleaded. "Mr. Pliny was so angry with me for selling it. He'd never been angry with me before. It was terrible. It was awful."

It had never occurred to me that Pliny would even know she had sold the piece; but now I remembered the passions of the trade and the stored-up lust that seems to pass between things and men like Pliny. He wouldn't forgive. He would be savage.

"Did he do something to you? He didn't hit you, did he?"

Isabel did not answer.

"What did he do?"

I remembered how frantic Pliny had been and how violent he had sounded when he told me to get out of his shop.

"He cried," she said. "He cried and he cried. He went down on his knees and he would not stop crying. I was wicked to sell it. I am the most precious thing he has. Please bring it. It will make him better."

"Is he still angry?"

"It has made him ill," she said.

"Let me come in," I said.

"Will you promise?"

"I swear I'll bring it," I said.

"For a minute," she said, "but not in the shop."

I followed her down a dark passage into the store and was so close that I could smell her hair.

Pliny crying! At first I took this to be one of Isabel's fancies. Then I thought of tall, clumsy, servant-like Pliny—expert at sales with his long-nosed face pouring out water like a pump—acting repentant, remorseful, agonized like an animal to a pretty girl. Why? Just because she had sold something? Isabel loved to sell things. He must have had some other reason. I remembered Castle of Westbury's story. What had he done to the girl? Only a cruel man could have gone in for such an orgy of self-love. He had the long face on which tears would be a blackmail. He would be like a horse crying because it had lost a race.

Yet those tears were memorable to Isabel and she so firmly called him "Mr. Pliny." In bed, did she still call him "Mr. Pliny"? I have often thought since that she did: it would have given her a power—perhaps cowed him.

At night the cold, whitewashed storeroom was silent under the light of its single bulb and the place was mostly in shadow; only the tops of stacked furniture stood out in the yellow light, some of them like buildings. The foundations of the stacks were tables or chests, desks on which chairs or small cabinets were piled. We walked down alleys between the stacks. It was like walking through a dead, silent city, abandoned by everyone who once lived there. There was the sour smell of upholstery; in one part there was a sort of plaza where two large dining tables stood with their chairs set around and a pile of dessert plates on them. Isabel was walking confidently. She stopped by a dressing table with a mirror on it next to a group of wardrobes and turning round to face it, she said proudly, "Mr. Pliny gave it all to me. And the shop."

"All of this?"

"When he stopped crying," she said.

And then she turned about and we faced the wardrobes. There were six or seven, one in rosewood and an ugly yellow one, and they were so arranged here that they made a sort of alcove or room. The wardrobe at the corner of the alley was very heavy and leaned so that its doors were open in a manner of such empty hopelessness, showing its empty shelves, that it made me uneasy. Someone might have just taken his clothes from it in a hurry, perhaps that very minute, and gone off. He might be watching us. It was the wardrobe with the squeaking door which I had seen the customer open while the woman (whom I had thought to be Mrs. Pliny) stood by. Each piece of furniture seemed to watch—even the small things, like an umbrella stand or a tray left on a table. Isabel walked into the alcove, and there was a greenish-grey sofa with a screwed-up paper bag of toffees on it and on the floor beside it I saw, of all things, the lancer's helmet and the side drum and the bugle. The yellow light scarcely lit this corner.

"There's your drum," I said.

"This is my house," she said, gaily now. "Do you like it? When Mr. Pliny is away I come here in case August's men come . . ."

She looked at me doubtfully when she mentioned that name again.

"And you beat the drum to drive them away?" I said.

"Yes," she said stoutly.

I could not make out whether she was playing the artless child or not, yet she was a woman of twenty-five at least. I was bewildered.

"You are frightened here on your own, aren't you?"

"No, I am not. It's nice."

Then she said very firmly, "You will come here on Monday and give me the box back?"

I said, "I will if you'll let me kiss you. I love you, Isabel."

"Mr. Pliny loves me too," she said.

"Isab . . ." I said. That did move her.

I put my arm round her waist and she let me draw her to me. It was strange to hold her because I could feel her ribs, but her body was so limp and feeble that, loving her as I did, I was shocked and pulled her tightly against me. She turned her head weakly so that I could only kiss her cheek and see only one of her eyes, and I could not make out whether she was enticing me, simply curious about my embrace, or drooping in it without heart.

"You *are* one of August's men," she said, getting away from me. "He used to try and get into my bed. After that, I locked my door."

"Isabel," I said, "I am in love with you. I think you love me. Why did you marry a horrible old man like Pliny?"

"Mr. Pliny is not horrible," she said. "I love him. He never comes to my room."

"Then he doesn't love you," I said. "Leaving you locked up here. And you don't love him."

She listened in the manner of someone wanting to please, waiting for me to stop.

"He is not a real husband, a real lover," I said.

"Yes, he is," she said proudly. "He takes my clothes off before I go to bed. He likes to look at me. I am the most precious thing he has."

"That isn't love, Isabel," I said.

"It is," she said with warmth. "You don't love me. You cheated me. Mr. Pliny said so. And you don't want to look at me. You don't think I'm precious."

I went to take her in my arms again and held her.

"I love you. I want you. You are beautiful. I didn't cheat you. Pliny is cheating you, not me," I said. "He is not with his sister. He's in bed with a woman in Brixton. I saw them in a pub. Everyone knows it."

"No, he is not. I *know* he is not. He doesn't like it. He promised his mother," she said.

The voice in which she said this was not her playful voice: the girl vanished and a woman had taken her place—not a distressed woman, not a contemptuous or a disappointed one.

"He worships me," she said, and in the squalid store of dead junk she seemed to be illumined by the simple knowledge of her own value and looked at my love as if it were nothing at all.

I looked at the sofa and was so mad that I thought of grabbing her and pulling her down there. What made me hesitate was the crumpled bag of toffees on it. I was as nonplussed and perhaps as impotent as Pliny must have been. In that moment of hesitation she picked up her bugle, and standing in the aisle, she blew it hard, her cheeks going out full, and the noise and echoes seemed to make the shadows jump. I have never heard a bugle call that scared me so much. It killed my desire.

"I told you not to come in," she said. "Go away."

And she walked into the aisle between the furniture, swinging her key to the door.

"Come back," I said as I followed her.

I saw her face in the dressing-table mirror we had passed before, then I saw my own face, red and sweating on the upper lip and my mouth helplessly open. And then in the mirror I saw another face following mine—Pliny's. Pliny must have seen me in the pub.

In that oblong frame of mahogany with its line of yellow inlay, Pliny's head looked winged by his ears and he was coming at me, his head down, his mouth with its yellowing teeth open under the moustache and his eyes stained in the bad light. He looked like an animal. The mirror concentrated him, and before I could do more than half turn he had jumped in a clumsy way at me and jammed one of my shoulders against a tallboy.

"What are you doing here?" he shouted.

The shouts echoed over the store.

"I warned you. I'll get the police on you. You leave my wife alone. Get out. You thought you'd get her on her own and swindle her again."

I hated to touch a white-haired man, but in pain I shoved him back hard. We were, as I have said, close to the wardrobe, and he staggered back so far that he hit the shelves and the door swung towards him, so that he was half out of my sight for a second. I kicked the door hard with my left foot and it swung to and hit him in the face. He jumped out with blood on his nose. But I had had time to topple the pile of little cane chairs into the alleyway between us. Isabel saw this and ran round the block of furniture and reached him, and when I saw her she was standing with the bugle raised like a weapon in her hand to defend the old man from me. He was wiping his face. She looked triumphant.

"Don't you touch Mr. Pliny," she shouted at me. "He's ill."

He *was* ill. He staggered. I pushed my way through the fallen chairs and I picked up one and said, "Pliny, sit down on this." Pliny with the bleeding face glared and she forced him to sit down. He was panting. And then a new voice joined us: the tobacconist came down the alley.

"I heard the bugle," he said. "Anything wrong? Oh, Gawd, look at his face. What happened, Pliny? Mrs. Pliny, you all right?" And then he saw me. All the native shadiness of the London streets, all the gossip of the neighbourhood, came into his face.

"I said to my wife," he said, "something's wrong at Pliny's."

"I came to offer Mr. Pliny a piece of Dresden," I said, "but he was out at Brixton seeing his sister, his wife said. He came back and thought I'd broken in and hit himself on the wardrobe."

"You oughtn't to leave Mrs. Pliny alone with all this valuable stock, Mr. Pliny. Saturday night too," the tobacconist said.

Tears had started rolling down Pliny's cheeks very suddenly when I mentioned Brixton and he looked at me and the tobacconist in panic.

"I'm not interested in Dresden," he managed to say.

Isabel dabbed his face and sent the tobacconist for a glass of water.

"No, dear, you're not," said Isabel.

And to me she said, "We're not interested."

That was the end. I found myself walking in the street. How unreal people looked in the sodium light.

The Diver

In a side street on the Right Bank of the Seine where the river divides at the Île de la Cité, there is a yellow and red brick building shared by a firm of leather merchants. When I was twenty I worked there. The hours were long, the pay was low, and the place smelt of cigarettes and boots. I hated it. I had come to Paris to be a writer, but my money had run out and in this office I had to stick. How often I looked across the river, envying the free lives of the artists and writers on the other bank. Being English, I was the joke of the office. The sight of my fat pink innocent face and fair hair made everyone laugh; my accent was bad, for I could not pronounce a full "o"; worst of all, like a fool, I not only admitted I hadn't got a mistress, but boasted about it. To the office boys this news was extravagant. It doubled them up. It was a favourite trick of theirs, and even of the salesman, a man called Claudel with whom I had to work, to call me to the street door at lunchtime and then, if any girl or woman passed, they would give me a punch and shout, "How much to sleep with this one? Twenty? Forty? A hundred?" I put on a grin, but to tell the truth, a sheet of glass seemed to come down between me and any female I saw.

About one woman the lads did not play this game. She was a woman between thirty and forty, I suppose: Mme. Chamson, who kept the menders and cleaners down the street. You could hear her heels as she came, half running, to see Claudel, with jackets and trousers of his on her arm. He had some arrangement with her for getting his suits cleaned and repaired on the cheap. In return—well, there was a lot of talk. She had sinfully tinted hair built up high over arching, exclaiming eyebrows, hard as varnish, and when she got near our door there was always a joke coming out of the side of her mouth. She would bounce into the office in her tight navy-blue skirt, call the boys and Claudel together, shake hands with them all, and tell them some tale which always ended, with a dirty glance round, in whispering. Then she stood back and shouted with laughter. I was never in this secret circle, and if I happened to grin she gave me a severe and offended look and marched out scowling. One day, when one of her tales was over, she called back from the door, "Standing all day in that gallery with all those naked women, he comes home done for, finished."

The office boys squeezed each other with pleasure. She was talking about her husband, who was an attendant at the Louvre, a small moist-looking fellow whom we sometimes saw with her, a man fond of fishing, whose breath smelt of white wine. Because of her arrangement with Claudel, and her stories, she was a very respected woman.

I did not like Mme. Chamson: she looked to me like some predatory bird; but I could not take my eyes off her pushing bosom and her crooked mouth. I was afraid of her tongue. She caught on quickly to the fact that I was the office joke, but when they told her that on top of this I wanted to be a writer, any curiosity she had about me was finished. "I could tell him a tale," she said. For her I didn't exist. She didn't even bother to shake hands with me.

Streets and avenues in Paris are named after writers; there are statues to poets, novelists, and dramatists, making gestures to the birds, nurse-maids, and children in the gardens. How was it these men had become famous? How had they begun? For myself, it was impossible to begin. I walked about packed with stories, but when I sat in cafés or in my room with a pen in my hand and a bare sheet of paper before me, I could not touch it. I seemed to swell in the head, the chest, the arms and legs, as if I were trying to heave an enormous load onto the page and could not move. The portentous moment had not yet come. And there was another reason. The longer I worked in the leather trade and talked to the office boys, the typists there and Claudel, the more I acquired a double personality: when I left the office and walked to the Métro, I practiced French to myself. In this bizarre language the stories inside me flared up, I was acting and speaking them as I walked, often in the subjunctive, but when I sat before my paper the English language closed its sullen mouth.

And what were these stories? Impossible to say. I would set off in the morning and see the grey, ill-painted buildings of the older quarters leaning together like people, their shutters thrown back, so that the open windows looked like black and empty eyes. In the mornings the bedding was thrown over the sills to air and hung out, wagging like tongues about what goes on in the night between men and women. The houses looked sunken-shouldered, exhausted, by what they told; and crowning the city was the church of Sacré-Coeur, very white, standing like some dry Byzantine bird, to my mind hollow-eyed and without conscience, presiding over the habits of the flesh and—to judge by what I read in newspapers—its crimes also; its murders, rapes, its shootings for jealousy and robbery. As my French improved, the secrets of Paris grew worse. It amazed me that the crowds I saw on the street had survived the night, and many indeed looked as sleepless as the houses.

After I had been a little more than a year in Paris—fourteen months, in fact—a drama broke the monotonous life of our office. A consignment of dressed skins had been sent to us from Rouen. It had been sent by barge—not the usual method in our business. The barge was an old one and was carrying a mixed cargo, and within a few hundred yards from our warehouse it was rammed and sunk one misty morning by a Dutch boat taking the wrong channel. The manager, the whole office, especially Claudel, who saw his commission go to the bottom, were outraged. Fortunately the barge had gone down slowly near the bank, close to us; the water was not too deep. A crane was brought down on another barge to the water's edge and soon, in an exciting week, a diver was let down to salvage what he could. Claudel and I had to go to the quay, and if a bale of our stuff came up, we had to get it into the warehouse and see what the damage was.

Anything to get out of the office. For me the diver was the hero of the week. He stood in his round helmet and suit on a wide tray of wood hanging from four chains, and then the motor spat, the chains rattled, and down he went with great dignity under the water. While the diver was underwater, Claudel would be reckoning his commission over again —would it be calculated only on the sale price or on what was saved? "Five bales so far," he would mutter fanatically. "One and a half per cent." His teeth and his eyes were agitated with changing figures. I, in imagination, was groping in the gloom of the riverbed with my hero. Then we'd step forward; the diver was coming up. Claudel would hold

my arm as the man appeared with a tray of sodden bales and the brown
water streaming off them. He would step off the plank onto the barge,
where the crane was installed, and look like a swollen frog. A workman
unscrewed his helmet, the visor was raised, and then we saw the young
diver's rosy, cheerful face. A workman lit a cigarette and gave it to him,
and out of the helmet came a long surprising jet of smoke. There was
always a crowd watching from the quay wall, and when he did this, they
all smiled and many laughed. "See that?" they would say. "He is having
a puff." And the diver grinned and waved to the crowd.

Our job was to grab the stuff. Claudel would check the numbers of
the bales on his list. Then we saw them wheeled to our warehouse,
dripping all the way, and there I had to hang up the skins on poles.
It was like hanging up drowned animals—even, I thought, human
beings.

On the Friday afternoon of that week, when everyone was tired and
even the crowd looking down from the street wall had thinned to next
to nothing, Claudel and I were still down on the quay waiting for the
last load. The diver had come up. We were seeing him for the last time
before the weekend. I was waiting to watch what I had not yet seen:
how he got out of his suit. I walked down nearer at the quay's edge to
get a good view. Claudel shouted to me to get on with the job, and as
he shouted I heard a whizzing noise above my head and then felt a
large, heavy slopping lump hit me on the shoulders. I turned round and,
the next thing, I was flying in the air, arms outspread with wonder.
Paris turned upside down. A second later, I crashed into cold darkness,
water was running up my legs swallowing me. I had fallen into the river.

The wall of the quay was not high. In a couple of strokes I came up
spitting mud and caught an iron ring on the quay wall. Two men pulled
my hands. Everyone was laughing as I climbed out.

I stood there drenched and mud-smeared, with straw in my hair,
pouring water into a puddle that came from me, getting larger and
larger.

"Didn't you hear me shout?" said Claudel.

Laughing and arguing, two or three men led me to the shelter of the
wall, where I began to wring out my jacket and shirt and squeeze the
water out of my trousers. It was a warm day, and I stood in the sun
and saw my trousers steam and heard my shoes squelch.

"Give him a hot rum," someone said. Claudel was torn between
looking after our few bales left on the quay and taking me across the
street to a bar. But checking the numbers and muttering a few more

figures to himself, he decided to enjoy the drama and go with me. He called out that we'd be back in a minute.

We got to the bar and Claudel saw to it that my arrival was a sensation. Always nagging at me in the office, he was now proud of me.

"He fell into the river. He nearly drowned. I warned him. I shouted. Didn't I?"

The one or two customers admired me. The barman brought me the rum. I could not get my hand into my pocket because it was wet.

"You pay me tomorrow," said Claudel, putting a coin on the counter.

"Drink it quickly," said the barman.

I was laughing and explaining now.

"One moment he was on dry land, the next he was flying in the air, then plonk in the water. Three elements," said Claudel.

"Only fire is missing," said the barman.

They argued about how many elements there were. A whole history of swimming feats, drowning stories, bodies found, murders in the Seine sprung up. Someone said the morgue used to be full of corpses. And then an argument started, as it sometimes did in this part of Paris, about the exact date at which the morgue was moved from the island. I joined in, but my teeth had begun to chatter.

"Another rum," the barman said.

And then I felt a hand fingering my jacket and my trousers. It was the hand of Mme. Chamson. She had been down at the quay once or twice during the week to have a word with Claudel. She had seen what had happened.

"He ought to go home and change into dry things at once," she said in a firm voice. "You ought to take him home."

"I can't do that. We've left five bales on the quay," said Claudel.

"He can't go back," said Mme. Chamson. "He's shivering."

I sneezed.

"You'll catch pneumonia," she said. And to Claudel: "You ought to have kept an eye on him. He might have drowned."

She was very stern with him.

"Where do you live?" she said to me.

I told her.

"It will take you an hour," she said.

Everyone was silent before the decisive voice of Mme. Chamson.

"Come with me to the shop," she ordered and pulled me brusquely by the arm. She led me out of the bar and said as we walked away, my boots squeaking and squelching, "That man thinks of nothing but money. Who'd pay for your funeral? Not he!"

Twice, as she got me, her prisoner, past the shops, she called out to people at their doors, "They nearly let him drown."

Three girls used to sit mending in the window of her shop and behind them was usually a man pressing clothes. But it was half past six now and the shop was closed. Everyone had gone. I was relieved. This place had disturbed me. When I first went to work for our firm Claudel had told me he could fix me up with one of the mending girls: if we shared a room it would halve our expenses and she could cook and look after my clothes. That was what started the office joke about my not having a mistress. When we got to the shop Mme. Chamson led me down a passage, inside which was muggy with the smell of dozens of dresses and suits hanging there, into a dim parlour beyond. It looked out onto the smeared grey wall of a courtyard.

"Stay here," said Mme. Chamson, planting me by a sofa. "Don't sit on it in those wet things. Take them off."

I took off my jacket.

"No. Don't wring it. Give it to me. I'll get a towel."

I started drying my hair.

"All of them," she said.

Mme. Chamson looked shorter in her room, her hair looked duller, her eyebrows less dramatic. I had never really seen her closely. She had become a plain, domestic woman; her mouth had straightened. There was not a joke in her. Her bosom filled with management. The rumour that she was Claudel's mistress was obviously an office tale.

"I'll see what I can find for you. You can't wear these."

I waited for her to leave the room and then I took off my shirt and dried my chest, picking off the bits of straw from the river that had stuck to my skin. She came back.

"Off with your trousers, I said. Give them to me. What size are they?"

My head went into the towel. I pretended not to hear. I could not bring myself to undress before Mme. Chamson. But while I hesitated she bent down and her sharp fingernails were at my belt.

"I'll do it," I said anxiously.

Our hands touched and our fingers mixed as I unhitched my belt. Impatiently she began on my buttons, but I pushed her hands away.

She stood back, blank-faced and peremptory in her stare. It was the blankness of her face, her indifference to me, her ordinary womanliness, the touch of her practical fingers that left me without defence. She was not the ribald, coquettish, dangerous woman who came wagging her hips to our office, not one of my Paris fantasies of sex and danger. She was simply a woman. The realization of this was disastrous to me. An unbelievable change was throbbing in my body. It was uncontrollable. My eyes angrily, helplessly asked her to go away. She stood there implacably. I half turned, bending to conceal my enormity as I lowered my trousers, but as I lowered them inch by inch so the throbbing manifestation increased. I got my foot out of one leg but my shoe caught in the other. On one leg I tried to dance my other trouser leg off. The towel slipped and I glanced at her in red-faced angry appeal. My trouble was only too clear. I was stiff with terror. I was almost in tears.

The change in Mme. Chamson was quick. From busy indifference she went to anger.

"Young man," she said. "Cover yourself. How dare you. What indecency. How dare you insult me!"

"I'm sorry. I couldn't help . . ." I said.

Mme. Chamson's bosom became a bellows puffing outrage.

"What manners," she said. "I am not one of your tarts. I am a respectable woman. This is what I get for helping you. What would your parents say? If my husband were here!"

She had got my trousers in her hand. The shoe that had betrayed me now fell out of the leg to the floor.

She bent down coolly and picked it up.

"In any case," she said, and now I saw for the first time this afternoon the strange twist of her mouth return to her as she nodded at my now concealing towel, "that is nothing to boast about."

My blush had gone. I was nearly fainting. I felt the curious, brainless stupidity that goes with the state nature had put me in. A miracle saved me. I sneezed and then sneezed again—the second time with force.

"What did I tell you!" said Mme. Chamson, passing now to angry self-congratulation. She flounced out to the passage that led to the shop, and coming back with a pair of trousers she threw them at me and, red in the face, said, "Try those. If they don't fit I don't know what you'll do. I'll get a shirt," and she went past me to the door of the room beyond, saying, "You can thank your lucky stars my husband has gone fishing."

I heard her muttering as she opened drawers. She did not return. There was silence.

In the airless little salon, looking out (as if it were a cell in which I was caught) on the stained smeared grey wall of the courtyard, the silence lengthened. It began to seem that Mme. Chamson had shut herself away in her disgust and was going to have no more to do with me. I saw a chance of getting out, but she had taken away my wet clothes. I pulled on the pair of trousers she had thrown; they were too long but I could tuck them in. I should look an even bigger fool if I went out in the street dressed only in these. What was Mme. Chamson doing? Was she torturing me? Fortunately my impromptu disorder had passed. I stood listening. I studied the mantelpiece, where I saw what I supposed was a photograph of Mme. Chamson as a girl in the veil of her first communion. Presently I heard her voice. "Young man," she called harshly, "do you expect me to wait on you. Come and fetch your things."

Putting on a polite and apologetic look, I went to the inner door which led into a short passage only a yard long. She was not there.

"In here," she said curtly.

I pushed the next door open. This room was dim also, and the first thing I saw was the end of a bed and in the corner a chair with a dark skirt on it and a stocking hanging from the arm, and on the floor a pair of shoes, one of them on its side. Then suddenly I saw at the end of the bed a pair of bare feet. I looked at the toes; how had they got there? And then I saw: without a stitch of clothing on her, Mme. Chamson —but could this naked body be she?—was lying on the bed, her chin propped on her hand, her lips parted as they always were when she came in on the point of laughing to the office, but now with no sound coming from them; her eyes, generally wide open, were now half closed, watching me with the stillness of some large white cat. I looked away and then I saw two other large brown eyes gazing at me, two other faces: her breasts. It was the first time in my life I had ever seen a naked woman, and it astonished me to see the rise of a haunch, the slope of her belly and the black hair like a moustache beneath it. Mme. Chamson's face was always strongly made up with some almost orange colour, and it astonished me to see how white her body was from the neck down—not the white of statues, but some sallow colour of white and shadow, marked at the waist by the tightness of the clothes she had taken off. I had thought of her as old, but she was not: her body was young and idle.

The sight of her transfixed me. It did not stir me. I simply stood there gaping. My heart seemed to have stopped. I wanted to rush from the room, but I could not. She was so very near. My horror must have been on my face, but she seemed not to notice that, but simply stared at me. There was a small movement of her lips and I dreaded that she was going to laugh, but she did not; slowly she closed her lips and said at last between her teeth in a voice low and mocking: "Is this the first time you have seen a woman?"

And after she said this a sad look came into her face.

I could not answer.

She lay on her back and put out her hand and smiled fully. "Well?" she said. And she moved her hips.

"I," I began, but I could not go on. All the fantasies of my walks about Paris as I practiced French rushed into my head. This was the secret of all those open windows of Paris, of the vulture-like head of Sacré-Coeur looking down on it. In a room like this, with a wardrobe in the corner and with clothes thrown on a chair, was enacted—what? Everything—but above all, to my panicking mind, the crimes I read about in the newspapers. I was desperate as her hand went out.

"You have never seen a woman before?" she said again.

I moved a little and out of reach of her hand I said fiercely, "Yes, I have." I was amazed at myself.

"Ah!" she said, and when I did not answer, she laughed. "Where was that? Who was she?"

It was her laughter, so dreaded by me, that released something in me. I said something terrible. The talk of the morgue at the bar jumped into my head.

I said coldly, "She was dead. In London."

"Oh my God," said Mme. Chamson, sitting up and pulling at the coverlet, but it was caught and she could only cover her feet.

It was her turn to be frightened. Across my brain, newspaper head-lines were tapping out.

"She was murdered," I said. I hesitated. I was playing for time. Then it came out. "She was strangled."

"Oh, no!" she said, and she pulled the coverlet violently up with both hands until she had got some of it to her breast.

"I saw her," I said. "On her bed."

"You *saw* her? *How* did you see her?" she said. "Where was this?"

Suddenly the story sprang out of me, it unrolled as I spoke.

It was in London, I said. In our street. The woman was a neighbour of ours, we knew her well. She used to pass our window every morning on her way up from the bank.

"She was robbed!" said Mme. Chamson. Her mouth buckled with horror.

I saw I had caught her.

"Yes," I said. "She kept a shop."

"Oh my God, my God," said Mme. Chamson, looking at the door behind me, then anxiously round the room.

It was a sweetshop, I said, where we bought our papers too.

"Killed in her shop," groaned Mme. Chamson. "Where was her husband?"

"No," I said, "in her bedroom at the back. Her husband was out at work all day and this man must have been watching for him to go. Well, we knew he did. He was the laundryman. He used to go in there twice a week. She'd been carrying on with him. She was lying there with her head on one side and a scarf twisted round her neck."

Mme. Chamson dropped the coverlet and hid her face in her hands; then she lowered them and said suspiciously, "But how did *you* see her like this?"

"Well," I said, "it happened like this. My little sister had been whining after breakfast and wouldn't eat anything and Mother said, 'That kid will drive me out of my mind. Go up to Mrs. Blake's—that was her name—'and get her a bar of chocolate, milk chocolate, no nuts, she only spits them out.' And Mother said, 'You may as well tell her we don't want any papers after Friday because we're going to Brighton. Wait, I haven't finished yet—here, take this money and pay the bill. Don't forget that, you forgot last year and the papers were littering up my hall. We owe for a month' . . ."

Mme. Chamson nodded at this detail. She had forgotten she was naked. She was the shopkeeper and she glanced again at the door as if listening for some customer to come in.

"I went up to the shop and there was no one there when I got in—"

"A woman alone!" said Mme. Chamson.

"So I called 'Mrs. Blake,' but there was no answer. I went to the inner door and called up a small flight of stairs, 'Mrs. Blake'—Mother had been on at me as I said, about paying the bill. So I went up."

"You went up?" said Mme. Chamson, shocked.

"I'd often been up there with Mother, once when she was ill. We knew the family. Well—there she was. As I said, lying on the bed, naked, strangled, dead."

Mme. Chamson gazed at me. She looked me slowly up and down from my hair, then my face and then down my body to my feet. I had come barefooted into the room. And then she looked at my bare arms, until she came to my hands. She gazed at these as if she had never seen hands before. I rubbed them on my trousers, for she confused me.

"Is this true?" she accused me.

"Yes," I said, "I opened the door and there—"

"How old were you?"

I hadn't thought of that, but I quickly decided.

"Twelve," I said.

Mme. Chamson gave a deep sigh. She had been sitting taut, holding her breath. It was a sigh in which I could detect just a twinge of disappointment. I felt my story had lost its hold.

"I ran home," I said quickly, "and said to my mother, 'Someone has killed Mrs. Blake.' Mother didn't believe me. She couldn't realize it. I had to tell her again and again. 'Go and see for yourself,' I said."

"Naturally," said Mme. Chamson. "You were only a child."

"We rang the police," I said.

At the word "police" Mme. Chamson groaned peacefully.

"There is a woman at the laundry," she said, "who was in the hospital with eight stitches in her head. She had been struck with an iron. But that was her husband. The police did nothing. But what does my husband do? He stands in the Louvre all day. Then he goes fishing, like this evening. Anyone," she said vehemently to me, "could break in here."

She was looking through me into some imagined scene and it was a long time before she came out of it. Then she saw her own bare shoulder and, pouting, she said slowly, "Is it true you were only twelve?"

"Yes."

She studied me for a long time.

"You poor boy," she said. "Your poor mother."

And she put her hand to my arm and let her hand slide down it gently to my wrist; then she put out her other hand to my other arm and took that hand, too, as the coverlet slipped a little from her. She looked at my hands and lowered her head. Then she looked up slyly at me.

"*You* didn't do it, did you?" she said.

"No," I said indignantly, pulling back my hands, but she held on to them. My story vanished from my head.

"It is a bad memory," she said. She looked to me once more as she had looked when I had first come with her into her salon soaking wet —a soft, ordinary, decent woman. My blood began to throb.

"You must forget about it," she said. And then, after a long pause, she pulled me to her. I was done for, lying on the bed.

"Ah," she laughed, pulling at my trousers. "The diver's come up again. Forget. Forget."

And then there was no more laughter. Once, in the height of our struggle, I caught sight of her eyes: the pupils had disappeared and there were only the blind whites and she cried out, "Kill me. Kill me," from her twisted mouth.

Afterwards we lay talking. She asked if it was true I was going to be a writer, and when I said yes, she said, "You want talent for that. Stay where you are. It's a good firm. Claudel has been there for twelve years. And now get up. My little husband will be back."

She got off the bed. Quickly she gave me a complete suit belonging to one of her customers, a grey one, the jacket rather tight.

"It suits you," she said. "Get a grey one next time."

I was looking at myself in a mirror when her husband came in, carrying his fishing rod and basket. He did not seem surprised. She picked up my sodden clothes and rushed angrily at him. "Look at these. Soaked. That fool Claudel let this boy fall in the river. He brought him here."

Her husband simply stared.

"And where have you been? Leaving me alone like this," she carried on. "Anyone could break in. This boy saw a woman strangled in her bed in London. She had a shop. Isn't that it? A man came in and murdered her. What d'you say to that?"

Her husband stepped back and looked with appeal at me.

"Did you catch anything?" she said to him, still accusing.

"No," said her husband.

"Well, not like me," she said, mocking me. "I caught this one."

"Will you have a drop of something?" said her husband.

"No, he won't," said Mme. Chamson. "He'd better go straight home to bed."

So we shook hands. M. Chamson let me out through the shop door while Mme. Chamson called down the passage to me, "Bring the suit back tomorrow. It belongs to a customer."

Everything was changed for me after this. At the office I was a hero.

"Is it true that you saw a murder?" the office boys said.

And when Mme. Chamson came along and I gave her back the suit, she said, "Ah, here he is—my fish."

And then boldly: "When are you coming to collect your things?"

And then she went over to whisper to Claudel and ran out.

"You know what she said just now," said Claudel to me, looking very shrewd. "She said, 'I am afraid of that young Englishman. Have you seen his hands?' "

Did You Invite Me?

Rachel first met Gilbert at David and Sarah's, or it may have been at
Richard and Phoebe's—she could not remember—but she did remember that he stood like a touchy exclamation mark and talked in a
shotgun manner about his dog. His talk jumped, so that she got confused: the dog was his wife's dog but was he talking about his dog or
his wife? He blinked very fast when he talked of either. Then she
remembered what David (or maybe Richard) had told her. His wife was
dead. Rachel had a dog, too, but Gilbert was not interested.

The bond between all of them was that they owned small white
stuccoed houses, not quite alike—hers alone, for example, had Gothic
churchy windows, which, she felt, gave her point—on different sides
of the park. Another bond was that they had reached middle life and
said nothing about it, except that Gilbert sharply pretended to be
younger than the rest of them in order to remind them they had arrived
at that time when one year passes into the next unnoticed, leaving
among the dregs an insinuation that they had not done what they
intended. When this thought struck them they would all—if they had
the time—look out of their sedate windows at the park, the tame and
once princely oasis where the trees looked womanish on the island in
the lake or marched in grave married processions along the avenues in
the late summer, or in the winter were starkly widowed. They could

watch the weekend crowds or the solitary walkers on the public grass,
see the duck flying over in the evenings, hear the keeper's whistle and
his shout "All out!" when the gates of the park closed an hour after
sunset; and at night, hearing the animals at the zoo, they could send
out silent cries of their own upon the place and evoke their ghosts.

But not Gilbert. His cry would be a howl and audible, a joint howl
of himself and this dog he talked about. Rachel had never seen a man
so howling naked. Something must be done about him, she thought
every time she met him. Two years ago, Sonia, his famous and chancy
wife, had died—"on the stage," the headlines in the London newspapers said, which was nearly true—and his eyes were red-rimmed as if
she had died yesterday, his angry face was raw with drink or the unjust
marks of guilt and grief. He was a tall man, all bones, and even his wrists
coming out of a jacket that was too short in the sleeve seemed to be
crying. He had also the look of a man who had decided not to buy
another suit in his life, to let cloth go on gleaming with its private
malice. It was well known—for he boasted of it himself—that his wife
had been much older than he, that they had quarrelled continually, and
that he still adored her.

Rachel had been naked, too, in her time when, six or seven years
before, she had divorced her husband. Gilbert is "in the middle of it,"
she thought. She had been "through it" and had "come out of it," and
was not hurt or lonely any more and had crowded her life with public
troubles. She was married to a newspaper column.

"Something really *must* be done about him," she at last said out loud
to David and Sarah as she tried to follow Gilbert's conversation that
was full of traps and false exit lines. For his part, he sniffed when he
spoke to them of Rachel.

"Very attractive woman. Very boring. All women are boring. Sonia
was a terrible bore sometimes, carrying on, silly cow. What of it? You
may have remarked it: I'm a bore. I must go. Thank you, Sarah and
David, for inviting me and offering me your friendship. You did invite
me, didn't you? You did? I'm glad. I have no friends. The friends Sonia
and I invited to the house were hers, not mine. Old codgers. I must
go home and feed her dog."

They watched him go off stiffly, a forty-year-old.

An outsider he was, of course, because of loss. One feels the east
wind—she knew that. But it was clear—as she decided to add him to
her worries—that he must always have been that. He behaved me-
chanically, click, click, click, like a puppet or an orphan, homelessness

being his vanity. This came out when David had asked Gilbert about his father and mother in her presence. From David's glances at his wife, Rachel knew they had heard what he said many times before. Out came his shot, the long lashes of his childish eyes blinking fast: "Never met the people."

He was showing contempt for a wound. He was born in Singapore, he said. One gathered the birth had no connection with either father or mother. She tried to be intelligent about the city.

"Never saw the place," he said. The father became a prisoner of the Japanese: the mother took him to India. Rachel tried to be intelligent about India.

"Don't remember it," he said.

"The old girl," his mother, sent him home to schools and holiday schools. He spent his boyhood in camps and dormitories, his Army life in Nissen huts. He was twenty when he really "met" his parents. At the sight of him they separated for good.

No further answers. Life had been doled out to him like spoonfuls of medicine, one at a time; he returned the compliment by doing the same and then erected silences like packs of cards, watching people wait for them to fall down.

How, Rachel asked, did the raw young man come to be married to Sonia, an actress at the top of the tree, fifteen years older than he? "The old girl knew her," he said; she was his mother's friend. Rachel worried away at it. She saw, correctly, a dramatic woman with a clever mouth, a surrogate mother—but a mother astute in acting the part among her scores of grand and famous friends. Rachel had one or two famous friends too, but he snubbed her with his automatic phrase: "Never met him." Or: "Never met her."

And then Rachel, again correctly, saw him standing in the doorway of Sonia's drawing-room or bringing drinks perhaps to the crowd, like an uncouth son; those wrists were the wrists of a growing boy who silently jeered at the guests. She heard Sonia dressing him down for his Nissen-hut language and his bad manners—which, however, she encouraged. This was her third marriage and it had to be original. That was the heart of the Gilbert problem: Sonia had invented him; he had no innate right to be what he appeared to be.

So Rachel, who happened to be writing an article on broken homes, asked him to come round and have a drink. He walked across the park from his house to hers. At the door he spoke his usual phrase, "Thank you for inviting me. You did invite me, didn't you? Well, I thank you.

We live on opposite sides of the park. Very convenient. Not too near."

He came in.

"Your house is white and your dog is white," he said.

Rachel owned a dog. A very white fox terrier came barking at him on a high, glassy note, showing a ratter's teeth. Rachel was wearing a long pale-blue dress from her throat to the tips of her shoes and led him into the sitting-room. He sank into a soft silky sofa with his knees together and politely inspected her as an interesting collection of bones.

"Shall I ever get up from this?" he said, patting the sofa. "Silly question. Yes, I shall, of course. I have come, shortly I shall go." He was mocking someone's manners. Perhaps hers. The fox terrier, which had followed him into the small and sunny room, sniffed long at Gilbert's shoes and his trouser legs and stiffened when he stroked its head. The dog growled.

"Pretty head," he said. "I like dogs' heads." He was staring at Rachel's head. Her hair was smooth, neat and fair.

"I remarked his feet on the hall floor, tick, tick, tick. Your hall must be tiled. Mine is carpeted."

"Don't be so aggressive, Sam," said Rachel gravely to the dog.

"Leave him alone," said Gilbert. "He can smell Tom, Sonia's bull terrier. That's who you can smell, isn't it? He can smell an enemy."

"Sam is a problem," she said. "Everyone in the street hates you, Sam, don't they? When you get out in the garden you bark and bark, people open their windows and shout at you. You chase cats, you killed the Gregory boy's rabbit and bit the Jackson child. You drive the doctor mad. He throws flowerpots at you."

"Stop nagging the poor animal," said Gilbert. And to the dog he said, "Good for you. Be a nuisance. Be yourself. Everyone needs an enemy. Absolutely."

And he said to himself, She hasn't forgiven her husband. In her long dress she had the composure of the completely smoothed-over person who might well have nothing on underneath. Gilbert appreciated this, but she became prudish and argumentative.

"Why do you say 'absolutely,' " she said, seeing a distracting point for discussion here. "Isn't that relative?"

"No," said Gilbert with enjoyment. He loved a row. "I've got an enemy at my office. Nasty little creepy fellow. He wants my job. He watches me. There's a new job going—promotion—and he thinks I want it. So he watches. He sits on the other side of the room and is peeing himself with anxiety every time I move. Peeing himself, yes. If I leave the room he goes to the door to see if I'm going to the director's office. If I do he sweats. He makes an excuse to go to the director to see if he can find out what we've been talking about. When I am working on a scheme he comes over to look at it. If I'm working out costs he stares with agony at the layout and the figures. 'Is that Jameson's?' He can't contain himself. 'No, I'm doing my income tax,' I tell him. He's very shocked at my doing that in office hours and goes away relieved. He'll report that to the director. Then a suspicion strikes him when he is halfway back to his desk and he turns round and comes over again panting. He doesn't believe me. 'I'm turning inches into centimetres,' I say. He still doesn't believe me. Poor silly bugger." He laughed.

"Wasn't that rather cruel?" she said. "Why centimetres?"

"Why not? He wants the French job. Boring little man. Boring office. Yes."

Gilbert constructed one of his long silences. Rachel saw skyscrapers, pagodas, the Eiffel Tower, and this little man creeping up them like an ant. After a while Gilbert went on and the vision collapsed. "He was the only one who came from the office to Sonia's funeral. He brought his wife—never met her before—and she cried. The only person who did. Yes. He'd never missed a show Sonia was in."

"So he isn't an enemy. Doesn't that prove my point?" she said solemnly. Gilbert ignored this.

"They'd never met poor Sonia," he said. And he blinked very fast.

"I never met your wife either, you know," said Rachel earnestly. She hoped he would describe her; but he described her doctors, the lawyers that assemble after death.

"What a farce," he said. "She had a stroke in the theatre. Her words came out backwards. I wrote to her two husbands. Only one replied. The theatre sent her to hospital in an ambulance—the damn fools. If you go to hospital you die of pneumonia, bloody hospital won't give you enough pillows, you lie flat and you can't get your breath. What a farce. Her brother came and talked, one of those fat men. Never liked the fellow."

She said how terrible it must have been. "Did she recover her speech? They sometimes do."

"Asked," he said, "for the dog. Called it God."

He got up suddenly from the sofa.

"There! I have got up. I am standing on my feet. I am a bore," he said. "I shall go."

As he left the room the terrier came sniffing at his heels.

"Country dogs. Good ratters. Ought to be on a farm."

She plunged into a confidence to make him stay longer.

"He used to be a country dog. My husband bought him for me when we lived in the country. I know"—she luxuriated in a worry—"how important environment is to animals and I was going to let him stay, but when you are living alone in a city like London—well—there are a lot of burglaries here."

"Why did you divorce your husband?" he asked as he opened the front door. "I shouldn't have asked. Bad manners. I apologize. I was rude. Sonia was always on to me about that."

"He went off with a girl at his office," she said staunchly.

"Silly man," said Gilbert, looking at the dog. "Thank you. Good-bye. Do we shake hands? You invited me, now it is my turn to invite you. That is the right thing, of course it is. We must do the right thing. I shall."

Weeks passed before Gilbert invited Rachel. There were difficulties. Whatever he decided by day was destroyed at night. At night Sonia would seem to come flying out of the park saying the house had belonged to her. She had paid for it. She enumerated the furniture item by item. She had the slow, languid walk of her stage appearances as she went suspiciously from room to room, asking what he had done with her fur coats and where her shoes were. "You've given them to some woman." She said he had a woman in the house. He said he asked only David and Sarah; she said she didn't trust Sarah. He pleaded he had kept the dog. When he said that, her ghost vanished saying he starved the poor thing. One night he said to her, "I'm going to ask Rachel, but you'll be there." "I damn well will," she said. And this became such a dogma that when at last he asked Rachel to come, he disliked her.

His house was not as sedate as hers, which had been repainted that year—his not. His windows seemed to him—and to her—to sob. There was grit on the frames. When he opened the door to her she noted the brass knocker had not been polished and inside there was the immediate cold odour of old food. The hall and walls echoed their voices and the air was very still. In the sitting-room the seats of the chairs, one could see, had not been sat on for a long time, there was dust on the theatrical wallpaper. Hearing her, Sonia's dog, Tom, came scrabbling downstairs and rushed into the room hysterically at both of them, skidding on rugs, snuffling, snorting, whimpering, and made at once for her skirts, got under her legs, and was driven off onto a sofa of green silk, rather like hers, but now frayed where the dog's claws had caught.

"Off the sofa, Tom," said Gilbert. The dog ignored this and snuffled from its squat nose and gazed from wet eyes that were like enormous marbles. Gilbert picked up a rubber bone and threw it to the dog. Down it came and the racing round the room began again. Rachel held her glass in the air for safety's sake and the dog jumped at it and made her spill whisky on her dress. In this confusion they tried to talk.

"Sonia liked being photographed with Tom," he said.

"I only saw her on the stage once. She was very beautiful," she said. "It must have been twelve years ago. Gielgud and another actor called Slade were in it. Was it Slade? Oh, dear! My memory!"

"Her second husband," he said.

He picked up the dog's rubber bone. The dog rushed to him and seized it. Man and dog pulled at the bone.

"You want it. You won't get it," said Gilbert while she seemed to hear her husband say: "Why can't you keep your mouth shut if you can't remember things?" And Gilbert, grinning in his struggle with the dog, said, "Sonia always had Tom to sleep on our bed. He still does. Won't leave it. He's on it even when I come back from the office."

"He sleeps with you?" she said with a shudder.

"I come home. I want someone to talk to."

"What d'you do with him when you go to your office?" The dog pulled and snorted.

"The woman who comes in and cleans looks after the dog," he said. And went on: "Your house has three storeys, mine has two, otherwise the same. I've got a basement full of rubbish. I was going to turn it into a flat but Sonia got worse. Futile. Yes, life is futile. Why not sell the damn place. No point. No point in anything. I go to the office, come back, feed the dog, and get drunk. Why not? Why go on? Why do *you* go on? Just habit. No sense in it."

"You *do* go on," she said.

"The dog," he said.

I must find some people for him to meet. He can't live like this, she thought. It is ghastly.

When she left he stood on the doorstep and said, "My house. Your house. They're worth four times what we gave for them. There it is."

She decided to invite him to dinner to meet some people—but whom could she ask? He was prickly. She knew dozens of people, but as she thought of them there seemed, for the first time, to be something wrong with all of them. In the end she invited no one to meet him.

On a diet, silly cow, he thought when she came to the door, but he fell back on his usual phrase as he looked about the empty room. "Did you invite me? Or shall I go away? You *did* invite me. Thank you. Thank you."

"I've been in Vienna with the Fladgates. She is a singer. Friends of David and Sarah."

"Fladgates? Never heard of the people," he said. "Sonia insulted someone in Vienna. I was drunk. Sonia never drank anything—that made her insults worse. Did your husband drink?"

"Indeed not."

He sat down on the sofa. The evening—Sonia's time. He expected Sonia to fly in and sit there watching this woman with all her "problems" hidden chastely except for one foot which tipped up and down in her shoe under her long dress. But to his surprise Sonia did not come. The terrier sat at Rachel's feet.

"How is your enemy?" she said as they drank. "The man in the office."

"He and his wife asked me to dinner," he said.

"That's kind," she said.

"People are kind," he said. "I've remarked that."

"Does he still watch you?"

"Yes. You know what it was? He thinks I drink too much. He thinks I've got a bottle in my desk. It wasn't the job that was worrying him. We are wrong about people. I am. You are. Everyone is."

When they went into dinner, candles were on the table.

Bloody silly having candles, he said to himself. And when she came in with the soup, he said, "We had candles. Poor Sonia threw them out of the window once. She had to do it in a play."

The soup was iced and white and there was something in it that he could not make out. But no salt. That's it, he thought, no salt in this woman. Writing about politics and things all day and forgets the salt. The next course was white too, something chopped or minced with something peculiar, goodness knew what. It got into his teeth. Minced newsprint, he thought.

"Poor Sonia couldn't cook at all," he said, pushing his food about, proud of Sonia. "She put dishes on the floor near the stove, terrible muddle, and rushed back to hear what people were saying and then an awful bloody stink came from the kitchen. I used to go down and the potatoes had burned dry and Tom had cleared the plates. Bloody starvation. No dinner."

"Oh, no!" she said.

"I live on chops now. Yes," he said. "One, sometimes two, every day, say ten a week. Am I being a bore? Shall I go?"

Rachel had a face that had been set for years in the same concerned expression. That expression now fell to pieces from her forehead to her throat. Against her will she laughed. The laugh shook her and was loud; she felt herself being whirled into a helpless state from the toes upward. Her blood whirled too.

"You laughed!" he shouted. "You did not protest. You did not write an article. You laughed. I could see your teeth. Very good. I've never seen you laugh before."

And the dog barked at them.

"She laughed," he shouted at the dog.

She went out to make coffee, very annoyed at being trapped into laughing. While he waited, the dog sat undecided, ears pricked, listening for her and watching him like a sentry.

"Rats," whispered Gilbert to the dog. It stood up sharply.

"Poor bastard. What a life," he said.

The dog barked angrily at him, and when she came in he said, "I told your dog he ought to be on a farm."

"You said that before," she said. "Let us have coffee next door." They moved into the next room and she sat on the sofa while she poured the coffee.

"Now *you* are sitting on the sofa. I'm in this armchair," he said, thinking of life tactically. "Sonia moved about too. I used to watch her going into a room. Where will she sit next? Damned if I ever got it right. The same in restaurants. Let us sit here, she'd say, and then when the waiter came to her chair, she'd say, 'No, not here. Over there.' Never knew where she was going to settle. Like a fly. She wanted attention. Of course. That was it. Quite right."

"Well," she said coldly, "she was an actress."

"Nothing to do with it," he said. "Woman."

"Nonsense," she said, hating to be called a woman, and thought, It's my turn now.

"My husband," she said, "travelled the whole time. Moscow, Germany, Copenhagen, South Africa, but when he got home he was never still, posing to the animals on the farm, showing off to barns, fences, talking French and German to birds, pretending to be a country gentleman."

"Let the poor man alone," he said. "Is he still alive?"

"I told you," she said. "I won't bore you with it all."

She was astonished to find herself using his word and that the full story of her husband and herself she had planned to tell and which she had told so many people suddenly lost interest for her. And yet, anyway, she thought, why shouldn't I tell this man about it? So she started, but she made a muddle of it. She got lost in the details. The evening, she saw, was a failure. He yawned.

If there was one thing Rachel could honestly say, it was that she had not thought of her husband for years. She had not forgotten, but he had become a generality in the busyness of her life. But now, after the evening when Gilbert came to dinner, her husband came to life and plagued her. If an aeroplane came down whistling across the wide London sky, she saw him sitting in it—back from Moscow, Cape Town, Copenhagen—descending not upon her, but on another woman. If she took the dog for a run in the park, the cuddling couples on the grass became him and that young girl; if babies screamed in their prams they were his children; if a man threw a ball it was he; if men in white flannels were playing cricket, she wondered if he was among them. She imagined sudden, cold meetings and ran through tirades of hot dialogue. One day she saw a procession of dogs tails up and panting, following a bitch, with a foolish grin of wet teeth in their jaws, and Sam rushed after them; she went red in the face shouting at him. And yet she had gone to the park in order to calm herself and to be alone. The worst thing that could happen would be to meet Gilbert, the cause of this, but like all malevolent causes, he never showed his face. She had wished to do her duty and be sorry for him, but not for him to become a man. She feared she might be on the point of talking about this to a woman, not a woman she knew well—that would be disastrous—but, say, to some woman or girl sitting alone on a park seat or some woman in a shop: a confidence she would regret all her life. She was touchy in these days and had a row with the doctor who threw flowerpots at her dog. She petted the animal. "Your head is handsome," she said, stroking its head, "but why did you go after that silly bitch?" The dog adored her when she said this. "You're vain," she said to it.

Gilbert *did* go to the park, but only on Saturdays, when the crowds came. He liked seeing the picnics, the litter on the grass; he stood still with pleasure when babies screamed or ice cream dripped. He grinned at boys throwing water from drinking fountains and families trudging, drunks lying asleep, and fat girls lying half on top of their young men and tickling their faces with grass. The place is a damn bedroom. Why not? Where else can they go? Lucky, boring people. I've got a bedroom and no one in it.

One Saturday, after three days of rain, he took his dog there and—would you believe it?—there the whole crowd was again, still at it, on the wet grass. The trouble with Sonia was that she thought the park was vulgar and would never go there—went once and never again, hadn't brought the right shoes.

He remarked this to his dog as he let it off its leash. The animal scampered round him in wide circles; came back to him and then raced off again in circles getting wider and wider until it saw a man with string in his hand trying to fly a kite. The kite was flopping on the ground, rose twenty or thirty feet in the air and then dived again. The dog rushed at the kite, but the man got it up again, higher this time. Gilbert walked towards the man. "Poor devil, can't get it up," he said as he walked. He got near the man and watched his struggles.

Then the kite shot up high and Gilbert watched it waving there until suddenly it swept away higher still. Gilbert said, "Good for him." The boredom of the grey afternoon was sweet. He lit a cigarette and threw the empty packet on the grass and then he found he had lost sight of the dog. When he saw it again it was racing in a straight line towards a group of trees by the lake. It was racing towards another dog. A few yards away from the dog it stopped and pranced. The dog was a terrier and stopped dead, then came forward. They stood sniffing at each other's tails and then jumped round muzzle to muzzle. They were growling, the terrier barked, and then the two dogs flew at each other's necks. Their play had turned to a war, their jaws were at each other's necks and ears. Gilbert saw at once it was Rachel's dog, indeed Rachel was running up shouting, "Sam! Sam!" The fight was savage and Tom had his teeth in.

"Stop them!" Rachel was shouting. "Stop them! They'll kill each other. He's got him by the throat."

And then she saw Gilbert. "You!"

Gilbert was enjoying the fight. He looked round and picked up a stick that had fallen from a tree.

"Stop them," she shouted.

"Get yours by the collar, I'll get mine," he shouted to her.

"I can't. Sam! Sam! They're bleeding."

She was dancing about in terror, trying to catch Sam by the legs.

"Not by the legs. By the collar, like this, woman," he shouted. "Don't put your arms round him, you idiot. Like this. Stop dancing about."

He caught Tom by the collar and lifted him as both dogs hung on to each other.

"You're strangling him. I can't, I can't," she said. Gilbert brought his stick down hard on the muzzles of the dogs, just as she was trying to grasp Sam again.

"You'll kill them."

He brought the stick down hard again. The dogs yelped with pain and separated.

"Get the leash on," he said, "you fool."

Somehow she managed it and the two dogs now strained to get at each other. The terrier's white neck and body were spotted with blood, and smears of it were on her hands.

Gilbert wiped their spit off his sleeve.

They pulled their dogs yards apart and she stared at him. It infuriated her that he was laughing at her with pure pleasure. In their stares they saw each other clearly and as they had never seen each other before. To him, in her short skirt and her shoes muddied by the wet grass, her hair disordered and the blood risen to her pale face, she was a woman. The grass had changed her. To her he was not a pitiable arrangement of widower's tricks, but a man on his own. And the park itself changed him in her eyes: in the park he, like everyone else there, seemed to be human. The dogs gave one more heave to get at each other.

"Lie down, Sam," Gilbert shouted.

She lifted her chin and was free to hate him for shouting at her animal.

"Look after yours. He's dangerous," she called back, angered by the friendliness of his face.

"Damn silly dogs enjoyed it. Good for them. Are you all right? Go up to the kiosk and get a drink—if I may, I'll follow you up—see you're all right."

"No, no," she put out a loud moan—far too loud. "He's bleeding. I'll take him home," and she turned to look at the park. "What a mess people make." And now, walking away, shouted a final accusation: "I didn't know you brought your dog here."

He watched her go. She turned away and dragged the struggling terrier over the grass uphill from the lake. He watched her walking unsteadily.

Very attractive figure, he thought. Silly cow. Better go home and ring her up.

He turned and on the way back to his house he could still see her dancing about on the grass and shouting. He went over the scene again and repeated his conclusion. "She's got legs. Never saw them before. A woman. Must be. Full of life." She was still dancing about as he put a bowl of water down for the dog. It drank noisily and he gave it another bowl and then he washed the dog's neck and looked at its ear. "Nothing much wrong with you," he said. He fed the animal, and soon it jumped on the sofa and was instantly snorting, whimpering and shaking into sleep.

"I must ring her up, yes, that is what I must do."

But a neighbour answered and said Rachel had gone to the vet and had come back in a terrible state and had gone to bed with one of her migraines.

"Don't bother her," he said. "I just rang to ask how the dog was."

Rachel was not in bed. She was standing beside the neighbour, and when the call was over she said, "What did he say?"

"He asked about the dog."

"Is that all?"

"Yes."

This flabbergasted her.

In the middle of the night she woke up, and when her stupefaction passed she damn well wished he was there so that she could say, "It didn't occur to you to apologize. I don't like being called a fool. You assume too much. Don't think I care a damn about *your* dog." She was annoyed to feel a shudder pass through her. She got out of bed, and looking out of her window at the black trees, saw herself racing across the park to his house and pulling that dog of his off his bed. The things she said! The language she used! She kicked the dog out of the room and it went howling downstairs. She went back to bed weak and surprised at herself because, before she realized it, Sam became Tom in her hand. She lay there stiff, awake, alone. Which dog had she kicked? Sam or Tom?

In his house Gilbert locked up, poured himself a strong whisky, then a second, then a third. Uncertain of whom he was addressing, Rachel or Sonia, he said, "Silly cow," and blundered drunkish to bed. He woke up at five very cold. No dog. The bed was empty. He got out of bed and went downstairs. For the first time since Sonia had died the dog was asleep on the sofa. He had forgotten to leave his door open.

In the morning he was startled to hear Sonia's voice saying to him in her stage voice, "Send her some flowers. Ask her to dinner."

So he sent the flowers, and when Rachel rang to thank him he asked her to dinner—at a restaurant.

"Your house. My house," he said. "Two dogs."

There was a long silence and he could hear her breath bristling.

"Yes, I think it has to be somewhere else," she said. And added, "As you say, we have a problem."

And after this dinner and the next, she said, "There are so many problems. I don't really know you."

They talked all summer, and people who came regularly to the restaurant made up stories about them and were quite put out when in October they stopped coming. All the proprietor had heard was that they had sold their houses—in fact he knew what they'd got for them. The proprietor had bought Sonia's dog. There was a terrier, too, he said, but he didn't know what had happened to that.

The Marvellous Girl

The official ceremony was coming to an end. Under the sugary chandeliers of what had once been the ballroom of the mansion to which the Institute had moved, the faces of the large audience yellowed and aged as they listened to the last speeches and made one more effort of chin and shoulder to live up to the gilt, the brocaded panels of the walls, and the ceiling, where cherubs, clouds, and naked goddesses romped. Oh, to be up there among them, thought the young man sitting at the back, but on the platform the director was passing from the eternal values of art to the "gratifying presence of the minister," to "Lady Brigson's untiring energies," the "labours of Professor Exeter and his panel" in the exhibition on the floor below. When he was named the professor looked with delight at the audience and played with a thin gold chain he had taken from his pocket. The three chandeliers gave a small, united flicker as if covering the yawns of the crowd. The young man sitting at the back stared at the platform once more, and then, with his hands on his knees, his elbows out, his eye turned to the nearest door. He was getting ready to push past the people sitting next to him and to be the first out—to get out before his wife, who was on the platform with the speakers. By ill luck he had run into her before the meeting and had been trapped into sitting for nearly two hours, a spectator of his marriage that had come to an end. His very presence there seemed to him an unsought return to one of those patient suicides he used to commit, day after day, out of drift and habit.

To live alone is to expose oneself to accident. He had been drawing on and off all day in his studio and not until the evening had he realized that he had forgotten to eat. Hunger excited him. He took a bus down to an Italian restaurant. It was one of those places where the proprietor came out from time to time to perform a private ballet. He tossed pancakes almost up to the ceiling and then dropped them into a blaze of brandy in the pan—a diversion that often helped the young man with the girls he now sometimes took there. The proprietor was just at the blazing point when two women came into the restaurant in their winter coats and stood still, looking as if they were on fire. The young man quickly gulped down the last of a few coils of spaghetti and stood up and wiped his mouth. The older and smaller of the two women was his wife and she was wearing a wide hat of black fur that made her look shorter than he remembered her. Free of him, she had become bizarre and smaller. Even her eyes had become smaller and, like mice, saw him at once and gave him an alert and busy smile. With her was the tall, calm girl with dark-blue eyes from their office at the Institute, the one she excitedly called "the marvellous girl," the "only one I have ever been able to get on with."

More than two years had gone by since he and his wife had lived together. The marriage was one of those prickly friendships that never succeeded—to *his* astonishment, at any rate—in turning into love, but are kept going by curiosity. It had become at once something called "our situation": a duet by a pair of annoyed hands. What kept them going was an exasperated interest in each other's love affairs, but even unhappiness loses its tenderness and fascination. They broke. At first they saw each other occasionally, but now rarely—except at the Institute, where his drawings were shown. They were connected only by the telephone wire which ran under the London pavements and worried its way under the window ledge of his studio. She would ring up, usually late at night.

"I hope it's all right," she'd say wistfully. "Are you alone?"

But getting nothing out of him on that score, she would become brisk and ask for something out of the debris of their marriage, for if marriages come to an end, paraphernalia hangs on. There were two or three divans, a painted cupboard, some rugs rolled up, boxes of saucepans and frying pans, lamps—useful things, stored in the garage under his studio. But as if to revive an intimacy, she always asked for some damaged object; she had a child's fidelity to what was broken: a lamp-shade that was scorched, an antique coal bucket with one loose leg, or a rug that had been stained by her dog, Leopold, whose paws were always in trouble. Leopold's limp had come to seem to the young man as the animal's response to their hopeless marriage. The only sound object she had ever wanted—and got into a temper about it—was a screwdriver that had belonged to her father, whom she detested.

Now, in the restaurant, she put up a friendly fight from under the wide-brimmed hat.

"I didn't know you still came here," she said.

"I come now and again."

"You must be going to the opening at the Institute."

"No," he said. "I haven't heard of it."

"But I sent you a card," she said. "You must go. Your drawings are in the exhibition. It's important."

"Three drawings," said the girl warmly.

"Come with us," his wife said.

"No. I can't. I'm just going to pay my bill."

A lie, of course. She peered at his plate as if hoping to read his fortune, to guess at what he was up to. He turned to the girl and said with feeling, "Are you better now?"

"I haven't been ill," said the girl.

"You said she'd been in hospital," he said to his wife.

"No, I didn't," she said. "She went to Scotland for a wedding."

A quite dramatic look of disappointment on the young man's face made the girl laugh and look curiously at him. He had seen her only two or three times and knew nothing much about her, but she was indeed "marvellous." She was not in hospital, she was beautiful and alive. Astounding. Even, in a bewildering way, disappointing.

The waiter saved him and moved them away.

"Enjoy yourselves," said the young man. "I'm going home."

"Good-bye." The girl turned to wave to him as she followed his wife to the table.

It was that good-bye that did it for him. It was a radiant good-bye, half laughing; he had seen her tongue and her even teeth as she laughed. Simply seeing him go had brought life to her face. He went out of the restaurant and in the leathery damp of the street he could see the face following him from lamp to lamp. "Good-bye, good-bye," it was still saying. And that was when he changed his mind. An extraordinary force pulled his scattered mind together: he determined to go to the meeting and to send to her, if he could see her in the crowd, a blinding, laughing, absolute good-bye forever, as radiant as hers.

Now, as he sat there in the crowded hall, there was no sign of her. He had worn his eyes out looking for her. She was not on the platform with his wife and the speakers, of course. The director, whose voice suggested chocolate, was still thanking away when suddenly the young man did see her. For the light of the chandeliers quivered again, dimmed to a red cindery glow, and then went out, and as people gasped "Oh," came on strongly again, and one or two giggled. In that flash when everyone looked up and round, there was a gap between the ranks of heads and shoulders and he saw her brown hair and her broad pale face with its white-rose look, its good-humoured chin and the laugh beginning on it. She turned round and she saw him as he saw her. There are glances that are collisions, scattering the air between like glass. Her expression was headlong in open conniving joy at the sight of things going wrong. She was sitting about ten rows in front of him, but he was not quick enough to wave, for now, *plonk,* the lights went out for good. The audience dropped en masse into the blackness, the hall sank gurgling to the bottom of the sea and was swamped. Then, outside, a door banged, a telephone rang, feet shuffled, and a slow animal grunting and chattering started everywhere and broke into irreverent squeals of laughter.

Men clicked on their lighters or struck matches, and long anarchic shadows shot over the walls. There was the sudden heat of breath, wool, fur, and flesh, as if the audience had become one body.

"Keep your seats for a moment," the director said from the darkness like God.

Now was the time to go. Darkness had wiped out the people on the platform. For the young man they had become too intimate. It had seemed to him that his wife, who sat next to her old lover, Duncan, was offering too lavish a sight of the new life she was proposing to live nowadays. Duncan was white-faced and bitter, and they were at their old game of quarrelling publicly under their breath while she was tormenting him openly by making eyes at the professor, who was responding by making his gold chain spin round faster and faster. The wife of the director was studying all this and preparing to defend her husband in case the longing in those female eyes went beyond the professor and settled on him.

How wrong I was about my wife's character, the young man thought. Who would have thought such wistful virginity could become so rampant. The young man said, "Pull yourself together, Duncan. Tell her you won't stand any more of it. Threaten her with Irmgard . . ."

Darkness had abolished it all.

It was not the darkness of the night outside. This darkness had no flabby wet sky in it. It was dry. It extinguished everything. It stripped the eyes of sight: even the solid human rows were lumped together invisibly. One was suddenly naked in the dark from the boots upward. One could feel the hair on one's body growing and in the chatter one could hear men's voices grunting, women's voices going fast, breath going in and out, muscles changing, hearts beating. Many people stood up. Surrounded by animals like himself he, too, stood up, to hunt with the pack, to get out. Where was the girl? Inaccessible, known, near but invisible. Someone had brought a single candle to the desk at which the director stood like a spectre. He said, "It would seem, ladies and gentlemen, that there has been a failure of the . . . I fear the . . . hope to procure the . . ."

There was a rough animal laugh from the audience, and all standing up now, they began to shuffle slowly for the doors.

"Get out of my way. Please let me pass," the young man shouted in a stentorian voice which no one heard, for he was shouting inside himself. "I have got to get to a girl over there. I haven't seen her for nearly a year. I've got to say good-bye to her for the last time."

And the crowd stuck out their bottoms and their elbows, broadened their backs and grew taller all round him, saying, "Don't push."

A man, addressing the darkness in an educated voice, said, "It is remarkable how calm an English crowd is. One saw it in the Blitz."

The young man knocked over a chair in the next row and in the next, shoving his way into any gap he could find in the clotted mass of fur and wool, and muttering, "I've only spoken to her three times in my life. She is wearing blue and has a broad nose. She lives somewhere in London—I don't know where—all I know is that I thought she was ill but it turns out that she went to a wedding in Scotland. I heard she is going to marry a young man in Canada. Think of a girl like that with a face as composed as a white rose—but a rose that can laugh—taking her low voice to Canada and lying at night among thousands of fir trees and a continent of flies and snow. I have got to get to the door and catch her there and say good-bye."

He broke through four rows of chairs, trod on feet and pushed, but the crowd was slow and stacked up solid. Hundreds of feet scraped. Useless to say to them, "A fox is among you. I knew when I first saw this girl that she was to be dreaded. I said just now in a poetic way that her skin is the colour of a white rose, but it isn't. Her hair has the gloss of a young creature's, her forehead is wide and her eyebrows are soft and arching, her eyes are dark blue and her lips warm and helpless. The skin is really like bread. A marvellous girl—everyone says so—but the sure sign of it is that when I first saw her I was terrified of her. She was standing by an office window watching people in the street below and talking on the telephone and laughing and the laughter seemed to swim all over her dress and her breasts seemed to join in and her waist too, even her long young legs that were continuing the dance she had been at—she was saying—the night before. It was when she turned and saw me that my sadness began.

"My wife was there—it was her office—and she said to me in a whisper, 'She is marvellous, isn't she? The child enjoys herself and she's right. But what fools girls are. Sleep with all the boys you like, don't get married yet, it's a trap, I keep telling her.'

"I decided never to go to that office again."

The crowd shuffled on in the dark. He was choking in the smell of fur coats, clamouring to get past, to get to the door, angrily begging someone to light one more match—"What? Has the world run out of matches and lighters?"—so that he could see her, but they had stopped lighting matches now. He wanted to get his teeth into the coat of a large broad woman in front of him. He trod on her heels.

"I'm sorry," he wanted to say. "I'm just trying to say good-bye to someone. I couldn't do it before—think of my situation. I didn't care —it didn't matter to me—but there was trouble at the office. My wife had broken with that wretched man Duncan, who had gone off with a girl called Irmgard, and when my wife heard of it she made him throw Irmgard over and took him back, and once she'd got him she took up with the professor—you saw him twiddling his gold chain. In my opinion it's a surprise that the exhibition ever got going, what with the professor and Duncan playing Cox and Box in the office. But I had to deliver my drawings. And so I saw this girl a second time. I also took a rug with me, a rug my wife had asked for from the debris. Oh, yes, I've got debris.

"The girl got up quickly from her desk when she saw me. I say *quickly.* She was alone and my sadness went. She pointed to the glass door at the end of the room. 'There's a committee meeting. She's in there with her husband and the others.'

"I said—and this will make you laugh, Mrs. Whatever-your-name-is, please move on—I said, 'But *I* am her husband,' I said.

"With what went on in that office how could the girl have known? I laughed when I said this, laughing at myself. The girl did not blush; she studied me and then she laughed too. Then she took three steps towards me, almost as if she was running—I counted those steps—for she came near enough to touch me on the sleeve of my raincoat. Soft as her face was, she had a broad strong nose. In those three steps she became a woman in my eyes, not a vision, not a sight to fear, a friendly creature, well shaped.

" 'I ought to have known by your voice—when you telephone,' she said. Her mistake made her face shine.

" 'Is the parcel for the exhibition?' he said.

"I had put it on a chair.

" 'No, it's a rug. It weighs a ton. It's Leopold's rug.

" 'I've got to go,' I said. 'Just say, "It's Leopold's." Leopold is a dog.'

" 'Oh,' she said. 'I thought you meant a friend.'

" 'No. Leopold wants it, apparently. I've got a lot of rugs. I keep them in the garage at my studio. You don't want a rug, do you? As fast as I get rid of them some girl comes along and says, "How bare your floor is. It needs a rug," and brings me one. I bet when I get back I'll find a new one. Or I could let you have a box of saucepans, a Hoover, a handsaw, a chest of drawers, fire tongs, a towel rail . . .'

"I said this to see her laugh, to see her teeth and her tongue again and to see her body move under its blue dress, which was light blue on that day. And to show her what a distance lay between her life and mine.

" 'I've got to go,' I said again, but at the door I said, 'Beds too. When you get married. All in the garage.'

"She followed me to the door and I waved back to her."

To the back of the fur-coated woman he said, "I can be fascinating. It's a way of wiping oneself out. I wish you'd wipe yourself out and let me pass. I shall never see her again."

And until this night he had not seen her again. He started on a large design which he called The Cornucopia. It was, first of all, a small comic sketch of a dustbin which contained chunks of the rubbish in his garage—very clever and silly. He scrapped it, and now he made a large design and the vessel was rather like the girl's head, but when he came to drawing the fruits of the earth they were fruits of geometry —hexagons, octagons, cubes, with something like a hedgehog on top, so he made the vessel less like a girl's head; the thing drove him mad the more he worked on it.

September passed into October in the parks and once or twice cats on the glass roof of the studio lost their balance and came sliding down in a screech of claws in the hurly-burly of love.

One night his wife telephoned him.

"Oh, God. Trouble," he said when he heard her plaintive voice. He had kept out of her way for months.

"Is it all right? Are you alone?" she said. "Something awful has happened. Duncan's going to get married again. Irmgard has got her claws into him. I rang Alex—he always said I could ring—but he won't come. Why am I rejected? And you remember that girl—she's gone. The work piles up."

"To Canada?" he said.

"What on earth makes you say that?" she said in her fighting voice.

"You said she was."

"You're always putting words into my mouth. She's in hospital."

"Ill," he said. "How awful. Where is she?"

"How do I know?" she said. "Leopold!"—and now she was giggling. "Leopold's making a mess again. I must ring off."

"I'm sorry," he said.

Ill! In hospital! The picture of the girl running towards him in the office came back to him and his eyes were smeared with tears. He felt on his arms and legs a lick of ice and a lick of fire. His body filled with a fever that passed and then came back so violently that he lost his breath. His knees had gone as weak as string. He was in love with the girl. The love seemed to come up from events thousands of years old. The girl herself, he thought, was not young but ancient. Perhaps Egyptian. The skin of her face was not rose-like, nor like bread, but like stone roughened by centuries. "I am feeling love," he said, "for the whole of a woman for the first time. No other woman exists. I feel love not only for her face, her body, her voice, her hands and feet, but for the street she lives in, the place she was born, her dresses and stockings, her bus journeys, her handbags, her parties, her dances. I don't know where she is. How can I find out? Why didn't I realize this before?"

Squeezed like a rag between the crowd he got to the doorway, and there the crowd bulged and carried him through it backward because he was turning to look for her. Outside the door was an ambitious landing. The crowd was cautiously taking the first steps down the long sweep of this staircase. There was a glimmer of light here from the marble of the walls, and that educated man gripped his arm and said "Mind the steps down" and barred the young man's way. He fought free of the grip and stood against the wall. "Don't be a damn fool," said the educated man, waving his arms about. "If anyone slips down there, the rest of you will pile on top of him." The man now sounded mad. "I saw it in the war. A few at a time. A few at a time," he screamed. And the young man felt the man's spit on his face. The crowd passed him like mourners, undecipherable, but a huge woman turned on him and held him by the sleeves with both hands. "Thornee! Thornee! Where are you? You're leaving me," she whimpered. "Dear girl," said a man behind her. "I am here." She let go, swung round and collided with her husband and grabbed him. "You had your arm round that woman," she said. They faded past. The young man looked for a face. Up the stairs, pushing against the procession going down, a man came up sidling against the wall. Every two or three steps he shouted "Mr. Zagacheck?" Zagacheck, Zagacheck, Zagacheck came nearer and suddenly a mouth bawled into the young man's face with a blast of heavily spiced breath.

"Mr. Zagacheck?"

"I am not Mr. Zagacheck," said the young man in a cold, clear voice, and as he said it the man was knocked sideways.

A woman took the young man's hand and said, "Francis!" and she laughed. She had *named* him. It was the girl, of course. "Isn't this wild? Isn't it marvellous? I saw you. I've been looking for you," she said.

"I have been looking for *you.*"

He interlaced his fingers with her warm fingers and held her arm against his body.

"Are you with your wife?" she said.

"No," he said.

She squeezed his hand, she lifted it and held it under her arm.

"Are you alone?" he said.

"Yes."

"Good," he said. "I thought you'd gone." Under her arm he could feel her breast. "I mean for good, left the country. I came to say good-bye."

"Oh, yes!" she said with enthusiasm and rubbed herself against him. "Why didn't you come to the office?"

He let go of her hand and put his arm round her waist.

"I'll tell you later. We'll go somewhere."

"Yes!" she said again.

"There's another way out. We'll wait here and then slip out by the back way."

The crowd pressed against them. And then he heard his wife's voice, only a foot away from him. She was saying, "I'm not making a scene. It's you. I wonder what has happened to the girl."

"I don't know and I don't care," the man said. "Stop trying to change the subject. Yes or no? Are you?"

The young man stiffened: "This is the test. If the girl speaks the miracle crashes."

She took his arm from her waist and gripped his hand fiercely. They clenched, sticking their nails into each other, as if trying to wound. He heard one of the large buttons on his wife's coat click against a button of his coat. She was there for a few seconds: it seemed to him as long as their marriage. He had not been as close to his wife for years. Then the crowd moved on, the buttons clicked again and he heard her say, "There's only Leopold there."

In a puff of smoke from her cigarette she vanished. The hands of the girl and Francis softened, and he pressed hard against her.

"Now," he whispered. "I know the way."

They sidled round the long wall of the landing, passing a glimmering bust—"Mr. Zagacheck," he said—and came to the corner of a corridor, long and empty, faintly lit by a tall window at the end. They almost ran down it, hand in hand. Twice he stopped to try the door of a room. A third door opened.

"In here," he said.

He pulled her into a large dark room where the curtains had not been drawn, a room that smelt of new carpet, new paint, and new furniture. There was the gleam of a desk. They groped to the window. Below was a square with its winter trees and the headlights of cars playing upon them and the crowd scattering across the roads. He put his arms round her and kissed her on the mouth and she kissed him. Her hands were as wild as his.

"You're mad," she said, "this is the director's room," as he pushed her onto the sofa, but when his hands were on the skin of her leg she said, "Let's go."

"When did you start to love me?" he said.

"I don't know. Just now. When you didn't come. I don't know. Don't ask me. Just now, when you said you loved me."

"But before?"

"I don't know," she said.

And then the lights in the building came on and the lights on the desk and they got up, scared, hot-faced, hot-eyed, hating the light.

"Come on. We must get out," he said.

And they hurried from the lighted room to get into the darkness of the city.

The Spree

The old man—but when does old age begin?—the old man turned over in bed and putting out his hand to the crest of his wife's beautiful white rising hip and comforting bottom, hit the wall with his knuckles and woke up. More than once during the two years since she had died he had done this and knew that if old age vanished in the morning it came on at night, filling the bedroom with people until, switching on the light, he saw it staring at him; then it shuffled off and left him looking at the face of the clock. Three hours until breakfast: the hunger of loss yawned under his ribs. Trying to make out the figures on the clock, he dropped off to sleep again and was walking up Regent Street seeing, on the other side of it, a very high-bred white dog, long in the legs and distinguished in its step, hurrying up to Oxford Circus, pausing at each street corner in doubt, looking up at each person as he passed and whimpering politely to them: "Me? Me? Me?" and going on when they did not answer. A valuable dog like that, lost! Someone will pick it up, lead it off, sell it to the hospital, and doctors will cut it up! The old man woke up with a shout to stop the crime and then he saw daylight in the room and heard bare feet running past his room and the shouts of his three grandchildren and his daughter-in-law calling "Ssh! Don't wake Grandpa."

The old man got out of bed and stood looking indignantly at the mirror over the washbasin and at his empty gums. It was awful to think, as he put his teeth in to cover the horror of his mouth, that twelve or fourteen hours of London daylight were stacked up meaninglessly waiting for him. He pulled himself together. As he washed, listening to the noises of the house, he made up a speech to say to his son, who must be downstairs by now.

"I am not saying I am ungrateful. But old and young are not meant to be together. You've got your life. I've got mine. The children are sweet—you're too sharp with them—but I can't stand the noise. I don't want to live at your expense. I want a place of my own. Where I can breathe. Like Frenchy." And as he said this, speaking into the towel and listening to the tap running, he could see and hear Frenchy, who was his dentist but who looked like a rascally prophet in his white coat and was seventy if he was a day, saying to him as he looked down into his mouth and as if he was really tinkering with a property there, "You ought to do what I've done. Get a house by the sea. It keeps you young."

Frenchy vanished, leaving him ten years younger. The old man got into his shirt and trousers and was carefully spreading and puffing up his sparse black-and-grey hair across his head when in came his daughter-in-law, accusing him—why did she accuse? "Grandpa! You're up!"

She was like a soft Jersey cow with eyes too big and reproachful. She was bringing him tea, the dear sweet tiresome woman.

"Of course I'm up," he said.

One glance at the tea showed him it was not like the tea he used to make for his wife when she was alive, but had too much milk in it, always tepid, left standing somewhere. He held his hairbrush up and he suddenly said, asserting his right to live, to get out of the house, in air he could breathe, "I'm going into London to get my hair cut."

"Are you sure you'll be all right?"

"Why do you say that?" he said severely. "I've got several things I want to do."

And when she had gone, he heard her say on the stairs, "He's going to get his hair cut!"

And his son saying, "Not again!"

This business, this defiance of the haircut! For the old man it was not a mere scissoring and clipping of the hair. It was a ceremonial of freedom; it had the whiff of orgy, the incitement of a ritual. As the years went by, leaving him in such a financial mess that he was now down to not much more than a pension, it signified desire—but what desire? To be memorable in some streets of London, or at least as evocative as an incense. The desire would come to him, on summer days like this, when he walked in his son's suburban garden, to sniff and to pick a rose for his buttonhole; and then, already intoxicated, he marched out of the garden gate onto the street and to the bus stop, upright and vigorous, carrying his weight well and pink in the face. The scents of the barber's had been creeping into his nostrils, his chest, even went down to his legs. To be clipped, oiled, and perfumed was to be free.

So on this decent July morning in the sun-shot and acid suburban mist, he stood in a queue for the bus, and if anyone had spoken to him he would have gladly said, to put them in their place, "Times have changed. Before I retired, when Kate was alive—though I must honestly say we often had words about it—I always took a cab."

The bus came and whooshed him down to Knightsbridge, to his temple—the most expensive of the big shops. There, reborn on miles of carpet, he paused and sauntered, sauntered and paused. He was inflamed by hall after hall of women's dresses and hats, by cosmetics and jewellery. Scores of women were there. Glad to be cooled off, he passed into the echoing hall of provisions. He saw the game, the salmon, and the cheese. He ate them and moved on to lose twenty years in the men's clothing department, where, among ties and brilliant shirts and jackets, his stern yet bashful pink face woke up to the loot and his ears heard the voices of the rich, the grave chorus of male self-approval. He went to the end where the oak stairs led down to the barber's; there, cool as clergy, they stood gossiping in their white coats. One came forward, seated him, and dressed him up like a baby. And then—nothing happened. He was the only customer, and the barber took a few steps back towards the group, saying, "He wasn't at the staff meeting."

The old man tapped his finger irritably under his sheet. Barbers did not cut hair, it seemed. They went to staff meetings. One called back, "Mr. Holderness seconded it."

Who was Holderness?

"Where is Charles?" said the old man to call the barbers to order. Obsequiously the man began that pretty music with his scissors.

"Charles?" said the barber.

"Yes. Charles. He shaved me for twenty years."

"He retired."

Another emptiness, another cavern, opened inside the old man.

"Retired? He was a child!"

"All the old ones have retired."

The barber had lost his priestly look. He looked sinful, even criminal, certainly hypocritical.

And although the old man's head was being washed by lotions and oils and there was a tickling freshness about the ears and his nostrils quickened, there was something uneasy about the experience. In days gone by, the place had been baronial; now it seemed not quite to gleam. One could not be a sultan among a miserable remnant of men who held staff meetings. When the old man left, the woman at the desk went on talking as she took his money and did not know his name. When he went upstairs, he paused to look back—no, the place was a palace of pleasure no longer. It was the place where—except for the staff— no one was known.

And that was what struck him as he stepped out of the glancing swing-doors of the shop, glad to be out in the July sun: that he was a sultan, cool, scented, and light-headed, extraordinary in a way, sacred almost, ready for anything—but cut off from expectancy, unknown nowadays to anybody, free for nothing, liberty evaporating out of the tips of his shoes. He stepped out on the pavement dissembling leisure. His walk became slower and gliding. For an hour, shop windows distracted him; new shops where old had been shocked him. But, he said, pulling himself together, I must not fall into *that* trap: old people live in the past. And I am not old! Old I am not! So he stopped gliding and stepped out wilfully, looking so stern and with mouth turned down, so corrupt and purposeful with success, that he was unnoticeable. Who notices success?

It was always—he didn't like to admit it—like this on these days when he made the great stand for his haircut and the exquisite smell. He would set out with a vision, it crumbled into a rambling dream. He fell back, like a country hare, on his habitual run, to the shops which had bought his goods years ago, to see what they were selling and where he knew no one now; to a café which had changed its décor, where he ate a sandwich and drank a cup of coffee; but as the dream consoled, it dissolved into final melancholy. He with his appetite for everything, who could not pass a shop window, or an estate agent's, or a fine house, without greed watering in his mouth, could buy nothing. He hadn't the cash.

There was always this moment when the bottom began to fall out of his haircut days. He denied that his legs were tired, but he did slow down. It would occur to him suddenly in Piccadilly that he knew no one now in the city. He had been a buyer and seller, not a man for friends: he knew buildings, lifts, offices, but not people. There would be nothing for it but to return home. He would drag his way to the inevitable bus stop of defeat, and stand, as so many Londoners did, with surrender on their faces. He delayed it as long as he could, stopping at a street corner or gazing at a passing girl and looking round with that dishonest look a dog has when it is pretending not to hear its master's whistle. There was only one straw to clutch at. There was nothing wrong with his teeth, but he could ring up his dentist. He could ring up Frenchy. He could ring him and say, "Frenchy? How's tricks?" sportily, and (a man for smells) he could almost smell the starch in Frenchy's white coat, the keen, chemical, hygienic smell of his room. The old gentleman considered this and then went down a couple of disheartened side streets. In a short cul-de-sac, standing outside a urinal and a few doors from a dead-looking pub, there was a telephone box. An oldish brown motor-coach was parked empty at the kerb by it, its doors closed, a small crowd waiting beside it. There was a man in the telephone box, but he came out in a temper, shouting something to the crowd. The old man went into the box. He had thought of something to say: "Hullo, Frenchy! Where is that house you were going to find me, you old rascal?"

For Frenchy came up from the sea every day. It was true that Frenchy was a rascal, especially with the women, one after the other, but looking down into the old man's mouth and chipping at a tooth, he seemed to be looking into your soul.

The old man got out his coins. He was tired but eagerness revived him as he dialled.

"Hullo, Frenchy," he said. But the voice that replied was not Frenchy's. It was a child's. The child was calling out, "Mum. Mum." The old man banged down the telephone and stared at the dial. His heart thumped. He had, he realized, not dialled Frenchy's number but the number of his old house, the one he had sold after Kate had died.

The old gentleman backed out of the box and stared, tottering with horror, at it. His legs went weak, his breath had gone, and sweat bubbled on his face. He steadied himself by the brick wall. He edged away from the bus and the crowd so as not to be seen. He thought he was going to faint. He moved to a doorway. There was a loud laugh from the crowd as a young man with long black hair gave the back of the bus a kick. And then suddenly he and a few others rushed towards the old man, shouting and laughing.

"Excuse us," someone said and pushed him aside. He saw he was standing in the doorway of the pub.

"That's true," the old man murmured to himself. "Brandy is what I need." And at that, the rest of the little crowd pushed into him or past him. One of them was a young girl with fair hair who paused as her young man pulled her by the hand and said kindly to the old man, "After you."

There he was, being elbowed, travelling backwards into the little bar. It was the small private bar of the pub and the old man found himself against the counter. The young people were stretching their arms across him and calling out orders for drinks and shouting. He was wedged among them. The wild young man with the piratical look was on one side of him, the girl and her young man on the other. The wild young man called to the others, "Wait a minute. What's yours, dad?"

The old man was bewildered. "Brandy."

"Brandy," shouted the young man across the bar.

"That's right," said the girl to the old man, studying his face. "You have one. You ought to have got on the first coach."

"You'd have been halfway to bloody Brighton by now," said the wild young man. "The first bloody outing this firm's had in its whole bloody history and they bloody forgot the driver. Are you the driver?"

Someone called out, "No, he's not the driver."

"I had a shock," the old man began, but crowded against the bar no one heard him.

"Drink it up, then," the girl said to him, and startled by her kindness, he drank. The brandy burned and in a minute fire went up into his head, and his face lost its hard bewildered look and it loosened into a smile. He heard their young voices flying about him. They were going to Brighton. No, the other side of Brighton. No, this side—well, to bloody Hampton's mansion, estate, something. The new chairman—he'd thrown the place open. Bloody thrown it, laughed the wild man, to the works and the office and, as usual, "the works get the first coach." The young girl leaned down to smell the rose in the old man's button-hole and said to her young man, "It's lovely. Smell it." His arm was round her waist and there were the two of them bowing to the rose.

"From your garden?" said the girl.

The old man heard himself, to his astonishment, tell a lie.

"I grew it," he said.

"We shan't bloody start for hours," someone said. "Drink up."

The old man looked at his watch: a tragic look. Soon they'd be gone. Someone said, "Which department are you in?" "He's in the works," someone said. "No, I've retired," said the old man, not to cause a fuss. "Have another, dad," said the young man. "My turn."

Three of them bent their heads to hear him say again, "I have retired," and one of them said, "It was passed at the meeting. Anyone retired entitled to come."

"You've made a mistake," the old man began to explain to them. "I was just telephoning to my dentist . . ."

"No," said one of the bending young men, turning to someone in the crowd. "That bastard Fowkes talked a lot of bull but it passed."

"You're all right," the girl said to the old man.

"He's all right," said another and handed the old man another drink. If only they would stop shouting, the old man thought, I could explain.

"A mistake . . ." he began again.

"It won't do you any harm," someone said. "Drink up."

Then someone shouted from the door. "He's here. The driver."

The girl pulled the old man by the arm and he found himself being hustled to the door.

"My glass," he said.

He was pushed, holding his half-empty glass, into the street. They rushed past him and he stood there, glass in hand, trying to say good-bye and then he followed them, still holding his glass, to explain. They shouted to him, "Come on," and he politely followed to the door of the bus where they were pushing to get in.

But at the door of the bus everything changed. A woman wearing a flowered dress with a red belt, a woman as stout as himself, had a foot on the step of the bus and was trying to heave herself up while people ahead of her blocked the door. She nearly fell.

The old man, all smiles and sadness, put on a dignified anger. He pushed his way towards her. He turned forbiddingly on the youngsters.

"Allow me, madam," he said and took the woman's cool fat elbow and helped her up the step, putting his own foot on the lower one. Fatal. He was shoved up and himself pushed inside, the brandy spilling down his suit. He could not turn round. He was in, driven in deeply, to wait till the procession stopped. "I'm getting out," he said.

He flopped into the seat behind the woman.

"Young people are always in a rush," she turned to say to him.

The last to get in were the young couple.

"Break it up," said the driver. They were slow, for they were enlaced and wanted to squeeze in united.

The old man waited for them to be seated and then stood up, glass in hand, as if offering a toast, as he moved forward to get out.

"Would you mind sitting down," said the driver. He was counting the passengers, and one, seeing the old man with the glass in his hand, said, "Cheers."

For the first time in his adult life, the old man indignantly obeyed an order. He sat down, was about to explain his glass, heard himself counted, got up. He was too late. The driver pulled a bar, slammed the door, spread his arms over the wheel and off they went, to a noise that bashed people's eyeballs.

At every change of the gears, as the coach gulped out of the narrow streets, a change took place in the old man. Shaken in the kidneys, he looked around in protest, put his glass out of sight on the floor, and blushed. He was glad no one was sitting beside him, for his first idea was to scramble to the window and jump through it at the first traffic lights. The girl who had her arm round her young man looked round and smiled. Then he too looked round at all these unknown people, belonging to a firm he had never heard of, going to a destination unknown to him, and he had the inflated sensations of an enormous illegality. He had been kidnapped. He tipped back his hat and looked bounderish. The bus was hot and seemed to be frying in the packed traffic when it stopped at the lights. People had to shout to be heard. Under cover of the general shouting, he too shouted to a couple of women across the gangway, "Do we pass the Oval?"

The woman asked her friend, who asked the man in front, who asked the young couple. Blocks of offices went by in lumps. No one knew except someone who said, "Must do." The old man nodded. The moment the Oval cricket ground came into sight, he planned to go to the driver and tell him to let him off. So he kept his eyes open, thinking, What a lark. What a thing to tell them at home. Guess what? Had a free ride. "Cheek, my boy" (he'd say to his son), "that's what you need. Let me give you a bit of advice. You'll get nowhere without cheek."

His pink face beamed with shrewd frivolity as the coach groaned over the Thames that had never looked so wide and sly. Distantly a power station swerved to the west, then to the east, then rocked like a cradle as the young girl—restless like Kate she was—got out of her young man's arms and got him back into hers, in a tighter embrace. Three containers passed, the coach slackened, then choked forward so suddenly that the old man's head nearly hit the back of the head of the fat lady in front. He studied it and noticed the way the woman's thick hair, gold with grey in it, was darker as it came out of her neck like a growing plant and he thought, as he had often done, how much better a woman's head looks from behind—the face interferes with it in front. And then his own chin went slack and he began a voluptuous journey down corridors. One more look at the power station, which had become several jumping power stations, giving higher and higher leaps in the air, and he was asleep.

A snore came from him. The talking woman across the gangway was annoyed by this soliloquizing noise which seemed to offer a rival narrative; but others admired it for its steadiness, which peacefully mocked the unsteady recovery and spitting and fading energy of the coach and the desperation of the driver. Between their shouts at the driver, many glanced admiringly at the sleeper. He was swinging in some private barber's shop that swerved through space, sometimes in some airy corridor, at other times circling beneficently round a cricket match in which Frenchy, the umpire, in his white linen coat, was offering him a plate of cold salmon which his daughter-in-law was trying to stop him from eating; he was off the coach, striking his way home on foot at the tail of the longest funeral procession he had ever seen, going uphill for miles into fields that were getting greener and colder and emptier as snow came on and he sat down, plonk, out of breath, waking to hear the weeping of the crowds, all weeping for him, and then, still waking, he saw himself outside the tall glass walls of a hospital. It must be a hospital, for inside two men in white could be clearly seen in a glass-enclosed room, one of them the driver, getting ready to carry him in on a stretcher. He gasped, now fully awake. There was absolute silence. The coach had stopped; it was empty—he was alone in it, except for the woman, who, thank God, was still sitting in front of him, the hair still growing from the back of her neck.

"Where . . ." he began. Then he saw the hospital was in fact a garage. The passengers had got out, garagemen were looking under the hood of the bus. The woman turned round. He saw a mild face, without makeup.

"We've broken down," she said.

How grateful he was for her mild face. He had thought he was dead.

"I've been asleep," he said. "Where are we?"

He nearly said, "Have we passed the Oval?" but swallowed that silly question.

"Quarter past three," he said. Meaning thirty miles out, stuck fast in derelict country at a crossroads, with a few villas sticking out in fields, eating into the grass among a few trees, with a billboard on the far side of the highway saying blatantly, MORTGAGES, and the cars dashing by in flights like birds, twenty at a time, still sweeping away westward into space.

The woman had turned to study him, and when he got up, flustered, she said in a strict but lofty voice, "Sit down."

He sat down.

"Don't you move," she said. "I'm not going to move. They've made a mess of it. Let them put it right."

She had twisted round and he saw her face, wide and full now, as meaty as an obstinate country girl's, and with a smile that made her look as though she were evaporating.

"This is Hampton's doing," she said. "Anything to save money. I am going to tell him what I think of him when I see him. No one in charge. Not even the driver—listen to him. Treat staff like cattle. They've got to send another coach. Don't you move until it comes."

Having said this, she was happy.

"When my husband was on the board nothing like this happened. Do you know anyone here? I don't. Everything's changed."

She studied his grey hair.

The old man clung for the moment to the fact that he and she were united in not knowing anybody. His secretiveness was coming back.

"I've retired," he said.

The woman leaned further over the back of the seat and looked around the empty bus and then back at him as if she had captured him. Her full lips were the resting lips of a stout woman between meals.

"I must have seen you at the works with John," she said. "It was always a family in those days. Or were you in the office?"

I must get out of this, the old man was thinking, and he sat forward nearer to her, getting ready to get out once more. I must find out the name of this place, get a train or a bus or something, get back home. The place looked nameless.

But since his wife had died he had never been as near to a strange woman's face. It was a wide, ordinary, baby-like face damp in the skin, with big blue eyes under fair, skimpy eyebrows, and she studied him as a soft, plump child would—for no reason beyond an assumption that he and she were together in this: they weren't such fools, at their ages, to get off the coach. It was less the nearness of the face than her voice that kept him there.

It was a soft, high voice that seemed to blow away like a child's and was far too young for her, even sounded so purely truthful as to be false. It came out in deep breaths drawn up from soft but heavy breasts that could, he imagined, kick up a hullabaloo, a voice which suggested that by some silly inconsequent right she would say whatever came into her head. It was the kind of voice that made the old man swell with a polite, immensely intimate desire to knock the nonsense out of her.

"I can smell your rose from here," she said. "There are not many left who knew the firm in John's time. It was John's lifework."

He smiled complacently. He had his secret.

She paused and then the childish voice went suddenly higher. She was not simply addressing him. She was addressing a meeting.

"I told him that when he let Hampton flatter him he'd be out in a year. I said to John, 'He's jealous. He's been jealous all the time.'"

The woman paused. Then her chin and her lips stuck out, and her eyes that had looked so vague began to bulge and her voice went suddenly deep, rumbling with prophecy.

"'He wants to kill you,' I said. You," said the woman to the old man, "must have seen it. And he did kill him. We went on a trip round the world: America, Japan, India"—her voice sailed across countries—"that's where he died. If Hampton thinks he can wipe it out by throwing his place open to the staff and getting me down there on show, he's wrong."

My God, she's as dotty as Kate's sister used to get after her husband died, thought the old man. I'm sitting behind a madwoman.

"Dawson," she said and abruptly stood up as the old man rose too. "Oh," she said in her high regal style, gazing away out of the window of the bus. "I remember your name now. You had that row, that terrible row—oh, yes," she said eagerly, the conspirator. "*You* ring up Hampton. He's afraid of you. He'll listen. I've got the number here. You tell him there are twenty-seven of his employees stranded on the Brighton road."

The old man sighed. He gave up all idea of slipping out. When a woman orders you about, what do you do? He thought she looked rather fine standing there prophetically. The one thing to do in such cases was to be memorable. When is a man most memorable? When he says no.

"No, I wouldn't think of it," he said curtly. "Mr. Hampton and I are not on speaking terms."

"Why?" said the woman, distracted by curiosity.

"Mr. Hampton and I," he began, and he looked very gravely at her for a long time. "I have never heard of him. Who is he? I'm not on the staff. I've never heard of the firm." And then like a conjurer waving a handkerchief, he spread his face into a smile that had often got him an order in the old days.

"I just got on the coach for the ride. Someone said, 'Brighton.' 'Day at the sea,' I said. 'Suits me.' "

The woman's face went the colour of liver with rage and disbelief. One for the law, all the rage she had just been feeling about Hampton now switched to the old man. She was unbelieving.

"No one checked?" she said, her voice throbbing. She was boiling up like the police.

The old gentleman just shook his head gently. "No one checked"— it was a definition of paradise. If he had wings he would have spread them, taken to the air, and flown round her three times, saying, "Not a soul! Not a soul!"

She was looking him up and down. He stood with a plump man's dignity, but what saved him in her eyes were his smart, well-cut clothes, his trim hair, and the jaunty rose: he looked like an old rip, a racing man, probably a crook—at any rate, a bit of a rogue on the spree, yet innocent too. She studied his shoes and he moved a foot and kicked the brandy glass. It rolled into the gangway and he smiled slightly.

"You've got a nerve," she said, her smile spreading.

"Sick of sitting at home," he said. Weighing her up—not so much her character but her body—he said, "I've been living with my daughter-in-law since my wife died."

He burst out with confidence, for he saw he had almost conquered her. "Young and old don't mix. Brighton would suit me. I thought I would have a look around for a house."

Her eyes were still busily going over him.

"You're a spark," she said, still staring. Then she saw the glass and bent down to pick it up. As she straightened she leaned on the back of the seat and laughed out loud.

"You just got on. Oh, dear." She laughed loudly, helplessly. "Serves Hampton right.

"Sit down," she said. He sat down. She sat down on the seat opposite. He was astonished and even shy to see his peculiar case appreciated, and his peculiarity grew in his mind from a joke to a poem, from a poem to a dogma.

"I meant to get off at the Oval, but I dropped off to sleep." He laughed.

"Going to see the cricket?" she said.

"No," he said. "Home—I mean my son's place."

The whole thing began to appear lovely to him. He felt as she laughed at him, as she still held the glass, twiddling it by the stem, that he was remarkable.

"Years ago I did it once before," he said, multiplying his marvels. "When my wife was alive. I got a late train from London, went to sleep, and woke up in Bath. I did. I really did. Stayed at the Royal. Saw a customer next day. He was so surprised to see me he gave me an order worth three hundred pounds. My wife didn't believe me."

"Well, can you blame her?" the woman said.

The driver walked from the office of the garage and put his head into the coach and called out, "They're sending a new bus. Be here four o'clock."

The old man turned. "By the way, I'm getting off," he shouted to the driver.

"Aren't you going on?" said the woman. "I thought you said you were having a trip to the sea."

She wanted him to stay.

"To be frank," said the old man. "These youngsters—we'd been having a drink—they meant no harm—pushed me on when I was giving you a hand. I was in the pub. I had had a bit of a shock. I did something foolish. Painful really."

"What was that?" she said.

"Well," said the old man, swanking in his embarrassment and going very red, "I went to this telephone box, you know, where the coach started from, to ring up my dentist—Frenchy. I sometimes ring him up, but I got through to the wrong number. You know what I did? I rang the number of my old house, when Kate—when my wife—was alive. Some girl answered—maybe a boy—I don't know. It gave me a turn, doing a thing like that. I thought my mind had gone."

"Well, the number would have changed."

"I thought, I really did think, for a second, it was my wife."

The traffic on the main road sobbed or whistled as they talked. Containers, private cars, police cars, breakdown vans, cars with boats on their roofs—all sobbing their hearts out in a panic to get somewhere else.

"When did your wife die?" said the woman. "Just recently?"

"Two years ago," he said.

"It was grief. That is what it was—grief," she said gravely and looked away from him into the sky outside and to the derelict bit of country.

That voice of hers, by turns childish, silly, passing to the higher notes of the exalted and belligerent widow—all that talk of partners killing each other!—had become, as his wife's used to do after some tantrum, simply plain.

Grief. Yes, it was. He blinked away the threat of tears before her understanding. In these two years he seemed, because of his loneliness, to be dragging an increasing load of unsaid things behind him, things he had no one to tell. With his son and his daughter-in-law and their young friends he sat with his mouth open ready to speak, but he could never get a word out. The words simply fell back down his throat. He had a load of what people called boring things which he could not say: he had loved his wife; she had bored him; it had become a bond. What he needed was not friends, for since so many friends had died he had become a stranger; he needed another stranger. Perhaps like this woman whose face was as blank as his was, time having worn all expression from it. Because of that, you could see she looked now, if not as old as he was, full of life; but she had joined his lonely race and had the lost look of going nowhere. He lowered his eyes and became shy. Grief—what was it? A craving. Yet not for a face or even a voice or even for love, but for a body. But dressed. Say, in a flowered dress.

To get his mind off a thought so bold he uttered one of his boring things, a sort of sample of what he would have said to his wife. "Last night I had a dream about a dog," he began, to test her out as a stranger to whom you could say any damn silly thing. A friend would never listen to damn silly things.

The woman repeated, going back to what she had already said, as women do, "Remembering the telephone number—it was grief."

And then went off at a tangent, roughly. "Don't mention dreams to me. Last week at the bungalow I saw my husband walk across the sitting-room clean through the electric fire and the mirror over the mantelpiece and stand on the other side of it, not looking at me, but saying something to me that I couldn't hear—asking for a box of matches, I expect."

"Imagination," said the old man, sternly correcting her. He had no desire to hear of her dead husband's antics, but he did feel that warm, already possessive desire, to knock sense into her. It was a pleasant feeling.

"It wasn't imagination," she said, squaring up to him. "I packed my things and went to London at once. I couldn't stand it. I drove in to

Brighton, left the car at the station, and came up to London for a few days. That is why when I heard about Hampton's party at the office I took this coach.

"Saved the train fare. Why shouldn't Hampton pay?" She grinned. "I told him I'd come to the party, but I'm not going. I'm picking up the car at Brighton and going home to the bungalow. It's only seven miles away."

She waited to see if he would laugh at their being so cunningly in the same boat. He did not laugh and that impressed her, but she frowned. Her husband would not have laughed either.

"I dread going back," she said sulkily.

"I sold my place," he said. "I know the feeling."

"You were right," said the woman. "That's what I ought to do. Sell the place. I'd get a good price for it, too. I'm not exactly looking forward to going back there this evening. It's very isolated—but the cat's there."

He said nothing. Earnestly she said, "You've got your son and daughter-in-law waiting for you," giving him a pat on the knee. "Someone to talk to. You're lucky."

The driver put his head into the door and said, "All out. The other coach is here."

"That's us," said the woman.

The crowd outside were indeed getting into the new coach. The old man followed her out and looked back at the empty seats with regret. At the door he stepped past her and handed her out. She was stout but landed light as a feather. The wild young man and his friends were shouting, full of new beer, bottles in their pockets. The others trooped in.

"Good-bye," said the old man, doing his memorable turn.

"You're not coming with us?" said the woman. And then she said quietly, looking round secretively, "I won't say anything. You can't give up now. You're worried about your daughter-in-law. I know," she said.

The old man resented that.

"That doesn't worry me," he said.

"You ought to think of them," she said. "You ought to."

There was a shout of vulgar laughter from the wild young man and his friends. They had seen the two young lovers a long way off walking slowly, with all the time in the world, towards the coach. They had been off on their own.

"Worn yourselves out up in the fields?" bawled the wild young man, and he got the driver to sound the horn on the wheel insistently at them.

"You can ring from my place," said the woman.

The old man put on his air of being offended.

"You might buy my house," she tempted.

The two lovers arrived and everyone laughed. The girl—so like his wife when she was young—smiled at him.

"No. I can get the train back from Brighton," the old man said.

"Get in," called the driver.

The old man assembled seventy years of dignity. He did this because dignity seemed to make him invisible. He gave a lift to the woman's elbow, he followed her, he looked for a seat, and when she made room for him beside her, invisibly he sat there. She laughed hungrily, show-ing all her teeth. He gave a very wide sudden smile. The coach load chattered and some began to sing and shout and the young couple, getting into the clinch again, slept. The coach started and shook off the last of the towny places, whipped through short villages, passed pubs with animal names, The Fox, The Red Lion, The Dog and Duck, The Greyhound, and one with a new sign, The Dragon. It tunnelled under miles of trees, breathed afresh in scampering fields and thirty miles of greenery, public and private, until slowly, in an hour or so, the bald hills near the sea came up and, under them, distant slabs of chalk. Further and further the coach went and the bald hills grew taller and nearer.

The woman gazed disapprovingly at the young couple and was about to say something to the old man when suddenly, at the sight of his spry profile, she began to think—in freezing panic—of criminals. A man like this was just the kind—outwardly respectable—who would go down to Hampton's garden party to case the place, as she had read, pass as a member of the staff, steal jewellery, or plan a huge burglary. Or come to her house and bash her. The people who lived only a mile and a half from where she lived had had burglars when they were away: someone had been watching the house. They believed it was someone who had heard the house was for sale. Beside her own front door, behind a bush, she kept an iron bar. She always picked it up before she got her key out—in case. She saw herself now suddenly hitting out with it passion-ately, so that her heart raced; then having bashed the old man, she calmed down, or rather, she sailed into one of her exalted moods. She was wearing a heavy silver ring with a large brown stone in it, a stone which looked violet in some lights, and she said in her most genteel, faraway voice, "When I was in India, an Indian prince gave this ring to me when my husband died. It is very rare. It is one of those rings they wear for protection. He loved my husband. He gave it to me. They believe in magic."

She took it off and gave it to the old man.

"I always wear it. The people down the road were burgled."

The old man looked at the ring. It was very ugly and he gave it back to her.

What fools women are, he thought, and felt a huge access of strength. But aloud he said, "Very nice." And not to be outdone, he said, "My wife died in the Azores."

She took a deep breath. The coach had broken through the hills, and now cliffs of red houses had built up on either side and the city trees and gardens grew thicker and richer. The sunlight seemed to splash down in waves between them and over them. She grasped his arm.

"I can smell the sea already!" she said. "What are you going to tell your daughter-in-law when you ring up? I told the driver to stop at the station."

"Tell them?" said the old man. A brilliant idea occurred to him.

"I'll tell them I just dropped in on the Canary Islands," he said.

The woman let go of his arm, and after one glance, choked with laughter.

"Why not?" he said, grinning. "They ask too many questions. Where have you been? What are you doing? Or I might say Boulogne. Why not?"

"Well, it's nearer," she said. "But you must explain."

The wild young man suddenly shouted, "Where's he taking us now?" as the coach turned off the main road.

"He's dropping us at the station," the woman called out boldly. And indeed, speeding no more, grunting down side streets, the coach made for the station and stopped at the entrance to the station yard.

"Here we are," she said. "I'll get my car."

She pulled him by the sleeve to the door and he helped her out.

They stood on the pavement, surprised to see the houses and shops of the city stand still, every window looking at them. Brusquely cutting them off, the coach drove away at once downhill and left them to watch it pass out of sight. The old man blinked, staring at the last of the coach, and the woman's face aged.

It was the moment to be memorable, but he was so taken aback by her heavy look that he said, "You ought to have stayed on, gone to the party."

"No," she said, shaking brightness onto the face. "I'll get my car. It was just seeing your life drive off—don't you feel that sometimes?"

"No," he said. "Not mine. Theirs." And he straightened up, looked at his watch and then down the long hill. He put out his hand.

"I'm going to have a look at the sea."

And indeed, in a pale-blue wall on this July day, the sea showed between the houses. Or perhaps it was the sky. Hard to tell which.

She said, "Wait for me. I'll drive you down. I tell you what—I'll get my car. We'll drive to my house and have a cup of tea or a drink, and then you can telephone from there and I'll bring you back in for your train."

He still hesitated.

"I dreaded that journey. You made me laugh," she said.

And that is what they did. He admired her managing arms and knees as she drove out of the city into the confusing lanes.

"It's nice of you to come. I get nervous going back," she said as they turned into the drive of one of the ugliest bungalows he had ever seen, on top of the Downs, close to a couple of ragged firs torn and bent by the wind. A cat raced them to the door. She showed him the iron bar she kept close to it, behind the bush. A few miles away between a dip in the Downs was the pale-blue sea again, shaped like her lower lip.

There were her brass Indian objects on the wall of the sitting-room; on the mantelpiece and leaning against the mirror he had walked through was the photograph of her husband. Pull down a few walls, reface the front, move out the furniture, he thought, that's what you'd have to do, when she went off to another room, and wearing a white dress with red poppies on it came back with the tea tray.

"Now telephone," she said. "I'll get the number." But she did not give him the instrument until she heard a child answer it. That killed her last suspicion. She heard him speak to his daughter-in-law, and when he put the telephone down she said grandly, "I want thirty-one thousand pounds for the house."

The sum was so preposterous that it seemed to explode in his head and made him spill his tea in his saucer.

"If I decide to sell," she said, noticing his shock.

"If anyone offers you that," he said dryly, "I advise you to jump at it."

They regarded each other with disappointment.

"I'll show you the garden. My husband worked hard in it," she said. "Are you a gardener?"

"Not any longer," he said as he followed her sulking across the lawn. She was sulking too. A thin film of cloud came over the late afternoon sky.

"Well, if you're ever interested let me know," she said. "I'll drive you to the station."

And she did, taking him the long way round the coast road, and there indeed was the sea, the real sea, all of it, spread out like the skirt of some lazy old landlady with children playing all along the fringes on the beaches. He liked being with the woman in the car, but he was sad his day was ending.

"I feel better," she said. "I think I'll go to Hampton's after all," she said, watching him. "I feel like a spree."

But he did not rise. Thirty-one thousand! The ideas women have! At the station he shook hands and she said, "Next time you come to Brighton . . ." and she touched his rose with her finger. The rose was drooping. He got on the train.

"Who is this lady friend who keeps ringing you up from Brighton?" his daughter-in-law asked in her lowing voice several times in the following weeks. Always questions.

"A couple I met at Frenchy's," he said on the spur of the moment.

"You didn't say you'd seen Frenchy. How is he?" his son said.

"Didn't I?" said the old man. "I might go down to see them next week. But I don't know. Frenchy's heard of a house."

But the old man knew that what he needed was not a house.

The Lady from
Guatemala

Friday afternoon about four o'clock, the week's work done, time to kill:
the editor disliked this characterless hour when everyone except his
secretary had left the building. Into his briefcase he had slipped some
notes for a short talk he was going to give in a cheap London hall, worn
by two generations of protest against this injustice or that, before he
left by the night plane for Copenhagen. There his real lecture tour
would begin and turn into a short holiday. Like a bored cardplayer, he
sat shuffling his papers and resented that there was no one except his
rude, hard-working secretary to give him a game.

The only company he had in his room—and it was a moody friend
—was his portrait hanging behind him on the wall. He liked cunningly
to draw people to say something reassuring about the picture. It was
"terribly good," as they say; he wanted to hear them say it lived up to
him. There was a strange air of rivalry in it. It rather overdid the
handsome mixture of sunburned satyr-like pagan and shady jealous
Christian saint under the happy storm of white hair. His hair had been
grey at thirty: at forty-seven, by a stroke of luck, it was silken white.
His face was an actor's, the nose carved for dramatic occasions, the lips
for the public platform. It was a face both elated and ravaged by the
highest beliefs and doubts. He was energized by meeting this image in
the morning and, enviously, he said good-bye to it at night. Its nights

would be less tormented than his own. Now he was leaving it to run the paper in his absence.

"Here are your tickets." His secretary breezed into the room. "Copenhagen, Stockholm, Oslo, Berlin, Hamburg, Munich—the lot," she said. She was mannerless to the point of being a curiosity.

She stepped away and wobbled her tongue in her cheek. She understood his restless state. She adored him: he drove her mad and she longed for him to go.

"Would you like to know what I've got outside?" she said. She had a malicious streak. "A lady. A lady from Guatemala. Miss Mendoza. She has got a present for you. She worships you. I said you were busy. Shall I tell her to buzz off?"

The editor was proud of his tolerance in employing a girl so sportive and so familiar; her fair hair was thin and looked harassed, her spotty face set off the knowledge of his own handsomeness in face and behaviour.

"Guatemala! Of course I must see her!" he exclaimed. "What *are* you thinking about? We ran three articles on Guatemala. Show her in."

"It's your funeral," said the girl and gave a vulgar click with her tongue. The editor was, in her words, "a sucker for foreigners"; she was reminding him that the world was packed with native girls like herself as well.

All kinds of men and women came to see Julian Drood: politicians who spoke to him as if he were a meeting, quarrelling writers, people with causes, cranks and accusers, even criminals and the mad. They were opinions to him and he did not often notice what they were like. He knew they studied him and that they would go away boasting: "I saw Julian Drood today and he said . . ." Still, he had never seen any person quite like the one who now walked in. At first, because of her tweed hat, he thought she was a man and would have said she had a moustache. She was a stump, as square as a box, with tarry chopped-off hair, heavy eyebrows, and yellow eyes set in her sallow skin like cut glass. She looked like some unsexed and obdurate statement about the future—or was it the beginning?—of the human race, long in the body, short in the legs, and made of wood. She was wearing on this hot day a thick bottle-green velvet dress. Indian blood obviously: he had seen such women in Mexico. She put out a wide hand to him; it could have held a shovel—in fact she was carrying a crumpled brown-paper bag.

"Please sit down," he said. A pair of heavy feet moved her with a surprisingly light skip to a chair. She sat down stiffly and stared without expression, like geography.

"I know you are a very busy man," she said. "Thank you for sparing a minute for an unknown person." She looked formidably unknown.

The words were nothing—but the voice! He had expected Spanish or broken English of some grating kind, but instead he heard the small, whispering, bird-like monotone of a shy English child.

"Yes, I *am* very busy," he said. "I've got to give a talk in an hour and then I'm off to lecture in Copenhagen . . . What can I do for you?"

"Copenhagen," she said, noting it.

"Yes, yes, yes," said the editor. "I'm lecturing on apartheid."

There are people who listen; there are people for whom anything said seems not to be heard but rather to be stamped on or printed. She was also receiving the impress of the walls, the books, the desk, the carpet, the windows of the room, memorizing every object. At last, like a breathless child, she said, "In Guatemala I have dreamt of this for years. I'm saying to myself, 'Even if I could just see the *building* where it all happens!' I didn't dare think I would be able to *speak* to Julian Drood. It is like a dream to me. 'If I see him I will tell him,' I said, 'what this building and what his articles have done for my country.'"

"It's a bad building. Too small," he said. "We're thinking of selling it."

"Oh, no," she said. "I have flown across the ocean to see it. And to thank you."

The word "thank" came out like a kiss.

"From Guatemala? To thank me?" The editor smiled.

"To thank you from the bottom of our hearts for those articles." The little voice seemed to sing.

"So people read the paper in Guatemala," said the editor, congratulating that country and moving a manuscript to another pile on his desk.

"Only a few," she said. "The important few. You are keeping us alive in all these dark years. You are holding the torch of freedom burning. You are a beacon of civilization in our darkness."

The editor sat taller in his chair. Certainly he was vain, but he was a good man. Virtue is not often rewarded. A nationalist? Or not? he wondered. He looked at the ceiling, where, as usual—for he knew everything—he found the main items of the Guatemalan situation. He ran over them like a tune on the piano. "Financial colonialism," he said, "foreign monopoly, uprooted peasants, rise of nationalism, the dilemma of the mountain people, the problem of the coast. Bananas.

"It is years since I've eaten a banana," he said.

The woman's yellow eyes were not looking at him directly yet. She was still memorizing the room, and her gaze now moved to his portrait. He was dabbling in the figures of the single-crop problem when she interrupted him.

"The women of Guatemala," she said, addressing the portrait, "will never be able to repay their debt to you."

"The women?"

He could not remember: was there anything about women in those articles?

"It gives us hope. 'Now,' I am saying, 'the world will listen,' " she said. "We are slaves. Man-made laws, the priests, bad traditions hold us down. *We* are the victims of apartheid, too."

And now she looked directly at him.

"Ah," said the editor, for interruptions bored him. "Tell me about that."

"I know from experience," said the woman. "My father was Mexican, my mother was an English governess. I know what she suffered."

"And what do you *do*?" said the editor. "I gather you are not married?"

At this sentence, the editor saw that something like a coat of varnish glistened on the woman's wooden face.

"Not after what I saw of my mother's life. There were ten of us. When my father had to go away on business, he locked her and all of us in the house. She used to shout for help from the window, but no one did anything. People just came down the street and stood outside and stared and then walked away. She brought us up. She was worn out. When I was fifteen, he came home drunk and beat her terribly. She was used to that, but this time she died."

"What a terrible story. Why didn't she go to the consul? Why—"

"He beat her because she had dyed her hair. She had fair hair and she thought if she dyed her hair black like the other women he went with, he would love her again," said the childish voice.

"Because she dyed her hair?" said the editor.

The editor never really listened to astonishing stories of private life. They seemed frivolous to him. What happened publicly in the modern world was far more extravagant. So he only half listened to this tale. Quickly, whatever he heard turned into paragraphs about something else and moved on to general questions. He was wondering if Miss

Mendoza had the vote and which party she voted for. Was there an Indian bloc? He looked at his watch. He knew how to appear to listen, to charm, ask a jolly question and then lead his visitors to the door before they knew the interview was over.

"It was a murder," said the woman complacently.

The editor suddenly woke up to what she was saying.

"But you are telling me she was *murdered*!" he exclaimed.

She nodded. The fact seemed of no further interest to her. She was pleased she had made an impression. She picked up her paper bag and out of it she pulled a tin of biscuits and put it on his desk.

"I have brought you a present," she said, "with the gratitude of the women of Guatemala. It is Scottish shortbread. From Guatemala." She smiled proudly at the oddity of this fact. "Open it."

"Shall I open it? Yes, I will. Let me offer you one," he humoured her.

"No," she said. "They are for you."

Murder. Biscuits, he thought. She *is* mad.

The editor opened the tin and took out a biscuit and began to nibble. She watched his teeth as he bit; once more, she was memorizing what she saw. She was keeping watch. Just as he was going to get up and make a last speech to her, she put out a short arm and pointed to his portrait.

"That is not you," she pronounced. Having made him eat, she was in command of him.

"But it is," he said. "I think it is very good. Don't you?"

"It is wrong," she said.

"Oh." He was offended and that brought out his saintly look.

"There is something missing," she said. "Now I am seeing you I know what it is."

She got up.

"Don't go," said the editor. "Tell me what you miss. It was in the academy, you know."

He was beginning to think she was a fortune-teller.

"I am a poet," she said. "I see vision in you. I see a leader. That picture is the picture of two people, not one. But you are one man. You are a god to us. You understand that apartheid exists for women too."

She held out her prophetic hand. The editor switched to his wise, pagan look and his sunny hand held hers.

"May I come to your lecture this evening?" she said. "I asked your secretary about it."

"Of course, of course, of course. Yes, yes, yes," he said, and walked with her to the outer door of the office. There they said good-bye. He watched her march away slowly, on her thick legs, like troops.

The editor went into his secretary's room. The girl was putting the cover on her typewriter.

"Do you know," he said, "that woman's father killed her mother because she dyed her hair?"

"She told me. You copped something there, didn't you? What d'you bet me she doesn't turn up in Copenhagen tomorrow, two rows from the front?" the rude girl said.

She was wrong. Miss Mendoza was in the fifth row at Copenhagen. He had not noticed her at the London talk and he certainly had not seen her on the plane; but there she was, looking squat, simple, and tarry among the tall fair Danes. The editor had been puzzled to know who she was, for he had a poor visual memory. For him, people's faces merged into the general plain lineaments of the convinced. But he did become aware of her when he got down from the platform and when she stood, well planted, on the edge of the small circle where his white head was bobbing to people who were asking him questions. She listened, turning her head possessively and critically to each questioner and then to him, expectantly. She nodded with reproof at the questioner when he replied. She owned him. Closer and closer she came, into the inner circle. He was aware of a smell like nutmeg. She was beside him. She had a long envelope in her hand. The chairman was saying to him, "I think we should take you to the party now." Then people went off in three cars. There she was at the party.

"We have arranged for your friend . . ." said the host, "we have arranged for you to sit next to your friend."

"Which friend?" the editor began. Then he saw her, sitting beside him. The Dane lit a candle before them. Her skin took on, to the editor's surprised eye, the gleam of an idol. He was bored: he liked new women to be beautiful when he was abroad.

"Haven't we met somewhere?" he said. "Oh, yes. I remember. You came to see me. Are you on holiday here?"

"No," she said. "I drink at the fount."

He imagined she was taking the waters.

"Fount?" said the editor, turning to others at the table. "Are there many spas here?" He was no good at metaphors.

He forgot her and was talking to the company. She said no more during the evening until she left with the other guests, but he could hear her deep breath beside him.

"I have a present for you," she said before she went, giving him the envelope.

"More biscuits?" he said waggishly.

"It is the opening canto of my poem," she said.

"I'm afraid," said the editor, "we rarely publish poetry."

"It is not for publication. It is dedicated to you."

And she went off.

"Extraordinary," said the editor, watching her go, and, appealing to his hosts, "That woman gave me a poem."

He was put out by their polite, knowing laughter. It often puzzled him when people laughed.

The poem went into his pocket and he forgot it until he got to Stockholm. She was standing at the door of the lecture hall there as he left. He said, "We seem to be following each other around." And to a minister who was wearing a white tie: "Do you know Miss Mendoza from Guatemala? She is a poet," and escaped while they were bowing.

Two days later, she was at his lecture in Oslo. She had moved to the front row. He saw her after he had been speaking for a quarter of an hour. He was so irritated that he stumbled over his words. A rogue phrase had jumped into his mind—"murdered his wife"—and his voice, always high, went up one more semitone and he very nearly told the story. Some ladies in the audience were propping their cheeks on their forefingers as they leaned their heads to regard his profile. He made a scornful gesture at his audience. He had remembered what was wrong. It had nothing to do with murder: he had simply forgotten to read her poem.

Poets, the editor knew, were remorseless. The one sure way of getting rid of them was to read their poems at once. They stared at you with pity and contempt as you read, and argued with offence when you told them which lines you admired. He decided to face her. After the lecture he went up to her.

"How lucky," he said. "I thought you said you were going to Hamburg. Where are you staying? Your poem is on my conscience."

"Yes?" the small girl's voice said. "When will you come and see me?"

"I'll ring you up," he said, drawing back.

"I'm going to hear you in Berlin," she said with meaning.

The editor considered her. There was a look of magnetized inhuman committal in her eyes. They were not so much looking at him as reading him. She knew his future.

Back in the hotel, he read the poem. The message was plain. It began:

> I have seen the liberator
> The foe of servitude
> The godhead.

He read on, skipping two pages, and put out his hand for the telephone. First he heard a childish intake of breath, and then the small determined voice. He smiled at the instrument; he told her in a forgiving voice how good the poem was. The breathing became heavy, like the sound of the ocean. She was steaming or flying to him across the Caribbean, across the Atlantic.

"You have understood my theme," she said. "Women are being history. I am the history of my country."

She went on and boredom settled on him. His cultivated face turned to stone.

"Yes, yes, I see. Isn't there an old Indian belief that a white god will come from the east to liberate the people? Extraordinary, quite extraordinary. When you get back to Guatemala you must go on with your poem."

"I am doing it now. In my room," she said. "You are my inspiration. I am working every night since I saw you."

"Shall I post this copy to your hotel in Berlin?" he said.

"No, give it to me when we meet there."

"Berlin!" the editor exclaimed. Without thinking, without realizing what he was saying, the editor said, "But I'm *not* going to Berlin. I'm going back to London at once."

"When?" said the woman's voice. "Could I come and talk to you now?"

"I'm afraid not. I'm leaving in half an hour," said the editor. Only when he put the telephone receiver back did the editor realize that he was sweating and that he had told a lie. He had lost his head. Worse, in Berlin, if she was there, he would have to invent another lie.

It *was* worse than that. When he got to Berlin she was not there. It was perverse of him—but he was alarmed. He was ashamed. The shadiness of the saint replaced the pagan on his handsome face; indeed, on the race question after his lecture a man in the audience said he was evasive.

But in Hamburg at the end of the week, her voice spoke up from the back of the hall: "I would like to ask the great man who is filling all our hearts this evening whether he is thinking that the worst racists are the oppressors and deceivers of women."

She delivered her blow and sat down, disappearing behind the shoulders of bulky German men.

The editor's clever smiles went; he jerked back his heroic head as if he had been shot: he balanced himself by touching the table with the tips of his fingers. He lowered his head and drank a glass of water, splashing it on his tie. He looked for help.

"My friends," he wanted to say, "that woman is following me. She has followed me all over Scandinavia and Germany. I had to tell a lie to escape from her in Berlin. She is pursuing me. She is writing a poem. She is trying to force me to read it. She murdered her father—I mean, her father murdered her mother. She is mad. Someone must get me out of this."

But he pulled himself together and sank to that point of desperation to which the mere amateurs and hams of public speaking sink.

"A good question," he said. Two irreverent laughs came from the audience, probably from the American or English colony. He had made a fool of himself again. Floundering, he at last fell back on one of those drifting historical generalizations that so often rescued him. He heard his voice sailing into the eighteenth century, throwing in Rousseau, gliding on to Tom Paine and *The Rights of Man.*

"Is there a way out at the back of this hall?" he said to the chairman afterward. "Could someone keep an eye on that woman? She is following me."

They got him out by a back door.

At his hotel a poem was slipped under his door.

> Suckled on Rousseau
> Strong in the divine message of Nature
> Clasp Guatemala in your arms.

"Room 363" was written at the end. She was staying in the same hotel! He rang down to the desk, said he would receive no calls and demanded to be put on the lowest floor, close to the main stairs and near the exit. Safe in his new room he changed the time of his flight to Munich.

There was a note for him at the desk.

"Miss Mendoza left this for you," said the clerk, "when she left for Munich this morning."

Attached to the note was a poem. It began:

> Ravenous in the long night of the centuries
> I waited for my liberator
> He shall not escape me.

His hand was shaking as he tore up the note and the poem and made for the door. The page boy came running after him with the receipt for his bill which he had left on the desk.

The editor was a well-known man. Reporters visited him. He was often recognized in hotels. People spoke his name aloud when they saw it on passenger lists. Cartoonists were apt to lengthen his neck when they drew him, for they had caught his habit of stretching it at parties or meetings, hoping to see and be seen.

But not on the flight to Munich. He kept his hat on and lowered his chin. He longed for anonymity. He had a sensation he had not had for years, not, indeed, since the pre-thaw days in Russia: that he was being followed not simply by one person but by dozens. Who were all those passengers on the plane? Had those two men in raincoats been at his hotel?

He made for the first cab he saw at the airport. At the hotel he went to the desk.

"Mr. and Mrs. Julian Drood," the clerk said. "Yes. Four fifteen. Your wife has arrived."

"My wife!" In any small group the actor in him woke up. He turned from the clerk to a stranger standing at the desk beside him and gave a yelp of hilarity. "But I am not married!" The stranger drew away. The editor turned to a couple also standing there. "I'm saying I am not married," he said. He turned about to see if he could gather more listeners.

"This is ludicrous," he said. No one was interested, and loudly to the clerk he said, "Let me see the register. There is no Mrs. Drood."

The clerk put on a worldly look to soothe any concern about the respectability of the hotel in the people who were waiting. But there on the card, in her writing, were the words: Mr. and Mrs. J. Drood— London.

The editor turned dramatically to the group.

"A forgery," he cried. He laughed, inviting all to join the comedy. "A woman travelling under my name."

The clerk and the strangers turned away. In travel, one can rely on there being one mad Englishman everywhere.

The editor's face darkened when he saw he had exhausted human interest.

"Four fifteen. Baggage," called the clerk.

A young porter came up quick as a lizard and picked up the editor's bags.

"Wait. Wait," said the editor. Before a young man so smoothly uniformed he had the sudden sensation of standing there with most of his clothes off. When you arrived at the Day of Judgement there would be some worldly youth humming a tune you didn't know the name of, carrying not only your sins but your virtues indifferently in a couple of bags and gleaming with concealed knowledge.

"I have to telephone," the editor said.

"Over there," said the young man as he put the bags down. The editor did not walk to the telephone but to the main door of the hotel. He considered the freedom of the street. The sensible thing to do was to leave the hotel at once, but he knew that the woman would be at his lecture that night. He would have to settle the matter once and for all now. So he turned back to the telephone booth. It stood there empty, like a trap. He walked past it. He hated the glazed, whorish, hypocritically impersonal look of telephone booths. They were always unpleasantly warmed by the random emotions left behind in them. He turned back: the thing was still empty. "Surely," he wanted to address the people coming and going in the foyer, "someone among you wants to telephone?" It was wounding that not one person there was interested in his case. It was as if he had written an article that no one had read. Even the porter had gone. His two bags rested against the desk. He and they had ceased to be news.

He began to walk up and down quickly, but this stirred no one. He stopped in every observable position, not quite ignored now; because his handsome hair always made people turn.

The editor silently addressed them again. "You've entirely missed the point of my position. Everyone who has read what I have written knows that I am opposed on principle to the whole idea of marriage. That is what makes this woman's behaviour so ridiculous. To think of getting *married* in a world that is in one of the most ghastly phases of its history is puerile."

He gave a short sarcastic laugh. The audience was indifferent.

The editor went into the telephone booth, and leaving the door open for all to hear, he rang her room.

"Julian Drood," he said brusquely. "It is important that I should see you at once, privately, in your room."

He heard her breathing. The way the human race thought it was enough if they breathed! Ask an important question and what happens? Breath. Then he heard the small voice: it made a splashing, confusing sound.

"Oh," it said. And more breath: "Yes."

The two words were the top of a wave that is about to topple and come thumping over onto the sand and then draws back with a long, insidious hiss.

"Please," she added. And the word was the long, thirsty hiss.

The editor was surprised that his brusque manner was so wistfully treated.

Good heavens, he thought, she *is* in that room! And because she was invisible and because of the distance of the wire between them, he felt she was pouring down it, head first, mouth open, swamping him. When he put the telephone down, he scratched his ear; a piece of her seemed to be coiled there. The editor's ear had heard passion. And passion at its climax.

He had often heard of passion. He had often been told of it. He had seen it in opera. He had friends—who usually came to him for advice —who were entangled in it. He had never felt it and he did not feel it now; but when he walked from the telephone booth to the lift, he saw his role had changed. The woman was not a mere nuisance—she was something out of *Tosca*. The pagan became doggish, the saint furtive as he entered the lift.

"Ah," the editor burst out aloud to the liftman, *"les femmes."* The German did not understand French.

The editor got out of the lift, and passing one watchful white door after another, came to 415. He knocked twice. When there was no answer he opened the door.

He seemed to blunder into an invisible wall of spice and scent and stepped back, thinking he had made a mistake. A long-legged rag doll with big blue eyes looked at him from the bed, a half-unpacked suitcase was on the floor with curious clothes hanging out of it. A woman's shoes were tipped out on the sofa.

And then, with her back to a small desk where she had been writing, stood Miss Mendoza. Or, rather, the bottle-green dress, the box-like figure were Miss Mendoza's: the head was not. Her hair was no longer black: it was golden. The idol's head had been chopped off and was replaced by a woman's. There was no expression on the face until the shock on the editor's face passed to hers, then a searching look of horror seized her, then of one caught in an outrage. She lowered her head, cowed and frightened. She quickly grabbed a stocking she had left on the bed and held it behind her back.

"You are angry with me," she said, holding her head down like an obstinate child.

"You are in *my* room. You have no right to be here. I *am* very angry with you. What do you mean by registering in my name—apart from anything else, it is illegal. You know that, don't you? I must ask you to go or I shall have to take steps . . ."

Her head was still lowered. Perhaps he ought not to have said the last sentence. The blond hair made her look pathetic.

"Why did you do this?"

"Because you would not see me," she said. "You have been cruel to me."

"But don't you realize, Miss Mendoza, what you are doing? I hardly know you. You have followed me all over Europe; you have badgered me. You take my room. You pretend to be my wife . . ."

"Do you hate me?" she muttered.

Damn, thought the editor. I ought to have changed my hotel at once.

"I know nothing about you," he said.

"Don't you want to know about me? What I am like? I know everything about you," she said, raising her head.

The editor was confused by the rebuke. His fit of acting passed. He looked at his watch.

"A reporter is coming to see me in half an hour," he said.

"I shall not be in the way," she said. "I will go out."

"*You* will go out!" said the editor.

Then he understood where he was wrong. He had forgotten—perhaps being abroad addressing meetings, speaking to audiences with only one mass face had done this—forgotten how to deal with difficult people.

He pushed the shoes to one end of the sofa to find himself a place. One shoe fell to the floor, but after all, it was his room, he had a right to sit down.

"Miss Mendoza, you are ill," he said.

She looked down quickly at the carpet.

"I am not," she said.

"You are ill and, I think, very unhappy." He put on his wise voice.

"No," she said in a low voice. "Happy. You are talking to me."

"You are a very intelligent woman," he said. "And you will understand what I am going to say. Gifted people like yourself are very vulnerable. You live in the imagination, and that exposes one. I know that."

"Yes," she said. "You see all the injustices of the world. You bleed from them."

"I? Yes," said the editor with his saint's smile. But he recovered from the flattery. "I am saying something else. Your imagination is part of your gift as a poet, but in real life it has deluded you."

"It hasn't done that. I see you as you are."

"Please sit down," said the editor. He could not bear her standing over him. "Close the window, there is too much noise."

She obeyed. The editor was alarmed to see the zipper of her dress was half undone and he could see the top of some garment with ominous lace on it. He could not bear untidy women. He saw his case was urgent. He made a greater effort to be kind.

"It was very kind of you to come to my lectures. I hope you found them interesting. I think they went down all right—good questions. One never knows, of course. One arrives in a strange place and one sees a hall full of people one doesn't know—and you won't believe me perhaps because I've done it scores of times—but one likes to see a face that one recognizes. One feels lost, at first . . ."

She looked hopeful.

This was untrue. The editor never felt lost. Once on his feet he had the sensation that he was talking to the human race. He suffered with it. It was the general human suffering that had ravaged his face.

"But you know," he said sternly, "our feelings deceive us. Especially at certain times of life. I was worried about you. I saw that something was wrong. These things happen very suddenly. God knows why. You see someone whom you admire perhaps—it seems to happen to women more than men—and you project some forgotten love on him. You think you love him, but it is really some forgotten image. In your case, I would say, probably some image of your father, whom you have hated all these years for what he did when you were a child. And so, as people say, one becomes obsessed or infatuated. I don't like the word. What we mean is that one is not in love with a real man or woman but a vision sent out by oneself. One can think of many examples . . ."

The editor was sweating. He wished he hadn't asked her to close the window. He knew his mind was drifting towards historic instances. He wondered if he would tell her the story of Jane Carlyle, the wife of the historian, who had gone to hear the famous Father Matthew speak at a temperance meeting and how, hysterical and exalted, she had rushed to the platform to kiss his boots. Or there were other instances. For the moment he couldn't remember them. He decided on Mrs. Carlyle. It was a mistake.

"Who is Mrs. Carlyle?" said Miss Mendoza suspiciously. "I would never kiss any man's feet."

"Boots," said the editor. "It was on a public platform."

"Or boots," Miss Mendoza burst out. "Why are you torturing me? You are saying I am mad."

The editor was surprised by the turn of the conversation. It had seemed to be going well.

"Of course you're not mad," he said. "A madwoman could not have written that great poem. I am just saying that I value your feeling, but you must understand that I unfortunately do not love you. But you *are* ill. You have exhausted yourself."

Miss Mendoza's yellow eyes became brilliant as she listened to him.

"So," she said grandly, "I am a mere nuisance."

She got up from her chair and he saw she was trembling.

"If that is so, why don't you leave this room at once?" she said.

"But," said the editor with a laugh, "if I may mention it, it is mine."

"I signed the register," said Miss Mendoza.

"Well," said the editor, smiling, "that is not the point, is it?"

The boredom, the sense of the sheer waste of time (when one thought of the massacres, the bombings, the imprisonments in the world) in personal questions, overcame him. It amazed him that at some awful crisis—the Cuban, for example—how many people left their husbands, wives, or lovers, in a general post: the extraordinary, irresponsible persistence of outbreaks of love. A kind of guerrilla war in another context. Here he was in the midst of it. What could he do? He looked around the room for help. The noise of the traffic outside in the street, the dim sight of people moving behind office windows opposite, an advertisement for beer were no help. Humanity had deserted him. The nearest thing to the human—now it took his eye—was the doll on the bed, an absurd marionette from the cabaret, the raffle, or the nursery. It had a mop of red hair, silly red cheeks, and popping blue eyes with long cotton lashes. It wore a short skirt and had long insane legs in checked stockings. How childish women were. Of course (it now occurred to him), Miss Mendoza was as childish as her voice. The editor said playfully, "I see you have a little friend. Very pretty. Does she come from Guatemala?" And frivolously, because he disliked the thing, he took a step or two towards it. Miss Mendoza pushed past him at once and grabbed it.

"Don't touch it," she said with tiny fierceness.

She picked up the doll, and hugging it with fear, she looked for somewhere to put it out of his reach. She went to the door, then changed her mind and rushed to the window with it. She opened the window, and as the curtains blew in, she looked as if a desperate idea had occurred to her—to throw herself and it out of the window. She turned to fight him off. He was too bewildered to move, and when she saw that he stood still her frightened face changed. Suddenly she threw the doll on the floor, and half falling onto a chair near it, her shoulders rounded, she covered her face with her hands and sobbed, shaking her head from side to side. Tears crawled through her fingers down the backs of her hands. Then she took her hands away and, soft and shapeless, she rushed to the editor and clawed at his jacket.

"Go away. Go away," she cried. "Forgive me. Forgive. I'm sorry." She began to laugh and cry at once. "As you said—ill. Oh, please forgive. I don't understand why I did this. For a week I haven't eaten anything. I must have been out of my mind to do this to you. Why? I can't think. You've been so kind. You could have been cruel. You were right. You had the courage to tell me the truth. I feel so ashamed, so ashamed. What can I do?"

She was holding on to his jacket. Her tears were on his hands. She was pleading. She looked up.

"I've been such a fool," she said.

"Come and sit here," said the editor, trying to move her to the sofa. "You are not a fool. You have done nothing. There is nothing to be ashamed of."

"I can't bear it."

"Come and sit here," he said, putting his arm on her shoulder. "I was very proud when I read your poem. Look," he said, "you are a very gifted and attractive woman."

He was surprised that such a heavy woman was not like iron to the touch but light and soft. He could feel her skin, hot through her dress.

Her breath was hot. Agony was hot. Grief was hot. Above all, her clothes were hot. It was perhaps because of the heat of her clothes that for the first time in years he had the sensation of holding a human being. He had never felt this when, on a few occasions, he had held a woman naked in her bed. He did something then that was incredible to himself. He gently kissed the top of her head on the blonde hair he did not like. It was like kissing a heated mat and it smelt of burning.

At his kiss she clawed no longer and her tears stopped. She moved away from him in awe.

"Thank you," she said gravely, and he found himself being studied, even memorized, as she had done when she had first come to his office. The look of the idol was set on her again. Then she uttered a revelation. "You do not love anyone but yourself." And worse, she smiled. He had thought with dread that she was waiting to be kissed again, but now he couldn't bear what she said. It was a loss.

"We must meet," he said recklessly. "We *shall* meet at the lecture tonight."

The shadow of her future passed over her face.

"Oh, no," she said. She was free. She was warning him not to hope to exploit her pain.

"This afternoon?" he said, trying to catch her hand, but she drew it away. And then, to his bewilderment, she was dodging round him. She was packing. She began stuffing her few clothes into her suitcase. She went to the bathroom, and while she was there the porter came in with his two bags.

"Wait," said the editor.

She came out of the bathroom looking very pale and put the remaining things into her suitcase.

"I asked him to wait," the editor said.

The kiss, the golden hair, the heat of her head, seemed to be flying round in the editor's head.

"I don't want you to leave like this," the editor said.

"I heard what you said to the man," she said, hurriedly shutting the suitcase. "Good-bye. And thank you. You are saving me from something dreadful."

The editor could not move when he saw her go. He could not believe she had gone. He could feel the stir of her scent in the air, and he sat down exhausted but arguing with his conscience. Why had she said that about loving only himself? What else could he have done? He wished there were people there to whom he could explain, whom he could ask. He was feeling loneliness for one of the few times in his life.

He went to the window to look down at the people. Then, looking back to the bed, he was astounded by a thought: I have never had an adventure in my life. And with that he left the room and went down to the desk. Was she still in the hotel?

"No," said the desk clerk. "Mrs. Drood went off in a taxi."

"I am asking for Miss Mendoza."

"No one of that name."

"Extraordinary," lied the editor. "She was to meet me here."

"Perhaps she is at the Hofgarten—it's the same management."

For the next hour he was on the telephone, trying all the hotels. He got a cab to the station; he tried the airlines and then, in the afternoon, went out to the airport. He knew it was hopeless. I must be mad too, he thought. He looked at every golden-haired woman he could see— the city was full of golden-haired women. As the noisy city afternoon moved by, he gave up. He liked to talk about himself, but here was a day he could never describe to anyone. He could not return to his room but sat in the lounge trying to read a paper, wrangling with himself and looking up at every woman who passed. He could not eat or even drink, and when he went out to his lecture he walked all the way to the hall on the chance of seeing her. He had the fancy once or twice, which he laughed at bitterly, that she had just passed and had left two or three of her footprints on the pavement. The extraordinary thing was that she was exactly the kind of woman he could not bear: squat, ugly. How awful she must look without clothes on. He tried to exorcise her by obscene images. They vanished and some transformed idealized vision of her came back. He began to see her tall and dark or young and fair: her eyes changing colour, her body voluptuously rounded, athletically slim. As he sat on the lecture platform, listening to the introduction, he made faces that astonished the audience with a mechanical display of eagerness followed by scorn as his gaze went systematically from row to row, looking for her. He got up to speak. "Ladies and gentlemen," he began. He knew it would be the best lecture he had ever given. It was. Urging, appealing, agonizing, eloquent. It was an appeal to her to come back.

And then, after a lot of discussion which he hardly heard, he re-turned to the hotel. He had now to face the mockery of the room. He let himself in and it did mock. The maid had turned the bed back and on it lay the doll, its legs tidied, its big ridiculous eyes staring at him. They seemed to him to blink. She had forgotten it. She had left her childhood behind.

The Fig Tree

I checked the greenhouses, saw the hose taps were turned off, fed the Alsatian, and then put the bar on the main gate to the Nursery and left by the side door for my flat. As I changed out of my working clothes I looked down on the rows of labelled fresh green plants. What a pleasure to see such an orderly population of growing things gambling for life—how surprising that twenty years ago the sight of so much husbandry would have bored me.

When I was drying myself in the bathroom I noticed Sally's bathcap hanging there and I took the thing to the closet in the bedroom, and then in half an hour I picked up Mother at her hotel and drove her to Duggie and Sally's house, where we were to have dinner. I supposed Mother must have seen Sally's bathcap, for as we passed the Zoo she said, "I do wish you would get married again and settle down."

"Dutch elm disease," I replied, pointing to the crosses on one of two trees in the Park.

The Zoo is my halfway mark when I go to Duggie and Sally's—what vestiges of embarrassment I feel become irrelevant when I have passed it.

"It worries your father," Mother said.

Mother is not "failing." She is in her late seventies and Father was killed in the war thirty years ago, but he comes to life in a random way, as if time were circular for her. Father seems to be wafted by, and sows the only important guilt I have—I have so little memory of him. Duggie has said once or twice to Sally that though I am in my early forties, there are still signs that I lacked a father's discipline. Duggie, a speculative man, puts the early whiteness of my hair down to this. Obviously, he says, I was a late child, probably low in vitality.

Several times during this week's visit I have taken Mother round the shops she likes in London. She moves fast on her thin legs, and if age has shortened her by giving her a small hump on her shoulders, this adds to her sharp-eyed, foraging appearance. She was rude, as usual, to the shop assistants, who seemed to admire this—perhaps because it reminded them of what they had heard of "the good old days." And she dressed with taste, her makeup was delicate, and if her skin had aged, it was fine as silk; her nose was young, her eyes as neat as violets. The week had been hot, but she was cool and slightly scented.

"Not as hot as we had it in Cairo when your father was alive," she said in her mannish voice.

Time was restored: Father had returned to his grave.

After being gashed by bombs during the war, the corner of early-Victorian London where Duggie and Sally live has "gone up." Once a neighbourhood of bed-sitters, now the small houses are expensive and trim; enormous plane trees, fast-growing sycamores, old apple and pear trees bearing uneatable fruit, crowd the large gardens. It was to see the garden and to meet Duggie, who was over from Brussels on one of his monthly trips, that Mother had really come: in the country she is an indefatigable gardener. So is Sally, who opened the door to us. One of the unspoken rules of Sally and myself is that we do not kiss when I go to her house; her eyes were as polite as glass (and without the quiver to the pupils they usually have in them) as she gave her hand to my mother. She had drawn her fair hair severely back.

"Duggie is down in the garden," Sally said to Mother and made a fuss about the steps that lead down from her sitting-room balcony. "These steps my husband put in are shaky—let me help you."

"I got used to companionways going to Egypt," said Mother in her experienced voice. "We always went by sea, of course. What a lovely garden."

"Very wild," said Sally. "There used to be a lawn here. It was no good, so we dug it up."

"No one can afford lawns nowadays," said my mother. "We have three. Much better to let nature take its course."

It is a clever garden of the romantic kind, half of it a green cavern under the large trees where the sun can still flicker in the higher branches. You duck your way under untidy climbing roses; there is a foreground, according to season, of overgrown marguerites, tobacco plants, dahlias, irises, lilies, ferns—a garden of wild, contrived masses. Our progress was slow as Mother paused to botanize until we got to a wide, flagged circle which is shaded by a muscular fig tree. Duggie was standing by the chairs with a drink in his hand, waiting for us. He moved a chair for Mother.

"No, I must see it all first," Mother said. "Nice little magnolia."

I was glad she noticed that.

There was a further tour of plants that "do well in the shade"— "Dear Solomon's-seal," she said politely, as if the plant were a person. A bird or two darted off into other gardens with the news—and then we returned to the chairs set out on the paved circle. Duggie handed drinks to us, with the small bow of a tall man. He is lazily well-made, a bufferish fellow in his late fifties, his drooping grey moustache is affable—"honourable" is how I would describe the broad road of sun-burned baldness going over his head. His nose is just a touch bottled, which gives him the gentlemanly air of an old club servant, or rather of being not one man but a whole club, uttering impressions of this and that. Out of this club his private face will appear, a face that puts on a sudden, fishy-eyed stare, in the middle of one of his long sentences. It is the stare of a man in a brief state of shock who has found himself suspended over a hole that has opened at his feet. His job takes him abroad a good deal and his stare is also that of an Englishman abroad who has sighted another Englishman he cannot quite place. Not being able to get a word in while the two women were talking, he turned this stare on me. "I missed you the last time I was home," he said.

Again, it is my rule that I don't go to the house unless he is there.

"How is that chest of yours?"

I gave a small cough and he gave me a dominating look. He likes to worry about my health.

"The best thing your uncle ever did for you was to get you out of the city. You needed an open-air life."

Duggie, who has had to make his own way, rather admires me for having had a rich uncle.

Was he shooting a barb into me? I don't think so. We always have this conversation: he was born to repeat himself—one more sign of his honourableness.

Duggie takes pride in a possessive knowledge of my career. He often says to Sally, "He ought to put on weight—white hair at his age—but what do you expect? Jazz bands in Paris and London, hanging round Chelsea bars, playing at all that literary stuff, going into that bank— all that sort of nonsense." Then he goes on, "Mother's boy—marrying a woman twelve years older than himself. Sad that she died," he adds. "Must have done something to him—that breakdown, a year in the sanatorium, he probably gambled. Still, the Nursery has pulled him together. Characteristic, of course, that most of the staff are girls."

"It's doing well," he said in a loud confidential voice, nodding at the fig tree by the south wall, close to us.

"What a lovely tree," Mother said. "Does it bear? My husband will only eat figs fresh from the tree."

"One or two little ones. But they turn yellow and drop off in June," said Sally.

"What it needs," Duggie said, "is the Mediterranean sun. It ought to be in Turkey, that is where you get the best figs."

"The sun isn't enough. The fig needs good drainage and has to be fertilized," Mother said.

"All fruit needs that," said Duggie.

"The fig needs two flies—the Blastophaga and, let me see, is it the Sycophaga? I think so—anyway, they are Hymenoptera," Mother said.

Duggie gazed with admiration at my mother. He loves experts. He had been begging me for years to bring her over to his house.

"Well, we saved its life, didn't we, Teddy?" he said to me and boasted on his behalf and mine. "We flagged the area. There was nothing but a lake of muddy water here. How many years ago was that?"

"Four or five," I said.

"No!" said Duggie. "Only three."

Was he coming into the open at last and telling me that he knew that this was the time when Sally and I became lovers? I think not. The stare dropped out of his face. His honourable look returned.

Sally and Duggie were what I call "Monday people" at the Nursery. There is a rush of customers on the weekend. They are the instant gardeners who drive in, especially in the spring and autumn, to buy everything, from plants already in bud and flowers, the potted plants, for balconies of flats. The crowd swarms and our girls are busy at the counter we had to install to save costs as the business grew. (The counter was Duggie's idea: he could not resist seeing the Nursery as one of his colonies.) But on Monday the few fanatic gardeners come, and I first became aware of Sally because she was very early, usually alone, a slight woman in her late thirties with her straw-blond hair drawn back from a high forehead in those days, a severe look of polite, silent impatience which would turn into a wide, fastidious grimace like the yawn of a cat if anyone spoke to her. She would take a short step back and consider one's voice. She looked almost reckless and younger when she put on glasses to read what was on the sacks and packets of soil, compost, and fertilizer in the store next to the office, happiest in our warm greenhouses, a woman best seen under glass. Her eyebrows were softer, more downily intimate than anything else about her. They reminded me when I first saw her of the disturbing eyebrows of an aunt of mine which used to make me blush when I was a boy. Hair disturbs me.

One day she brought Duggie to the Nursery when I was unloading boxes of plants that came from the growers and I heard her snap at him, "Wait here. If you see the manager, ask about grass seed and stop following me round. You fuss me."

For the next half-hour she looked round the seedlings or went into the greenhouses while Duggie stood where he was told to stand. I was near him when the lorry drove off.

"Are you being attended to?" I said. "I'll call a girl."

He was in his suspended state. "No, I was thinking," he said in the lazy voice of a man who, home from abroad and with nothing to do, was hoping to find out if there were any fellow thinkers about. "I was thinking, vegetation is a curious thing," he said with the predatory look of a man who had an interesting empire of subjects to offer. "I mean, one notices when one gets back to London there is more vegetation than brick. Trees," he said. "Plants and shrubs, creeper, moss, ivy," he went on, "grass, of course. Why this and not that? Climate, I suppose. You have laurels here, but no oleander, yet it's all over the Mediterranean and Mexico. You get your fig or your castor-oil plant, but no banana, no ginkgo, no datura. The vine used to swarm in Elizabethan times, but rare now, but I hear they're making wine again. It must be thin. The climate changed when the Romans cut down the forests." For a moment he became a Roman and then drifted on, "Or the Normans. We all come down to grass in the end."

He looked at our greenhouses.

"My job takes me away a lot. I spend half the year abroad," he said. "Oil. Kuwait."

He nodded to the distant figure of his wife. She was bending over a bed of tobacco plants.

"We spent our honeymoon in Yucatán," he said with some modest pomp. He was one of those colonizing talkers, talking over new territory.

"But that is not the point," he said. "We can't get the right grass seed. She sows every year, but half of it dies by the time summer comes. Yet look at the Argentina pampas." He was imposing another geography, some personal flora of his own, on my Nursery. Clearly not a gardener: a thinker at large.

I gave him the usual advice. I took him to a shed to show him sacks of chemicals. His wife came back from the flower beds and found us. "I've been looking for you everywhere," she said to him. "I told you to wait where you were." She sounded to be an irritable woman.

He said to me, in an aloof, conspiring way, ignoring her, "I suppose you wouldn't have time to drop round and have a look at our lawn? I mean, in the next week or two—"

"It will be too late by then," she interrupted. "The grass will be dead. Come along," and she made that grimace—a grimace that now struck me as a confidence, an off-hand intimation.

He made an apologetic gesture to me and followed her obediently out of the Nursery.

I often had a word or two with Sally when she came alone: grass seed seemed to be the couple's obsession. She said it was his; he said it was hers. I was a kind of umpire to whom they appealed when we met.

So one afternoon in November when I was delivering laurels to a neighbour of theirs down the street, I dropped in at their house.

A fat young man was sitting sedately on a motorbike outside it, slowly taking off a fine pair of gauntlets. Sitting behind the screen of the machine, he might have been admiring himself at a dressing-table mirror. In his white crash helmet he looked like a doll, but one with a small black moustache.

"Those lads get themselves up, don't they?" I said to Duggie, who came to the door.

"Our tenant," Duggie said. "He has the flat in the basement. He uses the side entrance. Under our agreement he does not use the garden. That is reserved for ourselves. Come through—I had these iron steps put in so that my wife has strictly private access to the garden without our interfering with him or he with us. My wife would have preferred a young married couple, but as I pointed out, there would be children. One has to weigh one thing against another in this life—don't you find?"

We went down to the garden. Their trouble was plain. The trees were bare. Half of the place was lifeless soil, London-black and empty. The damp yellow leaves of the fig tree hung down like wretched rags, and the rest had fallen flat as plates into a very large pool of muddy water that stretched from one side of the garden to the other. Overnight, in November, a fig collapses like some Victorian heroine. Here —as if she were about to drown herself. I said this to Duggie, who said, "Heroine? I don't follow."

"You'll never grow a lawn here. Too much shade. You could cut the trees down . . ."

At this moment Sally came down and said, "I won't have my trees cut down. It's the water that's killing everything."

I said that whole districts of London were floating on water. Springs everywhere, and the clay held it.

"And also, the old Fleet River runs underground in this district," I said. "The only thing you can do is to put paving down."

"The Fleet River? News to me," said Duggie, and he looked about us at other gardens and houses as if eager to call out all his neighbours and tell them. "Pave it, you say? You mean with stones?"

"What else?" said Sally curtly and walked away. The garden was hers.

"But, my dear," he called after her, "the point is—what stones? Portland? Limestone?"

The colonizer of vegetation was also a collector of rock. A load of geology poured out of him. He ran through sandstone, millstone, grit, until we moved on to the whinstone the Romans used on Hadrian's Wall, went on to the marble quarries of Italy and came back to the low brick wall of their garden, which had been damaged during the war.

Presently there was the howling and thumping of jazz music from the basement flat.

"I told you that man has girls down there," Sally said angrily to her husband. "He's just come in. He's turning the place into a discothèque. Tell him to stop—it's intolerable."

And she looked coldly at me as if I too were a trespasser, the sort of man who would kick up a shindy with girls in a quiet house. I left. Not a happy pair.

I sent him an estimate for paving part of the garden. Several months passed; there was no reply and his wife stopped coming to the Nursery.

I thought they were abroad. Then in the spring Duggie came to the Nursery with his daughter, a schoolgirl, who went off to make up confidently to a van driver.

Duggie watched her and then said to me, "About those paving stones. My wife has been ill. I had a cable and flew home."

"I hope it was not serious?"

He studied me, considering whether to tell me the details, but evidently—and with that kind of reluctance which suggests all—changed his mind. "The iniquitous Rent Act," he said disparagingly, "was at the bottom of it."

He gave an outline of the Act, with comments on rents in general.

"Our tenant—that boy was impossible, every kind of impertinence. We tried to get rid of him but we couldn't. The fellow took us to court."

"Did you get an order against him?" I asked.

Duggie's voice hurried. "No. Poor fellow was killed. Drove his motorbike head-on into a lorry, a girl with him too. Both killed. Horrible. Naturally, it upset my wife: she blames herself. Imagination," he apologized. Duggie spoke of the imagination accusingly.

"The man with the little black moustache?" I asked.

"She wouldn't have a married couple there," he said.

"I remember," I said. "You mentioned it."

"Did I?" he said. He was cheered by my remembering that.

"You see," he said. "It was clearly laid down in the agreement that he was not to go into the garden under any pretext, but he did. However, that is not what I came about. We're going to pave that place, as you suggested. It will take her mind off it all." He nodded to the house. "By the way, you won't say anything to her, will you? I'm away so much the garden is everything to her."

Shortly after this I took one of our men over to the house. Duggie was stirred at the end of the first day when he came home from his London office to see we had dug up a lot of brick rubble—chunks of the garden wall which had been knocked down by blast during the war. On the second day he came back early in the afternoon and stood watching. He was longing to get hold of my man's pickaxe. The man put it down and I had turned around when I heard the dead sound of steel on stone and a shout of "Christ!" from Duggie. He had taken the pickaxe and brought it down hard on a large slab of concrete and was doubled up, gripping his wrists between his legs, in agony. Sally came to the balcony and then hurried down the steps. Her appearance had changed. She was plumper than she had been, there was no sign of illness, and she had done her hair in a new way: it was loosened and she often pushed it back from her cheeks.

"You are a fool, Duggie," she said.

The man was shovelling earth clear of the slab of concrete, which tilted down deep into the earth.

"It's all right. It's all right. Go away. I'm all right," said Duggie.

"What is it?" he said.

"Bleeding air-raid shelter," my gardener said. "There's one or two left in the gardens round here. A gentleman down the road turned his into a lily pond."

He went on shovelling and dug a hole. The concrete ended in a tangle of wire and stone. It had been smashed. He kneeled down on the ground and said, "The end wall has caved in, full of wet muck." He got up and said, disappointed, "No one in it. Saved some poor bloke's life. If he copped it, he wouldn't have known, anyway."

Sally made a face of horror at the gardener. "Those poor people," she said. "Come indoors. What a fool you are, Duggie."

Duggie refused to go. Pain had put him in a trance: one could almost see bits of his mind travelling out of him as he called triumphantly to her, "Don't you see what we've got, my dearest?" he cried, excitement driving out his pain. He was a man whose mind was stored with a number of exotic words: "We've got a *cenote.*"

How often we were to hear that word in the next few days! For months after this he must have continued startling people with it in his office, on buses, men in clubs, whoever was sitting next to him in aircraft on his way to Kuwait.

"What is a cenote?" I said, no doubt as they did.

"It's an underground cistern," he said. "You remember Yucatán, Sally—all those forests, yet no water. No big rivers. You said, 'How did the Mayas survive?' The answer was that the Maya civilization floated on underground cisterns."

Duggie turned to me, calling me Teddy for the first time. "I remember what you said about London floating on underground rivers—it's been on my mind ever since you said it. Something was there at the back of my mind, some memory, I couldn't get it. There it is: a cenote. That's where your fig tree has been drinking, Sally. You plant your fig tree on a tank of water and the rubble drains it.

"Sally and I saw dozens of cenotes, all sizes, some hundred feet deep on our honeymoon," he confided to me.

Sally's eyes went hard.

"The Mayans worshipped them: you can see why. Once a year the priests used to cut out the heart of a virgin and throw it into the water. Propitiation," he said.

"It's an act for tourists at the nightclubs there," said Sally drearily.

"Yes," Duggie explained to us and added to me, "Fake, of course."

Sally said, "Those poor people. I shall never go into this garden again."

In the next few days she did not come down while we turned the ruin into a foundation, and the following week Duggie superintended the laying of the stones. His right arm was in a sling.

When the job was finished Duggie was proud of the wide circle of stones we had laid down.

"You've turned my garden into a cemetery. I've seen it from the window," Sally said.

Duggie and I looked at each other: two men agreeing to share the unfair blame. She had been ill; we had done this job for her and it had made things worse.

Imagination, as Duggie had said. Difficult for him. And I had thought of her as a calm, sensible woman.

It happened at this time I had to go to the Town Hall about a contract for replanting one of the neglected squares in the borough, and while I was there and thinking of Duggie and Sally I tried to find out who had lived in their house and whether there was any record of air-raid casualties. I went from office to office and discovered nothing. Probably the wrong place to go to. Old cities are piled on layer after layer of unrecorded human lives and things. Then Duggie sent a cheque for our work, more promptly too than most of our customers do. I thought of my buried wife and the rot of the grave as I made out a receipt. It occurred to me that it would be decent to do something for Duggie. I was walking around the Nursery one morning when I saw a small strong magnolia, a plant three feet high and already in bud. It was risky to replant it at this time, but I bound it, packed it, and put it in a large tub and drove to their house one Saturday with it, to surprise them. Sally came to the door with a pen in her hand and looked put-out by my sudden call. I told her I had the plant in the van.

"We didn't order anything. My husband is in Kuwait—he would have told me. There must be a mistake."

The pen in her raised hand was like a funny hostile weapon, and seeing me smile at it, she lowered her hand.

"It's not an order. It's a present. In the van," I said. She looked unbelieving at the van and then back at me. In the awkward pause my mind gave an unintended leap. I forgot about Duggie.

"For you," I said. I seemed to sail away, off my feet.

"For me?" she said. "Why for me?"

I was astonished. Her face went as white as paper and I thought she was going to faint. She stood there, trembling. The pen dropped out of her hand to the floor and she turned round and bent to pick it up and stood up again with a flustered blush as if she had been caught doing something wrong.

"You're the gardener," I said. "Come and look."

She did not move, so I started off down the few steps to the gate. She followed me and I saw her glance, as if calling for protection to the houses on either side of her own.

"Why should you do this?" she said in an unnatural voice. I opened the gate, but she made me go through first.

The swollen rusty-pink and skin-white buds of the plant were as bright as candles in the darkness of the van.

"Advertising," I said with a salesman's laugh. She frowned, reproaching me doubtfully. But when she saw the plant she said, "How lovely!"

My tongue raced. I said I had been thinking of the paved circle in the middle of the garden; the magnolia would stand there and flower before the trees shaded the place, and that it could be moved out of the tub wherever she wanted it in the garden later in the year.

"You mean that?" she said.

So I got out a trolley, put up a board, and wheeled the plant down from the van carefully. It was very heavy.

"Be careful," she said. She opened the side entrance to the garden and followed me there.

"No muddy puddle now. It's gone," I boasted. It was a struggle getting the heavy tub in place and she helped me.

"You've got a gardener's strong hands," I said.

I looked around and then up at the trees. Her wide mouth opened with delight at the plant.

"How kind you are," she said. "Duggie will love it."

I had never been alone with her in this garden and, I remember, this was privileged ground. She walked around and around the plant as if she were dancing.

"It will be in full bloom in ten days," I said. "It will cheer up the fig tree. It's trying to bud."

"This time of the year," she said, despising it, "that tree looks like a chunk of machinery."

A half-hour passed. We went back to the house and she thanked me again as I pushed the trolley.

"Leave it there," she said. "I must give you some tea or a drink. How lucky I was in. You should have telephoned."

In the sitting-room she laughed as she looked back at the plant from the window. It was, I realized, the first time I had heard her laugh. It was surprising not to hear Duggie's voice. She went off to make tea and I sat in an armchair and remembered not to put my dirty hands on the arms. Then I saw my footmarks coming across the carpet to me. I felt I had started on a journey.

I noticed she frowned at them and the cups skidded on the tray when she came back with the tea.

I said apologetically, "My boots!"

Strange words, now that I think of it, for the beginning of a love affair; even she gaped at them as if they had given me away.

When she had only half filled my cup she banged the teapot down, got up and came across to squeeze my hand.

"Oh, you are so *kind, kind*," she said and then stepped back to her chair quickly.

"You *are* a friend," she said.

And then I saw tears were dropping down her cheeks. Her happy face had collapsed and was ugly. "I'm sorry to be so silly, Mr. Ormerod," she said, trying to laugh.

Ten shelves of Duggie's books looked down, their titles dumb, but listening with all ears as I sat not knowing what to do, for, trying to laugh, she sobbed even more and she had to get up and turn her back to me and look out of the window.

"It's all right," she said with her back to me. "Don't let your tea get cold. My husband wanted to put an urn there," she said. "I suppose he told you."

Duggie had not been able to control his drifting mind.

"This is the first time I've been in the garden since you were here last," she said, turning round.

"By the way," I said, "if you're worrying about the shelter, I can tell you—I've looked up the records at the Town Hall. There were no casualties here. There was no one in the shelter."

I did not tell her no records could be traced. Her tears had made my mind leap again.

"Why on earth did you do that?" she said, and she sat down again.

"I had the idea it was worrying you," I said.

"No, not at all," she said, shaking after her cry, and she put on an off-hand manner and did not look at me.

"The shelter? Oh, that didn't worry me," she said. "The war was thirty years ago, wasn't it? One doesn't have to wait for bombs to kill people. They die in hospital, don't they? Things prey on my husband's mind. He's a very emotional man; you mightn't think it. I don't know whether he told you, we had trouble with a young man, a tenant. It made Duggie quite ill. They flew him home from Kuwait."

I was baffled. She had exactly reversed the story Duggie had told me.

She said with the firm complacency of a married woman, "He talks himself into things, you know."

After she said this there was a question in her eyes, a movement like a small signal, daring me for a moment. I was silent and she began talking about everyday things, in a nervous way, and intimacy vanished.

She stood at the door and gave a half wave as I left, a scarcely visible wave, like a beckon. It destroyed me. Damn that stupid man, I thought when I got home and stood at the stove getting a meal together. The telephone rang and I turned the stove off. I thought the call was from my mother—it was her hour—but the voice was Sally's, firm but apologetic. "You've left your trolley. I thought you might need it."

O blessed trolley! I said I'd come at once. She said curtly she was going out. That, and the hope that she was not interrupting my dinner, were the only coherent, complete sentences she spoke in one of the longest calls I have ever had. On her side it was a collection of unfinished phrases with long silences between them, so that once or twice she seemed to have gone away—silences in which she appeared to be wrestling with nouns, pronouns, and verbs that circled round an apology and explanation that was no explanation, about making "that silly scene." No sooner was she at the point of explanation than she drifted off it. It struck me that listening to her husband so much, she had lost the power of talking.

There was something which, "sometime in the future," she would like to ask me, but it had gone from her mind. "If there is a future," she added too brightly. Her silences dangled and stirred me. The manner was so like Duggie's: it half exasperated me and I asked her if she would have dinner with me one day. "Dinner?" This puzzled her. She asked if I had had my dinner. The idea died and so did the conversation. What affectation, I thought afterwards. Not on my side: desire had been born.

But on the following day I saw her waiting in one of our greenhouses. She was warmer under glass. I had collected my trolley. That, for some reason, pleased her. She agreed to have dinner with me.

"Where on earth are we going?" she said when we drove off.

"Away from the Nursery," I said. I was determined to amuse her. "To get away from the thieves."

"What thieves?" she said.

"The old ladies," I said.

It is well known, if you run a nursery, that very nice old ladies sometimes nip off a stem for a cutting or slip small plants into their bags. Stealing a little gives them the thrill of flirtation. I said that only this week one of them had come to me when I was alone in a greenhouse and said, "Can I whisper something to you? I have a *dreadful* confession to make. I have been very naughty. I *stole* a snippet of geranium from you in the summer and it has struck!"

Sally said, "And what about old men? Don't they steal?"

My fancy took a leap. "Yes, we've got one," I said, "but he goes in for big stuff."

There was a myth at our Nursery that when a box of plants was missing or some rare expensive shrub had been dug up and was gone, this was the work of a not altogether imaginary person called Thompson who lived in a big house where the garden abutted on our wall. Three camellias went one day, and because of the price he was somehow promoted by the girls and became known as "Colonel" Thompson. He had been seen standing on a stepladder and looking over our wall. I invented a face for the colonel when I told Sally about this. I gave him a ripe nose, a bald head, a drooping moustache; unconsciously I was describing Duggie. I went further: I had caught the colonel with one leg over the wall, and when I challenged him he said, "Looking for my dog. Have you seen my dog?"

Sally said, "I don't believe you."

This was promising. A deep seriousness settled on us when we got to the restaurant. It was a small place. People were talking loudly, so that bits of their lives seemed to be flying around us, and we soon noticed we were the quietest talkers there, talking about ourselves, but to our plates or the tablecloth, crumbling bread and then looking up with sudden questions. She ate very fast; a hungry woman, I thought.

How long, she asked suddenly, raising a fork to her mouth, how long had I known my wife before we were married? Four months, I said. She put her fork down.

"That was a rush," she said. "It took Duggie and me seven years."

"Why was that?"

"I didn't want to get married, of course," she said.

"You mean you lived together?" I said.

"Indeed not. We might not even have married *then*," she said, "but his firm was sending him to Mexico for three years. We knew each other very well, you know. Actually," she mumbled now, "I was in love with someone else." She now spoke up boldly, "Gratitude is more important than love, isn't it?"

"Is that the question you wanted to ask me," I said, "when you telephoned?"

"I don't think I said that," she said.

I was falling in love with her. I listened but hardly heard what she said. I was listening only to my desire.

"Gratitude? No, I don't," I said. "Not when one is young. Why don't you go with him on his jobs?"

"He likes travel, I don't," she said. "We like each other. I don't mind being alone. I prefer it. You're alone, aren't you?"

Our conversation stopped. A leaden boredom settled on us like a stifling thundercloud. I whispered, looking around first to be sure no one heard me, and in a voice I scarcely recognized as my own, "I want you."

"I know," she said. "It's no good," she said, fidgeting in her chair and looking down at the cloth. Her movement encouraged me.

"I've loved you ever since—"

She looked up.

"—since you started coming to the Nursery," I said.

"Thank you, but I can't," she said. "I don't go to bed with people. I gave that up when my daughter was born."

"It's Duggie?" I said.

She was startled and I saw the grimace I knew.

She thought a long time.

"Can't you guess?" she said. And then she leaned across and touched my hand. "Don't look so gloomy. It's no good with me."

I was not gloomy. That half wave of the hand, the boredom, the monotony of our voices, even the fact that the people at the next table had found us so interesting that they too had started whispering, made me certain of how our evening would end.

"Let us go," I said.

I called a waiter and she watched me pay the bill and said, "What an enormous tip." In our heavy state, this practical remark lightened us. And for me it had possessive overtones that were encouraging; she stood outside, waiting for me to bring the car with that air women have of pretending not to be there. We drove off and when I turned into a shopping street almost empty at this hour I saw our heads and shoulders reflected in the windows of a big shop, mocking us as we glided by: two other people. I turned into a street of villas; we were alone again and I leaned to kiss her on the neck. She did not move, but presently she glanced at me and said, "Are you a friend?"

"No," I said. "I'm not."

"I think I ought to like that," she said. And she gripped my arm violently and did not let it go.

"Not at my house," she said.

We got to my flat and there she walked across the sitting-room straight to the window and looked down at the long greenhouses gleaming in the dark.

"Which is Colonel Thompson's house?" she said.

I came up behind her and put my arms round her and she watched my daring hands play on her breasts with that curiosity and love of themselves that women have, but there was a look of horror on her face when I kissed her on the mouth, a hate that came (I know now) from the years of her marriage. In the next hours it ebbed away, her face emptied, and her wide lips parted with greed.

"I don't do things like this," she said.

The next day she came to me; on the third day she pulled me back as I was getting out of bed and said, "Duggie's coming home. I have something bad to tell you, something shameful." She spoke into my shoulder. "Something I tried to tell you when I telephoned, the day you came with the plant, but I couldn't. Do you remember I telephoned to you?

"I told a lie to Duggie about that young man, I told Duggie he attacked me." She said, "It wasn't true. I saw him and his girl at night from my bedroom window going into the garden with their arms round each other, to the end of it, under the trees. They were there a long time. I imagined what they were doing. I could have killed that girl.

I was mad with jealousy—I think I was really mad. I went out into the garden many nights to stop them, and in the afternoons I worked there to provoke him and even peeped into their window. It was terrible. So I told Duggie. I told him the boy had come up behind me and pulled at my clothes and tried to rape me. I tore my blouse to prove it. I sent a cable to Duggie. Poor Duggie, he believed me. He came back. I made Duggie throw the boy out. You know what happened. When the boy was killed I thought I would go out of my mind."

"I thought you said Duggie was ill," I said.

"That is what I'm ashamed of," she said. "But I was mad. You know, I hated you too when Duggie brought you in to do those stones. I really hated anyone being in the garden. That is why I made that scene when you brought the magnolia. When you came to the door I thought for an awful moment it was the boy's father coming for his things; he did come once."

I was less shocked than unnerved. I said, "The real trouble was that you were lying to yourself." I saw myself as the rescuer for a moment.

"Do you think he believed you?" I said.

She put on the distant look she used to have when I first met her, almost a look of polite annoyance at being distracted from her story. Then she said something that was true. "Duggie doesn't allow himself to believe what he doesn't want to believe. He never believes what he sees. One day I found him in the sitting-room, and he started to pull a book out of the bookcase and closed it with a bang and wiped his eyes. 'Dust,' he said. 'Bad as Mexico.' Afterwards I thought, He's been crying."

"That was because he knew he was to blame," I said.

I went to my window and looked at the sky. In the night he would be coming across it.

"What are we going to do?" I said. "When shall I see you? Are you going to tell him?"

She was very surprised. "Of course not," she said, getting out of bed.

"But we must. If you don't, I shall."

She picked up her dress and half covered herself with it. "If you do," she said, "I'll never see you again, Colonel Thompson."

"He'll find out. I want to marry you."

"I've got a daughter. You forget that. He's my husband."

"He's probably got some girl," I said lightly.

The gentleness went out of our conversation.

"You're not to say that," she said vehemently. We were on the edge of a quarrel.

"I have got to go," she said. "Judy's coming home. I've got to get his suits from the cleaners and there are some of yours."

My suits and Duggie's hanging up on nasty little wire hangers at the cleaners!

We had a crowd of customers at the Nursery and that took my mind off our parting, but when I got back to my flat the air was still and soundless. I walked round my three rooms expecting to see her, but the one or two pictures stared out of my past life. I washed up our empty glasses. Well, there it is, I thought cynically. All over. What do you expect? And I remembered someone saying, "Have an affair with a married woman if you like, but for God's sake don't start wanting to marry her."

It was a help that my secretary was on holiday and I had to do all the paperwork at night. I also had my contract for re-planting the square the council had neglected and did a lot of the digging myself. As I dug I doubted Sally and went over what I knew about her life. How did she and Duggie meet? What did they say? Was Sally flaunting herself before her husband, surprising and enticing him? I was burned by jealousy. Then, at the end of the week, before I left for the square at half past eight, I heard her steps on the stairs to my office. She had a busy smile on her face.

"I've brought your suits," she said. "I'm in a rush." And she went to hang them in their plastic covers on the door, but I had her in my arms and the suits fell to the floor.

"Is it all right?" I said.

"How do you mean?" she said.

"Duggie," I said.

"Of course," she said complacently.

I locked the door. In a few minutes her doubts and mine were gone. Our quarrel was over. She looked at me with surprise as she straightened her skirt.

Happiness! I took one of our girls with me to the square and stood by lazily watching her get on with her work.

After lunch I was back at the Nursery and I was alarmed to see Duggie's bald head among the climbing greenery of our hothouse. He was stooping there, striped by sunlight, like some affable tiger. I hoped to slip by unseen, but he heard me and the tiger skin dropped off as he came out, all normality, calling, "Just the man! I've been away."

I gave what must have been the first of the small coughs, the first of a long series with which I would always greet him and which made him put concern into his voice. I came to call it my "perennial hybrid" —a phrase that struck him and which he added to his vocabulary of phrases and even to his reflections on coughs in general, on Arab spitting and Mexican hawking.

"I came over to thank you for that wonderful magnolia. That was very kind. I missed it in flower but Sally says it was wonderful. You don't know what it did for her. I don't know whether you have noticed, she's completely changed. She looks years younger. All her energy has come back." Then in a louder voice: "She has forgotten all that trouble. You must have seen it. She tells me she has been giving you a hand, your girl's away."

"She was very kind. She took my suits to the cleaners."

He ignored this. We walked together across the Nursery and he waved his hand to the flower beds. Did I say that his daughter was with him? She was then a fat girl of thirteen or fourteen with fair hair like her mother's.

"Fetched them," said the pedantic child, and from that time her gaze was like a judgement. I picked a flower for her as they followed me to the door of my office.

"By the way," he said, "what did you do about that fellow who gets over the wall? Sally told me. Which wall was it?"

Sally seemed to tell him everything.

"He's stopped. That one over there."

He stood still and considered it. "What you need is a wire fence, with a three-inch mesh to it; if it was wider, the fellow could get his toe in. It would be worth the outlay—no need to go in for one of those spiked steel fences we put up round our refineries." He went on to the general question of fences: he had always been against people who put broken glass on walls. "Unfair," he said. He looked lofty—"Cruel, too. Chap who did that ought to be sent off the field.

"Come and have a drink with us this evening," Duggie said.

I could think of no excuse; in fact I felt confident and bold now, but the first person I saw at the house was Duggie wearing a jacket far too small for him. It was my jacket. She had left his suits at my office and taken mine to her own house.

Duggie laughed loudly. "Very fishy, I thought, when I saw this on my bed. Ha-ha! What's going on? It would be funnier still if you'd worn mine."

Sally said demurely she saw nothing funny in that. She had only been trying to help.

"Be careful when Sally tries to help." He was still laughing. The comedy was a bond. And we kept going back to it. Judy, her daughter, enjoyed this so much that she called out, "Why doesn't Mr. Ormerod take our flat?"

Our laughter stopped. Children recklessly bring up past incidents in their parents' lives. Duggie was about to pour wine into Sally's glass and he stopped, holding the bottle in the air. Sally gave that passing grimace of hers and Duggie shrank into instant protective concern and to me he seemed to beg us all for silence. But he recovered quickly and laughed again, noisily—too noisily, I thought.

"He has to live near the Nursery, don't you, Teddy? Colonel Thompson and all that."

"Of course," said Sally easily. "Duggie, don't pour the wine on the carpet, please."

It was a pleasant evening. We moved to the sitting-room and Sally sat on the sofa with the child, who gazed and gazed at me. Sally put her arm round her.

Three years have passed since that evening when Judy spoke out. When I look back, those years seem to be veiled or to sparkle with the mists of an October day. How can one describe happiness? In due time Duggie would leave and once more for months on end Sally and I would be free, and despite our bickerings and jealousies, our arguments about whether Duggie knew or did not know, we fell into a routine and made our rules. The stamp of passion was on us, yet there was always in my mind the picture of her sitting on the sofa with her daughter. I came to swear I would do nothing that would trouble her. And she and I seemed able to forget our bodies when we were all together. Perhaps that first comedy had saved us. My notion was that Duggie invented me, as he had invented her. I spend my time, she says, inventing Duggie. She invented neither of us.

Now I have changed my mind. After that evening when the child Judy said, "Why doesn't Mr. Ormerod take our flat?" I am convinced that Duggie *knew*—because of his care for Sally, even because he knew more than either of us about Sally and that tenant of theirs who was so horribly killed on his motorbike. When he turned us into fictions he perhaps thought the fiction would soon end. It did not. He became like a weary, indulgent, and distant emperor when he was home.

But those words of Judy's were another matter. For Duggie, Judy was not a fiction. She was his daughter, absolutely his, he made her. She was the contradiction of his failure. About her he would not pretend or compromise. I am now sure of this after one or two trivial events that occurred that year. One afternoon the day before he was due home —one of those enamelled misleading October days, indeed—Sally was tidying the bedroom at my flat. I was in the sitting-room putting the drinks away and I happened to glance down at the Nursery. I saw a young woman there, with fair hair, just like Sally's, shading her eyes from the sun, and waving. For a moment I thought it was Sally who had secretly slipped away to avoid the sad awkwardness of those business-like partings of ours. Then I saw the woman was a young girl— Judy. I stepped back out of sight. I called Sally and she came with a broom in her hand.

"Don't go near the window like that"—she was not even wearing a bra—"look!"

"It's Judy! What is she up to? How long has she been there?" she said.

"She's watching us," I said. "She knows!"

Sally made that old grimace I now so rarely see.

"The little bitch," she said. "I left her at home with two of her school friends. She can't know I'm here."

"She must do," I said. "She's spying."

Sally said crisply, "Your paranoia is a rotten cover. Do you think I didn't know that girl's got a crush on you, my sweetheart? Try not to be such a cute old man."

"Me? Try?" I said jauntily.

And then, in the practical manner of one secure in the higher air of unruffled love, she said, "Anyway, she can't see my car from there. She can't see through walls. Don't stand there looking at her."

She went back to tidying the flat and my mind drifted into remembering a time when I was a boy throwing pebbles at the window of the girl next door. What a row there was with her mother!

I forgot Judy's waving arm. Duggie came home and I was not surprised to see him wandering about the Nursery two days later like a dog on one of his favourite rounds, circling round me from a distance, for I was busy with a customer, waiting for his chance. He had brought Judy with him. She was solemnly studying the girls, who with their order books and pencils were following undecided customers or directing the lost to our self-service counter inside the building. Judy was murmuring to herself as if imagining the words they said. She was admiring the way one of the girls ordered a youth to wheel a trolley-load of chrysanthemums to the main gate.

When I was free Duggie came quickly to me. "That counter works well," he said. He was congratulating himself, for the counter had been his idea, one item in his dreamy possession of the place. "It has cut down the labour costs. I've been counting. You've got rid of three girls, haven't you?"

"Four," I said. "My secretary left last week to get married."

Judy had stopped watching and came up with him. Yes, she had grown. The child whose face had looked as lumpish as a coffee mug, colourless too, had suddenly got a figure, and her face was rounded. Her eyes were moist with the new light of youth, mingling charmingly with an attempt at the look of important experience. She gazed at me until Duggie stopped talking, and then she said, "I saw you the day before yesterday"—to show she had started to become an old hand—"at your window. I waved to you."

"Did you?" I said.

"You weren't in your office," she said.

Cautiously I said, "I didn't see you."

"You were ironing your shirts."

A relief.

"Not me. I never iron my shirts," I said. "You must have seen the man who lives in the flat below. He's always ironing his shirts, poor fellow. He usually does it at night."

"On the third floor," the girl said.

"I live on the fourth, dear," I said.

"How awful of me," the girl said.

To save her face Duggie said, "I like to see women scrubbing clothes on stone—on a riverbank."

"That's not ironing, Daddy," she said.

There was the usual invitation to come to his house for a drink now that he was back. I did my cough and said I might drop in, though as he could see, we were in a rush. When I got to his house I found a chance to tell Sally. "Clever of her," I said. "It was a scheme to find out which floor I live on."

"It was not what you think," Sally said.

The evening was dull and Sally looked unwell and went to bed early. Duggie and I were left to ourselves and he listened to me in an absent-minded way when I told him again about my secretary leaving. He said grumpily, "You ought leave the girls alone and go in for older women," and went on to say that his sister-in-law was coming to stay, suggesting that married life also had its troubles. Suddenly he woke up, and as if opportunity had been revealed to him in a massive way he said, "Come and have dinner with me at my club tomorrow."

The invitation was half plea, half threat. *He* was being punished. Why not myself also?

Duggie's club! Was this to be a showdown? The club was not a bolt-hole for Duggie. It was an imperial institution in his life and almost sacred. One had to understand that, although rarely mentioned, it was headquarters, the only place in England where he was irrefutably himself and at home with his mysteries. He did not despise me for not having a club myself, but it did explain why I had something of the homeless dog about me. That clubs bored me suggested a moral weakness. I rose slightly in his esteem once when I told him that years ago my uncle used to take me to *his* club. (He used to give me a lot to drink and lecture me on my feckless habits and even introduced me to one or two members—I suppose to put stamina in me.) These invitations came after my wife's death, so that clubs came to seem to me places where marriages were casketed and hidden by the heavy curtains on the high windows.

There was something formidable in Duggie's invitation, and when I got to his club my impression was that he had put on weight or had received a quiet authority from being only among men, among husbands, in mufti. It was a place where the shabby armchairs seemed made of assumptions in leather and questions long ago disposed of. In this natural home Duggie was no longer inventive or garrulous. Nods and grunts to the members showed that he was on his true ground.

We dined at a private table. Duggie sat with his back to an old brocade curtain in which I saw some vegetable design that perhaps had allayed or taken over the fantasies of the members.

A couple of drinks in the bar downstairs and a decanter of wine on the table eased Duggie, who said the old chef had had a stroke and that he thought the new chef had not got his hand in yet. The sweetbreads had been runny the last time; maybe it would be better to risk the beef.

Then he became confessional to put me at my ease: he always came here when his sister-in-law came to stay. A difficult woman—he always said to Sally, "Can't you put her off? You'll only get one of your migraines after she has been."

"I thought Sally didn't look too well," I said.

"She's having a worrying time with Judy," he said. "Young girls grow up. She's going through a phase."

"She is very lovely."

He ignored this. "Freedom, you know! Wants to leave school. Doesn't work. Messed up her exams."

"Sex, I suppose," I said.

"Why does everyone talk about sex?" said Duggie, looking stormy. "She wants to get away, get a flat of her own, get a job, earn her living, sick of the old folks. But a flat of her own—at sixteen! I ask you."

"Girls have changed."

Duggie studied me and made a decision. I now understood why I had been asked.

"I wondered," said Duggie, "has she ever said anything to you—parents are the last to hear anything."

"To me?"

"Friend of the family—I just wondered."

"I hardly ever see her. Only when Sally or you bring her to the Nursery. I can't see the young confiding in me. Not a word."

Duggie was disappointed. He found it hard to lose one of his favourite fancies: that among all those girls at the Nursery I had sublimated the spent desires of my youth. He said, taking an injured pride in a fate, "That's it. I married into a family of gardeners."

And then he came out with it—the purpose of this dinner: "The girl's mad to get a job in your nursery. I thought she might have been sounding you out—I mean, waving to that fellow ironing his shirt."

"No. Nothing," I said.

"Mad idea. You're turning people away! I told her. By the way, I don't want to embarrass you. I'm not suggesting you should take her on. Girls get these ideas. Actually, we're going to take her away from that school and send her to school in Switzerland. Alps, skiing. Her French and German are a mess. Abroad! That is what she needs."

Abroad! The most responsive string in Duggie's nature had been struck. He meant what he said.

"That will be hard on Sally," I said. "She'd miss her terribly."

"We've got to do the best for the girl. She knows that," said Duggie.

And without warning the old stare, but now it was the stare of the interrogator's lamp, turned on my face, and his manner changed from the brisk and business-like to the commandingly off-hand.

"Ironical," he said. "Now, if Sally had wanted a job at your nursery, that would be understandable. After all, you deal with all those Dutch and French, and so on. Her German's perfect. But poor Judy, she can't utter."

"Sally!" I laughed. "She'd hate it."

Duggie filled my glass and then his own very slowly, but as he raised the decanter he kept his eye on me: quite a small feat, indeed like a minor conjuring trick, for a man who more than once had knocked a glass over at home and made Sally rush to the kitchen for a cloth.

"You're quite wrong," he said. "I happen to know."

Know what? "You mean *she's* mentioned it," I said.

"No, no, of course not," he said. "But if you said the word, I'm certain of it. Not last year, perhaps. But if Judy goes to Switzerland, she'll be alone. She'd jump at it."

Now the wine began to work on him—and on me, too—and Duggie's conversation lost its crisp manner. He moved on to one of his trailing geographical trances; we moved through time and space. The club became subtropical, giant ferns burst out of the club curtains, liana hung from the white pillars of the dining-room, the other members seemed to be in native dress, and threading through it all was the figure of Sally, notebook in hand. She followed us downstairs to the bar, which became a greenhouse, as we drank our port. No longer wretched because her daughter had gone, no longer fretting about the disastrous mess she had made of her life when she was young, without a mother's experience to guide her. I heard Duggie say, "I know they're moving me to Brussels in a few months and of course I'll be over every weekend —but a woman wants her own life. Frankly," he said with awe in his voice, "we *bore* them."

The club resumed its usual appearance, though with an air of exhaustion. The leather chairs yawned. The carpets died. A lost member rose from the grave and stopped by Duggie and said, "We need a fourth at bridge."

"Sorry, old boy," said Duggie.

The man went off to die elsewhere.

"And no danger," said Duggie, "of her leaving to get married."

And now, drunkish as we were, we brought our momentous peace conference to an end. The interrogator's lamp was switched on again just before we got to our feet and he seemed to be boring his way into my head and to say, "You've taken my wife, but you're bloody well not going to get my daughter into your pokey little fourth-floor flat ironing your shirts."

I saw the passion in his mottled face and the powerful gleam of his honourable head.

After Sally had put up a fight and I had said that sending Judy away was his revenge, Sally came to work for me. Duggie had married us and I became as nervous and obsequious as a groom. There was the awkwardness of a honeymoon. She dressed differently. She became sedate —no strokings and squeezes of love were allowed: she frowned and twisted away like a woman who had been a secretary all her life. She looked as young and cross as a virgin. She went back to her straight-back hair style; I was back in the period when I was disturbed by the soft hair of her eyebrows. Her voice was all telephone calls, invoices, orders, and snapping at things I had forgotten to do. She walked in a stately way to the filing cabinet. Only to that object did she bend: she said what a mess her predecessor or I had left it in. If she went downstairs to the yard when the lorries arrived, she had papers in her hand. The drivers were cocky at first and then were scared of her. And in time she destroyed our legend—the only unpopular thing she did—the legend of Colonel Thompson. Dog or no dog, he had never come over the wall. The thief, she discovered, had been one of our gardeners. So Colonel Thompson retired to our private life.

Before this, our life had been one of beginnings, sudden partings, unexpected renewals. Now it hummed plainly along from day to day. The roles of Duggie and myself were reversed: when Duggie came home once a week now from Brussels, it was he who seemed to be the lover and I the husband. Sally grew very sharp with both of us and Duggie and I stood apart, on our dignity.

I have done one thing for him. I took my mother to dine with him, as I have said.

"What a saintly man," she said as we drove away. "Just like your father. He's coming to see me next time they're at their cottage."

On the Edge
of the Cliff

The sea fog began to lift towards noon. It had been blowing in, thin
and loose for two days, smudging the tops of the trees up the ravine
where the house stood. "Like the cold breath of old men," Rowena
wrote in an attempt at a poem, but changed the line, out of kindness,
to "the breath of ghosts," because Harry might take it personally. The
truth was that his breath was not foggy at all, but smelt of the dozens
of cigarettes he smoked all day. He would walk about, taking little steps,
with his hand outstretched, tapping the ash off as he talked. This gave
an abstracted searching elegance which his heavy face and long sentences needed. In her dressing gown Rowena went to his room. His
glasses were off and he had finished shaving and he turned a face
savaged to the point of saintliness by age, but with a heavy underlip
that made him look helplessly brutal. She laughed at the soap in his
ears.

"The ghosts have gone," she said poetically. "We can go to Withy
Hole! I'll drive by the Guilleth road, there's a fair there. They'll tell our
fortunes."

"Dull place," he said. "It used to be full of witches in the sixteenth
century."

"I'm a witch," she said. "I want to go to the fair. I saw the poster.
It starts today."

"We'll go," he said, suspicious, but giving in.

He was seventyish, and with a young girl of twenty-five one had, of course, to pretend to be suspicious. There are rules for old men who are in love with young girls, all the stricter when the young girls are in love with them. It has to be played as a game.

"The sea pinks will be out on the cliffs," he said.

"You old botanist!" she said.

He was about to say "I know that" and go on to say that girls were like flowers with voices and that he had spent a lot of his life collecting both, but he had said these things to her often before and at his age one had to avoid repeating oneself, if possible. Anyway, it was more effective as a compliment when other people were there and they would turn to look at her. When young girls turned into women they lost his interest: he had always lived for reverie.

"So it's settled," she said.

Now he looked tragic as he gazed at her. Waving his razor, he began his nervous trick of taking a few dance-like steps and she gave him one of her light hugs and ran out of the room.

What with his organizing fusses and her habit of vanishing to do something to a drawing she was working on, the start was late.

"We'll have to eat something," she said, giving an order.

But it was his house, not hers. He'd lived alone long enough not to be able to stand a woman in his kitchen, could not bear to see her cut a loaf or muddle the knives and forks or choke the sink with tea leaves.

"Rowena and I," he said to people who came to see them, in his military voice, "eat very little. We see no one."

This was not true, but like a general with a literary turn, he organized his imagination. He was much guided by literature. His wife had gone mad and had killed herself. So in the house he saw himself as a Mr. Rochester, or in the car as Count Mosca with the young duchess in *La Chartreuse de Parme;* if they met people, as Tolstoy's worldly aunt. This was another game: it educated the girl.

While he fussed between the kitchen and the room they ate in, she came down late and idled, throwing back her long black hair, lassoing him with smiles and side glances thrown out and rushed at him while he had a butter plate in his hand and gave him another of her light engulfing hugs and laughed at the plate he waved in the air.

"Rowena!" he shouted, for she had gone off again. "Get the car out."

The house was halfway up the long ravine, backed and faced by an army of ash trees and beeches. There was the terrace and the ingenious steep garden and the plants that occupied him most of the day, and down from the terrace he had had to cut the twenty or thirty steps himself, heaving his pickaxe. Rowena had watched his thick stack of coarse grey hair and his really rather brutal face and his pushed-out lips, as he hacked and the pick hit the stones. He worked with such anger and pride, but he looked up at her sometimes with appealing, brilliant eyes. His furious ancient's face contained pain naturally.

She knew he hated to be told to be careful when he came down the steps. She knew the ceremony of getting him into the car, for he was a tall, angular man and had to fold himself in, his knees nearly touching his chin, to which the long deep despondent lines of his face ran heavily down. It was exciting for her to drive the old man dangerously fast down the long circling lane through the trees, to show how dangerous she could be, while he talked. He would talk nonstop for the next hour, beginning, of course, with the country fair.

"It's no good. Plastic, like cheap food. Not worth seeing. The twentieth century has packaged everything."

And he was on to the pre-Roman times, the ancient spirit of carnival, Celtic gods and devils, as they drove out of the ravine into deep lanes, where he could name the ferns in the stone walls, and the twisting hills and corners that shook the teeth and the spine. Historical instances poured out of him. He was, she said, Old Father Time himself, but he did not take that as a joke, though he humoured her with a small laugh. It was part of the game. He was not Father Time, for in one's seventies, one is a miser of time, putting it by, hiding the minutes, while she spent fast, not knowing she was living in time at all.

Guilleth was a dull, dusty, Methodistical little town with geraniums in the windows of the houses. Sammy's Fair was in a rough field just outside it, where dogs and children ran about. There was only one shooting gallery; they were still putting up the back canvas of the coconut shy. There were hoopla stalls, a lot of shouting and few customers. But the small roundabout gave out its engine whistle and the children packed the vulgar circle of spotted cows with huge pink udders, the rocking horses, the pigs, the tigers and a pair of giraffes.

The professor regarded it as a cultural pathos. He feared Rowena. She was quite childishly cruel to him. With a beautiful arrogance that mocked him, she got out of the car and headed for ice cream. He had to head her off the goldfish in their bowls. She'd probably want to bring one home.

"Give me some money," she said, going to the roundabout. There was a small crowd near that. "I'm going on the giraffe. Come on."

"I'll watch you," he complained and cleaned his glasses.

There she was, riding a giraffe already, tall and like a schoolmistress among the town children, with her long hair, which she kept on throwing back as she whirled round, a young miracle, getting younger and younger. There were other girls. There were town youths and there was an idiotic young man riding backwards on a cow, kicking out his legs and every now and then waving to the crowd. Rowena on her giraffe did not smile, but as she came round sedately, waved to the old man as she sailed by.

He looked at his watch. How much longer?

"I'm going on again," she called, and did not get off.

He found himself absurdly among the other patient watchers, older than all, better dressed too, on his dignity, all curiosity gone. He moved away to separate himself from his bunch of them, but he had the impression they all moved with him. There was a young woman in a bright-red coat who always seemed to be in the next bunch he joined. Round came the giraffe: round came the young man on the cow. The young woman in red waved. Seeing that to wave was the correct thing, the old man too waved at the giraffe. The woman waved again a moment later and stared at him as if annoyed. He moved a yard from her, then five yards, then to the other side of the roundabout. Here he could wave without being conspicuous, yet the woman was standing close to him once more. She was small with reddish hair, her chin up, looking at him.

"You don't remember me," she accused him in a high voice. Her small eyes were impudent. He stepped back, gaping.

"Daisy Pyke," she said.

Pyke? Pyke? He gaped at her briefly, his mind was sailing round with Rowena.

"George's wife," she said, challenging his stupidity.

"George . . ." But he stopped. George Pyke's wife must be fifty by now. This woman could not be more than thirty. Her daughter—had they had a daughter?

"Have I changed as much as that?" she said. Her manner was urchin-like and she grinned with pleasure at his confusion and then her mouth drooped at the corners plaintively, begging. Nowadays he thought only of Rowena's wide mouth, which made all other women vague to him. And then the hard little begging, pushing mouth and its high voice broke into his memory. He stepped back with embarrassment and a short stare of horror which he covered quickly, his feet dancing a few steps, and saying with foolish smiles, "Daisy! I thought . . . I was watching that thing. What are you doing here?"

Now that he remembered, he could not conceal a note of indignation and he stood still, his eyes peered coldly. He could see this had its effect on her.

"The same as you," she said in that curt off-hand voice. "Waiting. Waiting for them to come off." And she turned away from him, offended, waved wildly at the roundabout and shouted, "Stephen, you fool!" The young man riding backwards on the cow waved back and shouted to her.

What an appalling thing! But there it is—one must expect it when one is old: the map in one's head, indeed the literal map of the country empties and loses its contours, towns and villages, and people sink out of sight. The protective faces of friends vanish and one is suddenly alone, naked and exposed. The population ranked between oneself and old enemies suddenly dissolves and the enemy stands before one. Daisy Pyke!

The old man could not get away. He said as politely as he could manage, "I thought you went abroad. How is George?"

"We did. George," she said, "died in Spain." And added briskly, "On a golf course."

"I'm sorry. I didn't know."

She looked back at the roundabout and turned again to say to him, "I know all about *you*. You've got a new house at Colfe. I've still got the old house, though actually it's let."

Forty miles lay between Colfe and Daisy Pyke—but no people in between! Now the roundabout stopped. There was a scramble of children getting on and getting off, and the local watchers moved forward too.

"I must get Rowena," he said ruthlessly and he hurried off, calling out in his peremptory voice, "Rowena!"

He knew that Daisy Pyke was watching him as he held out a hand to help Rowena off, but Rowena ignored it and jumped off herself.

"Rowena. We must go."

"Why? It was lovely. Did you see that ridiculous young man?"

"No, Rowena," he said. "Where?"

"Over there," she said, "with the girl in red, the one you were chatting up, you old rip. I saw you!" She laughed and took his arm. "You're blushing."

"She's not a girl," he said. "She's a woman I used to know in London twenty years ago. It was rather awful! I didn't recognize her. I used to know her husband. She used to be a friend of Violet's."

"Violet's!" said Rowena. "But you *must* introduce me." She was always eager to know, as if to possess, everyone he had ever known, to have all of him, even the dead. Above all Violet, his wife. Rowena longed to be as old as that dead woman.

"Really, Harry, you are frightful with people."

"Oh, well . . . But she's appalling. We had a terrible row."

"One of your old loves," she teased.

"I had to throw her out of the house," he said. "She's a liar."

"Then I *must* see her," said Rowena. "How thrilling."

"I think they've gone," he said.

"No," said Rowena. "There they are. Take me over."

And she pulled him towards the hoopla stall where Daisy Pyke and the young man were standing. There lay the delightfulness of Rowena: she freed him from the boredom into which his memories had set and hardened. He had known many young girls who in this situation would be eagerly storing opportunities for jealousy of his past life. Rowena was not like that.

At the stall, with its cunningly arranged bowls, jugs, and toys, the young man with the yellow curling hair was pitching rings onto the table, telling Daisy to try and altering the angle of the ring in her hand.

"Choose what you want, hold the ring level and lightly, don't skim fast. Don't bowl it like that! Like this."

Daisy's boldness had gone. She was fond and serious, glancing at the young man before she threw.

"Daisy," said the old man, putting on a shady and formal manner as if he were at a party, "I have brought Rowena to meet you."

And Rowena stepped forward gushingly. "How d'you do! I was telling Harry about the young man on the cow."

"Here he is," said Daisy stiffly. "Stephen!"

The young man turned and said "Hello" and went on throwing rings. "Like that," he said.

Rowena watched him mockingly.

"We are just off," said Harry.

"I've heard a lot about you," said Daisy to Rowena.

"We're going to walk along the cliffs," said Harry.

"To Withy Hole," said Rowena.

"It was extraordinary meeting you here," said Harry.

"Perhaps," said Daisy, "we'll meet again."

"Oh, well—you know we hardly see anyone now," said Harry.

Daisy studied Rowena impudently and she laughed at the boy, who had failed again.

"I won a goldfish once," said Rowena, laughing. "It died on the way home."

"Extraordinary," the old man said as he and Rowena walked away. "That must be George's son, but taller. George was short."

When she got him back into the car she saw by his leaden look that the subject was closed. She had met one more of his friends—that was the main thing.

The hills seemed to pile up and the sea to get farther and farther away and then, suddenly, as they got over the last long hill, they passed the caravan sites that were empty at this time of the year and looked like those flat white Andalusian towns he remembered, from a distance. The old man was saying, "But we have this new rootless civilization, anarchic but standardized"—suddenly the sea appeared between the dunes below, not grey and choppy, but deep blue, all candour, like a young mouth, between the dunes and beyond it, wide and still and sleepily serene. The old man was suddenly in command, fussing about the exact place where they could leave the car, struggling over the sand dunes dotted with last year's litter, on to the huge cliffs. At the top there they could look back and see on the wide bay the shallow sea breaking idly, in changing lines of surf, like lips speaking lines that broke unfinished and could not be heard. A long way off a dozen surfers were wading out, deeper and deeper, towards the bigger waves as if they were leaving the land for good and might be trying to reach the horizon. Rowena stopped to gaze at them, waiting for one of them to come in on a long glissade, but the old man urged her on to the close turf of the cliffs. That is what he had come for: boundlessness, distance. For thirty miles on a clear day in May like this, one could walk without meeting a soul, from headland to headland, gazing through the hum of the wind and under the cries of the dashing gulls, at what seemed to be an unending procession of fading promontories, each dropping to its sandy cove, yet still riding out into the water. The wind did not move the old man's tough thatch of hair but made his big ears stick out. Rowena bound her loose hair with a scarf. From low cliff to high cliff, over the cropped turf, which was like a carpet, where the millions of sea pinks and daisies were scattered, mile after mile in their colonies, the old man led the way, digging his knees into the air, gesticulating, talking, pointing to a kestrel above or a cormorant black as soot on a rock, while she followed lazily yards behind him. He stopped impatiently to show her some small cushioned plant or stood on the cliff's edge, like a prophet, pointing down to the falls of rock, the canyons, caverns, and tunnels into which the green water poured in black and was sucked out into green again and spilled in waterfalls down the outer rocks. The old man was a strong walker, bending to it, but when he stopped he straightened, and Rowena smiled at his air of detachment as he gazed at distant things as if he knew them. To her he looked like a frightening mixture of pagan saint and toiling animal. They would rest at the crest of a black cliff for a few minutes, feel the sun burn their skin, and then on they went.

"We can't see the bay any more," she said. She was thinking of the surf-riders.

"The cliff after the next is the Hole," he said and pulled her to her feet.

"Yes, the Hole," she said.

He had a kind of mania about the Hole. This was the walk he liked best and so did she, except for that ugly final horror. The sea had tunnelled under the rock in several places along this wild coast and had sucked out enormous slaty craters fifty yards across and this one a hundred and eighty feet deep, so that even at the edge one could not see the water pouring in. One stood listening for the bump of hidden water on a quiet day: on wild ones it seethed in the bottom of the pot. The place terrified Rowena and she held back, but he stumbled through the rough grasses to the edge, calling back bits of geology and navigation—and to amuse her, explained how smugglers had had to wait for the low wave to take them in.

Now, once more, they were looking at the great meaningless wound. As he stood at the edge he seemed to her to be at one with it. It reminded her of his mouth when she had once seen it (with a horror she tried to wipe from her mind) before he had put his dentures in. Of her father's too.

Well, the objective was achieved. They found a bank on the seaward side out of the wind where the sun burned and they rested.

"Heaven," she said and closed her eyes.

They sat in silence for a long time but he gazed at the rising floor of eventless water. Far out, from time to time, in some small eddy of the wind, little families of whitecaps would appear. They were like faces popping up or perhaps white hands shooting out and disappearing pointlessly. Yes, they were the pointless dead.

"What are you thinking about?" she asked without opening her eyes.

He was going to say "At my age one is always thinking about death," but he said "You."

"What about me?" she said with that shamelessness of girls.

"Your ears," he said.

"You are a liar," she said. "You're thinking about Daisy Pyke."

"Not now," he said.

"But you must be," she said. She pointed. "Isn't the cove just below where you all used to bathe with nothing on? Did she come?"

"Round the corner," he said, correcting her. "Violet and I used to bathe there. Everyone came. Daisy came once when George was on the golf course. She swam up and down, hour after hour, as cold as a fish. Hopeless on dry land. Gordon and Vera came, but Daisy only once. She didn't fit in—very conventional—sat telling dirty stories. Then she went swimming, to clean up. George was playing golf all day and bridge all evening; that didn't go down well. They had a dartboard in their house: the target was a naked woman. A pretty awful, jokey couple. You can guess the bull's-eye."

"What was this row?" she said.

"She told lies," he said, turning to her. And he said this with a hiss of finality which she knew. She waited for one of his stories, but it did not come.

"I want to swim in the cove," said Rowena.

"It's too cold this time of the year," he said.

"I want to go," she said.

"It's a long way down and hard coming back."

"Yes, but I want to go—where you all used to go."

She was obstinate about this, and of course he liked that.

"All right," he said, getting up. Like all girls she wanted to leave her mark on places. He noticed how she was impelled to touch pictures in galleries when he had taken her to Italy. Ownership! Power! He used to dislike that but now he did not; the change was a symptom of his adoration of her. And she did want to go. She did want to assert her presence on that empty sand, to make the sand feel her mark.

They scrambled the long way down the rocks until the torn cliffs were gigantic above them. On the smooth sand she ran barefoot to the edge of the sea rippling in.

"It's ice!" she screamed.

He stood there, hunched. There was a litter of last year's rags and cartons near the rocks. Summer crowds now swarmed into the place, which had been secret. He glowered with anger at the debris.

"I'm going to pee," he said.

She watched the sea, for he was a long time gone.

"That was a big one," she shouted.

But he was not there. He was out on the rocks, he had pulled off his clothes. He was standing there, his body furred with grey hair, his belly wrinkled, his thighs shrunk. Up went his bony arms.

"You're not to! It will kill you! Your heart!" she shouted.

He gave a wicked laugh, she saw his yellow teeth, and in he dived and was crawling and shouting in the water as he swam out farther, defying her, threshing the water, and then as she screamed at him, really frightened, he came crawling in like some ugly hairy sea animal, his skin reddened with cold, and stood dripping with his arms wide as if he was going to give a howl. He climbed over the rocks and back to the sand and got his clothes and was drying himself with his shirt.

"You're mad," she said. "You're not to put that wet thing on."

"It will dry in this sun," he said.

"What was all that for?" she said. "Did you find her?"

"Who?" he said, looking round in bewilderment. He had dived in boastfully and in a kind of rage, a rage against time, a rage against Daisy Pyke too. He did not answer, but looked at her with a glint of shrewdness in his eyes. She was flattered by the glitter in this look from a sometimes terrifying old man.

He was tired now and they took the short inland road to the car close to those awful caravans, and when she got him into the car again he fell asleep and snorted. He went to his room early but could not sleep; he had broken one of his rules for old men. For the first time he had let her see him naked. He was astounded when she came into his room and got into his bed: she had not done this before. "I've come to see the Ancient Mariner," she said.

How marvellous. She is jealous, after all. She loves me, he went about saying to himself in the next weeks. She drove to what they called "our town" to buy cakes. "I am so thin," she said.

The first time she returned saying she had seen his "dear friend Daisy." She was in the supermarket.

"What's she doing there?" he said. "She lives forty miles away. What did she say?"

"We did not speak. I mean, I don't think she saw me. Her son was with her. He said hello. He'd got the hood of the car up. She came out and gave me a nod—I don't think she likes me," she said with satisfaction.

The next week she went again to get petrol. The old man stayed at the house, shook one or two mats, and swept the sitting-room floor. It was his house and Rowena was untidy. Then he sat on the terrace, listening for her car, anxiously.

Presently he picked up the sound, much earlier than her usual time, and saw the distant glint in the trees as the car wound its way up. There she was, threading her beauty through the trees. He heard with alarm the sudden silences of the car at some turn in the hill, then heard it getting louder as it turned a corner, then passing into silence again. He put his book down and went inside in a dutiful panic to put the kettle on, and while he waited for it to boil he took the cups out pedantically, one by one, to the table on the terrace and stood listening again. Now it was on the last stretch, now he heard a crackling of wheels below. He ran in to heat the teapot and ran out with his usual phrase: "Did you get what you wanted?"

Then, puffing up the last steps, she came. But it was not she; it was a small woman, bare-legged and in sandals, with a swaggering urchin grin on her face, pulling a scarf off her head. Daisy!

"Gosh!" she said.

Harry skipped back a yard and stood, straightening and forbidding. "Daisy!" he said, annoyed, as if waving her off.

"Those steps! Harry!" she said. "Gosh, what a view."

She gave a dry dismissive laugh at it. She had, he remembered, always defied what she saw. The day when he had seen her at the fair seemed to slide away under his feet and years slid by, after that, following that day.

"What—" he began. Then in his military way, he jerked out, "Rowena's gone into town. I am waiting for her."

"I know," said Daisy. "Can I sit down and get my breath? I know. I saw her." And with a plotting satisfaction: "Not to speak to. She passed me. Ah, that's better."

"We never see people," said Harry sternly. "You see I am working. If the telephone rings, we don't answer it."

"The same with us. I hope I'm not interrupting. I thought—I'll dash up, just for a minute."

"And Rowena has her work . . ." he said. Daisy was always an interrupter.

"I gave you a surprise," said Daisy comfortably. "She is lovely. That's why I came. You're lucky—how d'you do it? Where did you find her? And what a place you've got here! I made Stephen go and see his friends. It was such a long time—years, isn't it? I had to come. You haven't changed, you know. But you didn't recognize me, did you? You were trying not to see me, weren't you?"

Her eyes and her nose were small. She is at her old game of shock tactics, he thought. He looked blankly at her.

"I explained that," he said nervously. "I must go and turn the kettle off," he said. He paused to listen for Rowena's car, but there was no sound.

"Well," she said. "There you are. Time goes on."

When he came back with a teapot and another cup, she said, "I knew you wouldn't come and see me, so I came to see you. Let me see," she said and took off the scarf from her head. "I told you George died, didn't I? Of course I did," she said briskly.

"Yes."

"Well . . ." she said. "Harry, I had to see you. You are the only wise man I know." She looked nervously at the garden and across to the army of trees stacked on the hill and then turned to him. "You're happy and I am happy, Harry. I didn't come to make a scene and drag it all up. I was in love with you, that was the trouble, but I'm not now. I was wrong about you, about you and Violet. I couldn't bear to see her suffer. I was out of my mind. I couldn't bear to see you grieving for her. I soon knew what it was when poor George died. Harry, I just don't want you to hate me any more. I mean, you're not still furious, are you? We do change. The past is past."

The little liar, he thought. What has she come up here for? To cause trouble between himself and Rowena as she had tried to do with his wife and himself. He remembered Daisy's favourite word: honesty. She was trying for some reason to confuse him about things he had settled a long time ago in his mind.

He changed the subject. "What is—"—he frowned—"I'm sorry, I can't remember names nowadays—your son doing?"

She was quick to notice the change, he saw. Nothing ever escaped Daisy.

"Oh, Tommy, the ridiculous Tommy. He's in Africa," she said, merrily dismissing him. "Well, it was better for him—problems. I'm a problem to him—George was so jealous too."

"He looks exactly like George," Harry said. "Taller, of course, the curly hair."

"What are you talking about? You haven't seen him since he was four." She laughed.

"Don't be stupid, Daisy, we saw him last week at that—what is the name of the place?—at the fair."

The blood went from Daisy's face. She raised her chin. "That's a nasty one," she said and gave her head a fierce shake. "You meant it to, didn't you? That was Stephen. I thought you'd be the last to think a thing like that, with your Rowena. I expect people say it and I don't care and if anyone said it to him he wouldn't know what they were talking about. Stephen's my lover."

The old sentimental wheedling Daisy was in the coy smile that quickly followed her sharpness. "He's mad about me," she said. "I may be old enough to be his mother, but he's sick of squealing, sulky girls of seventeen. If we had met years ago, he would have hated me. Seriously, Harry, I'd go down on my knees to him."

"I am sorry—I—that's why I didn't recognize you. You can ask Rowena. I said to her, 'That's Daisy Pyke's daughter,' " Harry said, "when I saw you."

Daisy gaped at him and slowly her lips curled up with delight. "Oh, good! Is that true? Is it? You always told the truth. You really thought that! Thank you, Harry, that's the nicest thing you ever said to me. I love you for it."

She leaned forward, appealing to him quietly.

"George never slept with me for seven years before he died. Don't ask me about it, but that's the truth. I'd forgotten what it was. When Stephen asked me I thought it was an insult—you know, all this rape about. I got into the car and slammed the door in his face and left him on the road—well, not on the road, but wherever it was—and drove off. I looked back. He was still standing there. Well, I mean, at my age! That next day—*you* know what it is with women better than anyone —I was in such a mood. When I got back to the house I shouted for George, howled for him to come back and poured myself a tumblerful of whisky and wandered about the house slopping it on the carpet." She laughed. "George would have killed me for *that* if he had come —and I went out into the garden and there was Stephen, you won't believe it, walking bold as brass up from the gate. He came up quickly and just took the glass from me very politely—the stuff was pouring down my dress—and put it on the grass and he wiped my blouse. That's what did it."

She paused thoughtfully and frowned. "Not there," she said prudishly, "not at the house, of course. I wanted to get away from it. I can't bear it. We went to the caravan camp. That's where he was living. I don't know why I'm telling you this. I mean, there's a lot more."

She paused. "Love is something at our age, isn't it? I mean, when I saw you and Rowena at Guilleth—I thought I must go and talk to you. Being in the same boat."

"We're not," he said, annoyed. "I am twenty years older than you."

"Thirty, if you don't mind," she said, opening her bag and looking into her mirror. When she had put it away with a snap she looked over the flowers in the steep garden to the woods. She was listening for the sound of a car. He realized he had stopped listening for it. He found himself enjoying this hour, despite his suspicions of her. It drove away the terrors that seemed to dissolve even the trees of the ravine. With women, nature returned to its place, the trees became real trees. One lived in a long moment in which time had stopped. He did not care for Daisy, but she had that power of enticement which lay in stirring one with the illusion that she was defying one to put her right. With Rowena he had thrown away his vanity; with Daisy it returned.

"Where did you and Rowena go the day we saw you?" she asked suddenly.

"Along the cliffs," he said.

"You didn't go to the cove, did you? It's a long way. And you can't swim at this time of the year."

"We went to the cove and I *did* swim," he said. "I wouldn't let Rowena."

"I should hope not! You don't forget old times, do you?" She laughed coolly. "I hope you didn't tell Rowena—young girls can be so jealous. I *was*—d'you remember? Gosh, I'm glad I'm not young still, aren't you?"

"Stop being so romantic, Daisy," said the old man.

"Oh, I'm not romantic any more," she said. "It doesn't pay else one would pity *them*, Rowena and Stephen. So you did go to the cove— did you think of me?"

"I only think of death now," he said.

"You always were an interesting man, the type that goes on to his nineties, like they do now," she said. "I never think about it. Stephen would have a fit. He doesn't even know what he's going to *do*. Last week he thought he'd be a beach guard. Or teach tennis. Or a singer! He was surfing on the beach when I first saw him. He was living at the camp."

She paused, offended. "Did you know they switch off the electric light at ten o'clock at the office in those places? No one protests. Like sheep. It would make me furious to be treated like that. You could hear everyone snoring at once. Not that we joined in, I must say. Actually, we're staying in his mother's house now, the bunks are too narrow in those caravans, but she's come back. So we're looking for something —I've let my house. The money is useful."

The old man was alarmed. He was still trying to make out the real reason for her visit. He remembered the old Daisy—there was always a hidden motive, something she was trying out. And he started listening urgently again for Rowena's car. I know what it is, he thought; she wants to move in here!

"I'm afraid it would be impossible to have you here," he said.

"Here, Harry?" she said, astonished. "None of that! That's not what I came for. Anyway," she said archly, "I wouldn't trust you."

But she considered the windows and the doors of the house and then the view. She gave a business-like sniff and said seriously, "You can't keep her a prisoner here. It won't last."

"Rowena is not a prisoner. She can come and go when she likes. We understand that."

"It depends what you mean by coming and going," said Daisy shrewdly. "You mean *you* are the prisoner. That is it! So am I!"

"Oh," said Harry. "Love is always like that. I live only for her."

"That is it! I will tell you why I came to see you, Harry. When I saw Rowena in town I kept out of her way. You won't believe it—I can be tactful."

She became very serious. "Because I don't want us to meet again." It was an open declaration. "I mean not see you for a long time, I mean all of us. You see, Rowena is so beautiful and Stephen—well, you've seen him. You and I would start talking about old times and people, and they'd be left out and drawn together—now, wouldn't they? I just couldn't bear to see him talking to her, looking at her. I wish we had not met down at the fair. It's all right now, he's with his surfing friends, but you understand?"

She got up and said, "I mean it, Harry. I know what would happen and so do you and I don't want to *see* it happen."

She went up to him because he had stood up and she tapped him hard on the chest with her firm bold finger. He could feel it on his skin, a determined blow, after she had stepped away.

"I know it can't last," she said. "And you know it can't. But I don't want *you* to see it happen," she said in her old hard taunting style. "We never really use your town anyway. I'll see *he* doesn't. Give me your word. We've got to do this for each other. We've managed quite well all these years, haven't we? And it's not saying we'll *never* meet someday, is it?"

"You're a bitch, Daisy," he said, and he smiled.

"Yes, I'm a bitch still, Harry," she said. "But I'm not a fool."

She put out her hand again and he feared she was going to dig that hard finger in his chest again, but she didn't. She tied her scarf round her hair. "If anything happened I'd throw myself down Withy Hole."

"Stop being so melodramatic, Daisy," he said.

"Well, I don't want you conniving," she said coarsely. "I don't want any of your little arrangements."

And she turned to the ravine and listened. "Car coming up," she said.

"Rowena," he said.

"I'll be off. Remember."

"Be careful at the turns," he said helplessly. "She drives fast. You'll pass her on the road."

They did not kiss or even shake hands. He listened to her cursing the steps as she went down and calling out, "I bet you dug out these bloody steps yourself."

He listened to the two cars whining their way towards each other as they circled below, now Rowena's car glinted, now Daisy's. At last Rowena's slowed down at the steps, spitting stones.

Rowena came up and said, "I've just passed Daisy on the road."

"Yes, she's been here. What a tale!"

She looked at the empty cups. "And you didn't give your dearest friend any tea, you wretch."

"Oh, tea—no—er—she didn't want any," he stammered.

"As gripping as all that, was it?" she laughed.

"Very," he said. "She's talking of marrying that young man. Stephen's not her son."

"You can't mean that," she said, putting on a very proper air. "She's old enough—" but she stopped, and instead of giving him one of her light hugs, she rumpled his hair. "People do confide in you, I must say," she said. "I don't think I like her coming up here. Tell me what she said."

A Family Man

Late in the afternoon, when she had given him up and had even
changed out of her pink dress into her smock and jeans and was working
once more at her bench, the doorbell rang. William had come, after
all. It was in the nature of their love affair that his visits were fitful:
he had a wife and children. To show that she understood the situation,
even found the curious satisfaction of reverie in his absences that lately
had lasted several weeks, Berenice dawdled yawning to the door. As she
slipped off the chain, she called back into the empty flat, "It's all right,
Father. I'll answer it."

William had told her to do this because she was a woman living on
her own: the call would show strangers that there was a man there to
defend her. Berenice's voice was mocking, for she thought his idea
possessive and ridiculous; not only that, she had been brought up by
Quakers and thought it wrong to tell or act a lie. Sometimes, when she
opened the door to him, she would say, "Well! Mr. Cork," to remind
him he was a married man. He had the kind of shadowed handsomeness that easily gleams with guilt, and for her this gave their affair its
piquancy.

But now—when she opened the door—no William, and the yawn,
its hopes and its irony, died on her mouth. A very large woman, taller
than herself, filled the doorway from top to bottom, an enormous blob

of pink jersey and green skirt, the jersey low and loose at the neck, a face and body inflated to the point of speechlessness. She even seemed to be asleep with her large blue eyes open.

"Yes?" said Berenice.

The woman woke up and looked unbelievingly at Berenice's feet, which were bare, for she liked to go about barefoot at home, and said, "Is this Miss Foster's place?"

Berenice was offended by the word "place." "This is Miss Foster's residence. I am she."

"Ah," said the woman, babyish no longer but sugary. "I was given your address at the College. You teach at the College, I believe? I've come about the repair."

"A repair? I make jewellery," said Berenice. "I do not do repairs."

"They told me at the College you were repairing my husband's flute. I am Mrs. Cork."

Berenice's heart stopped. Her wrist went weak and her hand drooped on the door handle, and a spurt of icy air shot up her body to her face and then turned to boiling heat as it shot back again. Her head suddenly filled with chattering voices saying, Oh, God. How frightful! William, you didn't tell her? Now, what are you, you, you going to do. And the word "Do, do" clattered on in her head.

"Cork?" said Berenice. "Flute?"

"Florence Cork," said the woman firmly, all sleepy sweetness gone.

"Oh, yes. I am sorry. Mrs. Cork. Of course, yes. Oh, do come in. I'm so sorry. We haven't met, how very nice to meet you. William's —Mr. Cork's—flute! His flute. Yes, I remember. How d'you do? How is he? He hasn't been to the College for months. Have you seen him lately—how silly, of course you have. Did you have a lovely holiday? Did the children enjoy it? I would have posted it, only I didn't know your address. Come in, please, come in."

"In here?" said Mrs. Cork and marched into the front room where Berenice worked. Here, in the direct glare of Berenice's working lamp, Florence Cork looked even larger and even pregnant. She seemed to occupy the whole of the room as she stood in it, memorizing everything —the bench, the pots of paintbrushes, the large designs pinned to the wall, the rolls of paper, the sofa covered with papers and letters and sewing, the pink dress which Berenice had thrown over a chair. She seemed to be consuming it all, drinking all the air.

But here, in the disorder of which she was very vain, which indeed fascinated her, and represented her talent, her independence, a girl's

right to a life of her own and, above all, being barefooted, helped
Berenice recover her breath.

"It is such a pleasure to meet you. Mr. Cork has often spoken of you
to us at the College. We're quite a family there. Please sit. I'll move
the dress. I was mending it."

But Mrs. Cork did not sit down. She gave a sudden lurch towards
the bench, and seeing her husband's flute there propped against the
wall, she grabbed it and swung it above her head as if it were a weapon.

"Yes," said Berenice, who was thinking, Oh, dear, the woman's
drunk, "I was working on it only this morning. I had never seen a flute
like that before. Such a beautiful silver scroll. I gather it's very old, a
German one, a presentation piece given to Mr. Cork's father. I believe
he played in a famous orchestra—where was it?—Bayreuth or Berlin?
You never see a scroll like that in England, not a delicate silver scroll
like that. It seems to have been dropped somewhere or have had a blow.
Mr. Cork told me he had played it in an orchestra himself once, Covent
Garden or somewhere . . ."

She watched Mrs. Cork flourish the flute in the air.

"A blow," cried Mrs. Cork, now in a rich voice. "I'll say it did. I
threw it at him."

And then she lowered her arm and stood swaying on her legs as she
confronted Berenice and said, "Where is he?"

"Who?" said Berenice in a fright.

"My husband!" Mrs. Cork shouted. "Don't try and soft-soap me
with all that twaddle. Playing in an orchestra! Is that what he has been
stuffing you up with? I know what you and he are up to. He comes every
Thursday. He's been here since half past two. I know. I have had this
place watched."

She swung round to the closed door of Berenice's bedroom. "What's
in there?" she shouted and advanced to it.

"Mrs. Cork," said Berenice as calmly as she could. "Please stop
shouting. I know nothing about your husband. I don't know what you
are talking about." And she placed herself before the door of the room.
"And please stop shouting. That is my father's room." And, excited by
Mrs. Cork's accusation, she said, "He is a very old man and he is not
well. He is asleep in there."

"In there?" said Mrs. Cork.

"Yes, in there."

"And what about the other rooms? Who lives upstairs?"

"There are no other rooms," said Berenice. "I live here with my
father. Upstairs? Some new people have moved in."

Berenice was astonished by these words of hers, for she was a truthful young woman and was astonished, even excited, by a lie so vast. It seemed to glitter in the air as she spoke it.

Mrs. Cork was checked. She flopped down on the chair on which Berenice had put her dress.

"My dress, if you please," said Berenice and pulled it away.

"If you don't do it here," said Mrs. Cork, quietening and with tears in her eyes, "you do it somewhere else."

"I don't know anything about your husband. I only see him at the College like the other teachers. I don't know anything about him. If you will give me the flute, I will pack it up for you and I must ask you to go."

"You can't deceive me. I know everything. You think because you are young you can do what you like," Mrs. Cork muttered to herself and began rummaging in her handbag.

For Berenice one of the attractions of William was that their meetings were erratic. The affair was like a game: she liked surprise above all. In the intervals when he was not there, the game continued for her. She liked imagining what he and his family were doing. She saw them as all glued together as if in some enduring and absurd photograph, perhaps sitting in their suburban garden, or standing beside a motorcar, always in the sun, but William himself, dark-faced and busy in his gravity, a step or two back from them.

"Is your wife beautiful?" she asked him once when they were in bed.

William in his slow serious way took a long time to answer. He said at last, "Very beautiful."

This had made Berenice feel exceedingly beautiful herself. She saw his wife as a raven-haired, dark-eyed woman and longed to meet her. The more she imagined her, the more she felt for her, the more she saw eye to eye with her in the pleasant busy middle ground of womanish feelings and moods, for as a woman living alone she felt a firm loyalty to her sex. During this last summer when the family were on holiday she had seen them glued together again as they sat with dozens of other families in the aeroplane that was taking them abroad, so that it seemed to her that the London sky was rumbling day after day, night after night, with matrimony thirty thousand feet above the city, the countryside, the sea and its beaches where she imagined the legs of their children running across the sand, William flushed with his responsibilities, his wife turning to brown her back in the sun. Berenice was often out and about with her many friends, most of whom were married. She loved the look of harassed contentment, even the tired faces

of the husbands, the alert looks of their spirited wives. Among the
married she felt her singularity. She listened to their endearments and
to their bickerings. She played with their children, who ran at once to
her. She could not bear the young men who approached her, talking
about themselves all the time, flashing with the slapdash egotism of
young men trying to bring her peculiarity to an end. Among families
she felt herself to be strange and necessary—a necessary secret. When
William had said his wife was beautiful, she felt so beautiful herself that
her bones seemed to turn to water.

But now the real Florence sat rummaging in her bag before her, this
balloon-like giant, first babyish and then shouting accusations, the
dreamt-of Florence vanished. This real Florence seemed unreal and
incredible. And William himself changed. His good looks began to look
commonplace and shady: his seriousness became furtive, his praise of
her calculating. He was shorter than his wife, his face now looked
hang-dog, and she saw him dragging his feet as obediently he followed
her. She resented that this woman had made her tell a lie, strangely
intoxicating though it was to do so, and had made her feel as ugly as
his wife was. For she must be, if Florence was what he called "beautiful." And not only ugly, but pathetic and without dignity.

Berenice watched warily as the woman took a letter from her handbag.

"Then what is this necklace?" she said, blowing herself out again.

"What necklace is this?" said Berenice.

"Read it. You wrote it."

Berenice smiled with astonishment: she knew she needed no longer
defend herself. She prided herself on fastidiousness: she had never in
her life written a letter to a lover—it would be like giving something
of herself away, it would be almost an indecency. She certainly felt it
to be very wrong to read anyone else's letters, as Mrs. Cork pushed the
letter at her. Berenice took it in two fingers, glanced and turned it over
to see the name of the writer.

"This is not my writing," she said. The hand was sprawling; her own
was scratchy and small. "Who is Bunny? Who is Rosie?"

Mrs. Cork snatched the letter and read in a booming voice that made
the words ridiculous: " 'I am longing for the necklace. Tell that girl to
hurry up. Do bring it next time. And darling, don't forget the flute!!!
Rosie.' What do you mean, who is Bunny?" Mrs. Cork said. "You know
very well. Bunny is my husband."

Berenice turned away and pointed to a small poster that was pinned to the wall. It contained a photograph of a necklace and three brooches she had shown at an exhibition in a very fashionable shop known for selling modern jewellery. At the bottom of the poster, elegantly printed, were the words

Created by Berenice

Berenice read the words aloud, reciting them as if they were a line from a poem: "My name is Berenice," she said.

It was strange to be speaking the truth. And it suddenly seemed to her, as she recited the words, that really William had never been to her flat, that he had never been her lover, and had never played his silly flute there, that indeed he was the most boring man at the College and that a chasm separated her from this woman, whom jealousy had made so ugly.

Mrs. Cork was still swelling with unbelief, but as she studied the poster, despair settled on her face. "I found it in his pocket," she said helplessly.

"We all make mistakes, Mrs. Cork," Berenice said coldly across the chasm. And then, to be generous in victory, she said, "Let me see the letter again."

Mrs. Cork gave her the letter and Berenice read it and at the word "flute" a doubt came into her head. Her hand began to tremble and quickly she gave the letter back. "Who gave you my address—I mean, at the College?" Berenice accused. "There is a rule that no addresses are given. Or telephone numbers."

"The girl," said Mrs. Cork, defending herself.

"Which girl? At Enquiries?"

"She fetched someone."

"Who was it?" said Berenice.

"I don't know. It began with a W, I think," said Mrs. Cork.

"Wheeler?" said Berenice. "There is a Mr. Wheeler."

"No, it wasn't a man. It was a young woman. With a W—Glowitz."

"That begins with a G," said Berenice.

"No," said Mrs. Cork out of her muddle, now afraid of Berenice. "Glowitz was the name."

"Glowitz," said Berenice, unbelieving. "Rosie Glowitz. She's not young."

"I didn't notice," said Mrs. Cork. "Is her name Rosie?"

Berenice felt giddy and cold. The chasm between herself and Mrs. Cork closed up.

"Yes," said Berenice and sat on the sofa, pushing letters and papers away from herself. She felt sick. "Did you show her the letter?" she said.

"No," said Mrs. Cork, looking masterful again for a moment. "She told me you were repairing the flute."

"Please go," Berenice wanted to say but she could not get her breath to say it. "You have been deceived. You are accusing the wrong person. I thought your husband's name was William. He never called himself Bunny. We all call him William at the College. Rosie Glowitz wrote this letter." But that sentence, "Bring the flute," was too much—she was suddenly on the side of this angry woman, she wished she could shout and break out into rage. She wanted to grab the flute that lay on Mrs. Cork's lap and throw it at the wall and smash it.

"I apologize, Miss Foster," said Mrs. Cork in a surly voice. The glister of tears in her eyes, the dampness on her face, dried. "I believe you. I have been worried out of my mind—you will understand."

Berenice's beauty had drained away. The behaviour of one or two of her lovers had always seemed self-satisfied to her, but William, the most unlikely one, was the oddest. He would not stay in bed and gossip but he was soon out staring at the garden, looking older, as if he were travelling back into his life: then, hardly saying anything, he dressed, turning to stare at the garden again as his head came out of his shirt or he put a leg into his trousers, in a manner that made her think he had completely forgotten. Then he would go into her front room, bring back the flute and go out to the garden seat and play it. She had done a cruel caricature of him once because he looked so comical, his long lip drawn down at the mouthpiece, his eyes lowered as the thin high notes, so sad and lascivious, seemed to curl away like wisps of smoke into the trees. Sometimes she laughed, sometimes she smiled, sometimes she was touched, sometimes angry and bewildered. One proud satisfaction was that the people upstairs had complained.

She was tempted, now that she and this clumsy woman were at one, to say to her, "Aren't men extraordinary! Is this what he does at home, does he rush out to your garden, bold as brass, to play that silly thing?" And then she was scornful. "To think of him going round to Rosie Glowitz's and half the gardens of London doing this!"

But she could not say this, of course. And so she looked at poor Mrs. Cork with triumphant sympathy. She longed to break Rosie Glowitz's neck and to think of some transcendent appeasing lie which would make Mrs. Cork happy again, but the clumsy woman went on making everything worse by asking to be forgiven. She said "I am truly sorry" and "When I saw your work in the shop I wanted to meet you. That is really why I came. My husband has often spoken of it."

Well, at least, Berenice thought, she can tell a lie too. Suppose I gave her everything I've got, she thought. Anything to get her to go. Berenice looked at the drawer of her bench, which was filled with beads and pieces of polished stone and crystal. She felt like getting handfuls of it and pouring it all on Mrs. Cork's lap.

"Do you work only in silver?" said Mrs. Cork, dabbing her eyes.

"I am," said Berenice, "working on something now."

And even as she said it, because of Mrs. Cork's overwhelming presence, the great appeasing lie came out of her, before she could stop herself. "A present," she said. "Actually," she said, "we all got together at the College. A present for Rosie Glowitz. She's getting married again. I expect that is what the letter is about. Mr. Cork arranged it. He is very kind and thoughtful."

She heard herself say this with wonder. Her other lies had glittered, but this one had the beauty of a newly discovered truth.

"You mean Bunny's collecting the money?" said Mrs. Cork.

"Yes," said Berenice.

A great laugh came out of Florence Cork. "The big spender," she said, laughing. "Collecting other people's money. He hasn't spent a penny on us for thirty years. And you're all giving this to that woman I talked to who has been married twice? Two wedding presents!"

Mrs. Cork sighed.

"You fools. Some women get away with it, I don't know why," said Mrs. Cork, still laughing. "But not with my Bunny," she said proudly and as if with alarming meaning. "He doesn't say much. He's deep, is my Bunny!"

"Would you like a cup of tea?" said Berenice politely, hoping she would say no and go.

"I think I will," Mrs. Cork said comfortably. "I'm so glad I came to see you. And," she added, glancing at the closed door, "what about your father? I expect he could do with a cup."

Mrs. Cork now seemed wide awake and it was Berenice who felt dazed, drunkish, and sleepy.

"I'll go and see," she said.

In the kitchen she recovered and came back trying to laugh, saying,

"He must have gone for his little walk in the afternoon, on the quiet."

"You have to keep an eye on them at that age," said Mrs. Cork.

They sat talking and Mrs. Cork said, "Fancy Mrs. Glowitz getting married again." And then absently, "I cannot understand why she says 'Bring the flute.' "

"Well," said Berenice agreeably, "he played it at the College party."

"Yes," said Mrs. Cork. "But at a wedding, it's a bit pushy. You wouldn't think it of my Bunny, but he *is* pushing."

They drank their tea and then Mrs. Cork left. Berenice felt an enormous kiss on her face and Mrs. Cork said, "Don't be jealous of Mrs. Glowitz, dear. You'll get your turn," as she went.

Berenice put the chain on the door and went to her bedroom and lay on the bed.

How awful married people are, she thought. So public, sprawling over everyone and everything, always lying to themselves and forcing you to lie to them. She got up and looked bitterly at the empty chair under the tree at first and then she laughed at it and went off to have a bath so as to wash all those lies off her truthful body. Afterwards she rang up a couple called Brewster who told her to come round. She loved the Brewsters, so perfectly conceited as they were, in the burdens they bore. She talked her head off. The children stared at her.

"She's getting odd. She ought to get married," Mrs. Brewster said. "I wish she wouldn't swoosh her hair around like that. She'd look better if she put it up."

Tea with Mrs. Bittell

She liked to say it was "inconvenient," on the general ground that a lady should appear to complain beautifully when doing a kindness to someone outside her own class; lately she had been keeping an afternoon for a rather "quaint" person, a young man called Sidney, one of a red-jacketed ballet who hopped about at the busy tea counter in Murgatroyd and Foot's. He often chatted with her to annoy the foreign tourists who pushed and shouted at his counter. She discovered that he came on Sundays to her own church. Such a lonely person he was, sitting in his raincoat among the furs and black suits and in such a sad situation: his father had been in the hospital for years now—a coal miner—he had that dreadful thing miners get. It was so *good* that the young man came to church with a friend, another young man from the tea counter, and waking up from her snooze during the service, she often frowned with pleasure. She would say to her atheistical sister, "The younger generation are hungry for Faith." The second young man stopped coming after a month or two, and only Sidney was left. She astounded him by asking him to tea.

Mrs. Bittell was sitting in her flat in the expensive block nearly opposite the church, among the wrongs and relics of her seventy years, when Sidney first came.

"Deliveries round the corner, second door," the doorman said.

"I'm a friend of Mrs. Bittell's," said Sidney.

The doorman's chestload of medals flashed. "Why didn't you say you were a friend?" he said, looking Sidney up and down. "Seventh floor."

"A very disagreeable man," said Mrs. Bittell when Sidney told her this, his wounded chin raised. She was a puddingy woman, reposing on a big sleepy belly; her hair was white and she had innocent blue eyes. She wore, as usual, a loosely knitted pink jersey, low in the neck, a heather-mixture skirt, flat-heeled shoes, and was very short. Her family had been Army people and at first she thought Sidney rather civilian in a disappointing way when he was not wearing the red jacket he wore in the shop, as she led him across the wide old-fashioned panelled hall of her flat into the full light of her large drawing-room, which, in addition to her furniture and pictures, owned a large part of the London sky where the clouds prospered: one looked down on the tops of three embassies and across to the creamy stucco of a long square.

Sidney sat looking at the distances between her sofas, her satiny chairs and other fine things. She remembered he had been so startled when she invited him to tea that he must be quite outside the concept of "invitations." Indeed, he had gone first of all to one of the large windows and searched the rooftops until he found the building where he and his family distantly lived. It was a high-rise block, a mile away, howling like cats, he told her, with the tenants' radios and television sets and children.

"We don't have anything to do with the neighbours," he said complacently. "Talk to the people next door, next thing they unscrew your front door or saw it off when you go out, and pinch the TV."

He turned his head slowly to Mrs. Bittell. He was a slow-talking young man, nearly handsome in a doleful way, and Mrs. Bittell liked this; she was slow and melancholy herself. He gave a droll laugh when he spoke of doors being sawn off and took a mild pride in the fact.

He also added something about the nearest roofs. "I can't stand slate," he said. "Slate is killing my father. The mine did it."

Mrs. Bittell murmured in her social way that, oh dear, she thought he had been a *coal* miner.

"No," he said. "Slate."

He spoke in short sentences between disconcerting pauses. "Dad took me down when I left school."

"You worked there?" said Mrs. Bittell.

"No," he said fastidiously. "Slate mines are cold. I don't like the cold."

There was a long pause.

"The deeper you go, the colder it gets," he said.

Mrs. Bittell said her sister Dolly had had the same impression of the catacombs outside Rome, even though wearing a coat.

"I've heard of them," he said.

From his account of the mine it seemed to her that he was describing the block of flats in which he was sitting with her, but upside down, under the earth. Yet the mine also seemed like a buried church with aisles, galleries, and side chapels, but in darkness and shaken by the noise of drilling holes for the sticks of dynamite and by the explosions in which the echoes pealed from cavern to cavern. The men worked with a stump of lighted candle on the peaks of their caps.

"Surely, Sidney, that is very dangerous, I've been told," said Mrs. Bittell. "Not lamps?"

"No gas in the slate mines," he said. But Sidney fell into a state of meditation. "Splinters," he said. "A splinter drops from the roof and goes clean through your skull. You have to wear a helmet. Dad never wore a helmet."

"Oh, dear, how thoughtless," said Mrs. Bittell.

"No. A splinter never got him."

Sidney had a taste for horrors which he displayed as part of his family's limited capital. "The dust got him," said Sidney. "He wouldn't wear a mask.

"So I went to work in 'the grocery.' "

Mrs. Bittell was offering him a second cup of tea from her silver teapot. She held the cup above the slop basin.

"I forget, d'you like to keep your remains?"

He thought about this; a funeral appeared to him to be passing through his mind.

"I always keep mine," she said.

"It's O.K., Mrs. Bittell," he said.

She was trying to think of a tactful way of saying the accent was on the second syllable of her name.

After that, talk became much easier. His long face still mooned but he warmed, although they got at cross purposes when she thought he was talking about the church when he was talking about the shop. He said he enjoyed the smell of furs, scent—they were like the smell of provisions. He looked at her piano and said, "Do you play it?"

Mrs. Bittell had a wide peaceful white forehead with fine lines on it, her eyes were delicately child-like and her voice was graceful, but now the peacefulness vanished. Her face became square and stubborn, and because his pauses were so long she was tempted to fill them with troubles and horrors of her own: her late husband's atrocious behaviour —he had once hit her with a bedside lamp; the selfishness of her daughters, who had made such "hopeless" marriages; the suspicions of her trustees, her income not a quarter of what it used to be; the wicked rise of taxes. Her wrongs settled like a migraine in fortified lumps on her forehead. But she did say to Sidney when he mentioned her piano that once one has got used to the big wrongs of life, little ones wake up, with their mean little teeth.

There had been a new wrong in her life in the last few months. The Misses Pattison on the floor below, she told him, the judge on the floor above, a Scottish "banker person," the general across the landing, had complained about her playing the piano. Several tenants had sent notes protesting: the landlord and even a solicitor had been dragged in to remind her of Clause 15 in her agreement about the hours when the playing of musical instruments was permitted. She had stonewalled, argued and evaded, tried tears, saying they were depriving an old lady of the only pleasure she had left in life. But she had had to give in: she was allowed to play between two and four in the afternoon. Even the doorman had turned against her. She supposed, she said, Sidney had seen, in the entrance hall to the flats, the board with a sliding slot indicating whether tenants were "In" or "Out." She was sure, she told Sidney, that the doorman changed her slot to "Out" when she was "In," and to "In" when she was "Out."

Sidney came to life when she said this; he exclaimed that the slot said "Out" when he had arrived. Mrs. Bittell had always loved a suspicion and she was impressed to find someone who shared one with her.

Before Sidney came to tea, on all his visits—Wednesday being his day off—Mrs. Bittell sat at her piano, a little distant from it because of her bold stomach, making one more attempt at a bit of Debussy. The notes came slowly from her fingers, for she was not one to vary her pace through life, and with occasional vehemence when she was uncertain. Biting her lips, she tried a little Chopin, but that went too fast, so she moved at last to one of those Hebridean songs she had known since she was a girl of fourteen. Now the fine lines on her forehead cleared and softened, her look became faraway and serene, her eyes became heavenly, and she felt herself to be gliding like a lonely bird over the rocky Atlantic shore at Cranach, her grandmother's great house. She was back in her childhood, keeping her father's boat straight in the sea-loch as he stood up and cast his line. She remembered chiefly his moustache like a burn. As the song began to fall away to its end she ventured to sing faintly, her voice coming out strong with longing as she lingered over the last line:

"Sad am I without thee!"

Who was "thee"? Certainly not her father with his shout of "Keep your oars straight, girl"; certainly not her husband, who had helped himself to her money for years and left her contemptuously and gone to live only a mile away across the park to play bridge with his military friends, and die. Certainly not a lover, though she had once thought the best man at her wedding rather attractive. Not the baby she had lost, or the daughters, who had made such unsuitable marriages. Sometimes she thought of "thee" as a girl—the self that had mysteriously slipped away when she was rushed into her marriage.

The buzzer sounded at the door. "Thee," of course, was not Sidney.

He took off his raincoat, folded it carefully and put it on the chest in the dim hall. They were on closer terms now.

"I heard you playing when I was coming up in the lift," he said.

"Oh, dear!" she said.

"Not to worry, Mrs. Bittell. They can't touch you. It's five to four: you've got another five minutes."

And he dawdled to allow her to dash back and get the last ounce of her rights.

He was at ease in the room now.

"Now tell me, how is your father today?" she said.

"The same," he said. "Round at the hospital. He goes three days a week. The doctors think the world of him; he's very popular." He added lazily, "X-rays. He must have had a hundred."

"The family depends on you," she said.

"Oh, no," he said. "There was the sickness benefit; the pension; the grant; he's an important case." Sidney seemed to regard the illness as a profession, an investment.

"What a worry for your mother—but you have a sister, haven't you? How old is she? Has she got a job?"

Sidney looked wounded at the suggestion. He was careful to let the peculiarity of his family sink in. "Seventeen," he said. "She sits on the sofa, sucking her thumb, like a baby, and looking at television. She's Mother's pet. They all sit looking at it. Dad too," he said.

This pleased him as he sat thinking about it and he laughed.

"Mother goes out," he said, "and always comes back with a special offer she sees on the commercials or something from Bingo.

"That," he added, studying the spaces between things in Mrs. Bittell's flat, in which the well-mannered chairs and tables kept their distance from one another, "is why we're so crowded in our place. You can't cross the room."

Mrs. Bittell said, politely evading comparison, "You have long legs."

"Yes," said Sidney, shaking his head. "Jennifer says, 'You're always on about my legs, what about yours?' "

Sidney offered this information in a bemused way. Suddenly he woke up out of his own life and asked, "Who is that gentleman over there?"

She was relieved to see he was looking at one of three portraits on the wall.

"Oh," she said solemnly, "I thought you meant someone had got into the flat."

"No, hanging on the wall," he said.

"Oh, that's just the old Judge. We call him the Judge—the red robe and the fur collar. It was from my mother's family," said Mrs. Bittell in a deprecating way. She had caught Sidney's taste for horrors: "I fear not a very nice man. They say he sentenced his own son to death."

"Oh," Sidney nodded. "History."

"I suppose it is," said Mrs. Bittell. "I like the next one to it, the boy in blue satin with his little sword—the Little Count. I don't know whether he was really a Little Count."

"Is he the one that was sentenced to death?" said Sidney.

"Oh, no," said Mrs. Bittell protectively. "The Little Count was the father of the Judge." She had her own pride in her family's crimes.

"Are you interested in pictures?" She got up and he followed her to look more closely.

"Antique," he said. "They must be valuable."

"So they say, but there is such a lot of that sort of thing about," she said.

He gazed a long time at the Little Count and again at the Judge. He gave a sigh. *The Battle of Waterloo* was on television last night. Did you see it?"

"I'm afraid not," Mrs. Bittell apologized. "I haven't a television. I believe the Misses Pattison have. I can hear it at night." Her wrongs woke up indignantly. "I don't know why they should complain of my piano."

Sidney ignored this. "Do you think the Duke of Wellington was sincere?" he said.

"They say he was very witty," said Mrs. Bittell.

"But do you think he was sincere?"

"Sincere?" said Mrs. Bittell. She was lost. "I've never thought of that," she said.

She saw he was struggling with a moral question, but what was it? She felt one of those violent sensations that swept through her nowadays since her quarrels about the piano. Did Sidney, who was older than she had at first thought, more than thirty, his dark hair receding, did Sidney feel too that sincerity, honesty, consideration, were wearing thin in modern life?

"I know what you mean," said Mrs. Bittell, who did not. She compared Sidney with her ancestors and even with the Duke of Wellington. Sidney was reaching towards the Light; she could not say her forebears had ever done so. She had known the family pictures all her life as furniture: they represented the boredom of centuries, of now meaningless anger. When her husband left her she had seen herself as a woman ruined by generations of reckless plunderers of land, putting down rebellions, fighting wars, gambling and drinking away their money, building big houses, losing their land to lawyers and farmers, grabbing the money of their wives and quarrelling with their children. She saw herself with unassuming pride as the victim of history. Even in the Mansions—her rising anger told her—her own class had betrayed her.

She calmed herself by showing him a photograph of a boy of ten. "My only grandson," she said. "Of course he's grown up now. Rupert."

"I've got a friend called Rupert," Sidney said.

"Really. Such a nice name," said Mrs. Bittell, putting the photograph down.

"He used to work at Murgatroyd's," he said, suddenly eager. "You must have seen him—tall, fair moustache. He left."

"I don't remember," she said. "But wait—didn't you bring him to the church?"

"That's it," said Sidney. "He brought me. You don't often meet a man who has had an education. Every Sunday we used to go to a different church—St. Paul's, Westminster Abbey. He knew about antiques too. Lunchtime and Saturdays we used to go to the National Gallery. He could see *into* pictures. If he was here now," he said, surveying her pictures and her furniture, "he'd have valued everything. It was very interesting."

"Very," said Mrs. Bittell.

"I was in the National Gallery this morning," he said. "It's my day off. I had the idea I might find him there. I've been everywhere we went. Holborn Baths too, we used to go swimming."

"And did you find him?" said Mrs. Bittell.

"No," said Sidney, looking aloof. "I don't know where he is. He walked out of the shop last August; not a word."

He paused in the midst of his mystery.

"He left the place where he lived. I went round, but he'd gone. The landlady didn't know. No address. Not a word."

"Too extraordinary," said Mrs. Bittell.

"I mean, you'd think a friend wouldn't go like that. I thought he was sincerely my friend." Sidney gazed at her for an answer. "After three years," he said.

He aged as he gazed. He sat there as if he were the last of a series of Sidneys who was now quite austerely alone, challenging her with a slight smile on his mouth, to see the distinction of his case.

"Oh, but there *must* be an explanation, Sidney," said Mrs. Bittell. She had an inspiration. "Was he married? I mean—or was he going to get married?"

Sidney looked at her disparagingly. "Rupert would never marry," he said. "I know that. It was ruin, he always said; you were better alone."

"If it's the wrong person," said Mrs. Bittell, nodding, "but in the Kingdom of Heaven there is neither marriage nor giving in marriage," she said. "As the Bible says." The tune of "Sad Am I Without Thee" went through her head. Her words brought her to the point of confidence, but she did not give in to it.

Sidney considered her. He held his hurt face high. "There was an American who used to come into Murgatroyd's. He was from the Bahamas," he said. "Or somewhere."

"Ah, the Bahamas!" said Mrs. Bittell. "Then perhaps that's where your friend went? My husband's best man went to live in the Bahamas. Have you enquired? Business may have taken him to the Bahamas."

Sidney's pale long face swelled and his mouth collapsed with agonized movements. Mrs. Bittell was embarrassed to see tears on his face.

"I can't bear it, Mrs. Bittell." A loud howl like a dog's howling at the moon came out of him. He was sobbing.

"Oh, Sidney, what is it?" said Mrs. Bittell, moving from her chair to the sofa where he sat.

The cry took her back years to a painful scene in Aldershot when a subaltern in her husband's regiment had suddenly sobbed like this about some wretched girl. He had actually cried on her shoulder.

Sidney did more than this: his head was on her bosom, weeping. His dark hair had a peculiar smell, just like the subaltern's smell. She patted Sidney on the head, but she was thinking, I mustn't tell my sister Dolly about this, or my daughters. It would be terrible if her grandson suddenly came; he often dropped in.

"I am sure you'll hear from him," she was saying.

"I loved him," Sidney wept.

"Love is never lost. In the Kingdom of Heaven, love is never lost, Sidney dear," said Mrs. Bittell. "I know how you feel. I have been through it too." She was thinking of her children.

He sat back away from her. He seemed to be saying that whatever she had been through, it was nothing to what he had been through. She also saw that in some kind of craven way he was worshipping her. And even while she felt compassion, she felt disturbed. Why had it never occurred to her, in her miserable troubles with her husband, long ago over, but for which her daughters blamed her, that there had been no "other woman"?

"We must turn to God," she said, though she knew that years ago she had done nothing of the sort, that outrage had possessed her.

"We must pray," she said. "The Kingdom of Heaven is within us, Sidney." And she declared, "There is no separation for the children of God."

Sidney looked round the room and then back to her, immovable in his gloom.

"We must not cling to our sorrows," she said, for he looked vain of his, but he nodded in a vacant fashion. She smiled beautifully, for she felt that there was some hope in that nod. As he got up to go Sidney changed too. He walked with her into the dim hall, at home in her company now. As he picked up his raincoat he saw himself reflected in the glass of a very large old picture, the full-length portrait of a girl, it seemed, though scarcely visible except for the face.

"Who is that?" he said.

"Oh, just a family thing. It used to be at Cranach. I'll switch on the light."

There was an overshadowing tree with leaves like hundreds of chattering tongues, a little stream in the foreground and a large grey mossy boulder. On it a sad, naked, wooden-looking nymph was sitting, the skin yellowed by time. In one corner of the picture was a little Cupid aiming an arrow at her.

Sidney gaped. "Is that you?" he said.

Questions took a long time sinking into Mrs. Bittell's head, which was clouded by kindness and manners and a pride in her relics. She herself had not "seen" the picture for years. It was glazed and was hardly more than a mirror in which she could give a last look at her hat before she went out. She was not surprised by Sidney's remark.

"It doesn't really belong to me, it's really my sister's, but she doesn't like it, so I put it there."

Sidney tried to cover his mistake. "That is what I meant. Your sister," he said.

"Oh, no," said Mrs. Bittell, waking up. "It's Psyche, the goddess, the nymph, I believe. The Greek legend, Psyche—the soul. I really must get one of those lights they fix to frames. It's so hard to know what to do with big pictures, don't you find? Do you like it?

"It's supposed to be by—Lely, is it?" said Mrs. Bittell nervously. "My husband said it was probably only a copy. My daughter tells me I ought to get it cleaned and hang it in the drawing-room, where one can see it more clearly."

The idea appeared to shock Sidney. "I've never seen one like that in a house before. In a gallery. Not in a house," he said censoriously.

"I mean," said Sidney. "The man who painted it, was he sincere?"

Mrs. Bittell was baffled again by the word and murmured politely. Her mind moved as slowly as her feet as she opened the door for him to leave and said, "You must call me Zuilmah, Sidney dear. Remember I will pray for you and Rupert. Ring for the lift," she said.

"I'll go down the stairs," said Sidney. He was bewildered.

She went to the bathroom after he had left and saw from the window the top of the distant block of flats where he lived. Now that the evening was coming on, the block was a tall panel of electric light, standing up in the sky. A thought struck her: How absurd to say it's a portrait of Dolly—no resemblance at all.

She flushed the toilet.

For Mrs. Bittell, Psyche was part of her furniture. She had not really looked at it since she was a girl at Cranach. Then she remembered that she and Dolly used to giggle and say it was Miss Potter, their governess, with nothing on. Mrs. Bittell had long stopped noticing that Psyche was naked, and if she had been asked, would have said that the figure was wearing one of those gauzy scarves that pictures of nymphs wore in books. She had never even thought of naked statues as being naked. Men, she supposed, might think they were—they were so animal.

It came to her that Sidney was a man.

"How embarrassing," she said. She imagined she had seen a hot, reddish cloud in Sidney's eyes. He had gaped, mouth open, at the picture, and his mouth looked angry and wet. She had once or twice seen her wretched husband looking at the picture, mouth open in the same way, though (as she remembered) he was short of money and said, "We'd get a tidy price for it at Christie's," and they had their lifelong quarrel. He was always itching to sell her things to pay his debts.

"You can't sell it, it's Dolly's," she had said to him.

"Your bloody sister," he said.

Now Mrs. Bittell's peaceful face changed into a lump of fear. Sidney slipped into her husband's place and became dangerous. He had had an empty, staring expression when he looked at that body. And he had thought it was she herself! Things she had read in the papers rushed into her mind, tales of men breaking into houses and attacking women, grappling with them, murdering them. Sidney had cried on her shoulder. He had touched her hand. His was hot. The scene became transformed. She saw the struggle. She would scream—she looked at her table with a lamp on it—yes, she would hit him with a lamp. That was what her husband had used on her.

Mrs. Bittell sat on the sofa opposite to the one Sidney and she had sat on and looked at the squashed cushions, her heart thumping. Slowly the panic quietened.

"How foolish," she said.

She recovered and went to her piano. She played three or four notes secretively and sulkily, and the illicit sound restored her.

Of course—Psyche was the soul, a "thee," the thee of her dead baby, herself as a young girl before she married, a loss, sadness. And Sidney too had a "thee." He must have been thinking of Rupert, poor young man.

I must pray. I must not let the Devil get hold of me, she thought. Sidney and Rupert are children of God made in His image and likeness.

And she closed her papery eyelids and prayed and pleasantly dropped off to sleep in the middle of the prayer.

For two weeks Sidney did not come to the church; then he reappeared and came to the flat again.

"I've been worrying about you," she said.

Sidney had changed. She noticed, once he had got out of the dim hall into her drawing-room, that his hair was different. It was combed

forward and he looked younger, leaner. She did not say anything;
perhaps her prayers had been answered.

"I've been worrying about you," she said again. "Have you any
news?"

"I made up my mind and packed the job in," he said. He looked
careless and grand.

"Sidney! From Murgatroyd's. Was that wise? Why did you do
that?" Mrs. Bittell was shocked.

"Undercurrents," he said.

Mrs. Bittell could understand that. There were undercurrents in the
Mansions. There were even undercurrents at the church.

"No consideration," he said lazily.

Mrs. Bittell could understand that, too. Why was her youngest
daughter so critical of her? Why did young people push past her in bus
queues?

"What are you going to do?" she said.

"I'm in no hurry," he said. "I might go back to Reception. Hotels."

"Is that better?" she said.

"Could be," he said.

"That is where I first met him—Rupert—hotel." He was off-hand,
cool, disdainful.

"Do sit down and tell me," she said.

He sat down. "It's all this stealing that goes on I can't stand. It's not
the customers—it's the staff. Food, clocks, rugs—anything. Six Persian
rugs last week. You can see it being wheeled off to delivery and loaded
onto vans in the bay. Tell the management, they don't want to know.
Insured. Rupert couldn't stand it. I think that's why he left."

"We live in a terrible world," said Mrs. Bittell.

"Bomb in that restaurant yesterday—did you read it in the paper?
A woman had her hand blown off," he said.

"How horrible," said Mrs. Bittell. His new haircut made it seem
more horrible. "Did they catch the men?"

"Tell the police, they don't want to know," said Sidney.

One of those sudden rages which seized her flared up and made her
heart thump; her stomach swelled and her sweet face became ugly.
Rage was lifting her into the air. Once more all her wrongs came back
to her. She felt herself to be united with him: he was no longer the
"quaint" young man. He was human and alone, as she was. And then
her rage declined. No, she mustn't give in to anger; one had to face
evil. A sentence from one of the vicar's sermons came back to her: she

loved the way he said it. "The darkest hour precedes the dawn." This was a dark hour for the world and for Sidney.

"When everything is dark, Sidney dear," she said, "we must pour in more love. We must open the floodgates." She was swimming in the growing exaltation of one who had sent out a message. She looked at his doubting face.

A vulgar buzzer went at the door, which startled her.

"Oh, dear," said Mrs. Bittell. "Now, who can that be? I hope it is not someone awkward."

How often in her life she had expected a prayer to be miraculously answered when she opened her eyes.

Sidney and she looked at each other. Then her face became stubborn. "How irritating," she said. "I'm losing my memory. It's Mr. Ferney. I'd forgotten him. He's a friend of my sister's and we've drunk all the tea. How silly of me."

"Shall I go to the door?" said Sidney possessively.

"No, I'll go. He's retired," she called back as she went. "Stay here. Would you do me a great kindness and put the kettle on? Wait—it's probably the doorman."

Mr. Ferney was at the door. Mr. Ferney was a meaty middle-aged man with two reproachful chins and a loud flourishing voice.

"Dear Zuilmah," he bawled. "Always the same. Like your Psyche, with a lily in your hand, waiting for Cupid's arrow. Am I late?"

"We didn't wait for you," said Mrs. Bittell.

Since he had retired Mr. Ferney's profession was having tea with ladies. He was on the verge of a belated search for a wife.

"You don't know Mr. Taplow, a dear friend," said Mrs. Bittell.

Mrs. Bittell went to make more tea.

"Tiplow," said Mr. Ferney. "Somerset Tiplows?"

"Taplow," said Sidney.

"Taplow, Tiplow, all Somerset names. Tiplawn, too. People couldn't spell in the past. You'll find Ferns, Fennys, de la Fresne and of course Ferness. I tell Mrs. Bittell that she was a Battle," he confided in a loud voice. "Bataille."

"What are you talking about?" said Mrs. Bittell, returning with her silver teapot.

"Your horrible family, my dear," said Mr. Ferney. "The rogues' gallery—that awful fellow." He pointed to the Judge.

"Mr. Taplow and I were talking about that the other day, weren't we, Sidney? Sidney was saying that History is coming back, wasn't that it? Tell Mr. Ferney."

"History always comes back. I can't afford it, can you?" said Mr. Ferney.

Sidney's face became swollen on one side and he said, "I'll be going, then. I've got to get Father," to Mrs. Bittell.

"Must you? Oh, dear. Of course you must," said Mrs. Bittell. "Mr. Taplow's father is in the hospital."

"Nothing serious, I hope."

"I'm afraid it is," said Mrs. Bittell.

"Such a tiresome man, I'm so sorry," she murmured as she took Sidney to the door. "Remember, Sidney dear, what I said. Open the floodgates. Don't forget to come to church on Sunday."

And seeing his unhappy look, she gave him a light kiss.

Sidney was shocked by the kiss.

"Who is that? What's he mean by 'then'? I've seen him somewhere. It'll come back to me . . . Treplawn," said Mr. Ferney.

"He used to work at Murgatroyd and Foot's," said Mrs. Bittell. "Terrible stories he's been telling me. I'm trying to help him."

"Oh, I see," said Mr. Ferney, relieved, and passed his cup. "What's he after? You do slave for people. I wish you'd slave for me."

Thieves in Murgatroyd and Foot's, a shop known all over the world for generations! The building itself became a long flaunting wrong and, for her, London changed overnight. Even the gardens in the squares became suspect to her. The doors of pillared terraces looked dubious, embassies were whited sepulchres, the cars outside hotels carried loads of criminals away. Walking in her quiet way, in the past she had floated sedately above curiosity, merely noticing that the young rushed. But now she saw that the city had become a swarming bazaar: swarms of foreigners of all colours—Arabs, Indians, Chinese, Japanese, and all people jabbering languages she had never heard—came in phalanges down the pavements, their eyes avid for loot. If she paused because she heard an English voice, she was pushed and trodden on, more than once laughed at. In the once quiet streets, such as the one in which her sister lived, there were empty bottles of whisky and brandy rolling in the gardens.

She noticed these things now because for three weeks Sidney had not been to church and when she was out walking she was looking at all the faces thinking she might see him. He had disappeared in the flood.

Yet the more impossible it was for her to know where he was or what he was doing or why he did not come, the calmer she became; inevitably the divine will would be manifested and, indeed, she went so far as to stop praying; in a modest way the sensation was exalting.

At church she gave up looking for Sidney in the congregation when the hymns were sung—she was too short to see far when she was sitting. It must have been on the fifth Sunday, as she stood up for the second hymn and heard the mouths of the well-dressed congregation shouting forth, that she noticed two men across the aisle who were holding their hymnbooks high and not singing. Sidney—and who was the other man? She hardly remembered him—it *must* be Rupert!

Mrs. Bittell stopped singing and said loudly, almost shouted "No" to the will of God. She flopped into her seat and her umbrella went to the floor. The church seemed to roll like a ship; the altar shot up into the air. The powerful odour of the fur coat of the woman in front of her was suffocating. The miracle had occurred. Rupert had returned. Sidney was standing beside him. Prayer had been answered: it had swept Rupert back across the Atlantic. All the old prayers of her life that had never been answered became like rubbish. A real miracle had been granted to her.

Flustered, she got to her feet and started singing the last verse and looked across the aisle. The two young men had heard her umbrella fall and now they were both singing, and singing at her, at least Rupert's mouth was open but Sidney was half hidden, and Rupert's teeth flashed. She nodded curtly; she had only one desire: to go at once across the aisle in anger and say, "Why didn't you tell Sidney you were going away? Why didn't you write? If he is sincerely your friend?"

When the service was over, they were ahead of her in the crowded aisle, but she found Sidney waiting for her on the pavement and Rupert a few yards away.

"He's back," said Sidney, beckoning to Rupert, who stood politely aside. For a moment the young man still looked unlike a real man but more like some photograph of a man.

"What did I tell you, Sidney?" she said as Rupert came nearer.

Sidney stood back, gazing up at the hero, his eyes begging her to admire.

"I remember you, Mrs. Bittell," Rupert said.

"What a time it has been," she said.

"What a time," he said.

"Our bus," said Sidney.

"You must tell me everything. Come to tea," she pleaded. "Monday? I don't want to lose you again."

They looked at each other and glanced at the bus and agreed. How flat she felt, but as they ran for the bus they turned back to wave—how delightful to see a miracle running.

Mrs. Bittell went beautifully and as if empowered to the door. There stood Sidney, so proud that he looked as if he would fall headfirst into the hall; behind him, stiffly controlled, stood Rupert, the answered prayer, perhaps rightly wearing dark glasses as if, as yet, shy of the spiritual life. She forgot to close the door and Rupert politely shut it for her.

"It gives a click," she called back to him.

"It clicked," he said.

Sidney went eagerly forward. They stood in the drawing-room.

"The Judge!" said Sidney, pointing to the picture. Rupert ignored this and looked round the room.

"Now," said Mrs. Bittell playfully, "where is your sunburn?"

"He has been ill," said Sidney. "He's only just out of hospital."

"I picked up one of those bugs," said Rupert.

"Oh, dear. I hope it was not serious," said Mrs. Bittell.

"Two months," said Sidney dramatically. What an emotional young man he was!

It was disappointing not to see the miracle in perfect health. His voice was hoarse, he brought a smell of cigarettes with him, and he had lost weight, so that his cocoa-coloured suit was loose on him. His thin face seemed to have a frost on it, and when he took his dark glasses off, he was obliged to narrow his eyes because of the light in the room. The thinness of the face made his mouth and lips too wide. There was grey in his hair. She noticed this because she had never been sure which of the young men at the tea counter he was. He sat so stiff and still, and despite his illness, his bones looked too heavy for the chair. He picked up one of the cups on the tea table and looked at the mark as Mrs. Bittell went off to get her silver teapot.

"Now tell us all about the Bahamas," said Mrs. Bittell as she came back, and out came her story that her husband's best man at their wedding had been aide-de-camp to the governor, whose name she could not remember; it was a long time ago, of course.

"Who is governor now?"

The question made Rupert smile thoughtfully. "McWhirter," he said at last. "He's retired, though—not very popular—the new man came after I left."

"I must ask my sister. She'll tell us," said Mrs. Bittell.

This was disappointing. And Rupert's account of the Bahamas was bewildering. No Government House, no beaches, no palm trees. All Victorians, he said. Full of English stuff left by early settlers. Harmoniums everywhere, he said, grandfather's clocks. Fox-hunting pictures.

Sidney said enthusiastically that Rupert was "in antiques."

Mrs. Bittell recovered. "There used to be Bittells in sugar—though I believe that was in Jamaica." She spoke disdainfully, admitting—to put Rupert at his ease—the shames that can occur in all families. She moved nearer home. "You must be very thankful you left Murgatroyd's," she said, admiring him. "There were undercurrents, Sidney tells me."

Rupert said, "You could put it that way."

"It takes courage," she said, and she meant this for Sidney, for it seemed to her that Rupert was a decisive man, one who had struck out on his own.

"You have interesting things," he said, nodding at her very fine bureau.

"Just old things from Cranach," said Mrs. Bittell, and she led them across the room.

"These are large flats," he said. "You've got a museum."

"And there's the big picture in the hall," said Sidney, the excited familiar of the place. "Lily."

They went out into the hall and Rupert looked closely at the picture. "It could be a Lely," he said.

An educated man!

And then Rupert said something which was not really very tactful. "It would pay you to have this cleaned," he said. "Six by four," he said, guessing the measurements. "It needn't cost too much if you go to the right firm—Dolland's, say—they do a good job. I mean, it would bring it out."

"I do not think my sister would care for that," Mrs. Bittell said. "It has never been cleaned. You see, it's always been in the family. I believe it was always like that."

She did not think Rupert knew her well enough to make suggestions about the tastes of the Bittells. They did not like things "brought out."

She certainly did not wish to do anything as "inconvenient" as that. It would be like asking Dolly to get herself "brought out."

"It's very suitable with the panelling," she said.

"That's true enough," said Rupert disparagingly.

And then Rupert made one more worrying remark about the picture. It was, she reported to her sister more than once afterwards, kindly meant, she was sure.

"That's interesting. There's one in the National Gallery like this, Sid." (He called Sidney "Sid"!) "See the Cupid down there in the corner? See how he's holding his bow? He's going to miss. He won't get her in the heart. He'll catch her in the—er—leg," he said. And he indicated the probable course of the arrow. And he gave a short laugh.

Over the years Mrs. Bittell had not particularly noticed that Psyche had a leg. Surely it was quite wrong to believe that the soul had legs.

And she could not understand why Rupert laughed.

She said, in her social voice, as one asking for information, "I always understood Cupid was blind."

Rupert stopped his laugh and she was amazed to see him turn to Sidney and do a most disconcerting thing: he winked at Sidney. The answer to prayer had winked. Even Sidney, she saw, was shocked by this.

Soon after this they said good-bye.

The miracle had vanished. The flat was empty now. Rupert had come back. Sidney was happy. There was nothing for her to do. He did not come to church. His visits stopped.

"Sad am I without thee"—whoever "thee" was—she sang on some days as she played her piano in the agreed hours. That last chord became more vehement. Mrs. Bittell put jealousy into the chord. Surely Sidney could spare her one afternoon? The hardest aspect of the case was that she had no one left to pray for, but she was stubborn in her sense of loss and she began to feel, as her jealousy grew, that wherever Sidney was, whatever he was doing, she could still pray for the freedom of his soul. Freedom, of course, from that very puzzling love of that strange young man who had, after all, not been sincere.

It was a prayer without urgency. It would come into her head at night when she saw the lights of the flats where Sidney lived, or when she was visiting her sister, or sitting on the train coming home from one of those trying visits to her daughter.

On one of her returns, on a Sunday too, when she had been obliged to miss her church, at six in the afternoon—she was expecting her grandson. She feared she was late. She got to her flat. She *was* late. The boy was there. His suitcase was in the hall, open, in his untidy way and —strange—his shoes beside it.

"Rupert darling," she called.

And when there was no answer, she called again. There was a strange smell in the flat. But then there were sounds; he must be in the bathroom. She went to the bathroom door and said quietly, "Rupert. It's Granny."

The door was open. He was not there. She went to her bedroom, where the door was half open, and there she saw a pair of stockinged feet and the cocoa-coloured trousers of a man kneeling at a drawer beside her bed.

"What *are* you doing, Rupert?" she said. The man got halfway to his feet.

She saw the face of Sidney's Rupert. His dark glasses were on her bed with some of her jewellery. A long smile split his face for a moment as he stood up. He had a bracelet in his hand.

"Put that down," said Mrs. Bittell. And called calmly, as if to her grandson, "Rupert, there's a man in my bedroom."

And with that she pulled the bedroom door to and turned the key in the lock.

"I've locked him in," she called.

The man was wrenching at the door handle. Then she heard him open the window.

But now Mrs. Bittell had exhausted the words she could speak. She opened her mouth to scream, but no sound came. Lead seemed to fill her legs, her heart thundered in her ears; she saw through the doorway of the drawing-room (miles away, it seemed) the telephone. She began a slow trudge that seemed to take hours, as in a dream, while the man returned to hammering at the door, shouting, "I'll break your bloody neck, you silly old bitch."

She was stupefied enough to turn and hear the sentence out. She got to the drawing-room, then to the hall, and what she saw there drove her back. Psyche was not there. The frame was empty. That sight drove her back, and giddily she went to her piano and banged away at the keys, defying the whole block of flats, banging as the man banged at the closed door. The telephone rang and rang, but still she banged and banged on the keys and then the man broke through the door and was coming at her, but in his stockinged feet; on the parquet at the edge of one of her rugs he skidded and fell flat on his back.

Mrs. Bittell saw this. She had often, in her quiet way, thought of what she would do if someone attacked her. She had always planned to speak gently and to ask them why they were so unhappy and had they forgotten they were children of God. But a terrible thing had happened. She had wet herself, like a child, all down her legs. Red with shame, as he rushed and fell and was trying to get up, she tipped the piano stool over as he jumped at her. He stumbled over it. And this was the moment she had often imagined. She became as strong as History; she picked up the brass table lamp and bashed him on the neck, the head, anywhere. Not once, but twice or three times. And then fell back and fainted.

That is how the doorman, the general from across the landing, the Misses Pattison and her grandson found her, as Rupert, bleeding in the head, was trying to put on his shoes in the hall and run for it.

"Tell Sidney to come," she was murmuring as they knelt beside her, and for a long time the telephone still went on ringing.

"A man called Sidney," said the doorman, answering it. "He's asking for her."

He turned to the crowd. "He says it's urgent."

No one replied.

With pomp the doorman returned to the telephone and said, "Mrs. Bittell is indisposed."

The Wedding

The market was over. Steaming in the warm rain of the June day, the last of the cattle and sheep were being loaded into lorries or driven off in scattered troupes through the side streets of the town which smelt of animals, beer, small shops, and ladies. The departing farmers left, the exhaust of their cars hanging in the air.

Tom Fletcher, the forty-year-old widower with a wilful twist of chestnut hair over his forehead where the skin had a knot of intention in it, drove off but got out at the open door of The Lion, and putting his head down as if threatening to charge into the crowd there, shouted, "Come on, Ted. Leave the women alone till Saturday," and Ted Archer came out and sat very tall in the car.

"That used to be a terrible place," Archer said. "The new people have done it up."

The pair drove twelve miles on the Langley road round the bottom of Scor, the hill which stuck up in a wooded lump over the slates of the town. To children of the town, Scor looked like the head of an old man, and that image sank into their minds like a kindness when they grew up. They thought the quarry carved out of the hill was his mouth. Today the rain ran off the woods into the streams that waggled below him.

Driving up the long rise to Poll Cross, the two men saw a woman come out of the larches, straight in the back and walking fast. She carried her head well.

"Effie Thomas must be hard up for it—going up the woods on a day like this," said Ted.

"Bugger," said Tom. He had the sly voice of someone enjoying a meal. "Someone got his knees wet. What's the matter with you, Ted? That's not Effie, with a back like that. That's Mrs. Jackson, the little bitch from the College, Mary's teacher. I'd give ten pounds to anyone who'd take her up Scor on a Sunday afternoon and pull her tights down. Filling my girl with a lot of parlez-vous. What's the good of French? Bugger, you can't talk French to your Herefords, Ted. Why don't you marry that teacher, Ted?"

"She's been married once already," said Ted.

"I know she has. She'll miss it, won't she then?" said Tom.

They caught up with her and made her skip up on the bank. The young woman had a rude look—very alluring.

"Jump in, you're getting your pretty hair wet, Mrs. Jackson," said Fletcher, very courtly. "Get in the back. We'll drop you. You'll be all right. I've got Ted in the front with me and I've tied his hands."

"I have been enjoying my constitutional; but, well, thank you. Yes, I will avail myself . . ."

"Avail yourself of everything while you can. We dropped the pig at the market."

"How do you do, Mrs. Jackson," said Ted when she got in and they drove on.

"Hear him?" said Tom. "He speaks French. You ought to see his heifers go off round the fields when they hear him. Like a horsefly under their tails."

"I can believe it," said Mrs. Jackson, who had a strict habit of giving a shake of her head for the sake of boldness. Fletcher was watching Mrs. Jackson in the mirror. Her fair hair was drawn straight back from her forehead into a bun at the back. It was the kind of hair that frizzes and is almost white. She was a thin, plain young woman; her blue eyes were small.

"You'll be coming to the wedding, missus, Saturday?" said Fletcher.

"I am looking forward to it," she said. "Most kind of you to ask me." Her pretty voice was cooled by all the knowledge in her head.

Fletcher dropped into country speech and said to Ted, "Tha was at school with me, warn't 'e, Ted? He's nobbut a rough farmer's boy, missus. Remember, Ted, poor old Lizzie Temple? Us dropping peppermints down her blouse?" And then to Mrs. Jackson: "He'd begun already. That's thirty-five years ago. Never ride in the back of a car with him."

"I will think of that when the temptation occurs," Mrs. Jackson said.

"When the temptation occurs. Did you hear that, Ted?"

Mrs. Jackson said she had never seen the country so green and Tom said he had never seen Mrs. Jackson's cheeks so blooming, which was a fancy, for she was as pale as a bone and her humour was dry.

They arrived at her little cottage, which stood back from the road on a short rise, and when she got out she thanked Fletcher and in her firm way she said, "I haven't given Mary up." The little blue eyes were determined.

Tom Fletcher gave one of his loud laughs and called to her as she crossed the road, "Run in quick, missus, or Ted'll chase you upstairs."

But when they drove off Ted said, "I can't stand so much forehead in a woman."

"It's the best part," said Tom. "But you wouldn't know that. But she's putting ideas into my Mary's head. It was all poor Doris's doing, sending the girl to a snobby college like that and now they want to send her to Oxford. Before Doris died I couldn't say anything, could I? But Doris has gone now. And Flo's getting married. I'll be alone in that house now, Ted, if I let Mary go."

"That's right, Tom. You will."

"It's all right for you, Ted, you dirty bugger, but I don't want my girl putting on airs and marrying a French professor. Where's the economics of it? Your family and mine, Ted, have farmed this land for two hundred years, haven't they? That's what I call economics. I want my girl at home talking English. And doing the wages. I've told old Mother Jackson so."

"How old is Mrs. Jackson?"

"Too old for you, Ted, you old bugger. Turned thirty, but I tell you if she hadn't been a friend of Doris's, I wouldn't have had her in the house, talking that classy stuff to Doris all day, about Louis IVth, the pair of them—they did, Ted, as if they were married to him. She wanted us to call one of my bulls Napoleon . . ." Fletcher's temper blew away into laughter. "No, I haven't anything against her. She's got a head on her. It's an education to listen to her. But her husband made a poor job of her. Ask me—she never had it. She sent me the bloody forms to fill up. I've got enough forms. Well—she's not going to get Mary."

They got to Ted's place and they went in to see the boxing on television. It annoyed Tom that although Ted hadn't got *his* money (for he often calculated that), Ted's house was a fine white place, fit for a gentleman, with peaches on its walled garden, well run.

"You bachelors look after yourselves," he said.

There was not a scratch on the paint inside the house, not a smear on the mahogany. If Ted hadn't won as many prize cups at the shows as he had, there was not a speck on his carpets. There were portraits of Ted's grandfather and grandmother on the wall of the dining-room; the decanters sparkled. A lot of money had gone down the drain in Ted's family, but the dining table could seat twenty-five and looked as if it was waiting for the whole tribe of Ted's forebears to come back and throw away more money if he reformed and got married.

"My place has been let go since Doris died," he said jealously as he watched the boxing. "Old Mrs. Prosser comes in but she's past it. That was a low one, see that?"

They were watching the middle of a fight.

"It will be all right after the wedding," said Ted.

"All right? What d'you mean? I'll be alone in the house like you, you bugger. His eye's cut."

"Mary's a good girl. She's got brains," Ted said. "You'll have to look around, Tom."

"Look at that—footwork, footwork. The lad'll never get anywhere with that. Hit him, boy. Look around? You haven't left much around, have you, you old sod."

"There's old Mrs. Arkwright. You'll have to do a deal," said Ted slyly.

"Bugger that for a deal," said Tom. "She's had one of my tractors for a month up there. I'd sooner old Mrs. Doggett. If she was twenty years younger, I'd have her. You remember how you lassoed her at Bill Hawkins's wedding? The old girl's got a kick on her."

"She did the cancan," shouted Ted, getting a drink. "I bet your Mrs. Jackson can do a cancan. She's been in Paris."

The laughter stopped. A mean look came into Fletcher's face. "She's been divorced," he said. He stuck out his lip. "They oughtn't to have a woman like that in the College. All the la-di-da did it. But we all know who she is."

"Old Charlie Tilly's daughter," said Ted.

"The seedsman who used to have The Lion till he drank it dry," said Tom.

The girl held the book in bewilderment.

"I shall tell your father you came for the book," Mrs. Jackson said.

She told the girl to read the book while she made some tea. It was called *Rambouillet: The Art of Conversation.*

"You wrote it!" exclaimed the girl.

"Yes, I did. I was going to bring it to give it to you at the wedding, but I forgot. Better late than never."

She drove the girl back to the farm, where Ted Archer was standing at the door.

"She's here," called Archer, and Fletcher came rushing out.

"Mrs. Jackson forgot to give me this," the girl said. "I've been to fetch it."

"At this hour?" said Fletcher as Mary kissed him.

"We've been all over the countryside looking for her," said Ted Archer quietly to Mrs. Jackson as they went inside. "They had words."

They sat on the large shabby chairs and Fletcher listened silently to Mrs. Jackson's chatter about the wedding, staring at her, and when at last she made him laugh she put on a prudish, busy face and got up to go at once.

"I'll be up tomorrow for my rope," he shouted from the doorstep as she switched on the car lights and drove off. It was the only time he spoke. His shout seemed to own the night.

When she got back to her cottage, she lay on her bed. "Oh, no," she said in the little hot room. A heavy night of throwing off bedclothes. Trivial dreams of voices and faces and Fletcher sitting in his chair and staring at her! And then—what a triumph—in the morning there was a mark on her waist: it had come up in the night. She would have liked to show it to him.

She had washed her hair and was sitting with a scarf around it, looking harsh and prim, when Fletcher came in the afternoon.

She put on an impudent mouth when he came to the door. She took the rope down from a hook. "Here is what you came for."

He took it and dropped it down outside on the step and then came in and sat down on the sofa.

"You've done something to this place since the old postman had it. It belonged to Randall; he was a fool to let it go. We got a bit rough, as Mary says. But I told her I could see you were on your way, and the best way to get a lady to stay is to stop her from going! I know, I know —the lads were rough."

"Well," said Mrs. Jackson. "I am not cattle. I suppose it was what one would have to call a country junket."

"I can't bear the stuff," said Fletcher innocently. "We used to give it to the girls, with prunes, when they wanted loosening."

Mrs. Jackson sat very upright on her chair.

"I had an engagement," she said.

"That's just what I said to Mary—she's been carrying on. I said you'd got an engagement."

"How is Mary?" said Mrs. Jackson.

"Girls get excited by weddings," he said. "You saw the heifers. News spreads. You've been married and so have I—it makes a difference. What's that?"

He pointed to a picture hanging on the wall beside the fireplace. It seemed to be a foam of pink cream and lace, and then he saw the vanishing chalk outline of a doll or a girl floating in the foam, possibly on a garden swing: there was a pink face, two indigo blurs for her eyes, the poppy-red of a drooping mouth. The creature was either just appearing or disappearing in the paint.

"It's a Vandenesse," she said, recovering her grand voice. "French."

He nodded. "Expensive, I expect," he said.

"My husband gave seven hundred and fifty pounds for it," said Mrs. Jackson coldly.

Fletcher was silent, then he said, "A rich man."

"Very," said Mrs. Jackson.

"Yes, that's what I heard."

Fletcher shifted on the sofa. "Bugger, I sold a bull last week for two thousand pounds. Who is it supposed to be?"

"It's a portrait of the Comtesse de Tillet," she said.

He nodded. "It would look funny in a farmhouse," he said.

"Yes, but this is not a farmhouse," she said.

Mrs. Jackson gave a shake of her head to change the subject. "I was writing you a letter," she said, pointing to the table by the window where she had been typing. "But you throw letters away, don't you, so coming here you've saved me a sheet of paper. I have been thinking of what you said to me yesterday about Mary. I've changed my mind since last night. I agree with you. Mary's better off at home."

"What's this?" said Fletcher, startled. "Turnabout, I see. Are you telling me she's not good enough?"

"Oh, she's a clever girl," said Mrs. Jackson. "Simply—I was mistaken."

"You're saying she's not good enough."

"Not at all. I've changed my mind."

His face was amiable. "I'll tell you what you are, missus. You're a bloody liar." He laughed. "And I'll tell you something else. That picture's not the countess of whatever you call her: it's you. Mary told me."

"It is the title of the picture. I have the catalogue," she said.

"It's you. Only he's taken all your bones out. He ought to have knocked something off for the price of that. When I am buying an animal I want to see how it stands. I look at its bones."

"I am sure you do," said Mrs. Jackson sharply. "But my husband was buying a work of art, not an animal. Don't you like it? The dress is very pretty, don't you think? I love the dress. I've got it upstairs. I was thinking of taking it to London tomorrow—very silly, of course, it's so out of date."

It was delightful to sit there, looking so plain, and to mock him. She got to her feet. "I'll get it," she said.

"No," he said, standing up, and he held both her arms. "Stay where you are. You and me have got to do a deal. I want you over at the farm."

"But I'm going to London. What deal? I know—you want me to clean all those cups."

"I did them myself this morning," he said intently. "I want you down at the farm and we'll do what you like about Mary."

In the cottage room the short man seemed to shut out the afternoon light. He was looking into her small blue eyes and she saw he dismissed the fight in them and in her chin. He let go of one arm and neatly pulled the scarf from her head, so that her damp fair hair straggled to her shoulders. She put on a face of horror that gave a twist to her parted lips, but the horror was growing into a pleasure in itself. It heated and was growing into a noise in her head as he stared at her, and yet in quick glances he was also taking in the room, the door, the furniture, the cushions, the books, and did not even spare the rugs on the floor. His stare was the stare of the hunt.

"Sit down. Please let me go," she said.

She was astonished, she was disappointed, when he sat down.

"Tom," she said. "Me. On a farm. Are you mad?"

"You know my name, anyway," he said. "I'm not mad." And then he said simply, "You brought Mary home."

"Of course I did. What do you imagine?" she said.

"You brought Mary home," he said again.

"You don't know anything about me," she said.

"I know everything about you." He nodded at the picture. "He's got your mouth."

"My mouth?" she said. She could not resist turning to the picture and looking at it with a moment's pride, and then the horror came back into her face and she mocked again. "You go by mouths, too," she said.

"Yes," he said and pulled her gently by the hand to the sofa, where she skilfully sat away from him.

"My hair is wet," she said, pushing it back over her ears. "What a sight I must be. Go on—what are you saying? You want a housekeeper? Now, there's Mrs. Arkwright—"

He did not let her finish the sentence. She was pushing his hands away, his arms, opening her mouth to speak, her ears full of din and her eyes scattering her hatred until, in a pause, her skin burned and her eyes dulled as his were dulled and her lips drooped, when his kissing stopped.

"At least," she said in a hard low voice into his coat, "at least lock the door."

There was a lot of talk at the shows that summer when Fletcher and she and sometimes Mary, too, drove off together. Ted Archer denied it all until Tom had his house repainted and Mrs. Jackson left the College and sold her cottage. Messell went about saying Vandenesse was a third-rate painter with a knack of catching girls inventing themselves but no good when they had turned thirty.

About the Author

V. S. PRITCHETT was born in 1900. In addition to being a short-story writer, he is a critic, autobiographer, biographer, novelist, and travel writer. Sir Victor is a foreign honorary member of the American Academy of Arts and Letters and of the Academy of Arts and Sciences. In 1975 he received a knighthood. He lives in London with his wife.